TOLKIEN
in Pawneeland

Essays
on the Inner Secrets
of Middle-earth

Roger Echo-Hawk

Tolkien in Pawneeland

Remastered Extended
Second Edition

© Copyright Roger Echo-Hawk
July 2016

The first edition of this book
was published December 2013

About
Tolkien in Pawneeland

The essays in this book explore various mostly invisible truths in the writings of JRR Tolkien. The first edition of *Tolkien in Pawneeland* (December 2013) set forth groundbreaking new insights, uncovering Tolkien's interest in North American mythology. I discovered that textual elements from a 1904 book called *Traditions of the Skidi Pawnee* had mysteriously found their way into *The Book of Lost Tales*, *The Hobbit*, and *The Lord of the Rings*. This new edition of *Tolkien in Pawneeland* amplifies those insights by revealing the brief flowering of English interest in Pawnee tradition and by shedding light on Tolkien's connections to the British folklore community.

Recent years have seen an increase in scholarship on Tolkien and race. Five of the newly added essays in this book consider in detail how the real-world traditions of race entered into the making of Middle-earth. The established consensus approach to this topic has relied on a handful of comments by Tolkien to dismiss contradictions in his legacy on race, while critics have underscored the social texturing of his invented realms – in that contested battleground, one must choose between comfortably entrenched polarized viewpoints. But both perspectives have typically ignored the broader record. Pondering the mechanisms of race in Middle-earth, I have considered Tolkien's opinions and his worldcraft, and I have mapped these onto the relevant historical contexts. This permits us to more precisely illuminate his thinking.

Tolkien often enough made mention of his inspirations, but he did not often go into detail. An extensive analytical literature has grown since the 1970s around his writings, appreciating his fictional worlds and shedding valuable light on his worldbuilding. Tolkien launched into mythmaking with the intention of creating a literature pertaining to English culture, and as time went on he expanded the scope of that agenda. But he never embraced a truly global vision despite his use of American source-materials. This book explores that legacy, showing how Tolkien wove a vast fictional narrative tapestry from diverse mythological and folkloric traditions, reconfiguring borrowed elements to create his own mythic tales and epic romance.

Roger Echo-Hawk
July 2016

Tolkien in Pawneeland
Essays on the Inner Secrets of Middle-earth

Roger Echo-Hawk

CONTENTS

Aryan Elves and the Nordic Roots of Númenor
1

The Taylorian Traditions
30

In the Land of Magic
48

Worlds of Song
55

Daughters of a Dark Moon
64

Saru and Sári and the Sun
72

The Mythology of Mischief
81

Coyote Bombadil
89

The Almost Forgotten Hobbits
108

Tolkien's Hobbit Origin Stories
120

Treasures of Tradition
138

British Folklore and Tolkien
142

Wizard of the Great Grasslands
150

Gollum the Mysterious Being
155

Beewolf and Beorn and the Bear-boy
165

To Distant Lands and Back Again
178

Unraveling Spider Silk
185

The Old Thrush's Secret
190

Messengers of Tirawa and Manwë
199

Bombadil Reborn
203

Holes and Houses and Hills
210

The Enchanted Feather
216

A Very Peculiar Letter
221

Olórin in the Uttermost West
230

Tolkien's Mongol-type Orcs
238

Tolkien's Black Men
289

The White Wizards
310

Companions in Shipwreck
319

Tolkien's Tree of Tales
328

Pawneeland in Middle-earth
339

The Future of Race
351

Endnotes
360

Cover Art

Eärendel and Night the Spider
May 2016 photo by Roger Echo-Hawk

Tolkien in Pawneeland

Essays

on the Inner Secrets
of Middle-earth

Tolkien in Pawneeland   ❧ ✳ ᘛ   Roger Echo-Hawk

Aryan Elves and the Nordic Roots of Númenor

Visitors to JRR Tolkien's Middle-earth sense both his immense creative vision and his reliance on literary tradition. He drew on European mythology, medieval literature, and fairytales for inspiration. For those who feel curious about the making of Middle-earth, decades of interesting scholarship have revealed the erudite artisan-scholar behind the talented novelist. Tolkien wove a specific vision of the cultural heritage of northern Europe into his legendarium – a vision rooted in his notions of "northernness." This cultural texturing also featured a subtle layering of racial thinking derived from European academic ideology of the time. This can be glimpsed in his early construction of Elvish history and in his later tales of Númenor. To understand what this means, we must visit realms that Tolkien knew well, but which have somewhat faded from view.

    Pondering the history of humankind, European intellectuals of the 19th century experimented with mingling the revelations of ancient myth and the insights of modern science. One trajectory of that project came to be known as Atlantology. As Joscelyn Godwin has shown, during the second half of the 19th century, Atlantologists promoted a fascinating cataclysmic vision of antiquity that linked Greek tales of Atlantis to the far North of the ancient world.[1] In one notable work, for example, William Warren postulated in *Paradise Found* (1885) that Eden and the birth of humankind occurred at the North Pole, an Atlantean realm drowned in the Deluge. And these first people were long-lived, but their descendants dwindled, becoming lesser folk in the world. With a steady stream of books like this, the shaping of the past seemed a matter that could be both rational and occult.

    By the time JRR Tolkien launched into his worldbuilding, mixtures of the fabrications of race and the study of language and mythology had become ascendant in European literature about antiquity. It is apparent that his early fantasy agenda unfolded as a culmination of this cultural imagery. As the 20th century moved onward, however, much of this historical context slowly faded into invisibility.

To get to that world, Tolkien could have taken many available paths, but it is arguable that he followed in the footsteps of an Oxford professor named John Rhys. In the late spring of 1886 Rhys gave an annual lecture series, the Hibbert Lectures, reading a set of papers on Celtic myth and Aryan cosmology. This research appeared in 1892 as *Celtic Heathendom*.[2] Tolkien knew of Rhys and his scholarship, and probably attended his lectures at Oxford University in 1914-1915.[3]

Three factors point to the influence of *Celtic Heathendom* on the writing of Tolkien's *The Book of Lost Tales*. The first can be framed as a kind of generalized cosmological aura. Rhys's project spelled out an array of commonalities among Celtic, Norse, and Greek divinities and myths, and we encounter a collection of deities who populate the cosmos under diverse names – this is a characteristic that Tolkien echoed in *The Book of Lost Tales*. This observation is not particularly helpful, however, because this kind of comparative mythography was common in the 19th century. A slightly more specific echo can be discerned in Rhys's brief commentary on minor Celtic deities and in Tolkien's early version of his lesser divinities who accompany the Valar to earth.

The strongest comparison can be made in Rhys's Arctic Circle and Tolkien's icy realms of the far north – a minor aside for Rhys, but a significant theme in Tolkien's history. In his discussion introducing us to the Arctic Circle, Rhys pondered winter / summer themes and the annual "yearly struggles" in myth, listing various Aryan mythic prophetic moments: "...the foreknowledge as to the final battle of Moytura..."; "the northern sybil could predict..."; and "the prophecy about the issue of the war with the giants..."[4] He drew two ideas from this survey. He observed that "we seem to be directed to the north as the original home of the Aryan nations..." And he pointed to a "cessation for a time of the vicissitude of day and night, as happens in midwinter within the Arctic circle."

It is apparent that Tolkien took this interpretation of Aryan history and inserted a cataclysmic shadow of it into the early version of his cosmos, and then he set a more intact version at the heart of his history of the Elves. Composing the unfolding of cosmic events, Tolkien mentioned "biting colds without moderation" devised by Melko, who is the great adversary of the Ainur divinities. And soon we see Melko in regions of "great cold and solitude" both North and South, and there is a great flood, and finally we see one more vast convulsion of the ocean floor.[5]

If this had been the total mention of Arctic-like spaces, we would have little reason to think that Tolkien ever gave thought to Arctic Circle mythmaking. But now enter the Elves, awakening in the world. They wander the Great Lands into the west. Several divisions of Elves ultimately make their home in far-off Valinor, and there they fall afoul of Melko, who raided them and then fled "back to the ice-kingdoms of the North."[6] And so the Noldoli abandon Valinor to pursue Melko.

They follow the "coasts of Eldamar" northward to "the confines of the Icy Realms," where "the Great Seas... dwindle to a narrow sound" full of grinding "islands of floating ice."[7] Here Tolkien paused to recall a recent time when "the North became clement for a while[.]" But when the Elves arrived on the scene, there came a chill moment of awful foretelling. A servant of the Valar issued to the Elves "the Prophesies of Amnos" warning of future "evil adventures." And with this tale, "Thus came the Noldoli into the world."

Experimenting here in 1919-1920 with great floods, ice-kingdoms, the coming of the Noldoli from the once-temperate North to the Great Lands, and prophetic history, Tolkien echoed the Rhys model of antiquity. He hoped to produce a mythology that would appeal to an audience born into a world where such storytelling really was deemed by many a matter of history. For this reason we must give thought to an interesting possibility. Did Tolkien have 19th century Aryan modeling in mind when he first constituted his Elves and their history?

We can readily see that Tolkien was not following a strict adherence to Rhys's synthesis. But we can hear a few shared narrative resonations. After suggesting an Arctic Circle origin for ancestral Aryans, Rhys went into some detail on the state of knowledge about Aryan philology. He told how Sanskrit had lost "its exaggerated weight" in philology as the "mother of the other Aryan languages[.]" And now "The ethnologist... finds that it is out of the question to suppose that the various peoples speaking Aryan languages to be of the same race." Tolkien's Elves from the start of their tale in *The Book of Lost Tales* prove diverse, with three divisions: the Teleri, Noldoli, and Solosimpi. They spoke a single language, but events separated the Solosimpi from the others. This brought the "sundering of that folk from the others both in speech and customs[.]"[8] The parallels here are weak, but focus similarly on the nature of divisions within an ancient language group.

Rhys and Tolkien also embraced a specific corresponding model of physical typology for Aryans and for Elves. Rhys contemplated the spread of Aryan culture by conquest, absorbing other racial groups, and for this reason "the various nations of the world speaking Aryan languages are not all equally Aryan in point of blood[.]" Given this observation, he wondered "what Aryan nation or nations most closely resemble the original stock of that name?" After careful thought he concluded that this "original stock" must be "the tall, blue-eyed, fair-skinned and light-haired inhabitants of Scandinavia and parts of north Germany."[9] Rhys also pointed out that Greek heroes were usually described as having blond hair – "golden as to the colour of their hair." And with the dethroning of Sanskrit from the place of Aryan pride, Hindus came to seem less Aryan, and "accordingly it is found that the least swarthy" of the Aryan nations "belong to the highest caste."

The ranking of "caste" through skin tone, eye color, and hair color was an established tenet of late 19th century racial ideology in Britain. But Tolkien divided his early Elves in *The Book of Lost Tales* by the nature of their singing and by qualities of mind and heart, and he made scant reference to the ranking criteria of traditional racial physical taxonomies. What little he did say, however, shows that from the beginning he set in place a moral equivalence of "swart" skin with an evil nature, while characters with white skin were morally pure and beautiful.

In "The Tale of Tinúviel" we encounter Queen Gwendeling / Wendelin, who is "very dark of hair" and "her skin was white and pale" and her daughter Tinúviel has "bare white feet[.]"[10] In "The Fall of Gondolin" we encounter a treacherous Elf named Meglin: "Less fair was he than most of this goodly folk, swart and of none too kindly mood, so that he won small love, and whispers there were that he had Orc's blood in his veins..."[11] And in this tale we see the birth of Eärendel who "was of greatest beauty; his skin was of a shining white and his eyes of a blue surpassing that of the sky..."

We also find in Gondolin a house of Elves known as "house of the Golden Flower" led by a particularly heroic Elf who is not described by skin tone, but as "golden Glorfindel" and "Glorfindel of the golden hair" with "yellow locks."[12] Glorfindel and his house clearly evoked John Rhys's Greek Aryan heroes, "golden as to the colour of their hair."

The study of hair and eye typology or "nigrescence" became widely established in physical anthropology of the late 19th century. Following this line of inquiry, John Beddoe asserted in 1885, "Ancient Irish poetry indicates... that blue eyes and yellow hair were most characteristic of the higher ranks, or ruling caste."[13] American scholar William Ripley disagreed with aspects of John Rhys's thinking about race and ancient history, but he offered his own thinking about blond hair, deeming it a matter of selection due to class distinctions.[14] As he concluded, "Both tall stature and blondness together constitute insignia of noble descent." He pictured an ancient royal class rising to become "the flaxen-haired and blue-eyed jarl or earl." Tolkien would have encountered this kind of symbolism around blond hair in any number of writings of the period. His choice to imagine a golden haired leader of a house of Elves cannot have been an act of pure independent invention.

Many years later Tolkien inserted a lingering subtle echo of this blond-haired racial imagery into the writing of the final chapters of *The Lord of the Rings*. In "The Grey Havens" Sam opened his gift from Galadriel and found that the box contained dust and a "golden-yellow" seed.[15] The finished chapter had Sam carefully distributing the grains of Elvish dust across the Shire, resulting in a spring "that surpassed his wildest hopes." And that year was filled with "a gleam of beauty beyond that of mortal summers" and "the children born or begotten in that year... were fair to see... and most of them had rich golden hair that had before been rare among hobbits."

Tolkien's original concept of Galadriel involved white hair, but he soon enough gave her the golden hair that made her famous in Elvendom.[16] Seven years later in 1948 he had his golden-haired Elf Queen bestow upon the Shire a gift of genetic magic that would transform their sturdy halfling hair into a symbol of an ebbing history – the slowly vanishing ages of the Elves. We can also surmise that for Tolkien, this magic "golden hair" came rooted in the same 19th century racial Aryan imagery that had inspired "Glorfindel of the golden hair."

This was a lifelong project for Tolkien. John Rhys favored the view that the Aryan "original stock" of long ages ago must have been "fair-skinned and light-haired" folk of "the highest caste." And during the final years of his life Tolkien would write of "the golden hair of the Vanyar" and "their noble and gentle temper[.]"[17] These ancestral royal attributes got passed down to Galadriel, an Elf Queen of the highest Aryan caste in those ancient days at the end of Tolkien's life.

In 1919-1920 Tolkien worked for the *Oxford English Dictionary* conducting research on words beginning with "w." At one point he prepared a slip on the word "wallop," illustrating its usage with a phrase that had entered British political parlance during the late 19th century: "the right to wallop one's own nigger."[18] This disconcerting academic research project may not necessarily shed light on Tolkien's private attitudes on race. But it is noteworthy since he was rummaging through books and documents to find examples of this usage during the same period when he was proceeding with a project in his mythological worldmaking to imbue skin and hair coloration with symbolic moral meaning.

The evidence is sparse but the messaging is clear enough. Tolkien employed a caste-like hierarchy among his Elves in which skin shading reflected a moral purity ranking. This was not a construction that received much emphasis, but it mattered to Tolkien enough for him to make occasional mention of it in his storytelling. And it underscored the general similarity of historical patterning between his world and the world envisioned by John Rhys.

Rhys cited a French scholar who posited in an 1883 publication that all humankind "originated on the shores of the Polar Sea at a time when the rest of the northern hemisphere was too hot to be inhabited by man." Tolkien had Melko chained in his ice-kingdom, and for a time "the North became clement[.]" For Rhys, Norse myth pointed to a connection "to some spot within the Arctic Circle" and those Aryans "descended into Scandinavia, settling, among other places, at Upsala"; while Tolkien's Aryan Elves marched to the Icy Realms and descended into the mythic Great Lands.

These Arctic folk were white. That is, they were fair-skinned Aryans to Rhys; to Tolkien they were white-skinned Elves of unearthly beauty. In their journey from the far North, we can see Tolkien's Elves following in the footsteps of the Arctic Aryan ancestors of Rhys's fair-skinned Scandinavians, and we find comparable mention of prophecy and a temperate North Pole. Tolkien's vision of the Arctic Circle and Rhys's vision overlap to such a significant degree that it does not seem coincidental.

We can assume that by circa 1919 Tolkien knew the history of "Aryan" as both a term of language and of race. Several decades later he carefully distinguished its racial meaning from its application to a language family. But in 1886 Rhys used the word in both senses. We can see Rhys fusing both language processes and race in his Aryans, and we can see Tolkien doing something similar with his Elves – in "The Music of the Ainur" his Elves and Men were described as "races," and in the mid-1920s he prepared a short text that repeated this description of his Elves as a "race of the Gnomes."[19] It is not clear that Tolkien intended for his Elves to replicate Rhys's Aryans, but it is plainly arguable that he drew inspiration from constructions of Aryan history, and we can see well-defined echoes of Rhys's Aryans in Tolkien's Elves. This is where matters stood at circa 1920 when Tolkien set aside *The Book of Lost Tales*.

In April 1933 a German dignitary named Alfred Rosenberg visited London and set a wreath at a memorial for WW1 soldiers and gave a Nazi salute.[20] This act inspired several very public protests in London, one of which resulted in the tossing of the wreath into the Thames. Tolkien would surely have noticed newspaper reports of these events. And we can also guess with some confidence that he already knew about Rosenberg from a book published in 1930.

I am aware of no direct evidence showing that Tolkien was familiar with Rosenberg's *The Myth of the Twentieth Century*. But it was extremely popular in Nazi Germany – Tolkien probably read it in German. It is also possible that during the 1930s he read similar writings by Herman Wirth, Rudolf John Gorsleben, Julius Evola and others, but *The Myth of the Twentieth Century* was particularly well-known.[21] Making frequent use of terms like "Aryan" and "Nordic," Rosenberg mingled scraps of myth with a rambling concoction of racialism, nationalism, and a vast sense of German exceptionalism – race provided the essential ingredient of Rosenberg's message. He hoped to create a Nordic mythology for Germany, and he was very successful.

To accomplish this goal, he crafted an elaborate edifice of esoteric history that began with a fascinating idea. Drawing on literature about Atlantis, Rosenberg theorized "that the north pole has shifted and that a much milder climate once prevailed..." Ancient Nordic essences, he determined, originated from Atlantis at the North Pole. "It seems far from impossible that in areas over which the Atlantic waves roll and giant icebergs float, a flourishing continent once rose above the waters, and upon it a creative race produced a far reaching culture and sent its children out into the world as seafarers and warriors."

A colorful sliver of information points to Tolkien's awareness in 1932 of Rosenberg's book. In his Father Christmas letter of that year he described the ancient caves of Cave Bear, and then Cave Bear told how "Men came along" and "there were lots about at one time, long ago, when the North Pole was somewhere else."[22] Father Christmas finished, "...I don't know if he is talking nonsense or not." Tolkien's tone was completely fanciful, but Rosenberg's nonsense theory about a shifting North Pole in antiquity helps to bring Cave Bear's ruminations into sharp focus.

During the years after Rosenberg's book made its huge splash in Germany, Tolkien came up with his own tale of Atlantis. The story that Tolkien told was that a conversation with his friend CS Lewis inspired him to invent his own version of the legend. Studying the early manuscripts of this material, Christopher Tolkien concluded that the conversations with Lewis probably happened in 1936, but he decided with more certainty that his father's new Atlantis tale had taken shape by November 1937.[23]

This dating of Tolkien's earliest Atlantis manuscripts is based on scant evidence. Tolkien's comments on the origin of the material can be found in various letters, but only one offered information useful for dating the project – a vague reference to when "C.S. Lewis and I tossed up" – this points to circa 1926 and the years immediately thereafter.[24] The mention of the North Pole in Tolkien's 1932 Father Christmas letter seems to suggest the early point of the possible dating spectrum; so circa 1935-1937 would not be too much of a stretch. We can guess that the impetus for Tolkien's Atlantis projects flowed not just from a conversation with CS Lewis, but also from awareness of Alfred Rosenberg's Nordic theory of German history.

Another piece of evidence shows that during the early to mid-1930s Tolkien was thinking of ancient cataclysmic myth – this can be seen in his reworking of the Norse *Lay of the Völsungs*, perhaps as early as the end of 1931.[25] In "Upphaf (Beginning)" we find "The mountains were moved, / mighty Ocean / surged and thundered[.]" Then the Gods war on their foes and we encounter "...roaring sea / and mountains of ice / on the margins of the world." Next appears a seer and "Of doom and death / dark words she spake[.]" There can be little doubt that during this period Tolkien had on his mind things Germanic, northernness, the icy reaches of the earth, prophetic legend, and oceanic catastrophism.

When Tolkien sat down to retell the legend of Atlantis, he began with various notes that set the story in the midst of his extant mythology. In his first outline, the gods situated the realm of Atalantë "in the great Western Sea" for "the Fathers of Men" who became "great mariners, and men of great skill and wisdom."[26] This model clearly drew from the Greek tradition, but it also echoed Rosenberg's "creative race" of Atlantean "seafarers and warriors." Tolkien and Rosenberg both had the residents of the realm follow the basic assumption of social compexity in the Greek model. And they both went beyond the model, crafting explicit differences in humankind that were only implied in the Greek Atlantis story.

Rosenberg had an "Indoaryan" Nordic wave swarming out across the world from Atlantis and encountering "dark alien peoples" and "black brown natives" and "racially inferior aborigines." Tolkien contrasted his men of Atalantë, the Númenórië, with "Wild Men" and "Faithless Men" who were not described but who took the Númenórië "for gods." And where Rosenberg spoke of a Nordic "adoration of light" and "the laws of light and heaven" Tolkien told of long-lived men "bathed in the radiance of Valinor."

One major difference is significant. Rosenberg portrayed Christian ideology as oppressive, as "lifeless and suffocating ideas which had come from Syria and Asia Minor and had brought about spiritual degeneracy." Tolkien's worldview surely took offense. His initial outline had a "battle of the Gods" in which "Men side largely with Morgoth." He struck out "Faithful men dwell in the Lands" (with "Lands" being a lingering precursor to "Middle-earth"). The will of the Gods and the violation of their decree constituted Tolkien's initial vision of the downfall of Atlantis – this rescued the story from the anti-Christian Nordic polar myth of timeless ancestral racial purity.

We can surmise that Tolkien's arguable primary objection to Rosenberg's Nordicism had to do with anti-Christian messaging, versus Tolkien's preferred theologized interpretation of history in which polluting evil and divine celestial intentions accounted for corrupted men. But both models provided well-defined rankings of humanity and culture. Tolkien was not noticeably attracted to Rosenberg's total enthusiasm for racialism, but rather than counter it, he settled on a religious basis for bestowing the logic of race on his Númenórië. In addition, to signal the independence of his vision, his Men would be Men of the West, not the Nordic north.

When Tolkien sat down to develop his notes into a more detailed narrative, he decided his project would portray a society blessed by divine gifts and damned by human failings – a story that adhered more closely to the Greek tradition of a moral fall from grace. Among the humans of the First Age, he began, were some who "took part with Morgoth" and "they brought evil into many places where wild Men dwelt..." But for those Men who had aided the Elves, "Fionwë son of Manwë... gave them wisdom, power and life stronger than any others..." These "Númenóreans" – as he now called them – were more like Elves "than any other races of Men that have been, yet less fair and wise than they, though greater in body."[27]

Tolkien incorporated race into his earliest two versions of "The Fall of Númenor." He didn't emphasize racial terms or constructions in these materials, but nor do we find explicit anti-race messaging of any kind. In terms of the hierarchical racial nature of humankind, the construction of Tolkien's storytelling tended to align with Rosenberg's Nazi creed, with both authors ranking humankind in terms of a privileged Atlantean caste versus lesser folk who populate the earth.

Tolkien's handling of race was subtle, but he inserted more explicit manifestations of race in his adaptation of this material for an unfinished book, *The Lost Road*, written at the same time as the early drafts of "The Fall of Númenor." And as we will see, this version of the story contained allegorical whisperings of Nazi Germany.

In *The Lost Road* Tolkien gave thought to "Englishmen and northerners" and to "the old days of the North" that have vanished "into Christendom."[28] The idea of "northernness" was something that Tolkien pondered from his early days as a student. Writing about Norse sagas in early 1911, Tolkien enthused about "marvels and miracles of the strange old Northern brand..."[29] This concept held deep meaning for him as a touchstone of identity, but it also referred to a spectrum of features deemed to infuse Norse and Germanic cultures – qualities that also served as ingredients in English identity, as noted by Marjorie Burns: "Northern Romanticism... allowed the English to see themselves basically as Norsemen only slightly diluted in race..." Tolkien's early notions of northernness were thus rooted in Scandinavian antiquity, racial ideology, and late Victorian English nationalism.

The contribution of racial thinking can be glimpsed in *The Lost Road*. The surviving text began with a conversation between Oswin Errol and his son Alboin, and we soon hear Oswin saying that he might have chosen the name Albinus for his son "[b]ut it is too Latin..." This is important since "you are not white or fair, boy, but dark." Other than being twelve years old and looking "rather bony" there is no further description of dark Alboin. But the boy pondered the idea of "Dark Alboin," wondering whether "there is any Latin in me." There isn't much, he concluded. A mention of "darkhaired people" seemed to hint that this was the source of his quality of being "dark."

Turning fifteen, Alboin learned "other languages, especially those of the North: Old English, Norse, Welsh, Irish." He "liked the flavour of the older northern languages" and the "things written in them." Nearing age eighteen Alboin had a conversation with his father, going into detail about ancestry, focusing on noses. "Anyway," he says, "I like to go back – and not with race only, or culture only, or language; but with all three." Oswin told him that you can go back through archaeology and philology, and Alboin added mythology to that. And going "back" via philology, Alboin sensed "another language" that seemed "related but quite different" and "much more – more Northern."

Race, language, myth, and northernness together set the tone for *The Lost Road*. Tolkien intended for this spectrum of ideas to serve as foundational concepts in the story he planned, a tale of ancient vanished Númenor. This sounds quite similar to the major ingredients that went into Rosenberg's *The Myth of the Twentieth Century*. Given the strong aura of an idealized autobiography in the opening chapter of Tolkien's book, these elements seem revealing in a personal sense.

There can be no doubt that Tolkien embraced the idea of race and that it played a role in his vision of Númenor. But some of his racial imagery sounds mysterious. What did he mean by "Dark Alboin"? In saying "not white or fair" did Tolkien mean that this character was racially black? This is highly unlikely. An explanation can be glimpsed when Alboin wondered about having "Latin" ancestry, and then we see mention of "darkhaired people."

In Tolkien's youth and early adulthood there was not just one European race. Efforts to racially categorize European populations during the late 19th century culminated with the identification of three races. In 1899 William Ripley listed these as Teutonic, (Celtic) Alpine, and Mediterranean.[30] This was an influential idea during Tolkien's early years, and as late as the 1930s these European subdivisions had evolved into Nordic, Eurasiatic, and Mediterranean groupings – this last was sometimes termed the "Brown Race."[31] The physical features commonly attributed to the Mediterranean subgroup included black hair, dark eyes, and a sallow to brown complexion. In one 1923 book on the Egyptians, the author found a striking "family likeness between the Early Neolithic peoples of the British Isles and the Mediterranean..." Perhaps Tolkien had such conceptions in mind when he pictured Alboin. This may not seem very familiar to us today, but it was a racial construction in Tolkien's day.

Moving the story to Númenor, we glimpse again Tolkien's fantasy hierarchy of Men, lesser and greater in nature. We hear that "in Middle-earth dwelt the lesser men..." But the Men of Númenor "have grown to be higher and greater than others of our race... We have knowledge, power, and life stronger than they." This is a religious hierarchy – innate nature based on the gifts of the gods textured by the temptations of evil.

But there is another detail of this storytelling that is quite significant for the light it sheds on Tolkien's thinking. Christina Scull and Wayne Hammond have observed that Tolkien's depiction of Númenor in *The Lost Road* "almost certainly owes something to then-current events in Nazi Germany."[32] This can indeed be glimpsed in Sauron's speechmaking: "And it seemed to men that Sauron was great; though they feared the light of his eyes." And "To many he appeared fair, to others terrible; but to some evil." Sauron's teachings "seemed good." He aided the people in building ships that "go without the wind, and many are made of metal..." And their "arms are multiplied as if for an agelong war" and their "shields are impenetrable" and their "darts are like thunder and pass over leagues unerring." And so Sauron "preached deliverance" and he urged the king of Númenor "to stretch forth his hand to Empire."

These descriptions of Sauron do sound very much like comments on Germany of the 1930s, with silhouettes of Hitler, the German rearmament program, and Hitler's expansionist agenda as it had begun to play out in the Saar Basin and the Rhineland. What logic inspired Tolkien to insert a real-world shadow of Nazi Germany into fictional Númenor? He said nothing that can directly answer this question. But this kind of subtle allegorical referencing makes perfect sense when we interpret Tolkien's Atlantis as a response to Alfred Rosenberg's Atlantis. Comparing Hitler to a satanist Sauron, Tolkien responded to the Nordic claim of a glorious racial destiny with a darker tale of spiritual downfall.

The concept of "Northern" culture was a topic that fired Tolkien's imagination, and it also interested his colleagues. Humphrey Carpenter's sense of what "Northernness" meant in

Tolkien's life had to do with the literature and culture of ancient Scandinavia.[33] Carpenter applied it to the friendship between Tolkien and CS Lewis and their mutual love for Norse mythology and saga. The meaning here, of course, is that that both men appreciated and discussed northernness as a cultural quality, and it was no doubt a term that came up in their talk.

Carpenter described an evening in September 1931 that has become famous in Tolkiendom. Tolkien, Lewis, and Hugo Dyson spent a long Saturday evening together at dinner, strolling around Addison's Walk, and finishing the night with further talk in Lewis' rooms. Tolkien felt inspired to compose a long poem, "Mythopoeia," which Carpenter has treated as a record of their discourse that night.[34] Lewis wrote to a friend a few weeks later reporting that this long evening inspired him to become a Christian.

We have only vague glimpses of the actual content of the talk that night. But it wandered at length through myth and religion. If we follow Carpenter's suggestion and treat Tolkien's "Mythopoeia" as a kind of record of the night at Addison's Walk, it is interesting that the idea of "northern courage" can be observed in two lines of the poem: "They have seen Death and ultimate defeat, / and yet they would not in despair retreat[.]" Outlining Tolkien's conception of "Northern courage," Carl Phelpstead showed that it had to do with a pre-Christian "theory of courage" in the face of inevitable defeat.[35] It has been argued that Tolkien gave considerable thought to how such values helped to precipitate World War Two and consequently became discredited.

We can outline a trajectory of events that ultimately precipitated the invention of Númenor. In the summer of 1931 Tolkien had an academic focus on German and related languages – in June he was listed as a member of a committee managing students working on "Germanic" requirements.[36] This seems a likely period for him to have had his first encounter with Alfred Rosenberg's *The Myth of the Twentieth Century*. It is also possible that Rosenberg's treatment of myth played a role in Tolkien's long night spent with Lewis and Dyson in September 1931 – it is clear enough that Tolkien's energy that night had to do with a critical examination of how myth and religion interact. And judging by "Mythopoeia," he could well have brought up a comparison of English Northernness and German Nordicism, setting his preferred Christianized interpretive perspective against Rosenberg's Nordic alternate reality and its anti-Christian message.

In the course of writing an essay circa 1930-1931 Tolkien included an interesting reference to "wood sprites" and "foam-fays" as "the white people of the shores of Elfland[.]"[37] This description illustrates the aesthetic lens that Tolkien had in hand during the time when is likely to have first read *The Myth of the Twentieth Century*. He no doubt intended to reference pale skin, a poetic emphasis of his established preferential color association for Elves and Men. But he would have had little reason to avoid a deliberate echo of racial whiteness, and he had no reason to call into question Rosenberg's basic embrace of race.

We can date Tolkien's probable awareness of Rosenberg more clearly at the end of 1932 when he inserted into his annual Father Christmas letter a mysterious comment on the North Pole – a comment that can be explained as a reference to Rosenberg's shifting North Pole. Tolkien saw how Rosenberg used the ingredients of race and myth to bestow a sense of antiquity on Nordic Aryans, the purpose of which was to encourage Germans to invest in a sense of fateful destiny. This German logic was comparable to the English identity agenda that shaped Tolkien's *The Book of Lost Tales*, but Rosenberg's path rejected Christian values. And sometime between 1932 and 1936 Tolkien had a conversation with CS Lewis that precipitated his invention of Númenor.

To invent his Atlantis tale, Tolkien started off preparing a manuscript about the shaping of the world, "The Ambarkanta"; then he set down a few notes for a story. With this material he introduced an interesting change into his older mythology. In *The Book of Lost Tales* he had Melko first setting foot in the middle of the world, but in "The Ambarkanta" he had the Valar alighting "first upon Middle-earth at its centre, save Melko who descended in the furthest North."[38]

Tolkien's Father Christmas letter of December 23, 1932 reported the odd doings of the North Pole and it also introduced goblins to the far north, found by North Polar Bear. We might wonder whether these new associations of the North Pole with Melko and goblins reflected a sense of distaste for the modeling of ancient history by Alfred Rosenberg and other Germans, who made the Polar North the center from which the Nordic race spread. But Tolkien also re-situated the realm where the first Elves awoke to "the North beside the waters of Helkar." This seemed to emphasize once again the general equivalence in *The Book of Lost Tales* between his Elves and John Rhys's Aryans of the Arctic Circle. Whatever interest he had in the Nazi project to create a Nordic antiquity, he preferred to focus on his own agenda.

Over the following months (or years) he created two intertwined projects, "The Fall of Númenor" and *The Lost Road*. In his vision of Atlantis, Tolkien's foremost response to Rosenberg was to craft a narrative centered on religious conceptions, an affirming meditation on pre-Christian manifestations of divine blessing, sin, and redemption. And for the first time he produced in Middle-earth a hierarchical ranking of humankind. His Elves in *The Book of Lost Tales* displayed skin tones that embodied moral differentiation, but now the gods of Middle-earth gave his Númenórië inner racial essences that set them off from lesser wild Men. Tolkien believed in race; he had no apparent interest in raising a direct counter to Rosenberg's racially ranked Nordic Atlanteans. It is also evident that his Númenor narrative extended and complemented his long-standing interest in the Arctic Circle and the origins of both Aryans and Elves.

Tolkien tried to publish his thinking on cataclysm and myth; in November 1937 he submitted *The Lost Road* to his publisher.[39] They responded that the project would be of interest primarily to other academics, not to a popular audience. This criticism Tolkien seems to have taken to heart because he soon dropped his Atlantis tale and launched into a new project, a sequel to *The Hobbit*.

The next summer Tolkien wrote several letters that commented directly on Nazi Germany. A German publisher gave consideration to issuing *The Hobbit* and wrote to inquire about Tolkien's Aryan ancestry.[40] Describing a requested formal "certificate of 'arisch' [Aryan] origin" as an "impertinence" of "their lunatic laws" Tolkien wrote that he had "many Jewish friends, and should regret giving any colour to the notion that I subscribed to the wholly pernicious and unscientific race-doctrine." He enclosed to his publisher two responses, of which only one has survived.[41]

In this response – which was not sent to the German publisher – Tolkien took on the use of *arisch* as a racial term, countering it with a more limited linguistic usage, saying he was "not of *Aryan* extraction: that is Indo-iranian" with no ancestors who "spoke Hindustani, Persian, Gypsy, or any related dialects." He then touched on his own ancestry, "...I regret that I appear to have *no* ancestors of that gifted people." If German publishers continue down this road, said Tolkien, "then the time is not far distant when a German name will no longer be a source of pride."

This response reflected Tolkien's general awareness of Nazi "race-doctrine." Pondering this awareness, Christine Chism felt that Tolkien "questioned the work of created mythologies" during World War Two because "he had before him a... spectacle of world-creation gone wrong..."[42] Assuming he was aware of Rosenberg's book and its Nazi mythography, Chism wondered, "How could Tolkien disinfect his own mythologies, his own scholarship, which drew from the same materials as Rosenberg?" She cited nothing that Tolkien is explicitly known to have read on Nazi Germany, and Rosenberg was not alone in his Nordic Atlantis mythmaking, but his stature in Nazi literature and publishing gave him such a high profile that we can safely presume he was known to Tolkien by the early 1930s.

Dimitra Fimi believes Tolkien may have encountered a specific book on race that influenced his 1938 response to the German publisher.[43] In a 1935 publication by Julian Huxley and

Alfred Haddon titled *We Europeans: A Survey of 'Racial' Problems*, we find a fascinating discussion on the notion of an "Aryan race." They wrote that English and American scholars had by then dropped the phrase, but German writers had adopted it "to appear very flattering to local vanity..."[44]

They cited a philologist whose work Tolkien knew well. Friedrich Max Müller, said Huxley and Haddon, introduced "the unlucky term *Aryan*" in 1853 and spoke of "a corresponding 'Aryan race.'" But they noted that in 1888 Müller retracted the racial basis for the term, writing that "Aryas are those who speak Aryan languages, whatever their colour, whatever their blood." He now considered it a great sin to speak "of Aryan race, Aryan blood, Aryan eyes and hair..." Huxley and Haddon added their own denunciation of the racialization of the term, mentioning the phrase "Indo-Persian" – virtually the same term used by Tolkien in 1938, "Indo-iranian." Huxley and Haddon also disparaged the German legalism of establishing "a pedigree clear of 'non-Aryan' – i.e. Jewish – elements for several generations back."[45] All the significant elements in Tolkien's 1938 letter can be found in *We Europeans*. This tends to support Fimi's suggestion that Tolkien probably read the book.

It seems evident that the best explanation for the 1938 letter was that he had indeed read *We Europeans*. We can assume, at least, that he was not merely expressing his own view; he was also embracing what he took to be the new British academic status quo. The conventions of race had undergone a major recalibration with the publication of *We Europeans*. But analysis of Tolkien's use of race in *The Lord of the Rings* and other writings shows that he did not fully embrace this change in racial culture. This may have been due in some degree to the fact that he had never made race a major focus of his stories. But it is also likely that his sensibility in the 1938 letter was influenced less by the academic rejection of race as an idea, and more by his distaste for Rosenberg's hostility toward Christianity and the resulting Nazi fusion of myth, nationalism, and race.

If we assume that *We Europeans* was somewhat fresh on Tolkien's mind in March 1938, this would point to a possible explanation for a minor evolution of phrasing in his successive manuscripts of "The Fall of Númenor." The phrase "races of Men" appeared in the first versions of the story, dating (most broadly) to circa 1933-1937, but in a later revision which Christopher Tolkien dated to circa 1938-1942, "races of Men" became "kindreds of Men."[46] It is possible that this change reflected some awareness of the fundamental message of *We Europeans*. But it was more likely just a minor wording preference – one that left intact the race-like hierarchical ordering of humankind.

To summarize, we can glimpse Tolkien's likely use of the category of "Aryan" in his early formulation of Elves and Elvish history. And during the mid-1930s he responded to German Nordic logic with his invention of Númenóreans, promoting a Christianized alternative to the anti-Christian message advanced by Rosenberg. Tolkien also stayed on course with his quasi-racial hierarchy that set his Númenóreans at the human apex as "a great people" who were "more like the [Elves] than any other races of Men[.]" A few years later Tolkien changed "races" to "kindreds," but he retained intact his original idea of elevating his Númenóreans over lesser Men.

Other evidence supports the view that Tolkien showed little inclination to truly abandon the interpretive lens of race. In one 1961 letter he wrote that his Númenóreans "knew more about heredity than other people."[47] Through "the common symbol of blood" they understood that "in spite of intermarriages, some characteristics would appear in pure form in later generations." This was, of course, pseudo-history, a fantasy formulation. But this view contemplated a diminishing of pure "blood" through miscegenation, the very essence of racial thinking; that is, the diminishment of greater folk through intermarriage with lesser people. Tolkien's comment elucidated an assertion by Aragorn, "I am... of the race of the West unmingled." Denethor – as Tolkien reminded us next – came from a "much less well preserved house" and yet "had come out as almost purely Númenórean."

Huxley and Haddon have a chapter in *We Europeans* that seems potentially relevant to Tolkien's thinking on this point.[48]

They outline the doings of recessive and dominant genes, with a discussion about "a type" being "apparently 'pure'" and with an "intermediate type" that "is always 'impure.'" The chapter went on to consider "the offspring of a cross between a white man and a half-breed coloured woman" which could produce children who are "fair and almost black" as "a result of recombination." But when they applied these processes to race, they concluded that "it is, in the present state of knowledge, impossible to disentangle the genetic from the environmental factors in matters of 'racial traits,' 'national character,' and the like."

Unfortunately, this does not help Aragorn. If Huxley and Haddon played any role in shaping Tolkien's thinking about heredity and Aragorn's sudden racial purity, he did not read the book very closely. In the end, perhaps it is best to see Tolkien's choice in this matter as driven by a wish to have race work in Middle-earth in a way that it didn't work on Planet Earth. But this does not help the argument that Tolkien was anti-race. His thinking here stands in stark contrast to his 1938 declaration that he did not subscribe "to the wholly pernicious and unscientific race-doctrine."

As I described earlier, in the years just previous to his 1938 declaration rejecting race, Tolkien had the gods bestowing special "wisdom" upon the Númenóreans, and this led to shipbuilding and they "became mariners whose like shall never be again" – with other lesser men seeing them as gods. This was retained in its entirety in a second manuscript of the period. A third was prepared during World War Two and it also repeated the above descriptions. These formulations also appeared in the version of the story edited and issued by Christopher Tolkien in *The Silmarillion* (1977).

Rosenberg portrayed a "Nordic longing for distance to conquer" and "Atlantic men" who "moved by water in their swan and dragon ships" to the Mediterranean, Asia, and Africa. The Aryans evolved a "worldview which, for range and depth, cannot be surpassed by any philosophy even today." Huxley and Haddon addressed the idea of "Nordic genius" and "exploration" in the context of "the orthodox Nazi view" and they pointed out that the ancient Greeks viewed "the Nordic barbarians" as "wanting in intelligence and skill"; while one scholar showed that "hardly any of the great British explorers were fair-haired or of the Nordic type."

Given these perspectives, one would expect that if Tolkien truly embraced an anti-race worldview, the logic of his worldbuilding would sound more like Huxley and Haddon and less like Rosenberg. But this is not the case. Even though Tolkien plainly despised German Nordicism, the fact remains that his fantasy mythmaking sounds curiously Nordic.

To expect Tolkien's version of northernness to exist entirely divested of racial connotations would be unusual, given the fact that race sat at the center of the idea of Aryan and Nordic cultural constructions. Elly Truitt has noted that "ever since the 19th and early 20th centuries, the idea of 'Northernness' that is so central to white supremacy has become an inextricable element of our Fantasy North."[49] Tolkien's perspective on northernness deserves to be seen with more nuance than Truitt's generalization might imply. But any effort to divorce his fantasy north from the general racial context of "northernness" deserves skepticism and careful scrutiny.

Tolkien's hostility to Nordicism seems to have had less to do with rejecting racial hierarchical rankings and more to do with other objections. In terms of Rosenberg's treatment of race, Tolkien didn't really object to the inner essences of racial thinking, but instead found distasteful the total reliance on racial modeling that informed the entirety of the German Nordic worldview. To the degree that we can match his early Elves to notions of Aryan purity, we can see that Tolkien did not make this a major narrative point. It was instead a peripheral underlying matter that he took for granted. He surely found Rosenberg's constant racial centering not much to his own taste. His aesthetic displeasure was further fueled by Rosenberg's disrespect for Christianity and by the objectionable treatment of Jews in Nazi Germany.

By 1941 World War Two was in full swing. In March of that year Tolkien wrote again on the topic of German racial usages.[50] In a letter to son Michael, Tolkien said that throughout his adult life he had studied "Germanic matters" and during his undergraduate years was "much attracted" to the "'Germanic' ideal." He said he knew "better than most what is the truth about this 'Nordic' nonsense." And he now had "a burning private grudge... against that ruddy little ignoramus Adolf Hitler... Ruining, perverting, misapplying, and making for ever accursed, that noble northern spirit, a supreme contribution to Europe, which I have ever loved, and tried to present in its true light."

During that same period – the midst of World War Two – Tolkien had decided to transfer the dehumanizing ingredients of race to his orcs, giving their already horrible character an even more degraded demeanor. While so doing, he paused to write to his son Michael to speak of his resentment toward Hitler's perversion of the Northernness that he treasured. And yet his actual writings tend to indicate that he was not opposed to the basic idea of racial distinctions.

This 1941 letter showed that Tolkien greatly valued what he termed "the noble northern spirit" and in his mind this northern spirit flowed from the same wellspring of culture that gave rise to Nazi German Nordicism. Tolkien's complaint was not that the Nazis had manufactured an entirely false cultural construct, but instead, as he saw matters, they had distorted the "true light" of his treasured Northern essences.

In 1955 he enthused again about "the North-western temper and temperature."[51] He described this as an "inevitable... evolvement of the birth-given." And it encompassed "linguistic pattern" and "the passionate love of growing things" and "the deep response to legends..." And later in that letter he asserted that "linguistic taste" was "as good or better a test of ancestry as blood-groups."

This juxtapositioning of an esoteric "birth-given" quality of mind with "ancestry as blood-groups" echoed notions of racial cultural inheritance. Tolkien seemed to stir a hazy quality into the boundary between biology and preferences of culture. Rosenberg spoke of "the commands of the blood" summoning Nordic Europe to "the subtle welling up of the ancient sap of life and values." And he concluded: "Racial history is therefore simultaneously natural history and soul mystique." This was his prelude to his brief discussion of the Aryan North Pole and Atlantis. Both mythmakers saw culture as a kind of mystical ingredient in ancestral blood-community.

In 1937 George Orwell published an essay on "northern" consciousness in England.[52] Born in 1903, he recollected, "The histories I was given when I was a little boy generally started off by explaining in the naivest way that a cold climate made people energetic..." The English, he said, "evolved the pleasing theory that the further north you live the more virtuous you become." A Northerner was "a hefty, vigorous chap with blond moustaches and pure morals..." And describing this virtuous "Northerner" he mentioned several interchangeable terms: "Teutonic" and "Nordic." It is impossible to miss both the racial quality of English northernness and the resonance with Tolkien's sense of it.

Tolkien's conception of inner Northern character was rooted to a notable degree in the logic of race, drawing from the same sustaining essences as Nazi Nordicism. This was why he found so offensive the Nazi version of it. In his tales of Middle-earth he took an essentialist notion of race for granted, but it served as the unobtrusive physical human foundation for a more expansive aesthetic spectrum of attitude and culture. In contrast, the Nazi version elevated race into the central defining fetish.

We can assume that Tolkien's mention of "this 'Nordic' nonsense" could well have been another comment on Rosenberg's *The Myth of the Twentieth Century* – it is fair, at least, to read it as a denunciation of the Nazi version of "the 'Germanic' ideal" and "that noble northern spirit" – the mythmaking propounded by Rosenberg and Herman Wirth and other German intellectuals. Tolkien's final observation in the 1941 letter seemed to counter the belittling of the influence of Christianity that we find in both Rosenberg and Wirth: "Nowhere incidentally, was it nobler than in England, nor more early sanctified and Christianized..."

Preparing *The Lord of the Rings*, Tolkien said he had "not put in, or have cut out, practically all references to anything like 'religion'..."[53] But in various writings he made quite plain his deliberate intention to infuse Christian ideology into Númenor. In one 1954 letter he had Sauron introducing a "Satanist religion" among the Númenóreans, with the survival of "the Faithful" positioned "in a kind of Noachian situation[.]"[54] Tolkien did not simply retell the Greek story. He produced a Christianized myth. I believe he intended to counter Alfred Rosenberg's anti-Christian Nordic Atlantean history.

A few months after Tolkien's 1941 mention of "noble northern spirit," his friend CS Lewis spelled out his own ideas in early May 1941 in a recorded lecture titled "The Norse Spirit in English Literature." This was produced for the British Joint Broadcasting Committee – a project of the Secret Intelligence Service. As explained by Hal Poe, this recording was designed to appeal to shared cultural values between Iceland and Britain, aimed at cultivating goodwill from Icelanders recently under German rule.[55]

As Poe described it, Lewis spoke about his love of Norse mythology and study of Icelandic – one of the most poetic languages known to Lewis. He listed a number of British writers influenced by Norse literature. He mentioned the Norse suspicion of politicians, the Norse objection to governance by medieval kings, and the sense of independence shared by the Norse and the British – a spirit not found elsewhere in Europe. It is a value system of loyalty to a worthy leader, a relationship founded on honest character. Lewis labeled this philosophy "personal realism." We can imagine that this kind of talk regularly entered into discussions between Lewis and Tolkien.

I have touched on the aspect of "northernness" that pertained, in Tolkien's view, to courage in the face of defeat. But this cultural "northern" quality carried other nuances pertaining to moral and social formulations. Preparing lecture notes on *Beowulf* during the 1930s, Tolkien united barrow-wights, necromancy, and the Old English term *orcnéas* into a matrix expressing "that terrible northern imagination[.]"[56] This esoteric construction seemed to impart upon "northernness" a more fantastic frame of mind, a magnification of monstrosity. Tolkien gave thought to this hazy geography of fright throughout his life.

In a 1966 interview with Charlotte and Denis Plimmer, he mysteriously referred to spiders as "the particular terror of northern imaginations."[57]

Pondering a draft of the 1966 Plimmer interview, Tolkien wrote of his dislike for the word "Nordic" as associated "with racialist theories." Tolkien's Middle-earth was not strictly a "Northern" realm, he said, not "geographically or spiritually" – and it is roughly equivalent to Europe, which "is not a purely 'Nordic' area in any sense." And his affection for the "North-west of Europe" had nothing to do with any "sacred" quality of the place. In fact, the North, he said, "was the seat of the fortresses of the Devil."

Nordic nationalism took root in Germany and blossomed during the 1930s, and Tolkien came to feel a vast sense of dismay that grew over time. He saw his notion of "northern spirit" at risk, as something to defend – perhaps a hopeless defense, but a fateful struggle. By the 1960s it seems unlikely that he would have forgotten his engagement with the geographic North in his early version of Elvish history, in his Númenor – these usages went well beyond making the North "the seat of the fortresses of the Devil." But by then, the imagery of Nazi Germany had made Northernness a matter of disrepute, and Tolkien had no wish for his invented world to be seen in that light.

The 1966 Plimmer interview drew from Tolkien a comparative critique of Nordicism and Northernness, and it is not coincidental that this also got him thinking about both the icy North and his Atlantis tale. After denouncing the term "Nordic," he continued with his corrections, saying that his early effort to write about Atlantis sprang from his interest in writing "a new version of the Atlantis legend."

Tolkien didn't ever publish his Atlantis tale in full. A summary appeared in "Appendix A" of *The Return of the King* with scattered notes in other appendices. Christina Scull and Wayne Hammond have prepared a detailed survey of Tolkien's manuscripts on Númenor, showing that after his early version of the story was rejected by Allen & Unwin, he continued work on the story, cultivating it into a major Middle-earth narrative – "the only part of Tolkien's legendarium in which Men are the main... focus of attention."[58]

Scull and Hammond also present a commentary prepared by Christopher Tolkien on unfolding events in *The Lost Road*. They note, "The picture Tolkien draws of Númenor... almost certainly owes something to then-current events in Nazi Germany."[59] They mean to propose that Tolkien deliberately inserted a somewhat oblique reference to Nazi Germany in his description of Sauron's seduction of the Númenóreans. This was not carried forward into later versions of the story. But the tale kept intact its flavorings of race, its hierarchy of greater and lesser Men.

In general, this tale reflected his fascination with a succession of narrative themes implicitly related to Northernness. Early on, we find a notable equivalence between John Rhys's Aryan Arctic Circle and Tolkien's march of Aryan-like Elves into the Great Lands from the ice-kingdoms of the far north. This translated into further vistas during the 1930s. The German Nordic mythmaking of Alfred Rosenberg and others raised Tolkien's religious hackles, and it wasn't long before his storytelling confronted Nordic Germany, with Nazi Sauron acting in allegorical service to an evil Satan-like overlord. Tolkien spent the rest of his life tinkering with his Atlantean Númenor.

Tolkien wrote a note sometime around 1942 that may add some clarity to the nature of his project.[60] Observing that Britain has "an intricate complex history racially and culturally" he decried "false simplifications in the service of this or that theory." Not wanting to be mistaken for "a secret Nazi" who had "gone all Nordic" he wrote that he wished "to emphasize certain things which the bewildered and tragic nonsense talked in modern Germany has made suspect." Whatever it was that he had in mind, this point certainly seems applicable to his Atlantis project – to his love of Northernness and Christianity. As I argue, Tolkien's Númenor arose from the sea partly in response to Rosenberg, particularly in offering a counter-message of regard for a religious morality versus a total preoccupation for racial destiny.

He understood the academic challenge to race as a "wholly pernicious and unscientific" idea, and he had never given race major duties in his writings. But it is clear that he felt little interest in rethinking the cultural assumptions that sustained the concept of Northernness, including his Eurocentric concern with essentialist notions of nation and selfhood that also enliven racialism. If we attribute to Tolkien a personal rejection of race, we must explain why so much of it endured in Middle-earth. In the end, the uncomfortable fact remains that to a notable degree Tolkien's assumptions about the nature of humankind matched those that Rosenberg advanced.

Tolkien wrote to one correspondent in 1961 that he drew his tales of Númenor from "the Atlantis legend" due to "a special personal concern with this tradition of the culture-bearing men of the Sea, which so profoundly affected the imagination of peoples of Europe with westward-shores."[61] This "special personal concern" probably referred to a dream that Tolkien described in a 1955 letter to WH Auden.[62] Speculating that the dream was somehow inherited from his parents, he went on to describe it as a "terrible recurrent dream... of the Great Wave, towering up, and coming in ineluctably over the trees and green fields." This dream ceased after he set down "The Downfall of Númenor." And just months after he wrote to Auden, he wrote another note saying he had surrendered that dream to Faramir in *The Lord of the Rings*.[63]

Discussing Atlantis and Númenor, Tolkien never mentioned Alfred Rosenberg or any other German proponent of the Atlantean Nordic myth. He never overtly connected his Atlantis of the West to Rosenberg's polar Atlantis. But his mention of "the imagination of peoples of Europe" being "so profoundly affected" by "the Atlantis legend" would certainly pertain to the imagination of Nazi Germany.

Tolkien took his overwhelming dream and made it a matter of myth. He chose to wield his dream against an extreme form of mythmaking that he found distasteful and offensive – yet it was mythmaking that bore significant compatibilities with his own storytelling. His tale of Atlantis – as we know it in *The*

Silmarillion – is a beautifully written story that expanded the narrative depth of Middle-earth. But it was a story that he never finished retelling. Falling for the rest of his life into the churning chasms of a world that kept changing its assumptions about race and hierarchy and Christianity, JRR Tolkien at last suffered the Doom of Men.

The Taylorian Traditions

An interesting report appeared on the first page of the June 1908 issue of the quarterly journal of the British Folk-Lore Society: "Dr. A. C. Haddon gave a lantern lecture on 'The Morning Star Ceremony of the Pownee,' and in the discussion which followed Mr. Calderon, Mr. N. W. Thomas, and the Chairman took part."[64] By the light of a magic lantern, Haddon discussed his visit in September 1906 to an obscure town in the rolling American countryside. An anthropologist named George Dorsey took Haddon and several other colleagues to Pawnee, Oklahoma to witness an all-night performance of the Skidi Pawnee Morning Star ceremony. Haddon told the Folk-Lore Society that this experience was "one of the most interesting and instructive experiences of my lifetime."

It was not the first time he gave this talk. He had read the same paper before a meeting of the Cambridge Antiquarian Society in late May 1907.[65] These presentations are not much remembered today, but at the time Alfred Cort Haddon was a major figure in British anthropology. He served in 1902 and 1905 as the president of the anthropology section of the British Association for the Advancement of Science. And he had a general interest in Pawnee ceremonialism, publishing a review that touched on Alice Fletcher's 1904 volume, *The Hako: A Pawnee Ceremony*.[66]

Lecturing on the Skidi Pawnees, Haddon knew about a 1904 book published by Dorsey, *Traditions of the Skidi Pawnee*.[67] The typescript of his lecture does not reveal that he drew from the volume in any way, but it is clear that he relied heavily on the insights of George Dorsey and James R. Murie. Murie was a Skidi Pawnee who learned English in American boarding schools, and he worked extensively with various ethnographers, beginning with George Bird Grinnell in 1889. In the 1906 ceremony Murie served as one of five priests, and he "performed a beautiful pipe-smoking ceremony... in an impressive manner."

In 1908 Haddon was serving as a vice-president of the British Folk-Lore Society along with such notables as Andrew Lang, Alfred Nutt, John Rhys, EB Tylor, AH Sayce, and other leading lights of the British academic folklore establishment. Many of these men were likely on hand when Haddon lectured on Skidi Pawnee ceremonialism. Rhys described Haddon as a friend, crediting him in one book for certain ideas about fairies.[68] And it is notable that the ensuing discussion included Northcote Thomas. In 1905 Thomas published a review of *Traditions of the Skidi Pawnee*.[69] This period is unique in the history of British academia for the extent to which Pawnee mythology was a matter of interest and comment.

In its heyday the British Folk-Lore Society focused on the family and community traditions of the British Isles. But there was also a pronounced international dimension. In 1904 David Nutt and Company served as the official publisher of the Folk-Lore Society, and that firm issued Dorsey's *Traditions of the Skidi Pawnee*. The volume was immediately reviewed by Thomas in the journal of the Folk-Lore Society, which was also published by David Nutt. The Dorsey volume was deemed significant in part because it marked the resumption of the American folklore publication program. As Thomas noted, "After an interval of five years the American Folklore Society has again begun to issue its Memoirs..."

In 1906 George Dorsey and co-author James R. Murie published a second volume of Pawnee traditional literature, *The Pawnee: Mythology*. Since the book was not issued by any British publisher, it was probably not as readily available in England as *Traditions of the Skidi Pawnee*, which could be found in British bookstores and library collections. One point is clear. The 1905 review of the volume in *Folk-Lore: A Quarterly Review* and AC Haddon's various lectures helped to create awareness of the book in Britain, especially within British folklore circles.

This means that during the years of JRR Tolkien's youth, this volume of Skidi Pawnee mythology sat near at hand on British bookshelves. We know that Tolkien patronized local bookstores in this period – Christina Scull and Wayne Hammond have reported that in the fall of 1907 Tolkien began "to buy books secondhand" and in 1913 he discovered "secondhand book catalogues[.]"[70] Tolkien could have readily encountered a new or used copy of Dorsey's *Traditions of the Skidi Pawnee* during the years before he stepped onto the path to Middle-earth.

By the time Tolkien appeared at Oxford in 1911, it is impossible to measure British academic awareness of *Traditions of the Skidi Pawnee*. The heyday of its repute in Britain ultimately left few noticeable traces in academia and literature. But various leading figures in the Folk-Lore Society were professors at Oxford. Archibald Sayce and John Rhys were both likely to have attended Haddon's lecture in 1908, and both were likely to have glimpsed Thomas's review in 1905.

Tolkien's personal connections to Sayce and Rhys are tenuous, but he was close to Oxford professor William Craigie, Lecturer in the Scandinavian Languages at the Taylor Institution.[71] Beginning in April 1913 Craigie tutored Tolkien in Scandinavian Philology. During the late 1890s Craigie had been an active member of the Folk-Lore Society – he might well have attended Haddon's talk on the Skidi Pawnee in 1908, and he probably saw the review of *Traditions of the Skidi Pawnee* by NW Thomas. And Tolkien must have known of Craigie's interest in folklore since Craigie contributed a number of translations of Swedish and Danish folktales to Andrew Lang's *The Pink Fairy Book* (1897). Craigie arranged for Tolkien's first post-WW1 job at the *Oxford English Dictionary*.

It is obvious that during his years as a student at Oxford Tolkien had plenty of opportunity to encounter *Traditions of the Skidi Pawnee*. This point matters because it is difficult to explain another fact. Careful analysis of Tolkien's Middle-earth legendarium reveals that during his student days at Oxford he somehow became aware of Skidi traditional literature. And during the years that followed, he made ongoing use of that literature in his fictional writings. This was something he never discussed.

I don't know exactly when I first noticed something peculiar about the origin of Middle-earth. A strange perception took shape, slowly floating into focus. It didn't feel very real – I can't picture that moment with much clarity because the very oddness of it gave it an aura of complete chance coincidence.
It's this: Tolkien's "Ainulindalë: The Music of the Ainur" in *The Silmarillion* made me think of a Skidi Pawnee creation story that appeared in the pages of George Dorsey's *Traditions of the Skidi Pawnee*. Becoming a fan of Middle-earth in 1967, and then becoming a student of Pawnee traditional literature in 1979, I found it surprising that the creation stories of both legendariums involved singing.
For many years I gave little further thought to this insight. In graduate school, studying creation stories worldwide, I realized that the idea of singing the cosmos into existence was not a common theme. I wondered what it might mean, but it just seemed improbable that Tolkien would have known anything about the Skidi story. There seemed little point in giving this curious coincidence any serious attention.
One day many years later I decided to look into the matter more closely. Still assuming the impossibility of any connection, in 2012 I skimmed Tolkien's original creation story and the Skidi narrative. I felt troubled. I found more to ponder than I had expected. Finally, in early 2013 I sat down to settle the matter.
The stories had many obvious differences, with Tolkien's tale focused on the original sowing of discord in the celestial community, and with the Skidi story focused on the making of community in the celestial world and the human world. But to my surprise, clear correspondences slowly emerged. As parallels accumulated, I realized something interesting. Despite the similarities in the stories, it still didn't feel rational to think that Tolkien had ever encountered the Skidi story. And if he had somehow seen the book somewhere, it was surely unlikely that he

would have had any reason to give it even a moment of serious thought.

Thinking back over my life, Middle-earth and Pawneeland occupied entirely different realms in my inner world. They had no reason to overlap in any meaningful way. But one thing I knew for certain. The Skidi story had first appeared in the wide world when Tolkien was on the verge of becoming a teenager. And it could be found in certain libraries and bookstores all through his youth and through his early adulthood and through all the years that followed.

The tales of Pawneeland may seem remote from the shores of British mythology and folklore. But this is an illusion. As I discuss in detail in this book, Tolkien grew up with an appreciation of fairy stories and he entered his youth with an awareness of British folklore as a field of literature. This also means he had both reason and opportunity to give thought to what he called "Red Indians" and their folk traditions. His familiarity with the cultural agenda of British folkloric studies and his personal interest in the tales of "Red Indians" must have predisposed him toward curiosity when he first encountered *Traditions of the Skidi Pawnee*.

Preparing in 1943 an extended version of his essay "On Fairy-stories," Tolkien reminisced about his childhood experience of reading fairytales and the works of Andrew Lang. After dismissing *Alice in Wonderland* and *Treasure Island*, he recalled, "Red Indians were better: there were bows and arrows (I had and have a wholly unsatisfied desire to shoot well with a bow), and strange languages, and glimpses of an archaic mode of life, and, above all, forests in such stories."[72] Since Red Indians were not a major focus of Lang's fairytale collections, Tolkien must have sought Red Indians in other readings during the years of his youth.

Tolkien's acknowledged encounters with what he termed "Red Indians" are sparse and general; his writings contain only a few explicit references to racial Indians. One can be found in notes dating to his research for his essay "On Fairy-stories."[73]

Sometime between 1938 and 1943 Tolkien consulted Andrew Lang's 1894 *The Yellow Fairy Book* and he notated one story: "Red Indian."

What this note signified is unclear. It does reflect Tolkien's awareness of "Red Indian" storytelling as a part of Lang's legacy, but perhaps it also indicated his familiarity with Lang's "Preface" to *The Yellow Fairy Book*. This preface is interesting because it connected the British Folk-Lore Society and Red Indians several times. Given the likelihood that Tolkien read *The Yellow Fairy Book* in his youth, he must have taken into his early adulthood some awareness of the British Folk-Lore Society, as well as a sense that the tales of Red Indians were of interest to folklorists.

The spark that most directly lit Tolkien's imagination and set his feet firmly on fantasy paths came in 1910. Tolkien's official biography tells us that in April 1910 Tolkien attended a production of JN Barrie's *Peter Pan* – a play that featured a fairy, pirates, and "Red Indians."[74] Tolkien felt moved to note in his diary, "Indescribable but shall never forget it as long as I live." Just a few months later he wrote "Wood-sunshine," a poem that mentioned "ye light fairy things" and "Sprites of the wood[.]"[75] This was his first known piece of writing about fairies.

With his imagination ignited by *Peter Pan*, we can guess that all through the late spring and summer of 1910 Tolkien's visits to bookshops might have included some interest in books on Red Indians. Tolkien's later expertise in philology, Old English, and Norse literature arose from his prior interest in fairytales and folklore and mythological traditions, and it is reasonable to assume that at circa 1910 Tolkien would have had at least an incipient interest in global mythologies. Tolkien source scholarship has clearly established one fact. His creative process of inventing Middle-earth would soon enough become rooted in diverse literary soils.

The earliest explicit evidence of Tolkien's interest in "Red Indians" in his own writings came as early as 1914. In an essay prepared in late 1914 and early 1915, Tolkien pondered the use of the Finnish *Kalevala* by Henry Wadsworth Longfellow in his poem

The Song of Hiawatha.[76] Studying this commentary, John Garth has identified similarities of names, plot, and circumstance between Longfellow's poem and a story that Tolkien began to write in 1914 and never finished.[77] This interest in America was underscored in that same 1914-1915 essay by mention of "Vinland the good," the Norse name for a region in North America.[78]

During the same period another reference to Vinland can be identified in a set of undated notes pertaining to a character he named Eärendel.[79] As I describe later in this book, Tolkien's notes sent Eärendel on a voyage to a realm that is best interpreted as Vinland, and there the mariner became enmeshed in the webs of a spider named Night. This was the origin of Ungoliant.

In my original edition of *Tolkien in Pawneeland* (December 2013), I described parallels between a Skidi Pawnee story and Tolkien's circa 1919 tale of Ungoliont. But I overlooked the Eärendel note. The note preserves an abandoned link between Vinland / America and Tolkien's initial conception of a spider monster – a creature that would soon enter *The Book of Lost Tales* as Ungoliont.

We have no clue from Tolkien himself as to why he would look to America for the makings of a monstrous spider. Spider divinities can be found in mythological storytelling across North America, but these are tricksters or beneficent deities, not creatures of dark intent, and I have seen no evidence that Tolkien had any substantive familiarity with North American traditional literatures. In Pawneeland, however, we find a monstrous version of such a deity. Making the suggestion that Tolkien found a model for Night the Spider in Pawneeland necessarily means that in 1914 Tolkien had already begun to make use of *Traditions of the Skidi Pawnee*.

As early as the end of 1916 Tolkien launched into the stories that eventually comprised his first book-length prose manuscript, *The Book of Lost Tales* – the original incarnation of his Middle-earth legendarium.[80] His first detailed use of Pawnee myth came when he sat down to write his creation story, "The Music of the Ainur," sometime during the first half of 1919.[81] Focused on his new mission as a mythmaker, it is safe to assume that he would have had a lively appreciation for world mythology during this period. In my 2013 edition of *Tolkien in Pawneeland* I argued that JRR Tolkien consulted a variety of Skidi Pawnee texts in the course of authoring his Middle-earth legendarium. Inspired by Pawnee mythological greenery, he colorized Middle-earth with what he thought of as an authentic aura of "primitive undergrowth."

Comparison of unique and substantive textual material has convinced me that Tolkien made use of *Traditions of the Skidi Pawnee* in the course of envisioning Night the Spider (circa 1914), and in writing *The Book of Lost Tales* (in early 1919), *The Hobbit* (in 1930-1932), and *The Lord of the Rings* (in 1938 and 1942). And in the original version of *Tolkien in Pawneeland* I put forth the view (p. 140-165) that Tolkien had reasons for deliberately keeping secret his use of obscure Skidi tradition.

Tolkien's interest in Pawnee myth was sporadic, but he had life-long access to a copy of the book. The evidence for this insight is circumstantial, based on the identification of shared textual elements rather than any information confirming that he consulted any specific copy of *Traditions of the Skidi Pawnee* over the years. I have seen no evidence that Tolkien or any member of his family owned a copy of the book; I have no basis for supposing that a friend had a convenient copy. Moreover, I do not have a clear idea as to the general availability of the book in England during the early 20th century. It does seem safe to presume that the book was available from various British booksellers and libraries even if it was not widely distributed.

To make use of *Traditions of the Skidi Pawnee* as source-material, it was not necessary for Tolkien to own a copy of the book. About 1905 an excellent candidate for the precise volume that he likely consulted found its way into the collections of Oxford University.

One day in early 2013 I found an online listing in the collections of the Oxford University libraries for *Traditions of the Skidi Pawnee*, but with no indication of its date of acquisition. That July I gave a paper on my initial findings at the annual conference of the Mythopoeic Society – one audience member introduced me to Tolkien scholar Verlyn Flieger. She felt curious about my work, and in August 2013 she traveled to London and tracked down *Traditions of the Skidi Pawnee* in the collections of the Taylor Institution Library at Oxford University.[82] Flieger confirmed that the book was acquired by the library in 1904, the year of its publication. This was well before Tolkien's tenure as a student (beginning in 1911), as a researcher for the Oxford dictionary (1919-1920), and as a professor (beginning in late 1925).

Christina Scull and Wayne Hammond's authoritative *The JRR Tolkien Companion and Guide: Reader's Guide* (2006, p. 709) described the Taylorian as "the centre for the study of modern European languages and literatures at Oxford." I do not know why a book on Pawnee tradition ended up in this library collection at Oxford. Perhaps this had to do with the fact that certain narratives in the volume contain passages written in Latin. But one thing is clear. The presence of *Traditions of the Skidi Pawnee* on the shelves of the Taylorian made it an excellent candidate to have been the copy that Tolkien consulted over the years. This possibility finds support in the chronology of Tolkien's association with the Taylorian and the appearance of Pawnee elements in his writings.

In 1911 Tolkien enrolled at Oxford University in Classical studies – he studied Latin and further developed his interest in mythology.[83] That fall he "attended lectures at the Taylor Institution" every Tuesday and Thursday, and thereafter on frequent occasions through 1914 he could be found at the Taylorian.[84] One area of particular focus for Tolkien during this period was "Medieval and Modern European Languages."[85] This means that he not only took classes at the Taylorian, he also had good reason to spend time researching the collections of that library. Beginning in April 1913 Tolkien could be found regularly at the Taylorian where he was tutored by William Craigie – Craigie had been active in the Folk-Lore Society during the late 1890s.[86]

Corresponding with the Taylorian staff in 2013 I learned their files contain no evidence that Tolkien ever borrowed their copy of *Traditions of the Skidi Pawnee*.[87] And their fragmentary records do not show that he ever checked out any book from their library. If this is actually the case, we should surmise that during his student days he spent considerable time at the Taylorian consulting the collections, roaming among the shelves, selecting materials to study, and preparing notes. As he wrote in an October 1914 letter, "I have got to go to the library now and get filthy amongst dusty books[.]"[88] It was in 1914 that the earliest arguable evident influence from Skidi stories appeared in Tolkien's writing.

In January 1919, with the help of William Craigie, Tolkien returned to Oxford to begin a new job for the *Oxford English Dictionary* researching words beginning with "w."[89] This means he had access to the Oxford University libraries, and he must have made use of them for this research. His knowledge of the Taylorian collections must have helped. By 1919 he had already spent a few years working on early versions of several of his mythological tales. Visiting the familiar collections of the Taylorian to do his *OED* research, he now had a special motive as a budding mythmaker to peruse *Traditions of the Skidi Pawnee*. Picking it up and skimming through it in early 1919, he found inspiration for his creation story and he developed his ideas for Ungoliant.

After 1925 Tolkien could be found once again at Oxford, this time as a professor. In May and June of 1930 he lectured on "Germanic Numerals" – it would have logical for him to visit the Taylorian at some point to look for language materials to help prepare his lecture notes.[90] Recalling the usefulness of *Traditions of the Skidi Pawnee* in 1919, Tolkien revisited the volume at some point. Again he found it helpful. He drew from three Skidi "Animal Tales" to envision four episodes that appear in a poem that was in existence by 1931, "The Adventures of Tom Bombadil." This experience also shaped various details of his new project, *The Hobbit*.

Beginning in January 1932 Tolkien's schedule included two lectures held every Tuesday and Friday at the Taylor Institution.[91] Sometime in the course of 1932 he paused once more to open the pages of *Traditions of the Skidi Pawnee*. He had taken a long break from writing *The Hobbit*, and perhaps he sought inspiration of the same sort that had helped him on two previous occasions already. Now he encountered a Pawnee story that helped him to chart a course into the story of Beorn the shapeshifter and into the story of spider-infested Mirkwood.

Tolkien next consulted *Traditions of the Skidi Pawnee* during the late summer of 1938. In May of that year he received an appointment to serve as "an elector to the Taylorian Professorship of German Language and literature."[92] He would have had reason to stop by the library on occasion during the months that followed. Now hard at work on *The Lord of the Rings*, one day he decided to consult *Traditions of the Skidi Pawnee* for help in situating Tom Bombadil in Middle-earth – he looked once more at one of the tales that had inspired his poem about Bombadil in 1931. This took him deep into the darkest recesses of "The Old Forest."

Beginning in early January of 1942 – and from late April to late June – Tolkien's lectures brought him to the Taylorian every Tuesday and Thursday.[93] It was then that he made his final foray into *Traditions of the Skidi Pawnee*. He encountered a story that helped to shape his account of the death and resurrection of Gandalf in "The White Rider."

Non-trivial parallel textual elements are shared by Tolkien's legendarium and the Skidi Pawnee stories. A theory of chance independent invention is highly unlikely. While no direct evidence has come forward to show that Tolkien opened any specific copy of *Traditions of the Skidi Pawnee*, he had ample opportunity to examine the Taylorian copy at his leisure throughout the course of his academic life at Oxford University. The established chronology of Tolkien's known associations with the Taylorian contains meaningful overlap with the chronology of his evident use of *Traditions of the Skidi Pawnee*.

As an academician Tolkien had access to global mythological literature, and at Oxford he had access to *Traditions of the Skidi Pawnee*. But the world of Tolkien studies has paid scant attention to this fact. In the extensive literature of Tolkien source scholarship that has emerged since his death, Tolkien came to be treated as a comfortably parochial author who knew next to nothing about world mythological traditions.

The David Nutt publishing house and the British Folk-Lore Society imported Skidi Pawnee mythology to Britain, and Tolkien the mythologist took notice. While it is certainly surprising to learn that he secretly drew on Skidi Pawnee traditions to colorize the mythological textures of Middle-earth, it should not be surprising to anyone that he would feel curiosity about the wide world beyond mythic Europe. Tolkien treated all his source-material in accordance with creative strategies that he adopted early in his career as a writer. He took in hand diverse mythological threads and he wove them together to invent his own vision of a legendary past, his tales of Middle-earth.

Exploring this mysterious dimension of JRR Tolkien's legacy as a novelist, in 2013 I issued the original version of *Tolkien in Pawneeland*. I argued that the shaping of his tales of Middle-earth owed a debt to North American myth – comparison of textual elements revealed a surprising spectrum of details with parallels in Skidi Pawnee traditions, consisting of both weak echoes and well-defined resonations too strong to easily dismiss. This research wasn't a comfortable path to follow. I couldn't imagine why Tolkien would have any reason to spend time thinking about Pawnee tradition. I also knew that the idea would rightly be met with a lot of skepticism in the world of Tolkien fandom and scholarship – a world that holds a settled view of Tolkien as a Eurocentric medievalist who knew almost nothing about the rest of the planet.

Pursuing this research, a further question soon arose. Why did Tolkien keep silent about the Pawnee narratives that he found interesting? It is necessarily a speculative enterprise to probe Tolkien's reasons for drawing from Pawnee traditions and then declining to disclose this use. It is important to raise the matter because questions and establishing processes of inquiry can be just as useful as answers, particularly when dealing with a cultural icon with the stature of JRR Tolkien.

As a mythmaker, it is evident that Tolkien appreciated mythological literature in part for its antiquarian tones. It seems logical enough to presume that he made use of Pawnee myth because he wished to texture his mythological narratives with a sense of primitive antiquity. And given his agenda of appealing to English and European sensibilities, it is also logical that he must have seen his literary mission as incompatible with his use of North American mythology – the logic of his Eurocentric mythological agenda did not permit him to acknowledge his use of Pawnee literature. This is what I concluded in my first edition of *Tolkien in Pawneeland*.

The next year after I published *Tolkien in Pawneeland*, John Garth published a paper that identified a set of connections between Tolkien's legendarium and Henry Wadsworth Longfellow's *The Song of Hiawatha*.[94] Garth argued that Tolkien made repeated use of Longfellow's poem over a long period. This pattern began with a seminal 1914 project and culminated in the early 1930s with the making of the death of Smaug in *The Hobbit* – inspirations from Longfellow may also help to account for a few details in later Tolkien writings.

As with the Pawnee connections, Tolkien never made any mention of Longfellow as an inspiration for *The Hobbit*, though he often touched on the source-materials that inspired him. Garth made no inquiry into this fact. But one thing is clear. When Tolkien spoke of the literatures that helped to give rise to Middle-earth, he consistently said nothing of his interest in North American myth.

Tolkien's youthful fascination with North American racial Indians – "Red Indians" as he termed them – is well-known. Pondering this interest, Tom Shippey casually speculated about the possible influence of James Fenimore Cooper on certain scenes in *The Lord of the Rings*.[95] But to my knowledge, prior to *Tolkien in Pawneeland* no detailed studies argued for any American mythological inspirations for Middle-earth. Now it is evident that Tolkien did give thought to North America in the course of his mythmaking. It is also clear that he chose to say nothing about such inspirations.

Why did he make this choice to say so little about North American influences? Investigation of this question brought me to preparation of this new edition of *Tolkien in Pawneeland*. I have expanded the focus beyond Pawneeland to include a broader survey of matters that Tolkien kept to himself. The project of peering under the surfaces of Middle-earth is useful not just to reveal secrets, but because we can observe Tolkien's creative processes, the making of the hidden world beneath the visible world of Middle-earth. Plenty of other good books on Tolkien explore the visible geography of Middle-earth, but this book strays from the familiar paths of traditional Eurocentric Tolkien studies to explore the twilight of things dimly glimpsed.

In this present book I explore instances where Tolkien implemented a pattern of derivative invention and source-secrecy. Although he often enough pointed out his literary influences, he didn't always feel inclined to explain either the processes of his mythmaking or the actual spectrum of the materials he mined. Launching into the production of his legendarium, JRR Tolkien intended for his mythological storytelling to express a sense of English national identity and to embody the cultural values of what he termed "Northernness." To produce these dimensions of meaning, he deliberately wove elements of his magic from existing tradition and literature.

Examples of this creative process appear early in his writings. John Garth has shown how Tolkien composed a seminal poem in 1914 by weaving together material from an Anglo-Saxon poem and from a poem by Percy Bysshe Shelley.[96] Garth rightly concluded that this observation matters in understanding Tolkien's legendarium since the "exploration of intertextual relations... follows naturally and logically" from Tolkien's own admissions about influences, and from the textual evolution of Tolkien's manuscripts as they flowed into each other. Garth asserted that his research served to "counter an all-too-easy acceptance of the idea (sometimes promoted by Tolkien himself) that his creations are an alloy of nothing but native genius and professional medieval expertise."

The next year in 1915, writing a poem about the Man in the Moon, Tolkien drew inspiration from British folklore and from a poem of the late 1830s.[97] We glimpse diverse sources behind the veil of these verses as Tolkien wove together "silver shoon," "St. Peter," "Norwich," and other elements into his own vision of the Man in the Moon. Mark Atherton has referenced Tom Shippey's explanation of "Mon in the Mone" and has suggested that Tolkien recycled "shoon" from a friend's poem.[98] But the "silver shoon" in first line of the poem can be found in a 1913 poem about the moon by Walter de la Mare: "Silver," in *Peacock Pie*. It is arguable that Tolkien read the de la Mare poem and decided he had a better use for "silver shoon." He could have drawn on numerous examples of British folkloric verses about the Man in the Moon – one such example occurs in an obscure volume known as *The Denham Tracts* – a publication which I will consider in more detail in relation to hobbits.[99] The creative process that gave rise to Tolkien's 1915 Man in the Moon poem produced a result that he liked enough to publish several times.

Launching his career as a writer, Tolkien learned early the art of weaving together threads from diverse materials, and this served as a major authorial procedure throughout his life. Remarking much later on his Rohirrim, Tolkien offered a comment that reflected a primary process of invention for him throughout his authorship: "I must profess that I have never attempted to 're-create' anything. My aim has been the basically more modest, and certainly the more laborious one of trying to make something new."[100] This may explain some of his reluctance to cite inspirational materials. He did not necessarily wish to be held too closely to the sources, to be compared, to be deemed a borrower rather than a laborious maker of new things.

He openly pointed out some of the sources for his first major creative publication, *The Hobbit* (1937). As we will soon see, it is evident that he started with an empty Welsh term, "hobbit," and a vaguely described English traditional concept – a "hob hole." Launching into the first chapter of the book, he filled these three words with meaning drawn from Old English literature, Norse mythology, and his own rich imagination.

In the course of writing *The Lord of the Rings* Tolkien again revisited Pawnee tradition. Despite the long period of his use of *Traditions of the Skidi Pawnee*, he had no interest in cultivating any deep knowledge about Pawnee history and culture. But he no doubt viewed the Pawnee people through the lens of race, seeing them as Red Indians, members of the Mongolic category. In the late 1930s he now gave this particular racial category special attention. Inspired by the traditions of British folklore, he decided to colorize his orcs, recasting them into what he called "Mongol-types." The late 1930s and early 1940s seems to have been the period when he gave most thought to matters of race. It was then that he inserted the real world ideology of race into Middle-earth.

Tolkien had a lifetime of opportunity to shed light on his literary inspirations. He occasionally made mention of such material, but he did not very often feel inclined to go into detail, and he deliberately kept certain matters secret. Source scholarship has focused almost exclusively on Tolkien's erudition in European literatures. In recent years, however, it has slowly become clear that he drew occasional inspiration from literature worldwide.

What does it mean that Tolkien made use of global myth to colorize his own creative vision? This is an important question for all who idealize the imagination as a culturally inclusive realm of mind and heart. Following Tolkien's immense influence, fantasy literature in the late 20th century took on the trappings of medieval Europe and became distinguished from science fiction through a comparative list of traits that focused on castles rather than spaceships, wizards rather than pilot-engineers, swords rather than laser pistols.

Chosing to keep secret his use of details from Pawnee myth, this strategy ultimately had the long-term effect of narrowing fantasy possibilities. Under his spell, fantasy tales became a 20th century genre that focused on medieval Eurocentric fairytales and not the Coyote tales of Pawneeland. Understanding now what happened, we must necessarily ponder the degree to which Tolkien's project should be read as a form of surreptitious exploitation that Europeanized the boundaries of the imagined universe.

If we make this leap, we can move beyond questions of cultural exploitation. A next step suddenly comes into view – an expansion of the horizons of our appreciation of fantasy. This is an inevitable consequence of divining Tom Bombadil's roots in the figure of Coyote, of glimpsing the Pawnee iteration of Spider Woman behind the veil of Ungoliant. The mythic world deserves to always bloom with unexpected possibility, unpredictable imaginings. We enrich our sense of self when our wandering becomes global. And when we glimpse a diversity of imaginal paths unfolding at our feet, we gain a kind of perspective that just naturally redefines our horizons.

This kind of magic is what Tolkien ultimately rejected.

In his early career as a writer and scholar JRR Tolkien aspired to produce from northern European traditions a coherent legendarium reflecting the mythic antiquity of England. Glimpsing frayed remnants of vanished worlds in ancient texts, he found he enjoyed weaving aspects of his personal life together with threads of literature and language into tales that pleased his sense of artistry and scholarship. For this reason, the sifting of Tolkien's source material usefully reveals the subtle scholar behind the renowned storyteller. We become explorers when we enter Middle-earth.

It is possible to study Tolkien's creative process as a matter of convenience due primarily to the labors of his son Christopher Tolkien, who has published extensive manuscript material. Those who feel curious can peer over JRR's shoulder to observe him at work, setting down his tales. And we can glimpse the weaving of obscure things that came to his hand in the making of his Middle-earth legacy. To study this process is to sense a subtle creativity, an engagement with the meanings of myth, a vast knowledge of word and language and literature, a careful structuring of artistry... and it is to examine the social meanings of the inner secrets of Tolkien's poetic magic. Making sophisticated use of Northern European traditions and literature in his writings, he surrounded himself with the archaic intellectual furnishings of Europe. And he had little apparent reason to visit other shores for inspiration.

Pondering Tolkien's legendarium one day in 2012, I found myself moving to the surprising conclusion that Tolkien deliberately hid an entire hemisphere inside his tales of Middle-earth. Setting my feet upon an almost invisible path, I slowly discovered a realm woven from spider silk, created from song, lit by lightning – a mysterious continent "whither few mariners of Men have ever come[.]" For Tolkien to do such a thing, and for no one to have noticed, is an interesting feat of literary legerdemain.

As the roots of his legendarium took shape in his first fantasy poems, Tolkien toyed with the idea of accounting for the existence of the world beyond Europe. This inclination never moved very far beyond the borrowing of assorted details – carefully selected details that helped to establish a specific cultural tone for his legendry. But in the end Tolkien lost interest in any inclination he had to bring the wider world more explicitly into Middle-earth. Instead, he set a hazy hidden continent within his legendarium – wafting vague hints of a shadowy realm into his mythmaking. And this secret endured through the growth of an extensive literature of scholarship inquiring into his source material.

Unveiling the existence of this mysterious world, we explore certain meanings of the mythology of Middle-earth that have never been openly disclosed. As we will discover, Tolkien visited this secret world not only to seek ways to enhance his creative vision, but his most mystical aspirations also gained definition from the contribution of this hidden realm to his legendarium.

In the Land of Magic

As a young writer JRR Tolkien wandered along a path that took him deep into fairy enchantment and mythological antiquity. Delving into literature of various kinds, he took note of elements he liked, and he taught himself how to weave together these borrowed moments into new tapestries of tales. This was the process that inspired his first fairytale monster, a deadly spider.

Tolkien told of being bitten by a tarantula during his childhood; and several family stories touch on incidents involving spiders.[101] Pondering Tolkien's fictional spiders, John Rateliff drew an interesting conclusion: "...Tolkien's spiders are his own creation, not quite like anything else in fantasy literature before or since."[102] He favored the possibility that Tolkien may have been influenced by two spiders that appeared in the fantasy tales of Lord Dunsany. Other potential inspirations could be found in fantasy literature in Britain and America, such as the giant spider that dwelt in a forest in *The Wonderful Wizard of Oz* (1900), slain by the Lion.[103] Rateliff's view was that Tolkien's monstrous spiders were modeled on actual arachnids – one spider that gets mentioned is the tarantula. But Rateliff's summary of Tolkien's spider monsters is notable for the absence of any explicit consideration of the first incarnation of the monster that later became Ungoliant.[104]

Tolkien's personal experiences and Dunsany's fantasy spiders no doubt have some relevance to the spiders that came to infest Middle-earth, but Tolkien connected his original conception of a monstrous spider to America. A direct inspiration can be identified in Skidi Pawnee tradition.

In an undated set of notes, the earliest incarnation of Tolkien's Ungoliant hailed from a realm that can be readily interpreted as a fantasy version of Vinland. Christopher Tolkien found an "isolated page" associated with a 1914 poem – the page outlined the original voyages of Eärendel.[105] The 1914 date is significant because John Garth has suggested that Tolkien's "The Story of Kullervo," written in the fall of 1914, borrowed names and plot details from Henry Wadworth Longfellow's *The Song of Hiawatha*.[106] This adds evidence that in 1914 Tolkien had North American racial Indians on his mind.

The Eärendel note sketched an epic sea adventure. Journeying past Iceland and beyond Greenland, Eärendel arrived at "the wild islands" where a rogue wave carried him farther west. Tolkien set here a mysterious note: "Land of strange men, land of magic." This was the "home of Night. The Spider." This spider had no other identifying features, but the association with night evoked the gloom that Tolkien later associated with Ungoliont. The story continued with Eärendel's escape "from the meshes of Night with a few comrades." We can surmise that Tolkien planned for Night the Spider to be some kind of monster.

It is impossible to know with any precision what Tolkien meant by "[l]and of strange men, land of magic." No further development of these men or this region appeared in his notes.[107] But a similar description can be found in an essay Tolkien wrote during this period, "On 'The Kalevala' or Land of Heroes," prepared in in late 1914. Writing here about the "amazing new excitement" of discovering the *Kalevala*, Tolkien drew an interesting comparison: "You feel like Columbus on a new Continent or Thorfinn in Vinland the Good."[108] Just a few sentences later he remarked on an "almost indefinable sense of newness and strangeness" and then he turned to the "natives" who he termed "strange people" with "new gods."

In this period "strange people" and a land of "strange men" both materialized in Tolkien's imagination in conjunction with mention of the *Kalevala* and the New World and Vinland in one instance, and in the second instance with mention of a mysterious "land of magic" located beyond Iceland and Greenland. Night the Spider had no substance at this early date. But the 1914 note had Eärendel escaping from Night into further

49

adventures and then departing from earth by sailing "west again to the lip of the world... He sets sail upon the sky..."

Tolkien's wrote his first poem about his mythical hero Eärendel in September 1914; it began with Éarendel springing up "From the door of Night..." and speeding "from Westerland."[109] This poem thus articulated Tolkien's original idea to have his hero visit a Vinland-like realm. And we also see that Tolkien's earliest notions of heroic departures into the unknown west were in fact rooted in his early experiment with imagining Vinland as a "land of magic." The possibility that "door of Night" referred to Night the Spider cannot be ruled out, given the coinciding time of creation for both the Eärendel poem and Eärendel's escape from Night.

Tolkien eventually became disenchanted with the idea of sending Eärendel to Vinland. Writing sometime around 1919-1921, he complained of "the unfortunate existence of America on the other side of a strictly limited Atlantic ocean" and "there are no magic islands in our Western sea[.]"[110] It was in 1919-1920 that he dropped the idea of situating a "new god" – his new spider monster – beyond the "wild islands" in a "land of magic[.]" Instead, he proceeded with storytelling about a divine spider monster "whom even the Valar know not whence... she came[.]"

Ever after, Tolkien had little to say about America. He briefly toyed with sending Númenórean aircraft to America. But this project went nowhere, and nothing explicitly attributed to America ever made it into his Middle-earth publications – with the exception of random vegetables and vegetation, transplanted without any explanation.

Night the Spider was a direct early experiment with America, a visit to Vinland. Beyond the circa 1914 note, Tolkien's explicit interest in Vinland / America has some sparse contemporary documentation. His 1914 essay on the *Kalevala* with his "amazing new excitement" at the sense of being "in a new world" seems to conflate Finland and Vinland into a revelation that it might be "rather jolly to live with this strange people and these new gods awhile[.]" This comparative alignment of the inner essence of the *Kalevala* with the inner essence of Vinland sheds an interesting light on what Tolkien made of myth.

In this early manuscript Tolkien wrote of the *Kalevala*: "We have here then a collection of mythological ballads full of that very primitive undergrowth that the litterature of Europe has on the whole been cutting away and reducing for centuries with different and earlier completeness in different peoples."[111] In a later typescript (circa 1919-1921) Tolkien added to this sentiment his own yearning for this lost mythic texturing: "...I am content to turn over the pages of these mythological ballads – full of that very primitive undergrowth that the literature of Europe has on the whole been steadily cutting away and reducing for many centuries with different and earlier completeness among different people[.] I would that we had more of it left – something of the same sort that belonged to the English..."[112]

This tells us that in the early evolution of his scholarly and literary agenda, Tolkien cultivated an interest in what he termed "primitive" mythology. He imbued this term with a particular character that he found absent from English culture, and this process shaped his formative agenda not only as a scholar but as a storyteller. Tolkien saw value in myth. But he felt particularly drawn to his notion of "primitive undergrowth."

If Finnish tradition and Norse sagas could display the kind of mythic underbrush that Tolkien treasured and deemed rare in England, we can surmise that such greenery worldwide held the same general connotations for him. He had no interest in the comparative ethnography of world traditions, mentioning in a dismissive tone the comparison of the *Kalevala* with Hausa and Andaman Island myth. He announced that he "wouldn't for the present move outside Europe" because the "uncivilized and primitive" tone of the *Kalevala* "belong essentially to Northern Europe" and he would much prefer to "emphasize that[.]"[113] But during that same period he was making plans to experiment with American mythological materials.

Tolkien left few details about Night the Spider, and yet it is arguable that when he created this monster in 1914 he was inspired by a Skidi Pawnee narrative called "The Death of Spider-

Woman."[114] The story portrayed Spider Woman as a murderous old Witch Woman who "had power from some mysterious animal in the earth." She had the habit of slipping poison into the food she served to guests and then decapitating and dismembering the bodies, removing the head to "take out the brains" and "cut the ears off..." And when people became aware of her gruesome manners, they stopped visiting her, so she "made her way to the villages and captured many and took them home." The celestial deity Tirawa took pity on the people and he "commanded the Sun and Moon to send their two boys to the village, saying that he wanted the Sun and Moon to help the people by destroying this Spider-Woman[.]" The celestial hero-boys descended to earth and embarked on a series of adventures involving snakes, mountain lions, and bears. Then they visited Spider Woman, who secretly vowed to decapitate them and use their skin for sacks. They prevailed in the end, exiling Spider Woman to the moon.

Every aspect of Tolkien's circa 1914 statements pertaining to Night the Spider could have been inspired by "The Death of Spider-Woman." Both spiders were adversarial in character; one was associated with Night and the other with the Moon; both were unsuccessful in encounters with heroic celestial opponents; and both dwelt in America. In Tolkien's circa 1914 note mentioning Night the Spider, he apparently planned for the spider to capture Eärendel, because the adventurer "escapes from the meshes of Night with a few comrades." This echoed the monstrous Skidi Spider Woman who "captured many."

Tolkien's minimal note on Night the Spider did not specify a sex for the monster. But surveying Tolkien's spiders, Christina Scull and Wayne Hammond noted that they are "invariably female" and that this might draw from spinning / weaving as "a female occupation" and perhaps from "the notorious black widow spider[.]"[115] This female identity, however, is notably consistent with assuming that the Skidi Spider Woman provided the underlying inspiration for Tolkien. The Skidi divinity is associated with the nighttime moon, with horrible murder, with ensnaring people, and she is defeated by celestial heroes – all details that materialized with the birth of Tolkien's first spider monster.

As a matter of authorial technique, in 1914 when Tolkien drew from a 1907 verse translation of the *Kalevala* to create his own prose retelling, this served as an important experiment – one that laid a useful foundation for his later fusions of pre-existing myth with his own creative vision.[116] This experience he deemed a "Northern European" enterprise. And a few years later, inspired by the same source to envision his own mythic storytelling, Tolkien developed a subtle touch in borrowing and utilizing such material. As Verlyn Fleiger has noted, "This was a period in Tolkien's life rich with discoveries that fuelled and fed each other."[117]

From such early creative experiences Tolkien learned the process of sifting through an extant piece of literature for details that could be remixed to fit his literary aspirations and preferences, adding moments of subtle coloration. And the rules he set for himself in such efforts were deliberate. Focusing on a Northern European sensibility, his work would appeal to a Northern European cultural identity; his invented legendarium would pertain exclusively to Northern Europe.

Tolkien scholarship has taken this focus to signify a carefully circumscribed field of view. Tolkienists generally believe that Tolkien had little interest in world mythologies, and that his legendarium subsequently reflected very little of the mythic world beyond Europe. For this reason, to get at Tolkien's broader experience of the world, it is useful to begin with Vinland, because this literary lens comports with the Eurocentrism that Tolkien himself encouraged.

The figure of Night the Spider, born in Vinland, embodied Tolkien's first arguable use of Pawnee source-material. Tolkien would ultimately draw this monster into his emerging legendarium as a deadly female spider divinity. But when he at last began to write the first legends of what would one day become his Middle-earth legendarium, he set aside this idea and turned to other stories.

His return to Pawneeland came when he sat down to give thought to the creation of the cosmos. Launching into the preparation of a coherent mythology, he now carefully studied the Skidi cosmogony. There he heard a curious music – a celestial singing wafting from the far shores of distant Vinland into Middle-earth.

Worlds of Song

The Skidi Pawnee creation story morphed into a written text during a transitional period in Pawnee history. In that era several American anthropologists worked with the Pawnee people to set down in writing ceremonial knowledge and oral narratives. This particular tradition was written in English sometime between 1899 and 1903, told by a prominent Skidi priest named Roaming Scout.

About 1839 Roaming Scout was born in Pawneeland in what would one day become known as the Great Plains of North America. He was a member of a royal family among the Skidi Pawnees, the son of a priest named Mud Bear, and he decided in his youth to embrace a religious life, learning the ceremonies and associated stories. We know he held the name Tah-whoo-kah-tah-wee-ah in his adulthood, and he took the name Roaming Scout about the time JRR Tolkien was born in 1892.[118] In those days Roaming Scout became a leading Skidi kurahus or priest.

We do not know exactly when Roaming Scout sat down with James R. Murie to recount story of the creation of the cosmos and humankind. Murie worked in those days with anthropologist George Dorsey, and they published *Traditions of the Skidi Pawnee* in 1904. This collection opened with Roaming Scout's creation story, "Dispersion of the Gods and the First People."[119] I am unaware of any record of manuscripts showing how the text achieved its final published form. The narrative can be divided into two parts: a cosmology explaining the creation of the universe, and a historical origin story of the founding of the Skidi Confederacy. It is likely that these two stories once existed as separate narratives.

Sharing his stories and the events of his life, Roaming Scout sought to pass along to future generations his priestly knowledge of Skidi tradition and mythology. He died in June

1914 while Tolkien was a student at Oxford – the very year that Tolkien arguably made first use of the book to invent Night the Spider.

Given the awareness in Britain of *Traditions of the Skidi Pawnee* and the availability of the book, Tolkien had ample opportunity to encounter it. Although we don't know when that happened, and we have no evidence pointing to his use of any specific copy of the book, we do know that after Tolkien began working as a researcher at Oxford in 1919 echoes of Roaming Scout's creation story entered Tolkien's first version of his own creation myth, "The Music of the Ainur."

Tolkien's first formal appreciation of cosmology probably arose through experience in his youth with Classical literature – meaning Greek and Roman mythologies. By the time he entered Oxford in the fall of 1911 we can surmise that he was familar with Hesiod's *Theogony*, Ovid's *Metamorphosis*, the Finnish *Kalevala*, and the Norse *Voluspa*. His own creation story, "The Music of the Ainur," seems to have first appeared in early 1919, though the dating of this manuscript is uncertain.[120]

By that date he had already written the early drafts of several of the legends that comprised his first major mythological history, *The Book of Lost Tales*. He decided this book would not just become a collection of tales, but would instead embody a grand mythic vision, and it would begin at the beginning. Looking at various European cosmogonic models, he settled on the idea of devising a pantheon of gods. Guided by a sense that England needed its own sense of pre-Christian mythological identity, Tolkien toyed with the notion of linking his pantheon with northern European divinities, but in the end he decided against reproducing well-known creation stories.

Rejecting the option of retelling a familiar cosmogony, Tolkien wanted an antiquity that would feel both familiar and yet not borrowed from the Norse or Finnish or Greek. And it couldn't sound purely literary, an obviously imagined fantasyland. Settling on the idea that his cosmogony had to be "primitive" in its tone, and it needed to sound vaguely European, he did something completely unexpected. He turned to another living cosmology to cultivate specific details to colorize his universe. He turned to the the Skidi Pawnee creation story in *Traditions of the Pawnee*. The evidence for this strategy can be seen in a spectrum of details.

In Roaming Scout's story, we encounter Tirawa and Atira and other gods, and "Tirawa spoke to the gods" giving them "stations in the heavens[.]" In Tolkien's creation story Ilúvatar "sang into being" the Ainur and "fashioned for them dwellings in the void" – the term "stations" appears in the next section when Eriol, a man, asks of the Elvish storyteller: "Whereof, tell me, are the Sun or the Moon or the Stars, and how came their courses and their stations?"[121] Eriol is asking a question that is perfectly applicable to the Skidi cosmic ordering. And it is fitting for the Skidi creator to make "stations in the heavens" for his lesser gods, who are, after all, stars and planets. But why did it seem logical to Tolkien to build "dwellings in the void" for Ilúvatar's lesser gods?

Preparing a summary version "some time in the 1930s" Tolkien dropped the dwellings in the void.[122] These dwellings do not return in the "Ainulindalë" of the 1930s, nor in the "Ainulindalë" of the 1950s.[123] The fact that Tolkien provided space stations for the earliest incarnation of his deities is a clue that when he envisioned the first version of his Ainur in 1919, somewhere in his thoughts he had an image of star deities like the Skidi gods.

In both creation stories all the celestial spiritual beings are represented as a pantheon of gods. In the Skidi story we are introduced to Tirawa and Atira and "[a]round them sat the gods in council." These lesser assisting celestial beings are consistently spoken of as gods. Tolkien similarly seems to envision the Ainur as gathered before Ilúvatar "about his throne"; and as Christopher Tolkien informs us: "The Valar are here referred to as 'Gods'... and this usage survived until far on in the development of the mythology."[124] Tolkien's Ainur started life as gods but he eventually demoted them to a lesser category of celestial spirit.

Roaming Scout's creation story opened with Tirawa providing a precise description of what will come. Tirawa's vision sets the cosmic plan in place, granting each god duties to come. In this sense, Tirawa offered a foretelling of the coming future, establishing the ordering of the gods and their roles, and giving four star gods the power to eventually create people. These four gods were "Stars of the Four Directions" under the authority of Evening Star, who is female, the "Mother of all things." She is the consort of Morning Star, who played a minor role in the great events of creation.

After this prologue of vision, Tirawa instructed Evening Star to command her four deities (now personified as Clouds, Winds, Lightnings, Thunders) to sing – these deities dropped a pebble that became the earth. Tirawa commanded another song to put life into the surface of the earth; then another song to create plants; then a song to create waterways; then a song for seeds. After the first girl and boy were made, a song delivered them to the earth; then a song to make them conscious; then a song to give gifts to the woman; then a song to give gifts to the man.

In the early version of his story, Tolkien also set forth the process of his version of creation-by-song as both a vision and a creative act: Ilúvatar "propounded a mighty design of his heart to the Ainur, unfolding a history..." Then Ilúvatar asks the gods to fashion a "great music."[125] And as the singing unfolded, Ilúvatar made the song manifest: "...those things that ye have sung and played, lo! I have caused to be – not in the musics that ye make in the heavenly regions... but rather to have shape and reality even as have ye Ainur..."[126] Then Ilúvatar revealed to the Ainur: "Even as ye played so of my will your music took shape, and lo! even now the world unfolds and its history begins..." The Ainur marvel to "see how the world was globed amid the void..." They saw the ocean, the winds, and the materials of earth, and three of the Ainur each contributed to the making of different aspects of this world.[127]

The grand design of the Skidi creation is exactly reproduced in Tolkien's creation, with singing generating the cosmic order. Tolkien had no interest in replicating the specific sequence of events in the Skidi story, but he did make use of the general cosmic origin and he then proceeded to extract various minor details. In one such example of borrowed parallel cosmological ordering, the preeminent stature of the four Skidi sky deities is echoed in Tolkien's earliest conception of four dominant Valar. As Christopher Tolkien explains: "Manwë, Melko, Ulmo, and Aulë are marked out as 'the four great ones'; ultimately the great Valar, the *Aratar*, came to be numbered nine[.]"[128]

The Skidi female-centered cosmic ordering positioned Evening Star as the prime enactor under Tirawa, with Morning Star as her male consort. This worldview is countered by Tolkien's male-centered universe. Ilúvatar sat at the top of the celestial order with Manwë described as "the greatest and chief of those four great ones" and Manwë's partner "Varda the Beautiful... his spouse... Queen of the Stars[.]"[129] Both Evening Star and Manwë had consorts who do little in the beginning.

Evening Star took charge of the four leading "Stars of the Four Directions" and Manwë acted as the leading god of "the four great ones." And Tirawa directed Evening Star to command her four deities to sing to create earth, while Ilúvatar asked the gods to fashion a "great music" and the songs of the four leading Ainur played special creative roles. The correspondence is strikingly parallel.

But there is an exact correspondence of associations between the gender-identified gods. Both Evening Star and Varda have charge of "stars," though not in the same way. And in the Skidi cosmology, Morning Star has an association with hawks, who serve as his messengers; while Manwë in Middle-earth is also associated with hawks as messengers.[130]

It is reasonable to interpret the similarities between the Skidi Pawnee creation story and Tolkien's creation story as more than a matter of curious coincidence. A deliberative process can be seen at work, ordering the meaningful array of corresponding details and structures. The most parsimonious explanation is that Tolkien read the Skidi story and used it as a model for his own creation story.

The differences between the two creation stories are legion in both tone and content, yet the two stories nevertheless share notable features, with an originating vision followed by singing as a generative act, with a leading god and lesser gods, with both leading gods creating star-like "stations" for the lesser gods, with exact pairings of dominant lesser gods, and with the major lesser gods numbering four. A fundamental parallel of celestial pairings is also evident: Evening Star the major goddess with Morning Star the minor god; Manwë the major god with Varda the minor goddess. And stars and hawks have exact gender-specific associations in both Pawneeland and Middle-earth.

These features appear in the earliest versions of Tolkien's story. And as Tolkien revised his creation story it slowly drifted away from these parallel constructions. He transformed the celestial singing from a creative act, as in the Skidi story, to a hymn of foretelling. As Christopher Tolkien explained: "...by far the most important difference [between early and later versions of this creation story] is that in the early form the Ainur's first sight of the World was in its actuality... not as a Vision that was taken away from them and only given existence in the words of Ilúvatar[.]"[131]

Surveying creation stories worldwide, tales of genesis that associate the act of creation with the act of singing are exceedingly rare. To my knowledge Tolkien did not replicate this theme from any European creation story. The closest echoes appear in the Finnish *Kalevala* and, to a lesser degree, Hesiod's *Theogony*. It is reasonable that these texts would be inspirational for Tolkien, but rather than reproduce the singing of the *Kalevala* or the *Theogony*, textual comparisons demonstrate that Tolkien instead drew from the more obscure Skidi model.

Tolkien could have produced a thinly veiled retelling of the *Kalevala* creation story, exactly as he did just a few years earlier with his Kullervo story. But he had no interest in that kind of project. The major features of Tolkien's version which resonate with the Skidi story cannot be explained by the *Kalevala*. For this reason, it seems problematic to theorize that Tolkien's creation plays a tune inspired by the *Kalevala* when his song of creation ended up sounding more directly Skidi.

It is clear, however, that Tolkien's lifelong fascination with myth featured a strong connection to song through his interest in the *Kalevala*. In a 1914 letter he wrote of introducing a friend to "the *Kalevala* the Finnish ballads."[132] And several of his earliest writings include an analytical essay on the *Kalevala* and a retelling of part of it.[133] The power of song attracted him, and early on he decided music would play a prominent role in his legendarium. For this reason alone he would have found the Skidi creation story compelling. Tolkien picked up *Traditions of the Skidi Pawnee* – possibly in the collections of the Taylor Institution Library – and he encountered the conjoining of song and creation, and he stood there reading that day, enchanted by the unexpected resonance with the *Kalevala*.

Analysts have suggested that Tolkien drew upon Christian cosmological source material for inspiration in crafting his creation story.[134] Given his life-long immersion in Christian myth, we should expect that Tolkien would formulate a story that would echo a theology familiar to him. But his cultural agenda as a mythmaker also involved a quest to summon archaic pre-Christian texturing for his legends of the First Age. He felt suspicious of Celtic Arthurian myth in part because it was too Christianized.[135] What this signified for him was that certain qualities had been sheared away and lost through the Christian revision of myth – he thought he saw this same process at work in the Christianization of Scandinavia.[136] For whatever reason, it is evident that Tolkien made the choice to refrain from explicitly modeling his creation on Judeo-Christian tradition. We can surmise that Tolkien would have read the Skidi creation story as a "primitive" tradition entirely free of Christian influence.

And we can assume that he did not have to become an expert on Pawnee cosmology in order to identify and extract details that interested him. Tolkien had no desire to retell the Pawnee cosmogony no more than he had any intent to reference northern European creation stories. Instead, he was selective about his choice of borrowed details. But the two accounts of creation are very different. In 1919 when Tolkien borrowed from Pawnee myth to create his own mythology, he ignored the character and cultural focus of the Pawnee stories – the focus on the peaceful integrative formation of celestial and earthly communities. He had to explain more cataclysmic truths. The extremities of his experience in the First World War needed a mythic context, and that was his agenda – all the intricacies of catastrophy that unfold on both a cosmic scale and at the level of individual experience.[137]

European pantheons no doubt account for the idea of creating a community of specific divinities in Middle-earth, but John Rateliff believes that Tolkien's Valar "were directly inspired" by *The Gods of Pegāna*, a 1905 book by Lord Dunsany.[138] I do not know whether his opinion also encompasses Tolkien's creation story, and if so, whether it is sustained by text comparisons and the identification of similar components. A casual review of Dunsany's creation tales in *The Gods of Pegāna* does not seem to point to substantive parallels. Instead, Tolkien's awareness of Dunsany's tales most arguably added to a certain kind of momentum – a momentum that brought Tolkien to plan an ambitious world that began in song.

Tolkien's pantheon and the genesis of his universe are unique artistic creations. But he intended for his cosmos to evoke familiar archetypes because it arose from his quest to summon a lost English mythic past. Tolkien wished to offer the folk of England a story that echoed the mythology of Norse tradition and the logic of Indo-European mythic storytelling.[139] "Echo" is the key idea, not "reproduce." To achieve this cultural texturing, he decided that he needed to plant some convincing "primitive undergrowth" – narrative greenery that felt indigenous, as if it had always been present, rooted in familiar soils. The fantastical inventions of Lord Dunsany showed him what he did not want to do – that is, to seem purely inventive in a literary sense. And he could not merely reproduce Norse or Celtic tradition. To mix together the ingredients of a new but still ancient mythology, Tolkien had to invent his own cosmological recipe. The dashes of cosmic spice imported from Pawneeland added living flavors he deemed essential.

Comparative evidence suggests that Tolkien drew both structure and detail from the Skidi Pawnee cosmogony. The shared parallels between Tolkien's creation story and the Skidi story are of such diversity and significance that it is reasonable to presume that Tolkien knew of the Skidi story and drew inspiration from it in a deliberative creative process. We must assume he had a motive for pursuing this course of action. As I have suggested, Tolkien asserted that in his early years he envisioned a specific cultural tone for his legendarium, and the Pawnee story does match his desired specifications.

The alternate interpretation, of course, is to decide that the Middle-earth parallels to Pawnee myth are wholly unrelated independent inventions, mere curiosities. In fact, it may well be useful to subjectively weigh the shared details, and to then decide whether they should be heard in either a major or minor key. It does not seem justifiable to treat the matter as impossible to prove – meaning that an arbitrary preferential level of freedom from doubt must be achieved, or some specific form of evidence must be found before acceptance can occur. Skepticism is merely an analytical tool; it is not a counterweight to actual circumstantial evidence.

The connections I have identified in the comparison of the creation stories of Middle-earth and Pawneeland are not unique or isolated. My insight that Tolkien drew on the Skidi creation story is supported by indications that he also drew from other narratives in *Traditions of the Skidi Pawnee*. By any measure, the traditional literature of Pawneeland provided JRR Tolkien with a greatly important body of mythological source-material in the making of Middle-earth.

Daughters of a Dark Moon

In late May of 1874 the two Manchester, England newspapers advertised a series of special performances at the Royal Pomona Palace and Gardens. One feature-article promised "an entertainment that is quite novel on this side of the Atlantic." According to historian Dan Jibréus, three Pawnee men "performed traditional songs and dances and also showed their skill with bow and arrow."[140] These were the Skidi Pawnee discoverers of Britain: White Fox, White Eagle, and Red Fox.

Red Fox was a member of one of the leading royal families of the Skidi. He held at least three Pawnee names during his life, and among the Americans he took the name John Box.[141] Almost three decades after performing in Britain, Box shared a number of stories with James R. Murie and George Dorsey. When *Traditions of the Skidi Pawnee* appeared in 1904 it contained thirteen of his narratives.[142] In 1906 when British anthropologist Alfred Haddon visited Pawneeland to witness a Skidi ceremony, it is quite possible that John Box was on hand for the proceedings that night.

Sometime between 1899 and 1903 John Box told a story that James R. Murie and George Dorsey titled "How the Buffalo Went South."[143] Textual evidence indicates that in early 1919 JRR Tolkien mined this story in the course of preparing his account of one of most memorable monsters in his legendarium – a spider divinity that would, in turn, inspire the horrible spiders of *The Hobbit* and give rise to deadly Shelob in *The Lord of the Rings*. In other words, John Box's account of Spider Woman accounts for a lineage of monsters that has shaped modern imaginations worldwide.

Not long after drawing from a Pawnee tradition for help in creating the cosmos, Tolkien turned his attention back to Night the Spider. In *The Book of Lost Tales* Tolkien told the tale of "The Theft of Melko and the Darkening of Valinor."[144] A monstrous spider divinity made its first appearance as Melko "wanders the dark plains of Eruman" and journeyed "farther south than anyone had ever yet penetrated" and there "he found a region of the deepest gloom[.]"[145] Melko "finds a dark cavern in the hills, and webs of darkness lie about so that the black air might be felt heavy and choking[.]"

In this southern realm "dwelt the primeval spirit Móru" who some believe to have been "bred of mists and darkness on the confines of the Shadowy Seas[.]" This was a female who took "the guise of an unlovely spider, spinning a gossamer of gloom that catches in its mesh stars and moons and all the bright things that sail the airs." Móru has other names, including "Ungwe Lianti the great spider who enmeshes" and "Ungoliont the spider."

And Tolkien soon called her "the Spider of Night," echoing his circa 1914 note on "Night... The Spider." Night the Spider hailed from a mysterious "land of magic" – a land which occupied the space in northern tradition that is otherwise known as "Vinland." Now here in 1919 we find Ungoliont "on the confines of the Shadowy Seas[.]" This rather vague geography can be read as a poetic remnant of Tolkien's original vision, an enduring silhouette of the roots of this story – an uncharted Vinland-like realm at the edges of what we know.

By the time Tolkien set down his first tale of Ungoliont in 1919, he had already written "The Music of the Ainur" with its numerous elements borrowed from the Skidi creation story. During the next few months he revisited Night the Spider to invent a more detailed "unlovely spider" and insert her into "The Theft of Melko and the Darkening of Valinor." Ungoliont eventually became Ungoliant / Ungoliantë, but she would always be rooted in Night the Spider – his first monster, a creature born from the dark tales of Pawneeland.

In an interview published by Charlotte and Denis Plimmer in 1968 Tolkien made a mysterious claim that spiders "are the particular terror of northern imaginations."[146] It does not appear that he ever illuminated this assertion with any insights about the making of his monstrous spiders or about the specific traditions of terror that moved him. If he remembered his original idea of a Vinland-like setting for Night the Spider, he made no mention of it.

It is unlikely that Tolkien took inspiration from Norse or Germanic sources for his abhorrent arachnid of primeval Middle-earth.[147] Finnish and Celtic mythologies do not feature much spider mythic imagery; those traditions seem to lack spider divinities, evil or otherwise.[148] In contrast, Spider Woman can be found in many mythologies in North America. It is also interesting that Tolkien's first conceptions of "Ungoliont the spider" hold various elements in common with John Box's "How the Buffalo Went South."

In this Skidi story the father of the buffalo stood in the "north," and this magic buffalo knew of another guardian of the earth's center, and he sent a delegation to obtain permission from this creature for the buffalo to move south. The delegates found a little girl who told her mother about the visitors. "The mother said: 'You need not mind, they are sent on purpose to see me; I have built my cobwebs in the centre of the earth, so they cannot pass.'"

This was Spider Woman. She was "one of those great red spiders, a tarantula... the daughter of Sun and Moon." The delegation returned north to report to the father buffalo "that it was the Spider-Woman in the centre of the earth, who had stretched cobwebs all along so that the buffalo could not pass[.]" The buffaloes finally lost patience with Spider Woman. In a rush they trampled her into the ground. In so doing, the buffaloes "turn her into a large root, so that a vine should grow from it" and "her cobwebs were trampled also" and "the vines should represent her webs[.]"

Both Spider Woman and Ungoliont were associated with "the south" in their various worlds.[149] In the Skidi story the phrase "in the centre of the earth" is ambiguous, but it certainly does evoke a cavern of some kind, and Tolkien's first home for

Ungoliont was a cavern. The Spider Woman in this Skidi story displayed an adversarial demeanor, while Tolkien's spider was unabashedly evil. Both partook of a shapeshifting quality, with both being female divinities in the guise of spiders. Both of these spider women had daughters. Tolkien was not clear about what kind of deity Ungoliont might be – perhaps we can assume she was another "daughter of Sun and Moon," a sister to Spider Woman.

An endnote to John Box's story explained that there were many Spider Women in the world, and they were "under the direct influence of the Moon" and inhabited "the sides of the mountains[.]"[150] It is interesting that Tolkien revised Ungoliont's early cavern into a later "deep cleft in the mountains[.]"[151] His Middle-earth spiders had no association with the moon, but in Tolkien's novelette "Roverandom," written for his children between 1927 and 1936, many monstrous spiders resided on the moon where they spun "enormous silver nets... from mountain to mountain[.]"[152]

In the Skidi story Spider Woman's cobwebs became vines, and Tolkien's etymology for Ungoliont equated spider silk with vines. He prepared a lexicon during the same period when he wrote *The Book of Lost Tales*. And for "Ungwë Lianti, Ungweliant(ë)" he rendered the second part of this name as "from root Li+ya 'entwine,' with derivatives *lia* 'twine,' *liantë* 'tendril,' *liantassë* 'vine'."[153]

At first glance it seems an unusual choice for Tolkien to draw a connection between the idea of a monstrous spider and a vine. But keeping in mind that Ungoliont was further associated with the far south of Middle-earth, within the next few years after devising this conception, Tolkien invented Dor-Winion as a region associated with "the burning South" and with "vine-clad valleys[.]"[154] He did not specify a more exact location for this region, but the Skidi Spider Woman, Ungoliont, Dorwinion, and Vinland were all entangled with vague notions of the south, and all were more specifically entwined with vines.

Tolkien could have found adequate inspiration for his deadly "primeval spirit" spider in extant fantasy literature of his time. But it is difficult to see in any of those tales substantive parallels that establish unique indicators of a well-defined arguable connection. In contrast, "How the Buffalo Went South" displays a spectrum of unique shared details with Tolkien's tale of Ungoliont. James R. Murie and George Dorsey included the tale as the seventh Skidi "Cosmogonic" narrative.

The eighth narrative, "The Death of Spider-Woman," portrayed Spider Woman as a murderous old Witch Woman.[155] As I described earlier, in this story Spider Woman was defeated by the sons of Sun and Moon. The boys ultimately vanquished her, singing songs about the Sun and Moon and exiling Spider Woman to the Moon. In the course of these adventures, Spider Woman revealed her power to summon clouds: "When she sang about the dark clouds nearing, the dark clouds were at hand." Tolkien's spider was called Gloomweaver because she can spin "lightless webs and ill-enchanted shades" that resemble another Valar's "great mists and darkness[.]" Under the cover of this "woven night" Tolkien's Spider performed great evil, for she was "ahungered of that brightness" of gems offered by Melko, and she set her lips to the tree Laurelin. And Spider Woman felt hungry too, saying at one point "...I am hungry..."

Spider Woman is an ancient figure in North American traditions – she is occasionally portrayed as somewhat dangerous, but she is a benevolent deity, never murderous.[156] Murie and Dorsey categorized both of the John Box stories as "Cosmogonic" tales, pertaining to mythological history. "How the Buffalo Went South" established a portrayal that would fall within the spectrum of stories depicting Spider Woman as a benign goddess; in contrast, the tone of "The Death of Spider-Woman" registered a rather severe moral social judgment, framing her as a violent and deadly enemy.[157]

Reviewing "How the Buffalo Went South" and skimming "The Death of Spider-Woman," Tolkien would probably not have noticed such nuance. But he would have found plenty of inspiration for a monstrous spider-deity. And he had no need to study the Skidi Spider Woman in any detail; he had no need to know anything about Spider Woman stories in other American traditional literatures; he had no interest in reproducing Spider Woman in Middle-earth.

Tolkien harvested details and ideas from the Skidi stories, but he relied on his own inventive genius to make use of that material. Tolkien associated Ungoliont with night, just as the Skidi Spider Woman is associated with the moon – in "The Death of Spider-Woman," two celestial heroes prevailed over her and exiled her to the moon. Both characters had power to darken the earth; both hungered; both were ultimately vanquished; and the webs of both Ungoliont and Spider Woman became associated with vines. And as with the celestial twins who defeated Spider Woman, Tolkien eventually planned for Eärendel, his own celestial hero, to defeat Ungoliont someday. But he never wrote that tale.

Tolkien gave much thought to spiders during the early 1930s. Carl Phelpstead has quoted briefly from one Tolkien poem dating back to 1930 which suggestively referred to a "witch... who webs could weave / to snare the heart and wits to reave / who span dark spells with spider-craft."[158] In the Skidi legendarium a sorceress named "Witch Woman" figured very prominently.[159] Even though we are warned that she "is not to be confounded with the Spider-Woman" Tolkien was not bound by such legalistic niceties in his borrowing of myth. This can only add to the argument that Tolkien had some kind of fling with the Skidi Spider Woman.

Sometime in 1938, writing the first version of "In the House of Bombadil," Tolkien set down several interesting ideas about barrow-wights: "A dark shadow came up out of the middle of the world" and "a dark shadow came up out of the South."[160] These conceptions reverberate with Ungoliont's early association with a cavern and the south, and echo from afar the Skidi description of Spider Woman as dwelling "in the centre of the earth" where she forbids passage to the south.

Another conjunction occurred in the evolution of a poem titled "Errantry." An early version was published in 1933 and sometime after that date Tolkien began working on a longer version.[161] This new draft for a time included these lines: "Ungoliant abiding there / in Spider-lair her thread entwined; / for endless years a gloom she spun / the Sun and Moon in web to wind."[162] The Skidi Spider Woman in one story is "the daughter of Sun and Moon," and in the second story she is defeated by the sons of "the Sun and Moon." The phrase "Sun and Moon" is common enough in world literature, but in these instances it exists in both Tolkien's tale and in both of John Box's Skidi stories in association with a spider divinity and with exactly repeated capitalizations.

If these striking parallels between the Skidi Spider Woman and Tolkien's spider monsters are all coincidence, they exist as remarkable accidents of invention. It is more arguable that here we catch a glimpse of Tolkien the mythologist opening *Traditions of the Skidi Pawnee* and finding a moment that interested him.

The Skidi Spider Woman inspired him when he made his first notes on Night the Spider. And several years later he again revisited Spider Woman when he sat down to compose the story of Ungoliont the spider. These details of creative inspiration never entered Tolkien's later origin stories. Settling into his own preferred mythology of the making of Middle-earth, by the 1960s he chose to speak of his spiders as infesting "northern imaginations"; he never mentioned Vinland, the Skidi Pawnees, or Spider Woman.

Writing of Ungoliont's first appearance in his legendarium, Tolkien's observations were telling: "here dwelt the primeval spirit Móru whom even the Valar know not whence... she came..."[163] But we can now surmise what the Valar never knew. Ungoliont came to Middle-earth from Pawneeland.

In May 1874 John Box and his two relatives traveled from Pawneeland to perform in Manchester, England at the Royal Pomona Palace and Gardens, dancing and shooting arrows before an English audience. People from around the region visited these gardens and enjoyed the entertainments in the exhibition hall.

JRR Tolkien's father, Arthur, was a young man living near Birmingham, just a short train-ride away from Manchester; and JRR's mother, Mabel Suffield, was a little girl living in another suburb.[164] We have no reason to believe that the Tolkiens or Suffields ever took note of the doings of the Pawnee performers who visited nearby Manchester in 1874.

But it is interesting to think that they could have paused in their lives, glimpsing a newspaper article, a poster – overhearing a casual conversation about the Pawnees and their demonstrations of bowmanship. And it is interesting that many years later Tolkien would say that his interest in "Red Indians" left him with "a wholly unsatisfied desire to shoot well with a bow..."[165]

That spring the three Skidi Pawnee discoverers of Britain came and went. They were no doubt long remembered by many who witnessed their performances, even as those moments slipped away down a long grey firth into the memory of history.

Saru and Sári and the Sun

After creating Ungoliont and installing her in the south of Middle-earth, Tolkien prepared "The Tale of the Sun and Moon" for *The Book of Lost Tales*.[166] The early versions of this story appear to have been written in 1919.[167] As I noted in the first edition of *Tolkien in Pawneeland*, in this tale we find a name that Tolkien originally used circa 1914, but which also bears a striking resemblance to a Skidi name. And that name has a complex history, but the contextual details resonate with certain Skidi cosmological echoes.

Studying the *Kalevala*, Tolkien felt particularly drawn to Runo XLVII "Robbery of the Moon and Sun."[168] In his 1914-1915 essay on the *Kalevala* he briefly mentioned this Runo and its scene of "the sun and moon being shut up in a mountain" as reflecting an "unhazy unromantic momentariness and presentness that quite startles you" as if "splashed onto a clean bare canvas by a sudden hand[.]"[169] He could have retold the story, but he instead drew a more subtle inspiration from it, preferring to splash his own colors onto the canvas of his own account of the sun and moon.

He may well have consulted his unfinished "The Story of Kullervo" from late 1914. Studying that manuscript, John Garth has noted Tolkien's use of the word "sari" in various forms as a "byname" for Kullervo, observing that "the first element of *Sārihonto* is identical to Sári, the name for the Sun in *The Book of Lost Tales*..."[170] He suggested that it probably held the same meaning, something to do with heat, but Tolkien attached no specific meaning to the word in this 1914 manuscript. Nor does the manuscript offer any hint as to whether any word in any language helped to inspire the term.

In "The Tale of the Sun and Moon" after Ungoliont destroyed the Two Trees in Valinor, the gods gathered to exert their magic.[171] Yavanna "put forth" her power and "sang the songs of unfading growth" and swooned from the exertion. But the tears of Vána and her song of joyful lamentation caused a shoot to emerge from one tree, and in this manner, "Light hath returned." From one golden blossom of this magic shoot Aulë built a "ship of light." And "[t]hen did the Gods name that ship, and they called her Sári which is the Sun[.]"[172] This ship was piloted by Urwendi, "the mistress of the Sun" and her maidens. A similar tale spoke of the magic origin of the Moon, piloted by Ilsinor who is jealous of the sun.[173] Tolkien planned a story called the "Tale of Qorinómi" as a love story between Urwendi and Fionwë, a son of Manwë and Varda.[174]

Tolkien characterized humankind in these tales as the "Children of Ilúvatar" and as "Children of Men" – the appearance of humankind in Middle-earth was the subject of a tale that Tolkien started but never finished: "Gilfanon's Tale: The Travail of the Noldoli."[175] Here an Elf wandered and found a sleeping folk and "all who slumbered there were children"; Tolkien's notes indicated that the first human to awaken would witness the first sunrise.[176]

Tolkien next returned to the origin of humankind in what Christopher Tolkien called "The Earliest 'Silmarillion'" written in 1926 and subsequently much-revised.[177] Here Tolkien envisioned the making of the sun and moon and "At the rising of the first Sun the younger children of earth awoke in the far East."[178] In 1930 in "The Quenta" Tolkien again revisited this scene, adding more detail and repeating the rivalry of the sun and moon and describing humankind as "the younger children of earth."[179] These brief summaries dropped the term Sári as the name given by the gods to the sun.

Several other manuscripts dating to the same period touched on the origin of the sun and moon but provided little detail.[180] Sometime during the 1930s Tolkien prepared a manuscript that is now called "The Earliest Annals of Valinor."[181] A second draft of this manuscript contained an interesting statement: "Men, the Younger Children of Ilúvatar, awoke in the East of the world at the first Sunrise; hence they are also called the Children of the Sun."[182] This designation "Children of the Sun" appeared here for the first time.

Tolkien prepared a short text titled "The Ambarkanta" sometime during the mid-1930s, possibly circa 1936, and this featured an interesting new twist. It contained a short description of the orbits of the moon and sun and how the moon "pursues ever after the Sun, and overtakes her seldom, and then is consumed and darkened in her flame."[183] This sounds somewhat like a solar eclipse, and it seemed to reference the previous characterizations of rivalry and jealousy. But sometimes the Moon "comes above Valinor ere the Sun has left it, and then he descends and meets his beloved, and Valinor is filled with mingled light as of silver and gold...." Here the Moon regarded the Sun as "his beloved."

Tolkien's new ideas about the sun and moon of the 1930s became more fully articulated in late 1937 and early 1938 with preparation of the "Quenta Silmarillion."[184] Here Tilion at the helm of the moon "was wayward... and at times sought to tarry Arien [the sun], whom he loved[.]" Tolkien also wrote of the solar eclipse: "at times they are both in the sky together, and still at times he draws nigh to her, and there is a darkness amid the day." But Tillion in his vessel of the moon sometimes "descends and meets his beloved, for they leave their vessels for a space; and then there is great joy[.]" Here we see mentioned "the Younger Children of Ilúvatar." And just a few pages later we find a description of the first awakening of humankind: "At the first rising of the Sun above the earth the younger children of the world awoke in the land of Hildórien in the uttermost East of Middle-earth that lies beside the eastern sea[.]" Tolkien added a footnote here listing names bestowed by the Eldar upon humankind, including "the Children of the Sun."

Between 1919 and 1938 Tolkien experimented with the names of various characters and groups, but he consistently used the term "children" to refer to humankind. At the beginning, circa 1919, the sun was given the name Sári by the Gods, and this term appeared in several tales composed in that period. Tolkien came up with various names for the two deities who captain the ship of the moon and the ship of the sun, and the sun remained a female dominion and the moon a male one. Over the next several decades a trajectory of relations occurred between the sun and moon. Rivalry marked the original relationship, but this gave way during the early 1930s to love between the two celestial deities, punctuated by solar eclipses. At some point during the 1930s humankind received the name "Children of the Sun"; but the fullest articulation of this new phase came in 1937-1938 with the conjoining of solar eclipses and the celestial bond of love – humans were again termed "Children of the Sun."

This evolution of the sun and moon is interesting because it bore very little evident relationship to the narrative details pertaining to these celestial bodies in the *Kalevala*, but it did echo certain elements in Skidi narratives in *Traditions of the Skidi Pawnee*. Two narratives told by Roaming Scout are particularly noteworthy.

One cosmogonic narrative began, "In olden times there was a society known as the Saru, or Children-of-the-Sun."[185] An endnote specified that the term "saru" was "often bestowed by old people upon children, to indicate that they are acting in a child-like manner, and consequently foolishly."[186] This story concerned a fraternal organization consisting of young men who "were supposed to be children of the Sun."

In Roaming Scout's creation story the Sun was a male deity.[187] Tirawa instructed the Sun: "Now, when you have taken your place in the heavens, I give you my permission for you to overtake the Moon, so that you can be with the Moon. At this time she will disappear. In the years to come a boy shall be born unto you, Sun and Moon." This passage featured a solar eclipse in conjunction with a romantic relationship between Sun and Moon, followed by the birth of the first boy "in the summer-time."[188] And mention of this son of Sun and Moon was specifically referenced in the Skidi story about the Children of the Sun: "The name 'Children-of-the-Sun Society' seems to have been derived from the Son of the Sun."[189]

Interesting congruences exist between various elements found in these two Skidi cosmogonical stories and in Tolkien's cosmology. In one Skidi narrative the term "Saru" means "Children of the Sun"; in Tolkien's cosmos "Sári" is the name of the Sun, bestowed by the gods. The Skidi narrative applied the term "Saru" as a special reference to the first son of the Sun and Moon; Tolkien applied the term "Sári" to the Sun, and the awakening of the first Men accompanied the first dawn of the Sun. In the Skidi cosmos, the Sun and Moon were romantically involved; Tolkien's sun and moon began with jealousy and a sidebar love story, but by the 1930s the Sun and Moon had found true love. In the Skidi love story the Sun overtook the Moon and a solar eclipse marked their meeting, their sexual union; in Tolkien's love story the Moon overtook the Sun and a solar eclipse marked their trysts. In both Skidi tradition and in Tolkien's storytelling we find Children of the Sun. In the Skidi sense, the Children of the Sun were a group of young men named by elders; in Tolkien's usage, the Children of the Sun is a name bestowed by the Eldar upon humankind, the Younger Children of Ilúvatar.

As Tolkien wrote *The Book of Lost Tales* between 1916 and 1920 he made extensive notes on names and terms devised in two Elvish languages.[190] The word *sári* did not appear in either of the notebooks he used for this purpose.[191] But it seems related to terms in both languages. In Qenya "the root SAHA/SAHYA yields *sâ* 'fire,' *saiwa* 'hot,' *Sahóra* 'the South'"; and Goldogrin "has *sâ* 'fire' (poetic form *sai*), *sairen* 'fiery,' *saiwen* 'summer,' and other words." It is not clear exactly when Tolkien came up with these terms and meanings.

The name Sāri appeared in "The Story of Kullervo" – Tolkien's retelling of a story in the *Kalevala*, dating to circa 1914.[192] As explained by editor Verlyn Flieger, Tolkien inserted into this retelling "his own invented names or nicknames" and Sāri appeared as a nickname for Kullervo, the main character of the story. This nickname could have been inspired by a waterway mentioned in the *Kalevala*: the "Sound of Saari" – a name meaning "island."[193]

Tolkien did not provide any translation of his name Sāri, so it is not clear whether he borrowed the term or invented a name with a chance resemblance to a Finnish word. It seems unlikely that he would study the *Kalevala*, write a story based on it, and independently invent a word that is also found in the text. But if he did borrow the term, he abandoned its original meaning. To nickname his main character "Island" would seem an odd fit. Whatever Tolkien intended, when he wrote "The Tale of the Sun and Moon" for *The Book of Lost Tales* it does seem apparent that he borrowed Sāri from his earlier "The Story of Kullervo," and this time he attached his own new meaning to the word. It would now be the name for the sun.

John Garth wondered whether Tolkien's circa 1914 use of Sāri had a more fundamental connection with this later usage as a name for the sun, guessing that in 1914 perhaps he intended to refer in some manner to heat or fire.[194] This speculation made no mention of the possibility that Tolkien borrowed the term from the Sound of Saari in the *Kalevala*. In the end, it isn't clear what meaning Tolkien attached to the circa 1914 version of this term. Nor is it clear whether he intentionally transferred that term to "The Tale of the Sun and Moon" as a name for the sun. This confusing trajectory hints at a complex history in Tolkien's mind.

In Tolkien's tale of the sun's origin, it was first a fruit, then a globe of fire, and finally a ship.[195] It doesn't seem to fit for Tolkien to apply the Finnish term for "island" to the sun, but in this same account the moon is first a flower and then a ship that is "like an island of pure glass[.]"[196] And the Finnish term appeared in a Runo that is concerned with the sun and moon. This tends to support the idea that Tolkien borrowed from Finnish *saari* for his "Sári which is the Sun."

But if Tolkien encountered the Skidi *saru* and this inspired him to repurpose his older name Sāri into the term Sári, then an almost invisible matrix of associations rises into sudden focus. His connection between *sári* and *Sahóra* "the South," for example, would accrue special significance. During this period Tolkien invented Ungoliont's association with the south – echoing Spider Woman's connection with the south – and he also created Dorwinion and its association with "the burning South[.]"[197] The south was burning here because both "south" and "fire" derived from the same Elvish roots. And in the context of Dorwinion, the south also enclosed a subtle reference to the Vinland saga and a land of vines in the south. In addition, the birth of the Skidi son of Sun and Moon occurred in summer, and Tolkien's term "*saiwen* 'summer'" was related to Sári, the Sun.

The Elvish term for fire, *sâ*, acquired a particularly interesting association in its relationship to Tolkien's "Sári which is the Sun." In *Traditions of the Skidi Pawnee* we find a further discussion on a Pawnee word related to *saru*. The introduction by George Dorsey listed "Sun, Sakuru (Light-Bringer)."[198] Sun was a male deity who "furnishes light during the day, the fire for which must be renewed each night in the garden of the Evening-Star in the west." In *The Book of Lost Tales* the original galleon of the Sun required similar rejuvenation. Yavanna set a spell upon the golden basin that the Gods placed in the mound of the former Two Trees and "it became a bath of fire."[199] This was the "Bath of the Setting Sun" and when the Sunship brought the first sunset "the ship was drawn down and its radiance refreshed against new voyagings on the morrow[.]"

Since Evening Star's garden and Yavanna's bath of fire both served to rejuvenate Sun's fire, it is logical to compare Yavanna and Evening Star. In Middle-earth Yavanna is also known as Palúrien "whose delights were richness and fruits of the earth[.]"[200] And the Skidi Evening Star "maintains a garden in which... spring all streams of life."[201] In the Skidi creation story Evening Star is commanded to put life in the "timbers and underbrush that make the land gray."[202] Evening Star's four stardeities pass over these plants and "then was there life in the timber." After the building of Valinor "Palúrien Yavanna fared forth from her fruitful gardens... and wandered the dark continents sowing seed[.]"[203] But "fungus and strange growths... and lichens and mosses crept stealthily... and the creeping plants died in the dust" and Yavanna wept. But she and her son "put forth all their might, and Oromë blew great blasts upon his horn as though he would awake the grey rocks to life" and "all the trees of dark leaf came to being, and the world was shaggy with a growth of pines[.]" Here the Skidi gray land and the "grey rocks" of Middle-earth are made to give life through the efforts of Evening Star and Yavanna. Finally, Evening Star has charge of lesser deities in the form of Winds, Rains, Lightnings, and Thunders; while Palúrien has charge of a host of brownies, fays, pixies, and leprawns, termed "the great companies of the children of Palúrien[.]"[204] Yavanna is not a thinly veiled Evening Star, but aspects of the two goddesses are similar.

Yavanna's name Palúrien has interesting geographic associations. A form of the name seems to have appeared early in Tolkien's listing of Qenya terms. Christopher Tolkien has explained that its root PALA had derivatives that convey "a common sense of 'flatness'."[205] And in Gnomish "the corresponding name is *Belaurin, B(a)laurin*; but she is also called *Bladorwen* 'the wide earth, the world and its plants and fruits, Mother Earth' (related words are *blant* 'flat, open, expansive, candid,' blath 'floor,' *bladwen* 'a plain')." As a goddess whose name referred to a "plain" Yavanna / Palúrien / Bladorwen suddenly draws around her the aura of a thinly veiled Skidi Evening Star – these are goddesses of the Pawnee Great Plains and of the plains of Middle-earth.

The evolution of these elements of Tolkien's cosmology gains a particular kind of mythological clarity when we hinge it upon an ongoing relationship between Middle-earth and Pawneeland. It can be theorized that Tolkien was influenced by the Skidi material in 1914 and 1919, and he again drew from it for certain revisions of the 1930s. Tolkien's conceptions of the sun and moon reveal a lattice of correspondence to Pawnee cosmological conceptions.

One equivalence comes with Sári (the Sun) and Saru (the Children of the Sun). The Skidi Sakuru (the Sun) is a male deity and Tolkien's Sāri is a male protagonist, a magical son of a divinty

– and he is also called Sākehonto / Sāki. Tolkien could have formed the name Sāri from a Finnish word for island, Saari, but this is unclear. A few years later he repurposed Sāri into Sári (the Sun). Among the Skidi the Saru are the Children of the Sun, so it is noteworthy that eventually we find Tolkien dropping the name Sári and dubbing his first Men the Children of the Sun. Another set of parallels point to comparisons of Yavanna and Evening Star. And during the 1930s Tolkien made his creation more comparable to the Skidi cosmogony by discarding the jealous rivalry between his Sun and Moon and replacing it with a more courtly love story, with both cosmologies referring to solar eclipses.

The comparisons set forth here suggest that in the course of inventing his own cosmos, Tolkien sought inspiration from Pawnee mythology. We can guess that his interest in what he deemed "primitive" myth drew his attention to Skidi Pawnee tradition, but he had no wish to retell Pawnee stories, so we should not look for exact replications. Instead, we glimpse more subtle patterns. This was a typical practice for him, as Clive Tolley has suggested, "Tolkien changes his sources and uses them only cursorily, so that what is used is welded inextricably into the story, and the result is essentially original."[206]

Tolkien intended to enrich his invented world with mythic textures that fit both his aesthetic sense and his sense of poetic history. This authorial process of texturing was not a minor matter of incidental coloration. As we know from extensive scholarship on his use of Norse, Celtic, Finnish, and other sources, Tolkien's creative vision typically involved the mining of useful raw materials from pre-existing myth. This strategy clearly encompassed Skidi tradition.

The Mythology of Mischief

In Roaming Scout's "Lightning Visits the Earth" – the second cosmogonic narrative in *Traditions of the Skidi Pawnee* – the first "people" placed on the new earth were stars.[207] Morning Star gathered the stars and drove them to Evening Star: "These are my people," Morning Star informed Evening Star. And she "opened her sack, and all these stars rushed in." They gave this sack to Lightning the giant. Lightning traveled to the earth where he opened the sack to let out these star-folk, the first people on earth. But one deity felt envious and placed a wolf on earth.[208] When the star-people killed this wolf, Lightning chided them, saying they have brought death into the world, so now they would suffer death.

In *The Book of Lost Tales* Melko indulged his own "vain imagining" and inserted it into the celestial singing.[209] This was "the mischief of Melko," the source of evil in Tolkien's creation. In a later narrative Melko attacked the homeland of the Elves – the first people – to steal the Silmarils, in the course of which he slew some Elves, and Manwë, one of the Valar, declared: "...my wisdom teaches me that because of the death of Bruithwir and his comrades shall the greatest evils fall on Gods and Elves, and Men to be."[210]

These two stories account for evil and death in very different ways. But in both stories the first killing of an innocent sentient creature brought doom upon all the people of earth. In the Pawnee story, the star-people did the killing; and in Tolkien's story, it was one of the gods. Murder and the violation of innocence is a shared theme in both, but comparison of these cosmogonic tales yields only superficial connections between the mythologies of Middle-earth and Pawneeland. As we will soon see, however, these realms do not stand very far apart in certain aspects of their treatment of human mortality.

In "The Coming of the Valar and the Building of Valinor," written in 1919, Tolkien set forth in detail the fate of the dead.[211] Vefántur Mandos has a hall beneath the Mountains of Valinor – vast caverns full of shadows and echoes and "lit only with a single vessel placed in the centre, wherin there lay some gleaming drops of the pale dew of Silpion[.]" Here is where Elves come when they die, "dreaming of their past deeds" in the dark until they become reincarnated "into their children[.]"

His wife Fui governs her own hall. "Thither came the sons of Men to hear their doom[.]" Many of these Men "she sends aboard the black ship Mornië" from its "dark harbour of the North[.]" When laden with the souls of Men this ship "spreads her sable sails" and journeys along the shores of Valinor. "Then do all aboard as they come South cast looks of utter longing" upon Valinor until they arrive at "the wide plains of Arvalin" where they disembark and "wander in the dark, camping as they may... till the Great End come."

"The Hiding of Valinor," also written in 1919, framed death for both Elves and Men as a mystical soul journey.[212] After envisioning rainbows as "Ilweran the Bridge of Heaven" (fashioned by Oromë to connect Valinor and Middle-earth) Tolkien constructed a second path for Elves and Men. This is a "very dark" and "very short" path – "the shortest and swiftest of all roads, and very rough"; "Qalvanda is it called, the Road of Death, and it leads only to the Halls of Mandos and Fui." This road is "[t]wofold... and one way tread the Elves and the other the souls of Men, and never do they mingle."

In *Traditions of the Skidi Pawnee* the Milky Way served a similar function. A star in the north took the dead on a journey to the Milky Way and another star stood at the southern end of the Milky Way and received the spirits of the dead.[213] As with Tolkien's Qalvanda, this path was twofold. "If the dead man had been a warrior, he was put on the dim Milky Way; if he died of old age, or if it was a woman, they were put upon the wide travelled road." For humankind in Middle-earth, the short dark path of death similarly leads to a second journey. Aboard a black ship the dead sail from the North to the South, just as the dead in Pawneeland journey from north to south.

Astronomer Kristine Larsen has carefully studied Tolkien's constellations and stars, and she came to an interesting conclusion: "One of the most curious aspects of Tolkien's cosmology is that he neglects to utilize the Milky Way in any obvious way..."[214] Gazing carefully at Tolkien's stars, Larsen suggested that a celestial map of the Milky Way can be discerned in a set of constellations that first materialized in Tolkien's legendarium about 1951.[215] This implied that Tolkien gave no thought to the Milky Way until then, and even then his thinking was a little nebulous.

But early in his construction of Middle-earth, Tolkien did give thought to the Milky Way and English tradition. In his early conception of Fëanor he reconstructed a lost English tradition as suggested by an ancient highway known as Watling Street – a name that referred to the Milky Way.[216] This tale did not make it into the collection of legends that became *The Book of Lost Tales*. Instead, Tolkien substituted an oblique reference to the Milky Way, hidden within his "Qalvanda... the Road of Death." Rather than set the Milky Way over Middle-earth for all to see, he ultimately decided to make more mystical use of this celestial path. But it cannot be seen as a manifestation of the Milky Way until one understands the hidden connection to the Pawnee conception of the Milky Way.

Envisioning the Milky Way through a Pawnee lens helps to make sense of another esoteric minor detail. The hall of Vefántur Mandos in *The Book of Lost Tales* is lit in part by "gleaming drops of the pale dew of Silpion[.]"[217] Of the magic ingredients that gave rise to this Tree, "a small star Varda cast" into the pit.[218] In 1951 – the year when the Milky Way at last came into focus in a series of new constellations above Middle-earth – Tolkien tasked Varda with creating stars and constellations using "silver dews from the vats of Telperion[.]"[219] Telperion and Silpion are names for the same Tree in Valinor.

Lighting the dark halls of Mandos with starlight, and contemplating mortality in Middle-earth, Tolkien did something interesting. He equated stars and starlight with the mysticism of death, setting an enchanted form of starlight as a fascinating aura around the mystery of mortality. Under this starlight dead Elves gather, having traversed the Road of Death, the Skidi Milky Way. They are immortal, yet their inner secret lives are bound to stars and starlight, and so to the deeper mysticism of death. In this manner, in the poetry of his secondary sub-creation, Tolkien secretly referenced a living traditional belief system.

The Skidi notion of stars as the first people might have planted a seed in Tolkien's mind. Tolkien's term for the Elves eventually came to mean "People of the Stars," but as explained by Christopher Tolkien, it didn't start off with that meaning: "The name *Eldar* was already in existence in Valinor before the Awakening, and the story of its being given by Oromë ('the People of the Stars') had not arisen... *Eldar* had a quite different etymology at this time."[220] He also noted that the term "Eldar" went back even before *The Book of Lost Tales* when it meant "a beach-fay" or "a being from outside" from *eg* "far away, distant."[221] He concluded: "The association of Eldar with the stars does not go back to the beginning."

It isn't clear when this change occurred. But by the mid-1930s Tolkien had shifted the meaning of Eldar to its more well-known translation. In a note on the revisions to a manuscript published in *The Lost Road and Other Writings* Christopher Tolkien observed: "With the emendation made to *Lhammas B* we meet at last the ideas that it was Oromë who named the Elves Eldar, that Eldar meant 'Star-folk'..."[222] He added that the texts in this volume were written "up to the time at the end of 1937 and the beginning of 1938 when he set them for long aside."[223] These were "texts of the later 1930s[.]"

In this case, Tolkien's shift of the meaning of "Eldar" made his tales of the Elves slightly more congruent with the Skidi notion of the first folk on earth as star-people. If Tolkien drew inspiration from the Skidi cosmology for this conception, it makes sense that he would have done so during the period 1930-1932 when he arguably looked at *Traditions of the Skidi Pawnee* for help in writing "The Adventures of Tom Bombadidl" and *The Hobbit*. Taking note of Roaming Scout's story, "Lightning Visits the Earth," Tolkien subsequently shifted the meaning of "Eldar" as part of his continuing project to impart to his legendarium an aura of "primitive" cultural undergrowth.

Lightning carried people in a bag, so it may be significant that Tolkien began *The Hobbit* by having the wizard Bladorthin visit "Baggins" who lives at "Bag-End"; and it is the wizard's intention to send this hobbit forth from Bag-End. He later had Bilbo pose a riddle for Smaug: "I am come from the end of a bag, but no bag went over me."[224] This riddle referred to the fact that the first adventure in the book involved the stuffing of the adventurers into bags. The exploits of "Baggins" concluded with his return to the end of his bag, and there he found himself "Presumed Dead"[225] – the Skidi story of Lightning and his bag was about the origin of death.

Tolkien borrowed "Bag End" from his family history – it was the name of an aunt's farm.[226] With Bag End already in his mind, encountering the Skidi story, "Lightning Visits the Earth," the imagery of star-people who were brought to earth in a bag would have attracted his attention. In later years Tolkien wrote that Bag End was "meant to be associated (by hobbits) with the end of a 'bag'."[227]

Tolkien must have relished the idea of hiding Lightning's mythical bag behind prosaic Bag End. This may explain why he found more than one use for elements of "Lightning Visits the Earth" in writing *The Hobbit*. We next encounter the Skidi story when Tolkien introduced Bilbo to "stone-giants," a class of creatures that make no other appearance in Middle-earth. Up to this point in his work, Tolkien found several scattered occasions to mention giants in his legendarium, but they did not appear in person in any Middle-earth story until his expedition of Dwarves entered the Misty Mountains.

John Rateliff and Douglas Anderson reasonably suggested that Tolkien may have drawn on German folklore to invent his stone-giants.[228] But the Andrew Lang story they cite concerns a "mountain Gnome" who is not a giant. For this reason it seems appropriate to consider other candidates, and in the Skidi story we do have a more likely giant – one who can shed real light on the origin of Tolkien's stone-giants.

"One day," wrote Tolkien of his wayfaring Dwarves in the Misty Mountains, "they met a thunderstorm..."[229] Tolkien described "how terrific a really big thunderstorm can be down in the land and in a river-valley; perhaps you have seen thunder and lightening [sic] in the mountains at night" and "lightning splinters on the peaks[.]" Bilbo "peeped out and in the lightning-flashes he saw that across the valley the stone-giants were out" playing a game. "Then came a wind and a rain, and the wind whipped the rain and hail about..."

In "Lightning Visits the Earth," told by Roaming Scout, Evening Star "commanded Lightning to visit the earth. The Wind rose. Clouds came. The Thunders sounded and Lightning came. As the storm arose Bright-Star commanded Lightning to go into a cloud, so that he could be placed upon the earth. Now Lightning was a giant."[230] Evening Star promises, "By my power I shall send Winds, Clouds, the Rain, and the Lightning[.]" And so Lightning the Giant is placed on earth, and after fulfilling his mission, "He returned to the west, upon high mountains... He was sitting upon a high mountain, with a mountain at his side, a stream of water in front, with a grassy valley."

Both stories situated their giants among mountains and rivers and valleys, among thunder, lightning, rain, and wind. But it is particularly interesting that Tolkien made sure to reveal his giants to Bilbo Baggins and to readers for the first time in conjunction with lightning: "in the lightning-flashes he saw... across the valley the stone-giants[.]" To emphasize this moment, in an illustration Tolkien drew "The Mountain-Path," showing a path in steep mountains lit by a great stroke of lightning. And it was in the months or years after he wrote down this scene, after he sketched the scene of mountain lightning – drawing from

Lightning the Giant, who carries a sack full of people who are really stars – that Tolkien transformed the meaning of the term Eldar away from "beach-fay" to "People of the Stars."

Tolkien bestowed upon the stone-giants a somewhat misty but suggestive history. Speaking of the shape-shifter Beorn, Gandalf informed the Dwarves: "Whether he is a bear descended from the great bears of the mountains that lived here before the giants came, or a man descended from the old men who lived there before Smaug invaded the land and the goblins came into the hills out of the North, I can't say."[231] The stone-giants thus "came" to the Misty Mountains at some point in the past, just as Lightning the Giant journeyed from elsewhere to his high mountains. And Tolkien later changed "the old men" into "the first men," which would further conjoin them and the stone-giants as figures in a misty ancient age, suggestive of Lightning the Giant and his sack full of the first people. In this manner, Tolkien's historical glimpse of the stone-giants contained a faint echo of the Skidi version of distant antiquity.

This echo was amplified by the fact that Skidi tradition contained giants who dwelt upon the earth in antiquity.[232] These giants were rude creatures – just as Tolkien's stone-giants were not very decent – and for their sins they are destroyed by flood. Tirawa sent several rain clouds to the land of the giants and finally managed to drown them, and it is notable that we encounter Tolkien's stone-giants under a cloudburst. But most noteworthy is the fact that Tolkien did not have to invent the term "stone-giants." One endnote in *Traditions of the Skidi Pawnee* contained this interesting comment: "At the time of the flood the giants were turned into stone."[233]

In a letter written in 1961 Tolkien briefly mentioned that his "thunder-battle" in *The Hobbit* drew from his experiences in the Swiss Alps in his youth. This "thunder-battle" was derived from "a bad night in which we lost our way and slept in a cattle-shed[.]"[234] If we take at face value Tolkien's 1961 memory of a thunderstorm in the Swiss Alps, this means that when he encountered the Skidi story of Lightning and the Skidi giants who were turned into stone, these moments surely resonated with his personal experience. For this reason he felt moved to imagine and invent his stone-giants.

But the Skidi stone-giants and the Skidi god Lightning could never expect to receive explicit acknowledgement in Middle-earth. Tolkien's agenda as a mythologist had nothing to do with promoting the mythology of Pawneeland and everything to do with evoking a mythical past for England and northern Europe. And so when Gandalf the Grey pondered the origin of the stone-giants, the wizard concluded his musings with "I can't say."

Coyote Bombadil

The eccentric charm of JRR Tolkien's Tom Bombadil has puzzled and entertained millions of readers since publication of *The Lord of the Rings*. Responding to inquiries from intrigued readers, Tolkien adopted a mysterious air about the origin of this character, writing in a 1954 letter that "even in a mythical Age there must be some enigmas" and "Bombadil is one (intentionally)."[235]

Tolkien's tales involving Bombadil first arose during the late 1920s in storytelling sessions with his children – the adventures of a Dutch doll the family once owned.[236] The earliest known Bombadil text is a short poem written about 1930. The original manuscript does not survive; Tolkien transcribed the poem late in life with the note "Date unknown – germ of Tom Bombadil so evidently in mid 1930s[.]"[237] He followed with a second poem, "The Adventures of Tom Bombadil"; excerpts from this poem were written in a script dated circa 1931.[238] This second poem was subsequently published in February 1934.

In the first edition of *Tolkien in Pawneeland* (2013, p. 57-64) I set forth various parallels to show that Tolkien drew on three Skidi Pawnee fantasy tales to create the incidents that appear in "The Adventures of Tom Bombadil." I argued that Tolkien consciously studied these Pawnee traditions and consciously used them to colorize his Bombadil poem.

Sitting down to write "The Adventures of Tom Bombadil," Tolkien wove together elements borrowed from diverse sources to create the scenes. This was his usual practice in dealing with traditional materials. But to understand the making of this poem and the making of Tom Bombadil, we must scroll back to Tolkien's early writings, back to the text of his Middle-earth creation story.

In "The Music of the Ainur" (dating to 1919-1920), after the making of Middle-earth, "many of the most beautiful and wisest of the Ainur, craved leave of Ilúvatar to dwell within the world."[239] These "great ones" entered the world and became gods known as the Valar, but they came accompanied by lesser spirits described as "sprites of trees and woods, of dale and forest and mountain-side": "These are the... brownies, fays, pixies, leprawns, and what else are they not called, for their number is very great: yet they must not be confused with the Eldar, for they were born before the world and are older than its oldest, and are not of it, but laugh at it much, for had they not somewhat to do with its making, so that it is for the most part a play for them[.]"[240]

Describing these semi-divinities as "sprites of trees and woods, of dale and forest and mountain-side" Tolkien could have drawn inspiration here from any number of mythological traditions. But this passage sounds very much like a specific description by John Rhys, describing "spirits" of antiquity that "vulgar imagination peopled all the Celtic lands..."[241] "The number of these minor divinities was legion..." he wrote. And they "included the spirits of particular forests, mountain tops, rocks, lakes, rivers, river-sources, and all springs of water..." Rhys thought these spirits very ancient, and "as to the innumerable divinities attached, so to say, to the soil, the great majority of them were very possibly the creations of the peoples here before the Celts."

Tolkien had his sprites, brownies, fays, pixies, and leprawns entering Middle-earth in company with the gods. Their exact natures were not set forth in the creation story, but they are not gods themselves, nor are they Elves. Tolkien associated these merry creatures with two Valar, Aulë and Palúrien. Deploying so many names for them, he perhaps envisioned some kind of diversity among them and he may have had some intention to devise more exact classifications and characteristics in later tales. He included the class of "fays" on an early chart of seven categories of creatures.[242]

In writings that soon followed, Tolkien began inserting these fays into his tales. In "The Chaining of Melko" he introduced Tinfang Warble or Timpinen, noting "this quaint spirit is neither wholly of the Valar nor of the Eldar, but is half a fay of the woods and dells, one of the great companies of the children of Palúrien, and half a Gnome or a Shoreland Piper."[243] This character originated in a 1914 poem, where he is described as a "leprawn," and in an early glossary of terms he is a "fay."[244]

In this same tale appeared a second such creature: "...the lonely twilight spirit (Tindriel) Wendelin dancing in a glade of beeches."[245] This "spirit" is known in *The Book of Lost Tales* under many names (Wendelin, Gwendelin, Gwendeling, Gwedheling, Gwenethlin, Gwenniel), but Tolkien eventually settled on the name Melian. She was also variously described as "a sprite come long ago from the quiet gardens of Lórien" and also as "the fay Wendelin."[246] In "The Tale of Tinúviel" Queen Wendelin "was a sprite that escaped from Lórien's gardens"; and later on the same page she is Gwendeling, "for indeed Gwendeling was not elf or woman but of the children of the gods..." And a few pages later she is again "a fay, a daughter of the Gods..."[247]

Tolkien seemed to use these terms interchangeably in *The Book of Lost Tales* with no clear demarcations of definition, other than to distinguish these creatures as a group apart from the Valar and from the Eldar. They are notable for their ability to exert forms of magic in Middle-earth: "...the magics of Gwendeling the fay, and she wove spells about the paths..." and "...that fay Gwedheling the queen [wove] much magic and mystery and such power of spells as can come only from Valinor[.]"[248]

It is also interesting that in these early writings Tolkien associated the quality of fearlessness with Melian's two children: "Even at night when the moon shone pale still would they play and dance, and they were not afraid as I should be, for the rule of Tinwelint and of Gwendeling held evil from the woods and Melko troubled them not as yet, and Men were hemmed beyond the hills."[249]

In summary, Tolkien created a special class of creatures and applied to them a spectrum of terms that included spirits, sprites, fays, leprawns, brownies, pixies, and children of the gods. These beings were divinities of some kind, but they were not gods, nor were they Elves. It might also be inferred that these creatures could take on Elvish forms, and they had qualities of playful laughter, fearlessness, and magical abilities. They came to Middle-earth in company with the Valar and were particularly associated with a Vala called Palúrien, also known as Yavanna, and her associate Lórien.

Through the early to mid-1920s Tolkien turned his tales of Middle-earth into long poems, but in 1926 he returned to prose with his "Sketch of the Mythology" – there he briefly mentioned Melian, referring to her as a queen "of divine race" who wields "divine magic."[250] Then in the *Quenta*, a more comprehensive manuscript written in 1930, Tolkien prepared a compendium based on *The Book of Lost Tales*. In this text he revisited the special class of divinities he had created in 1919-1920: "Many spirits [this becomes Many lesser spirits] they brought in their train, both great and small, and some of these Men have confused with the Eldar or Elves: but wrongly, for they were before the world, but Elves and Men awoke first in the world after the coming of the Valar."[251]

He has here reduced the group from a seeming diversity of spirits to a single group termed "lesser spirits," though a little later he again referred to Melian as a fay.[252] This was echoed in "The Earliest Annals of Valinor," written circa 1930-1931, where he added this: "With them [the Valar] came many lesser spirits, their children, or beings of their own kind but of less might; these are the Valarindi."[253]

This is where matters stood in Tolkien's Middle-earth cosmos when he turned to the invention of Tom Bombadil. Envisioning distinguishable classes of sentient beings for Middle-earth, Tolkien set forth a ranked gradation of creatures, with the Valar, who are gods; followed by divine "spirits," who go by many names at first; and then the Eldar, and finally humankind.

In the first Bombadil poem we find Tom rowing a boat upon a river with a friend, seeking other friends.[254] There are willows and reeds and wind and ripples, and this short poem displayed a cheerful tone, ending with "let laughter run a-ringing!" It is difficult to see this poem and its protagonist as fitting into Middle-earth. The poem reflected most strongly the kind of storytelling that Tolkien devised to entertain his sons, referring to a doll rowing upon a river.

One aspect is clear. Tolkien had by this time invented a name for the Dutch figurine. But where did this name arise? This mystery he chose to leave unexplained. Refusing to shed light on the naming of Bombadil, Tolkien was not being coy. As a linguist he had learned a special pleasure of philology, piecing together vague linguistic puzzles. He knew the pleasure of seeing strange little shapes click into meaningful configurations, for lost scenes to materialize from oblivion. Inventing a persona for the Dutch doll, Tolkien drew from this sensibility to make a name.

Linguist Mark T. Hooker made an interesting discovery one day. He learned that a bell in the Tom Tower of Christ Church at Oxford University is known as the "Great Tom" bell.[255] It had originally featured an odd inscription in Latin: "In Thomae laude resono Bim Bom sine fraude," meaning "In praise of Thomas I ring out Ding Dong truly." This dedication to St. Thomas of Canterbury was erased in 1680 when the bell was recast, but record of it endured. In 1926 Tolkien took up a professorship at Oxford University, and Hooker suggested that Tolkien came across a record of the old inscription and drew from that to invent a name for the Dutch doll: Tom Bombadil. As fellow "dictionary diver" Jason Fisher remarked, Hooker's argument has "a genuine ring of truth."[256]

Tolkien wrote the original version of "The Adventures of Tom Bombadil" – his second Bombadil poem – sometime around 1931.[257] This poem featured a sequence of incidents involving a "Riverwoman's daughter" named Goldberry, a "Willow-man," a "Badger-brock," and "Barrow-wight." None of these characters were drawn from any previous text associated with Middle-earth. To some degree, Tolkien composed "The Adventures of Tom Bombadil" with his children in mind. He must have been inspired by Kenneth Grahame's *The Wind in the Willows* (1908) with its river setting, its Wild Wood, its Badger, and the willows in the title – Grahame's influence on Tolkien is more commonly noted with regard to *The Hobbit*. Devising adventures for Tom Bombadil in his storytelling, Tolkien knew his children would enjoy hearing echoes of *The Wind in the Willows*.

The magic of Goldberry reflected a new configuration of characterization for Tolkien. As a "water-lady" who dwelt with her mother in a shady pool, no one like her could yet be found in Tolkien's writings. And he never shed any explicit light on the specific inspirations for any of the details that shaped Goldberry, but he had many inspirational models near at hand. One 1851 publication contrasted folkloric kelpies and "the water-wraith," noting that kelpies had "the form of a young horse" while the water-wraith resembled "a very tall woman, dressed in green..."[258]

The John Rhys 1901 collection of Welsh and Manx folklore featured a lengthy section on just such a character in Welsh tradition, beginning with the story of a beautiful woman who dwelt with her family in a lake.[259] Rhys went on to provide an extended consideration of fairy / human intermarriage. More recently John Bowers has pointed to medieval literature for a possible model for Goldberry.[260] A 14th century English lyric associated a maid with a marsh and with lilies, and this text would have been known to Tolkien. Bower also cited a 1968 publication by Peter Dronke setting forth references in German legends to moor-maidens as a kind of water-sprite associated with well-springs. And Bower noted English "water-hags" like Peg Powler as a possible influence.

By 1930-1931 Tolkien's Cauldron of Story included a substantial body of his own writings, and these hovered near at hand as he crafted the Bombadil poem, as they did during this same period for *The Hobbit*. As a character Goldberry aligns well with Tolkien's evolving class of "lesser spirits," who had by then become the Valarindi, with the term "fay" lingering where the other labels had vanished. Tolkien would later find himself connecting *The Hobbit* to Middle-earth, and it would have been just as easy for him to follow this same path in creating Goldberry.

In other words, Goldberry represents a natural evolution from Tolkien's already-extant "lesser spirits" and "fays."[261]

In the view of Mark Hooker, Tolkien assembled Goldberry's name by weaving together complex threads of scholarship.[262] Hooker referred to one of Tolkien's terms for "gold," *mal*, and related it to a Welsh word, *mael*, used for gold. And he suggested that "berry" appears in various forms in British place-names, referring to a meadow or heath. He related this to the name of a daughter of a Welsh river goddess, Maelan, "The Gold," and a Welsh place-name, Rhosmaelan or Maelan's Meadow.

In *The Welsh People* John Rhys made mention of "an old woman of fabulous age called Bera, Béara, or Béirre" who attained "the status of a witch or wise woman... not quite to that of a goddess."[263] This could be evidence that Tolkien drew from Rhys to construct the name "Goldberry" but Bera does not seem much like Goldberry, and there are no further notable parallels of the text to "The Adventures of Tom Bombadil."

Another possibility is that the name "Goldberry" emerged as a modification of the Old English term *goldwine* in *Beowulf*. Tolkien translated this word as "goldfriend... a lord or king" who is "generous in gifts of treasure to his kin and loyal knights."[264] Not only did Goldberry have a generous quality, this particular source also has the authority of a more direct English ancestry – a good ingredient for a character who Tolkien later identified as a spirit of the English countryside. He would have had to merely change his "wine" into "berry." But if we accept a Welsh inspiration for the name "Goldberry" – and following from an influence of the Rhys publications on Welsh folklore – then it fits that Tolkien would turn to Celtic tradition to help devise elements of Goldberry's character.

A folklorist named RC Maclagan published a paper on Scottish folklore in 1914 that featured a folkloric figure who seems to prefigure Goldberry.[265] Writing of a Washer Woman or "Bean Nigheachain, otherwise Bean Nighidh," Maclagan described her as a "water nymph" who "is of small size" and resembles a woman and wears a green dress. But she is not a woman. Her feet are "webbed like a duck's." She is "a Washer Woman, and what she washes is described as 'clothes of the battle' and shrouds (aodach matrbh, ais-leine)."

She is not malevolent, but she can seem dangerous, as one story tells: "A lad who saw one and went down to her was dipped by her in the river, she abusing him for going too near her. An onlooker who sees the Washer Woman first has nothing to fear, but if she sees him first she will get the better of him."

In the Bombadil poem Goldberry wears a "green gown" and is "robed all in silver-green" like the Washer Woman.[266] The Scottish lad who got dipped by a Washer Woman in the river could have provided the model for Goldberry pulling Tom by his beard into the river. But in contrast to the lad, Tom has nothing to fear, and he eventually gets the better of her.

Tolkien returned to Goldberry in 1938, and he again dressed her in a "green gown" – and he would bestow upon her even more aspects of the Maclagan Washer Woman.[267] Whether Tolkien saw the Maclagan publication or one very like it, it is plainly arguable that he chose to weave distinctive echoes of this Scottish source material into his circa 1931 poem and later into *The Fellowship of the Ring*.

Pondering his version of a British water fairy, Tolkien could have chosen to retell the Welsh tale of the Lady of Lyn y Fan Fach; he could have described her as the "maid of the moor" rather than as the "river-daughter"; he could have named her Peg Powler rather than Goldberry. Tolkien chose instead to follow his own mythic path, but it was a path rooted in British mythological soils.

What about Tom, the Dutch figurine? The making of Goldberry might well have led Tolkien to steer Tom Bombadil out of his family folklore and toward the edges of his growing legendarium. Nothing in the two early Bombadil poems overtly referenced his mythology, but the experimentation with a fairy marriage echoed Tolkien's interest in pondering the union of Men and Elves. The early Bombadil materials more clearly reflected Tolkien's creative project of weaving together diverse mythic fabrics into new stories.

As I wrote in the first edition of *Tolkien in Pawneeland*, I believe that Tolkien colorized "The Adventures of Tom Bombadil" with elements drawn from *Traditions of the Skidi Pawnee*.[268] The book featured a collection of narratives that editor George Dorsey termed "Animal Tales." These Coyote stories were a form of Pawnee storytelling that embodied an ancient North American fantasy literary heritage.

The first three Coyote stories in *Traditions of the Skidi Pawnee* contain incidents that parallel the four adventures that Tom Bombadil experienced in Tolkien's poem. The first of the tales, "The Story of Coyote" contributed to Tom's encounter with Goldberry. The same Skidi tradition inspired the entrapment of Tom in the crack of a tree, Old Willow-man. The second Skidi Coyote story shaped Tom's badger adventure. And the third Skidi Coyote story helped to inspire Tom's adventure with a deadly barrow-wight.

My argument is that Tolkien read all three Skidi Coyote stories sometime in 1930 or early 1931, and he borrowed elements that he then mixed into his Bombadil poem. The four incidents in the Bombadil poem and the four incidents in the Pawnee stories exist in precise alignment. This indicates that Tolkien studied the stories in sequence and extracted elements of interest and worked them into the Bombadil poem in exact sequence.

It is not possible that this process of authorship could have been independently enacted by JRR Tolkien with no awareness of the Skidi stories. It is not possible that Tolkien could have accidentally reproduced such faithful corresponding elements on his own with no knowledge of the Skidi stories.

The first Coyote story in *Traditions of the Skidi Pawnee* is Cheyenne Chief's "The Story of Coyote," and certain elements of this story echo certain details of Tom's adventure with Goldberry.[269] In this tale a boy hero decided to win the hand of the Leader's daughter and eventually the Leader invited the boy hero to marry one of his daughters. The boy hero took the youngest daughter to a pond, "I am going upon this pond, and shall be gone for some time." In the center of the water he dove. "The boy dived, disappeared, and stayed a long time under the water." When he came up from the water, he was dressed in fine clothing and wore a cap "made of woodpeckers' heads, the heads placed in front, and the feathers behind."

In the 1934 poem, "The Adventures of Tom Bombadil," Tom wore a "feather-hat" adorned with a peacock feather, and Goldberry pulled him by his beard into the river and "he went a-wallowing / under the water-lilies, bubbling and a-swallowing." Goldberry teased him, accusing him of "frightening the finny fish and the brown water-rat, / startling the dabchicks, and drowning your feather-hat!" In their various waters, both Tom and the Skidi boy are heroes wearing hats with bird feathers – hats that get drenched in the course of the stories.

Both men entered the water for the sake of a woman, and both stories result in marriage. This theme is present in the Welsh tales collected by John Rhys – there we find various fairy wives associated with lakes. These fairy women agree to conditional marriages with mortal men and vanish after the conditions have been violated. But this element of courtship is absent from the Scottish Washer Woman traditions, as is the drowning of a feather-hat.

Creating Tom Bombadil's adventure with Goldberry, Tolkien wove together a spectrum of threads from Welsh and Scottish and Pawnee tradition. Envisioning Tom Bombadil as an adventurer in a realm of the imagination, Tolkien had no interest in duplicating any specific mythological character. He instead consulted tales from various traditional literatures to borrow details that he found interesting, and it is also likely that he kept in mind his own evolving class of magical fays.

The second adventure in the Bombadil poem involved a tree that traps Tom. In the poem Willow-man magically sang Bombadil to sleep, and "in a crack caught him tight: quiet it closed together, / trapped Tom Bombadil, coat and hat and feather." Willow-man teased Tom, and the tree finally relented: "Willow-man let him loose, when he heard him speaking[.]" We next find

Tom sitting "a-listening." "On the boughs piping birds were chirruping and whistling." And "Tom called the conies out, till the sun was sinking." This last detail appeared in the 1934 version of the poem, but Tolkien deleted it from the version published in the 1960s.

The Skidi story began with a bird that all the young men are hunting, and it "sat on the dry limb of a high tree" and in the evening flew west "as the sun went down." The Skidi boy-hero demonstrated his magic by shooting another bird through his tipi entrance; then shooting several rabbits. He soon embarked on an adventure in which Coyote tricked him out of his robe and feather-hat and maneuvered him into climbing a magic tree. Coyote caused the tree to swiftly grow, carrying away the young man, who escaped with help of birds. In contrast to the Skidi boy-hero, Tom was "trapped" but kept his "coat and hat and feather."

Cheyenne Chief's tale transitioned into an account of Coyote's adventures.[270] After killing a bear, Coyote noticed "two elm-trees standing there, which were rubbing one another, so that when the wind blew these two trees would make a squeaking noise, and that would frighten Coyote." He climbed one tree and put his hand upon the squeak. "While he was feeling with his hand, the trees came together again and his hand was caught. So he was held fast. He tried to get away, but he could not." At last "the trees parted and let Coyote loose."

In the same Skidi story we find mention of singing and a further mishap involving a tree.[271] Coyote met a medicine-man with a Coyote Bundle. This bundle spoke about singing and dancing, and it taught the song and dance to Coyote. Coyote killed the medicine-man and soon got into trouble, escaping with the help of two buzzards. But these birds dropped Coyote "so that he fell into a hollow log, and down he went, screaming and yelling." This tree "was cracked at the base, so Coyote took his knife out and made a hole in it." And he tricked some women into cutting down the tree to free him. Reading the Skidi stories, Tolkien had a choice of adventures involving trees.

The stories do have many substantive differences, but the list of parallels between this specific Bombadil adventure and the

Skidi story include the shared presence of birds, conies, sunset, a focus on comparable clothing, singing, and imprisonment inside a tree. A more general equivalency comes in the character of the Skidi boy hero / Coyote and Bombadil as adventuresome characters who overcome difficulties. These unique and diverse elements point to deliberate borrowing. It would be quite a stretch to deem these parallels unrelated coincidence.

Humphrey Carpenter reported that Bombadil's adventure with a tree in this poem "probably came in part from Arthur Rackham's tree-drawings[.]"[272] Other scholars have suggested that Tolkien found his tree-adventure in a story by George MacDonald, *The Golden Key*. In that fairytale a little girl escapes through a wood at sunset and is briefly captured by tree-branches and then liberated by a magic "air-fish" – it is also possible that the MacDonald story helped to inspire aspects of Goldberry.

If the MacDonald story with its nominal associations can be taken seriously as an inspiration to Tolkien in writing "The Adventures of Tom Bombadil," then it is important to acknowledge source material with much stronger parallels. The parallels between the Pawnee Coyote story and the Bombadil adventure with Old Man Willow are much stronger than the parallels that can be seen in the MacDonald story.

One notable difference in between the Bombadil poem and the Pawnee story involves the species of tree. The trees that trapped Coyote were elms, but the tree that enchanted Bombadil was a willow. Tolkien's decision to make Tom's adversarial tree a willow is probably rooted in English folklore – he must have known about a folk song called "The Bitter Withy." A collection published by Cecil Sharp in 1911, *English Folk-Carols*, featured a version of this song.[273] Sharp collected versions of "The Bitter Withy" from various places, including a variant from Buckland in Gloucestershire. In the song a young Jesus took three friends on an adventure in which all three were drowned, and Mary punished Jesus by laying him across her knee and whipping him with "green withy twigs." Jesus cursed the tree, saying, "...the withy shall be the very first tree / That shall perish at the heart!"

In the early 1930s Tolkien had not yet invented either Buckland in the Shire or the Withywindle. But he could have consulted *English Folk-Carols* again in 1938 when he decided to send four adventurers from his newly created Buckland to the Withywindle for an encounter with Old Man Willow. The British Withy song explains why willows rot at the heart, and when we return to Old Man Willow in *The Fellowship of the Ring*, we learn that Old Man Willow's "heart was rotten[.]" Tolkien did not retell the Bitter Withy story, but instead drew elements from it.

To write his 1934 poem Tolkien took folk elements from English and Pawnee tradition and skillfully wove them together to create Tom Bombadil's adventure. And he returned to the folksong's four adventurers in 1938 to help inspire an adventure of four friends in Middle-earth. It was Tolkien's habit to draw together disparate threads into a coherent and new tapestry.

Tolkien's decision to insert a badger adventure into "The Adventures of Tom Bombadil" could have been inspired by the badger in *The Wind in the Willows* or by Tommy Brock in Beatrix Potter's popular 1912 novel *The Tale of Mr. Tod*. But it is difficult to identify any traces of these sources in the poem. In contrast, clear parallels exist in the second Coyote story in the Skidi collection: "Coyote Rescues a Maiden" told by Newly Made Chief Woman.[274]

In this story Coyote must rescue his daughter from some buffalo who use her for a round gaming ring; in "The Adventures of Tom Bombadil" Tom hurried in the rain with "round rings spattering in the running river." Coyote rescued his daughter and escaped with the help of a badger who "began to dig the ground, Coyote following him." And "old Tom Bombadil crept into a shelter." There "Badger-brock" and "his wife and many sons" captured Tom, and they "pulled him inside the hole, down their tunnels…" Coyote took shelter in Badger's home, while Badger dug many tunnels and exit holes to deceive the buffalo. The badgers told Tom, "You'll never find it out, the way that we have brought you!" But "Coyote said he had done his duty, and he wanted now to live in the hole and make it his dwelling-place[.]"

Even so, Tom has frightened the badgerfolk and they "hid themselves a-shivering and a-shaking / ...earth together raking"; and in Pawneeland the badger "being frightened... had digged into the ground" and "he thought it would be better for him to live in the ground[.]"

It is notable that up to this point, each of Tom Bombadil's adventures unfolded in exact sequence to parallel incidents in the Pawnee stories. The protagonist in the first incident is a heroic youth who Coyote seeks to overcome. In the second and third adventures, however, Coyote's adventures become the adventures of Tom Bombadil. For the fourth adventure, Tolkien turned to Norse tradition, but certain essences resonate with the third Skidi Coyote story.

Tom's fourth adventure in "The Adventures of Tom Bombadil" involved an undead creature that was probably borrowed from a description by Andrew Lang: "In the graves where treasures were hoarded the Barrowwights dwelt, ghosts that were sentinels over the gold..."[275] Lang here mentioned the Icelandic saga of Njal and "dead Gunnar" who "sang within his cairn..." And on the previous page Lang referred to Grettir who battled "dead bodies that arose and wrought horrible things..."

Sometime during the 1930s, in the course of preparing lecture notes on Beowulf, Tolkien mentioned barrow-wights: "'Necromancy' will suggest something of the horrible associations of this word [orcnéas]. I think that what is here meant is that terrible northern imagination to which I have ventured to give the name 'barrow-wights.' The 'undead.' Those dreadful creatures that inhabit tombs and mounds. They are not living: they have left humanity, but they are 'undead.' With superhuman strength and malice they can strangle men and rend them. Glamr in the story of Grettir the Strong is a well-known example."[276] Tolkien's barrow-wights were doubtless inspired by Lang's essay on Norse sagas, but Tolkien chose not to term his barrow-wights "draugr" or some version of "ghost."

In the 1934 poem, "The Adventures of Tom Bombadil," this barrow-wight creature dwelt "in the old mound / up there atop the hill with the ring of stones round."[277] It is dangerous and threatens to kill Tom. It seems to have form of some kind, but very vague, with mention only of "gleaming eyes." This was Tolkien's first use of the term "barrow-wight." We also know that Tolkien was thinking about the term "wight" during the period 1930-1934 when he prepared an essay on Chaucer and translated the term as "swift."[278] The Chaucer tale in question included two different usages of that term, with one in the sense of "person" and the other in the sense of "swift."

The word "wight" in 19th century England did not typically refer to a ghost; nor was it associated with barrows. The term was most often applied to people. In James Halliwell's 1846 *A Dictionary of Archaic and Provincial Words* the term "wight" is listed with five meanings: a person; active, swift; weight; white; a small space of time; a witch.[279] Some of these are clearly alternate spellings of terms; none seem particularly promising as the source for an undead tomb monster.

The lengthy list of British folklore creatures in the 1895 *The Denham Tracts* did not include the word "wight," but "witless wight" does appear elsewhere in the tracts as a term of derision for a man. Joseph Wright's *English Dialect Dictionary* defined the word as "used contemptuously," with a second definition related to vigor, power, and strength.[280] In his Beowulf note Tolkien endowed barrow-wights with "superhuman strength." This follows the meaning in Halliwell of "active, swift"; but it closely aligned with Wright's definitions related to strength and power, suggesting that Tolkien's wight was more closely aligned with Wright's dictionary. Tolkien's later description of a barrow-wight in *The Fellowship of the Ring* retained this aspect of strength; there Frodo gets caught in "a grip stronger and colder than iron[.]"

Wights in English usage do not seem associated with tombs of any kind. But *The Denham Tracts* contains several references to standing stones as "sepulchral."[281] The identification of standing stones as mortuary monuments seems stronger elsewhere in Northern Europe. Tolkien mentioned a particular Norse story as an influence on his wight – a story that describes a man who rises undead from his grave. But this tale has no specific association with standing stones.

Tolkien's decision to conjoin his undead monster with standing stones could have been inspired in part by a Pawnee tradition about Coyote and a dangerous stone living atop a hill. In the course of creating adventures for Tom Bombadil, Tolkien drew from the first two Skidi Pawnee Coyote tales for details that appear in the first three Bombadil adventures. To formulate his final adventure, the Pawnee story brought to mind Lang's barrowwight and standing stones, but it nevertheless echoed elements in the third Skidi Coyote story.

In "Coyote and the Rolling Stone," Coyote "climbed up on some hills and came to a big stone" that is "round and smooth, and Coyote thought to himself... that stones were wonderful..."[282] And Tom went home and there he encountered "Barrow-wight dwelling in the old mound / up there a-top the hill with the ring of stones round." Coyote prayed to the round stone and gave it a knife but soon took back his gift. The angry stone began to chase Coyote. And Barrow-wight is quite a threatening figure, "Poor Tom Bombadil, pale and cold he'll make you!" Wildcats and mountain lions and bears and a whirlwind-man and a witch-woman can't help poor Coyote. Bull-bats help, destroying the dangerous stone, but they get angry and reassemble the rolling stone and it kills Coyote.

Unlike Coyote, Tom proved victorious. He returned home where he married Goldberry, the River-daughter, a fairy creature of Scotland. Dorsey's introduction to *Traditions of the Skidi Pawnee* called Coyote "a wonderful fellow" and Tom is "a merry fellow"; and Coyote is "very tricky" and Tom is "a clever fellow"; and since Coyote is "rarely ever finally vanquished" Tom surpasses the wiles of Old Man Willow, Badger-brock, and Barrow-wight, and "[n]one ever caught old Tom..."

I can imagine Tolkien sitting with his sons and ending a tale of Tom Bombadil with the same message that Skidi listeners took away from the telling of Coyote stories: "...when... a story is told in which Coyote, or some culture-hero overcomes his enemy, the teller thereby indicates his desire that he also may be equally successful."[283] This is, in fact, exactly the kind of story that appealed to Tolkien as a father during the writing of *The Hobbit*. His son Michael disliked and feared spiders, and he always believed that the chapter "Flies and Spiders" was written by his father "almost entirely for my benefit to show however big a spider was, he could, in fact be overcome."[284]

Barrow-wights first entered Tolkien's writings as fairytale monsters not associated with his Middle-earth legendarium. But in 1938 he decided to situate them in Middle-earth – at first he toyed with the idea of making his black riders mounted barrow-wights. But he ultimately retained the association of his barrow-wights with Tom Bombadil.

The early drafting of this adventure in 1938 mentioned a barrow but no standing stones; then a "stone pillar" entered the adventure, and finally "dark rocks" and "standing rocks."[285] Tolkien eventually decided to have the hobbits arrive at "a hill whose top was wide and flattened, like a shallow saucer with a green mounded rim." Within this hilltop hollow "there stood a single stone, standing tall under the sun...." The hobbits rested against this single stone and all became drowsy. This scene is certainly reminiscent of the Skidi story with its single "big stone" located "up on some hills."

Numerous elements in "The Adventures of Tom Bombadil" exist in sequence in three Skidi Coyote stories. Tom Bombadil and the Skidi hero-boy wear hats adorned with bird feathers; both hats get drenched; both men enter a body of water for the sake of a woman; and both stories result in marriage. The first Skidi story and the Bombadil poem both feature birds, conies, sunset, a focus on clothing, singing, and imprisonment inside a tree. The second Skidi Coyote story involves a badger, as does the third adventure of the Bombadil poem. In both appear round rings; Coyote and Bombadil both take shelter in badger homes; both mention "tunnels" and deceptive exits; in both accounts the badgers become frightened and dig to hide. In the third Skidi Coyote story, atop some hills rests a stone described as "wonderful" and deadly, while Tom's home stands near a hilltop with a "ring of stones" and a barrow-wight who threatens Tom with death.

These parallels are numerous and substantial. They occur in precise alignment. It is not helpful to ignore these corresponding parallels and their exact positioning. It is not rational to favor the impossible notion that these parallels might be an accident of chance invention. This assumption would stretch the notion of coincidence beyond reasonable probability.

To create his Bombadil poem, Tolkien read the Pawnee tales and drew from them various elements which he wove together with details from Scottish tradition, Norse sagas, and other material. And as I describe later, further resonations with Skidi myth occurred in the later 1938 drafting of the Bombadil / Goldberry tales for *The Fellowship of the Ring*. This creative process involved the careful interweaving of very diverse threads – a typical pattern of invention for Tolkien.

As for Tom Bombadil's origins, it is not clear at circa 1931 that Tolkien drew from his "lesser spirits" or from his Valar to invent Tom for the two early poems. Aside from the enigmatic transfer of excerpts of the poem into Elvish text, there is no other obvious or arguable association of Bombadil with Middle-earth. Only very minor hints in these early texts suggest that he might be something more than a human, a "merry fellow." But these hints are so slight that if the two early poems had been his only materialization in Tolkien's writings, no one would see Tom as anything other than a clever human who had managed to capture the heart of a "fay" wife.

By the beginning of 1931 Tolkien had launched into the writing of *The Hobbit*. It isn't clear exactly how far he had progressed in this project when he sat down to write "The Adventures of Tom Bombadil" or whether the poem preceded *The Hobbit*. In the first edition of *Tolkien in Pawneeland* (p. 65-114) I argued that in 1930-1931 Tolkien consulted *Traditions of the Skidi Pawnee* and he drew inspiration and details of coloration for *The Hobbit*. I outlined textual comparisons to show that he drew from several Skidi stories to help invent the character of Bladorthin / Gandalf and to create the stone-giants of the Misty Mountains. And during the period dating from 1931 to 1932 Tolkien also drew inspiration from the Skidi stories to tell the story of Beorn and to help finalize the death of Smaug.

We must guess at how Tolkien proceeded in this usage of Pawnee material. But the extent to which Pawnee details entered *The Hobbit* tends to favor the view that Tolkien sat down during this period on at least two different occasions and consulted the Skidi stories in question. He did not necessarily have to study the stories closely, but he did read them, and he did give thought to what he read. And this was not a new procedure for Tolkien. He drew from the same volume of Skidi narratives to help write his creation story in 1919, to develop Ungoliont the spider, and to draw other details into *The Book of Lost Tales*.

My argument is that Tolkien was a mythologist. He focused on European traditions, but he also had a casual interest in world mythological traditions and he had a youthful fascination with "Red Indians." We know very little about what he read on this topic, what experiences shaped this interest in his life. It is reasonable to propose that he became aware of *Traditions of the Skidi Pawnee* through his more general interest in British fairytale folklore. He could have first found the book on the shelves of the Taylorian or some other library in a random encounter. He could have learned about it in the mythology section of a bookstore. But one thing is clear. Textual comparisons show that JRR Tolkien did make use of *Traditions of the Skidi Pawnee*.

The Almost Forgotten Hobbits

Just a few years after the death of JRR Tolkien, a discovery by folklorist Katharine Briggs intrigued researchers at the *Oxford English Dictionary* and left a minor wrinkle in the fabric of Tolkien scholarship. She found the term "hobbit" in an obscure 1895 book called *The Denham Tracts*.[286] The existence of a hobbit in that book posed an interesting problem because it pre-dated the period when Tolkien said he invented the term. It established the fact that Tolkien was not the first to use the word "hobbit" for a humanlike creature of British folklore. This opened a puzzling possibility. Perhaps he found the term. Maybe he didn't invent it in an idle moment, as he said.

In its day *The Denham Tracts* materialized during a period when British folklore was a vibrant field of study at its zenith. But by the time Tolkien began experimenting with hobbits, British folklore studies had gone into decline. Its miscellany had faded into a forgetful twilight; the Denham hobbit had vanished.

The Briggs reference to a forgotten folkloric hobbit came immediately to the attention of the Tolkien world, but it wasn't until 1989 that Donald O'Brien's groundbreaking study of the term appeared.[287] Tom Shippey would eventually set the tone in Tolkienland for how one should best interpret the discovery. He decided that an ascerbic dismissal was warranted: "It is somehow typical that the *OED* should have claimed... to have identified Tolkien's 'source' and 'inspiration' in J. Hardy's edition of *The Denham Tracts*, Vol. II (1895), which declares that 'the whole earth was overrun with ghosts, boggles... hobbits, hobgoblins.' The word 'hobbit' is there, but in a run of distinctly insubstantial creatures which hardly correspond to Tolkien's almost pig-headedly solid and earthbound race."[288] Shippey cited here a news report dated May 31, 1977 on the *Oxford English Dictionary* and the newly rediscovered Denham hobbit. The *OED* decided that Tolkien independently invented the word – my 1993 edition of the *New Shorter Oxford English Dictionary* listed the word as a Tolkien invention. And it made no mention of the word as a minor term of English folklore.[289]

Tolkien claimed that his 1930 "hobbit" did not derive from any previous "hobbit." On various occasions he described the circumstances under which he came to use the term "hobbit." Formulating what would become a widely embraced hobbit origin story, his accounts made no mention of borrowing any old forgotten word, such as the hobbit of *The Denham Tracts*. Tolkien wished for everyone to see his "hobbit" as his own creature, not derived in any manner from pre-existing folklore.

Shippey's tone warned that it would be discourteous to challenge Tolkien's account without good cause. But the discovery of the Denham hobbit raised questions that eventually began to attract inquiry. In so doing, as we shall see, it has slowly become apparent that certain major circumstances of Tolkien's hobbit origin story were mysteriously inconsistent, while other aspects were indeed consistent with his hobbit as a borrowed creature.

The dismissive quality of Shippey's tone and of the *OED* response both seem designed to insulate from scrutiny Tolkien's claim of independent invention. But Shippey's detailed and insightful expositions on Middle-earth have helped to establish our understanding of Tolkien's well-known strategy of reconstruction – a process that typically took extant terms for mythological creatures and reconfigured them. In the end, Shippey's assertion that the Denham hobbit does not correspond to Tolkien's hobbit diminishes the degree to which they do correspond.

The project to insulate Tolkien from inquiry soon ran into more problems. The Denham hobbit was not the only pre-Tolkien hobbit in Britain. It was already long-established that various kinds of "hobs" populated British folklore during the 19th century, but in 1989 Donald O'Brien showed that at least one other "hobbit" was extant in Britain long before Tolkien's hobbit first appeared in Middle-earth. Given the prior existence of these various British hobbits before *The Hobbit*, it is both appropriate and necessary to scrutinize Tolkien's hobbit origin story carefully, rather than accept it at face value.

To investigate the making of Tolkien's first hobbit, we can begin by separating these circumstances into interlocked elements. First, it is appropriate to review the term "hobbit" and some of its manifestations in British literature prior to Tolkien's adoption of the word at circa 1930. This history reveals that it is highly unlikely that Tolkien invented his Middle-earth hobbit as he claimed. Instead, his hobbit was more likely born from the mingling of two dictionary entries authored by his mentor and friend, Joseph Wright.

Second, adapting the term "hobbit," Tolkien followed his usual practice in filling the creature up with his own usages. This was a straightforward reconstructive strategy for Tolkien, but his journey took an unexpected turn. Instead of acknowledging his process of creative reweaving of tradition, he produced an origin story in which he took credit for unilateral invention of the term.

In 19th century Britain the term "hobbet" and its variants enjoyed widespread usage as a measurement of weight of agricultural products. The word seems to have arisen as a Welsh term, but its history is not very clear.[290] The variant form "hobbit" appeared in British publications as early as the 1863 edition of John Morton's *A Cyclopedia of Agriculture*.[291] An earlier edition published in 1855 did not contain the term. Morton's Welsh "hobbit" and definition was subsequently reprinted in various publications: "Hobbit (N. Wales), of wheat, weighs 168 lbs.; of beans, 180; of barley, 147, of oats, 105; being 2 1/2 bushels imperial."[292] This hobbit then appeared in Joseph Wright's *English Dialect Dictionary*.[293] All these sources defined a hobbit as an agricultural unit of weight and volume.

In 1892 and 1895 a publishing company called David Nutt issued two volumes of collected chapbooks and newspaper articles originally published in the 1840s and 1850s, gathered by Michael Denham.[294] These volumes were a project of the British

Folk-Lore Society, managed by two prominent members of the society. James Hardy prepared the tracts for publication and G. Laurence Gomme completed the editing of the second volume. Gomme's preface to the second volume of *The Denham Tracts* drew attention to a particularly interesting list of terms (p. ix):

> The names for the different classes of spirits (on p. 77-78) is very full, and needs some investigation philologically and mythologically, because, although there are names derived from obvious misconceptions of the popular mind, there are others which seem to me to contain important indications of early God-names. Apparitions, ghosts, and spirits make up a large element in north English folk-lore, for which the geographical and climatic conditions are no doubt chiefly answerable.

The cited list included the term "hobbits." Here it is in full: "...ghosts, boggles, bloody-bones, spirits, demons, ignis fatui, brownies, bugbears, black dogs, specters, shellycoats, scarecrows, witches, wizards, barguests, Robin-Goodfellows, hags, night-bats, scrags, breaknecks, fantasms, hobgoblins, hobhoulards, boggy-boes, dobbies, hob-thrusts, fetches, kelpies, warlocks, mock-beggars, mum-pokers, Jemmy-burties, urchins, satyrs, pans, fauns, sirens, tritons, centaurs, calcars, nymphs, imps, incubusses, spoorns, men-in-the-oak, hell-wains, fire-drakes, kit-a-can-sticks, Tom-tumblers, melch-dicks, larrs, kitty-witches, hobby-lanthorns, Dick-a-Tuesdays, Elf-fires, Gyl-burnt-tales, knockers, elves, rawheads, Meg-with-the-wads, old-shocks, ouphs, pad-fooits, pixies, pictrees, giants, dwafs, Tom-pokers, tutgots, snapdragons, sprets, spunks, conjurers, thurses, spurns, tantarrabobs, swaithes, tints, tod-lowries, Jack-in-the-Wads, mormos, changelings, redcaps, yeth-hounds, colt-pixies, Tom-thumbs, black-bugs, boggarts, scar-bugs, shag-foals, hodge-pochers, hob-thrushes, bugs, bull-beggars, bygorns, bolls, caddies, bomen, brags, wraithes, waffs, flay-boggarts, fiends, gallytrots, imps, gytrashes, patches, hob-and-lanthorns, gringes, boguests, bonelesses, Peg-powlers, pucks, fays, kidnappers, gallybeggars, hudskins, nickers, madcaps, trolls, robinets, friars' lanthorns, silkies, cauld-lads, death-hearses, goblins, hob-headlesses, buggaboes, kows, or cowes, nickies, nacks, [necks] waiths, miffies, buckies, gholes, sylphs, guests, swarths, freiths, freits, gy-carlins [Gyre-carling], pigmies, chittifaces, nixies, Jinny-burnt-tails, dudmen, hell-hounds, dopple-gangers, boggleboes, bogies, redmen, portunes, grants, hobbits, hobgoblins, brown-men, cowies, dunnies, wirrikows, alholdes, mannikins, follets, korreds, lubberkins, cluricauns, kobolds, leprechauns, kors, mares, korreds, puckles korigans, sylvans, succubuses, black-men, shadows, banshees, lian-hanshees, clabbernappers, Gabriel-hounds, mawkins, doubles, corpse lights or candles, scrats, mahounds, trows, gnomes, sprites, fates, fiends, sibyls, nicknevins, whitewomen, fairies, thrummy-caps, cutties, and nisses..."[295]

    The index listed many of these creatures under the generic label of "a class of spirits," and this included the term "hobbit" (p. 388): "Hobbits, a class of spirits."[296] No direct evidence exists to show that Tolkien ever consulted either volume of *The Denham Tracts*. Circumstantial clues add little on this point.

    In one 1951 letter Tolkien made mention of having "always been seeking material, things of a certain tone and air" which he "found (as an ingredient) in legends of other lands"; and he listed there the various mythological literatures that he found interesting "but nothing English, save impoverished chap-book stuff."[297] He shed no specific light here on what he meant by "impoverished chap-book stuff" though he did make mention of chapbook materials in his draft essay (circa 1938-1943) of "On Fairy-stories."[298] The context of his 1951 statement pertained to mythic fairytale materials distorted by Christianization, so the "impoverished chap-book stuff" must refer to English materials that he had encountered in pamphlet form and studied with a sense of disappointment. This could refer to any number of publications in British literature. It could also refer to more recent folkloric materials, such as a series of booklets launched by Alfred Nutt and the British Folk-Lore Society in 1899, *Popular Studies in Mythology, Romance and Folk-Lore*.[299] It also fits the material found in *The Denham Tracts*.

The various hobs in *The Denham Tracts* are striking but sketchy – none came with much definition. On p. 355-356 of volume 2 of *The Denham Tracts* we find discussion of a Hob Thrush as a sprite that is "a sort of a brownie" or "a goblin or spirit generally coupled with Robin Good-fellow." This brief note is interesting because Tolkien's 1922 "A Middle English Vocabulary" listed "Hobbe," defined as a "familiar form of Robert (used contemptuously)..."[300] The word "hobbe" could have inspired Tolkien's "hobbit." But as a term of insult, hobbe does not seem very promising as construction material for a new kind of small folkloric person. Tolkien never made mention of this potential connection, and if this hobbe served as the basis for his hobbit, it is difficult to understand why he would choose to keep silent on this point. The likely explanation is that Tolkien's Middle English hobbe did not contribute to the making of his hobbit. It is more likely that various Victorian-age hobs took on that job.

The Denham list featured a number of creatures whose names include the word "hob," and John Rateliff summarized the folklore on hobs: "The traditional hob of English folklore was a solitary creature, sometimes described as a little brown man a few feet high..."[301] He further noted that Tolkien's typical usage involved philological and mythological investigation of folkloric terms, adapting "actual folklore survivals just like the elves, dwarfs... wizards, goblins, giants, fire-drakes... trolls and hob-goblins, all of which occur both in *The Hobbit* and in Denham's list and all of which are given distinctly Tolkienian interpretations." Rateliff seemed to suggest that had Tolkien encountered the Denham hobbit, he might have seen this mysterious creature as another kind of "hob." Rateliff ultimately favored the view that Tolkien "probably never knew" of the Denham hobbit, but had Tolkien peered into *The Denham Tracts*, "he would almost certainly have discovered Denham's list[.]"[302] Believing that that no such encounter ever happened, Rateliff offered no insight into any potential context under which Tolkien would have encountered *The Denham Tracts* or any of the many hobs that appear in British folklore literature.

An example of these British hobs can be found in an 1840 dictionary.[303] This work listed a number of hobs: hobbil, hobgobbin, hob-hald, hob-thrush, hobgoblin, hob-thrust, and hobby-lanthorn. None were clearly defined as small magical creatures, and some were defined as derogatory terms for people, but this list reflected the kind of terms that were in play early in the century. Another dictionary of the period listed similar terms: hob, hobbil, hobby-lanthorn, hoberd, hobgobbin, hobgoblin, hobhoulard, and hob-thrush.[304] Again, only a few of these terms were defined as referencing magical creatures, and none were described. If "hobbit" ever served as another kind of hob in British tradition, it was a minor term that didn't see widespread use. The Denham hobbit was nowhere described or discussed in the Denham papers or elsewhere, but if we follow Rateliff's suggestion, it is most reasonably classed as some form of hob – as he described it: "a little brown man a few feet high[.]" Given the likeness, it seems reasonable that Tolkien could have borrowed his hobbit from the Denham list.

What is not speculative is the fact that Tolkien's literary interests were noticeably influenced by the British folklore community. Three authors who shaped Tolkien's lifelong interests were Andrew Lang, WS Kirby, and John Rhys – all were established figures in the British folklore scene. As a student at Oxford, Tolkien was tutored by William Craigie, a prominent member of the British folklore world during the 1890s.[305] Another personal connection existed through Tolkien's friendship with Raymond Chambers, who became a member of the Folk-Lore Society in 1912, and who Tolkien described in 1937 as "an old and kindhearted friend."[306] This was the same academic organization that published the 1905 review of George Dorsey's *Traditions of the Skidi Pawnee*.

Tolkien's connections to the British folklore community are clear. Given the fact of his awareness of British folklore and its associated literature, and given his creative strategy of mining mythological traditions for material that could be reconfigured into his own legendarium, it would be very surprising for Tolkien to independently improvise a hobbit that bears a merely coincidental likeness to an already extant folkloric British hob / hobbit. John Rateliff speculated that Tolkien could have had reason to glance at *The Denham Tracts* on various occasions between 1911 and 1923. This could just as easily have happened in 1930. But it is important to point out that Tolkien was one of the foremost scholars of British folklore in his time.

In short, it is not a stretch to assume that *The Denham Tracts* came to Tolkien's hand at some point, and that the Denham hobbit served as the unacknowledged inspiration for his own hobbit, and this history shaped *The Hobbit*. But as we will see, it is even more strongly arguable that in 1930 Tolkien became aware of the Welsh hobbit and English hobs. An empty folkloric term, an agricultural unit of weight, and vaguely described folkloric creatures do not seem particularly relevant to Middle-earth hobbits, but good reasons exist to believe that Tolkien found his hobbit in extant literature and configured it to suit his purposes.

It is also evident that in later years he deliberately declined to acknowledge this history. This choice on Tolkien's part – to withhold the true origin of his hobbit – has been widely accommodated in Tolkien studies. Recent publications on Tolkien and Wales make no mention of the Welsh hobbit despite acknowledgement of the extensive use of Welsh sources for diverse materials, such as his dragon Chrysophylax, his hobbit *Red Book*, various hobbit place names and family names, and other materials.[307] This circumstance should be read as respectful deference to Tolkien's widely disseminated representation of the history of his hobbit.

A particularly significant aspect of British folklore hobs can be found in the association of the creature with holes in the ground. The first volume of *The Denham Tracts* contains a brief mention of a 1772 report of hobgoblins inhabiting a cave.[308] But an 1895 paper published in an American philology journal went into considerable detail.

In "The Devil and his Imps: an Etymological Inquisition" Charles Scott listed many of the known kinds of hobs and also gave details about their character.[309] A "hob," for example, was "a rural spirit or goblin" also called a "Hobgoblin"; and these creatures were "countryside goblins" with the name applied to "any goblin, elf, or domestic spirit." And "hobs haunted caves, holes, crofts, fields, and other special places, which came to be known accordingly, Hob's Cave, Hob-croft, Hob-field, Hob-yard. It was so likewise with Hob-Thurst, Hob-Hurst, and Thurse..." Scott listed a "Hob's Cave at Mulgrave."

For "Hob-hole" Scott quoted from 1637 report of "...Hobb Hoyle lying in Sheffield soake." Scott explained that "hoyle is a dialectal variant of hole." He next quoted an 1867 book: "...there is a Hob Hole at Runswick, a Hob Hole near Kempswithen, a Hob's Cave at Mulgrave, Hobt'rush Rook on the Farndale Moors, and so on." For "Hob-House" he cited the "Hob of Runswick" and gave this 1855 account of it: "A hobgoblin haunting Hobholes, a cave in the cliff at Runswick, a fishing village near Whitby. He was famous for curing children of the hooping-cough or kin cough, when thus invoked by those who took them in – Hob hole hob! my bairn's gotten t'kin cough, / Tak 't off, tak 't off."

It is reasonable to suspect that Tolkien could have encountered Charles Scott's 1895 publication in the transactions of the American Philological Association. But it is more likely that Tolkien found his hobbit and hob hole in the pages of Joseph Wright's multivolume *English Dialect Dictionary*.

Wright's influence on Tolkien was substantial.[310] In his youth Tolkien encountered a book on Gothic by Wright that inspired his later interests as an academic philologist. When Tolkien attended Oxford University in 1911-1915 Wright was serving as Professor of Comparative Philology, and they developed a warm mutual appreciation that evolved into a close colleagueship. Tolkien's first post-WW1 job as a researcher for the *Oxford English Dictionary* gave him reason to familiarize himself with Wright's *English Dialect Dictionary*. In 1923 Tolkien wrote to Wright's wife an interesting letter in which he mentioned the *English Dialect Dictionary*, noting, "E.D.D. is certainly indispensible, or 'unentbehrlich' as really comes more natural to the philological mind, and I encourage people to browze in it."[311]

When Wright died on February 27, 1930, Tolkien served as executor of his estate.[312] Scholarship on the date that Tolkien first set down the word "hobbit" is not in complete agreement, but the most likely timing for the moment was the summer of 1930 – the very period that Tolkien had reason to give considerable thought to Wright's legacy and writings. In one volume of Wright's dictionary we find the Welsh hobbit and "hob's hole" just pages apart, as well as the suggestion that a hob was something like a man. For Tolkien to take notice of this Welsh hobbit in 1930 is consistent with the momentum of his existing scholarship on Celtic materials. In January 1929 he gave a lecture titled "Celts and Teutons in the Early World," and in his draft notes he stated, "I will mark myself as a Celtophile..."[313]

Tolkien already knew something about hobs by 1930. We know, at least, that he enjoyed browsing through Joseph Wright's *English Dialect Dictionary* during the early 1920s. For him to recollect in 1930 the collective imagery and terminology surrounding hobs from a casual encounter ten years earlier seems unlikely. But a new factor entered the picture in 1930. Now he was seeking material he could work into tales for his children. We can surmise that sometime in early 1930 Tolkien came across the terms "hob" and "hob hole" and "hobbit" in the course of browsing Wright's *English Dialect Dictionary*, and this precipitated his own version of a hob.

The dictionary contains a lengthy entry on "Hob."[314] Most notably, Wright mentioned that "Obthrush Rook, as well as Hob's Hole and the Cave at Mulgrave" were "haunted by the goblin." Wright told how the "Hob of the Cave at Runswick" cured children of illness, while the "Hob at Hart Hall, in Glaisdale" performed farmwork. These hobs went about "nak't," and when offered the wrong sort of clothing, determined to "come nae mair nowther..." Another township had stories of various hobs, including a "giant Hobb." Wright's survey of hobs ended with a comment that evoked Tolkien's Baggins / Bag-End: "Each elf-man or hobman had his habitation, to which he gave his name." This entry was followed by a short entry on "Hobbit," with a definition that repeated Morton's Welsh agricultural measure.

Wright knew of *The Denham Tracts*, citing it in his definition for "hob-lantern."[315] But his exhaustive survey of hobs and his entry for hobbit overlooked the Denham hobbit. It is also possible that he did not include any hobbit as a form of hob because he could find no evidence attesting to this identification in his sources, so he focused instead on the more established agricultural usage of the term.

Numerous British publications held etymological and folkloric material that could readily inspire Tolkien's hobbit. All of this material fell within the purview of Tolkien's professional interests. Given these circumstances, it is indeed reasonable to assume that he drew his hobbit from extant British source-materials, taking a term that seemed empty of mythological significance and reconfiguring it to suit his purposes. The Wright dictionary offers a particularly strong candidate for the precise source that inspired Tolkien's first hobbit.

In the course of writing *The Hobbit,* Tolkien also made use of another term related to hob. The word "hobthrush" can be found in all the sources that discuss English hobs. This hob entered mid-19th century dictionaries under various names – most often as a hobthrush or hobthrust.[316] A comprehensive survey of the folkloric material on this form of hob was provided by Charles Scott in his 1895 paper.[317] Joseph Wright's *English Dialect Dictionary* featured a detailed entry for "hob-thrust," listing it as "hob-thross, hob-thrush, hob-thurst, hob-trush, hog-thrush."[318] He defined this hob as a "hobgoblin, sprite, elf, 'thurse'" that was also known as a Robin Goodfellow. It was a solitary hob often associated with domesticity, a "hobgoblin having the repute of doing much useful work unseen and unheard during the night, if not interfered with; but discontinuing or doing mischief if crossed or watched, or if endeavours are made to coax or bribe him to work in any way but his own[.]" Wright also defined the term "thrush" as a "sprite, boggle"; and "thurse" was "an apparition; a goblin," with a "thurse-hole" as "a hollow vault in a rock or hill which served for a dwelling."[319] He described "thurse" as derived from an Anglo-Saxon term meaning "giant, demon."

It is arguable that this folkloric hobthrush put in an appearance in *The Hobbit* as a minor but significant character. At the Lonely Mountain Bilbo sat before the hidden door in a "grassy bay" when he hears "a sharp crack" and turned to see "a large thrush" cracking snails against a stone.[320] The dwarves gathered: "The old thrush which had been watching from a high perch with beady eyes & head cocked on one side gave a sudden trill." A flake fell off the rock-face, revealing the keyhole of the hidden door. This was a very helpful thrush, and it was first noticed by a hobbit. It seems that Tolkien here adapted the hobthrush and made use of its aspect of "doing much useful work" because this Erebor thrush has useful work to do in *The Hobbit*.

The bird reappeared later to hear Bilbo's account of his meeting with Smaug, and Thorin noted, "The thrushes are friendly – this is a very old bird, probably one of those that used to live here tame to the hands of my father and grandfather – they were a long lived and magical breed."[321] The magic Erebor thrushes were more than long-lived; they were also very helpful creatures – Thorin added that the birds were used as messengers because both the dwarves and the men of Dale could understand the thrush-language. This particular magic hardworking thrush subsequently landed on Bard's shoulder and advised him where best to take aim at Smaug.[322]

This thrush clearly evoked the Wright hobthrush – a "hobgoblin having the repute of doing much useful work..." And Tolkien's thrush and Wright's hobthrush were both associated with rocky places. Tolkien had no interest in borrowing the English hobthrush intact, but instead took the term and invented his own magical breed of bird.

Tolkien's Hobbit Origin Stories

The likely candidate for the primary source of Tolkien's hobbit exists in the writings of Joseph Wright, Tolkien's mentor and friend. The circumstances suggest that Tolkien found the term "hobbit" while browsing through the pages of Wright's *English Dialect Dictionary*, and it does not seem at all likely that he invented his hobbit one day in an idle moment of inspiration. Yet this was what he encouraged us to believe.

Tolkien's first explicit discussion on the external origin of his hobbit occurred within months of publication of *The Hobbit*. In January 1938 a letter posted under the name of "Habit" appeared in an English newspaper. Habit reported that a woman recalled "an old fairy tale called 'The Hobbit' in a collection read about 1904," and this story featured a creature that was "definitely frightening."[323] Habit wanted to know the "inspiration for Professor Tolkien's attractive hobbit[.]" Tolkien replied: "I do not remember anything about the name and inception of the hero. I could guess, of course, but the guesses would have no more authority than those of future researchers, and I leave the game to them." He went on to assert that he had "no waking recollection... of any Hobbit bogey in print by 1904."

Tolkien then expressed his sense of certainty that his hobbit and any earlier hobbit surely bore no meaningful resemblance – his comment on this point sounds very much as if he had the Welsh agricultural hobbit in mind: "the two hobbits are accidental homophones, and... they are not... synonyms." Tolkien predicted here that any "Hobbit" predecessor would not be his kind of hobbit. This prediction would apply to the Welsh hobbit, but the equivalence of the Denham hobbit to Tolkien's hobbit is evident, and the two hobbits are more clearly in the realm of synonyms than homophones and are not "accidental homophones" by any stretch of this description.[324] Perhaps these circumstances could be read as indicating that Tolkien did not know of the Denham hobbit.

In January 1938 Tolkien's response to Habit sounded quite adamant and definitive. He declared that he had no memory of the specific circumstances surrounding the origin of either his term "hobbit" or of the origin of Bilbo Baggins as "the hobbit." Nor could he recall any instance of encountering the word "hobbit" in his previous readings. Even so, he soon wrote to his publisher, saying that his response to Habit was in the spirit of a "jesting reply" propounded as an "ill-considered joke."[325] It isn't clear exactly how this characterization applied to his remarks about the origin of the term "hobbit." Setting the record straight with his publisher, however, Tolkien did not correct any specific element of his January 1938 story. And he did not offer then the account of the origin of his hobbit that later became accepted as canon in Tolkien studies.

Given the likelihood that Tolkien borrowed his hobbit from Joseph Wright and the Welsh hobbit of British agriculture, is it possible that he forgot this origin by 1938? This is the position favored by some Tolkien scholars. It is indeed a reasonable view because it respectfully defers to Tolkien's own statements. This view assumes that Tolkien's first use of the word "hobbit" may not have been particularly memorable, and so the contextual elements of the moment could easily have evaporated over the years.

In addition, John Rateliff posits that Tolkien's independent invention of the term hobbit reflects his "gift for... creating words that sounded like real ones..."[326] In other words, Tolkien could have invented "hobbit" as a word that merely echoed "hobgoblin" or some related term. Both of these theories assume that Tolkien did not borrow the word. But I presume that Tolkien in 1938 knew exactly where the term originated. This is evidenced by his continuing use of Joseph Wright's *English Dialect Dictionary* in constructing hobbit culture – a project that commenced within months of his reply to Habit.

Tolkien's early uses of the term "hobbit" reflect very little, if any, sense of the Welsh hobbit in its original agricultural context. In *The Hobbit* manuscripts, the nature of hobbit society is not rendered in any detail. The sketchy narrative emphasis seems more concerned with portraying class than with any referencing of countryside or agriculture. But Tolkien set down the sole possible reference linking hobbits to an agrarian context when he had Bilbo announce, "Tell me what you wish me to do and I will try it – if I have to walk from here to the Great Desert of Gobi and fight the Wild Wire worms of the Chinese."[327] Wireworms apear in 19th century English agricultural texts as a common nuisance insect, a voracious animal, yellowish in color, very difficult to control.[328] We encounter here a private joke; Tolkien found it amusing to pit his Welsh agricultural hobbit against this pest of the farm field, deadly to wheat, corn, turnips, and other crops. This joke, however, does not support the idea that at this early stage he envisioned hobbit society as a farming culture.

There is no evidence in *The Hobbit* that Tolkien saw his first hobbits as a society of agrarian country-folk. But when he sat down to write *The Lord of the Rings* he developed hobbit society more completely, and he decided then to emphasize the agrarian nature of hobbit culture. The earliest possible references to the agricultural roots of the term "hobbit" came in Tolkien's late 1937 draft of the first chapter of what would become *The Fellowship of the Ring*.[329] After Bilbo's farewell party, "Gardeners came (by appointment) and cleared away in wheelbarrows those that had inadvertently remained." This is subtle but amusing when we think of this scene as one in which gardeners are carting off not just hobbits, but rather Welsh agricultural hobbits. And the second draft of his first chapter mentions "a quantity of Tooks" being invited to Bilbo's farewell birthday party.[330] These statements are so subtle that they can be easily overlooked, not readily perceived as secret referencing of the Welsh hobbit, a measure of weight and volume for agricultural produce.

In his correspondence of the 1950s Tolkien acknowledged the pastoral nature of his hobbit world. In a letter dated to 1951 Tolkien described hobbit life in the Shire as a "simple and rural life"; and he noted in a 1955 letter that he envisioned the Shire as "more or less a Warwickshire village of about the period of the Diamond Jubilee[.] [1897]"[331] In 1956 he objected to certain translations and insisted, "'The Shire' is based on rural England"; and its toponymy and inhabitants represent a "parody" of "rural England[.]"[332] In a 1958 letter he wrote: "I am in fact a *Hobbit* (in all but size). I like gardens, trees and unmechanized farmlands[.]"[333]

Tolkien's descriptions of "simple and rural" and "Warwickshire village" and "farmlands" sound straightforward, but we are left with a somewhat empty picture. In point of fact, one finds no mention in the rich literature on Tolkien that would shed any light on any specific steps he took to produce an agrarian world in The Shire. But we can clarify certain matters on this point. Circumstantial evidence shows, for example, that he was interested in words pertaining to farm life. This is apparent when we consider the term "Crickhollow." Tolkien described the word as composed of "an obsolete element" and "the known word *hollow*."[334] What are we to make of this? The list was intended to aid translators, but "obsolete element" offered no help whatsoever.

We can make an informed guess as to the likely origin of both the mysterious term "crick" and "Crickhollow." We can deduce that it originated from a term described by John Rhys, who wrote that "the [Irish] word *cruach* might mean a heap of anything, and it is attested as a rick of hay or the like; the Welsh *crûg* admits of much the same use..."[335] He then described a place in Wales known as "*Crûg Hywel*, Anglicized Crickhowel." This particular source was arguably available to Tolkien, and since he often made use of words in exactly this way, "Crickhollow" seems a deliberate choice. I don't know when Tolkien added that name to "A Conspiracy Unmasked." But he described Frodo's new home as an "old-fashioned countrified house, as much like a hobbit-hole as possible..." Just an hour of slow riding from that countrified house brings us to a great hedge known as the High Hay. Crickhollow is more than a countrified word; in its reference to a Welsh term for a rick of hay, it was particularly apt for his Welsh agricultural hobbits.

Tolkien's first arguable use of the Wright dictionary for *The Lord of the Rings* came when he coined the name "Withywindle" in August 1938.[336] It represents a fusion of two words that appeared together in the Wright dictionary, "withywind and "withy."[337] Tolkien listed "Withywindle" in his 1967 "Nomenclature," acknowledging that it originated from "withywind," the term for bindweed.[338] Tolkien didn't provide the specific source he consulted, but "withywind" is exactly how the term appeared in Wright's dictionary, and on the previous page appeared the term "withy," which refers to willows. Since "withywind" often appears as "withwind" in other sources, this tends to support the assumption that Tolkien consulted Wright for the term.

Immediately after Tolkien constructed Withywindle, he took his hobbits to Bree and there explicitly instituted his vision of hobbits as rustic creatures of a bucolic countryside. He also began to bury secret clues in the text that acknowledged the Welsh agricultural hobbit. In 1930 Tolkien clearly borrowed his hobbit from extant folkloric sources that included the Welsh hobbit, but little evident intention can be found in *The Hobbit* to reference this origin via the use of agricultural imagery or by constructing a bucolic hobbit country society. But now, taking the Shire hobbits to Bree, Tolkien wove a variety of terms into his narrative from Wright's *English Dialect Dictionary* and possibly other sources. This insertion of British farming words occurred in August 1938 and later.

Tolkien originally envisioned the "Bree-folk" as mainly "Big People" with a mingling of hobbits, and these hobbits were termed "Outsiders" who were "a rustic, not to say (though in the Shire it was often said) uncivilized sort."[339] But Tolkien immediately revised this portrayal and made all the residents of Bree into rustic hobbits. Keeping in mind the definition of "hobbit" as an agricultural term of weight and volume, it would fit for Tolkien to derive these Bree terms from dialectical terms of the English countryside and from "old farming words."

Toward this end, the terms Combe, Archet, Staddle, and Lob / Nob appeared in his new project for the first time.[340] This conjunction suggests that Tolkien actively sought useful names for places and people that reflected an agrarian context for his hobbits. It is possible – and perhaps even likely – that more than one source came to hand, and so the suggestion that any particular volume served as a source must remain merely a suggestion. A good candidate for an alternate source of useful material is Walter W. Skeat and James Britten's *Reprinted Glossaries and Old Farming Words*, a book that also contained the Welsh agricultural hobbit.[341]

Tolkien was familiar with the work of Walter Skeat. In early 1914 at Oxford he attended lectures on a publication co-edited by Skeat, *Specimens of Early English*, and he was also awarded the Skeat Prize for English, of which he wrote years later that "...the shade of Walter Skeat, I surmise, was shocked" when he spent his prize money on a Welsh grammar.[342] Joseph Wright dedicated his *English Dialect Dictionary* to Skeat, describing him as "Founder and President of the English Dialect Society."[343] By 1922 Tolkien was a member of the Yorkshire Dialect Society and he wrote a foreword to a glossary of dialectical terms published in 1928.[344]

Sending his four hobbits into Bree, Tolkien immediately mentioned a nearby village called Staddle.[345] This term appeared with numerous meanings in Wright's dictionary, with a number related to the construction of a stand for a rick of hay.[346] Tolkien mentioned Staddle in his 1967 "Nomenclature" as a term "now dialectical" – a likely reference to Wright's dictionary.[347] He specifically noted its meaning as a foundation for "buildings, sheds, ricks..."

Archet is another village near Bree.[348] This term does not appear in Wright's dictionary, but in Skeat and Britten's collection of farming words "Archet" is defined as an orchard.[349] In Tolkien's 1967 "Nomenclature" Archet is listed as "an English place-name of Celtic origin" with the term "chet" meaning "wood."[350] This inclusion of a Welsh term is notable, given the origin of "hobbit" as a farming term used in Wales.

Near Bree we also find "the valley of Combe" which soon became a village.[351] In Wright's dictionary "Combe" was defined as a "narrow valley, between two hills, with only one inlet; the head of a valley" and as a wooded hillside; Tolkien's "Nomenclature" defined Coomb as a "deep (but usually not very large) valley."[352] The term in his Bree chapter drafts and final version is consistently "Combe," but in his "Nomenclature" it is "Coomb." In Wright's dictionary Coomb appeared with three meanings as a brewing-vat, as a measure of four bushels of grain, and as a tub, cistern, or large ladle for bailing out a boat.[353] In Skeat and Britten the terms combe, comb, and coom have various meanings as associated with window construction, as a bin for corn and hay horse-feed, as a reference to four bushels, and as a ridge in a road "between the horse-path and rut."[354]

At the Prancing Pony in Bree we soon meet a character who Tolkien dubbed Lob but who then became Nob.[355] Lob appeared in Wright's dictionary as a lump, as a clumsy clownish fellow, as drooping leaves, as a loser in a race, and as other meanings; Lob was defined by Skeat and Britten as a "kick on the seat of honour."[356] Nob can be found in Wright's dictionary defined as a lump of coal, a round hill, a head / headache, a toe, a young colt, and several other meanings; and Nob appeared in Skeat and Britten as a "flower-head of clover."[357] Nob was not listed in Tolkien's "Nomenclature." But at his first mention in 1938, Butterbur referred to him as a "woolly-footed slowcoach," perhaps evoking a clownish loser in a race – Wright's lob.

Skeat and Britten's fourth entry after "Hobbit" is "Hundred Weight," an agricultural measure of weight, applied to cheese.[358] Throughout the British countryside it typically equated to 120 pounds in weight, except in Leicester where it came out as 100, 112, or 120 pounds. "Hundredweight" also appeared in Wright's dictionary as a "measure... of 120 lbs., but varying in different districts according to the article weighed" – particularly "cheese and hay."[359] Wright mentioned various numbers associated with this weight, including 112.

"Hundred-weight" is given in *The Fellowship of the Ring* as the name for a special observance held the year after Bilbo's departure from The Shire. In what Christopher Tolkien has characterized as the "Second Phase" of the manuscript, written in the early fall of 1938, the gathering was called the "Hundredweight Party" even though "only a few friends were invited and they hardly ate a hundredweight between them."[360] In the final text Frodo "refused to go into mourning; and the next year he gave a party in honour of Bilbo's hundred-and-twelfth birthday, which he called a Hundred-weight Feast." Tolkien joked here that 112 "was short of the mark..." Tolkien's wry choice of a farm term for the hobbit feast is knowingly subtle because his hobbits were themselves a unit of agricultural measure.

In the spring of 1944 Tolkien introduced a new term into *The Lord of the Rings* – a special term for hobbits. In the course of writing about the meeting of Frodo and Sam with Faramir in Ithilien, Tolkien adopted the term "halfling" as a word used by Faramir for hobbits.[361] This replaced "half-high." Consistent with this usage, Tolkien defined "halfling" as "half the height of normal Men."[362] Christopher Tolkien offered no elucidation for the revision of "half-high" into "halfling." Keeping in mind the Morton definition of "hobbit" and "hundred-weight" as agricultural terms, as well as Tolkien's coloring of the environs of Bree with British "farming words," it is interesting that Joseph Wright's *English Dialect Dictionary* defined "halfling" in a similar context: "A half-grown boy, a stripling, a boy employed upon a farm or in a stable..."[363]

It is clear that the original meanings of both hobbit and halfling pertain to British usage as farm terminology. But it is less clear what this signified to Tolkien and what he intended in his use of the terms. We know that in the course of writing *The Lord of the Rings* he bestowed upon hobbit culture a deliberate rusticity – this could have been on his mind from the very beginning, but it is not particularly apparent or even arguable from the surviving texts of *The Hobbit*.

To sum up the evidence, in 1938 Tolkien deemed it useful to set the aura of the British countryside around his hobbits, and he did this in part by cultivating a sense of terminological depth in The Shire, just as he did with other aspects of his world-building. In 1944 he experimented with a secondary term for his hobbits, "half-high," but in the course of that year he decided to replace it with "halfling." The appropriateness of this choice becomes fully evident when we view both hobbit and halfling in their original usages as agrarian terms, and when we understand that these usages were framed in the work of Tolkien's mentor and friend, Joseph Wright. Seen this way, we can suggest that Tolkien's hobbits memorialize that friendship.

In this light it is interesting that in 1944, sometime after adopting the term "halfling," Tolkien also set down the description of Frodo as "a little halfling from the Shire, a simple hobbit of the quiet countryside..."[364] This description draws together the threads of these meanings, referencing creatures of rustic English folklore and agrarian Welsh agricultural terminology.

No direct evidence affirms that Tolkien consulted Skeat and Britten's *Reprinted Glossaries and Old Farming Words*. Of the farming / countryside terms that appear early in the writing of *The Fellowship of the Ring*, Archet is the only that appeared solely in Skeat and Britten; the other terms are common to both Skeat and Britten and to Wright's dictionary. But it cannot be coincidence to find in *The Fellowship of the Ring* a close association between hobbit and hundred-weight; between Combe and Archet and Staddle and Nob and Lob; and between Withywind and Withy. Tolkien used all of these terms during 1938, the first year of his work on *The Fellowship of the Ring*. And he would eventually find a use in 1942 for Quick-beam and Moots / Moot.

It is evident that Tolkien made use of the Wright source, and possible that he consulted Skeat and Britten. He did so in the course of secretly embedding his Middle-earth hobbits in an almost invisible context. When he decided in August 1938 to colorize his hobbits as rustic folk of the countryside, he was consciously referencing their hidden history as Welsh agricultural hobbits, drawn from Joseph Wright's *English Dialect Dictionary*.

During the fall of 1942, crafting an appropriate Rohirric linguistic background for "hobbit," Tolkien came up with two options: the words "holbytla" and "hoppettan."³⁶⁵ Christopher Tolkien identified *hoppettan* as an Old English verb meaning "to hop, leap, jump for joy." But Tolkien ultimately settled on "*holbytlan* that dwell in holes in sand-dunes..." Christopher Tolkien observed of the 1942 text: "This is where the word *Holbytla* arose." He translated it as "Hole-builder." As Tom Shippey explains, *hol-bytla* is not attested in Old English, but is, rather, a compound term that Tolkien constructed in accordance with linguistic principles as a plausible Old English word.³⁶⁶

This experimentation in 1942 with terms and the construction of a feigned history to explain the term "hobbit" tends to undermine the presumption that Tolkien derived "hobbit" from hole at circa 1930. But Tolkien must have toyed with *hoppettan* while keeping in mind the actual relationship of hobbit and hob-hole. In other words, in 1942 Tolkien experimented briefly with creating a feigned etymology for "hobbit" that derived the word from "hop," but he decided to go with hole instead, conscious of the external history in which "hob-hole" and "hobbit" occurred together in British folk literature.

In a manuscript dating to the late 1940s a new twist entered the picture. Tolkien seemed to take credit for inventing the word "hobbit": "This, I confess, is my own invention; but not one devised at random."³⁶⁷ But he then provided an origin completely internal to the logic of Middle-earth: "This is its origin. It is, for one thing, not wholly unlike the actual word in the Shire, which was *cūbuc* (plural *cūbugin*). **** Some Hobbit-historians have held that *cūbuc* was an ancient native word, perhaps the last survivor of their own forgotten language. **** It appears to be derived from an obsolete *cūbug* 'hole-dweller'... In support of this I would point to the fact that Meriadoc himself actually records that the King of Rohan used the word *cūbagu* 'hole-dweller'..." And in the summer of 1948 Tolkien further specified that "hobbit"

129

was a "corruption" or a "shortening" of the term holbytla or "hole dweller."[368]

Here we find Tolkien in the midst of a project to establish his own invented linguistic background for his hobbit – a background wholly appropriate for Middle-earth but also compatible with his conscious recollection of the role played by "hob-hole" in the invention of his first hobbit. A likely progression of development can be outlined. Tolkien said on various occasions that when he began writing *The Hobbit* he had no plan in mind to associate it with his extant Middle-earth legendarium. In the summer of 1930 "hob," "hob-hole," and "hobbit" drew his interest as potential material for a new fireside story for his children, and when he set down his first integration of these terms he had no intention to invent a story that partook of his evolving Elvish legendarium. Between 1938 and 1944 Tolkien developed his hobbits as agrarian folk, tied closely to farm terminology. And in the late 1940s he devised his own Rohirric term that went back to hob-hole for inspiration.

By 1955 the entirety of *The Lord of the Rings* had appeared in print, and Tolkien now made a decision to craft a hobbit origin story. He set forth the earliest known account of the external origin of the word "hobbit" in a letter to a reviewer.[369] There he wrote of "correcting School Certificate papers" and on "a blank leaf" he wrote the first sentence of *The Hobbit*: "In a hole in the ground there lived a hobbit." In this account, it is notable that Tolkien stopped short of claiming credit for inventing the term "hobbit."

Later that same month, writing to his American publisher, he amended this account from composing the entire first sentence to merely jotting down a single word: "I once scribbled 'hobbit' on a blank page of some boring school exam paper in the early 1930's."[370] This account is interesting because it was not prepared in private correspondence, but rather as an official account of his authorship. This means that we can take this as his first stab at an official formal explanation for his first hobbit. Once again, Tolkien did not take credit for inventing the word. He instead noted, "It was some time before I discovered what it referred to!" Tolkien here made no mention of deriving his hobbit from any folkloric source, but this comment was entirely consistent with derivation of "hobbit" from *The Denham Tracts*, where it is merely listed and not described, or from Joseph Wright's *English Dialect Dictionary*, where it makes no reference to any sort of creature but can be readily associated with traditional folkloric hobs under their various names.

In a 1957 interview with Ruth Harshaw, Tolkien's hobbit origin story returned to the composition of what amounted to the first sentence: "...he was in the midst of correcting 286 examination papers one day when he suddenly turned over one of the papers and wrote: 'At the edge of his hole stood the Hobbit.'"[371] In this version, "he later tried to think just who and what this Hobbit was..." This is, again, entirely consistent with a scenario in which Tolkien found the word rather than invented it.

By this point in time, we know of four separate accounts of his hobbit origin story, and all four provide differing accounts of the essential specifics of his first use of the word "hobbit." The first account of 1938 asserted that Tolkien had no memory of the circumstances under which he first used the term. The second account came in 1955 and there he described setting down the first sentence of *The Hobbit*. The next account, also in 1955, mentioned the single word "hobbit" and not the first sentence. The fourth known account in 1957 gave a version of the first sentence. None of these varying origin stories took credit for inventing the term.

In an unpublished 1958 letter Tolkien made his first clear claim regarding the origin of his hobbit as his own invention: "I invented the word hobbit, and can say no more about it than it seemed to me to fit the creatures that I had already in mind."[372] On the margin of this letter he added a note: "Or rather it generated them: they grew to fit it." Tolkien says here that he had some kind of creature in mind at circa 1930, and after he devised for it the name "hobbit," this newly coined name helped to inspire the later evolution of his invented creature. This was a letter to a private correspondent, not written for publication, but it is his first effort to lay claim to invention of the term "hobbit." This account could be read to indicate that Tolkien had been thinking of hobs as a class of folkloric creatures, and when he settled on "hobbit," the word ultimately gave rise to Bilbo Baggins.

An undated note of the late 1950s or 1960s repeated his exam story: "I came across a blessed blank page and scrawled on it (without conscious reflection or effort of invention) *In a hole in the ground lived a Hobbit.*"[373] It is difficult to know what Tolkien meant by "without conscious reflection or effort of invention" but it seems to suggest that the entire sentence came to him suddenly. In addition, it isn't clear in this account whether he intended to give the impression that "hobbit" was also his own invention. If we include this undated mention, by this time six separate accounts of this story existed – only one specified in any definitive way that Tolkien invented the word. None specified that he drew on any folkloric source for his hobbit.

In 1966 Tolkien gave an interview that appeared in an American magazine. There he set forth his exam paper origin story once again. He used language that seemed to reference an empty term, as with the Denham folkloric hobbit, but he also said he had never before encountered the word: "I had no idea what a Hobbit was. Or perhaps I did sense it was a little creature of some sort. But I had never heard the word and had never used it."[374] Tolkien once again stopped short of a claim of independent invention. But sensing in his hobbit "a little creature of some sort," his hobbit also stepped into synonym territory. The Denham hobbit was a mere word devoid of attributes, appearing in a list that included numerous other hobs, "little creatures of some sort." It would be remarkable for Tolkien to fortuitously write down a word yielding the same attributes of a word already written, and for this to be purely coincidental.

In another interview conducted in late 1966 and published in early 1968 Tolkien repeated his story of setting down the first sentence of *The Hobbit*, and he now added a reference to an American novel: "I knew no more about the creatures than that... I don't know where the word came from. You can't catch your mind out. It might have been associated with Sinclair Lewis's Babbit."[375] This new addition to the story strongly implied that

Tolkien himself fashioned his first hobbit – perhaps, as he now said, under the influence of a Sinclair Lewis novel. We are given to believe that he might well have fashioned the word "hobbit" as an echo of "Babbit."

This would suggest that his term "hobbit" was a newly constructed word, devoid of folkloric context and terminological ancestry. With this account, Tolkien propounded the story that "hobbit" was a term he invented and set down with no clear British associations of any kind, except for an implied borrowing from a character in an American novel, a character, who, as Tolkien noted, came from a "limited" world and who "has the same bourgeois smugness that hobbits do."

In a film interview conducted by the BBC in early February 1968 Tolkien again repeated his story of setting down the first line of the book on a blank exam page.[376] "So I scribbled on it, I can't think why, 'In a hole in the ground there lived a hobbit.'" Tolkien expressed discomfort with the BBC interview, but he nevertheless made an effort to accommodate the project.

In short, Tolkien's correspondence and interviews from 1938 to 1968 most consistently show that he most often avoided taking clear and direct credit for inventing the word "hobbit." On only one occasion did he make an explicit claim of fully independent invention; this occurred in a private letter not for publication. In one interview Tolkien suggested a possible inspiration from an American novel for both the word "hobbit" and for an associated cultural context. But it is notable that his most typical contextual comments comport with a history in which he found the word in Wright's *English Dialect Dictionary* and / or in *The Denham Tracts*.

A new twist entered the story when Tolkien was contacted in 1970 by a former student who had joined the *Oxford English Dictionary* staff. The *OED* wished to know more about the origin of the word "hobbit." Promising a detailed response (which he never provided), Tolkien issued an odd warning: "don't look into things, unless you are looking for trouble: they nearly always turn out to be less simple than you thought."[377] He amplified this strange statement with another enigmatic comment: "...I am having the matter of the etymology: 'invented by J.R.R. Tolkien': investigated by experts. I knew that the claim was not clear, but I had not troubled to look into it, until faced by the inclusion of *hobbit* in the Supplement." This seemed to offer another clear statement of invention, but it is curiously evasive, asserting that the claim for the word being "invented by J.R.R. Tolkien" was "not clear" and was now being "investigated by experts."

He followed this letter four months later with an explicit declaration that he invented the term. But this clarity came embedded in a somewhat dubious context. In early January 1971 he sent a detailed statement to a former student "to justify my claim to have invented the word."[378] After dismissing three vaguely similar terms from folklore sources, Tolkien asserted now "that the only E. word that influenced the invention was 'hole'; that granted the description of hobbits..."

This could be read in two ways. First, it seems to reference the usage of "hob-hole" in the Wright dictionary and other sources. And second, it could suggest that Tolkien in his final years became convinced that his manufactured Old English term, *holbytla*, played a role in his invention of "hobbit." But no contemporaneous evidence exists that he had *holbytla* in mind in 1930 when he wrote down his first "hobbit." In this letter he made an interesting admission: "one cannot exclude the possibility that buried childhood memories might suddenly rise to the surface... though they might be quite differently applied." He ended by delicately probing, "I do not suppose you have found a name precisely *hobbit* or you would have mentioned it."

This is what we know of the confusing history of Tolkien's hobbit. It is especially notable that the evolution of his account included comments portraying his hobbit as empty of pre-existing meaning. This comports exactly with the word as it appears in Wright's *English Dialect Dictionary*, in *The Denham Tracts*, and in other sources that all fell within the purview of Tolkien's professional interests.

John Rateliff studied the matter in some detail and concluded that it was possible, though unlikely, that Tolkien knew of *The Denham Tracts*.[379] He noted that if Tolkien encountered the book "it must have been during his early years [1911-1915, 1918, or 1922-1925]" but Tolkien "had forgotten about it completely by 1930 when he actually came to write down that solitary sentence *In a hole in the ground lived a hobbit*." Rateliff characterized Tolkien's "own account of how he created the name" as "repeated over and over with great consistency over a number of years[.]" With this interpretation in mind, he favored the view that the term "hobbit" was indeed Tolkien's "own coinage."[380]

It is useful to see Rateliff's position as a meaningful effort to defer to Tolkien's varying assertions. But given the nature of the actual textual history of Tolkien's origin story, it is less useful to accept unquestioned any implication that Tolkien never encountered the term "hobbit" in his wide readings of dictionaries, literature, and folklore. He left no indication of having derived his hobbit from any folkloric source. But to a large degree, the most consistent aspects of his various accounts comport with an inspiration from the Welsh agricultural hobbit, the Wright hob-hole, and / or the Denham folkloric hobbit.

And Tolkien's origin story is best described as an evolution of implication mixed with assertion. The early iterations of Tolkien's hobbit origin story were noticeably bereft of any claim of independent invention. When a clear statement of independent invention at last entered the story, it was followed with an obvious effort to associate the origin of his hobbit with a hole – consistent with folkloric hob-hole references. Tolkien's collective commentary does not establish a history of "great consistency" as John Rateliff has asserted.

As best as we can determine from the evidence, Tolkien's first use of the word "hobbit" came during the summer of 1930 in the form of an idle scrawl of either the isolated word or some version of what became the first sentence of *The Hobbit*. This scribble came just a few months after Tolkien became the executor of the estate of a mentor, Joseph Wright – giving Tolkien reason to ponder Wright's *English Dialect Dictionary* with its Welsh hobbit, its hobs, and its English hob-hole. A moment of casual surfing through the dictionary offers the most likely scenario to explain Tolkien's scribbled note. At the end of 1930 Tolkien revisited that note and launched into making something of his borrowed hobbit.

In early 1938 Tolkien wrote that he had no specific memory of inventing the term, claiming, "I do not remember anything about the name and inception of the hero."[381] The evidence indicates that this mischaracterized what actually happened. During that same year, in the course of writing *The Fellowship of the Ring*, he made use of additional material from the Wright dictionary and perhaps from Skeat and Britten's *Reprinted Glossaries and Old Farming Words*. These usages situated his hobbit in an agrarian context, and this in turn reflected the true origin of the word "hobbit" as a Welsh agricultural term.

And during the 1940s he invented a logic and linguistic context for the internal fit of this term in his Middle-earth legendarium. He settled on "hole" as the defining idea after rejecting a connection to "hop." Then he propounded from Old English elements a manufactured word for hole-dweller / hole-builder. These choices consciously reference the external history of "hob-holes" in the making of his hobbit.

In June 1955, nine months after the release of the final volume of *The Lord of the Rings*, Tolkien now set forth two different stories of the origin of his hobbit. In one account he told of having written the first sentence of what eventually became *The Hobbit*, and in the second account he said he merely wrote down the word "hobbit." After that point, the story of the spontaneous composition of the first sentence in its entirety settled in as his standard external history to explain his hobbit – this development came with varying degrees of assertive clarity and occasional explicit claims of independent invention.

Pressed for an authoritative statement on this point in 1970, Tolkien chose to issue an odd warning about "looking for trouble" and some kind of mysterious complexity. The next year he asserted that "the only E. word that influenced the invention was 'hole'" – this was partly true, but he chose to say nothing of the hob-hole in Wright's *English Dialect Dictionary*.

The most reasonable conclusion to draw from this analysis is that JRR Tolkien did not invent the term "hobbit." He instead found an intriguing and mostly empty word that closely echoed an existing folkloric creature. He took the word "hobbit" and reimagined it as a version of a hob, and he filled it up with his own enchantment.

We can only guess why he then chose to construct an origin story that invited listeners to assume he invented the term. But to understand the actual history of the term sheds an interesting light on Tolkien's creative processes and preferences, revealing how he assembled elements of tradition in the making of Middle-earth, and clarifying his subsequent reluctance to shed light on the specifics of his method of invention.

Treasures of Tradition

Tolkien began his first hobbit project with two ideas fused into a single image. The Welsh agricultural hobbit sounded enough like a hob that it wasn't too far of a journey from a traditional English hob hole to a hobbit standing beside a hole. But pondering this initial imagery, Tolkien did not have any immediate answer for the question of what to do next. A few months later, when he decided to turn to traditional materials for help, he resisted the idea of merely retelling any specific story. To develop his own tale, Tolkien took up certain threads that he had already woven into a poem of the early 1920s, and he borrowed a vague character-sketch from ancient English literature.

Christina Scull and Wayne Hammond's edition of *The Adventures of Tom Bombadil* presents a poem by JRR Tolkien titled "Iúmonna Gold Galdre Bewunden" – a title derived from *Beowulf*.[382] This poem was written about 1922 and published in 1923, and it mentioned a dwarf and "an old dragon under old stone" who "dreamed of the woe" it would wish upon thieves who "ever set finger on one small ring" of its hoard. The parallels in this poem to aspects of *The Hobbit* are clear. Tolkien acknowledged in a 1938 letter that he had *Beowulf* vaguely in mind when he crafted the taking of a goblet from Smaug's hoard.[383] When he began to write *The Hobbit* in 1930, he started the book by conjoining dwarves, a dragon, and a hoard – and as the earliest surviving manuscript shows, he also decided at the outset that Bilbo Baggins would be a thief.[384] In short, the story of the Beowulf thief greatly interested Tolkien, and it inspired elements of both "Iúmonna Gold Galdre Bewunden" and *The Hobbit*.

Tolkien completed his initial translation of *Beowulf* in 1926, and he continued to work on it through the 1930s. In his *Beowulf*, a "nameless man" crept along "a path little known to men" and "seized a goblet..."[385] Tolkien translated references to this nameless man as "thief" and "thrall." This thief had felt in "dire need" and had not intended to steal the goblet, and did so "burdened with guilt." The thief then "bore to his liege-lord a goldplated goblet, beseeching truce and pardon..." The dragon deployed its sense of smell to discover the thief's visit – just as Smaug does after Bilbo steals a goblet.[386] Tolkien portrayed the *Beowulf* dragon hoard as "laden with history" – a history that unfolds into a tale that is "somber, tragic, sinister, curiously real." This history is fragmentary, but rich with meanings and hints of magic. Tolkien asserted that the "quintessence" of this dragon's treasure can be encapsulated in *iúmonna gold galdre bewunden*, which means "the gold of bygone men was wound about with spells."

His commentary on the *Beowulf* theft incident described the thief as a "wretched fugitive" and a "fugitive slave" for whom the *Beowulf* author felt a sense of sympathy.[387] The status of this thief as a slave does not match Bilbo, but it is nevertheless clear that the *Beowulf* theft incident was on Tolkien's mind when he drew his new hobbit into a tale. Echoing the wretched fugitive thief in the story of *Beowulf*, Bilbo's taking of an item from a dragon hoard gave him his own wretched moment when an angry Thorin Oakenshield denounced him, "You miserable hobbit, you you burglar..."[388] As Tolkien noted, the passage on the theft incident in the *Beowulf* manuscript was "badly spoilt" and "practically unintelligible." The tattered quality of the manuscript and the threadbare nature of the story of the thief interested Tolkien enough to insert Bilbo Baggins into that "badly spoilt" space.

Bilbo the hobbit came to Tolkien's hand mostly empty of meaning. Sometime in the spring or summer of 1930 it appears that Tolkien took note of "hob" and "hob-hole" in a dictionary published by a colleague, and he conjoined this hob to "hobbit," a Welsh term pertaining to an agricultural measure of weight.[389] This process of invention gave rise during the summer of 1930 to the evocative opening sentence of *The Hobbit*. For months it remained empty of substance. Pondering this vacuum, Tolkien eventually filled this empty mythological British hob with the fragmentary tale of the thief in *Beowulf*.

But in 1938 when an insightful letter-writer self-dubbed "Habit" inquired of his use of *Beowulf* as a source for *The Hobbit*, Tolkien did something very curious. He suggested that the *Beowulf* tale "was not consciously present to the mind in the process of writing" but "the episode of the theft arose naturally... almost inevitably" as the story grew.[390]

This account is curious because it cannot be true. *Beowulf* was consciously present in Tolkien's mind from the very beginning as he sat down to compose the opening chapter of *The Hobbit*. The story began as a prose retelling of aspects of his poem "Iúmonna Gold Galdre Bewunden," with dwarves, a dragon, a hoard, and a thief. The mostly empty thief of *Beowulf* inspired the writing in 1922-1923 of "Iúmonna Gold Galdre Bewunden," and this same mostly empty thief a few years later animated Tolkien's hobbit-burglar, setting his feet upon a deliberately formulated narrative trajectory – a path that led Bilbo Baggins to Smaug's hoard and a golden cup.

In 1938 Tolkien declined to fully acknowledge this obvious process of invention. And he declined to make any mention whatsoever of the origin of his hob / hobbit. But it is clear that he started with the idea of a British hob-hole, and he altered this slightly by pasting "hobbit" over "hob." To fill this creature with a story, he gave thought to the *Beowulf* thief and he decided to follow the example of the *Beowulf* poet who, as Tolkien said, "leaps straight into the dragon-story and the thrilling adventure of the fugitive hiding in a cave..."[391] Leaping into the story of *The Hobbit*, Tolkien pasted over "fugitive hiding in a cave" with a hobbit living in a hole in the ground.

And it is also quite significant that Tolkien took this wisp of a story and merged it with a listing of Norse names from *Voluspa* in the *Poetic Edda* – names that come empty of depth, devoid of character. Tolkien wrote in one letter that he filled these names with "conventional and inconsistent Grimm's fairy-tale dwarves..."[392] This means that in the first draft of the first chapter of *The Hobbit*, Tolkien wove together a variety of ingredients to create his tale, including a Welsh hobbit, an English hob-hole, the *Beowulf* thief, the Norse *Voluspa*, and Grimm's fairytales. This intricate process of interwoven invention would serve him well throughout the making of his mythology.

This creative process interests me because in this case Tolkien never deemed it useful to set forth a complete record of his source-materials. He preferred to keep invisible the elaborate details of his world-building. Perhaps this helps to explain why, when responding in 1938 to a letter-writer known to us as "Habit," Tolkien decided to minimize the true extent of the seminal influence of *Beowulf* on *The Hobbit*.

The 1938 "Habit" letter made reference to a possible pre-existing hobbit, and after Tolkien's death a story called "The Hobyahs" was identified as the likely candidate. The earliest note on this seems to be by David Cofield in a 1983 publication – Katherine Briggs observed in her 1976 book that "The Hobyahs" was published in an American folklore journal in 1891 and reprinted a few years later in Joseph Jacobs' collection *More English Fairy Tales* – a follow-up to *English Fairy Tales*.[393]

Both of the Jacobs fairytale collections were published by David Nutt and Company. Under the leadership of Alfred Nutt, this publishing firm set itself up as a central pillar in the establishment of a formal British folklore community during the late 19th century and early 20th century. A variety of circumstances reveal Tolkien's awareness and interest in this particular neighborhood of the academic world.

British Folklore and Tolkien

Tolkien was a specialist in European languages and a scholar of European traditional literature. These two passions together ultimately gave rise to various primary elements of his fictional Middle-earth legendarium. But to get to philology and medieval literature, Tolkien first followed narrative paths pioneered by British folklorists.

In his childhood and youth he encountered the fairytale collections of Andrew Lang, a leading figure in the British folklore community. And during Tolkien's student university years he encountered and absorbed both the Finnish language and the *Kalevala*, a collection of Finnish mythological ballads that had recently been translated into English by WF Kirby. Kirby, like Lang, was a member of the British Folk-Lore Society – this organization sponsored books, held meetings, and published a journal called *Folk-Lore: A Quarterly Review*. Tolkien also became familiar with the work of such prominent British folklorists as John Francis Campbell, George Dasent, and Edwin Hartland.[394]

Through the decades before the First World War, the Folk-Lore Society sponsored a prolific publication program. Under the management of Alfred Nutt – a key figure in the society until his death in 1910 – the firm of David Nutt and Company published numerous volumes prepared by members of the Folk-Lore Society, as well as issuing their quarterly journal. But an interesting notice appeared in 1914: "The Council, after long and anxious consideration, have severed their connection with the firm of D. Nutt, and have entered into an agreement with Messrs. Sidgwick & Jackson... who since the 1st July have been the Society's publishers."[395] Just two years later JRR Tolkien submitted his first book to Sidgwick & Jackson.[396] Given the Folk-Lore Society's emphasis on fairytales and British fairy traditions, this choice tends to show that Tolkien had a comfortable familiarity with the publications of the Folk-Lore Society.[397]

Tolkien's evolving hobbit origin story never made mention of *The Denham Tracts* and folklore literature as sources for his hobbit. His 1938 letter responding to a letter-writer with the pseudonym "Habit" has a particularly intriguing tone in this light. Contemplating an innocent and friendly inquiry as to the origin of his hobbit, Tolkien chose to issue a puzzling, "I do not remember... I could guess... I leave the game to [future researchers]." He had here an immediate opportunity to speak on the origin of his hobbit, and it hardly seems likely that he would fail to recall then the story that eventually materialized seventeen years later. But he deliberately chose otherwise. He crafted a flippant denial and issued an obtuse hint at some kind of source for "future researchers" to find.

It is unlikely that Tolkien invented the term "hobbit," given its widespread use as a term in British literature. It seems most likely that he first encountered the hobbit in Joseph Wright's *English Dialect Dictionary*, and perhaps in *The Denham Tracts*. But what drew Tolkien's interest was the resonance with "hob" – folkloric English hobs standing beside their hob-holes lacked definition from tradition. This hob sounded ancient, but it was an empty creature that Tolkien could fill up with his own imagination.

With a named creature in hand with few guiding traits, Tolkien could say of his hobbit, as he did in one interview, "Names always generate a story in my mind."[398] Developing the cultural setting for his hobbit, in time Tolkien made an interesting decision. He envisioned the Shire at circa 1897 as "more or less a Warwickshire village of about the period of the Diamond Jubilee[.]"[399] Since the Denham hobbit was unearthed from the English countryside and listed in an 1895 publication, and the Welsh hobbit and Wright hobs could be found populating British publications of the late 19th century, it is interesting that Tolkien chose for his hobbits the environs of the English countryside at circa 1897.

If we reject his claim of independent invention and accept that he found his hobbit in Wright's *English Dialect Dictionary*, and perhaps in *The Denham Tracts*, this raises an important question. What explains the absence of any acknowledgement of these previous folk hobbits? Rateliff points to the possibility that Tolkien perhaps glimpsed the passage in *The Denham Tracts* and it became lodged as a vague detail that shook loose suddenly in 1930. This is certainly possible. But his continuing use in 1938 of Wright's dictionary – and possibly Skeat and Britten's *Reprinted Glossaries and Old Farming Words* – surely meant that he had not forgotten the folkloric source-materials that gave rise to his first hobbit in 1930.

And if Tolkien truly forgot the specific sources, once he became focused on the term, and once his hobbit became a matter of public interest, why wouldn't he embark on any review of English folklore? Surely he knew the literature as well as anyone at circa 1940 – perhaps even better than most of his academic contemporaries. At the time of Habit's inquiry in 1938, Tolkien stood poised on the verge of a research project in which he did examine numerous texts in British folklore literature. In the end, it does not appear that he ever made any effort to clarify the source of his hobbit.

The evidence suggests that in 1938 Tolkien did not lack the relevant memories. Instead, he chose to say nothing about his folkloric source-material. I believe Tolkien did make use of the Wright dictionary material in 1930, drawing from it a hob-hole and a hobbit, and he may well have known about the Denham hobbit. But in all his versions of his hobbit origin story he made no mention of these key influences. It seems highly unlikely that in 1938 or in the 1950s he would have forgotten the key role of the dictionary entries prepared by Joseph Wright, his mentor and old friend. An erratic memory seems less plausible than intentional editing of his origin story.

So why would Tolkien decide not to credit these sources as the inspiration for his hobbits? Why would this history become a matter for Tolkien to keep secret, to ignore, to forget? He must have had some good reason for declining to report the true history, for deciding instead to misdirect attention away from the actual origins of his hobbits, and to craft a narrative that told only part of the story.

The Welsh hobbit, the Denham hobbit, and the Wright hob-holes provided Tolkien with empty silhouettes, mere suggestive figures that could be infused with color and narrative life. So Tolkien eventually decided that material from two ancient mythological sources would be useful toward coloring in the empty silhouette of his new hobbit. He drew from *Beowulf* and from Norse tradition for material that went into the first chapter of *The Hobbit*. This established his hobbit as a thief drawn from a nameless character who briefly appeared in *Beowulf*, and it brought in dwarves who appeared in Norse tradition only as an empty listing of names.

As I explained in the first edition of *Tolkien in Pawneeland*, Tolkien's mythological agenda had to do with cultivating in his legendarium a tone that he deemed "primitive." Norse mythological materials fit this standard, as did aspects of the mythological material in *Beowulf*. Pointing to this agenda, I argued that Tolkien found useful mythological substances to fill his hobbit not in Old English – as he claimed in 1971 – but rather across the water in America, in Skidi Pawnee tradition. The new research in this present book provides a more precise analysis on this point.

I have never thought it likely that any Pawnee influence accounted for the term "hobbit." But I linked the writing of an early Tom Bombadil poem to Pawnee tradition, and one of those traditions ended with the birth of a "little bit of a man with hair on." This led me to another Pawnee story about an old hairy man living in a cave. I identified six parallels between the Pawnee hairy man story and Tolkien's initial description of hobbits. I thought the Pawnee material sufficient to have given rise to Tolkien's initial line situating his hobbit beside a hole in the ground. While this model remains possible, it is much more likely that Tolkien relied on Joseph Wright's *English Dialect Dictionary* and its listing for "hobbit" and its mention of a hob-hole. Pondering this inspiration, Tolkien set down some kind of note or sentence – perhaps even the first line of what later became the opening sentence of *The Hobbit*. Then a period of months passed.

When Tolkien sat down to sort out ideas to build his note / sentence into a story, he took ideas from Norse and Old English sources. These sources explain the narrative trjectory of the story that emerged, but not any of the elements that correspond to Pawnee tradition. A key component of my original thinking about the Pawnee contribution to the origin of *The Hobbit* lay with the authorship of a Tom Bombadil poem – a poem that can be dated to circa 1931.

After Tolkien invented his hobbit, it is possible that months later, in the course of writing his Bombadil poem, he encountered the Skidi stories of small hairy folk and a hairy man living in a hole in the ground. At that point he had in mind an intention to write a story for his sons – a children's tale like the one told in 1928 by E.A. Wyke-Smith in *The Marvelous Land of the Snergs*.[400] And eventually he took his hobbit and situated him into the fragmentary tale of the *Beowulf* thief. But the *Beowulf* thief was not a small hairy man who dwelt in a hole in the ground. The elements that correspond between Skidi tradition and Tolkien's opening discussion of his first hobbit cannot be attributed to either *Beowulf* or to the Norse tradition from which Tolkien took his dwarves.

Skidi tradition could have helped to shape a variety of elements in the first chapter of *The Hobbit*, including the characterization of Bilbo as a small person with hairy feet, the long fingers of hobbits, the presence of a river near the hobbit's hole, and other details. I also argued in the first edition of *Tolkien in Pawneeland* that Pawnee tradition influenced Tolkien's new wizard, Bladorthin, a grey master of lightning from a grassy plain. The tale that unfolded started as another exercise in creative storytelling for his sons – it drew random terms and ideas from his growing legendarium of Middle-earth. The resulting manuscript held sufficient interest as a piece of well-crafted storytelling that it inadvertently found its way into the hands of a publisher. When it saw print in late 1937, it became an immediate minor hit.

Simon Cook has offered an alternate theory for Tolkien's characterization of hobbits. Cook draws on the hobbits of *The Lord of the Rings* to make his case, but he implied that his insights also pertain to *The Hobbit*. Cook pointed to two main influences on Tolkien. A 1900 paper by John Rhys linked Britain's ancient indigenous population to descriptions of archaeological remnants and to portrayals of fairy folk in Celtic tradition. This source, proposed Cook, seems to account for hobbit holes and for hobbit stature; he suggests that Tolkien was drawn to it due to his interest in creating a mythological history reflecting the actual British past.[401] Another source identified by Cook was the fiction of John Buchan, which Tolkien admired. In a novelette first published in 1902 Buchan has an ancient community of indigenes lingering in a cave in Scotland.[402] A visitor to the Scottish highlands meets a man who is "little and squat and dark" and "so rough with hair that it wore the appearance of a skin-covered being."[403] The actual parallels are limited and do not explain much of Tolkien's hobbits, but Buchan's description does evoke hobbits to a minor degree, and Tolkien could have drawn some influence from it.

Another publication by John Rhys can also explain Tolkien's hobbit as a hairy creature based on tradition. In *Celtic Folklore: Welsh and Manx*, Rhys described a Manx brownie termed the "fenodyree" who was "described as a hairy and apparently clumsy fellow..."[404] This was a solitary creature, and one Manx dictionary defined its name "to mean one who has hair for stockings or hose." Rhys deemed the name to be a Norse construction describing a "hairy satyr" perhaps related to the English hobgoblin and the Celtic glashtyn – a goblin that is "half human, half beast." Tolkien's hobbits do not seem much in evidence in the fenodyree, but Tolkien was not prone to reproduction of folkloric creatures; he instead drew details that he found interesting. It is possible that to Tolkien's first hobbit did get from the hairy Manx fenodyree a set of feet covered with "thick warm brown hair like the stuff on their heads (which is curly)..."[405]

Cook seems to propose that Tolkien in 1930-1931 had in mind both Rhys and Buchan when he formulated his first hobbits. In my analysis of *The Hobbit*, however, I think it is most useful to separate the invention of the first line of the book from the material that followed – in other words, Tolkien's invention of hobbits occurred in stages and must be assessed in that form. Toward this end, I have the impression that it is most strongly arguable that Tolkien drew upon Joseph Wright's *English Dialect Dictionary*, and perhaps *The Denham Tracts* to invent his hobbit and its hole in the ground. Some months later he filled this empty new creature with details drawn from traditional literatures, and he sent this hobbit into a story borrowed from *Beowulf* and Norse tradition.

At this point, an important problem arises. Tolkien never made mention of any influence of either Rhys or Buchan in the making of his hobbits or in the story that followed. Given the nature of Cook's argument – that Tolkien's hobbits emerged from his longstanding interest in crafting an ancient mythological backdrop for British historical identity, it is mystifying why Tolkien would decline to mention the materials that he used to create his hobbits if he drew on the squarely British inspirations of Rhys and Buchan for his hobbits. This vast silence deserves some effort at explanation. To the degree that we decide to give serious consideration to Cook's argument, we must also ponder why Tolkien never gave credit to these writings.

Tolkien's January 1938 decision to decline to clarify the origin of his hobbit is especially puzzling if it arose from British inspirations. It is possible to explain this response as a mere quirk of character, an "ill-considered" impulse that got out of hand. But Tolkien had decades of further opportunity and encouragement to shed precise light on the origins of his hobbit, and he made sure to repeat his origin story on various occasions, but the totality of references to inpirational source materials is quite sparse.

One circumstance helped to shape Tolkien's response. I believe that Tolkien's choice had to do in some part with his reluctance to reveal the American contributions to *The Hobbit*. Tolkien began making use of Pawnee materials as early as 1914, consulting *Traditions of the Skidi Pawnee* by George Dorsey. He typically set into place discursive hints about mysterious unknown origins for many of the narrative details that came from Pawnee sources. And he also decried and discouraged source hunting as not useful for appreciating the significance of his legendarium. Any revelation of far-off Pawnee sources would collide with his lingering agenda of creating tales that would appeal to an English sense of myth and history.

Tolkien had any number of possible folkloric models to draw upon in filling his hobbit with physical detail and cultural character. This makes it difficult to determine whether some observed parallels are reasonable versus merely coincidental. But when a spectrum of parallels can be identified, and when shared details are unique, and when clusters of parallels appear together in texts, then we can assume that a reasonable level of confidence has been met.

Toward this end, it is useful to analyse materials in detail and to identify the range of corresponding elements. My arguments that Pawnee materials ended up in Middle-earth touch on likenesses and parallels that are strong and unique, while others are only weakly arguable. All deserve consideration.

Wizard of the Great Grasslands

In Tolkien's legendarium the wizard Gandalf provides a crucial link between *The Hobbit* and *The Lord of the Rings*. A handful of vague but suggestive hints show that Tolkien had *Traditions of the Skidi Pawnee* in mind at the very beginning of his construction of the character of Gandalf. The indistinct quality of these hints reflects the fact that he only extracted subtle cultural colorations from the Pawnee stories, and he had no wish for clarity when it came to his use of Pawnee source material.

When Tolkien launched into writing *The Hobbit*, he bestowed upon Gandalf the name Bladorthin.[406] Tolkien left no translation of this name, but John Rateliff has suggested that *thin* is probably Sindarin for "grey" and that *blador* "probably applies to wide open country." He offered several possible ways to interpret the name as a whole, including "the Grey Country," "Grey Plains Fay," and "Grey Master of the Plains."

Rateliff also mentioned two other extant uses of the term *blador* in the names *Bladorwen* and *Bladorion*. The first name refers to "Yavanna, the goddess of the earth and all growing things." The second is a place-name which seems to have materialized during the period when Tolkien was writing *The Hobbit*. "Bladorion," noted Rateliff "is the name given to the great grassy plain dividing Thangorodrim from the elven realms to the south[.]"[407]

Bladorion first appeared in Tolkien's legendarium circa 1930 as a name for a grassland in Beleriand.[408] And in one document from this period, Tolkien used the description "great plains of Bladorion[.]"[409] We can surmise from this usage that since Tolkien originally conceived of Bladorion as a "great plains" it is appropriate to view this as a useful interpretation of the name.

Tolkien envisioned the Great Plains of Bladorion as a place where the Elves "rode often... and their horses multiplied for the grass was good."[410] And "Of those horses many of the sires came from Valinor." Horses imported from across an ocean galloped in this grassland, this Great Plains – just as horses from across an ocean galloped in the Great Plains of Pawneeland.

The Great Plains of Bladorion became a battleground and the region got "turned into a great desert[.]"[411] It is no doubt coincidental that the North American Great Plains became known during the 19th century as the Great American Desert. Tolkien intended for the destruction of his Great Plains to happen as a result of "[r]ivers of fire... from Thangorodrim" and the first appearance of "Glómund the golden, Father of Dragons[.]" He could also have had in mind the Skidi story "Death of the Flint-Monster: Origin of Birds" which associated a dragon-like beast with a burned grassland where "even the ground was red, and seemed to be baked."[412]

The names Bladorthin and Bladorion offer hints about what was in Tolkien's mind when he invented his new wizard for *The Hobbit*. By 1930 he had already made use of material from *Traditions of the Skidi Pawnee* to produce his creation story and to invent Ungoliant, and it was around this time that he made use of Skidi stories to craft adventures for Tom Bombadil. So when we find him that year envisioning a grassland in Beleriand while inventing a wizard with a similar name, it is reasonable to wonder whether he intended some kind of oblique reference to the Great Plains and Pawneeland.

Tolkien had by then created Tû the wizard, the Lord of Gloaming in *The Book of Lost Tales*, and he had also invented the two *Roverandom* wizards, Artaxerxes and Psamathos Psamathides.[413] For his next wizard we know he drew inspiration for Gandalf in part from a late 1920s postcard reproduction of a painting by Josef Madlener.[414] But Tolkien also wanted something more godlike.

In a 1946 letter Tolkien recorded his conception of Gandalf as an "Odinic wanderer" – his association of "Odinic" imagery with Gandalf probably dated back to circa 1930 since Tolkien used the phrase "Odinic magician" in a note dating to the early 1930s.[415] But Gandalf was not merely a thinly veiled version of Odin. Instead, Tolkien developed Gandalf from his imaginative stirring of what he called the "Cauldron of Story," so it is fitting for us to wonder what other source ingredients went into his recipe for the wizard.

Tolkien stirred into his recipe for Bladorthin an association with lightning. At Bag End, after Bladorthin "struck a blue light on the end of his magic staff" we find Bilbo cowering: "Then he fell flat and kept on calling out 'struck by lightning, struck by lightning' over and over again."[416] In an endnote John Rateliff drew a relationship between Bladorthin's act and Bilbo's response, inviting us to think of two later scenes in which Bladorthin produced "a terrific flash of lightning" to kill several goblins in the Misty Mountains, and the subsequent report of surviving goblins that "[s]everal of our people were struck by magic lightning in the cave… and are dead as stones."[417] To this we can add the scene at the beginning of the Battle of Five Armies in which Gandalf (Bladorthin has become Gandalf by this point in the narrative) stops the impending conflict: "'Halt!' he cried and his staff blazed with a sudden flash."[418]

In *The Hobbit* Bladorthin wielded lightning through his staff. His staff seemed somewhat Odinic in this regard, since Odin is associated in Norse myth with a spear used to stir passion for battle, and Bladorthin killed goblins with his staff by making it produce lightning. As he told Beorn: "I killed a goblin or two with a flash[.]"[419] But the wizard also used his magic lightning to halt a senseless war. In brief, Tolkien originally envisioned Bladorthin as a wise wielder of lightning, a godlike wizard with a name referencing a great grassland.

I read this as a hidden reference to the Skidi story told by Roaming Scout, "Lightning Visits the Earth" – a story containing elements that Tolkien would have viewed as Odinic. Lightning roamed the earth after its creation, carrying a sack full of star-folk. In this sack we find "two warriors, guardians of the earth… the Dawn and the Night" and these guardians are "each given a lance, the weapon of a soldier."[420] And Gandalf is an Odinic wanderer who wields lightning through his magic staff, an Odinic spear. Soon after Gandalf at last became "Gandalf" in the manuscript for *The Hobbit*, Tolkien salvaged the name "Bladorthin" in association with spears: "There they sat and the talk drifted on to things they remembered... the spears that were made for the armies of Bladorthin, each with a thrice forged head, each shaft... with cunning gold[.]"[421]

Tolkien took note of how Lightning wandered the earth with his magic "lance men," Night and Dawn, in his sack. These were warriors who carry spears. Bladorthin / Gandalf carried what is best viewed as an Odinic spear, and this magic spear is associated with Lightning. And Lightning carried his "army" – two warriors with spears – in his sack, and Tolkien ultimately transformed Bladorthin into a fabled keeper of an army for whom the dwarves crafted spears.

Tolkien pictured "great plains" at the outset when he invented Bladorthin the wizard because he had read the Skidi story "Lightning Visits the Earth." For this reason, it wasn't very long in *The Hobbit* until we saw Tolkien's dwarves, in their first adventure after leaving the Shire, getting slipped into troll sacks.[422] And the trolls even mentioned the Skidi lance men, Night and Dawn: "[T]he night's getting on and the dawn comes early." And then Bladorthin cried out, "Dawn take you both..." This incident drew from Norse tradition for certain elements, but those sources do not explain the elements borrowed from "Lightning Visits the Earth."[423]

This scene can be read as an act of battle in which the trolls were destroyed by Gandalf's Odinic wisdom and by the hidden power of Lightning's lance-men. In this tale, Gandalf is Bladorthin, a wandering Odinic "Grey Master of the Plains." And after his victory Bladorthin must "untie the sacks and let out the dwarves." In untying the sacks, at that moment Bladorthin becomes Lightning, a Great Plains deity carrying a sack filled with people.

A few chapters after Tolkien's wizard outwitted the trolls, Tolkien again drew on "Lightning Visits the Earth" to colorize his story with stone-giants in a lightning storm. And there we also witness Bladorthin becoming Odinic, striking down several hapless goblins in a cave in the Misty Mountains. As his staff issues a bolt of lightning, in the blinding flash we glimpse Lightning, visiting from Pawneeland.

This scene in the Misty Mountains is also notable as the sole instance of the word "flint" in *The Hobbit*. Goblins take captive the dwarves and haul them away "before you could have said 'tinder and flint'."[424] A moment later in this same paragraph "there was a terrific flash like lightning" – Bladorthin's lightning. In *Traditions of the Skidi Pawnee* we find a report that flint has a "magic power... owing to its intimate relation to the lightning."[425] When attached to a bow, the bow becomes "a weapon of last resort of considerable magic power." This magic has to do with "the belief that the power of the lightning rests in the flint, and that the flint in turn is able to produce lightning." Bladorthin indeed released his deadly lightning as "a weapon of last resort of considerable magic power."

It is noteworthy that Tolkien referred to Gandalf as "Odinic," because in a lecture that could date to the years around 1930 he described Odin – so quintessentially Norse – as an alien import: "...he is really important – for the astonishing fact that he is clearly un-Scandinavian in origin cannot alter the fact that he became the greatest of the Northern gods."[426] The secret of Gandalf is that he is indeed Odinic. Like Odin, Gandalf had some exotic roots since his origin, in part, lay in distant Pawneeland.

Tolkien in Pawneeland   ✶   Roger Echo-Hawk

Gollum the Mysterious Being

In the first Skidi "Animal Tale" that shaped the making of Tom Bombadil's adventures, an interesting incident concluded the narrative. Cheyenne Chief's "The Story of Coyote" ended with Coyote's immolation and a strange birth.[427] The people brought wood and captured Coyote and set him on the woodpile and lit it. "Coyote burned up, and as he was burning, his belly burst open – like thunder – and made a loud report." The onlookers next "saw him as a little bit of a man with hair on." This little man became known among the Skidi as "Mysterious-Being" and was said to belong to a "kind of people... known to exist in the timber." These little folk were dangerous. People encountering them would "become sick, some nearly dying."

What this means is that in the course of writing "The Adventures of Tom Bombadil" Tolkien drew inspiration for this poem from a story that ended with the appearance of "a little bit of a man with hair on." This Mysterious Being was not described in detail and materialized in the tale as a vague, suggestive creature. But since the association of the words "little" and "man" and "hair" do evoke Tolkien's hobbits, it is reasonable to wonder whether Tolkien's hobbits originated in some part from Skidi sources.

This leads us to another Skidi tradition, a very short narrative also told by Cheyenne Chief titled "The Hairy Man."[428] In this story a hunter and his dogs encounter "an old man" living in a cave. This man is termed a "hairy man" and he has short legs, wrinkled skin, long fingernails, long teeth, and gray hair. That night the hunter dreams of this hairy man, who says he makes his home "under the bank of the river" and he doesn't ever "come out from the ground." His fingernails are long to help him "dig inside of the earth for food[.]" Leaving gifts for this hairy man at the mouth of the cave, the hunter "lived a long life and died of old age."

It is logical to suggest that Tolkien encountered the Skidi Mysterious Being while composing his poem about Tom Bombadil, and that he also took note of the story about Hairy Man. But granting this model, it is less clear what kind of impact the Pawnee narratives had on Tolkien's imagination, if any. In my first thoughts on this topic, I wondered whether this Skidi material have influenced the origin of *The Hobbit*.[429] I now think that Tolkien drew entirely on Joseph Wright's *English Dialect Dictionary* for the term "hobbit" and for the idea of associating this hobbit with a "hob-hole." This gave rise to the first sentence of what would eventually become *The Hobbit*, and for a period of months had no idea how to fill these concepts, how to proceed.

It is possible that the ideas finally began to flow in conjunction with his invention of Tom Bombadil. The authorship of both "The Adventures of Tom Bombadil" and *The Hobbit* are difficult to date with any precision. As I outline earlier, the original version of the Bombadil poem could have been written in 1930 and more certainly by sometime in 1931. This vague date of initial composition pertained to "a fine manuscript of the poem in Tengwar" – so it is not a first draft. It is possible, at least, that Tolkien wrote the poem in late 1930 just as he was beginning to write *The Hobbit*.[430]

Douglas Anderson has carefully studied the extant evidence pertaining to the writing of *The Hobbit*.[431] He concluded that "the earliest [Tolkien] could have written the first sentence would have been the summer of 1928" and more broadly during the summer "in one of three years from 1928 to 1930." He also noted "Tolkien himself dated the beginning of the writing of *The Hobbit* to 1930." Sometime after writing the first sentence Tolkien wrote the first chapter of the book, and after an "unknown amount of time" he took the story to the Lonely Mountain by January 1933.

Christina Scull and Wayne Hammond have also set forth the extant evidence for dating *The Hobbit*.[432] Tolkien's earliest recollection of the initial inspiration for *The Hobbit* can be found in a letter written in 1955. He said he wrote the first line and "did nothing about it, for a long time[.]" And "for some years I got no further than the production of Thror's Map." A few weeks later in 1955 he wrote he had "once scribbled 'hobbit' on a blank page" and "it was some time before I discovered what it referred to!" In another note dating from roughly the same period, Tolkien's account again involved writing the first line of the book. And in a 1957 interview Tolkien thought that only "some months" intervened between writing the first line and launching into the first chapter of the book. Tolkien's son John dated his early hearing of hobbit tales before 1930 and perhaps as early as "1926 or 1927." Son Christopher also believed that *The Hobbit* originated before 1930. Scull and Hammond concluded that the book can be most broadly dated no earlier than 1926; they seem to favor the book's origin as "perhaps in 1928 or 1929."

John Rateliff also reviewed the original extant manuscript and evidence pertaining to the date of authorship, observing that "Tolkien did not remember the exact date, but he did retain a strong visual image of the scene."[433] Based on Tolkien's "strong visual memory" and the known date that he moved from one house to another, Rateliff concluded that the original first sentence for *The Hobbit* came to Tolkien's hand "no earlier than the summer of 1930."

Based on this record, and comparing the analyses of Anderson, Scull and Hammond, and Rateliff, I find Rateliff's argument most compelling. By this logic, during the summer of 1930 Tolkien wrote the first line of the book; and at the end of 1930 he wrote at least the first chapter of it. This timing is significant because it is consistent with the possibility that the Skidi Mysterious Person and Hairy Man could have influenced *The Hobbit* via Tom Bombadil. In other words, Tolkien probably wrote the first chapter of *The Hobbit* during the period when he wrote "The Adventures of Tom Bombadil," weaving together a variety of materials, including material drawn from Skidi Coyote stories.

Tolkien mingled many waters to create his mythic elixirs. In the case of Bilbo Baggins, Tolkien started with an empty image of a "hobbit" standing beside a hob-hole. In this regard, it is interesting that the Skidi account of Hairy Man begins with a description of hunting with dogs to "find beaver and otter holes along the banks of the rivers."[434] Thus, the story starts with a hole in the ground. This is notable because Tolkien already had his new hobbit standing beside a hole in the ground, and now he found another mythical creature and another hole in the ground. In the opening scenes of *The Hobbit* we soon learn that Tolkien's hobbit hole is located "across the Water." No hint is given that this is a river, but it is a river, just as in the Skidi story.

Tolkien now needed to develop this character. Considering what he would do and what he would look like, Tolkien eventually decided to turn to *Beowulf* and the sparsely sketched dragon-hoard thief for both a character and a storyline. But rather than tell a thinly veiled tale of Anglo-Saxon England, he chose to summon a kind of fairytale antiquity, what he deemed a more primitive realm of the imagination.

To appropriately texture this storytelling, it is arguable that he drew subtle influences from Pawnee tradition. The Skidi hairy man with short legs lived in a hole in the ground where he found plenty to eat with his long fingernails; while in the third paragraph of Tolkien's story, hobbits turn out to be "small people" whose feet grow "thick warm brown hair like the stuff on their heads" and these folk have "long clever brown fingers[.]" In the Skidi Coyote story about the Mysterious Being, a little hairy man is said to be of a "kind of people"; Tolkien's hobbit is not a singular creature or a solitary one, but is identified immediately as a member of a community of hobbits.

At this point, at least six corresponding details can be drawn between the Skidi stories and Tolkien's story: a focus on a little folk; a focus on holes as homes; a focus on unusual hair; a focus on fingers; a focus on rivers; and a focus on eating. In addition, the Skidi Mysterious Being is small in stature but deemed dangerous in some unspecified way, capable of inducing great harm to people. Hobbits do not seem dangerous, but in the earliest fragment of text – what John Rateliff terms "The Pryftan Fragment" – Bladorthin the wizard terms Bilbo "fierce as a dragon in a pinch" and Bilbo indeed feels an impulse "to be thought fierce[.]"[435]

Finally, in the Skidi story the hunter dreamed of the hairy man and left gifts for him, consisting of "a robe and some tobacco." The action in Tolkien's story opens with Bilbo smoking "a pipe of baccy" just as a man appears wearing "a long grey cloak" – this "baccy" is tobacco that originated in America. The discussion between these two characters turns on "adventure." We have already learned that our particular hobbit is descended from the family of "the Old Took" and "there was something not entirely hobbitlike about them" – perhaps due to an alleged marriage with a "fairy family." And these "Took hobbits would go and have adventures and the family hushed it up[.]"[436]

This clearly echoes "The Adventures of Tom Bombadil" and his liaison with Goldberry. She is a kind of fairy wife, rooted partly in Scottish fairy tradition and emulating Welsh tradition – it is clear that in 1930-1931 Tolkien had fairy intermarriage on his mind since this entered both the composition of the Bombadil poem and the opening chapter of *The Hobbit*. Tolkien had a long-standing fascination with marriage between his various classes of creatures, perhaps sparked by John Rhys and his retelling of Welsh tales on this theme. And the Rhys description of the Manx "fenodyree" depicts a brownie who was "a hairy and apparently clumsy fellow…"[437]

But Tolkien did not want to simply retell Celtic or English fairytales. He had every opportunity to do that, but we can readily see parallels that have nothing to do with Welsh hobbits or hob-holes, but do evoke Skidi story-materials. And he did not dream up his hobbit in a narrative vacuum. Tom Bombadil's adventures and his marriage to Goldberry also arose during that same period, and those moments drew many details from Skidi Coyote stories. So when the hero of *The Hobbit*, Bilbo Baggins, is given "something a bit queer from the Tooks" it could be argued that Tolkien hid here a very subtle reference to something Pawnee entering the making of Bilbo.

We can speculate that it was in 1929 or early 1930 when Tolkien wrote his first Bombadil poem. This poem reveals no influence from any arguable Skidi text, nor does it mention Goldberry. But during the summer or fall of 1930 Tolkien wrote his second Bombadil poem – we can favor 1930 as the likely date rather than 1929 because it was in 1930 that he fine-tuned a class of divinities in his legendarium that seem to account for Goldberry. These are variously termed "spirits" and "lesser spirits" and "fays" in the *Quenta*, written in 1930.[438]

For his second Bombadil poem Tolkien drew a portrait of Goldberry as a fay, modeling her in part on a text from Scottish tradition. And he took inspiration from threee Skidi Coyote stories to construct a series of adventures for Tom. In the course of selecting and formulating Tom's adventures, Tolkien encountered the Skidi Mysterious Being, who is described as a member of an enigmatic "kind of people... known to exist in the timber." Tolkien was intrigued and next found the Skidi story about "The Hairy Man" – an odd little fellow who dwelt in a cave. He had already set down a curious sentence one summer day in 1930 while grading papers: "In a hole in the ground there lived a hobbit." Now the strange imagery of this opening line took on definition as Tolkien summoned imagery from a diverse stew of sources. At the end of 1930 he began writing *The Hobbit*.

A gathering momentum of images from English, Celtic, and Pawnee sources led to the formulation of Tolkien's first hobbits, not any singular folkloric model. To fully explain this collection of sources would have entailed a complicated sorting process that might have mainly served to distract readers from Tolkien's creative genius – his magical weaving together of disparate threads into a coherent new mythic tapestry. This fact may explain Tolkien's reluctance to clarify the folkloric foundations of his new hobbit.

But most importantly, for him to make even the slightest mention of Pawnee tradition would be to open his work to examination against the content of the Skidi texts. This would forever open the door to future source-scrutiny across his legendarium as it already existed in numerous manuscripts. Tolkien could never mention *Traditions of the Skidi Pawnee*.

Not long after inventing a hobbit living in a hole in the ground, Tolkien drew from the same Skidi source-material to create one of his most memorable characters. I came to this awareness when one of my friends wondered whether the Skidi references to Mysterious Being and Hairy Man might fit Gollum better than Bilbo.

Gollum "lived with his grandmother in a hole in a bank by a river"; Hairy Man's tale opens with a discussion of finding "beaver and otter holes along the banks of the rivers."[439] Gollum "had been underground a long long while"; Hairy Man tells the Skidi hunter, "I never come out from the ground." Gollum is termed in his first mention as "old Gollum"; Hairy Man is "an old man." Gollum has "long fingers, as quick as thinking"; Hairy Man's fingernails are "very long[.]" Gollum uses his long fingers to grab fish and throttle goblins; Hairy Man uses his fingernails to "dig inside the earth for food." Gollum is also like Mysterious Being, very dangerous to encounter, "something not quite nice"; when people encounter Mysterious Being they can "become sick, some nearly dying."

And just a few pages before we encounter Hairy Man in *Traditions of the Skidi Pawnee*, we meet "Speak-Riddles and Wise-Spirit."[440] In this story Speak Riddles tells Wise Spirit, "now that we have met, I want to give you a riddle to make out, for I understand that you know how to solve riddles that are given to you by other people." He tells a story, but Wise Spirit "could not make it out." This is a dangerous game with very high stakes. Wise Spirit "began to have a headache and got very sick" and he decided "he was dying." He finally summoned Speak Riddles, who explained the riddle and Wise Spirit slowly recovered. Finally he said, "I am now a well man." Gollum's riddle game is also a perilous contest, but Bilbo survives.

The next Skidi story is "Contest Between Witch-Woman and Beaver."[441] In this story a cannibal witch issued challenges to every stranger who "came into the village." The challenge involved some kind of a body of water, and "the witch had a cave to go to, under a bank." And "a little boy" managed to defeat her. Tolkien has Gollum residing in a cave and when Bilbo – who is the size of a little boy – finds himself lost in a cave, he encounters a body of water but "[h]e didn't know whether it was just a pool in the path, or the edge of an underground stream[.]"[442] Gollum is horrible and hungry and sees Bilbo as "a tasty morsel[.]" But Bilbo prevails and defeats the cannibal witch.

John Rateliff referred to Gollum as "[o]ne of Tolkien's greatest characters[.]"[443] He asserted that "all the details of his description argue against his being of hobbit-kin." Rateliff accepted the suggestion of Douglas Anderson that Gollum entered *The Hobbit* from "Glip," a poem they tentatively date at 1928.[444] But I would suggest that the poem more likely dates to 1930-1931 and not 1928, and Glip was born in conjunction with Tolkien's invention of Bilbo and Gollum. Glip is "a slimy little thing" who dwells "in a little cave" near the sea where he keeps "[a] white bone that is gnawed quite clean[.]" It is interesting that "out he crawls / All long and wet with slime" while we find the Skidi Hairy Man in one scene "crawling up to his tipi[.]"

In the course of writing *The Lord of the Rings*, Tolkien returned to Gollum's character, and Rateliff suggested it was then that he had "the inspiration to make Gollum a hobbit." But I believe Tolkien kept in mind all along that a hidden connection existed between Bilbo and Gollum. Since they had shared Skidi roots from Mysterious Being and Hairy Man, it was logical to Tolkien to make more explicit their common ancestral origin. Tolkien didn't need help from Skidi storytellers to imagine a wholly new creature and to then situate it in a hole in the ground. But comparative evidence from Skidi tradition suggests that Tolkien found aspects of Gollum and Bilbo in Pawneeland.

Tolkien's return to the character of Gollum came in early 1938 – the first new details were that Gollum was "an ancient sort of hobbit" and of a "wise, cleverhanded and quietfooted little family" and he "disappeared underground."[445] And this new Gollum is a kind of goblinish hobbit – "some sort of distant kinsman of the goblin sort."[446] Tolkien selected Dígol as Gollum's original name – Old English for "secret, hidden."[447]

It was Tolkien's typical practice to merge diverse construction materials. One novel that Tolkien mentioned as an inspiration for *The Hobbit* is *The Marvelous Land of the Snergs*. In October 1937 Tolkien mentioned this book in conversation with his publisher.[448] And a few years later in a draft of his 1938-1939 essay "On Fairy-stories" Tolkien wrote, "I should like to record my own love and my children's love of E.A. Wyke-Smith's *Marvellous Land of Snergs*..."[449] Much later in 1955 he suggested that this book "was probably an unconscious source-book! for the Hobbits, not of anything else."[450]

In Wyke-Smith's book snergs are described as "a race of people only slightly taller than the average table but broad in the shoulders and of great strength."[451] They are explained as an "offshoot of the pixies who once inhabited the hills and forests of England[.]" And they wear "little round leather caps" and are "gregarious" and "are great on feasts." To some degree these snergs surely helped give rise to Tolkien's original idea for a hobbit. Tolkien may have toyed with the idea suggested by the use of the term "pixies" since this was a term that appears about 1919-1920 in his legendarium. But he framed the specific influence of snergs as "unconscious" and gave no other more direct source for his hobbits. Most importantly, in terms of the influence of snergs on the scene in Tolkien's opening sentence, the comparison is weak; snergs did not help Tolkien in any noticeable way.

In January 1938 Tolkien took a moment to discuss the sources of *The Hobbit*. Responding to queries in a letter in a local newspaper, Tolkien denied any derivation of his hobbits from African folklore and asserted, "I do not remember anything about the name and inception of the hero."[452] Regarding his source-material for the tale that followed, Tolkien wrote that he "had not thought of future researchers" and added that he had "been made to see Mr. Baggins's adventures as the subject of future inquiry[.]" He acknowledged that aspects of "the rest of the tale... derived from (previously digested) epic, mythology, and fairy-story" and that *Beowulf* was a valued though unconscious source, as well as Norse mythology.

Notably absent from this 1938 acknowledgement is any mention of Wyke-Smith's *The Marvelous Land of the Snergs* or Sinclair Lewis' *Babbit;* nor do we find any hints pointing to Welsh folklore via John Rhys or Joseph Wright's *English Dialect Dictionary*. Tolkien had no evident reason to treat any of these sources as secret. But he was firm about one point: "My tale is not consciously based on any other book[.]"

Beewolf and Beorn and the Bear-boy

Tolkien's strategy of derivative invention shaped "Sellic Spell," his reconstruction of the lost folktale that gave rise to the *Beowulf* poem.[453] Considering in detail the creative process behind the story – dating to circa 1943 – we glimpse Tolkien enriching his creative productions by weaving together carefully selected elements from pre-existing source-materials. The genesis of "Sellic Spell" emerged primarily from his study of ancient English literature, but he also drew from other sources. Fascinated with the lingering glow of fading realms glimpsed but long-lost, Tolkien wondered whether he could "reconstruct the Anglo-Saxon tale that lies behind the folk-tale element in *Beowulf*."

The study of the transmission of verbal documents over long time periods is necessarily an art, not a science. He knew this kind of project could not be accomplished "with certainty," but he thought he could do a rendering that would reflect "the difference of style, tone and atmosphere if the particular heroic or *historical* is cut out." He seemed to mean here that references to historical events crept into the original folktale, as well as a heroic dimension, and if these elements were deleted, one might well have in hand an ancient folktale – the ancient tale that at some point morphed into a historically minded heroic elegy.

To envision and recreate the forgotten story that led to *Beowulf*, Tolkien pondered a widespread folktale called the "bear's son tale." He followed a trajectory of logic that he described in 1943 as "turning... the bear-boy into the knight Beowulf..."[454] And he had at hand a substantial body of literature to study. We might presume that the back-engineering of the substance of a lost tradition would be based on the systematic review of surviving descendant narratives among related literary traditions, but it does not appear that Tolkien left notes reflecting any such study of relevant textual materials.

In 1943 in the course of expanding his essay, "On Fairy-stories," Tolkien conducted a wide-ranging survey of fairytale / mythological literature.[455] This was the same period when he is believed to have written "Sellic Spell," and in fact Tolkien made mention of the bear's son tale in this essay with the statement, "We read that *Beowulf* 'is only a version of *Dat Erdmänneken*...'"[456] Verlyn Flieger and Douglas Anderson note that this is a reference to a Brothers Grimm story which "bears virtually no resemblance to *Beowulf*."[457] But the story in question, retitled as "The Elves," is a typical tale of the bear's son legend complex, and when compared to "Sellic Spell," the resemblances are clear.[458] Beewolf uses the word "mannikin" to describe Unfriend, an opponent who betrayed him, and this term also appears in *Dat Erdmänneken* / "The Elves." Beyond this term, it is difficult to identify other unique corresponding details between the two stories.

The section of "On Fairy-stories" where Tolkien made mention of *Dat Erdmänneken* is interesting because he gave it the heading of "Origins." There he dismissed the work of folklorists and anthropologists as "people using the stories not as they were meant to be used, but as a quarry from which to dig evidence, or information, about matters in which they are interested." But we should read this criticism through Tolkien's own preferred lens – a lens through which he peered at textual material in search of useful details to set into his own stories. And Tolkien knew to look at *Dat Erdmänneken* due to the analytical research of a greatly esteemed colleague and friend, RW Chambers, who briefly mentioned the story in his study of *Beowulf* – Chambers cited the story as an example of the bear's son tale, together with another Grimm story from the same collection.[459]

This second story, "Strong Hans," is interesting because it mentioned the taking of a "great meal-sack" stuffed with gold and silver from a cave, and Tolkien had Beewolf take from Grinder's cave "such treasure beside of gold and gems as he could pack in Grinder's bag[.]"[460] "Strong Hans" also had Hans taking a ring from a dwarf and setting it on his finger. When he "turned it round on his finger" there appeared spirits in the air "who told him he was their master[.]" They aided him twice when he turned the ring. In a passage deleted from "Sellic Spell," Beewolf was given a ring by the Queen of the Golden Hall, who told him, "turn it on your finger and your call for help will be answered..."[461] It seems clear that Tolkien made use of this story – his reason must have had to do with the status of "Strong Hans" as a bear's son tale.

Flieger and Anderson present a list of publications consulted by Tolkien in preparing "On Fairy-stories," and this list contains references to two additional works cited by Chambers in his consideration of the bear's son legend complex: George Dasent's *Popular Tales from the Norse* and JF Campbell's *Popular Tales of the West Highlands*.[462] In the course of doing research for "On Fairy-stories" Tolkien wondered if he could find some version of the *Beowulf* tale in fairytale collections. Verlyn Flieger and Douglas Anderson found two notes in the draft manuscripts for the essay showing that Tolkien searched through Andrew Lang's fairy books for a story that resembled *Beowulf*.[463] When this search failed to turn up a likely candidate, he noted, "It should be retold as a fairy-story." Tolkien's research for "On Fairy-stories" and "Sellic Spell" thus overlapped, and the seeming absence of research notes for the latter probably means that as his work unfolded for "On Fairy-stories" he found sufficient material to prepare "Sellic Spell" to his satisfaction.

Tolkien's understanding of the connection of *Beowulf* to the bear's son tradition was amplified by the work of RW Chambers.[464] Chambers cited previous research pointing to the likelihood that an ancient version of the bear's son tale gave rise to certain aspects of both *Beowulf* and a related Norse tradition, *Grettis Saga*. He outlined eight versions of the bear's son tale found in various European traditional literatures, and he included an abstract of a Russian version from the early 1860s, "Ivashko Medvedko."[465] This drew Tolkien's notice, but Anderson noted that he was not "known to have been adept in Russian."[466]

In the end it is apparent that Tolkien turned to an English translation of this Russian tradition for help, drawing from Post

Wheeler's "Little Bear's-Son" in *Russian Wonder Tales*, a 1912 collection that drew from Ifanasief's Russian folktales.[467] Textual comparisons show a number of elements that match between "Sellic Spell" and "Little Bear's-Son." Some of these parallels are general defining features and so must be common to many versions. Tolkien knew well the Norse *Grettis Saga* – we can guess that he reviewed it in the course of writing "Sellic Spell," and it must have been helpful in various ways, but there is no clear indication that he borrowed anything unique from the saga. In fact, since Tolkien left no record of the research he did for this project, we can only identify a handful of texts that he arguably consulted aside from *Beowulf*, and this includes the Russian story. We can see notable textual convergences between "Sellic Spell" and "Little Bear's-Son."

In the Russian story a peasant who hunted bears and wolves "tracked a bear to its den, and having killed it, he found there to his astonishment a little boy three years old, naked and sturdy, whom the bear had stolen and had been rearing like a cub." Tolkien has huntsmen encounter a bear, and they "tracked him to his lair and killed him, and in his den they found a man-child" and they "marveled much, for it was a fine child, about three years old, and in good health," and the huntsmen thought "it must have been fostered by the bears, for it growled like a cub."

In the Russian story "[t]he lad grew" and "did not realize his own strength... as he played with the other lads of his village..." But his strength was dangerous and the neighbors complained. Tolkien wrote that "Beewolf grew, and as he grew he became stronger, until first the boys and lads and at length even the men began to fear him."

In the Russian story the bear-boy goes into exile and travels, encountering three strong giants who he befriends as companions, including one called "Oak-man." Tolkien has Beewolf set forth from his home, and he falls in with several companions who have magical strength, including one named "Ashwood."

The Russian story has the new friends setting up a home, and each of the giants takes a turn watching the home, but each is worsted by a horrible enemy. Tolkien has Beewolf and his two companions appear at Heorot, and the two companions each take a turn at watch, and each is worsted and slain by a horrible enemy.

The Russian story has the bear-boy taking his turn and besting the horrible enemy, who escapes. Tolkien has Beewolf taking his turn and besting a horrible enemy, who escapes.

The Russian story has the bear-boy entering a hole in the ground, where the horrible enemy "is a hundred times more powerful... surrounded by her enchantments..." Tolkien has Beewolf enter a lake and an underground cave and there he meets a horrible enemy and "[v]ery strong she was, there in her own house over which many spells were woven."

The Russian story has the bear-boy eventually encountering the horrible enemy, and he beheads her with a sword. Tolkien has Beewolf confront the horrible enemy, and he beheads her with a sword.

The Russian story has a betrayal when the bear-boy climbs a rope out of the underworld and he falls back underground. Tolkien has Beewolf betrayed while climbing his rope, and he falls back into the lake.

The Russian story has the bear-boy receiving aid from a bird. Tolkien has Beewolf swimming in the lake looking to escape, "but there was no way up... save for birds."

The Russian story has the bear-boy eventually prevailing; the story ends with his marriage. Tolkien also has Beewolf prevailing and the story ends with his marriage.

John Rateliff's discussion of Medwed / Beorn in *The Hobbit* showed that Tolkien was thinking as early as circa 1932 of a reference to either a Russian term or a Russian source-story for the fantasy commingling of bear and man. Douglas Anderson felt it likely that Tolkien's formulation of Beorn reflected the Chambers publication on *Beowulf*, with its abstract of "Ivashko Medvedko."[468]

It is clear enough that Tolkien was indeed thinking of Russian tradition and "Ivashko Medvedko" during the writing of *The Hobbit*, given his use of Medwed as the original name of Beorn. But his storytelling contains nothing of the bear's son tradition. When Tolkien wrote *The Hobbit* he decided not to draw from Russian folklore for his portrayal of Medwed, and he eventually dropped the Russian name and replaced it with a Norse name.

As I explain in the first edition of *Tolkien in Pawneeland*, he nevertheless did make use of pre-existing myth to construct his tale of Beorn – in this case, I believe he drew upon a Pawnee tradition for raw material.[469] John Rateliff has suggested that Tolkien drew inspiration from a Norse story, *Hrolf Kraki's Saga*, which tells the story of a man who can enter a trance and generate a bear-warrior.[470] Rateliff pointed to Tolkien's likely interest in the fact that this story survived in a form recorded during the 14th century, and it was derived from a lost text that helped give rise to several Norse sagas and perhaps to *Beowulf*.

Tolkien's typical practice was to weave together diverse threads into a new story, and it is indeed likely that he had in mind *Hrolf Kraki's Saga* and *Beowulf* when he constructed his tale of Beorn. But as with "Sellic Spell," Tolkien sought for what he would have considered a "primitive" text from the bear's son complex for additional texturing. He found that mythological greenery in Pawneeland, and he transplanted into Middle-earth various details from a story in *Traditions of the Skidi Pawnee*.

"The Boy, the Bears, and White Crow" was told by James Yellow Calf, a Skidi ceremonialist and one of the Keepers of a leading Skidi Holy Bundle handed down from antiquity.[471] In this Skidi story a boy-hero follows a father grizzly bear to its cave-home in a cedar grove where he is given shape-shifting magic, the power to transform into a bear. In Tolkien's original manuscript the fellowship of the Dwarves comes down off the Carrock to meet in a cave where Medwed / Beorn – a man who can turn into a bear – "sometimes sleeps" and whose house is also located in a grove, "an oakwood[.]"[472]

Yellow Calf's story has a little black bear cub talking to the boy, giving him advice.[473] In the cave of the grizzly this bear cub is transformed into a "fine black horse" – a gray horse is also given to the boy and it is implied that this horse is actually a mountain lion. Tolkien's original manuscript for *The Hobbit* says that Medwed / Beorn "keeps... horses, which are nearly as marvellous as himself[.]"[474] This marvelous quality is nowhere specified; the story goes on to say that the horses talk, and we soon see "some horses... with very intelligent faces" giving Beorn advice. John Rateliff explained this as a reference to Doctor Doolittle.[475] But Beorn is a skinchanger, a werebear, both a man and a bear, and his horses are "nearly as marvellous as himself[.]" This is certainly true of the Pawnee werebear skinchanger and his marvelous horses, both of whom seem to be shape-shifters, and one of whom can transform into a bear.

In the Skidi story the young skinchanger returns to his community and encounters an evil leader and they fight, both turning into bears; and the magic gray horse helps the boy to kill the evil man-bear. After this incident, the people are understandably nervous about the dangerous character of the young skinchanger. The same sentiment of fear mingled with distrust accompanies Beorn. In Tolkien's original manuscript Gandalf warns the Dwarves about Beorn, "you *must* be careful not to annoy him[.] He can be appalling when angry... and he gets angry easily."[476]

In Yellow Calf's story the young skinchanger is offered a pipe to smoke. Accepting it and smoking this tobacco pipe, he becomes their leader and then he eats with his new wife. In Tolkien's original manuscript Gandalf (who is the actual leader of the Dwarves) takes a meal and then smokes his pipe in the house of Beorn – "a splendid place for smoke-rings!"[477] This is the second time Gandalf has lit his pipe. On both occasions tobacco isn't specifically identified by Tolkien, but it is strongly implied by his use of the word elsewhere in *The Hobbit*. It is worth noting that tobacco is not European; it is from America. At Bag End and at the house of Beorn, Gandalf more explicitly produces "smoke-rings." At Bag End his smoke-rings "would go green" and at

Beorn's house the wizard turns them "into all sorts of different colours... green, blue, red, silver-grey, yellow[.]"[478]

In another Skidi story about a magic bear ("Long-Tooth-Boy"), two boy-heroes approach a den and a bear emerged and "threw breath at them, and each breath was of a different color."[479] An endnote attached to this incident explains that the colored breath is used by this bear to "kill its enemies[.]"[480] And in Tolkien's 1932 Father Christmas letter to his children, Father Christmas sends his "patent green luminous smoke down the tunnel, and Polar Bear blew and blew it with our enormous kitchen bellows."[481] As with the weaponized colored breath of the Skidi magic bears, this green smoke is explicitly intended as a weapon to ward off enemy goblins.

In Tolkien's original manuscript Gandalf describes a Middle-earth bear dance: "I should say little bears, big bears, ordinary bears, and gigantic big bears must have been dancing outside from dark to nearly dawn."[482] And that night Bilbo "dreamed a dream of hundreds of black bears dancing slow heavy dances round and round in the moonlight in the courtyard." *Traditions of the Skidi Pawnee* describes a Pawnee bear dance:

> This dance is held very sacred. The day before the dance they go out and get a cedar-tree and set it up before the bear-lodge. They sing all night. Next morning they paint, put their bear claws around their necks. Three or four men put the bear robes about their shoulders. The four leaders then take four drums and sing, and as soon as they commence to dance, the outside people rush into the entrance and look on; this is why the boys and girls have congregated at this place.[483]

The Pawnee bear dance and the Middle-earth bear dance have interesting similarities. In both instances, the bear ceremonialism is not explained; instead, the dancing is imbued with mysterious purpose. Both are nocturnal events. The Middle-earth bear dance proceeds "from dark to nearly dawn" while the Pawnee ceremony involves singing "all night." There is also singing in Middle-earth – on the night of the Middle-earth bear dance, Bilbo "began to nod because he was very sleepy... until he woke with a start and heard the end of a song of the dwarves."[484]

In the Skidi story the young skinchanger prizes his horses and instructs everyone, "Seeing my ponies upon the hill, never touch or scold them." In Tolkien's original manuscript Beorn loans the Dwarves ponies and shadows them because "he loves his ponies as his children[.]"[485] This sentence has a powerful directness. Beorn's fatherly sentiment toward his horses becomes quite revealing when we connect it to the Skidi father grizzly who transforms his own cub into a horse.

In Yellow Calf's story, when someone happens to hit the young skinchanger's horse with a stick, both the young skinchanger and the horse turn into bears and they go berserk and slaughter many people. Tolkien's Beorn reveals his "appalling" brutal side when he captures, tortures, kills, and mutilates a goblin and a warg.[486]

In the Skidi story the young skinchanger and his horse-bear return to the home of the father grizzly bear in his cedar grove. In *The Hobbit* Gandalf tells the Dwarves, "I heard [Beorn] growl in the tongue of bears: 'The day will come when they will perish and I shall go back.'"

John Rateliff and Mark Hooker have identified various European sources that can account for many aspects of Tolkien's tale of Beorn.[487] These include useful reference to sources like *Hrolf Kraki's Saga*, the Doctor Dolittle stories, and the *Mabinogi*. Tolkien was influenced by the material that he loved and studied, and he made derivative uses of it in various ways in constructing his own legendarium, mingling such influences with the productions of his own imagination. But Tolkien never made any reference to *Hrolf Kraki's Saga*, the Doctor Dolittle stories, or the *Mabinogi* as source-materials for *The Hobbit* or for Beorn. He had plenty of opportunity to do so but chose to say nothing.

The resonations of European traditional materials added to his mythology, weaving a familiar cultural air around his world-making. Tolkien could have spent his entire career retelling known stories in the mode of Andrew Lang's fairy books and the

Brothers Grimm. But he wanted to create something both familiar and new.

Tolkien's authorial technique of weaving together disparate threads from his source-material could be applied to any kind of appropriately toned traditional materials, including the narratives of Pawneeland. For this reason, it is quite logical that numerous details in Tolkien's story so clearly echo details found in the Skidi tradition. It is highly unlikely that mere coincidence can carry the needed explanatory weight to account for this situation. Moreover, as I explain in more detail below, the use of the name Medwed for *The Hobbit* points to his interest in the bear's son legend complex, and "The Boy, the Bears, and White Crow" can be recognized as a story of that very complex.

A decade after Tolkien pondered the name Medwed for *The Hobbit*, it is evident that he consulted "Little Bear's-Son" in *Russian Wonder Tales* and decided to draw useful elements from it for "Sellic Spell." Borrowing pre-existing traditional elements and carefully weaving them into his narrative, Tolkien felt satisfied enough with the result that he was willing to affirm that indeed a "bear-boy" tradition served as the originating source for the story of *Beowulf*, as he wrote in a 1953 lecture: "...the Bear-boy lurks behind the heroic Beowulf..."[488] Pondering the "unhistorical" Beowulf, Tolkien pictured a "bear-man" and a "giant-killer" most at home in the world of fairytale.[489] And after stripping away what he considered to be a later accretion of heroic knighthood, he thought we should find a "lumpish and greedy bearboy, who is a trouble to keep and feed, but who is now offering to earn his keep..."[490] The end result is a regressive transformation of the Christianized Anglo-Saxon knight Beowulf into Beewolf, a "lumpish and greedy bearboy" who ultimately becomes "a great lord."[491] This reconstructed story is slightly Russianized, but Tolkien deemed it a useful representation of the kind of folktale that might be told at an Anglo-Saxon fireside of circa 700 CE.[492]

Tolkien's reservations regarding "Sellic Spell" did not stop him from offering it for publication, and when the project fell through, he never made any further effort to publish the story.

The textual history of the story is vague, but it doesn't appear that he ever returned to the story after the mid-1940s to improve it. It is possible that the problems he sensed could explain why he lost interest in the project. It is more certain, however, that "Sellic Spell" reached a point where it felt publishable, and even though Tolkien had reservations, these were minor concerns. He must have felt satisfied with this manuscript as a finished project.

In his eyes, "Sellic Spell" did achieve his intent to produce a story that could logically have been told long ago among his Anglo-Saxon ancestors. For Tolkien, the illuminating glow cast by "primitive culture" lit the way to this logic. Tolkien's creative agenda in part had to do with expressing what he deemed a "Northern spirit" related to English and Anglo-Saxon culture – that is, an esoteric defining quality that he associated most strongly with things Norse and Old English.[493] Russia lay somewhat askew from such associations. We can surmise that he deemed Slavic Russian tradition to lack the medieval "Northern" heroic quality that he valued – a quality of culture that characterized Beowulf the character and *Beowulf* the heroic elegy. This very quality had to be deleted from the story to give it a more ancient "primitive" texturing. In addition, Tolkien seems to have assumed that Slavic Russian tradition recorded at circa 1860 CE held some of the same cultural resonations that one might find in ancient Anglo-Saxon tradition of the 7th century CE.

Choosing between the likelihood of unconnected coincidental similarity versus the likelihood of purposeful borrowing, it is more arguable that Tolkien did reconfigure elements from Wheeler's "Little Bear's Son" to fit his story. He didn't cut and paste; nor did he simply retell the Russian tale. Borrowing material from a Russian tradition, he added details to "Sellic Spell" that he felt would impart a tone of antiquity, a primitive quality.

This was also the composition procedure Tolkien followed in his use of Pawnee tradition. Pawneeland could never have an explicit place on any map of Tolkienian Northernness, but its cultural tones could be useful. Pawnee tradition could help guide his efforts to craft details that harkened back to the primitive cultural tones of ancient ancestral Europeans.

When Tolkien decided to make use of a Skidi Pawnee story to colorize the story of Beorn in *The Hobbit*, he chose "The Boy, the Bears, and White Crow" because it featured recognizable traces of the bear's son tale. He knew about the wide European distribution of the bear's son tale from a long history of scholarship on the topic, including from RW Chambers 1921 edition of *Beowulf: An Introduction to the Study of the Poem*. This legend complex was not limited to Europe. Variants of the bear's son tale can also be found in traditional literatures throughout North America.

Tolkien launched into the making of Beorn from the starting point of the Russian name Medwed, and this tells us clearly that he was pondering the bear's son legend complex. We must guess at why he decided not to draw the Russian story into his tale of Beorn and to instead make use of a distant Pawnee bear's son legend. But the scope of the parallels indicate that he opened the pages of *Traditions of the Skidi Pawnee* and he made selective use of details from "The Boy, the Bears, and White Crow" to colorize the tale of Beorn. He had no interest in retelling the bear's son legend, so he made the story of Beorn unique, a marvelous weaving of tradition and creativity.

Tolkien drew together many threads to invent his tales. And he frequently chose to keep to himself this authorial procedure. In the case of "Sellic Spell," he found occasion to discuss Beowulf and the bear's son tale, but he never disclosed his use of Russian tradition. And in the case of Beorn, he found occasion to discuss various sources for *The Hobbit*, but he never made mention of any Pawnee contribution.

All the traditions of the world lay near to hand for JRR Tolkien, and he used them to tell his stories, weaving together their magic. And he found the traditions of Pawneeland useful, just as he found the traditions of Europe useful. Details from Pawnee tradition could colorize his vision of Middle-earth. And observing him at work weaving very diverse sources into his legendarium, we must learn to re-envision the significance of

Middle-earth as a place made of the whole world. When we peer into the stories told by JRR Tolkien, we glimpse strange secret rumors and hidden whispers, and we see that he truly was a teller of marvelous tales.

Tolkien in Pawneeland   ✻   Roger Echo-Hawk

To Distant Lands and Back Again

Slender glimmers of evidence show that about 1931, in the course of writing *The Hobbit*, Tolkien made a secret visit to Vinland. This is arguable because we can identify fleeting glimpses of a specific Vinland narrative in *The Hobbit*, and we know that Tolkien occasionally gave thought to the New World, with traces of Pawneeland and Longfellow's *The Song of Hiawatha* making their way into Middle-earth. His interest in American mythologies can be fairly characterized as peripheral and often incidental, but it helped him to craft cultural nuances that advanced his agenda as a mythologist.

Tolkien's deep study of Norse literature left a rich array of impressions in the mythic soils of Middle-earth.[494] As I have described earlier, his crica 1914 note on Night the Spider can be read as referencing Vinland, and he made brief mention of the Norse Vinland sagas in his 1914-1915 paper, "On 'The Kalevala' or the Land of Heroes." A second explicit mention of Vinland can be found in Tolkien's later writings. After preparing the early manuscript version of *The Hobbit* in 1930-1932, Tolkien launched into writing a book called *The Lost Road*, probably about 1936-1937. He never finished this book, but in one set of notes he made reference to plans for a number of stories, including "a Norse story of ship-burial (Vinland)."[495]

In manuscripts dating to 1936-1937 Tolkien invented his first tales of Númenor, and there he envisioned visits of Númenórean airships to America. An outline briefly mentioned these airships and "ship burials" and "fleets of the Númenórië" that "sailed round the world; and Men took them for gods."[496] In the subsequent narrative manuscript, the airships visited "the lands of the New World" and "the east of the Old World" and "Men of Middle-earth looked on them with wonder and great fear, and took them to be gods[.]"[497] And in a revised second manuscript Tolkien again has these "Men of Middle-earth" looking up at the airships in wonder and fear and "they took the Númenóreans to be Gods[.]"[498] Tolkien decided the people of America would enter his legendarium as a folk who would feel awe, observing the Númenóreans as they stepped forth in majesty and power from magic airships.

These sparse mentions of America and Vinland reflect a very casual interest in the Western Hemisphere during the 1930s. But a few additional moments in his writings can be added to these explicit references to Vinland – a collection of slight textual traces indicating that Tolkien had in mind the two Norse Vinland sagas in other writings of the 1920s and 1930s, including *The Hobbit*.[499]

One of the two extant Norse Vinland sagas – the saga of Eric the Red – began with a woman whose grandfather and brother were named "Bjorn."[500] When some Norse travelers decided to journey out of the realm of Bjorn, they sought Vinland, and in their travels and travails, one member of their party was found dazed, and he later sang a song about "sweet wine." In the "south" they found a land of vines and a folk with whom they trade.

In *The Hobbit* Tolkien told a story in which travelers with Old Norse names journeyed from the realm of Beorn. In the course of their travels and travails, one member of their party became quite dazed, and the story soon told of Elves "fond of wine" who sang a song about sending wine barrels "South away" – they get their wine "from the vineyards of Men in distant lands." The Norse saga told how the travelers brought livestock to Vinland, including a bull. And the Elves in Mirkwood sang of sending wine barrels "back to mead / Where the kine and oxen feed[.]"

When the swooning Norseman appeared in the Vinland saga, the folk were hungry and they found a beached whale "and they ate it, but it made everyone ill."[501] Tolkien's original manuscript description of Mirkwood mentioned "black squirrels in that wood"; and later in the story the hungry dwarves with Norse names shot a squirrel and cooked it but "it proved horrible to taste, and they shot no more squirrels."[502] Soon thereafter Bombur fell into an enchanted swoon, just as the Norse saga had a swooning man "staring skyward..." The color of Tolkien's unsavory Mirkwood squirrel was not mentioned, but in the final version of the chapter, the black squirrels and the squirrel hunting incident were brought closer together, hinting strongly that Tolkien pictured the dwarves as shooting and eating a black squirrel.

This conjunction of imagery is interesting because black squirrels were imported to England from North America during the late 19th century. Sightings of these American black squirrels in English forests began as early as 1912. It isn't clear that Tolkien knew anything about them; it seems doubtful that he had in mind any actual model for his Mirkwood squirrel. But there is no doubt that the awful-tasting black squirrels in Mirkwood were not drawn from any European bestiary. And it is interesting that an obvious parallel existed between the Norse-named dwarves eating a black squirrel "horrible to taste" and the Norse visitors to Vinland eating a beached whale that "made everyone ill."

In the course of the Dwarves' visit to Mirkwood, Tolkien described the imported wine of the Elves: "The wine, and other goods, were brought from far away, from their kinsfolk in the South, or from the vineyards of Men in distant lands." In an early version of *The Hobbit*, Tolkien bestowed a specific and unexplained name upon the land of vineyards: "But this... was the heady brew of the great gardens of Dorwinion in the warm south..."[503] In the later published version he retained this mysterious name: "The wine of Dorwinion brings deep and pleasant dreams."

The first appearance of Dorwinion occurred in "The Lay of the Children of Húrin" – Tolkien began writing this long poem perhaps as early as 1918 but more likely about 1920.[504] At line 224-225 Tolkien referred to "a flask of leather   full filled with wine / that is bruised from the berries   of the burning South[.]" This wine is known to the Elves who import it to their realm in the

North. At line 229-230, "their heads were mazed / by the wine of Dor-Winion" and "they soundly slept[.]"[505]

The second version of this poem apparently dates from circa 1923 to circa 1925.[506] It expands Tolkien's conception of this wine as made from "berries   of the burning South" and "from Nogrod the Dwarves / by long ways lead it   to the lands of the North / for the Elves in exile   who by evil fate / the vine-clad valleys   now view no more / in the land of the Gods."[507] Here the wine of Dorwinion reminds the Elves of the wine of Valinor.

Tolkien provided no translation of "Dor-Winion" in "The Lay of the Children of Húrin" or *The Hobbit*. But the context indicates that at first it applied to a place in the warm "south" where wine was produced, and a few years later this place was further specified as a realm of "vine-clad valleys." This wine came to the Elves through trade with Dwarves.

When Tolkien wrote *The Hobbit* in 1931-1932 he revisited Dorwinion and placed it within reach of the Elves in Mirkwood via trade with "Men in distant lands." The continuing association of wine, south, and vineyards very vaguely echoes the Vinland of the Norse sagas. But if Tolkien had in mind any framing of Dorwinion with a silhouette of Vinland, the concept receded when he placed Dorwinion within reach of the Elves in Mirkwood. To be sure, there is no explicit clarification of the term "Dorwinion" – no name on any map yet, no translation, and no other specificity.

Sometime before 1937, launching into a new version of a work now titled *Quenta Silmarillion*, Tolkien at last determined his initial location for Dorwinion as "…the Lonely Isle, Tol Eressëa, whither few mariners of Men have ever come, save once or twice in a long age when some man of Eärendel's race hath passed beyond the lands of mortal sight and seen the glimmer of the lamps upon the quays of Avallon, and smelt afar the undying flowers in the meads of Dorwinion."[508]

Placing Dorwinion in a far land across the ocean in the West, Tolkien pictured it as an exotic region that "few mariners of Men" have visited. This would certainly suffice as a description of the character of Vinland in the Norse sagas, a realm that few

Norse seamen had ever seen. So in the evolution of Dorwinion, we see "the vine-clad valleys" (circa 1923-1925) becoming (by circa 1931-1932) "the vineyards of Men in distant lands," and next becoming (prior to 1937) a legendary place glimpsed on remote shores by only the farthest seafarers among Men.

It was not until decades later that Tolkien left a record specifying a preferred translation of Dorwinion, rendering the translation as "Young-land country."[509] And by the late 1960s he seems to have situated this realm near the Sea of Rhûn. The geography of Dorwinion evolved over time, and it is reasonable to suppose that its meaning could have also shifted. In an excellent synthesis of Tolkien's use of the term "Dorwinion," John Rateliff points out that the term "is easy to explicate: Dor, land... winion, wine: Wine-land or Vinland."[510] This would seem a reasonable conclusion about what was in Tolkien's mind when he invented and experimented with the term. But whatever Tolkien's original thinking, in later life when he considered the term, he decided to make sense of it in the context of what he had written in *The Hobbit*.

John Rateliff takes Tolkien's late translation as a reference to the Irish mythical realm "The Land of Youth." No clear evidence exists to show that in 1931-1932 Tolkien had in mind "Young-land country" as the translation of Dorwinion, and it isn't clear why Tolkien would situate Dorwinion anywhere near Mirkwood or the Sea of Rhûn if this was always the intended translation of the name. But during the 1930s he gave much thought to the nature of mythical realms in the west of Middle-earth. This is when Tolkien's invented islands of Valinor and Tol Eressëa were joined in his writings by Númenor / Atlantis and by Avalon of Arthurian legend – the latter name becoming interchangeable with Tol Eressëa.[511] It is fitting that he also gave thought to Vinland in those days.

With Vinland in Tolkien's notes for *The Lost Road* at circa 1936-1937 – together with Tolkien's explicit application of Dorwinion to Tol Eressëa in the same period – it is interesting that "New World" offers a rendering that seems at least as close to the spirit of "Young-land country" as Rateliff's suggestion of "The

Land of Youth." Vinland, The Land of Youth, and Tol Eressëa are all realms of tradition that are situated somewhere in the hazy West of the world. Tolkien could well have intended the ambiguity of referencing a mythical place in Irish tradition, while also evoking Vinland in the New World.

Tolkien had a long fascination with voyaging to the shores of a mythical West, but he preferred to stop short of envisioning this "West" as the Western Hemisphere. He was always careful to leave no question about his mythical destinations in the West; these were more esoteric destinations, more spiritual realms. Even so, it might have appealed to Tolkien to insert a vague rumor of Vinland into Middle-earth in his description of Dorwinion as a realm "whither few mariners of Men have ever come, save once or twice in a long age[.]" I am not suggesting that Tol Eressëa or Dorwinion ever served as literal reflections of Vinland. Rather, Vinland construction materials provided exactly the kind of mythic depth that interested Tolkien. But drawing from those associations to put them to work in the making of rumored realms in his legendarium, he would not have wished for Vinland to make headlines in Middle-earth.

One additional possible hint comes in the form of a name. The Norse saga of Eric the Red begins with a prominent woman named "Aud" who settled in Iceland. Aud's grandfather and brother were both named Beorn. In *The Lost Road* Tolkien specifically mentioned this name as a Lombard term that seems to refer to "Friend of fortune... or of fate, luck, wealth, blessedness...": "'I like *Aud*,' young Audoin had said – he was then about thirteen – 'if it means all that.'"[512] It should be recalled here that Tolkien intended for *The Lost Road* to contain a story about Vinland, so although he clearly wanted to reference Lombardic etymology, beyond "all that," the name could have held another resonance for him – an echo of the saga of Eric the Red and Vinland.

In a nearby passage Tolkien unfolds a sweeping vista: "...to see the lie of old and even forgotten lands, to behold ancient men walking, and hear their languages as they spoke them, in the days before days, when tongues of forgotten lineage were heard in kingdoms long fallen by the shores of the Atlantic."[513] This epic sense of history evokes the European vistas that preoccupied Tolkien, but his vision of the "shores of the Atlantic" also touched on distant Vinland.

Tolkien's misty traces of Vinland can seem merely coincidental, a chance collision of narrative accidents unworthy of further commentary. This conclusion would be logical because Tolkien had a well-known focus on Northern European literature, language, history, and mythology – he seemingly borrowed very little from America. Aside from black squirrels, tobacco is his most explicit import. But tobacco is interesting, in part, because it is "tobacco" on five occasions in *The Hobbit*, and only twice in *The Lord of the Rings* – there it has become "pipeweed." Whatever Tolkien chose to make of America in *The Hobbit*, by the time he filled the pipe-bowl in Frodo's hand, he did not wish for our thoughts to sail too far to the west.

Scholarship on the sources that inspired the making of Tolkien's Middle-earth is extensive and insightful, and to my knowledge no scholar has ever pointed to Norse Vinland sagas as material useful to Tolkien. The impressionistic nature of the evidence makes it speculative to wonder whether Tolkien intentionally hid hazy rumors of Vinland in *The Hobbit*. Why would Tolkien do such an odd thing? I think the answer has to do with the fact that he also wove into his tale of Mirkwood an encounter descended from his original evil monster, his circa 1914 Night the Spider.

Tolkien in Pawneeland   ❧ ✶ ☙   Roger Echo-Hawk

Unraveling Spider Silk

Tolkien situated his first fantasy monster – Night the Spider – in a fantasy version of Vinland, and his surviving notes contain clear parallels to aspects of a Skidi story about Spider Woman. A few years later he drew from the same Pawnee source-material to craft the story of Ungoliont in *The Book of Lost Tales*. A decade and a few years passed, and Tolkien decided he wasn't yet finished with spiders and the Skidi Pawnees.

In the course of writing *The Hobbit,* Tolkien paused to prepare what John Rateliff termed the "First Outline."[514] This outline contained a sparse list of ten ideas that Tolkien jotted down in preparation for introducing Beorn, then named "Medwed." The first seven notes clearly helped to shape the story that followed. The eighth note consisted of two words: "swans" and "Mirkwood" – a likely reference to swan-women in "The Lay of Volund," a poem in the Norse *Poetic Edda*.[515]

The next entry was "ball of twine[.]" Rateliff had no insight as to Tolkien's intentions regarding swans. And no ball of twine appeared in the first published edition of *The Hobbit*. But Rateliff discovered that Tolkien's original manuscript portrayal of the journey into Mirkwood preserved a deleted scene. In this scene Bilbo slew his first spider and the spider expelled a bunch of silk string in the course of the struggle.[516] Bilbo then "gathered the horrible string of the great spider's thread together" into "a huge ball[.]" He used this ball of string to leave a trail as he wandered in search of the Dwarves. As in the Skidi stories of Spider Woman and in his own story of Ungoliont, Tolkien made this first Mirkwood spider a female and later decided to edit away its gender.[517]

Rateliff offered the plausible speculation that Tolkien borrowed his spiders from the fantasy tales of Lord Dunsany; and he suggested that the ball of spider silk could refer to the story of Theseus and the Minotaur in Greek mythology.[518] Rateliff's explanations of Tolkien's sources seem convincing enough, especially when we chalk up the remaining unexplained elements to Tolkien's own rich imagination. But a stronger argument can be made that Tolkien found his spider silk in Pawneeland.

Two stories in *Traditions of the Skidi Pawnee* concerned the magical uses of a ball of spider silk. In one tale a "ball of spider-web" belonged to "an old witch-woman" and Long Tooth made her skin come alive and controlled her with the spider silk.[519] The second story, "The Boy, the Bears, and White Crow" told by James Yellow Calf, is particularly noteworthy for students of Middle-earth because it contributed so much to the story of Beorn.[520] It also contributed spider silk to Bilbo's adventure in Mirkwood.

In Yellow Calf's story the young Skidi skinchanger must capture a white bird that has been frightening buffalo away, and he does so using a ball of spider silk given to him by a tarantula. The magic spider silk became invisibly attached to the white bird, and the white bird could not "feel anything" and could see "nothing on the leg"; but the silk held it fast.

Tolkien apparently liked this magic because he used it in his poem "Errantry." It isn't clear exactly when this poem was written, but it was published in November 1933 and reprinted in *The Adventures of Tom Bombadil*, and the original version could date to 1930-1931.[521] Christopher Tolkien believed that the earliest surviving version was preceded by "preliminary workings" that have not survived.[522] He also noted that the "second" draft underwent later revisions, but these changes occurred only in the opening passages.

In the poem a mariner wove "a tissue airy-thin" and then captured a butterfly "with a filament of spider-thread"; this imagery does not appear in the first extant version.[523] This is because Tolkien probably wrote that version prior to reading the Skidi story, "The Boy, the Bears, and White Crow," circa 1932, when he borrowed its spider silk for *The Hobbit*. In the "second version" of "Errantry" the mariner "caught her in bewilderment /

in filament of spider-thread[.]" The word "bewilderment" echoes the bewilderment of the white bird in the Skidi story, held fast by something it cannot see. Further support for this composition history was the appearance in the "second version" of "webs of all the Attercops / he shattered them and sundered them[.]" This was surely written around the same time that Bilbo was battling Skidi spiders in Mirkwood and toting around a Skidi ball of spider silk.

Jason Fisher made a strong case that Tolkien's cobweb imagery in "Errantry" derived from *Nymphidia: The Court of Fayrie*, a poem written by Michael Drayton.[524] Fisher drew our attention to a line reading "A cobweb ouer them they throw[.]" Drayton's cobweb blanket seems sufficient as an inspiration for the spider thread in "Errantry," even if Tolkien came to detest *Nymphidia* as a fairytale – "one of the worst ever written."[525] While we have no need to seek further, Tolkien was not necessarily interested in wrapping his Elizabethan fairies in a cuddly cobweb. I believe that Tolkien found the Skidi "cobweb ball" with its unbreakable spider filament much more useful for capturing errant flying things.

The version published in 1933 added the "filament of spider-thread;" and in the later evolution of the poem the filament was dropped and replaced by "Ungoliant abiding there / in Spider-lair her thread entwined; / for endless years a gloom she spun / the Sun and Moon in web to wind."[526] In the Skidi story, "How the Buffalo Went South," Spider Woman was "the daughter of Sun and Moon" – Tolkien's phrase "Sun and Moon" echoed the Skidi phrasing, capitalizations intact.[527] The Skidi Spider Woman related to the Sun and Moon very differently than Ungoliant, but Tolkien had no interest in retelling the Pawnee story. Instead, he drew useful elements from it – and he also had in mind, no doubt, the *Kalevala* and its tale of Sun and Moon in captivity.

Tolkien monstrous spiders all arose from his 1914 note on Night the Spider. The connection of this spider to Vinland / America is inarguable. With this linkage in mind, two factors point onward to the traditions of Pawneeland. First, spider imagery in North America is benign and beneficial, not deadly and monstrous. But we find otherwise in Pawneeland. If we look only at *Traditions of the Skidi Pawnee*, we immediately encounter John Box's conceptions of a dark version of Spider Woman – this traditional portrayal of a spider divinity is unique in North America. And second, we can indeed see well-defined parallels in the Pawnee spider stories and Tolkien's spider stories.

Ungoliant emerged first from this origin. Born in 1919, Tolkien colorized his storytelling about Ungoliant with details from Pawneeland because he had conceived Night the Spider in 1914 from Pawnee tradition. Ungoliant eventually spawned many lesser offspring in Tolkien's storytelling. The mysterious swans in Tolkien's "First Outline" for *The Hobbit* never materialized, but the listed "ball of twine" turned out to be the silk of a giant Skidi spider – the offspring of Spider Woman and of Ungoliant. The Mirkwood scene of Bilbo Baggins carrying around a ball of spider silk offers unique and convincing evidence of Tolkien's use of Pawnee mythology. He might have sensed that he had been too blatant in this borrowing, because the moment was soon enough deleted from *The Hobbit*. But spiders and spider webs lingered in his workings of "Errantry," which was born alongside *The Hobbit*.

It is not apparent that Tolkien drew details from any Pawnee story for his account of Shelob in *The Lord of the Rings*, but nor did he set aside her literary ancestry. His first idea was to have Gollum lead Frodo and Sam across the Dead Marshes to "Kirith Ungol" or "Spider's Vale," and from there the story moved to Minas Arnor.[528] He next decided to drop Minas Arnor and instead associate Kirith Ungol with Minas Ithil, the Tower of the Moon.[529] This association lingered through further transformations of the tale and the emergence of Shelob.

Skidi Pawnee tradition has Spider Woman exiled to the moon. And so only ten years after she appeared in England, she inspired Night the Spider, a creature of fabled Vinland. Next came Ungoliant, "the Spider of Night"; and she birthed broods of spiders in the First Age of the world and in Mirkwood. And Ungoliant became the ancestor of Shelob... "She that walked in the darkness..." So we find Shelob lurking in her lightless lair beyond the Tower of the Moon. And when the impossibly strong threads of Spider Woman enter Middle-earth, they can't be easily severed by blades forged by Men.

All through the 20th century the magic webs spun long ago in Pawneeland eventually covered the earth. Tolkien rewove the magic Pawnee spider silk into Middle-earth, and readers worldwide found themselves getting caught up in their narrative grip. This is a special kind of cultural enchantment.

Elements from Yellow Calf's "The Boy, the Bears, and White Crow" entered into Tolkien's "Queer Lodgings" and "Flies and Spiders," and the Skidi story also helped to shape his colorful portrayal of crows in "The Gathering of Clouds." In the Skidi tale the white bird that frightened away buffalo was a crow. The young skinchanging hero of the story embarked on a quest to capture this pesky crow, using magic spider silk.

At one point the crow thought it was free. Unaware of the magic spider silk attached to its leg, the white crow offered some very rude opinions of the young skinchanger: "Come out of your tipi, you chief; you are nothing but a poor burnt-belly boy; you and your grandmother used to eat rawhide, and anything you could get hold of."[530]

In drafting *The Hobbit*, Tolkien's crows underwent an evolution into birds holding unspecified rude opinions of the Dwarves.[531] Sometime in 1931-1932 Tolkien decided that ravens and crows would play very different roles in *The Hobbit*. Referring to an earlier incident involving ravens in the original, but revised into crows later, Bilbo got the impression that Balin did not like ravens, and Balin clarified his views: "'Those were crows! said Balin, 'and nasty suspicious-looking ones at that, and rude as well. You must have heard the ugly things they were calling after us...'"[532]

Balin offered no specific hint of the "ugly things" said by the uncouth crows at the Lonely Mountain. But now we can make a pretty good guess as to what these ill-mannered birds said to the Dwarves: "You are nothing but poor burnt-belly boys, and you and your grandmothers used to eat rawhide!"

The Old Thrush's Secret

One day in Pawneeland a Skidi man named Curly Head told a story about an animal wearing an impenetrable coat, and when James Murie and George Dorsey published it, they gave it the title "Death of the Flint-Monster: Origin of Birds."[533] Curly Head related about six tales, and Murie translated them, and four appeared in *Traditions of the Skidi Pawnee*. The flint monster story became important in the 20th century because Tolkien drew from it in the course of deciding how best to slay Smaug in *The Hobbit*.

In the story a boy spoke of "an animal far in the southern country, that comes up and carries people away..." The boy and his sister took a long journey, meeting people in "a far-away country..." At several dances the animal carried off various warriors. The boy followed the path of the animal into what could be termed the Desolation of the Monster, a scorched and barren land. Going on, the boy saw smoke and he climbed a hilltop and there he saw "the animal coming." The animal spoke to the boy, warning him to leave. Finally, "the boy took his bow and arrow and shot the animal under the arm and shot it through the body, killing the animal." This monster had very unusual skin. "The boy went to the animal, and it did not look like any animal he had ever seen, for this animal was clothed with flints all over. The flint flakes looked like fish scales, but they were really flint."

Tolkien was age ten or so when Murie and Dorsey set down Curly Head's story. Years later he recalled that in boyhood he was "interested in traditional tales (especially those concerning dragons)[.]"[534] Various scholars have thoroughly described Tolkien's deep fascination with dragons – John Rateliff concluded that Tolkien's dragon tales ultimately "redeemed the dragon and re-established it as the greatest of all fantasy monsters."[535]

The death of Smaug in *The Hobbit* must certainly rank high on the list of memorable dragon scenes crafted by Tolkien. In his original manuscript an old thrush landed on the shoulder of Bard at Esgaroth.[536] The bird whispered, "Look for the hollow of the left breast as he flies and turns above you." With this magical knowledge in hand, Bard bent his bow and slew Smaug.

John Rateliff characterized the killing of Smaug in interesting terms: "Unlike traditional methods of dragon-slaying... so far as I have been able to discover the method Tolkien chose for slaying The Dragon is unprecedented in fairy-tale, English folktale, or Old English / Old Norse lore."[537] He concluded that a likely "parallel" came from tales of Hercules who killed the Dragon of the Hesperides "with an arrow or arrows."

In various plot notes, wrestling with how best to kill Smaug, Tolkien toyed with having Bilbo do the deed.[538] Had he chosen to rely on European tradition, he would have had a variety of options for slaying Smaug – options that would have been recognized as borrowings. After composing his initial notes, Tolkien came to another decision. I believe he turned to *Traditions of the Skidi Pawnee* and studied a scene that would never come to the attention of the experts he knew – the scene of the Skidi boy-hero slaying a flint-scaled monster with an arrow under the arm.

Curly Head's story made a very clear connection between the flint monster and its effect on the land, with the boy-hero encountering various paths made by the creature, and then a burned region: "The boy went on, and there he saw where the animal had gone, for even rocks were cut where the animal had gone. The grass was burned, and even the ground was red, and seemed to be baked."[539]

John Rateliff provided an excellent discussion on Tolkien's association of dragons with environmental "desolation."[540] Tolkien's original version of a dragon desolation in "Turambar and the Foalókë" could have been written as early as the end of 1917 and as late as mid-1919.[541] There Tolkien described his first dragon desolation with the land "all barren and... blasted... and the lands were scored with the great slots that the loathly worm made in his creeping."[542]

Seeking to explain this scene, the source material cited by Rateliff could acount for Tolkien's description, but the connection seems weak, consisting of what he terms "hints." A stronger candidate for the inspiration of the desolation idea has been suggested by John Garth, who compared Tolkien's earliest dragons in *The Book of Lost Tales* to "the tanks of the Somme" in World War I.[543] And citing the above dragon desolation from "Turambar and the Foalókë," Garth distinguished the dragon in question (Glorund) from Tolkien's earlier "mechanistic dragons." But we might nevertheless keep in mind at least a general equivalency between the devastations of dragons and tanks.[544]

Even so, Tolkien's dragon desolation was also clearly reminiscent of the Skidi story. With an existing comparison in Tolkien's mind between tank warfare and dragons, when he encountered the pre-war text of the Skidi story, he would have taken note. Skimming the pages of *Traditions of the Skidi Pawnee* in 1919 and again in 1930, he would have been drawn to the description of the Skidi flint monster terrorizing the countryside, carrying off various warriors – a coincidental echo of the story of Beowulf. And the Skidi flint monster spoke to the boy-hero, issuing a warning, just as Tolkien's dragons are talkative beasts who issue dire predictions and warnings.

The opening summary of the Skidi story described the monster as "a fiery creature covered with flint-armor[.]" In Tolkien's original manuscript he gave Smaug "iron scales and hard gems" for a waistcoat. And in a 1938 letter Tolkien responded to a reader's question about the origin of this "waistcoat" with a very interesting comment: "I am as susceptible as a dragon to flattery, and would gladly show off my diamond waistcoat, and even discuss its sources, since [the reader] has also asked where I got it from. But would not that be rather unfair to the research students? To save them trouble is to rob them of any excuse for existing."[545]

Tolkien may have been thinking entirely of his "dragons of fire and serpents of bronze and iron" in his 1919 legend "The Fall of Gondolin," but John Rateliff seemed to suggest that one source for Smaug's iron scales could have been the beast described in chapter 41 of *The Book of Job*.[546] Since Tolkien left no actual hints in any writings as to where he found Smaug's flesh and waistcoat, this leaves open the Skidi monster, "clothed with flints all over" – and unlike the other sources, the Skidi tradition also helps to explain the slaying of Smaug.

Tolkien would never have revealed this source, given the contradiction inherent in writing a tale with Northern European flavors but incorporating spices from America. Given the obscurity of the Skidi text by 1930, Tolkien could feel relatively confident that no researcher in his Eurocentric academic circle would ever stumble onto the Skidi flint monster.

In the end, Smaug's expensive waistcoat did not protect him from Bard the bowman – Bard slew Smaug with an arrow that seems to have special properties. Tolkien borrowed some of these properties from an Elvish arrow he invented during the 1920s.[547] But for *The Hobbit* Tolkien added something new. He colored the arrow black. The shooting of this special black arrow into Smaug is memorable: "The great bow twanged. The black arrow sped straight for the hollow by the left breast where his foreleg was flung wide."[548]

In a Skidi story that considered the special use of black arrows, a buffalo was killed in exactly the same way: "...as the buffalo threw out its front leg, the boy pulled his bow-string, loosed the arrow, and shot the buffalo in the soft place under the shoulder, so that the arrow went through the heart."[549] Smaug flung out his foreleg and was shot by Tolkien's black arrow, just as the buffalo in the Pawnee story threw out its front leg and got shot by a Pawnee arrow.

Both the Skidi flint monster and Tolkien's Smaug can each boast of being scaled creatures, scaled respectively with flint and with iron. Given the likelihood that Tolkien found part of his black arrow in Pawneeland, as well as the means to kill Smaug, other innocent-sounding details take on new significance. After the dragon tumbled into Long Lake, Tolkien had the dead dragon "lying cold as stone"; and later, as Bilbo journeyed homeward, the merry folk of Rivendell welcomed him back with an interesting jibe: "And your snores would wake a stone dragon" – this would serve as an excellent description of the Skidi flint monster, but it would hardly evoke any biblical monster or any armored vehicle of the First World War.[550]

These narrative references to stone sound merely poetic but make perfect sense to say of Smaug when we link them to the killing of a Skidi Pawnee monster clothed in flint. With these connections in mind, it is appropriate that Tolkien's first physical description of Bard the bowman mentioned that "his black hair hung wet over his shoulders; a fierce light was in his eyes."[551]

Finally, the aftermath of Smaug's death brought birds back to Erebor. In the words of Roäc the magic raven: "I bring tidings of joy... Behold the birds are gathering back again to the Mountain from South and East and West, for word has gone forth that Smaug is dead!"[552] In the Skidi tradition about the monster with stone scales, in that era, "There were no birds." After the slaying of the monster, some people then became birds – for this reason the Skidi story was titled "Death of the Flint-Monster: Origin of Birds."

Another dimension to this story entered the picture in 2014 with new insights from John Garth. Identifying a handful of interesting parallel textual elements between some of Tolkien's early writings and *The Song of Hiawatha* by Henry Wadsworth Longfellow, Garth suggested that Tolkien drew inspiration from the American epic poem between 1914 and circa 1920.[553] He made a strong case that Tolkien returned to the poem in the course of constructing Smaug's death scene in *The Hobbit*. In Longfellow's poem, Hiawatha was confronted with a flying monster named Megissogwon, clothed in a "magic shirt of wampum[.]" A woodpecker called to Hiawatha from a tree, advising him to take aim at the only vulnerable spot: a tuft of hair on the monster's head.

Tolkien did not clothe Smaug in either shell or stone material, but the idea of an impenetrable coat is a shared element in Longfellow's poem, in the Skidi story, and in Tolkien's tale of Smaug. Tolkien decided against slaying Smaug with an arrow to the head; instead, he selected a Skidi black arrow, and he shot it under a stretched foreleg, just as a Pawnee hunter would have done.

Garth deemed the Longfellow "match" as "most awkward to refute..." It is interesting that the Longfellow material contained elements that the Skidi story lacked, and the Skidi material featured material absent from the Longfellow story. These sources thus resemble pieces of a puzzle that fit together perfectly. In other words, we can make a clear argument that Tolkien looked at both sources and borrowed specific elements and seamlessly wove them together into the death of Smaug. This creative strategy was his typical practice. As Garth noted regarding the complex elements woven into one poem, "If all this cross-referencing of dictionaries and texts seems unlikely, it should not. This was an activity Tolkien pursued vigorously both for pleasure and for his studies."

Tolkien drew upon traditional European dragons to create Smaug. But if any source in European literature inspired the demise of Smaug, it has yet to be identified. To assemble the tale of this dragon-slaying, Tolkien merely had to spend a few moments skimming Longfellow's *The Song of Hiawatha* and two stories in *Traditions of the Skidi Pawnee*. Most importantly, the identification of several interwoven sources that explain the killing of Smaug comports with the fact that Tolkien himself mentioned "sources" in his enigmatic 1938 reference to Smaug's "waistcoat."

Tolkien made no mention of either Longfellow or the Skidi Pawnees in his numerous comments on the making of *The Hobbit*. Nor did John Garth offer any insights that might explain Tolkien's silence. But it is important to ponder what it signifies, because we now know that he drew from these two American sources in the course of constructing the tales of Middle-earth. Secretly visiting the literary traditions of Vinland, Tolkien became a surreptitious world mythologist. And when we glimpse him setting foot upon those particular circles of the world, we suddenly see that the enchanted seas of Middle-earth wash up against many hidden shores.

Reading *The Hobbit* in company with a Tolkien discussion group, we arrived at the end of the book in late May 2013. Our journey through the book took us on a path that became truly unexpected as I discovered connections between *The Hobbit* and *Traditions of the Skidi Pawnee*. Pondering Tolkien's mythmaking long ago, I wrote my book and issued it at the end of that year. But I didn't stop writing it, and over the months that followed I kept developing new material, eventually producing this second edition.

At our Tolkien meeting in May 2013 my friend Charles Conant pointed out an interesting resonance. "The Return Journey" begins with references to "cold" and "fire," and the chapter ends with "snow" and "fire." Could there be some kind of meaning behind this bracketing?

To this we can add the fact that Tolkien titled an earlier chapter "Fire and Water," with "fire" referring to Smaug and "water" referring to Esgaroth where Smaug is slain. This chapter ends with "oncoming winter" but this seems entirely incidental, a detail of the narrative not related to fire and water. And it also seems equally incidental that in the next chapter, "The Gathering of the Clouds," the dwarves in the Lonely Mountain sing a song that refers to "dragon-fire" and "mountains cold" – dragon-fire does not appear in Tolkien's draft of this poem; he imported it from the dwarf-song that appears in "An Unexpected Party."[554]

Tolkien consistently uses "fire" as a synecdoche for Smaug, so it stands to reason that "water" and "snow" and "cold" could have a similar metaphorical meaning. But even though "water" most clearly refers to Esgaroth and the folk of the lake-town and the death of Smaug, it would seem a stretch to include "winter" and "cold" and "snow" in this symmetrical symbolism. It is interesting that "The Return Journey" has Bilbo awakening on the battlefield "shaking with cold... but his head burned like fire."[555] Even so, here fire seems to have nothing to do with Smaug.

In the absence of a logical connection between these oppositions, the seeming association of fire and cold should be read as a purely descriptive enrichment of narration rather than as an intentional symbolic conjunction. This leaves us with the unanswered question, do the terms "cold" and "snow" hold any metaphorical significance? In the week before our Tolkien discussion group gathered for the final meeting on *The Hobbit*, I gave thought to how Tolkien brought together snow and fire.

At the end of "The Return Journey" Bilbo is homeward bound. Departing from Beorn's realm, the hobbit pauses atop the Misty Mountains to peer eastward. And glimpsing the distant peak of the Lonely Mountain with "snow yet unmelted" Bilbo murmurs, "So comes snow after fire[.]"[556] So the fire refers to Smaug, but it is awkwardly conjoined to "snow" because the snow has no thematic relevance to Smaug or dragon-fire or Smaug's death. This far-off snow just suddenly falls into the story. To link this snow in a symbolic sense to "oncoming winter" or to "mountains cold" and from there to Smaug, it would help if we could show that Tolkien had some kind of reference in mind related to dragons.

A possible explanation can be found in the Skidi story told by James Yellow Calf, "The Boy, the Bears, and White Crow."[557] Tolkien drew on this story to help colorize Beorn's tale and a deleted spider scene in *The Hobbit*. Since he never discussed his use of this material, it has a covert air, an invisible quality. In keeping with this quality, the conjoining of fire and snow offers a superficial balance of imagery which becomes slippery when you look directly at it. I think Tolkien intentionally crafted a referential mystery that seems to make sense in the story, but which doesn't really come into focus until you discover the Skidi source.

In the Skidi tale the young shape-shifting hero must capture a very annoying magical white crow. When he at last succeeds, the bird proves unrepentant, and it is killed and "put in the fire." The final sorcery of the white crow generates a massive snowstorm. In this manner, snow follows fire.

Tolkien deliberately took this Skidi narrative connection between fire and snow and hid it in Bilbo's otherwise odd comment, "So comes snow after fire." Here "fire" refers to both Smaug and a hidden white crow – they share an apt equivalency as evil flying creatures touched by fire. And "snow" offers an awkward symmetry to the "cold" that plagues Bilbo at the beginning of "The Return Journey," but it very gracefully connects to fire and to the death of the enchanted Skidi crow.

I outlined this logic to the Tolkien discussion group and the talk moved on to the end of the night. I pondered what "snow after fire" seemed to signify. The oblique quality of this reference can be read many ways. But when we acknowledge the Pawnee contribution to Middle-earth, we acknowledge that very diverse cultural productions entered Tolkien's "cauldron of story," and we can explore how this diversity of Middle-earth reflects the manifold human world.

Messengers of Tirawa and Manwë

In John Rateliff's fascinating consideration of Tolkien's eagles, he suggests that European "bestiary lore" and folk tradition may help account for certain aspects of the eagles in Middle-earth.[558] Rateliff nevertheless concluded that European sources seem to offer little raw material for such mythmaking: "Aside from American Indian traditions, there seems to have been little fairy-tale or folklore resonance to eagles[.]" He did not here intend to suggest that Tolkien had any known awareness of the resonance of eagles in "American Indian traditions." But in discussing creation stories, I have already pointed to one interesting resonance between the birds of Middle-earth and of Pawneeland.

In the Skidi creation story told by Roaming Scout, the singing gods bestow upon the first male a "Swift Hawk" which symbolizes military service to the community, and a note adds: "The hawk is sometimes spoken of as the messenger of the Morning-Star[.]"[559] Tolkien inserted into his creation story, "The Music of the Ainur," a very Skidi-like description of Manwë's home: "Hawks flew ever to and fro about that abode, whose eyes could see to the deeps of the sea... They brought him news from everywhere of everything..."[560] Both Morning Star and Manwë preferred hawks as messengers.

The Skidi traditions are replete with references to birds as messengers between humankind and deities.[561] And in one Skidi story an eagle who wished to be changed into a man said, "I am now an eagle. I carry messages for Tirawa."[562] In Middle-earth Sorontur the King of Eagles also carried messages for Manwë, saying, "... tidings have I also for thy ear..."[563]

Eagles carry other interesting resonances that bear comparison in both legendariums. The Skidi creation story bestowed upon the first man a hawk-skin and an eagle feather – this feather was symbolic of the Creator: "In the decoration of the different chiefs an eagle feather is placed above downy feathers, the whole symbolizing 'Tirawa standing above fleecy clouds.'"[564] Tolkien also designated both hawks and eagles as birds special to Manwë: "Thence did he speed his darting hawks and receive them on his return, and thither fared often in later days Sorontur King of Eagles whom Manwë gave much might and wisdom."[565] Eagles in both legendariums were associated with nobility and leadership. In the case of the Skidi, community leaders used eagle feathers, while Tolkien's first eagle was a king.

Tolkien added a mysterious dimension to his eagles in an unfinished novel of the late 1930s. In *The Lost Road*, he had a character named Alboin notice "great dark clouds" and when he said they "look like the eagles of the Lord of the West[,]" he "wondered why" he would say such an odd thing.[566] The Skidi symbolism of an eagle feather standing in downy feathers referred to both Tirawa and "fleecy clouds." Associating eagles, clouds, and deities in exact correspondence, it is reasonable to wonder whether Tolkien intentionally hid the Skidi god Tirawa behind his Lord of the West.

The Lost Road included a poem titled "King Sheave" that referred to "clouds greyhelméd... as mighty eagles" flying from the west to the east.[567] A ship came sailing with those clouds, and in it "there laid sleeping / a boy" and "his sleeping head was soft pillowed / on a sheaf of corn shimmering palely / as the fallow gold doth from far countries / west of Angol." In this poem "corn" refers to wheat and other grains, but given Tolkien's conjoined image of clouds and eagles, "far countries" held a hidden resonation with imagery of the Skidi clouds / eagles.

Tolkien never clarified the significance of clouds and eagles and the Lord of the West. Christopher Tolkien noted that his father intended for the imagery to appear in each tale in *The Lost Road* – including an unwritten tale about Vinland – and the meaning of this mysterious statement would be revealed at the end of the book.[568] Sorting through his father's notes regarding "the Eagles of the Lord of the West," Christopher Tolkien got the impression that "he was as puzzled by them as was Alboin[.]"[569] The uncertainty had to do with the identity of "the Lord of the West." Was this "the King of Númenor, or Manwë"? Tolkien experimented with a possible scenario involving "Sorontur King of Eagles" being "sent by Manwë[.]"

Tolkien's surviving papers contained no clue as to the source of the associated imagery of clouds, eagles, and deities. But we can see clarity in this imagery when we consider the Skidi link between an eagle feather and Tirawa, and between downy eagle feathers and clouds. These hidden echoes of Pawneeland eluded Christopher Tolkien as he delved into his father's papers.

Opening the pages of *Traditions of the Skidi Pawnee* Tolkien would have noticed that the book contained talking eagles.[570] It would soon have become clear that eagles were very powerful creatures. In one story, after a talking red eagle and many other eagles visited a man on a vision quest, a buffalo told him: "The eagle which you lately saw is the bird which controls all animals."[571] Another story referred to a golden eagle as an incarnation of Tirawa.[572] An endnote explained that the Skidi generally believed that "the red eagle is supposed to be the most powerful of all birds."[573] The idea of talking eagles stayed with Tolkien through the writing of *The Silmarillion*, *The Hobbit*, and *The Lord of the Rings*.

Douglas Anderson has noted that Tolkien's talking eagles in *The Hobbit* "recall a scene" in one of Chaucer's unfinished poems.[574] Anderson didn't offer any comparison between Chaucer's eagle and Tolkien's eagles – it is possible that Tolkien was entirely and exclusively influenced by this source. To be sure, magic birds can be found in traditional literature worldwide, and Tolkien could have drawn from any number of such sources for inspiration. And he didn't necessarily need pre-existing models to invent his own unique creatures for his worldscapes. But during the late 1950s he acknowledged that his talking animals and birds were "rather lightly adopted from less 'serious' mythologies..."[575]

It is interesting that in Tolkien's legendarium and in the Skidi legendarium certain birds acted as intermediaries between humans and the gods, and messenger hawks and talking eagles played special roles. And eagles that control all other birds and who symbolize Tirawa and can even be seen as incarnations of Tirawa are majestic in exactly the same way that Sorontur, King of Eagles, is majestic. And the exact deployment of eagles, clouds, and deities in both legendariums is noteworthy. If these corresponding manifestations of eagles existed as the only arguable parallels between Tolkien and the Skidi, this might be deemed a matter of curious coincidence. But we have many connections to consider.

Bombadil Reborn

With the publication in September 1937 of *The Hobbit*, a new factor suddenly entered Tolkien's world. His literary aspirations took on a new dimension when his publisher began writing to him with requests that he prepare a sequel to *The Hobbit*. Tolkien's initial response was that he felt "a little perturbed" because he couldn't "think of anything more to say about *hobbits*."[576]

But over the next few months Tolkien gave this matter much thought. His initial idea was to send his Silmarillion mythology to the publisher, but this plan met with rejection. He had to come up with another idea. He wrote a very interesting letter to Stanley Unwin: "Do you think Tom Bombadil, the spirit of the (vanishing) Oxford and Berkshire countryside, could be made into the hero of a story? Or is he, as I suspect, fully enshrined in the enclosed verses? Still I could enlarge the portrait."[577] When Tolkien sat down to plan a new hobbit project, Tom Bombadil came to mind because "The Adventures of Tom Bombadil" and *The Hobbit* were interlocked projects already – linked by mutual borrowings from Pawnee myth. Now Tom was back with fresh ideas for Tolkien's next project.

In this December 1937 letter Tolkien defined Tom Bombadil as a "spirit." In so doing, he made use here of terminology drawn from his evolving Silmarillion legends. But rather than place Tom in a Middle-earth context, Tolkien instead situated him in the "Oxford and Berkshire countryside." Up to this moment Tolkien was still hesitant to waft Bombadil into Middle-earth. But he had tentatively decided that Tom could easily become something more than a man, "a merry fellow." Perhaps he could be drawn into Goldberry's world. He could become a "lesser spirit." A fay.

So Tolkien launched into writing *The Lord of the Rings*. Tom would soon enough enter Middle-earth as a fay. By the 1930s the terminology for this class of semi-divinities had narrowed to just a few terms, but it was still a nebulous category – fays seem to have been envisioned through a trait list rather than by any specific definition.

As mentioned in *The Book of Lost Tales*, fays "were born before the world and are older than its oldest, and are not of it, but laugh at it much[.]" In Middle-earth Tom Bombadil would become Eldest and he would laugh much. And he would also become fearless in *The Lord of the Rings*, just as we find the children of the fay Melian: "Even at night when the moon shone pale still would they play and dance, and they were not afraid as I should be..."[578] And Tom would wield magic, just as Melian the fay wielded magic. Tom Bombadil and Goldberry might best be seen as quasi-fays – the kind of creature that Tolkien eventually transformed into the category of Maiar.

Two brief notes written in early 1938 marked the earliest entry of Bombadil into Tolkien's planning for *The Fellowship of the Ring*, indicating his decision to put Tom Bombadil into this new story.[579] This set of notes referenced the Old Forest, Willowman, Barrow-wights, and "T. Bombadil." Months passed, and it is not clear that Tolkien yet had any specific notions about what Willowman and Barrow-wights and T. Bombadil would do in his story. But referencing two of the four adventures that are drawn from Pawnee tradition, it would have been logical for Tolkien to think of the role played by *Traditions of the Skidi Pawnee* in shaping the 1930-1931 poem, "The Adventures of Tom Bombadil," and *The Hobbit*.

In late 1938 it is evident that Tolkien once again opened the pages of *Traditions of the Skidi Pawnee,* and he consulted one of the Skidi Coyote stories. He wrote a letter on August 31, 1938 describing an intense period of writing "in the last two or three days" in the course of an illness which required a "sanctioned neglect of duty" – meaning a pardon from his normal academic responsibilities.[580] According to the chronology of Tolkien's life prepared by Christina Scull and Wayne Hammond, Tolkien resumed his labors on *The Fellowship of the Ring* at this point.[581] As Scull and Hammond put it: "new ideas come to Tolkien in the process."

During this period of intense writing, Tolkien began setting down the material that eventually became "The Old Forest." After launching into a short beginning, he paused to prepare a set of notes that listed "Willowman," "Meeting with Tombombadil" and "Barrow-wights."[582] More detailed notes soon ensued. Here Tolkien envisioned two hobbits who "sit down with their backs to a great willow" and "Willowman traps Bingo and Odo." And "Suddenly a singing is heard in the distance." This was Tom Bombadil's premiere as a singer of songs of power – he sang at his wedding in the original 1934 poem, but now we witness the first mention by Tolkien of Tom's singing magic.

I believe that by this point Tolkien had consulted *Traditions of the Skidi Pawnee*. He reviewed in particular one of the Skidi traditions that had given rise to his original Bombadil poem, and this sparked "new ideas." "The Story of Coyote" told how Coyote had just "made a great fire" (p. 248) to cook meat when he is caught tight by two elm trees. This scene contributed details to the Bombadil poem of the early 1930s, but the Pawnee tale moved on to a subsequent adventure (p. 249-252) that involved singing and another mishap involving a tree.

Coyote meets a magician who has a Coyote Bundle. This bundle talks about singing and dancing and teaches the song and dance to Coyote. Coyote kills the magician and soon gets into trouble, escaping with the help of two buzzards, but these birds intentionally drop Coyote "so that he fell into a hollow log, and down he went, screaming and yelling." This tree "was cracked at the base, so Coyote took his knife out and made a hole in it." To escape, Coyote must trick some women into cutting down the tree.

With the inspiration of this story in hand, in late August 1938 Tolkien wrote the first draft of the material that would eventually become "The Old Forest" and "In the House of Tom Bombadil." Christopher Tolkien described a heavily edited manuscript that "reaches at a stroke the narrative as published..."

Since he did not present the draft text in its entirety, we can only presume that two minor details entered the text during this initial composition: mention of fire and wind. In "The Story of Coyote" Coyote built "a great fire" just before getting caught by two elms. In the Old Man Willow adventure the hobbits decided to build a fire to attempt to free their two captured companions. And then in "Coyote and the Rolling Stone" we meet "a man who represented the whirlwind" who couldn't help Coyote; while Tolkien had Tom threaten to raise a wind to blow off Old Man Willow's leaves. These are weak parallel echoes, but it is important to note that Tolkien drew details from his sources; he did not cut and paste intact Pawnee material.

As I have previously outlined, Tolkien's earliest incarnation of Goldberry contained echoes of RC Maclagan's 1914 paper on Scottish folklore.[583] Maclagan described the Scottish Washer Woman or "Bean Nigheachain, otherwise Bean Nighidh" as a "water nymph" who "is of small size" and resembles a woman and wears a green dress. But her feet are "webbed like a duck's." This creature washes "'clothes of the battle' and shrouds (aodach matrbh, ais-leine)."

In the Bombadil poem of the early 1930s Goldberry wore a "green gown" and was "robed all in silver-green" like the Washer Woman.[584] Returning now to Goldberry in 1938, Tolkien's initial note described her with "hair as yellow as the flag-lilies, her green gown and light feet."[585] Her feet were not webbed, as with the Washer Woman, but "her shoes were like fishes' mail."

Christopher Tolkien's presentation of the early draft notes and texts shined very little light on the evolution of Goldberry's characterization. Penciled notes changed the weather to include a "sudden rainy day" and a new revision took the story to a point "scarcely distinguishable" from the published version.[586] And now, like the Scottish Washer Woman who sat at the riverside and washed clothes, Goldberry has laundry to do. As Bombadil informed his hobbit-guests, "This is Goldberry's washing day[.]" The noise made by the Washer Woman was "like the splashing of water"; while the sound of Goldberry's feet became "like a stream falling gently away downhill..." Maclagan cited descriptive adjectives that he associated with the Washer Woman, and which also sound like Goldberry: innocent, free from sin, spotless, and pure.[587]

The parallels between Maclagan's Washer Woman and Tolkien's Goldberry are striking. Tolkien must have seen the 1914 folklore publication or one very like it, and he wove distinctive echoes of this Scottish source material into his circa 1931 poem. Then he revisited the same material to develop his Goldberry character for *The Fellowship of the Ring*.

The 1960s version of this Bombadil poem introduced a new verse that further emphasized the parallel between Goldberry and the Washer Woman. In the early version Goldberry's mother resided "in her deep weedy pool"; but now Goldberry sleeps "where the pools are shady / far below willow-roots" in "her mother's house in the deepest hollow[.]" And Goldberry is a "little water-lady" just as the Washer Woman is a water-nymph "of small size."

In essence, I believe that Tolkien kept returning to the same Scottish tradition for construction materials for Goldberry. He did not aim at exact replication of this Celtic traditional figure, and so Goldberry does not resemble the Washer Women found in most Celtic storytelling. But she very clearly echoed the specific characterization in the Maclagan 1914 text.

Tolkien drew details and inspiration from traditional stories, but he carefully wove these elements into his own magical world. When Old Man Willow trapped two hobbits, he was not reenacting a Pawnee story; rather, the Pawnee story aided in colorizing this Middle-earth adventure. The result is a powerful articulation of tradition and creativity. The landscape feels ancient because it draws from actual traditional textual source material. And Middle-earth feels enchanted because Tolkien was a wonderfully poetic writer.

Tolkien never revealed his use of Pawnee material. Situating Bombadil in a little realm in Middle-earth, Tolkien secretly sent Frodo and the Fellowship into Pawneeland.

Bombadil arose in part from the adventures of Coyote, but in 1938 he became fully transformed into a Middle-earth fay / Maia.

In Tolkien's later retrospective observations of the 1950s, it is not an accident that he declared his intention to keep Bombadil's origins secret, writing that "in a mythical Age there must be some enigmas" and "Bombadil is one (intentionally)."[588] As I noted in the first edition of *Tolkien in Pawneeland* (p. 153-157), this was an authorial strategy that he deployed often to obscure his use of Pawnee source material.

Inventing an adventure involving Tom Bombadil in August 1938, Tolkien also came up with a name for the river running through Tom's realm. Years later Tolkien acknowledged that "Withywindle" was "modelled on withywind, a name of the convolvulus or bindweed[.]"[589] And in the fall of 1938, preparing the "Second Phase" manuscript for *The Fellowship of the Ring*, giving further thought to the flora of Middle-earth, Tolkien now planted several American flowers in Bilbo's garden at Bag-End.[590] He has Bilbo and Gandalf gazing out of the window of the sitting-room into a sunny afternoon: "...the flowers were red and golden; snapdragons, and sunflowers, and nasturtians trailing all over the turf walls..."

Sunflowers and nasturtians were introduced into Europe from the Americas, and Tolkien acknowledged this fact with regard to nasturtians, which were sometimes called Indian Cress. When an editor tried to change nasturtians to nasturtiums, Tolkien objected: "I dug in my toes about nasturtians," he wrote in one letter.[591] He explained, "It seems to be a natural anglicization that started soon after the 'Indian Cress' was naturalized (from Peru, I think) in the 18th century..." It was during this same period of revision that Tolkien decided to make Gaffer Gamgee the gardener at Bag-End – a character upon whom he had already bestowed an association with potatoes, another American plant.[592]

Tolkien did not explain why he felt so adamant about importing nasturtians from America into the Shire. But it is clear that he had some awareness of horticultural history.[593] Perhaps he knew of John Gerard's 1636 book on plants, which said of "Indian Cresses" that "some have deemed it a kinde of *Convolvulus*, or Binde-weed..."[594] This description of nasturtians is worthy of mention because bindweed appeared in Joseph Wright's *English Dialect Dictionary* under the term "Withywind."[595] Within a few months after inventing the term "Withywindle" and using a Pawnee tradition to colorize an adventure along that river, Tolkien then planted American nasturtians and American sunflowers in Bilbo's garden.

Others have set forth the continuing evolution of Tom Bombadil as a character in *The Lord of the Rings*. Some have found compelling Gene Hargrove's contention that Tolkien configured Bombadil and Goldberry as incarnations of two Valar.[596] Comparisons between Tolkien's Yavanna and Goldberry can point to a few interesting parallels, as well as the reverential attitudes of the hobbits and of Tom Bombadil himself.[597] This is an interesting interpretation, but I see both characters as lightly rooted in Tolkien's evolving class of creatures he termed fays, and which ultimately became his Maiar – Tolkien would use this same process to re-invent his wizards as Maiar.

John Garth has pointed to certain Elvish terms of the 1930s that seem to "form a bridge between the 'fays' who accompany the Valar in *The Book of Lost Tales* and the Maiar who do so in later versions of the legendarium."[598] One term, *nindari*, referred to a "river-maid" and "particularly brings to mind Goldberry" who originated during the same period as a text listing the term.

Tom's power of song may derive in some degree from Finnish epic, while Goldberry grew from Scottish tradition. But both characters became firmly transplanted into the magic greenery of Middle-earth, and there they transcended their mortal roots, achieving immortality in myth.

Holes and Houses and Hills

When Tolkien sat down to write *The Hobbit*, he began by taking us into Bilbo's home. "In a hole in the ground there lived a hobbit." This was no "nasty dirty wet hole... it was a hobbit's hole, and that means comfort."[599] The door "opened onto a tubeshaped hall like a tunnel, but a very comfortable tunnel"; and this tunnel "wound on and on" and there was "no going upstairs for the hobbit[.]" Everything could be found "on the same floor, and indeed on the same passage." But we soon learn about a cellar where Bilbo stored his beer. Bilbo's home is referred to as the "Hill," and his address is "Mr. Baggins of Bag-End Under-Hill[.]" Illustrating this home, in the summer of 1937 Tolkien drew an interesting scene titled "The Hill: Hobbiton-across-the Water" – a landscape showing a dome-shaped hill.[600] "Under-Hill" was a picturesque way to say that Bilbo the hobbit dwelt inside this hill.

George Dorsey's introduction to *Traditions of the Skidi Pawnee* contained a description of a Pawnee architectural residential structure termed an "earth lodge."[601] This "dome-shaped structure" was entered through a "passageway" with the entire building covered by "a thick layer of sod and earth." An earthlodge had no upper story but did feature "a storage cellar for provisions[.]" Figure 2 is a photo showing one such dome-shaped earthlodge and its long entryway.

It is a curious coincidence that Tolkien's drawing of the Hill displayed almost the exact silhouette of the Pawnee earthlodge photo in Figure 2 of *Traditions of the Skidi Pawnee*. This means that Bilbo Baggins lives inside a hill shaped very much like a Pawnee earthlodge. And it is curious that Bilbo entered his house through a tunnel, just as a Pawnee would enter his hill-shaped home through a tunnel-like passageway, and in both residences everything could be found on one floor, except for cellars. I suggested in the first edition of *Tolkien in Pawneeland* that there might be a connection. But other source-materials seem more likely as inspirations for Tolkien.

Hob-holes can be found in a handful of scattered references in British folklore – but all of those references lacked detail. To whatever extent he borrowed from this vague concept, Tolkien still had to furnish the details from his own imagination. In the end he constructed his version of a hob-hole as a cozy home for his hobbit. Various publications that touched on the ancient architecture of the British Isles make mention of hillock-shaped grass-covered structures, so it is interesting that Tolkien would decide to situate a hill atop his hob-hole. And in the later writing of *The Lord of the Rings*, it is arguable that Tolkien then inserted a more definite silhouette of antiquity into Middle-earth.

In August 1938, taking the incipient Fellowship of the Ring to Bree, Tolkien's earliest surviving draft provided an interesting first glimpse of this "little village."[602] He described the "Bree-folk" as "an odd... community" made up of "brown-faced, dark-haired" people – and no one "knew why or when they had settled where they were."[603] The hobbits among the Bree-folk were "no better than tramps and wanderers, ready to dig a hole in any bank[.]" And the dwellings of these odd Bree-folk "seemed strange, large and tall (almost hillocks)[.]" Tolkien soon rewrote these people into hobbits who were "browner-skinned, darker-haired... than the average hobbit of the Shire." Continuing the tale, we soon meet "one of the wild folk" – a "brown-faced" hobbit ranger named Trotter who, as we learn in time, is "dark, long-haired."[604]

To understand Tolkien's creative choices at this point, we must step back a few days in time to his reworking of Tom Bombadil. As we have seen, in late 1937, just months after publication of *The Hobbit*, mulling over ideas for a sequel, Tolkien revisited Tom Bombadil, wondering if he could become "the hero of a story[.]"[605] And in early 1938, launching into writing *The Lord of the Rings*, Tolkien made notes to have his new story involve Tom Bombadil, Willowman, and Barrow-wights.[606]

The first appearance of Tom Bombadil in the tale came in August 1938.[607] This was followed by several very interesting notes. One indicated for the first time an enigmatic history for Tom in Middle-earth: "Tom Bombadil is an 'aborigine' – he knew the land before men, before hobbits, before barrow-wights, yes before the necromancer – before the elves came to this quarter of the world."[608] Tolkien's early version of Tom included a very striking idea, articulated by Tom in an autobiographical speech: "I am an Aborigine, that's what I am, the Aborigine of this land."[609] And Tom's speech ended with another interesting observation about how he "knew the dark under the stars when it was fearless – before the Dark Lord came from Outside."

A year after I issued the first edition of *Tolkien in Pawneeland* scholar Simon Cook argued that Tolkien found his hobbits in the writings of John Rhys.[610] In his student days Tolkien might have taken coursework from Rhys at Oxford, and in 1929-1930 while researching the name "Nodens" he made use of Rhys's work.[611] Given this chronology, it is certainly possible that Tolkien was inspired by Rhys when he invented his hobbits.

Cook suggested that when Tolkien wrote *The Hobbit* he decided to reference Rhys's ideas about pre-Celtic antiquity, conceiving "of ancient England as the green and pleasant Shire" with hobbits as a "representation of the little people that back in 1900 Rhys had identified as Britain's first farmers." Cook cited a paper published in 1900 by Rhys, and we are encouraged to conclude that Tolkien knew of this 1900 publication and read it closely circa 1930.[612]

A major problem with this argument is that the framing of hobbit culture as an agrarian farming society cannot be seen in the sparse details of *The Hobbit*. It is certainly possible to speculate that the full agrarian modeling that Tolkien produced for *The Lord of the Rings* was already in his mind by the end of 1930. But no notes, drafts, or other records can be cited to support this possibility. It seems more accurate to favor the view that in 1937-1938 Tolkien created an expanded vision of his hobbit realm, and it was then that we can begin to speak of hobbits as a bucolic folk of field and meadow.

It is important to note that Cook made no effort to consider Tolkien's silence on this Welsh material. Why would Tolkien formulate a Rhys-inspired farming antiquity and never make mention of this source? I point this out not as evidence of any shortcoming in Cook's logic, but just to emphasize that this suggested connection necessarily comes with the inherent implication that Tolkien had some reason to make no mention of it. There were numerous opportunities for Tolkien to mention Rhys and Welsh tradition, but he said nothing with regard to hobbits.

I believe that a different argument for Rhys and Tolkien and the modeling of British antiquity is more plausible. Some slight textual evidence shows that Cook's general argument is a better fit for Tolkien's 1938 construction of Tom Bombadil and Bree in *The Fellowship of the Ring*. Certain details of this period do fit the suggestion that Tolkien drew then from John Rhys's writings.

In *The Welsh People* Rhys outlined the Celtic ancestors of the Welsh and concluded that these "Aryans" were not the first settlers of ancient Britain.[613] Instead, there were folk he termed "the Aborigines of these islands" and an "Aboriginal race... here possibly thousands of years before the first Aryan arrived[.]" Rhys identified these aborignes as the Picts. This sounds very much like Tolkien's initial August 1938 notes on Tom Bombadil describing him as "an 'aborigine'" who "knew the land before men, before hobbits, before barrow-wights, yes before the necromancer – before the elves came to this quarter of the world." He soon toyed with having Bombadil say, "I am an Aborigine, that's what I am, the Aborigine of this land."[614]

An additional esoteric detail illuminates this connection. In a chapter on "The Pictish Question" Rhys pondered the evidence for matrilineal descent in Celtic antiquity, perhaps influenced by even older pre-Celtic Picts who, in Rhys's estimation, reckoned descent from birth, and for whom fatherhood was of no consequence. He pondered "a state of things in which the children were the children of the family, so to say, and owned no fathers in particular..."[615]

Rhys repeated this point in another book published about the same time as *The Welsh People* – a book thought by Simon Cook to have been consulted by Tolkien in the invention of his hobbits. In *Celtic Folklore* Rhys argued that Celtic fairy folklore preserved memoirs of the ancient aboriginal population of Britain, and this culture minimized the idea of fatherhood. He concluded that an even deeper primitive antiquity might have "some community so low in the scale of civilization as never to have had any notion whatsoever of paternity..."[616] This is interesting because years later, pondering Bombadil in the course of revising the Council of Elrond, Tolkien decided to have Elrond refer to Bombadil in similar terms: "Iarwain Ben-adar we called him, oldest and fatherless."[617]

Another hint that Tolkien consulted Rhys in 1938 rather than 1930 came in the first glimpses he formulated of Bree and the description of their houses as "strange, large and tall (almost hillocks)[.]" This brings to mind the Rhys lecture discussed by Simon Cook. In an address give before the Anthropology Section of the British Association for the Advancement of Science, Rhys cited research by David MacRitchie regarding "Pecht" dwellings that "appear from the outside like hillocks covered with grass" with inner cells that are "so small that their inmates must have been of very short stature, like our Welsh fairies."[618]

MacRitchie in 1890 published an account of ancient structures in Scotland that went by the name "Earth House."[619] This structure was a "long curved gallery,' and another type of this architecture he described as having "the appearance of a conical or rounded green hillock." MacRitchie pondered traditions about the ancient builders of these structures, associating them with dwarfs, fairies, and other magical beings.

The early version of Bree could well have been inspired by these references by Rhys and MacRitchie to hillock-like houses. It is at least evident that Tolkien's details align with the details put forward by Rhys and MacRitchie for British antiquity.

Mark Hooker suggests that Tolkien could have based his hobbit holes upon a Cornish structure known as a fogou, which one enters by crawling.[620] This is an apt suggestion, given that a fogou is an ancient structure of forgotten purpose – and it is a perfect size for very small folk. Hooker's suggestion is a relevant reminder that Tolkien could have gotten his hobbit holes from many possible sources, if not from his own fertile imagination. And Tolkien would doubtless much prefer to house his hobbits in some form of architecture indigenous to the British Isles.

Tolkien in Pawneeland   ~ * ~   Roger Echo-Hawk

The Enchanted Feather

Gandalf the Grey was born with a different name – a name that hinted at the mythology of Pawneeland, and as the events of *The Hobbit* took shape, that connection evaporated. But Tolkien was not finished with Pawneeland and Gandalf. Just a few years after publishing *The Hobbit* he would set the wizard's feet upon paths that would take him out of another Skidi story and into Middle-earth.

An aura of mystery and wonder surrounds Gandalf's nature, and this aura imbues Middle-earth with a special enchantment. Nowhere is this more evident than when he sheds his life as Gandalf the Grey and returns as Gandalf the White.

Tolkien's original fate for Gandalf at Moria had nothing to do with the mysticism of death and resurrection. Instead, he planned for Gandalf to overcome the Balrog, don mithril armor, slay trolls, and shine in sunlight, newly "clad in white."[621] Tolkien's second plan also did not clearly involve Gandalf's death, though it matches the final account in many ways.[622]

Sometime after preparing those various notes, Tolkien made the crucial decision to kill Gandalf the Grey and resurrect him as Gandalf the White. This decision came in 1942 between January and July when he wrote "The White Rider."[623] In this chapter Gandalf the White meets the remnant Fellowship in Fangorn and his friends ask him to provide an account of his fate at Moria. Tolkien here fashioned a powerfully compelling tale of death and resurrection.

I believe that a tale told in *Traditions of the Skidi Pawnee* influenced Tolkien's vision of Gandalf's death and resurrection. "The Man Who Visited Spirit Land" was told by a woman named Bright Eyes, and it appeared among the Skidi Pawnee "Cosmogonic" myths as a historical narrative.[624] In this Skidi tradition, a very ill man died and came back to life at graveside. A variety of details from this story match details in the tale that Gandalf told his companions in Fangorn.

In the Pawnee story the dead man observed a fire as it approached him, and "it seemed to get under my feet and around my legs and on my body; but I kept going." When Gandalf spoke of his battle with the Balrog, he also mentioned fire: "His fire was about me. I was burned." But he kept going, too.

The Skidi man who died and came back to life described his experience as a mystical journey upon mystical roads: "When I died I found myself walking toward the east, and I came to a big path, a very big wide path. The road was very dusty[.]" The man saw many footprints, but no people. Alone he climbed into a black kettle suspended from a black rope, and he was transported to "a different country." In that place he encountered four men and was instructed to look for four swans. One swan told him which path he could follow "to where Tirawa sits[.]" The man there encountered "a large golden eagle" and learned that this bird was an incarnation of Tirawa. The golden eagle described the next path he should choose among many branching paths.

Pondering Gandalf's fate at Moria, Tolkien decided to send the wizard on a spiritual journey not referenced in either of his early planning notes. In the published account in *The Two Towers*, Gandalf described his death in dreamlike visionary terms: "Then darkness took me, and I strayed out of thought and time, and I wandered far on roads that I will not tell." Refusing to speak of the mystical roads he followed, he nevertheless acknowledged the surreal mystery of the entire episode of his death and resurrection, musing, "by strange roads I came[.]"

One of these "strange roads" may refer to an idea that appeared in *The Book of Lost Tales*.[625] Written in 1919, "The Hiding of Valinor" frames death as a mystical soul journey for Elves and Men. This is "the shortest and swiftest of all roads"; "Qalvanda is it called, the Road of Death[.]" This road is "[t]wofold... and one way tread the Elves and the other the souls of Men, and never do they mingle." The term Qalvanda derives from two roots, with "qal" related to death and "vanda" related to "way, path[.]"[626]

The Milky Way serves a similar function in Skidi tradition. As with Tolkien's Qalvanda, this Skidi path is twofold. "If the dead man had been a warrior, he was put on the dim Milky Way; if he died of old age, or if it was a woman, they were put upon the wide travelled road."[627] It is possible that Tolkien intended to reflect the Skidi meaning of the Milky Way in his Qalvanda, and it is also possible that Gandalf's "strange roads" were meant to reference the Qalvanda of *The Book of Lost Tales*. Later versions of Tolkien's mythology dropped the Qalvanda and contain no further mention of any specific Road of Death.

Gandalf's death involved an aspect of visionary consciousness – a very dreamlike vision. When he lay upon Celebdil, "Faint to my ears came the gathered rumour of all lands: the springing and the dying, the song and the weeping, and the slow everlasting groan of overburdened stone." And in this state of mind, Gandalf mentions stars: "There I lay staring upward, while the stars wheeled over..." Tolkien's stars and mortality seem to have an invisible connection – a link to the Skidi identification of the Milky Way as a pathway of departed spirits. Perhaps this is one of Gandalf's secret paths.

In the story told by Bright Eyes, the young man's body is taken to a hilltop for burial and it is there upon the hill that he awakens from death. In Tolkien's original version of Gandalf's story, Gandalf says, "Naked I returned, and naked I lay upon the mountain-top."[628] Gandalf is rescued from "the pinnacle of the Silvertine" by Gwaihir the Windlord, a talking eagle. And lifting Gandalf in his talons, Gwaihir offers this poetic insight: "Light as a swan's feather in my claws you are." In the Skidi story there are swans and a talking eagle, and Tolkien has chosen to to put a swan's feather in the words of a talking eagle.

In the Skidi story told by Bright Eyes the golden eagle – who is Tirawa the Creator – directs the dead man to a community full of his deceased relatives. There his uncle bestows upon him "my title as a chief." The man is granted an enhanced mission in life and subsequently becomes "a great warrior, a medicine-man, and chief of the Pawnee." Gandalf was similarly "enhanced in power" in the course of his death experience; he was originally sent to Middle-earth to fulfill a plan of the Valar "but Authority had taken up [Gandalf's mission] and enlarged it[.]"[629] As Tolkien put it: "...Gandalf sacrificed himself, was accepted, and enhanced, and returned."

In the Skidi story the dead man's uncle bestows more than a mission upon his nephew. He also clothes his nephew in a robe and feathers: "That robe you have on you throw aside. I give you my robe... Now go back to your people."[630] The man stands up at the graveside and he says to the astonished mourners, "My uncle sent me back. I am sick no longer, but a well man." Gandalf uses similar language: "Naked I was sent back – for a brief time, until my task is done." And speaking of his timeless sojourn in Lothlórien, Gandalf says, "Healing I found, and I was clothed in white." An endnote to the Skidi story describes how a mourner "went off mourning with old clothes" until a sympathetic friend gave "the mourner a robe, leggings, and shirt."[631] The mourner then "laid his mourning clothes aside and put on clean clothes and ceased mourning."

Gandalf forsakes his vanquished grey robe and death, just as the Skidi man abandons his tattered robe and his death. Galadriel heals Gandalf and bestows upon him a white robe, just as the Skidi man is healed and given a new robe. The Skidi story mentions an enigmatic gift of feathers, while Gwaihir compares the wizard to a feather in the course of flying him to Lothlórien. These striking parallels, so diverse and unique, can be readily viewed as deliberate artifacts, as borrowings.

Tolkien was aware that he was drawing on the experiences of an actual person to shape what happened to Gandalf. As I will soon explain, I believe that this quality of the narrative is important because it subsequently shaped Tolkien's history as the creator of Middle-earth. Since Gandalf's death and resurrection was modeled on the death and resurrection of a Skidi Pawnee man, this experimental fusion of fiction and non-fiction set Tolkien's feet on a path that ultimately led him to elaborate his existing ideas about what he termed "subcreation."

In designing the details of Gandalf's uttermost mysticism, borrowing from a historical Skidi Pawnee tale of resurrection, Tolkien's poetry becomes wonderfully transcendent when it gathers "rumour of all lands" in Gandalf's ears. Surely Tolkien meant for this global murmuring to include rumor of Vinland far off – Vinland in the form of Pawneeland. But Tolkien wished for only the very faintest rumor of Pawneeland to come to our hearing. Of the roads that Olórin followed next, Gandalf would never speak. And Tolkien kept those paths secret, too. As we shall see, these turn out to be very strange roads.

Tolkien in Pawneeland ✦ Roger Echo-Hawk

A Very Peculiar Letter

During the early 1940s, in the aftermath of setting down the mysticism of Gandalf's spiritual journey upon Celebdil, Tolkien's theory of the role of vision and dream in Middle-earth took shape and cohered around the character of Gandalf. This materialized from the secret knowledge that Gandalf's death experience was derived from the actual death experience of a Skidi Pawnee. Given the role of Pawnee traditions in shaping aspects of the life and character of Gandalf, it is not surprising that Skidi philosophical constructions also had an apparent impact on Tolkien's ideas about dream and vision.

The careful parsing of visions and dream as the mystical grammar of consciousness can be found in *Traditions of the Skidi Pawnee*. The idea of a "vision" as distinguished from a "dream" appears in Roaming Scout's creation story, and the first dream-teaching comes from the Moon, while the first vision is associated with Evening Star.[632] A note attached to this vision provides a detailed explication of dream versus vision:

> The Pawnees make a distinction between dream and vision. The translation for the word "vision" is "learn by being touched." From the visit of some power a vision may occur during the day or night, but only when the individual is awake or is in a trance, brought upon through fasting or self-imposed hypnotism. In such a condition he is visited by some being who holds communication with him, and whose person the one in the vision is able to see distinctly. Thus, in a group of priests sitting in silence in a ceremony, one of them may in a vision see clearly some god or supernatural being and hold

discourse with it, while the other priests present are not aware of the presence of supernatural beings.[633]

In this theory of "vision" we find reference to "some god or supernatural being" of whom "other priests present are not aware[.]" This kind of vision is not an act of imagination or of fantasy, but rather of special spiritual insight. Reading this endnote, Tolkien encountered a belief system that took for granted a kind of mystical permeability between worlds. It suggested that in the Pawnee world the experience of "vision" reflected a socially respected acceptance of mystery – one which grants the possibility of ambiguity in the cultural production of the social boundary between spirituality and reason. Perhaps this resonated with the tension between Tolkien's religious temperament and his academic rationality.

It isn't clear when Tolkien formulated the various ideas in his legendarium about dreaming and vision. As early as the writing of "The Cottage of Lost Play" – composed in late 1916 or early 1917 – Tolkien wrote of dusk as "a time of joy to the children, for it was mostly at this hour that a new comrade would come down the lane called Olórë Mallë or the Path of Dreams."[634] In another tale from this manuscript called "The Coming of the Valar" Tolkien listed one Valar as "Fantur of Dreams who is Lórien Olofantur"; and later as "the lord of dreams and imaginings[.]"[635] A marvelously dreamlike description of Lórien's realm in Valinor also appears in this manuscript, and this mentions Lórien's experience of seeing "visions of mystery" upon a mirroring lake.[636]

Tolkien experimented with the imaginal boundary between dream and vision in *The Hobbit* when he described the half-dream and half-vision experiences of Bombur in Mirkwood. For his next major book project, *The Lost Road* (dating to about 1936-1937), he set the art of dreaming center stage. There dreams serve as a kind of transport to Middle-earth. And there is little philosophizing about the nature of dreaming, but at one point one character has the insight that his "last night's vision remained with him, something different from the common order of dreams."[637] And at another point he ponders the esoteric nature of his dreams as "not the usual sort, quite different: very vivid... a sort of phantom story with no explanations."[638]

It is curious that in the spring of 1942 a dream might have given rise to Tolkien's short story, "Leaf By Niggle."[639] A likely early mention of this story appears in a postcard Tolkien wrote in April 1943, but in 1945 he told of its origin: "I woke up one morning... with that odd thing virtually complete in my head." The story is interesting because it tells how a vision of artistry ultimately becomes manifest, and this vision becomes Niggle's ultimate destination for "a long journey" that he had to take but kept postponing.[640] It is unclear whether Tolkien had a dream that inspired the story, but it is more certain that he did author this story during the same period that he was composing "The White Rider," sorting out Gandalf's fate upon Celebdil and his "strange roads."

In the end, however, none of these writings offer a coherent formal theory or interpretation of the significance of dreaming. But I suggest that in the spring or early summer of 1942, in the course of seeking inspiration to sort out Gandlf's fate at Moria, Tolkien took notice of the Skidi Pawnee definitions of dream versus vision. This encounter inspired him to ponder the nature of reality versus fantasy. Whether this simply added to his own existing intellectual momentum or whether it actually precipitated this direction in his thinking, Tolkien set forth Gandalf's visionary fate, and his pondering of vision soon became evident in an extensive revision of "On Fairy-stories," an essay that he originally wrote in 1938-1939 as a lecture. Here he sorted out not just the character of fairytales, but also the essences of dreaming and vision.

"On Fairy-stories" underwent composition during at least two periods. Its birth came sometime in 1938 and progressed through to the delivery of Tolkien's lecture in March 1939. Two draft manuscripts seem to date to this period.[641] The second draft manuscript dates in part to circa 1939, but Tolkien used it as the basis for an extensive revision in 1943, and from this a third manuscript was prepared that same year.[642] These three manuscripts have been labeled by Verlyn Flieger and Douglas Anderson as "Manuscript A," "Manuscript B," and "Manuscript C." In 2008 Flieger and Anderson published A and B in *Tolkien On Fairy-stories*. "Manuscript B" contains material from both periods of composition, and it is described by Flieger and Anderson as "a very difficult text, a large proportion of which seems written for oral delivery [so dating to 1938-1939] but which also shows evidence of considerable revision undertaken probably in 1943."[643] Christina Scull and Wayne Hammond also provide evidence that during 1943 Tolkien added both the idea of "eucatastrophe" and the text of his epilogue.[644]

In "On Fairy-stories" Tolkien formally defined his view of "the machinery of Dream" as "only a thing imagined" and "a figment or illusion."[645] This definition does not appear in the original draft, "Manuscript A," dating to 1938-1939. Nor does it appear in "Manuscript B," written in 1938-1939 and revised in 1943. It must first appear in "Manuscript C" or in the typescript that followed – these later manuscripts are not presented by Flieger and Anderson, but it seems safe to assume that the "machinery of Dream" passage dates to 1943.[646]

There Tolkien writes, "In dreams strange powers of the mind may be unlocked."[647] But the nature of dreaming is such that it "cheats deliberately the primal desire" for "the realization, independent of the conceiving mind, of imagined wonder." To explain, he shifts from the illusions of dream to point out that traditional fairytales accept fairy folk as "not themselves illusions[.]" And such traditions exist in their most exalted form when "presented as 'true.'" Tolkien concludes that since dreams lack this kind of narrative truth, they cannot offer the most appropriate environment for a fairytale.

One thing is certain. Many of the Skidi stories I have mentioned in this study were told among the Pawnees as historical narratives. Tolkien's creation was rooted in the Skidi creation story, as was his story about Ungoliont in 1919, and his dragon wasteland, and his storytelling about the sun and moon, and his weaving together of hobbits in their holes, and his envisioning of Bladorthin the Master of the Great Plains, and the birth of Beorn, and the death of Smaug. These stories held the aura of history among the Pawnees, and Tolkien knew that. His own "invented" tales seem fictional, but they nevertheless have a secret aura, borrowed from Pawneeland. As the basis for his mythology for England, Tolkien's myths were not fanciful tales he whipped up to tell his children.

If dreams are fanciful, what is fantasy itself? Tolkien's consideration of fantasy in the essay begins with a description that sounds like the definition of a dream: "The human mind is capable of forming mental images of things not actually present."[648] But Flieger and Anderson show that he derived this language from "definition 4" for the term "fancy" in the first edition of the *Oxford English Dictionary*: "Imagination: the process and faculty of forming mental representations of things not actually present."[649] Tolkien's paraphrased version does not appear in "Manuscript A" or in "Manuscript B," so its initial appearance must date to "Manuscript C" in 1943. The OED definition ends with this: "...imagination is the power of giving to ideal creations the inner consistency of realities." Tolkien attached this statement mostly intact to the end of his opening paragraph on the topic of fantasy. An abbreviated version of it appears in "Manuscript B" on a sheet dated by the editors to 1943.[650] This shows that Tolkien was giving much thought to these matters in 1943 rather than in 1938-1939.

Inspired by the definition for "fancy" in the *Oxford English Dictionary*, Tolkien set forth an elaborate cognitive mechanism for creative vision. The faculty of conceiving "mental images of things not actually present," he says, has been termed "Imagination" but it is "Art" that provides "the operative link between Imagination and... Sub-creation."[651] And the term "Fantasy" is useful to "embrace both the Sub-creative Art in itself and a quality of strangeness and wonder in the Expression[.]" He then distinguishes Fantasy from dreaming, just as the Pawnee conception distinguishes "vision" from "dreaming." But Tolkien provides a highly obtuse meaning for "fantasy" as a term of artistry – with both fantasy and art emerging from the mysticism of what he termed "sub-creation."

It is in the 1943 epilogue to "On Fairy-stories" that Tolkien sketches his answer to the question of what is "true" in a fairy-story: "...in the 'eucatastrophe' we see in a brief vision that the answer may be greater – it may be a far-off gleam or echo of *evangelium* in the real world."[652] From this "brief vision" Tolkien muses, "It is not difficult to imagine the peculiar excitement and joy that one would feel, if any specially beautiful fairy-story were found to be 'primarily' true, its narrative to be history..." With such imagining in hand, Tolkien's joy centers on the prospect that "the Great Eucatastrophe" in God's plan for the world will mean that "Art has been verified." At this point it is apparent that Tolkien's uttermost hope is that his own art will become "hallowed" by the Christian evangelium and we will see that "God is Lord, of angels, and of men – and of elves." Tolkien's happy ending will find fulfillment when "Legend and History have met and fused."

And so we find Tolkien in 1943 deploying the word "vision" in a mystical fusion of the world of internal imagination and the world of external reality. In the Skidi Pawnee "distinction between dream and vision" the idea of vision does not derive its significance in terms of any distinction between fiction and non-fiction, between reality and fantasy. Rather, the idea is that reality is a construct that can be derived not just from ordinary insight, but also from mystical consciousness.

The erasure of a boundary between the fictive constructions of Tolkien's "secondary world" and the non-fiction truths of our "primary world" would be achieved as a religious act of grace, a Great Eucatastrophe. If the Skidi Pawnees could believe in a mystical gift of "vision" in which we "may in a vision see clearly," then perhaps this was something that Englishmen could also do, except do it through the precepts of Christianity. For this reason, Tolkien took seriously the formulation for his sub-created Elves and Maiar of an aspect of consciousness that could become embodied as a grand outcome of God's plan for humankind.

His discussion of "recovery" conveys these very teachings.[653] This concept appears in vague form in the original version of the essay, "Manuscript A," as "renewal," while the concept of a "Recovered Thing" receives brief mention in "Manuscript B": ""The Recovered Thing is not quite the same as the Thing-never-lost. It is often more precious. As Grace, recovered by repentance, is not the same as primitive Innocence, but it is not necessarily a poorer or worse state."[654] Tolkien's full disquisition on "recovery" must therefore appear in "Manuscript C" written in 1943.

Recovery, Tolkien explains, "is a re-gaining – regaining of a clear view." He continues: "I do not say 'seeing things as they are'... though I might venture to say 'seeing things as we are (or were) meant to see them' – as things apart from ourselves." The sin of "possessiveness" of beautiful things means that having acquired them, we have "ceased to look at them" and so we must "clean our windows" of this dross. Toward this end, recovery is a poetic form of liberation: "Creative fantasy, because it is mainly trying to do something else (make something new), may open your hoard and let all the locked things fly away like cage-birds."

These teachings held for Tolkien hope for transcendent visionary enchantment. Having set forth the logic behind this hope in "On Fairy-stories," he sought conscious moments of contemplative clarity in his everyday life. In late 1944 he wrote a letter describing the essay and focusing on eucatastrophe and vision as the "highest function of fairy-stories" because the experience of it offers "a sudden glimpse of Truth[.]"[655] He then goes on to describe three instances of such sudden clarities involving a waking epiphany, the joy of eucatastrophe, and "the most touching sight" of a "holy tramp." He knew these were esoteric matters, difficult to articulate and very personal: "This is becoming a very peculiar letter!" Ten years later, writing another letter, Tolkien mentioned that his Middle-earth was only "an incompletely imagined world" but perhaps "if it pleased the Creator" then it might well be given "(in a corrected form) Reality[.]"[656]

During the next year after writing his 1944 letter Tolkien set aside his work on *The Lord of the Rings* and launched into a new/old project – reviving certain conceptions of *The Lost Road* manuscript dating to circa 1932-1937. In 1945-1946 this took shape as *The Notion Club Papers*, another unfinished manuscript.[657] Verlyn Flieger has suggested that "[t]he mystical strain in Tolkien's nature is at its clearest in the para-psychological spin he puts on the characters in *The Notion Club Papers*..."[658] Quoting from letters written between 1941 and 1955, she showed that he delved into "reincarnation, genetic memory, and the concept of inherited memory of a homeland..." In one 1955 letter he wrote of his "recurrent dream" of an overwhelming "Great Wave" as "[p]ossibly inherited" from his parents, and then passed along through the same mystical means to his son Michael.[659] Flieger suggested that these were ideas that Tolkien held to be actualities of some kind, and she showed how they shaped the narrative logic of *The Notion Club Papers*.

Moreover, if such esoteric mysteries were not real, there was a god who could make them real. It is fascinating to consider Tolkien's hope that "the Creator" might give "Reality" to his fictional Middle-earth, and to ponder what this signified for him in his private life as a religious Catholic. It surely impacted his storytelling. Feeling that his worldmaking might well please his Christian god to such a degree that Middle-earth might be granted an ultimate completion, he gave much thought to the inner nature of his worldmaking. But our expectations should be open to nuance – surely Tolkien made different things of this mysticism and had many ways of relating to what it meant. This is implied by Tom Shippey's sense in *The Road to Middle-earth* that "For many years [Tolkien] had held to his theory of 'sub-creation,'" but "by the 1960s he was not so sure."[660] And Tolkien "no longer imagined himself rejoining his own creations after death[.]"

As I have argued in this book, Tolkien's mythmaking was partially historical to begin with – rooted in the borrowed details of narratives that set forth a mythological history of the Skidi Pawnees. This was the secret aura that Tolkien lit inside his own storytelling. In fact, this logic applies to the substance of all the mythological sources that inspired Tolkien – materials that arose in usage as historical texts, as telling of actual events.

Within just a few years of writing about his three "very peculiar" visionary experiences, Tolkien would add a very peculiar glimpse of such matters in *The Lord of the Rings*. Here the Pawnee note on vision is useful to revisit: "Thus, in a group of priests sitting in silence in a ceremony, one of them may in a vision see clearly some god or supernatural being and hold discourse with it, while the other priests present are not aware of the presence of supernatural beings."[661] In "Many Partings" Tolkien wrote in similar terms of the final converse among Gandalf, Galadriel, Celeborn, and Elrond: "...they would sit together under the stars, recalling the ages that were gone... And if any wanderer had chanced to pass, little would he have seen or heard, and it would have seemed to him only that he saw grey figures, carved in stone... For they did not move or speak with mouth, looking from mind to mind; and only their shining eyes stirred and kindled as their thoughts went to and fro."

During the 1940s Tolkien's ambitious theory of sub-creation shined with visionary clarities. As we will soon see, in 1944 one outcome of his thinking about dream and vision gave rise to a new aspect of Gandalf – the invention of Gandalf as Olórin the Maia. And this in turn permitted a further moment of insight and epiphany in the above mystical converse of Gandalf the Maia with the Elves. The making of this explicit dream/vision aspect of the character of Gandalf therefore represents a culmination of the period when Tolkien formally organized his thinking on dreams and vision. In the delicate spiritual mechanisms of visionary experience, Tolkien found a means of elucidating the mystery that moved in the mist between worlds, between the fictional realms of his Secondary world and the truths of the Primary world.

Olórin in the Uttermost West

In this realm of visionary contemplation, Tolkien found himself journeying upon a path perpendicular to history and into a hidden inward world. A lattice of intellectual and spiritual connections between what Tolkien termed the Primary World and the Secondary World helped to further in him the sense that the misty ambiguities that so often exist at the boundary separating the inner worlds of rationalism and spiritualism could be less formed from impenetrable materials and more composed of permeable esoteric truths. In contrast to the illusions of dream, the "true" elements of enchantment appropriate to Tolkien's kind of fairy-story needed to address a "primal desire" for "the realization, independent of the conceiving mind, of imagined wonder."[662] Tolkien summoned much dreaming into his writings, but a sense of fully realized "imagined wonder" had to come from something less idiosyncratic and fickle than a dream. He needed "vision."

Through 1943 Tolkien pondered the nature of "vision" and soon began to wonder how it might flavor the character of his legendarium. In early 1944 he turned to the mystery of Gandalf to brew this enchantment. He did so by giving the wizard a new name and a new past incarnation, retroactively conceiving him as a Maia in Valinor with the name Olórin.

This name apparently first appears in Tolkien's legendarium in the spring of 1944 with the writing of the chapter that became "The Window on the West" in Book IV of *The Two Towers*. In that chapter Faramir quotes from Gandalf, listing his various names. Tolkien's original version of Gandalf's name in Valinor was Olórion, soon revised to Olórin.[663] As evidenced in "On Fairy-stories," Tolkien was pondering dream as illusion in

1943, and this was followed early the next year by his invention of the name Olórin for Gandalf.

It was in this context of evolving ideas that he also set forth his perception of historical ideas about "visions" in his introduction to *Pearl*, a Middle English poem. It isn't clear exactly when he prepared that introduction, but it was after 1938 and probably sometime close to July 1947.[664] He wrote that in Middle English times people believed that "visions... allowed marvels to be placed within the real world... while providing them with an explanation in the phantasies of sleep..." and it was "a period when men, aware of the vagaries of dreams, still thought that amid their japes came visions of truth" and "...their waking imagination was strongly moved by symbols and the figures of allegory...."

Tolkien's surviving notes apparently say nothing more about the name Olórin until his earliest portrayal of Olórin the Maia sometime in early 1951.[665] There Tolkien characterizes Maiar as spirits who "appear seldom in forms visible" and this includes Olórin whose "bright visions drove away the imaginations of darkness" and "[t]hose who harkened to him arose from despair; and in their hearts the desire to heal and to renew awoke, and thoughts of fair things that had not yet been but might yet be made for the enrichment of Arda."

The idea that the Maiar exist as invisible spirits echoes a conception of the Valar that took an early form during the late 1930s, when the first hint of this aspect of the Valar first appears in the "Ainulindalë": "...their shape and form is greater and more lovely and it comes of the knowledge and desire of the substance of the world rather than of that substance itself, and it cannot always be perceived[.]"[666] This vague conception took on greater specificity and definition during the 1940s. Sorting out the confusing chronology of manuscripts of the "Ainulindalë," Christopher Tolkien concludes that "Version C*" of the creation story was prepared sometime before 1948.[667] This manuscript contains this passage on the Valar: "Moreover their shape comes of their knowledge and desire of the visible World, rather than of the World itself, and yet we may be naked and suffer no loss of our being. Therefore the Valar may walk unclad, as it were, and then even the Eldar cannot clearly perceive them."[668] Tolkien's thinking about Olórin continued to evolve in the late 1950s to the form published in *The Silmarillion*: "though he loved the Elves, he walked among them unseen, or in form as one of them, and they did not know whence came the fair visions or the promptings of wisdom that he put into their hearts."[669]

Collecting the extant information on the five wizards of Middle-earth – the Istari – for publication in *Unfinished Tales*, Christopher Tolkien included material from brief notes dating between 1953 and 1972.[670] His father seems to have prepared a synthesis about 1953, revisiting it in 1965.[671] But the extant composition history seems sparse and vague. Among some "rapid jottings" thought to date to 1953, Tolkien developed the meaning of the name Olórin as "a High-elven name" bestowed in Valinor.[672] The term *olor* "is a word often translated 'dream,' but that does not refer to (most) human 'dreams,' certainly not the dreams of sleep." Tolkien next offers a very esoteric definition: "To the Eldar it included the vivid contents of their *memory*, as of their *imagination*: it referred in fact to *clear vision*, in the mind, of things not physically present at the body's situation." This note concludes with an even more cryptic comment: "But not only to an idea, but to a full clothing of this in particular form and detail." In another undated "isolated" note Tolkien added a definition for "*olo-s*" as "vision, phantasy," which refers to the "[c]ommon Elvish name for 'construction of the mind[.]'"[673]

In this undated note, believed to date to circa 1953 we find the term "clear vision"; this surely arose from Tolkien's 1943 definition of "recovery" in "On Fairy-stories" as "a re-gaining – regaining of a clear view."[674] This language in turn may well derive from the Pawnee description of "vision" where we find the words "vision see clearly[.]"[675] The Pawnee idea of vision and the Elvish idea of vision sound very similar, and this similarity of concept is underscored by some corresponding language in the definitions. In addition, when Tolkien wrote in "On Fairy-stories" in 1943 "...in the 'eucatastrophe' we see in a brief vision..." it seems arguable that this provided the foundation for the spiritual insights of what he termed "clear vision" in 1953.[676] But for what reason did Tolkien devise such a mystical abstraction for the concept of a "dream"? The arts of dream and the meanings of dreaming enter his legendarium early and remain to the end of his storytelling. It can be wondered whether Tolkien experimented with defining "clear vision" as a mechanism for special insight on the part of Maiar and Elves in Middle-earth at the same time that he also devised, in "On Fairy-stories," a meaning for "fantasy" that involved "art" as the link between imagination and the mysticism of what he termed "sub-creation."[677]

In 1943 Tolkien studied the *Oxford English Dictionary* for help in sorting out his own thinking; and for "On Fairy-stories" he consequently drew from the definition an adaptation for "fancy" regarding "things not actually present."[678] In time this also provided the foundation for the note he wrote in 1953. In that note we find reference to "things not physically present[.]"[679] It is clearly indebted to material he prepared in 1943 for "On Fairy-stories," and since it pertains to the making of Gandalf's character, the 1953 note may well have originated during 1943 or 1944. In any case, these materials together helped to orient him to the ambiguities of fantasy experience versus true experience.

It is possible to trace the evolution of an interconnected web of ideas between 1942 and 1944. This is important because in my theory of Tolkien's use of Pawnee material, he consulted *Traditions of the Skidi Pawnee* on specific occasions and came away with usable ideas of coloration, and I think he looked at the book in 1942 and found interesting the Pawnee division between dream and vision. In the years that followed Tolkien decided that he needed a complex interpretive lens to see all that he wished to see in dreams and visions, and at some point he decided to link the geography of dreamlike visionary imaginal realms of consciousness to the enigma of Gandalf. He accomplished this through the lens of "vision" – a lens that permits us to see a further set of spiritual ideas that Tolkien held dear as a Christian, and which express the hidden religious philosophy that guided his aspiration as the maker of Middle-earth. This journey became embodied by Gandalf in his previous incarnation as Olórin, but it emerged from a broader set of writings and conceptions – and Pawnee ideas arguably play a role in launching this journey. Between 1942 and 1944, the ideas of "dream" and "vision" and the invisible nature of the Valar and Maiar as spiritual beings arose as various strands of thought. From these strands Tolkien wove together the inner essences of Gandalf.

In one of his last notes, dating to circa 1973, Tolkien made manifest his continuing interest regarding *"clear vision, in the mind, of things not physically present at the body's situation"* in a way that fully accords with the Skidi idea that such visions touch a person "during the day or night... when the individual is awake" and can "see clearly" the vision. Tolkien describes how Círdan the Shipwright declared his purpose to sail "into the West" and "received in his heart a message, which he knew to come from the Valar, though in his mind it was remembered as a voice speaking in his own tongue."[680] This voice issued a warning and "then it seemed to him that he saw (in a vision maybe) a shape like a white boat, shining above him[.]" This vision represents "a full clothing" of transcendent insight in the form of a vessel witnessed only by Círdan, foretelling his aid to Eärendil and the building of Vingelot. This marvelously dreamlike transcendent vision was witnessed only by Círdan, but it unfolded from Tolkien's hand as his final journey into the mysticism of dreams and visions.

If we embrace the idea that in 1942 Tolkien consulted *Traditions of the Skidi Pawnee* to colorize his story of the death and resurrection of Gandalf, then it is logical to presume that other influences could have slipped into his storytelling at that time. The Pawnee idea of a supernatural being who visits a visionary while unseen by others fits into a particular space in the chronology of Tolkien's evolving ideas not just about Olórin and the Maiar, but also about his more explicit religious ideas on eucatastrophe and the ultimate spiritual function of fairy story.

I have the impression that Tolkien first looked at *Traditions of the Skidi Pawnee* in 1919 when he composed his creation story, and again about 1930, so he could have encountered the Skidi ideas about dreams and visions very early in his career as a mythologist and storyteller. But I believe that strong circumstantial evidence supports the view that Tolkien visited the pages of *Traditions of the Skidi Pawnee* in 1942 when he settled Gandalf's fate at Moria. It was then that Tolkien noticed and found appealing the Pawnee conception of dream versus vision.

The Pawnee attitude toward dream and vision interested Tolkien in 1942 because he understood that such imaginal materials were not deemed to be the stuff of fictitious mythmaking, but rather the substance of an accepted mode of mindfulness. In the years that followed, he decided to separate the generative vision of his creation story from the act of creation. His reason for doing this is not clear, but must be related to his evolving sense of "vision" as an experience that is inherently definitional and not necessarily only validated by outward manifestations of "truth." Tolkien felt inspired to not only add a sense of mysticism to his literary creations, but to also experiment with his own introspective inner sense of mystical selfhood.

It is certainly possible that Tolkien wholly invented his own evolving ideas on these matters without any influence from Skidi tradition, but I believe Tolkien's interlocking ideas about Gandalf, Olórin, dream, and vision all took shape during the same period. This moment of invention begins with Gandalf's experience of death and resurrection, told in visionary terms: "Then darkness took me, and I strayed out of thought and time, and I wandered far on roads that I will not tell." This dreamlike journey was not metaphorical, nor was it a dream. It was instead a "clear vision" of the wizard's "waking imagination." For this key moment in Gandalf's story, having drawn already on a Pawnee tradition about an actual person who died and came back to life, it would seem reasonable to presume that it is not mere coincidence that Tolkien would also proceed to set forth his ideas pertaining to "vision" and "dream" and spirits sensed but unseen. The Pawnee material added momentum and certain details of coloration to his thinking, but in this regard, Tolkien proceeded under no enchantment but his own.

The fact that Gandalf journeys to Lothlórien after his resurrection is also interesting because the term *lórien* corresponds in meaning to his name, Olórin, with both words related to dreaming. And when Gwaihir compares Gandalf to a swan's feather, this metaphor emphasizes the "clear vision" of the magic eagle, who sees Gandalf as he is – wearing his "body's situation" as an embodiment of imagination that is connected "not only to an idea, but to a full clothing of this in particular form and detail." The fact that this language putatively dated to 1953 fits so well what Tolkien wrote in 1942 seems to strongly suggest for both a common origin point rooted partially in Skidi tradition – a moment of origin that then gave rise to the 1943 deliberations that form the spiritual heart of "On Fairy-stories," as well as to the evolution of Olórin in *The Lord of the Rings* and beyond.

The fusion of vision and myth and history attains transcendence in Gandalf's death because this is a moment not only of Tolkien's imagination, but also of Skidi history. A real person died and returned to life in the Skidi story. The vision of this mystical experience is hidden at the heart of Gandalf's death and resurrection. This means that Tolkien can seem to speak of this event as an act of subcreative imagination, but here "subcreative" enfolds a secret history, a real history. "Gandalf really died," wrote Tolkien in 1954.[681] "I am G. the *White*, who has returned from death" – this is how Tolkien should have written the tale, according to his own account. And Tolkien concluded, "I might say much more, but it would only be in... elucidation of the 'mythological' ideas in my mind[.]" Those mythological ideas, I suggest, have something to do with his use of Skidi mythology – an elucidation that can never be said.

It is difficult to believe that all the aspects and incidents pertaining to the character of Gandalf were wholly invented by Tolkien when so many of those details echo details found in *Traditions of the Skidi Pawnee*. It is more logical to believe that the variety of corresponding configurations means something beyond coincidence, and that there is a Pawnee wizard standing behind the feathery curtain of Gandalf the White. And it is also logical that Tolkien would wish for this Pawnee wizard to remain forever invisible, unseen behind the curtain.

Tolkien saw himself, to some degree, as a mythmaker engaged in constructing a lost pre-Christian ancient mythology, a Eurocentric mythology, a mythology full of primitive undergrowth. With this fact in hand, perhaps we can guess why he would have felt a professional interest in the Skidi Pawnee legendarium, and why he would have borrowed from it, and why he would do so in secret.

Tolkien's Mongol-type Orcs

The year that Tolkien entered Oxford University, one could find in local bookshops a volume newly published by the university – a book about fairies. This was not such an unusual thing to find in those days in England. But this book contained mention of the belief that in Cornwall along the "fringe of coast... are found today a strange and separate people of Mongol type..."[682] These strange people were "a little 'stuggy' dark folk" who "were commonly believed to be largely wizards and witches." This came in the midst of ruminations about "Picts" and "piskies," and we are encouraged to surmise that these strange "Mongol type" folk may well be a lingering remnant folk from ancient days. This was not such an odd moment to encounter in the literature of the day. But it is interesting because JRR Tolkien would one day make a mysterious decision – he decided to transform his monstrous orcs into something he would later describe as "Mongol-types."

The orcs of JRR Tolkien might well represent the least individualized of his invented fantasy folk – they come to us pressed out of a single loathsome mold. But there is a history to consider, an evolution of characterization. A survey of this history shows that Tolkien's orcs were not born fully constituted when they first entered his world as folkloric fantasy soldiery of evil. Their subsequent entry into *The Hobbit* did not substantially alter this characterization, though the intended tone of the story did introduce a minor shift of tonal emphasis, modifying these creatures slightly from nightmarish soldier-monsters toward a nightmarish fairytale mode.

Then in the early stages of writing *The Lord of the Rings*, Tolkien decided to substantially rewrite his orcs. He made a deliberate decision to racialize his fantasy soldiery of evil. And just a few years after this major revision appeared in print, he insisted that these racialized creatures should be explicitly portrayed in that new light. Writing a letter in 1958, he set forth his vision of these orcs as "squat, broad, flat-nosed, sallow-skinned, with wide mouths and slant eyes: in fact degraded and repulsive versions of the (to Europeans) least lovely Mongol-types."[683]

To fully understand this transformation, we must trace the evolution of Tolkien's orcs over several decades from their first appearance in his writings to their later incarnation as unlovely Mongol-types.[684] Following this trajectory, we glimpse a significant fact that deserves attention when we ponder Tolkien's intended racial messaging in Middle-earth. That is, as a matter of choice, Tolkien embraced the attitudes of his peers in British academia when it came to racial discourse on Jews, Celts, and Germanic peoples, but he also deliberately invoked a demeaning Asian racial stereotype in the construction of his Middle-earth orcs.

When Tolkien first began writing poems about a fairytale England, the term "goblin" in its various forms applied to a popular and well-established folkloric creature, a small magical creature somewhat interchangeable with fairies, brownies, and hobs. Tolkien's first goblins were just a kind of diminutive fairy. One of his early publications was a 1915 poem titled "Goblin Feet," and this poem used "goblin" as an alternate word for "enchanted leprechauns" and "gnomes" – a term he later applied to elves.[685]

Within just a few years Tolkien decided to transform his primitive fairy-like goblins into humanlike fairytale soldier-monsters that he also conflated with "orc," a more obscure term. A formative influence on his evolving goblins came from the writings of George MacDonald – Tolkien wrote in 1939 of MacDonald's "classic goblin" as a "mixture of German and Scottish flavours[.]"[686] Christina Scull and Wayne Hammond have pointed to the fact that "MacDonald describes his goblins as having been human originally."

In *The Book of Lost Tales*, written between 1916 and 1922, Tolkien listed various creatures of evil "and more fearsome still were the wandering bands of the goblins and the Orcs – foul broodlings of Melko who fared abroad doing his evil work, snaring and capturing beasts, and Men, and Elves, and dragging them to their lord."[687] He now described them as having "a squat and unlovely stature" with "most evil faces... and their voices and their laughter was as the clash of stone and metal."[688] Another description of these Orcs said "all that race were bred by Melko of the subterranean heats and slime" and "[t]heir hearts were of granite and their bodies deformed; foul their faces which smiled not, but their laugh that of the clash of metal" and they gladly served Melko. The Elves hated them and "named them Glamhoth, or folk of dreadful hate."[689] These Orcs had "ears of cats" and their eyes were "yellow and green like cats."[690]

These cat-like orcs of circa 1919 were more impressionistic than human, and they did not display precise alignments with racial stereotypes of the day. Between 1926 and 1930 Tolkien composed a sketch of his mythology which mentioned "Orcs (Goblins, also called Glamhoth or people of hate)"; and a new version of Tolkien's mythological history written circa 1930 continued the conception of "hordes of the Orcs" made by Morgoth "of stone" – again termed "Glamhoth, people of hate" and "Goblins they may be called[.]"[691] In an essay dated to circa 1930-1931 he termed orcs / goblins "the Stonefaces."[692] No hint of race can be found in these conceptions.

Ten years later, in the course of writing *The Hobbit*, Tolkien slightly redefined his goblins. Crafting a fairytale aimed at a young audience, he decided to experiment with segregating his goblins and orcs into two kinds of monsters, with goblins representing somewhat less grim creatures. This probably explains his minimal use of "orc" in *The Hobbit*, a decision that he carried forward into the early formulation of *The Lord of the Rings*. Christopher Tolkien observed of an early draft of *The Fellowship of the Ring* that "the rarity of the usage [of 'orc'] at this stage is remarkable" – he suggested that his father planned for his orcs to represent "a more formidable kind of 'Goblin'[.]"[693] In 1931-1932

Tolkien may have decided to assign goblins to a more fairytale setting while reserving orcs for his Middle-earth legends.

The original texts of *The Hobbit*, dating to circa 1931-1932, did not associate goblins / orcs with any color or obvious quality of race. But several drawings of goblins in Tolkien's *Letters from Father Christmas* (1933, 1938) depicted them as small black humanoid figures. This could be evidence of a newly emerging visualization – one that served as a transitional experiment between Tolkien's familiar goblins and his later orcs. Tolkien's fantasy productions overlapped and seeped into each other, but his Father Christmas goblins and the goblins in *The Hobbit* appeared in stories aimed at a younger audience. It is arguable that Tolkien merely modified his Middle-earth goblins to fit this circumstance.

Tolkien derived the term "orc" from *Beowulf*. There the Old English *orcnéas* appeared in a listing that Tolkien translated as "ogres and goblins and haunting shapes of hell..." In undated lecture notes on *Beowulf* he prepared an interesting explanation: "'Necromancy' will suggest something of the horrible associations of this word."[694] Tolkien analyzed this association by observing that "*orc* is found glossing Latin *Orcus*" meaning "Hell" or "Death"; and *neas* is a form of "the old (poetic) word *né* 'dead body'." He specified that "what is here meant is that terrible northern imagination to which I have ventured to give the name 'barrow-wights'." These are "undead" creatures with "superhuman strength and malice[.]"

This *Beowulf* note on *orcnéas* hinted at an intention to apply the word "orc" to an undead creature. Tolkien had inserted his first barrow-wight into "The Adventures of Tom Bombadil" – a poem dating to circa 1931 – and he may have considered using "orc" as an alternate term for barrow-wight. And by 1931 he had invented for *The Hobbit* a character he named the Necromancer. He apparently had in mind some experimental association of evil zombie wizardry with barrow-wights / orcs as undead creatures, differentiated from goblins. If so, the idea evaporated in the course of writing *The Hobbit*. Sitting down to write *The Lord of the Rings*, Tolkien eventually decided to stay on track with using the terms "goblin" and "orc" as interchangeable names for the same creature.

In various manuscripts dating to circa 1936-1937 he was still making use of concepts developed early in his Middle-earth legendarium, portraying orcs as creatures made by Morgoth as "mockeries of the creatures of Illúvatar" and "made of stone" with no new descriptive details.[695] It is notable that Tolkien used the phrase "black armies of the orcs" during the late 1930s, but it is not clear that this was meant to describe skin color.[696] The attachment of skin color to goblins and orcs evolved slowly during the 1930s, always focused on the color black.

By circa 1940 the unsmiling orcs of *The Book of Lost Tales* and the colorless goblins of *The Hobbit* had given way to black orcs. After the use of "black" to denote orc skin-color materialized, it endured through the writing of *The Lord of the Rings* – a text associated with the 1948 preparation of "The Land of Shadow" for *The Return of the King* described two orcs dressed in black who are "a small breed, black-skinned..."[697]

What accounts for this transformation? This is an important question that is difficult to answer. But tracing the evolution of Tolkien's goblins / orcs as they appear in his various writings, we can glimpse the influence of race on this process. This means that we can also survey the social context of race in Britain, and we can study what we know of Tolkien's attitudes.[698] The evidence shows that the orcs of Middle-earth began life as fantasy monsters born from nightmarish fairytale, but during World War Two Tolkien's orcs accrued new dimensions borrowed from the traditions of race.

European race theory during the mid-19th century embraced an influential idea that shaped the real world traditions of racial belief and had an impact on the thinking of JRR Tolkien. This idea was that interbreeding of lower and higher races led to a decline in the vitality of the higher race.[699] This notion became entwined with the evolving intersection of linguistics and bioracialism, inspiring new vistas on human history. As Asya Pereltsvaig and Martin W. Lewis have described, one point of contention had to do with the role of "Orientalism" in the shaping of the Indo-European family of languages and nations, with philologist Max Müller pointing to the influence of India and minimizing the influence of racial differences, and with other leading European intellectuals disparaging Müller's philological position and elevating the role of race.[700]

Pereltsvaig and Lewis portray Müller as harboring a "profound contempt" for the exclusive association of "an Aryan race with northern Europeans" and thus earning for himself the title of "Public Enemy Number One" among pro-race proponents of Aryan exceptionalism. Müller wrote in 1887 that there is no evidence "for saying that the nearer to Scandinavia... the purer would be its Aryan race and speech, while in Greece and Armenia, Persia and India, we should find mixture and decay[.]" In other words, Müller felt that the narrative of "Northernness" as an exposition of mystical racial purity was baseless.

Ivan Hannaford's assessment of Müller is that he came to regard the term "Aryan" as applicable only to language "and nothing but language" – and both languages and human groups were permeable mixtures, not rigidly segregated formations.[701] But denying that race existed in blood, Müller nevertheless sensed a spiritual essence of national will, a "living soul of the nation and race..."

Beyond the development of philology as a discipline, Müller's work also contributed to the vast ferment of ideas that gave shape to the production of race during the late 19th century. JP Mallory has credited Müller as a key figure in advancing "the use of Aryan to describe the ancient Indo-Europeans" and who ultimately became "annoyed by the madness he had helped to create..."[702] Mallory noted that Müller "blasted the anthropologists who spoke of an 'Aryan race, Aryan blood, Aryan eyes and hair' as a lunacy"; but by then "it was too late: the Indo-Europeans and racism had become inseparable in the minds of many scholars."

Müller won enormous popularity for his research on language and myth. He promoted the idea that distant Aryan ancestors passed through a "mythopoeic" age in which "the disease of language" mingled word meanings and cosmological metaphor, giving rise to mythology.[703] He drew on global myth to make his case. He argued at one point that "savages" like Andaman Islanders are not really fossilized "primitive" people; and then he turned around to frame "the most remote races" as following the same processes as those used by primitive Aryans in antiquity.

Tolkien gave thought to aspects of Müller's scholarship. In the course of preparing his essay "On Fairy stories" he took issue with Müller's modeling of the history of language and myth as evolving from an allegorical interpretation of natural phenomena – an interpretation that dominated the study of myth during the late 19th century.[704] But Tolkien made only observations in passing and offered no coherent critique relating to race and Northernness.

This history matters to the making of Middle-earth because Tolkien knew well the pitfalls of mixing language categories with race, and mingling nationalism with racialism. But he nevertheless toyed with a nebulous identity construction that he termed a "noble northern spirit."[705] This esoteric "Germanic" quality, as he termed it, had to do with an antiquarian conception of the moral and cultural climate of ancient northern Europe, and this meant that Tolkien followed pathways that wound in and out of the margins of race-based nationalism.

The final decades of the 19th century and the early 20th century race ideology brought about an important shift in European social and political relations. As Ivan Hannaford observed, "During the period from 1890 to 1915, race as an organizing idea claimed precedence over all previous formulations of nation and state."[706] Pro-race intellectuals were widely influential in Europe and America. In the British Isles, anthropologists filled their publications with careful measurements of local populations; the study of "negrescence" (hair and eye coloration), head shapes, and other physical attributes indicated to some that more than one race could be defined. In the halls of academia, the rise of an idea called "eugenics" fueled racial thinking by uniting random observations into a science-like discourse.

The traditions of race energized eugenics in the public mind, but race was also controversial in the academy. When American anthropologist Franz Boas published data that challenged the pro-race consensus, the head of the Anthropology Section of the British Association for the Advancement of Science, G. Elliot Smith, advised colleagues to "view his data and the inferences from them with the most profound suspicion."[707] In Smith's view, race helped to sustain hierarchical rankings in both the human intellect and in human culture: "Difference of race implies a real and deep-rooted distinction in physical, mental, and moral qualities; and the contrasts in the achievements of the various peoples cannot be explained away by lack of opportunities, in face of the patent fact that among the most backward races of the present day are some that first came into contact with, or even were founders of, civilisation, and were most favourably placed for acquiring culture and material supremacy." Tolkien came of age with ideas like this shaping the British academy.

Tolkien's English parents lived in South Africa when he was born in 1892, and according to his official biography, his mother objected in some fashion to "the Boer attitude" toward racial blacks, and in the Tolkien household "there was tolerance[.]"[708] No detail is available to further clarify this mysterious sliver of information, however, so it is difficult to know what kind of meaning to assign to it. Tolkien was too young to have formed his own opinions about either race or the nature of social attitudes in South Africa. But if we take this sparse statement at face value and credit it as a guiding factor in shaping the quality of Tolkien's early racial notions, we can assume that he grew up in a household that frowned on mistreatment of people on the basis of race.

It would have been highly unusual, however, for the Tolkien household to have completely eluded common English attitudes of the time toward racial blacks. Citing seven "authorities" – materials published between 1887 and 1905 – the 1911 *Encyclopedia Britannica* entry for "Negro" summarized extant anthropological literature on racial blacks. It provided an explicitly racist ranking system, asserting that "the negro would appear to stand on a lower evolutionary plane than the white man" and "[m]entally the negro is inferior to the white."[709] British youth of the 1890s grew up in a social world shaped by the widespread idea that racial blacks were intellectually inferior to whites.

Whatever attitudes shaped Tolkien's youth, his university years exposed him to intersecting currents of British racism and aloof aristocratic ethnocentrism. This was at least true of the experience of Alain Locke, an American who attended Oxford from 1907 to 1910 as the first African-American Rhodes Scholar.[710] Applying to Oxford with his scholarship in hand, five different colleges turned down his application for admission – Magdalen, Balliol, Merton, Brasenose, and Christ Church. Finally settling in at Oxford, Locke helped to found a racially diverse group called the Cosmopolitan Club, and he wrote of Oxford attitudes toward race as "indifference" colored by what one biography termed "benighted illusions about racial superiority."[711] Locke ultimately abandoned hope of obtaining a degree. He left the school feeling undecided about the exact role played by race in his difficulties but certain that it was a factor.

By the time Tolkien entered Oxford University in 1911, a new idea had taken root in British racial ideology. Eugenics advanced the idea that social institutions could be manipulated to help maintain racial purity, and the racial well-being of white people could be enforced by regulating population dynamics on the basis of race. The global eugenics movement was ideologically rooted in the pro-race intellectual currents of late 19th century Britain.[712] It was a British scientist named Francis Galton who formulated eugenics as an extension of race. Beginning in 1870 Victoria Woodhull popularized the concept in public lectures in America and Britain – she attended the First International Congress of Eugenics in London in July 1912 while Tolkien was a student at Oxford, and her participation was noted in the British press.[713] The idea of racial hygiene in Britain took inspiration from American thinking, and had deeply committed proponents in the United States and in Europe. But during the first decades of the 20th century the eugenic legislative and legal apparatus that took shape in the United States and Sweden was not replicated in Great Britain.

Eugenics in Britain grew in the public imagination in the years leading up to World War One, as noted by GK Chesterton, "It was a time when this theme was the topic of the hour..."[714] Chesterton was a notable critic of eugenics, publishing a set of scathing essays in 1922 in response to proposed eugenic legislation in Britain. As a popular Catholic intellectual and social commentator, Chesterton's thinking on eugenics might well have come to the notice of Tolkien, who later made use of other Chesterton writings in preparing "On Fairy-stories."[715] Chesterton denounced eugenics, but he believed in race, finding it useful to mention in this book a "mad negress with a hump back," "Red Indians," "Asiatic blood," and then denouncing the idea of treating the poor as a racial group "as if they were a colony of Jap or Chinese coolies."[716]

In 1914 a pressing issue of the British mercantile trade was the employment of "Chinamen and Asiatics." A speech made by a politician named Havelock Wilson on April 19 touched on one tenet of eugenics: "...one of the most degrading and abominable sights one could witness was to go down into the East End of London and see there Chinese hob-nobbing with our own women, marrying our own women, and bringing into the world mongrels of the very lowest type."[717] Another commentator, O'Connor Kessack, added his view on the "China-towns" springing up in English cities: "The areas where they live are rotten centres from which there emanates the most degrading and demoralising influences; and it would be futile to deny that many young women have been lured to destruction by the seductive suavity and treacherous lubricity of the Yellow Man."[718]

It seems likely that Tolkien encountered such attitudes throughout his youth. We can only guess as to his personal views – his notion of the "least lovely Mongol-types" in later life serves as our most direct guide as to how he might have felt about the Chinese in Britain. Another more general indicator, of course, can be teased out of his usages of eugenic and racial ideology in his legendarium. These sparse indicators may not shed much light on Tolkien's inner world, but we must consider them when we seek to understand the manifestations of race in Middle-earth.

Analysis of the social geography of Middle-earth provides evidence that Tolkien accepted certain general assumptions of early forms of British eugenics. To understand this point, it is useful to start with the original definition of eugenics that lay at the core of the later social project of mingling science and society. In 1883, Francis Galton, the British inventor of the term "eugenics" provided this definition of the term: "Eugenics is the science of improving stock, which is by no means confined to judicious mating, but which, especially in the case of man, takes cognisance of all influences that tend in however remote a degree to give the more suitable races or strains of blood a better chance of prevailing speedily over the less suitable than they otherwise would have had."[719] Several decades later, as eugenics grew in influence, Galton fine-tuned his definition of eugenics as "the study of agencies under social control that may improve or impair the racial qualities of future generation either physically or mentally."[720] Both definitions promote the idea of race as the foundation for eugenic thinking, and both turn on the idea of improvement versus impairment of humankind.

The logic of eugenics from the beginning followed two general patterns. "Positive eugenics" focused on encouraging "judicious mating" of "stock" deemed socially desirable to maintain and enhance "strains of blood." The other main trajectory was to decry a diminishment of "blood" by matings with "less suitable" stock; this gave rise to "negative eugenics," which focused on controlling the reproduction rights of those deemed unfit. Eugenics sought to set the imprint of the science of genetics on these notions, transforming an entirely subjective determination of race improvement into what sounded like quantifiable objective science. To identify these processes of logic at work in the world that followed, we should look for the existence of moral determinations about the elevation and diminishment of "blood" and "stock" and "race." That is, we should look for the existence of judgments of arbitrary superiority and inferiority of a racial genetic inheritance as a determining factor in the group character.

In the early version of his mythology Tolkien made use of "blood" as a carrier of genetic nobility.[721] This was an old idea, of course, not attributable only to eugenic thinking, but it does serve as a point of compatibility with eugenic theory. The question here is whether forms of eugenic ideology entered Tolkien's aesthetic, his vision of the character of sentient creatures, of humankind. Can we glimpse the assumptions of eugenics in his early mythological storytelling?

In that same collection of legends we find "The Tale of Tinúviel." In this story Tinúviel is the daughter of an Elf and of Gwendeling, one of the "children of the gods," also called "a fay, a daughter of the Gods" and so Tinúviel is "the most beautiful of all the maidens of the hidden Elves..."[722] Here we see that such a marriage adds an elevating luster to offspring; intermarriage of these separate kindreds serves to uplift the lesser. It is a beautifully told tale of how Tinúviel, robed in sable mist, enchanted Melko with her dancing, her singing filled with the voices of nightingales. Again, the outcome of this union of Elf and Fay does not seem particularly distinctive as a concept borrowed from eugenics, but the narrative logic is clearly compatible with eugenic thinking.

In "The Fall of Gondolin" we encounter Meglin, and "[l]ess fair was he than most of this goodly folk, swart and of none too kindly mood, so that he won small love, and whispers there were that he had Orc's blood in his veins, but I know not how this could be true."[723] This is interesting because ancestry is rumored as the cause not just of Meglin's swarthy coloration, but also of his "mood." Meglin is dark. Whatever the Elves might know of Meglin's parentage, his interior life bore an awful similarity to that of orcs, made by Melko. And in Gondolin the Elves were given to think that such darkness was heritable. This tale concerns brooding passions. Meglin's suit for Idril of the Silver Feet, a "daughter of Elfinesse," is doomed and he feels bitter envy at the birth of Eärendel to Idril and Tuor – Tuor is a man who dwells among the Elves. His son with Idril "was of greatest beauty; his skin was of a shining white..." Idril fears swart Meglin. And indeed, when swart Meglin gets captured by Orcs, it is inevitable that evil treason should enter his heart, and his betrayal leads to the fall of Gondolin. In these early writings the brooding dark passions that Tolkien associated with swartness had not yet made their way into the flesh of his goblin / orc monsters. But skin of "shining white" was already a matter of heroic legendry.

GK Chesterton wrote in 1922, "Round about the year 1913 Eugenics was turned from a fad into a fashion."[724] The topic "began to appear in big headlines in the daily Press[.]" Tolkien surely took notice – in 1913 he was a student at Oxford University. Between 1914 and 1922 he produced the foundations of his legendarium and *The Book of Lost Tales*. It is not surprising that these tales would reflect the central essences of eugenic thinking, a deferential attitude toward the linking of ancestry to disposition, intelligence, values, and the fate of whole societies. Tolkien's preferred aesthetic of skin coloration is also notable. The messaging of swart evil and white beauty came into focus for him in those days, and this color chart would never go away. Writing *The Book of Lost Tales*, Tolkien aimed at composing a mythological sense of legend and antiquity for England. And in that time English belief in racial essentialism was widespread, and when the British talked to one another in their daily newspapers, they spoke often of eugenic theory.

Tolkien's thematic formula of degradation and elevation of group character as an outcome of ancestry and intermarriage lingered in his storytelling. Writing a letter in 1954, Tolkien described intermarriage between Elves and humans as "a direct act of God" with an outcome that sounds quite eugenic: "The entering into Men of the Elven-strain is indeed represented as part of a Divine Plan for the ennoblement of the Human Race, from the beginning destined to replace the Elves."[725] Tolkien decided that divine intervention would be needed to set aside the distinction of Elvish immortality from human mortality, but divine blessings did serve to ennoble humankind on their road to inherit the earth. At minimum, we can trace the presence of this fantasy version of basic eugenic thought through all of Tolkien's Middle-earth novels.

Whatever Tolkien thought of eugenics and race, he hoped his mythology would appeal to the expectations and sensibilities of the social world he valued. Modern readers of Tolkien's legendarium keep wondering whether he was a racist. Given the nature of his preferential color chart of moral evil and moral good, there is a good reason why the issue keeps coming up. But whatever one makes of Tolkien's attitudes toward race, racial practice was real in his world, and his novels were aimed at the folk who engaged in those social practices. Understanding how eugenics shaped British society offers a lens through which we can also glimpse Tolkien's approach to matters of race.

Dimitra Fimi has characterized Tolkien's approach to cultural geography in his stratified fantasy world as "hierarchical." She also noted that during the period before World War Two "blacks were still viewed in a negative light and their intermixture with whites was regarded as disastrous both biologically and socially."[726] But even though racism is inherently hierarchical, Fimi stopped short of overtly connecting this cultural disposition with Tolkien's hierarchical world-making.

Tolkien's conceptions of race tended to reflect the tenets of the British academic establishment, which could treat the ideology of race as a matter of benign skeptical acceptance rather than in terms of unquestioning rigid allegiance. Even so, traces of pro-race ideology can be glimpsed in the lattice of Tolkien's attitudes about primitivism. The aloof British mind-set of assumed cultural superiority could accommodate the idea that racial blacks should do what they could with what they had, and the honorable task of colonial Britain was to guide the process of properly bestowing the benefits of white civilization upon less fortunate races. Such paternalism elevated the gentility of white British society by situating it upon a self-serving perception of noble generosity, while devaluing the cultural status of non-white races as primitives. This is also the essence of the hierarchy of cultural rankings that Tolkien favored in his world-making. It is a system that he carefully reproduced in the construction of his ranked fantasy races.

It can be argued that all racialism inevitably generates racist emissions, and in this sense Tolkien was no doubt just as racist as his colleagues in academic Britain. But Tolkien was not averse to embracing opinions that he saw as running counter to established thinking on race. In notes he assembled for a 1929 lecture titled "Celts and Teutons in the Early World" he acknowledged the stereotypic notion that "[a] Celt is in popular belief a queer irresponsible fellow" while "[t]he Teuton is a practical and blunt fellow... a stickler for his rights."[727] He then shared his personal view that the two putative racial groups "were indistinguishably alike" during the early Middle Ages, and he preferred to argue in favor of the unpopular notion that no basis existed for dividing the groups into two races bent on "perennial incompatibility and unceasing conflict."

This was Tolkien's position on a longstanding issue in 19th century British racial typology in which Celts and Teutons were treated as separate racial groups. At the end of the century an American scholar named William Ripley published a widely read book that further divided Europeans into three races: Teutonic, (Celtic) Alpine, and Mediterranean.[728] Tolkien's position echoed the opinion of John Rhys, an Oxford professor whose lectures he likely attended as a student. Rhys expressed the view in 1900 that the historical "mixture of races constituting each of the nations in the United Kingdom... disposes of the stock generalisations framed to flatter the German at the expense of the Celt."[729] This kind of racial discourse was common in late 19th century British historiography, but it was abandoned after 1900 in certain influential circles of academic history.[730]

Dimitra Fimi has suggested that just a few years after writing his 1929 lecture Tolkien became aware of a 1935 book on race by Alfred Haddon and Julian Huxley titled *We Europeans: A*

Survey of 'Racial' Problems. She characterized this book as designed "to show that claims about race in Germany were nothing but pseudoscience."[731] She noted that a pamphlet based on the book was published at Oxford, "aimed to popularize the scientific conviction that race is a myth, that the fallacy of the belief in an 'Aryan' or 'Nordic' race is dangerous and based on misunderstandings and totally unscientific." Fimi pointed out that Tolkien was acquainted with Julian Huxley, and that "Tolkien seems to have been aware of Huxley's anthropological work[.]" This means that as a man of his times, an academic scholar at Oxford, Tolkien's attitudes toward race can be usefully measured against the standard set by Huxley and Haddon – a standard contemporaneous with Tolkien's re-invention of orcs as "Mongol-types."

In its day, *We Europeans* was a groundbreaking book. According to historian Elazar Barkan, Alfred Haddon was contacted by publisher Jonathan Cape in 1932, and he was pressed into writing a book on race that would be, in his words, "a dispassionate strictly scientific book[.]"[732] But then Julien Huxley entered the picture and the project became a broader collaboration – they were soon joined by historian Charles Singer and anthropologist Charles Seligman. Huxley took the book into a direct critique of race as an idea, and Haddon's reputation as an established anthropologist helped to ensure that the book would not be dismissed by the status quo. According to Barkan, Haddon "represented the mainstream attitudes among English scientists" who "accepted advances in biology" but nevertheless hesitated to play a role "in the transformation of anthropological theories of race."

The introduction of *We Europeans* touched on "group sentiment" and "universal human brotherhood" and then suggests that the word "race" is a slippery term with "no exact meaning" and of uncertain origin with diverse historical usage.[733] The authors then note that "the vague idea of 'race'" is often associated with "the almost equally vague" idea of "blood." The reduction of social identity to genetic ancestry conflicts with well-established integrative processes in every society that transcend genetic kinship and employ permeable social boundaries that are only partially genetic in nature. And immigration and adoption and incorporation of new groups are well-understood social processes. "Group-sentiment" or culture, in other words, "proves to be based on something much broader but less definable than physical kinship."

This is just the introduction to *We Europeans*. What followed in its pages was a devastating confrontation of the idea that race and its arbitrary physical observations provide useful insights into human biological diversity. The issuing of this book in 1935 was a major event. The next year brought a joint meeting of the zoology and anthropology sections of the British Association to consider the whole concept of race and its politicized social usages.[734] This was not an obscure topic within the British academic world.

The issuing of *We Europeans* marked a turning point in the global production of the ideology of race. Elazar Barkan concluded that in "discrediting the scientific foundation of race" *We Europeans* represented "an important milestone in the evolution of non-racialist literature."[735] And biological anthropologist Jonathan Marks has characterized *We Europeans* as "the first full-length critique of racial science." In the years that followed, anthropologist Ashley Montagu led an effort to reconfigure race away from its status as a biological truth and toward its actual character as a cultural belief system. The momentum generated by *We Europeans* stalled in the early 1960s, but the academic rejection of race as a useful biological construction eventually achieved a convincing consensus in anthropology.[736]

A final question can be raised about one of the coauthors of *We Europeans*. As I discussed earlier, Alfred Haddon visited Pawneeland in 1906, and in Britain he was a prime promoter of anthropological awareness of the Pawnees. We do not know exactly how Tolkien learned of *Traditions of the Skidi Pawnee*; nor do we know how he first encountered *We Europeans*. We can only wonder whether Haddon played a role in bringing the Pawnee volume to Tolkien's attention, and whether this might have been a factor in Tolkien's later awareness of *We Europeans*.

The sophisticated anti-race viewpoint promoted in *We Europeans* helped to set a new standard of thinking within the British academic world by the time Tolkien sat down to begin writing *The Lord of the Rings*. We do not know for certain that he read the book, but we can surmise that he was aware of it because his ideas about Jews and race closely echoed the tenor of *We Europeans*.

Describing the integrative nature of Jewish identity, Huxley and Haddon asserted, "The result is that the Jews of different areas are not genetically equivalent, and that in each country the Jewish population overlaps with the non-Jewish in every conceivable character."[737] They went on to discredit the idea of Jews as a racial group, and then they confronted the pro-race criteria of stereotypic physical characteristics, pointing to diversity and variability and "ethnic mixture" as the actual norm.[738]

This perspective could well have influenced the tone of Tolkien's letter of July 1938 in which he responded to a German inquiry with scathing observations on "their lunatic laws" regarding Aryan ancestry.[739] Tolkien wrote that he had "many Jewish friends, and should regret giving any colour to the notion that I subscribed to the wholly pernicious and unscientific race-doctrine." This laudable attitude is difficult to square with his approach to "Mongol-types" just a few years later, but it does suggest that Tolkien was tuned in to academic debates on the nature of race as a false depiction of human diversity – especially as this academic discourse applied to the nature of Jewish identity.

Taking pains to confront Nazi racial propaganda on "the myth of Nordic superiority," Haddon and Huxley dismissed Nazi racial science as "ridiculous on scientific grounds" and having "no point of contact with biological science[.]"[740] This point would have had great appeal to Tolkien. His expressed primary concern about racial representation during the late 1930s arose from his distress over the Nazi Germany perversion of what he called the "northern spirit," of Germanic character.

In a 1941 letter Tolkien said that he was "much attracted" to the "'Germanic' ideal" in his youth.[741] And he now had "a burning private grudge... against that ruddy little ignoramus Adolf Hitler... Ruining, perverting, misapplying, and making for ever accursed, that noble northern spirit, a supreme contribution to Europe, which I have ever loved, and tried to present in its true light." In light of Tolkien's 1938 opinion of race as a "wholly pernicious and unscientific" doctrine, his embrace of what he terms a "noble northern spirit" could be taken as more cultural than racial. He objected to Hitler's perversion of this sense of northern European ethnic "spirit" into Nazi "Nordic" racialism. This aligns with Haddon and Huxley, rejecting race as a concept. In contrast to this seeming anti-race attitude, expressed in July 1938, during the several years that followed Tolkien made use of the racial taxonomy of "Mongol-types." To the extent that this usage relied upon reproducing a demeaning racial stereotype, it can be fairly viewed as evidence of a double-standard in his attitudes.

It is reasonable to evaluate what we know of Tolkien's thinking on race against the academic standards of his day. He rejected the racial basis for anti-Semitism; he pondered the racial division of Celtic versus Teutonic; and he gave thought to Nazi Germany. It seems evident that Tolkien's known perspective on race pertained most directly to elements that related to his Eurocentric sense of mission.

Christine Chism has argued that Tolkien "came to scrutinize his own world-creating enterprise because he had before him a parallel spectacle of world-creation gone wrong" in the National Socialist "cannibalization of medieval narratives and histories into pseudo-historical racialist mythologies."[742] In terms of race, Chism's viewpoint has a narrow focus that completely ignores Tolkien's Mongol-type orcs. But those orcs were born in the midst of World War Two, and as Chism noted, this was a period in his writing when the context of his time most influenced his creative choices: "Tolkien explicitly and persistently links the creation of fantastic and mythological worlds to the temptations of power, and never more so than during the war." Guided by her selective field of view, Chism favored the view that Tolkien was anti-race – she asserted that in one lecture "...Tolkien furiously dismantles the whole mythology of racialism..."[743]

Chism's idea that Tolkien favored dismantling "the whole mythology of racialism," is nevertheless interesting because it would be instructive if we were to measure this idealized anti-race Tolkien against the Tolkien who made the creative choice to racialize his orcs. In other words, to the extent that we can observe Tolkien reflecting the anti-race tenets of his peers, we can also identify a convenient contemporary standard by which to assess Tolkien the Mongol-typologist.

The fundamental problem with Chism's interpretation is that it cannot be reconciled to Tolkien's embrace of Mongol-types. He was not bent on dismantling race. It is more arguable that he merely conformed to British academic mainstream skepticism toward racial beliefs, but he also accepted the racial thinking that pervaded the wider social world. During the years when Tolkien was finishing *The Lord of the Rings* and making it ready for publication, race was a lively topic within the British eugenic community, with a spectrum of attitudes marked by challenges to race and eugenic racism, versus pronouncements favoring race-based anti-miscegenation.[744] Tolkien's pre-WW2 position invoked eugenics with its focus on breeding and purity of blood. But as the world plunged into war he followed mainstream academia in hesitating to rely on eugenic logic to indulge explicit racism.

As I pointed out earlier, in 1958 Tolkien contextualized his vision of orkish nature in terms of a racial narrative. It was in the course of correcting a film treatment that misconstrued his orcs that Tolkien advanced his racial logic: "The Orcs are definitely stated to be corruptions of the 'human' form seen in Elves and Men. They are (or were) squat, broad, flat-nosed, sallow-skinned, with wide mouths and slant eyes: in fact degraded and repulsive versions of the (to Europeans) least lovely Mongol-types."[745]

It is marginally possible that Tolkien simply meant to reference Mongols – this is what Michael Martinez concluded in his analysis of the comment, though he also acknowledged that this statement "may be the only clear evidence of racism in Tolkien's fiction – in that he uses a racist stereotype for one of his fantasy races."[746] But Dimitra Fimi came to a different view in her 2010 study, deciding that Tolkien "seems to reflect popular ideas of the traditional hierarchy of the three extreme human racial types: the Caucasoid, the Mongoloid and the Negroid."[747] Fimi also compared Tolkien's comment on "Mongol-types" to the late 19th century idea that Down's syndrome victims represented a regression to "Mongolian idiots." She noted that John Langdon Down's 1862 description of the condition contains some parallels to Tolkien's description of orcs: "The face is flat and broad... The eyes are obliquely placed... The lips are large and thick..." But these are parallels because both descriptions were derived from the same racial stereotype. Other Tolkien scholars have also seen the reproduction of stereotypic racial Asian features in his "half-orcs." This seems to have been the position reached by Sandra Straubhaar in her study of Tolkien and miscegenation – she mounted a defense of Tolkien's intentions, but acknowledged that his slant-eyed orcs represented a problem: "Tolkien seems to have exhibited a kind of racism perhaps not unremarkable in a mid-twentieth-century Western man[.]"[748]

Tolkien's 1958 description of "squat, broad, flat-nosed, sallow-skinned, with wide mouths and slant eyes" closely followed the 1911 *Encyclopedia Britannica* description for "Mongolic or Yellow Man": "His physical characteristics are a short squat body, a yellowish-brown or coppery complexion, hair lank, straight and black, flat small nose, broad skull, usually without prominent brow-ridges, and black oblique eyes."[749] This British portrayal of racial typology treated humankind as divisible into three groups: "Caucasic or White Man," "Mongolic or Yellow Man," and "Negroid or Black Man." A long listing of Mongolic folk accompanied the "Yellow division of mankind," including people as diverse as Finns, Chinese, Japanese, and "American races." No direct evidence exists to show that Tolkien ever read this entry in *Encyclopedia Britannica*, but we do know that Tolkien consulted the entry for "fairy" in some edition of that encyclopedia while researching "On Fairy-stories" circa 1938-1943.[750]

In August 1938 Tolkien introduced us to a character who appeared in company with a friend at Bree – they are described together as "not a well-favoured pair."[751] Sometime in late 1938 or early 1939 during the "Third Phase" of the writing of *The Fellowship of the Ring*, Tolkien took this pair and transformed one into a nameless character described now for the first time as "the squint-eyed southerner" – a description altered from "dark-eyed."[752] In Tolkien's final published version his squint-eyed character became "a squint-eyed ill-favoured fellow" and "the squint-eyed southerner" and "Bill Ferny's squint-eyed companion" who featured "a sallow face with sly, slanting eyes[.]" This character turned out eventually to be a man with orc ancestry, a "half-orc."

In my Oxford dictionary when the term sallow is applied to a person it means "having an unhealthy yellow or pale brown colour." And in John Rhys's collection of Welsh folklore, which was known to Tolkien, Welsh fairy folk were sometimes described as having "sallow" or "swarthy" flesh.[753] The choice of skin-color was not an incidental random detail for Tolkien. But it was not meant to indicate a sign of ill-health. It may have been incorporated into his orcs as faint evocation of Welsh fairytale traditions, but that was not its primary function.

Christopher Tolkien wrote that he was "not sure" what his father "meant to convey by the '*squint-eyed* Southerner' at Bree[.]"[754] Responding to the suggestion that it might refer to "narrow eyes" or "half-closed" eyes, he mentioned a "muscular disorder that causes the eye to look obliquely[.]" Following this suggestion, Wayne Hammond and Christina Scull pointed out that the term "squint" in England "denotes a disorder of the eye." An intention to denote a muscular disorder for orcs and half-orcs seems less likely than a pointed reference to established language pertaining to the Mongolic racial category, particularly since

Tolkien's own citation of "Mongol-types" was not at all applicable to a physical disability of the eye. It is also curious that, in seeking an explanation for Tolkien's use of "squint-eyed," Christopher Tolkien and Hammond and Scull made no mention of Tolkien's June 1958 letter in which he set forth his intended representation of orcs as "Mongol-types" with "slant eyes."

The term "squint-eyed" is most reasonably interpreted as Tolkien's modification of the English term "squinny-eyed." This term can be found in a fairytale published by Joseph Jacobs called "Fairy Ointment."[755] The story concerned a "strange, squinny-eyed little ugly old fellow" who turns out to be a pixie whose children were "flat-nosed imps with pointed ears." Given that this description echoes Tolkien's "flat-nosed" orcs, it is possible that Tolkien drew on this source for inspiration. But this is the only resemblance, and it is clear that Tolkien did not mean for his orcs to be taken as a reference to Jacobs' unlovely fairytale imps. He explicitly meant for his orcs to echo unlovely "Mongol-types."

By the time Tolkien entered Oxford, the idea of slanted eyes as a racial signifier was a universal convention of racial thinking in Britain and it also served as an idiomatic term of contempt. In Skeat and Britten's 1879 glossary we find the term "squinny" defined as "a contemptible fellow"; this is followed by "squinny-eyed" which is defined as "cross-eyed."[756] In an 1885 publication John Beddoe made mention of "the oblique or Chinese eye" as a marker of the "Mongoloid race" in England.[757] Joseph Wright's 1905 dictionary provided a detailed discussion of the dialectical usage of "squinny" and "squinny-eyed."[758] Here squinny appeared as "a contemptible fellow" and as a slender, undersized, shriveled physical condition. But most significantly, Wright's "squinny-eyed" referred either to the act of squinting or to "a person whose eyes are habitually half-closed" as illustrated by an 1885 quote: "We saw the queer Chineese... With little squinney eyes." A 1908 book affirmed an established association in British thinking between the Chinese and eye-shape, mentioning "the oblique or Chinese eye, with its almond-shaped opening and thick upper eyelid[.]"[759] This book was published under the imprint "Oxford at the Clarendon Press," meaning it was a scholarly book according to the highest standards of Oxford University.

Since Tolkien acknowledged that he had a "degraded" version of "Mongol-types" in mind when he designed his orcs for *The Lord of the Rings*, the terms "squint-eyed" and "sallow" are properly read in this context. And with this context in mind, the derivation of "squint-eyed" from "squinny-eyed" and "squinny" comes into focus, particularly given that Tolkien's description pertains to a contemptible fellow in *The Fellowship of the Ring*, exactly as a squinny is defined by Wright and by Skeat and Britten. And since there is an obvious alignment of Tolkien's "Mongol-types" with "slant eyes" and "the oblique or Chinese eye" and Wright's "queer Chineese" with their "little squinney eyes," it can be deemed likely that Tolkien drew his "squint-eyed" from Wright's "squinny-eyed." This adds momentum to the conclusion that he meant to reference the British racial terminology of "Mongolic or Yellow Man" in his construction of orcs. He underscored the racial connotations of this context when he added "sallow" to the mix. We can also guess that this imagery came to hand from the legacy of British attitudes that occasionally appeared in print, as in the 1914 commentary on the Chinese of East End London, where one could observe "Chinese hob-nobbing with our own women, marrying our own women, and bringing into the world mongrels of the very lowest type."[760]

The appearance at Bree of Tolkien's "squint-eyed southerner" reveals that his decision to recast his orcs as "Mongol-types" occurred in late 1938 or early 1939. In October 1938 Tolkien wrote that his new hobbit book was "more 'adult'" because "[t]he darkness of the present days has had some effect on it."[761] This is a reference to the growing global war, fueled by an alliance in 1937 among Germany, Italy, and Japan. Within a few months after noting this "darkness of the present days" Tolkien invented his "squint-eyed southerner." Through this character, Tolkien took his existing goblins / orcs and reconfigured them via his notion of the "least lovely Mongol-types," infusing them with "degraded and repulsive" aspects derived from an Asian racial stereotype.

Orcs did not appear in the drafting of *The Fellowship of the Ring* until after August 1940, when Tolkien first set forth the descent of the Fellowship into Moria. When they enter the story, their "Mongol-type" roots seem little in evidence, and instead the color black is constantly referenced. These first orcs enter the narrative with "a great rolling boom" and the blast of "a great horn" and "harsh cries" and hurrying feet.[762] The booming continues with "a rush of hoarse laughter[.]" Gandalf observes: "There are goblins: very many of them... Evil they look and large: black Orcs." These "black Orcs" eventually end up as "black Uruks of Mordor."[763] The orcs attack and one is described in some detail: "...a huge orc-chief, almost man-high, clad in black mail from head to foot, leaped through the door. **** His eyes were like coals of fire. He wielded a great spear. *** Then leaping with the speed of a snake he charged..."[764] A little later Frodo sees "the swarming black figures of many orcs" who "brandished spears and scimitars which shone red as blood." A second draft of this chapter has Gandalf's description of the orcs "talking their horrible secret language, which I never knew more than a word or two of."[765]

Aside from the "swarming" and the reference to an incomprehensible "secret language" these early renderings do not evoke Asian racial stereotypes. Even though Tolkien indicated some years later that his orcs had something to do with an Asian stereotype, he colorized these orcs of Moria as black, perhaps as a means of adding emphasis to an evil inner moral orientation – there are no decent black sentient creatures in Tolkien's Middle-earth, capable of real rectitude and truly humane nuance. These first black orcs do not seem Asian in any sense; nor do they seem particularly African. Tolkien instead seemed bent on portraying monstrous fantasy creatures warped by evil origin; fearful enemies fit only for heroic monster-slayers. But the final version of this incident featured a more clearly racialized orc. At some point after writing the early drafts – perhaps after about mid-1942 – Tolkien edited his description of the "huge orc-chieftain" to make him more racial: "His broad flat face was swart, his eyes were like coals, and his tongue was red..."

Sometime in 1941 Tolkien returned to his orcs to set down his first account of Frodo taken prisoner at Minas Morgul.[766] Gollum appeared, and "behind him came the black orcs[.]" One orc spoke with relish at the prospect of "Blood on blade and fire on hill, smoke in sky and tears on earth." Later Sam killed an orc wearing "black scale-like mail" and a "black iron cap" too large for Sam since "orcs have large heads for their size[.]" The size and shape of orc skulls did not much interest Tolkien, but anthropology of the 19th century was much concerned with measuring heads and skulls and drawing from them vast conclusions on things racial. The description of orc character and head-size provide very slight hints of what was in Tolkien's mind at this stage, but seem to indicate some kind of racial contouring was at hand with his orcs.

These circumstances are mildly reminiscent of certain depictions by Thomas Blundeville, an Englishman of the late 16th century who sought to portray geographic patterns of global human diversity. Historian Ivan Hannaford outlines Blundeville's view of the Chinese as having "broad faces, little eyes, flat noses, little beards" while the southernmost Africans "do not differ much from Oriental Indians" and "black Moors" are "yellowish in color."[767] Tolkien's treatment of his orcs in 1940 could echo the way Blundeville's pre-racial depiction of humankind reflected mixed skin coloration. Given Tolkien's knowledge of medieval literature, he probably knew of Blundeville, but the parallels are not sharp.

Another explanation can be identified with a higher level of certainty. In December 2014 scholar Simon Cook posted a fascinating theory on the origins of hobbits, arguing that Tolkien found them in the writings of John Rhys.[768] Tolkien might have taken coursework from Rhys at Oxford in 1914-1915, and he is known to have owned at least one book by Rhys – he also made use of Rhys's work for research in 1929-1930 on the name "Nodens."[769] Cook suggested that Tolkien studied Rhys's thinking on the pre-Celtic residents of Britain and when he wrote

The Hobbit, he decided to conceive "of ancient England as the green and pleasant Shire of the Hobbits" with reference to Rhys's ideas about pre-Celtic antiquity. Cook argued that "Hobbits are (a somewhat tongue-in-cheek) representation of the little people that back in 1900 Rhys had identified as Britain's first farmers." Cook cited a paper published in 1900 by Rhys.[770] We are encouraged to conclude that Tolkien knew of this 1900 publication and read it closely at some point, probably in 1930.

It is indeed likely that Tolkien read this 1900 paper or a 1901 book on Celtic mythology published by Rhys (or both), and that he did make use of some of the ideas he found there. But this is most arguable in his 1939 construction of Tom Bombadil and Bree in *The Fellowship of the Ring*. And given the arguable likelihood that he read the 1900 paper, an interesting set of reports appear in the same publication – reports that can account for Tolkien's black-skinned Mongol-type orcs in 1940. Just a few pages beyond the conclusion of Rhys' 1900 essay we find two reports associated with the Cambridge Exploring Expedition to the Malay Provinces of Lower Siam, also known as the Skeat Expedition. Tolkien may have sought the 1900 report to study the Rhys essay, and if so, his eye would have been drawn to the Skeat Expedition papers – he had won the Skeat Prize as a student in 1914, and he knew of Walter Skeat's stature in British folklore.[771]

A short report by WLH Duckworth set out some "Anthropological Observations" of "a skeleton of a native of the Pangan tribe[.]"[772] This was a skeleton from the Malay Peninsula – and so a racial Asian – but the "skull presents a combination of features commonly found in the skulls of negroes with those which characterise the crania of infants, the whole constituting evidence of the lowly physical type of the individual." Here was "a race of Malayan aborigines hitherto little investigated" and "the most interesting point to notice is the small average stature of the Pangans (about 5 feet for adult men)." The skeleton showed "signs of widespread disease" not further specified, but deemed "congenital." The skeleton was examined for resemblances to apes but "they present comparatively few anatomical features which can be claimed as evidence of an approximation to the ape." A second report by Duckworth contained observations on nine skulls taken from Rotuma, an island north of Fiji.[773] The skulls seemed to represent a fusion of three distinct groups: "These are in the first place a variety of the form of cranium usually found among Polynesian natives, though possessing certain characteristics which may almost be described as Mongolian; and in the second place the type of cranium characteristic of Melanesians[.]" Here were two 1900 reports from southeastern Asia and nearby Polynesia that brought together four populations listed as "negroes," "Melanesians," "Mongolian," and "Polynesian," with one repulsively "diseased" and with mention of a passing comment on resemblances to "the ape."

Designing new orcs for his hobbit sequel, Tolkien offered little physical description in these initial scenes. And it is a mystery why he first chose to colorize them as "black Orcs" if he had in mind "degraded and repulsive versions of the... least lovely Mongol-types" – as he asserted in his 1958 letter to Forrest Ackerman.[774] Why would orcs derived from an Asian racial stereotype display black skin? But if Tolkien in 1939 glanced at the Skeat Expedition reports on human remains from the Malay Peninsula and Rotuma, he could have readily framed a model for his 1940-1941 "black Orcs" from just these two brief reports. It is thus possible to see his color-choice as logically derived from anthropological sources, rather than as a wholly arbitrary decision.

In January 1942 Tolkien's interest in the Asian theater of World War Two became explicitly evident in notes he scribbled on the back of an examination sheet: "Chinese bombers" and "Muar River" and "Japanese attack in Malaya[.]"[775] Christopher Tolkien has dated these notes to "the winter of 1941-2" – the Japanese invasion of Malaya began on December 8, 1941, and the Muar River battles in Malaya took place in mid-January 1942, and British, Australian, and British Indian military forces suffered heavy casualties.[776] With these sparse notes in hand, we know that Tolkien in early 1942 was giving some kind of thought to the

Chinese, the Japanese, and to Malaya in the context of the now full-blown World War.

Tolkien's doodled references to the Asian theater of World War Two came as he sat down once again to insert orcs into his tale, composing notes on the material that became "The Departure of Boromir." In Christopher Tolkien's presentation of this material, the description of orcs is not detailed. Tolkien wrote now of "several orcs of large stature armed with short swords, not the curved scimitars usual with goblins, and with great bows greater than their custom." Here he distinguished his orcs through physical typology, but little detail is present. Along with this weaponry we glimpse the orkish frame of mind: "...they slash and hack and beat down growing things as they pass, as if the breaking of things delighted them."[777] The timing of these notes on the war in Malaya and the timing of Tolkien's second insertion of orcs into *The Lord of the Rings* is clear. It is also evident that Tolkien did not drop Japanese soldiers intact into Middle-earth, but instead had something more subtle in mind. The events in Malaya came as a sobering defeat for the British. And here we find Tolkien's orcs inflicting a notable defeat upon the Fellowship, killing the only member of the nine who is truly slain in the book.

Not long after this, Tolkien prepared "The Uruk-hai," launching into the making of what he now termed "great orcs." Christopher Tolkien's presentation of the drafting of this chapter is minimal, noting that "this chapter was achieved with far greater facility than any previous part of the story..."[778] In the final published text for this chapter, we encounter Orcs with "hideous faces" whose speech "sounded at all times full of hate and anger..." We soon meet three different kinds of orcs: a band of "long-armed crook-legged Orcs" from Mordor, "a grim dark band... of large, swart, slant-eyed Orcs" from Isengard, and "smaller goblins" from Moria. Pippin sees "a large black orc" and "a short crook-legged creature, very broad and with long arms that hung almost to the ground." The latter, Grishnákh of Mordor, uses an interesting insult for Uglúk, the "large black orc": "'Ape!' he snarled fiercely." These orcs refer to Rohirrim as

"Whiteskins" and this is preceded by a reference to "Saruman the Wise, the White Hand: the Hand that gives us man's-flesh to eat."

Tolkien had race on his mind; these horrible orcs make use of race. They speak in harsh tones with much derision of each other and everyone else in Middle-earth. They don't just believe in race; they embody race. And we now see a full flowering of racialized orcs in all their Mongol-type degraded repulsive glory. They are also envisioned for the first time as physically diverse, divisible into communities that differ in physical type. To describe these new orcs Tolkien made use of the terms black, ape, slant-eyed, and swart – and this clustering of terms hints at the 1900 Skeat Expedition negroes / apes, Mongolians, and Polynesians. This conjoining of Middle-earth and the Malay Peninsula occurred only a few months beyond Tolkien's brief contemporary scribbles: "Muar River" and "Japanese attack in Malaya" – scribbles that appear on the reverse of Tolkien's notes on orcs for "The Departure of Boromir."[779]

The Skeat Expedition notes on the Malay Peninsula in *Report of the Seventieth Meeting of the British Association for the Advancement of Science* are not detailed, and we do not have any clear indication that Tolkien looked more closely at any additional materials, such as Walter Skeat's ethnography, *Malay Magic*.[780] But we do know that Tolkien looked at *Encyclopedia Britannica* in 1938-1943, and the 1911 edition contained entries on the Malay. One entry mentioned "there are three races which have had their home in the Malay Peninsula. These are Semang or Pangan, the Sakai or Jakun, and the Malay."[781] The Pangan were here characterized as "Negritos – a small, very dark people, with features of the negroid type..." This diversity of "type" could have inspired Tolkien to devise a new portrayal of orcs with varying physical aspects, including black skin tone. The "two or three quite different tribes" of orcs that we encounter in *The Two Towers* certainly do echo the "three races" of the Malay Peninsula.[782]

This parallel between Tolkien's orcs and the Malays is further amplified by the next entry in the 1911 *Encyclopedia Britannica*. There we find an entry pondering past thinking about the Malay as "an offspring of the Mongol type" and then describing them "as famous almost exclusively for their piratical expeditions" and who "used to be described as the most cruel and treacherous people in the world, and they certainly are callous of the pain suffered by others, and regard any strategy of which their enemies are the victims with open admiration."[783] Tolkien had no interest in cutting Malay pirates out of the encyclopedia and pasting them into his Middle-earth orcs, so we should not look too much for exactly corresponding elements. But here I believe that we can indeed glimpse the meaning of Tolkien's intended use of the term "Mongol-types" – it references racial "Mongolic" terminology that we find in *Encyclopedia Britannica*, and it directly resonates with the description of the "piratical" Malay as "offspring of the Mongol type."

Scientific literature was not the only place where British readers could encounter Malay pirates. In a popular 1863 "sensation novel," *Hard Cash*, Charles Reade included chapters telling the tale of a British vessel sailing "among the Bornese and Malay islands" and there spying an oncoming ship. One character announces, "I think he is a Malay pirate[.]" In the ensuing battle we meet "the pirate's wild crew of yellow Malays, black chinless Papuans, and bronzed Portuguese..." And later we again encounter "the Papuans and Sooloos, their black faces livid and blue with horror... the yellow Malays and brown Portuguese..." Tolkien's assembly of diverse pirate-like orcs evokes this colorful mixture of pirates, and while we have no reason to think that he ever read *Hard Cash*, we do know of his youthful interest in pirates via *Treasure Island* and *Peter Pan*. One point is clear enough. Sometime in 1944 Tolkien had two orcs in *The Two Towers* make a plan to "slip off and set up somewhere... with a few trusty lads... where there's good loot nice and handy..."[784] The real world roots of these pirate orcs sail into focus when we align them with the British stereotype of piratical Malays – an alignment that is compatible with Tolkien's 1958 comment on orcs as "Mongol-types."

Very soon after producing his newly expanded portrayal of racialized orc folk in *The Two Towers*, a new group of squint-eyed sallow Mongol-types came into focus. When Tolkien turned his hand to describing "half-orcs" like Bill Ferny's friend, the squint-eyed southerner, the inspiration of a racial Asian stereotypic characterization became at last fully manifest in Middle-earth. In "Flotsam and Jetsam," written sometime during the late summer or fall of 1942, Tolkien had Merry offer this comment on the folk of Isengard: "...there were some others that were horrible: man-high, but with goblin-faces, sallow, leering, squint-eyed. Do you know, they reminded me at once of the Southerner at Bree; only he was not so obviously orc-like as most of these were." Aragorn agrees, mentioning "half-orcs" at Helm's Deep and terming them "evil folk."[785] Tolkien's squint-eyed southerner was only briefly mentioned when he first appeared in 1939. That is probably when Tolkien first envisioned this new class of creatures, but it wasn't until this writing in 1942 that he turned his hand to sketching in more details of his half-orcs, and the portrayal is clearly drawn from traditional racial Asian typology.[786]

Tolkien's reconfiguration of goblins into "Mongol-types" was convenient because it merely involved the addition of detail; but these details redefined the substance of his orcs. From the beginning Tolkien envisioned his goblin / orc beasts as sentient folkloric creatures, human-like but abjectly murderous. His construction of orcs explicitly intended the production of corrupted creatures, warped by their makers into monstrous soldier-beasts. These were not a variety of human. But now his Mongol-type orcs had a whole new aspect, birthed in the midst of World War Two from Tolkien's conception of the traditions of racial Asian typology. It is plainly arguable that he found stereotypic Malay imagery a useful place to harvest details that could enhance his monsters. Discussing his orcs as "folk made bad" in a letter written in 1944, Tolkien opined that "it must be admitted that there are human creatures that seem irredeemable short of a special miracle, and that there are probably abnormally many of such creatures in Deutschland and Nippon..."[787] Damning the World War Two enemies of Britain, Tolkien nevertheless granted the human diversity of Germans and

Japanese. But in his Middle-earth, even a casual survey of the folk colorized by Germanic elements reveals that same carefully sculptured moral texturing, and there is no similar moral diversity when it comes to his representation of "Mongol-types." In short, the project of bringing these Mongol-types into his legendarium establishes a useful contrast to Tolkien's carefully construed Germanic nuance.

Deciding how best to portray his half-orcs, it is evident that Tolkien made use of Joseph Wright's squinny-eyed contemptible fellow, a "queer Chineese" with "little squinney eyes." He drew from the kind of attitude that we find in the 1914 comments of Havelock Wilson, who noted with horror that one could visit the "East End of London and see there Chinese hobnobbing with our own women, marrying our own women, and bringing into the world mongrels of the very lowest type."[788] Inventing a class of these contemptible fellows and inserting them into *The Lord of the Rings*, Tolkien deliberately infused his half-orcs with ingredients drawn from the "least lovely Mongol-types," evocative of the most irredeemable creatures of WW2 Nippon. He used racial taxonomic language like that found in the *Encyclopedia Britannica* entry for "Mongolic or Yellow Man," borrowing "a short squat body, a yellowish-brown or coppery complexion... flat small nose... and black oblique eyes." These Mongol-types were bent on the pleasures of cruelty, like Malay pirates.

It can be argued that Tolkien's treatment of orcs only obliquely reflects his personal views on race, given that these creatures are meant to be non-human monsters. His characterization of orcs and goblins may not provide an ideal lens through which to discern his attitudes, but the important issue at hand is to consider Tolkien's use of race and the legacies of this usage in our communal dialogue on the significance of race in our lives. To trace the materialization of racial ideology in Tolkien's legendarium, I do not think it is particularly helpful to stay too focused on his more general occasional use of the term in describing his classes of folkloric creatures in Middle-earth. We must instead trace his own attitudes toward race in his social world, and assess how those attitudes shaped his storytelling.

During the same period (1942) when Tolkien implemented his vision of half-orcs as humans degraded with Mongol-type orkish ancestry, he also constructed the culture of Rohan from aspects of Anglo-Saxon culture. Comparing the moral nuance of his half-orcs and his Rohirrim, we find a broad spectrum of moral behavior in Rohan with at least one Anglo-Saxon-type man of Rohan who is morally degenerate. In contrast, no orcs, goblins, or half-orcs transcend their circumstances and display any serious depth of decency or complexity of rectitude. All are corrupt. Robert Tally gives weight to what he calls the "simple humanity" that Tolkien occasionally bestows upon his orcs, expressing "moral valuations" that reveal "quite human qualities."[789] But we are not really encouraged to find in any of Tolkien's orcs truly redeeming moral diversity – there are no orkish paragons of righteous virtue.

Efforts to discern the finer sensibilities of orcs as sentient creatures capable of limited moral character must necessarily set aside Tolkien's intentions. Writing to son Christopher in August 1944, Tolkien discussed allegory and the gradation between good and bad moral extremes, and then illustrated his point: "In real... life men are on both sides: which means a motley alliance of orcs, beasts, demons, plain naturally honest men, and angels."[790] He further noted, "But it does make some difference who are your captains and whether they are orc-like per se!" In other words, during the period when he was racializing his orcs Tolkien did not see them as morally nuanced. They instead served as exemplars of evil, degraded and unlovely always. And the plain fact that they are Mongol-types deserves contemplation when we ponder what Tolkien intended with his insertion of racial messaging into Middle-earth.

If we regard Tolkien as "a man of his times" then we must understand those times, and part of that understanding includes grasping the power of race to define social discourse in Britain. Clare Hanson's study of British eugenics suggests that the movement did succeed in reshaping British society during the

1930s and 1940s.[791] The social architecture of post-war Britain arose in part from a planning document called the Beveridge Report, authored by William Beveridge, a life-long supporter of the British Eugenics Society. In February 1943 – just months after Tolkien ensconced his half-orc Mongol-types in Middle-earth – Beveridge addressed the Eugenics Society at their annual meeting, observing that the British lower-classes were outbreeding the middle-class and upper-class.[792] According to Hanson, "the movement rapidly became entwined with the aims of an upwardly mobile middle-class."

In addition, a reformation of British eugenic thought occurred in response to the professionalizing of genetic science of the time, influenced in part by the thinking of Julian Huxley and JBS Haldane. John Haldane was a geneticist who wrote a popular column on science for the *Daily Worker*, a newspaper published by the British Communist Party, and Tolkien was aware of this newspaper, decrying it as sold "in the streets unmolested."[793] No direct evidence exists to show that Tolkien ever expressed overt sympathy for the eugenic end of the pro-race spectrum. But he was acquainted with Huxley and with Naomi Mitchison, who was a prominent member of the Eugenics Society and the sister of JBS Haldane.[794] A short biographical sketch on Mitchison in Scull and Hammond's guide to Tolkien's life does not mention her association with eugenics – it seems to indicate that the two writers were not particularly close friends.[795] But this acquaintance does support the presumption that Tolkien had plenty of opportunity to encounter the tenets of eugenic thinking in Britain during the 1940s.

This is also indicated by a comment he made in a draft letter written sometime in 1943. Talking about the need for a religious moral basis for regulating sexual behavior, Tolkien wrote, "From the biological-sociological point of view I gather (from Huxley and others) that monogamy is probably highly beneficial to a community."[796] Even though the source of this "biological-sociological point of view" isn't clear, this is certainly a reference to Julian Huxley, a zoologist and eugenicist who had a regular presence on the BBC during the early 1940s. Huxley wrote in 1916, "Do not think me fantastic if I say that, even in birds, I believe that the finest emotions and most comfortable happiness are, as in man, associated with that form of monogamy in which male and female bear equal parts."[797] He also subscribed to the idea that polygamy in "primitive societies" in "tribal times" eventually gave way to monogamy in societies shaped by "unrestricted commercialism."[798] It isn't clear exactly what Tolkien knew of Huxley and how this influenced his own thinking, but some kind of influence did occur.

During the 1930s and 1940s Huxley and Haldane were prominent figures in setting the tone for genetic science and British eugenics – a tone that rejected the racism of eugenic rhetoric.[799] Both men seemed to believe that genetic inheritance might well play a role in shaping the nature of human intelligence, perhaps even with some kind of quasi-racial component. But they challenged the racial basis of eugenics, and they rejected Nazi anti-Semitic racism just as Tolkien did. As I have already mentioned, in 1935 Huxley was a coauthor with anthropologist Alfred Cort Haddon of *We Europeans: A Survey of 'Racial' Problems*. This book asserted that the idea of race was problematic as a useful way to characterize human biological diversity – a challenge that eventually became an established tenet of both genetic science and anthropology during the late 20th century. Their uses of racial terminology are often qualified by notations on the problems of racial taxonomy.

The emphasis placed by Nazi Germany on using deadly forms of genetic engineering to benefit the white race showed that eugenics could empower racism, and racism could empower eugenics. But some British eugenicists wondered whether eugenics could transcend race. Huxley and Haldane helped to shift thinking about the relationship of genetics and the betterment of humankind away from race. The basic contention of what can be termed eugenic thinking in Britain became focused on the idea that the essences of humankind could be manipulated through social engineering aimed at economically defined social strata, and the interfacing of genetics and social systems could be beneficial to the communal long-term prospects of British society and humanity at large. Minimizing race in the logic of eugenics, British eugenics decided that the science of genetics could still play a role in the improvement of national social environments and global humanity. The problem of defining "improvement" would always plague this intersection of science and society, but British efforts to conjoin them persisted in the intellectual world that followed the fall of Nazi Germany.

There is no reason to suspect that Naomi Mitchison's involvement with eugenics played any role in orienting Tolkien's relationship with her, or that Julian Huxley's association with eugenics was particularly attractive to Tolkien. But we should assume that Tolkien was familiar with the concept of eugenics. More generally, we should assume that his engagement with race reflected some of the same complexity of racial thinking that surrounded him in British society. His sparse statements that explicitly mention race are meaningfully amplified by the evidence of race in his writings, and these points of consideration should be interpreted in the social context of his day. Taken together, we can see that both race and eugenics had an influence on the fantasy social formulations that engaged Tolkien's imagination.

Tolkien's various comments on race curiously echo his conflicting statements on religion. He made a point of asserting that he downplayed religion in the early writing of *The Lord of the Rings* and perhaps more generally in his Middle-earth legendarium. But he also acknowledged that religion was nevertheless significant. He didn't overtly set Christian theology in his mythology, but scholarship on Tolkien and Christianity is prolific, treating Middle-earth as rich with covert subject-matter. Taking into consideration Tolkien's statements about disliking race, my research here reveals that it is nevertheless useful to assume that the real world conventions of race did help to contour the fantasy social geography of Middle-earth.

This history of the construction of orcs unfolded to shape the foreground of Middle-earth by the time Tolkien returned to the backdrop of *The Silmarillion* during the 1950s. In the course of reconstituting his old goblin / orcs into new ones for *The Lord of the Rings*, he pondered whether to drop the idea that Morgoth made them from stone. Perhaps they had instead been corrupted somehow. Now in the wake of that insight he invented a different origin for his orcs. He reframed them as Elves tormented by Melkor and "corrupted" into "the hideous race of the Orkor..."[800] Then he wondered whether they might have been made from both Men and Elves, and this led to preparation of an interesting set of manuscripts composed between 1955 and 1960.[801] In these papers Tolkien experimented with making orcs corruptions of "the least of the Maiar' who became "more and more earthbound[.]" Perhaps they were beasts "of humanized shape" with maybe "an Elvish strain[.]" These notes do not indicate that Tolkien intended to continue formulating his orcs out of the traditions of race. He had drawn useful details from his notions of degraded "Mongol-types" for *The Lord of the Rings*, but by the end of the 1950s he seemed uninterested in continuing to draw from racial stereotyping.

Soon after Tolkien wrote his 1958 note on orcs as "degraded and repulsive versions of the (to Europeans) least lovely Mongol-types," he prepared another meditation on these creatures, dating to circa 1959-1960.[802] He wrote that Maiar who served as "servants of Melkor" had the power of "mocking and degrading the very forms of the Children."[803] Rumor had it that Melkor "captured and perverted" Men in early times. Orcs were "pitiless" and full of "cruelty" and "wickedness" and "they took pleasure in their deeds" and in the "doing of evil deeds... for their own sport[.]" Even after the defeat of Morgoth the orcs continued with "their business of ravaging and plundering[.]" Certain Maiar could take orkish form to captain the orcs. And "Men could... be reduced almost to the Orc-level... and then they would or could be made to mate with Orcs, producing new breeds, often larger and more cunning." Here Tolkien cited Saruman and "his wickedest deed: the interbreeding of Orcs and Men, producing both Men-Orcs large and cunning, and Orc-men treacherous and vile." Tolkien decided that it would be a "teaching of the Wise" that Men and Elves should show mercy to those few orcs who might surrender. Finally, Sauron had great success in mastering the orcs despite the "difficulties" presented by the "diversity of the Orcs in breed and language" and their "petty realms[.]"

Another manuscript that seems to be more clearly dated to circa 1958 painted the Orkor as a mystery to the Elves, who deemed them degraded Elves: "...Avari, maybe, that had become evil and savage in the wild."[804] In the text that followed these orcs regularly do battle with Elves, but none surrender and we find no mention of Elves showing these orcs any mercy.[805] Most notably, beyond their degenerate nature, these orcs lacked any distinguishing quality linking them to Tolkien's racialized orcs of *The Lord of the Rings* – they seem more clearly descended from his old-fashioned pre-Mongoloid orcs.

Aspects of Tolkien's meditations of the 1950s and 1960s represent new ideas, but other points do illuminate his thinking during earlier periods. His 1958 comment on Mongol-types was clearly intended to explain his portrayal of orcs in *The Lord of the Rings*. And his portrayal there can indeed be seen to conform to certain stereotypes of the racial Mongolic category and of Malay peoples as mentioned in English ethnography at circa 1900. Tolkien had no known expertise in anthropological or folkloric literature pertaining to either Asians or Southeast Asia. But he did not need such expertise in order to mine readily available textual sources for construction materials.

It is also useful to note that Tolkien's 1958 comments were composed for the benefit of Forrest Ackerman, an American publisher of imaginative literatures, who approached Tolkien in September 1957 with a film project in hand.[806] Tolkien expressed a willingness "to play ball" despite misgivings about the script. He prepared preliminary responses, some of which entered his later 1958 letter to Ackerman, and he contacted Rayner Unwin and his son Christopher about the matter.[807] In early 1958 Ackerman was given "a free option" to do a film, and in April Tolkien corresponded again with Unwin about the "stupid script!"[808] He prepared more detailed notes that eventually gave rise to the June letter to Ackerman.[809] In essence, Tolkien's comment on orcs as

"Mongol-types" was intended to shape a film portrayal; it was not a rejected draft experiment.

Why would Tolkien draw from a racial "Mongolic" model to colorize his orcs? We do not know for certain what motivated him. A possible triggering influence can be found in a book that Tolkien probably read in 1937-1938. In *We Europeans* Julian Huxley and Alfred Haddon made an odd point: "There is even a school of Nazi thought which would bring the Turks and the Japanese into the Nordic fold!"[810] Tolkien would have read about this curious Nazi notion during the same period when he decided to racialize his half-orcs and orcs with Mongol-type features – a point in time that followed the formal establishment of the Anti-Comintern Pact between Japan, Germany, and Italy in 1936 and 1937. It is clear, at least, that Tolkien's hatred of Nazi ideology was a full-blown attitude during the era when he decided to emphasize Asian racial features in his monstrous orcs.

It is possible that he entertained a specific bias against racial Asians, a sense of bigotry magnified by the events of World War Two. The actual moment of creating racialized orcs certainly points to this possibility – this act of invention came in the aftermath of the Japanese attacks on Pearl Harbor and Malaya. It is noteworthy that as a student at Oxford Tolkien bought some Japanese prints, and Michael Organ has pointed to the possible influence of this art on Tolkien's artistic style.[811] But this youthful appreciation and possibility of influence, even if it were less speculative and more definite, would merely complicate rather than foreclose the existence of a racial bias.

We don't know exactly what Tolkien knew of the spectrum of English attitudes toward Asians, but he surely encountered the kind of bias that existed during his Oxford days. Havelock Wilson's 1914 comments illustrated this kind of British prejudice against the Chinese and miscegenation: "...one of the most degrading and abominable sights one could witness was to go down into the East End of London and see there Chinese hob-nobbing with our own women, marrying our own women, and bringing into the world mongrels of the very lowest type."[812] The views of O'Connor Kessack on English "China-towns" amplified this perspective: "The areas where they live are rotten centres from which there emanates the most degrading and demoralising influences; and it would be futile to deny that many young women have been lured to destruction by the seductive suavity and treacherous lubricity of the Yellow Man."[813]

We should recall here Tolkien's language in 1958 regarding "degraded and repulsive versions of the (to Europeans) least lovely Mongol-types"as well as his note ten years later on Saruman and "his wickedest deed: the interbreeding of Orcs and Men, producing both Men-Orcs large and cunning, and Orc-men treacherous and vile."[814] The trajectory of negative imagery here from Wilson and Kessack in 1914 to Tolkien's fantasy Mongol-type orcs is noteworthy for its unbroken cultural and moral consistency. Those inclined to read this as coincidence might still wonder about the extent to which peers of Tolkien's generation would have connected his despised squint-eyed Men-Orcs to the despised slant-eyed "Yellow Man" found in English Chinatowns.

Another potential inspirational factor was an idea that became influential in 19th century European academic thinking and seeped into the annals of British folklore. William Ripley in his 1899 book on race summarized and rejected the model of a "Turanian" / "Mongoloid" population as originally widespread across Europe, becoming displaced by invading Aryans.[815]

English antiquarian history of the 19th century portrayed the European past as a misty cultural battleground. Tolkien's predecessors in philology and folklore sought glimpses of distant historical settings in words and mythography, and some experimented with racializing this history, transforming antiquity into a clash of races. Philologist Max Müller crafted a vision of European history that proved influential – a vision he later disavowed, but too late to stop the trajectory of logic that it inspired. Giving thought to "Aryan nations who pursued a north-westerly direction" he made some interesting assertions in a lecture first delivered in 1853.[816]

They have been the prominent actors in the great drama of history, and have carried to their fullest growth all the elements of active life with which our nature is endowed. They have perfected society and morals, and we learn from their literature and works of art the elements of science, the laws of art, and the principles of philosophy. In continual struggle with each other and with Semitic and Turanian races, these Aryan nations have become the rulers of history, and it seems to be their mission to link all parts of the world together by the chains of civilisation, commerce, and religion. In a word, they represent the Aryan man in his historical character.

This passage made its way into the introductory essay of a book that Tolkien read in 1938-1939 as he launched *The Lord of Rings*. He probably first encountered George Dasent's *Popular Tales of the Norse* during his student days at Oxford under the tutelage of William Craigie. Taking us through his version of Aryan history, Dasent quoted the above passage in full, altering "Turanian" to "Mongolian."[817] The key conception here was the supremacy of Aryan people who were locked in "continual struggle" with Mongolic folk – this dynamic can be observed in the model that Tolkien followed closely. In the course of racializing his orcs, he kept them in "continual struggle" with the folk of Middle-earth.

Dasent also envisioned a "mighty wedge of Aryan migration" as "driving its way through that prehistoric race, that nameless nationality, the traces of which we everywhere find underlying the intruders in their monuments and implements of bone and stone – a race akin, in all probability, to the Mongolian family, and whose miserable remnants we see pushed aside, and huddled up in the holes and corners of Europe, as Lapps, and Finns, and Basques..."[818] Tolkien's history certainly echoed this tone. It would be easy to see his Mongol-type orcs as "miserable remnants," a degraded folk who are "huddled up in the holes and corners" of Middle-earth. In *The Book of Lost Tales* it is not clear whether any orcs / goblins preceded the coming of his Elves and

Men into Middle-earth. But in 1926 Tolkien set forth his "Sketch of the Mythology" and just before mentioning the awakening of the first Elves, he placed Orcs in the far North of the Outer Lands, which would seem to make them an indigenous race that preceded the coming of Elves and Men.[819]

An 1890 book by David MacRitchie began with a chapter about "Finns" and "Finn-men" in the Scottish folklore of Shetland and Orkney.[820] MacRitchie postulated that these fabled folk "were of the Eskimo races." Building a case for this explanation of folkloric tradition, MacRitchie eventually linked widespread European tales of small hairy folk to a "race of Skraelings" residing in northern Norway – these people, he asserted, were also termed "goblins" in Norse traditions.[821] An appendix provided detail on these "pygmy" Skraelings of Norse tradition: "They were small, ugly men, with horrible heads of hair, great eyes, and broad cheek-bones[.]"[822]

Tolkien's orcs only vaguely echo MacRitchie's piratical Finn-men in kayaks. But the linking of Skraelings, pirate pygmies, and goblins could have motivated Tolkien to turn to the 1911 *Encyclopedia Britannica* and other sources for details that could be useful in reframing his existing goblins into "Mongol-types." This would invisibly link his monstrous Mongol-type orcs to the Mongolic folk of Scottish tradition.

As I have shown, I believe that Tolkien knew British folklore literature better than most of his contemporaries. MacRitchie's ideas in 1890 helped to give rise to an intellectual program in British folklore that sought for history in oral tradition – a tradition of inquiry that influenced at least one of Tolkien's professors at Oxford. John Rhys also looked at Celtic fairytales and wondered if he might be glimpsing a lingering antiquity. Walter Evans-Wentz then studied with Rhys and consulted with Andrew Lang, and in 1911 he published his occult thesis on fairy lore, a fascinating collection of Celtic traditions about fairies – a book that very briefly touched on a remnant "Mongol type" folk in Cornwall.[823]

Even as this book appeared in 1911, an intellectual shift was underway. British historians and anthropologist were turning the attention of the academy away from the study of oral tradition and toward the study of ancient texts and archaeology. And by the time Tolkien proceeded with the racialization of his orcs, decades of dust had gathered on the vast literature of British folklore in forgotten corners of university libraries. If Tolkien was familiar with MacRitchie's 1890 book, he never mentioned it.

This brings us to the process of invention that Tolkien followed in racializing his orcs during the 1940s. We do not know precisely how he proceeded. But through his youth and his early adulthood, he surely became aware of the British racial Asian stereotype, and it is likely that during his student years he came to know some of the arguments regarding the role of racial Mongolians versus Aryans in ancient European history. In late 1938 or early 1939, refreshing his familiarity with George Dasent's arguments on this point, Tolkien decided to draw on a Mongolic stereotype to add details to his half-orcs, a new class of monstrous servants of evil.

This decision first became manifest through his adaptation of the English dialectical term "squinny." The sprinkling of Asian features upon his half-orcs naturally gave rise to the recalibration of his orcs into Mongol-types. At that point it would have been logical for him to conduct research, gathering useful and somewhat obscure details. We can guess that he spent time skimming his *Encyclopedia Britannica* and paging through the Skeat Expedition papers and other materials; and in early 1942 his newly minted racialized orcs made their horrific début, marching into Middle-earth.

In 1958 as he pondered the Ackerman film script, he may have consulted *Encyclopedia Britannica* once again, planning to provide helpful guidelines for the film portrayal of his orcs. This would explain why his description at that time is an evident paraphrasing of the definition for "Mongolic or Yellow Man."

It is also possible that Tolkien received some kind of negative response in 1958 to his admitted racial characterization. This would help to explain why, in 1958-1960, resuming the construction of his orcs for *The Silmarillion*, he kept intact his pre-racial orcs and made no effort to weave racial elements into them – they would remain the fairytale soldiery of *The Book of Lost Tales*. Perhaps this would also explain his fleeting notion of including orcs capable of surrender. Had Tolkien actually completed *The Silmarillion* there is a slim possibility that we might have glimpsed a soldiery capable of laying down their arms and suing for peace in Middle-earth.

      Tolkien's choices regarding racial ideology did not occur in a timeless fantasy social vacuum. When *The Lord of the Rings* appeared in print, certain elements of academia were poised to confront the growing civil rights movement with a new commitment to race. This failed to stop the anti-race momentum that was already unfolding in the form of a slow abandonment of white racial bonding. This anti-race movement was generated to a large degree through the work of British and American anthropologists of the 1930s and 1940s. Through the final decades of the 20th century, as race spiraled toward the academic abyss, white racist attitudes were steadily centrifuged to the outer orbits of American social trends. And all through this period Middle-earth fandom launched into a substantive retroactive makeover of Tolkien's racial usages.

      Humphrey Carpenter's "authorized biography" of Tolkien appeared in 1977.[824] This book brought forth the distaste of Tolkien's mother toward South African Boer "attitudes" and his own revulsion toward Nazi Germany. And this official biography also pondered the Forrest Ackerman film proposal – the project that gave rise to Tolkien's comment on orcs. But Carpenter omitted mention of Mongol-type orcs. He later wrote that his first draft of the biography was "a long and sprawling thing, and was deemed unacceptable by the Tolkien family..."[825] His second version proved more acceptable. In hindsight, however, he felt he went too far to please the family: "What I'd actually done was castrated the book, cut out everything which was likely to be contentious."

      Patrick Curry's *Defending Middle-earth* touched on the accusation of racism and advised that we might best see Tolkien's orcs as evocative of medieval Huns.[826] We are urged to picture Tolkien the studious medieval scholar, pondering how to plug in allegorical Huns to match his allegorical Goths in Middle-earth. "Perhaps the worst you could say" – offered Curry – "is that Tolkien doesn't go out of his way to forestall the possibility of a racist interpretation." Given the fact that Curry made no mention of Tolkien's infamous 1958 comment about orcs as degraded Mongol-types, we might well suspect here a civil effort to discourage us from delving too deeply. We can guess that Curry was unwilling to delve very far into the matter because he thought there would be nothing to find.

In 2006 Christina Scull and Wayne Hammond issued an authoritative analysis that seemed to present Tolkien scholarship as holding a unified and settled view of Tolkien's racial orcs.[827] Concluding that Tolkien produced fantasy monsters in his orcs, and they should be seen as a fictional race corrupted by evil – a kind of "deadly virus or disease" – Scull and Hammond advised that we should absolve Tolkien from his use of race in this project for a very awkward reason: "If he were writing today, at a time of greater appreciation (or at least discussion) of diversity and racial sensitivity, he might well have chosen a more fantastic description which could not be related to any actual people." Holding Tolkien blameless for the orcs he invented, it is no wonder that Hammond and Scull just a year before this publication made no mention of Tolkien's Mongol-typology in discussing what he meant by "squint-eyed" and in their discussion of the chapter where orcs surge forth as racialized creatures.[828]

In 2007 Michael Drout's extensive compendium of essays included various contributions touching on race. In one essay Tom Shippey dismissed the charge that Tolkien can be "accused of 'racism'" partly on the grounds that Tolkien never used the word "in the modern sense used by official beauracracies (Caucasian, Asian, Hispanic, etc.)."[829] It is notable and disappointing that Shippey here somehow overlooked Tolkien's infamous racial use of "Mongol-types." It is also surprising that in this same volume three entries on "Race and Ethnicity in

Tolkien's Works," "Race in Tolkien Films," and "Racism, Charges of" all neglected to mention Tolkien's Mongol-type orcs.

The year 2010 brought several major publications on orcs and race. The journal of the Mythopoeic Society published a perplexing paper designed to both concede Tolkien's racial project and levitate him onto a pedestal above the fray. Robert Tally Jr propounded a complicated moral calculus of Tolkien's racialized orcs, teasing out and amplifying a few tepid ethical behaviors while acknowledging that it is understandable for one to feel a sense of offense at Tolkien's "swart" and "slant-eyed" descriptors.[830] And framing Tolkien's 1958 letter on "Mongol-types" as a "notorious... racial characterization" Tally encouraged us to feel some sympathy for those readers who might experience a sense of offense. But rejecting for himself the option "to accuse Tolkien of racism" Tally seemed to favor the view that Tolkien's narrative need for fictional villains ought to supercede our non-fictional sensibilities on race.

The project to officially excuse Tolkien's notorious use of race became established as a tenet of the Tolkien community with the 2010 publication of Dimitra Fimi's award-winning book, *Tolkien, Race and Cultural History: From Fairies to Hobbits*. Fimi gave considerable thought to race and Tolkien, but she prepared a very superficial consideration of his racialized orcs.[831] She outlined and then mysteriously set aside the anti-racism message of the 1935 book *We Europeans* in order to conclude that racism "as a construct deserving of ideological questioning is a later construct and accusing Tolkien of racism would decontextualize his writings from their historical period..."

Fimi's surprise ending here was warmly welcomed by many as a serviceable defense of Tolkien. Jason Fisher in a 2010 review eagerly siezed on the notion that Tolkien was a man of his times who simply cannot be held accountable for his actions: "Fimi does a fine job establishing context with the 'scientific' theories of race promulgated in the late Victorian period" – and he concluded with Fimi's quote that "accusing Tolkien of racism would decontextualize his writings from their historical period[.]"[832]

But the historical context is not ambiguous. Tolkien chose to make use of a racial stereotype. He applied it in the most unflattering way possible. This was intentional racism according to the standard of scholarship on race in his day. In addition, Tolkien's exploitation of a racist Asian stereotype is difficult to reconcile with the narrow glimpse we have of his childhood, growing up in a household where the South African "Boer attitude" was deemed insensitive, a social circumstance that "nearly always horrifies anyone going out from Britain..." These sparse bits of information suggest that Tolkien was raised to frown on overt racial belittlement.

When it came to the racial treatment of Jews and the racialist programs of Nazi Germany, Tolkien's thinking was guided by plenty of sensitivity for applicable moral standards of his day – standards widely held among peers who rejected racism and challenged race itself. He chose to disregard those same standards in order to borrow openly from a demeaning racial stereotype. Through the course of World War Two, Tolkien connected his Middle-earth fantasy orcs to a real world racial Asian stereotype – and he focused on odious qualities of that racial imagery to transform his orcs from fantasy soldiery of evil into degenerate racialized soldiery of evil.

Tolkien wished to keep the record straight on his intentions. Correcting an American film treatment that portrayed his orcs as fantasy monsters, he felt strongly that these proposed creatures had to be unlovely Mongol-types. This was his position in 1958 when civil rights and racism were matters of vast public interest in America and Britain. Even while pardoning Tolkien from blame as a man of his times, Dimitra Fimi noted that it was "after World War II that a greater awareness of racial offensiveness was expressed in Britain..." It is impossible to reconcile this point to the fact that *The Lord of the Rings* appeared in print during the early 1950s, well after WW2. Even if we accept at face value Fimi's willingness in this comment to overlook extensive evidence of academic anti-racism in Britain and the United States through the entire period of the writing of *The Lord of the Rings*, it was in 1958 when Tolkien sought to ensure the portrayal of his orcs as racialized creatures. As Fimi admitted, this was clearly a period of "greater awareness of racial offensiveness..."

In terms of the intellectual history of race, even if we completely ignore the impact of *We Europeans* during the mid-1930s, or dismiss it as a minor fluke of some kind, there is still the fact that a new momentum was underway even as Tolkien wrote the final chapters of *The Lord of the Rings* in 1948, sitting down to populate one chapter with evil half-orcs based on "Mongol-types." As bioanthropologist Jonathan Marks has noted: "After World War II, the critiques of race that had always been there from scholars like W.E.B. DuBois and Franz Boas gained more normative status; what had previously been invisible, or intellectually marginal, now became the dominant intellectual program in the study of human diversity."[833] Marks also cited a later memoir by Julian Huxley in which he observed of *We Europeans* that it "demonstrated conclusively that there was no such thing as a 'pure race' anywhere in the world..." But such demonstrations did not inspire any hesitation on Tolkien's part. He went on to racialize his orcs anyway, and he stood by that project in 1958.

It is also notable that while Dimitra Fimi excused Tolkien's racial usages, in a 2015 publication she issued a much harsher pronouncement on Peter Jackson's derivative version of Middle-earth.[834] Finding fault with Jackson's "evil" men because they display a "blend of non-European material cultures," Fimi decided sufficient cause existed to condemn his creative choice: "In a period of high tension between the Eastern and Western worlds, such cultural borrowings can be deemed purposefully offensive and ideological." One wonders how Tolkien managed to evade a similar verdict, given the fact that he crafted his racialized orcs while Britain was at war with Japan. Yet his more blatant use of race – acknowledged by Tolkien himself – somehow left Fimi unworried that any offense might well be purposeful and ideological.

Fimi's 2015 paper appeared in a collection of short essays by thirty-three professors who teach Tolkien. There I found two other contributors who brought up their methods for teaching on the topic of race – neither made mention of "Mongol-type" orcs. One contributor wrote that his students proved "reluctant at first to discuss the arguments about race in *The Lord of the Rings*."[835] Pointing them to a short movie review by John Yatt, a British National Party pamphlet, and an interview with actor John Rhys-Davies, the professor expected such material to generate "critical discussions" and "papers on race." But such superficial resources do not provide anything like in-depth insights or real guidance into the issues. This would seem to point to a need for more comprehensive critical analyses of the kind I have prepared in this book.

    Intent on the business of propounding fantasy monsters, JRR Tolkien deliberately concocted his orcs from the worst ideology of race. He consciously chose to embrace and enliven a negative racial stereotype. This may well be due in some degree to the inspiration of texts written before World War One that set Aryans against Mongolic peoples in ancient Europe. He may well have drawn inspiration from conventional medieval imagery. We can speculate that Tolkien's personal feelings about Mongolic peoples might have been guided more by an aloof insensitivity than by closeted bigotry, but we could also speculate that he was a closet racist. What is most clear is that race, racism, and Tolkien's worldmaking deserve exactly the kind of analysis I have provided.
    One could argue that his race-prejudice was not entirely monolithic, given his enjoyment of what he would have seen as a Mongolic element in Finland. But the evidence tends to favor the view that his inner attitudes did include some form of deep-seated lifelong cultural preference moderated by a commitment to social gentility. Whether Tolkien's antipathy toward "Mongol-types" simply reflected a situational insensitivity, or whether he actively despised racial Asians, the outcome is the same. His racialized orcs and his miscegenated half-orcs are irredeemably evil. Their wicked nature is swarthy, squint-eyed, degraded.

Whatever meaning we might each prefer to attach to this outcome, we must all ask an important question. What should "Mongol-type" readers around the world make of Tolkien's inventive use of race? This is a question that cannot be answered in any meaningful way until we make available an adequate body of research and analysis on this issue. But it is an obvious fact that Tolkien felt little evident concern for the sensibilities of any such readers who would pick up *The Lord of the Rings* or who would someday step into a movie theater and encounter there his racialized Mongol-type orcs. He did not believe his preferred readership would take offense or feel troubled.

In the end, when readers today encounter Tolkien's orcs and half-orcs in *The Lord of the Rings*, they deserve the opportunity to give informed consideration to his intentional deployment of a demeaning racial stereotype. If some readers consequently decide to see this creative choice as racist, this response does not warrant trivialization or dismissal. We should instead question those who see no problem with Tolkien's racial insensitivity or who would casually excuse and even hush up the truth about Tolkien's racial project.

Listing Tolkien's invented peoples in terms of their artistic aesthetic, Christine Chism touched on the Valar, Elves, and Dwarves – and she considered Orcs who "represent art gone wrong, warped to military service... a nightmare version of the work of art in an age of mechanical reproduction."[836] Tolkien's early orcs could be usefully deemed a kind of weaponized artifice twisted to ill purpose, but we should construe the orcs of *The Lord of the Rings* as racialized evil. These twisted orcs are not of Morgoth's making. Instead, these orcs were degraded by Tolkien's hand – manifestations of his own creative "art gone wrong[.]"

Tolkien in Pawneeland ⁓ ✳ ⋞ Roger Echo-Hawk

Tolkien's Black Men

To the degree that Tolkien's novelization of what he termed "northern spirit" can be observed in Middle-earth, it contributed to renderings of folk who display great moral diversity. He felt protective of the esoteric quality of "northernness," and it is just as clear that he felt no such protective impulse when it came to fictional characters he colorized as "black" or "sallow." In Tolkien's mythmaking, these colorations uniformly denote moral darkness. But to what extent did elements of racial thinking guide his use of the color?

In his youth and early professional life Tolkien certainly accepted the generalizations of race as a fact. This is briefly evidenced in an essay he prepared during the early 1930s, mentioning "common human taste or instinct" that would remain after "all sorts of local and racial differences are deducted' – and here he mentioned "an African's choice of colours" and whether "black is disliked because of night, or night because it is black?"[837] His recalibration of his goblin / orc demon-soldiers for *The Lord of the Rings* occurred in an explicitly racial context – he intended to make more monstrous his characters of evil by importing aspects of racial social ideology into Middle-earth. This was accomplished by attaching to his orcs black skin-color and other features derived from racial stereotypes.

Most importantly, the single clear referencing of black-skinned humans in *The Lord of the Rings* also denoted an essentializing generalization that was patently racial and intentionally demeaning. Even so, readers who search Tolkien's novels for evidence of racism must sort through the evidence with care. As we will see, for example, Tolkien labeled his Black Riders as "black men," and race typology played a role in this creative choice, but this specific usage is more directly derived from mythological folklore that came to his hand interwoven with racial tradition.

During the 1930s Tolkien's annual Christmas letters to his children occasionally featured goblins with black coloration – a detail suggesting a reconfiguration of his original colorless goblins / orcs.[838] And an interesting drawing appeared in the margin of his December 1935 letter. There we find a seated human figure with kinky hair, black skin, large lips, and round eyes. No explanation of this drawing is immediately evident in the text. The letter merely says: "Polar Bear... sends love to you – and to the Bingos and to Orange Teddy and to Jubilee..."[839]

The name "Jubilee" is nowhere explained. It seems to represent a doll's name. This possibility deserves consideration because during the early decades of the 20th century this term in Britain referred to popular "Negro" musical troupes visiting from America. Whatever this small 1935 drawing signified, it showed that Tolkien did not entirely ignore racial blacks during the years leading up to the writing of *The Lord of the Rings*.

In Tolkien's original August 1938 draft of the visit of the fellowship of hobbits to Bree, Nob was reported by Butterbur as having said: "It's another of they black Men..."[840] Tolkien gave this imagery careful thought. A later version of this chapter written in late 1938 or early 1939 contained four mentions of Black Riders as "black men."[841] Nob's comment appeared in rewritten form: "There's the Black Man at the door!" Butterbur says, "For these Black Men mean no good to anyone, I'll be bound." He added: "How came these Black Men to think Baggins was one of your party?" And Harry Goatleaf told Gandalf: "Black men on horses; and a lot of foreigners out of the South came up the Greenway at dusk."

All of these statements concerned Black Riders. Three mentions of these "black men" at Bree lingered into the published version of this chapter. The description was spoken twice by Butterbur and once by Strider. In 1948 Tolkien inserted one final mention of black men in "The Scouring of the Shire."

In 1895 *The Denham Tracts* featured a long list of folkloric creatures, and it mentioned two that, to my knowledge, are exclusive in the mid-20th century to Tolkien's writings: "hobbits" and "black-men."[842] As with the term "hobbit," black men also appeared in Joseph Wright's *English Dialect Dictionary*.[843] There the term was defined in various ways, but the first definition was "a supposed 'bogy,' a nursery terror." Three other more mundane usages were listed: licorice, a plant, and a go-between. Wright provided three examples of black men as frightening bogies, while *The Denham Tracts* offered no explicit example of the creature.[844] It is possible that Tolkien saw the term in the Denham list. But it is more likely that he found the term in Wright's dictionary sometime between 1930 and 1938, and he made use of it in constructing his Black Riders.

The list of folkloric creatures in *The Denham Tracts* included both "black-men" and "wraithes" and both were labeled in a generic way as "a class of spirits."[845] For Tolkien to frame his Black Riders as both wraiths and black men suggests that *The Denham Tracts* could have provided inspiration for the construction of his Black Riders. But it is even more relevant that "black men" became emphasized in the drafting of late 1938-1939 at the same time that the racialized "squint-eyed southerner" made his debut in Bree. This seems to indicate that Tolkien was culling folkloric sources for implicitly racial terms that were unusual and mostly empty of concrete meaning.

He was in fact conducting a far-reaching research project into folklore during that period – research that gave rise to his paper "On Fairy-stories." He already had experience in taking folkloric terms and filling them up with his own vision. The term "black men" is not defined in any evident way in *The Denham Tracts*, and it isn't much more detailed in Wright's *English Dialect Dictionary*.

It is interesting that the first appearance of "they black Men" in the writing of *The Fellowship of the Ring* came in August 1938. On June 22, 1938 a world-famous boxing match occurred in New York between Joe Louis and Max Schmeling. This was a major event because Schmeling had won an earlier match against Louis and that had served as an occasion for Nazi Germany to further the cause of white racial superiority. But with this rematch, in short order Louis won decisively. Louis trained hard for the event, feeling pressure that "the whole world was looking to this fight" because "Germany was tearing up Europe, and we were hearing more and more about the concentration camps for the Jews."[846] Louis heard that the Germans suppressed the news of his victory: "They didn't want their people to know that just a plain old nigger man was knocking the shit out of the Aryan Race."

It is difficult to know the degree of Tolkien's interest in news of the Louis-Schmeling fight, but it was a major story in Europe and America, and Tolkien was an avid reader of newspapers. If Tolkien gave any thought to the boxing match, he might well have recollected his days as a researcher for the *Oxford English Dictionary*. In those days, studying the word "wallop," he submitted to OED a slip on usage citing a phrase that had been common in Britain during the late 19th century: "the right to wallop one's own nigger."[847]

To find such a racially charged term in Tolkien's legacy is mystifying if we embrace the longstanding consensus in Tolkien scholarship that treats him as squarely opposed to racism. It is likely that he became interested in the phrase through its association with the Second Boer War.[848] For whatever reason, his slip on usage of "wallop" was rejected by his supervisors as racially offensive and not illustrative enough. A contrast can be seen in Joseph Wright's *English Dialect Dictionary* which contained a lengthy entry on the uses of "wallop" but did not cite the phrase "the right to wallop one's own nigger."

Just a month after the Louis-Schmeling boxing match, Tolkien was contacted regarding a German translation of *The Hobbit*. He was asked about his ancestry – the German publisher wished for him to fill out a legal form declaring whether he had any Jewish forebears. He wrote a scathing response to his publisher, denouncing Germany's "lunatic laws" and "the wholly pernicious and unscientific race-doctrine."[849] This has been taken by Dimitra Fimi to reflect Tolkien's awareness of anthropological thinking on race.[850] This seems likely enough, but it most clearly pertained to race-based anti-Semitism, to the quality of "Northernness," and to the incivility of overt social expressions of racism. Tolkien's comments must have reflected the kind of discourse that many of his Oxford colleagues held regarding Jews, Nazi Germany, and racial eugenics. A few years later in 1942 Tolkien mentioned his suspicion of the "false simplification" of Britain's "intricate complex history racially and culturally" and of his hatred of "the bewildered and tragic nonsense talked in modern Germany" concerning matters "Nordic."[851]

Writing *The Lord of the Rings*, it could be argued that Tolkien devised a way to express his concerns regarding the Nazi view of Jews. He turned to Jewish culture to colorize his Norse dwarves in *The Lord of the Rings*. In one 1955 letter he drew attention to elements of Jewishness in his Middle-earth Dwarf-culture, saying, "I do think of the 'Dwarves' like Jews"; and he observed in 1965 that "All their words are Semitic..."[852] Setting these Dwarves in conflict with his Elves, Tolkien resolved this polarized cultural opposition by having his main Dwarf-character and his main Elf-character overcome their differences and become fast friends.

Tolkien could have devised some sort of similar uplifting messaging with racial blacks and racial whites. He chose otherwise. He decided to impose an insurmountable divide between whiteness and blackness in Middle-earth, making systematic use of this color-scheme to denote good and evil, with whiteness attached to the possibility of moral diversity, and with a contrasting uniformity of evil attached to blackness. To the degree that Tolkien's semi-Semitic Dwarves bond with enemy Elves, we are meant to receive a transcendent moral social message. Tolkien's "they black Men" never acquired such narrative positioning.

The timing of this usage is noteworthy. It is not clear that any direct connection existed between the Louis / Schmeling fight and Tolkien's insertion of "black men" into his story during the summer of 1938. But it is reasonable to suspect a connection given the fact that only two months after the world-famous boxing match Tolkien sat down and wrote, "It's another of they black Men..." Given this timing, it is certainly arguable that the social narrative of contesting blackness versus whiteness spilled over in a minor way from world events into Middle-earth. Since we know that Tolkien treated race as a matter of marginal interest, we can suggest that in this instance Tolkien chose a path that overtly echoed English folkloric "black men" and covertly drew on the conventions of racial practice in his social world.

This usage was not necessarily borrowed as an explicit racial reference, but it cannot be read in isolation from the social context of race. The historical reality of anti-black British racism and the racial social context of Tolkien's immediate social world both have relevance that must be considered. Defending Tolkien, however, Patrick Curry deemed it sufficient to merely specify that Black Riders lack black skin.[853] It is disappointing that he neglected to mention the implications of "black men" as an alternate term for Black Riders, and he offered no consideration of the racial context for that usage.

Margaret Sinex has summarized the deeper roots of English and European meditations on physical diversity in humankind, showing that medieval traditional attitudes mingled skin-color, pre-racial modeling, and moral orientation, and that this narrative logic was echoed by Tolkien.[854] Sinex touched on Tolkien's more immediate cultural circumstance, but her argument implied that Tolkien drew for inspiration upon his readings of ancient and medieval literatures. In this view, Sinex tended to favor the idea that Tolkien's agenda reflected an intention to reconstitute medieval tradition in Middle-earth rather than articulate any private attitudes.

It is certainly appropriate to look for shadings of medieval Europe in Middle-earth, but bestowing a careful sense of weight upon Tolkien's scholarly understanding of literary tradition should not foreclose consideration of the real weight of his private notions regarding race. And it does not seem appropriate to entirely ignore the real world cultural spectrum of Tolkien's era.

It is not speculative to assert that the narratives of race do enter his literary agenda. This includes his use of the color black.

It is also clear that when Tolkien drew from source material his most typical intention was to use elements to colorize his fantasy fiction, not to retell that material. To say that Tolkien intended to echo medieval usages is to merely take note of inspirational materials that entered his world. The usage itself must then be evaluated on its own terms. This is the logic that is most appropriate to follow in analyzing the nature of his use of racial imagery. Investigations of Tolkien and race must consciously inquire into the extent to which Tolkien intended to echo and affirm the extant racial discourse as it was practiced and understood in his time. To the degree that we can align his usage with contemporary racial imagery, it doesn't matter if he drew inspiration from pre-racial medieval imagery.

It is important to understand that the racializing of swart skin color was not a medieval construction. As discussed by Audrey Smedley and Brian Smedley in their history of race, Winthrop Jordan in 1968 suggested that to the English the color black historically signified "an emotionally partisan color, the handmaid and symbol of baseness and evil, a sign of danger and repulsion."[855] Medieval inscriptions of color and meaning were not monolithic. Both dark and pale coloration could be viewed as morally complex skin shadings. As M. Lindsay Kaplan has explained, the dark skin color associated with a "melancholic" condition in medieval texts probably arose as a way of bestowing a negative moral judgment on Jews as "dominated by a malign influence."[856] Classical and Christian writings promoted the association of dark skin with inferiority and sin, but this was not a racial association.

This is indicated by the fact that a "melancholy condition" was also described in some texts as white, pallid, pale, tawny – even blue. In other words, a melancholic could display a variety of skin tones. Kaplan reminded us that even when the term "niger" (black) appeared "we don't necessarily know what that blackness was thought to look like." The modern color chart of race imposes an interpretive lens that seems to make everything clear, but that color chart was not fixed in medieval Europe. Nor was the idea of being "white" in racial terms a medieval concept. Elly Truitt addresses the modern idea that the Norse saw themselves as "white people" with the observation that "medieval Scandinavians were not concerned with racial purity or their own 'whiteness' – indeed, such concepts would have been foreign to them."[857]

There seems to have been a significant population of identifiable people from Sub-Saharan Africa in London by the early 1600s, but most historians believe that prior to the mid-17th century few folk elsewhere in England "had encounters with black persons..."[858] The English folkloric association of the color black with evil predated racial taxonomies, and arguably played a role in tuning social attitudes toward racial blackness, predisposing the English toward antipathy toward dark-skinned Africans. The implication is that the rise of racial thinking transformed a general historical signifier of moral debasement into a specifically racist judgment about the meaning of skin shading.

The defining concepts that we subsume under the term "race" were not medieval notions, and even as race took its first tentative steps into the world, the emerging idea of racial blackness as a negative demarcation was not consistent. A random stew of concepts swirled around dark skin. As Anu Korhonen has argued, during the 16th and 17th centuries powerful meanings were attached to skin coloration identified as black, but "the meanings of blackness... were without philosophical and scientific fixity."[859] Even so, she concluded that English ethnocentrism produced various cultural precursors of racial stereotyping that exerted a powerful influence on English and American proto-racial ideology. In the medieval lexicon the modern idea of race was not present, but prejudice associated with the color black was an old idea, and it ultimately helped to instill racialist attitudes that were very much alive in Tolkien's time.

Tolkien had the option to borrow the "black men" of British folklore and reconstitute the imagery in any number of ways. We can guess that he drew his black men from British folklore via the Wright dictionary or *The Denham Tracts*, but it is clear that decided to render a portrayal of "black men" that was not at all morally positive or neutral. His black men are evil creatures in the service of Sauron, the Dark Lord; they display no moral ambiguity whatsoever. With some exceptions, this reflected Tolkien's typical use of the color black. Noting the insertion of black swans in "The Great River" Wayne Hammond and Christina Scull observed: "Tolkien never indicates whether the swans are spies for Sauron, but that they are black suggests evil motives."[860]

The "black men" who appear in various folkloric texts and novels of the 19th century tended to reference either the Christian Devil or a kind of fearful monster. In Irish the term *fear dubh* is usually translated as "black man" and is often cited as a name for the Christian Devil. A Robert Louis Stevenson story titled "Thrawn Janet" (1881) concerns an encounter with a man sitting on a grave "of a great stature, an' black as hell" – this is the Devil, "the Accuser of the Brethren." A German folkloric monster is Der schwarze Mann (the black man). A tale in *Brothers Grimm's Household Tales* titled "The King of the Golden Mountain" tells of "a little black mannikin" or "black dwarf" or "black man" who attempts to ensnare a man's son.[861] Sometime in 1939-1943, during the period when Tolkien brought "black men" into *The Lord of the Rings*, he consulted this Brothers Grimm book in the course of researching "On Fairy-stories."[862]

The association of "black" and evil has some antiquity in European tales; it also has a presence in 19th century American literature. A Washington Irving story published in 1824 was titled "The Devil and Tom Walker," and it described the Devil as "a great black man" who was "neither negro nor Indian" with a face that was "neither black nor copper colour, but swarthy and dingy and begrimed with soot..." Nathaniel Hawthorne's 1850 novel, *The Scarlet Letter*, referred to the Devil as "the Black Man" and there it is told that "this scarlet letter was the Black Man's mark on thee, and that it glows like a red flame when thou meetest him at midnight, here in the dark wood."

Tolkien seemed inclined to compare both Morgoth and Sauron to Satan.[863] But his Black Riders are not angelic in any sense. Despite Tolkien's deployment of satanic symbolism, the Ringwraiths do not seem directly aligned with the Christian Devil or fallen angels. Tolkien's use of the term "wraith" for them, with "black men" as a colloquial label, seems to put these creatures in a folkloric light that was only loosely attached to racial thinking and Christian imagery. His "black men" could be said to echo European traditions that subsumed the Devil and assorted monstrous creatures as traditional figures of fright and evil – a cultural resonance that also hinted at the history of race and the intentions of racism. Tolkien never identified any specific source for his "black men," but they do resemble the black men in Wright's *English Dialect Dictionary* as "a supposed 'bogy,' a nursery terror."

In *The Lost Road*, a 1936-1937 manuscript, Tolkien included a poem, *King Sheave*, listing a number of Germanic groups and then "beyond Myrcwudu a mighty realm" – Christopher Tolkien explained that the intended reference was "to the Eastern Alps[.]"[864] Pondering the term "Mirkwood" Tolkien noted in 1966 that it is "a very ancient name, weighted with legendary associations."[865] He deemed this an old Germanic name "for the great mountainous forest regions that anciently formed a barrier to the south of the lands of Germanic expansion." The Germanic term *mirkiwidu* seemed to date as early as the 11th century, and the stem term, a reconstructed word for "dark" occurred in various languages. In Old English *mirce* was used as a poetic term for "'dark', or rather 'gloomy'" and "elsewhere only with the sense 'murky' > wicked, hellish." Tolkien concluded that the term "was never, I think, a mere 'colour' word: 'black', and was from the beginning weighted with the sense of 'gloom'..."

Inventing one of his Elvish languages, Tolkien created a number of words based on the root MORO, including the terms for night, dark, black, to hide – giving rise to words like Morgoth and Mordor.[866] Dimitra Fimi and Andrew Higgins have pointed out that the MORO-derived terms convey "a feeling of literal or metaphorical 'darkness'" – a sense evoked by "words of Indo-European languages such as 'murder,' 'murky,'" and others. There can be no doubt that Tolkien carefully coded the meanings that pertain to his color usages.

Tolkien set forth his understanding of the linguistic history of various terms related to the color black. During the early 1930s Tolkien published a two-part analysis of Old English references to Africa.[867] In this research Tolkien traced a trajectory of attitude and perspective on the part of Europeans toward Africans, and he concluded that the Old English term "Sigelwara" drew a connection between the sun and dark skin coloration. He reconstructed "Sigelhearwan" as a literal reference to "black people living in a hot region" but also as preserving an ancient monstrous creature from a time predating the Anglo-Saxon awareness of Ethiopia – perhaps a mythological demon like Norse fire giants. Later Anglo-Saxon perceptions drew on that imagery and went further, equating dark-skinned Ethiopians living in a hot clime and Christian conceptions of Hell and its denizens.

This layering of history and imagery appealed to his creative aesthetic – a point which raises an interesting question. To what extent did Tolkien model his Balrogs from his understanding of this linguistic backcloth? Is it possible to say that Balrogs might reference a fantasy version of racial black people – Africans reconfigured through a Norse / Anglo-Saxon-tinted fantasy lens?

Certain conclusions reached by Tom Shippey have a direct bearing on these questions.[868] Working through Tolkien's "Sigelwara Land," Shippey noted the argument that Anglo-Saxons attached their limited experiences with "Ethiopians" to older imagery and ultimately connected terms for "sun" and "jewel" and "soot" with the Norse fire giant Múspell. Tolkien argued that this process hinted at distant mythic ancestral figures "with red-hot eyes that emitted sparks, with faces black as soot." Shippey concluded that this flow of logic "helped to naturalise the 'Balrog' in the traditions of the North..." In other words, Shippey seems to conclude that Tolkien constructed his Balrogs from an analysis of linguistic history and Norse tradition and Anglo-Saxon conceptions of "Ethiopian" Africans.

Tolkien's Balrogs were not in any direct sense black Africans. But given Shippey's point, it is useful to examine Tolkien's fantasy Balrog monsters for glimpses of racially black Africans. Toward this end, such essences are not readily apparent in his original incarnation of Balrogs. In *The Book of Lost Tales* the characterization of Balrogs is vivid and sparse. They are giants – twice as tall as the Elves – and they wield steel claws and whips of fire.[869] If Tolkien's knowledge of Anglo-Saxon conceptions of Ethiopians was a factor in the making of Balrogs, we can see that they originally emerged from his creative forge as sketched creatures that didn't necessarily seem very human.

Balrogs next appeared in Tolkien's lays of the 1920s – poems that grew out of *The Book of Lost Tales*. There we find Balrogs and Orcs described as "black legions"; this vague description may or may not refer to flesh-tone, but Balrogs also acquire "fiery manes" and this new detail further diminished any hint of humanity and moved instead toward fantasy monstrosity.[870]

Yet we can now take note of a new and curious circumstance. Up to the decade of the 1920s we know of only one occasion when Tolkien made mention of racial black people. This occurred in his slip to the *Oxford English Dictionary* on the usage of "wallop" in his example of "the right to wallop one's own nigger." In some iterations of this saying, the word "whip" took the place of "wallop" – a detail that was likely known to Tolkien. Just a few years later we find him writing lays that featured Balrogs derived in some part from black Africans. Now we suddenly find them wielding whips upon "thy white flesh" and "thy white body" (meaning the flesh of captured Hurin).[871]

At that point in time, Tolkien's African-derived Balrogs weren't very humanlike; they were monstrous creatures with steel claws and manes of fire. They were demons, servants of evil who wielded whips of fire. One could say, nevertheless, that their evil master had given them the right to wallop the white flesh of their enemies. This much is clear.

Tolkien followed with another fantasy moment that is relevant to Tom Shippey's comments on "Sigelwara Land." That research, Shippey observed, "helped to create (or corroborate) the image of the *silmaril*, that fusion of 'sun' and 'jewel' in physical form." Circa 1930 we find Tolkien bestowing black hands on Morgoth as a result of touching the Silmarils: "It is said that his evil hands were burned black with the touch of those holy and enchanted things, and black they have been ever since..."[872] It was during this period or immediately thereafter that Tolkien set down his research on "Sigelwara Land." It is clearly arguable that he decided in this scene to summon up a mythologized hint of racial blackness, bestowing Ethiopian "black hands" onto evil Morgoth via the desecration of "holy and enchanted things." Here we glimpse Tolkien engaged in a subtle Africanizing of his satanic Morgoth.

More than a decade later we find Tolkien reconfiguring his Balrogs of old into something new for *The Lord of the Rings*. Bringing the Fellowship to Moria, he set down his first description of this freshly re-envisioned monster: "A figure strode to the fissure, no more than man-high... They could see the furnace-fire of its yellow eyes from afar; its arms were very long; it had a red [?tongue]."[873] This Balrog also has "streaming hair" and it wields a sword and "a whip of many thongs." Tolkien also decided to have Gandalf announce to this Balrog, "I am the master of the White Fire." And he soon decided to transform his wizard into "Gandalf the White," a character slain by a Balrog and brought back to life.[874]

This was Tolkien's most humanized Balrog. It was "man-high" with long hair and yellow eyes and a "red [?tongue]" – Christopher Tolkien guessed that "tongue" was probably the right word here. This pronounced humanization would get toned down, but Tolkien would also darken the Balrog's blazing essence into "a dark form, of man-shape maybe" and as a "dark figure streaming with fire[.]"

This humanized dark Balrog was not alone in Moria. Tolkien had Gandalf make mention of "black Orcs"; they attack and we encounter "a huge orc-chief, almost man-high" whose "eyes were like coals of fire."[875] At some point after writing this early draft – perhaps after about mid-1942 – Tolkien further racialized his "huge orc-chieftain" and gave him a red tongue: "His broad flat face was swart, his eyes were like coals, and his tongue was red..." Pondering this passage LJ Swain has noted that this particular Orc fits "both the Sigelware as Ethiopians (or at least medieval conceptions of them in literature) and the Sigelware as offspring of the fire giant."[876]

It would be inaccurate to conclude that explicit consideration of racial blackness was completely absent from Tolkien's choices regarding the color black. The list of candidates reflecting this process include his project to colorize his demonic orcs with black skin tones, the derivation of his Balrogs from sources that included black African imagery (which includes the turning of Morgoth's hands black), and the labeling of his Ringwraiths as "black men."

Keeping in mind Tolkien's preferred imagery about colorful eyes and red tongues, we can suddenly see another set of figures looming into view. In late 1944 he entered an explicit reference to racial black people in *The Lord of the Rings*. Writing "The Battle of the Pelennor Fields," he listed the forces of Mordor and crafted an infamous description: "...out of Far Harad black people like half-trolls with white eyes and red tongues."[877]

The conjunction of this red tongue imagery with African-derived Balrogs and with the swart Orc chieftain of Moria is enlightening, given the plain fact that Tolkien modeled the red tongued folk of Far Harad on a caricature of racial black Africans. We can guess that he first gave thought to the Anglo-Saxon term for Ethiopian Africans sometime before circa 1917, and this inspired his Balrogs. But at that point he had no interest in creating a humanlike Africanized monster. Ten years after writing "Sigelwara Land," when he next turned to a produce a more detailed portrayal of a Balrog, he now decided to both humanize it and Africanize it.

Tom Shippey has argued that Tolkien intended for the "black people" of Far Harad to reflect an Anglo-Saxon perspective and not his own attitude.[878] Acknowledging that Tolkien's brief description of the horrific brutish black people at Pelennor Fields "certainly sounds racist" he proposed that Tolkien was "trying to write like a medieval chronicler" conveying what amounts to a first encounter perception. Given Tolkien's professional focus on medieval literature, it is certainly reasonable for Shippey to offer this suggestion. But the absence of tonal texturing is absolute. Rather than moderate a shocked first impression with some subsequent hint of humanity, there is instead a move in the opposite direction. We soon notice that these "black people like half-trolls" disappear from the tale and in their place we find "troll-men" – even more monstrous creatures.

Shippey prefers that we interpret these black people as a folk who have been filtered through a medieval lens and not through a racist perspective. This approach also seems favored by Margaret Sinex, who has conveniently summarized the treatment of black skin tones in classical and medieval literature.[879] Outlining the binary representation of black skin in the hot south and white skin in the cold, she noted the associated attachment of folk character to that imagery. But there both taxonomies were equally "savage" and equally cowardly and bold. This equivalence of meaning is not a racial framing. Yet Sinex concluded that "medieval Europeans came by their use of binaries (Scythian / Ethiopian, white / black, saved / damned) to analyze racial differences honestly, which is to say, they inherited them from Antiquity." She later added that "we may study medieval theorizing about race dispassionately."

But the attachment of "blackness" to skin was not straightforward in medieval thinking, nor was it "racial." Instead, we find a more confusing stew of notions that are not conveniently arranged into a clear ideological trajectory, as we find with race after the late 18th century. Sinex conceded that medieval representations of Jews, at least, was not monolithic, citing another scholar in an endnote to the effect that "not every medieval representation of Jews was negative[.]"

This is evident in Tolkien's scholarship, too. In "Sigelwara Land" he quoted the mention of Ethiopians found in the Old English text "Wonders of the East." This manuscript offered a short listing of swart-colored Ethiopians that did not come with any identifiable notions of group character. We find nothing that can be read as a moral quality; the reference instead presented a very spare observation of human physical diversity. Tolkien had a menu of options at hand, and he selectively framed swart skin tones in the most negative available terms possible – in Middle-earth his swart folk lack any kind of classical / medieval parity with people who are not swarthy.

It can also be noted that Tolkien peopled Middle-earth in accordance with a very eclectic fantasy vision that cannot be readily aligned with medieval Europe. On the Pelennor battleground the characters come to us from a mingling of essences. We find Hobbits modeled in part from Victorian England, Homeric-tinted Anglo-Saxon Rohirrim, Orcs colorized by a racial Asian stereotype, an Elf rooted in an Aryan prehistory, a Dwarf composed in part from Jewish culture, a semi-Odinic wizard, and Gondorians who, as Tolkien noted, "resemble 'Egyptians'" with a "Hebraic" theology – and all this happened in Middle-earth in the mythic past, maybe 6,000 years ago.[880] Tolkien borrowed from his deep knowledge of medieval materials, but he did not reproduce medieval Europe in Middle-earth; he rejected the option of writing a strictly medievalist romance.

In the end, Tolkien's choice to portray the "black people" of Far Harad as "like half-trolls" stands alone as the sole overt reference to racial black humankind in Africa in *The Lord of the Rings*, *The Hobbit*, and *The Silmarillion*. It is fair to note the complete absence of moral diversity in this single explicit construction of racial blacks. It is fair to observe that all the creatures into which Tolkien painted covert elements of racial blackness can be seen as corrupt things of great evil with no positive connotations whatsoever.

The dearth of characters that we can identify as explicit racial blacks in Tolkien's fictional writings is puzzling given the fact that he was born in South Africa. But the actual range of black texturing within this "absence" comes into better focus when we identify the elements of racial blackness that Tolkien covertly wove into his Orcs, Balrogs, and Ringwraiths.

Just months before he inserted the sole mention of "black people like half-trolls" into the battle scene before Minas Tirith, Tolkien wrote about South Africa in a letter to son Christopher, then stationed there.[881] In this 1944 letter Tolkien recalled his mother talking about "'local' conditions" in South Africa and he had "ever since taken a special interest in that part of the world." He added, "The treatment of colour nearly always horrifies anyone going out from Britain" and it is unfortunate that "not many retain that generous sentiment for long."

In framing the horrifying "treatment of colour" as a "generous sentiment," this letter suggested that he had a moral objection to South African racial attitudes. It would be helpful to know what reports motivated Tolkien to mention "anyone going out from Britain"; by 1944 he had probably met various people who had visited South Africa, and we can assume that he had read accounts by travelers. Keeping in mind that his mother died in November 1904 and that it was her tales which sparked his "special interest," this means that his curiosity dated back at least as far as 1904, if not earlier. So it is quite possible that Tolkien learned in his youth about a 1905 travelogue by an Englishman named John Balfour-Browne.

That book featured a detailed discussion of racial dynamics observed in the course of his 1904 visit to South Africa.[882] It began by noting that genteel Englishmen at home had little understanding of the situation faced by English colonists in South Africa, beset by "partial civilization on the one hand, and ancient savagery on the other." Discussing the ethics of offering blacks the benefit of "good hard work" Browne described an account he heard from an Englishman who hired a group of blacks to accompany his trading expedition. The man found himself restraining and whipping a Zulu employee who had fomented "insurrection." The moral lesson for Balfour-Browne was that "it is necessary to govern the blacks with a strong hand, a strong command, and no mealy-mouthed talk of equality or brotherly love." And the finishing point made by the English colonist to Balfour-Browne was that "he would be as kind to a nigger as he would to a horse, and I believe him."

This was no doubt the kind of account that Tolkien had in mind when he wrote to Christopher about the the horrifying "treatment of colour" and the "generous sentiment" that "not many retain... for long." Just a few months after writing to his son about South Africa Tolkien sent his own "black people like half-trolls" marching to bring war from Far Harad to the noble folk of Minas Tirith. We are intended to visualize large brutish black people. It is interesting, though probably coincidence, that the Balfour-Browne story described the rebellious Zulu man as "mountainous" – "a huge black... cast in nature's largest mould."

In a January 1945 letter to his son Christopher – not long after inventing the brutish black folk of Far Harad – Tolkien made an intriguing reference to race. He had been reading an "enthralling" book called *Anglo-Saxon England*, and after observing that his "mind" was "wholly different" from that of the author, he wrote, "...it is the things of racial and linguistic significance that attract me and stick in my memory."[883] He wished to encourage Christopher to look into English history and the origins of "our peculiar people." And he reminded Christopher that, aside from the Tolkien-German ancestry, "you are a Mercian or Hwiccian (of Wychwood) on both sides."

This comment reminds us that Tolkien was not anti-race. In his personal conception of racial identity, one should seek meaning from something more specific than a generalized racial whiteness. Encouraging his son to ponder English ancestry through the focus of family history, he deemed such a project an inquiry into the meanings of race. His denunciations of racial hatreds toward Jews were clear. This sprang in some part from acceptance of attitudes that were widely shared in British academia during the late 1930s. But Tolkien believed in race as an appropriate lens for glimpsing the esoteric essences of humankind, and this belief system is not completely transparent to us today, yet it played a role in shaping Middle-earth.

Public attitudes in Britain during the 1950s harbored forms of racism that reflected an enduring social legacy from earlier generations. As Julian Huxley and Alfred Haddon wrote in the mid-1930s, "In Europe, the feeling against intermarriage with black or brown is far less marked among the Latin-speaking nations than in Britain."[884] Clare Hanson cited one survey of 100 female students at Oxford and Cambridge and noted that 84 reported "they would not be willing to marry an African" – an attitude echoed in the Notting Hill race riots of late August 1958.[885]

But by the late 1950s the spectrum of attitudes was in flux. A key factor for post-war British youth was the influence of American music, particularly music by racial blacks.[886] Just months after the Beatles inspired a national mania in Britain, Tolkien found the new British rock music scene little to his liking, describing the "noise" made in the rehearsals of one "Beatle Group" as "indescribable," and then a few years later opposing a plan by the Beatles to make a film based on *The Lord of the Rings*.[887]

Tolkien's preferential aesthetic of fair white skin as the ultimate standard of beauty materialized in his earliest mythology and apparently endured through his lifetime. This might be evident in a minor anecdote told by Joy Hill, Tolkien's secretary during the 1960s. A few years after his death she recalled his lively conversational style, saying he often held forth at length and "you'd get a fantastic nonstop half-hour lecture" on various topics like "the origin of a certain word" or "how you were a stupid girl to sit in the sun and how much better it was to have a white skin than a sunburnt one."[888] Whatever meaning we might attach to this recollection, it is worth mentioning because it evokes Tolkien's research in "Sigelwara Land" and his insights touching on medieval conceptions involving "faces black as soot" and "a race burned brown by the heat of the sun[.]"

Tolkien pursued his preferred professional agenda in a world in which a thin layer of anti-race academic attitudes floated on a sea of pro-race beliefs. Racial thinking was deeply rooted in both European tradition and in the social norms of his time. A long heritage of pre-racial imagery established in literature the moral shadings of color, and these shadings interacted with the emerging meanings that came to define racial imagery. The culture of race and Tolkien's symbolisms of color must be seen as intertwined and inseparable. But during the years just before he sat down to write *The Lord of the Rings*, the British academic community had launched an open challenge to both racism and race.

In Tolkien's imagination the connotations of whiteness and blackness could be readily sorted along a moral spectrum. Experimenting with this spectrum in his writings, it is obvious that Tolkien decided to construe his "black" characters as uniformly evil with little moral diversity in evidence. His portrayals of racially black characters are all monstrous and frightful.

Given the fact that he chose to travel down this path and imbue skin color with the same demeaning moral absolutes that were reflected in the racial culture of his time, it is proper that we should acknowledge the role that race holds in the social structures of Tolkien's fictional world. It is proper for us to conclude that Tolkien did not produce his fantasy colorations in a social vacuum. It isn't helpful to distort the record by insisting that Tolkien's deployment of the color black is race-neutral. It is misleading to decide that it merely references medieval imagery and folkloric characters. Tolkien's storytelling was not a reproduction of a medieval narrative; it was not designed to educate the public on the cultural nuances of medieval thinking. *The Lord of the Rings* was shaped to appeal to his contemporaries in Britain.

Whatever judgments we bring to our moral calibrations, one outcome is certain. Tolkien intentionally incorporated various subtleties of racial shadings into his worldscapes. We cannot dismiss these complexities of Middle-earth without doing violence to his intentions. Since he obviously hoped his preferred readership would embrace his choices, it is indeed proper for us to inquire into those choices, and to form meaningful opinions about the enactment of race in Tolkien's fantasy literature.

The White Wizards

As a term suffused with moral messaging, Tolkien's construction of "white" occasionally centered on racial ideology, but it most typically went beyond the mundane meanings attached to flesh-tone. He colorized the quality of whiteness with a magical spiritual essence that we can readily trace in the evolution of his Middle-earth wizards. Sitting down to write *The Lord of the Rings*, Tolkien decided that his wizards would contend for moral authority through the betrayal and bestowing of the mystical mantle of the color white.

According to John Rateliff, in the original version of *The Hobbit* the wizard Gandalf was not "Gandalf the Grey."[889] In the final chapter of that book, however, Tolkien set the foundation for the development of his later wizard color chart.[890] To counter the Necromancer, Tolkien invented "a council of many magicians and wise and learned men masters of lore and beneficial wizardry..." He soon altered "beneficial wizardy" to "white wizardry," and this eventually became "a great council of the white wizards, masters of lore and good magic..." It isn't clear from John Rateliff's analysis of the manuscripts for *The Hobbit* when this change was made.

The idea of "white wizards" was in place by 1937 in *The Hobbit*, but it is clear that the more detailed color chart of Middle-earth wizards evolved during the writing of *The Lord of the Rings*. Although it is difficult to follow the few indications of composition dates in the manuscripts, Christopher Tolkien seemed to indicate that it was in the fall of 1939 or later in 1940 during preparation of the "Fourth Phase" of the manuscripts that we find mention of "...the White Council in the South..."[891] What this meant at that time is not clear. Tolkien had not yet invented Saruman the White. But Gandalf was by then moving toward a new definition as "a grey-mantled figure..." and as "...the grey rider..."[892]

It was in 1940 that Tolkien at last convened the White Council, inventing a new wizard designated variously as "Saramond the White" and "Saramund the Grey."[893] This new wizard was envisioned as a fallen wizard who would betray Gandalf. And Gandalf then became known, for the first time, as "Gandalf the Grey."[894] Drafting a new version of "The Council of Elrond" sometime in late 1940, Tolkien wafted the wizard Radagast into the story from *The Hobbit*, assigning to him the color "Grey" and then "Brown," while bestowing upon Saruman the color white and electing him "chief of the White Council."[895] These three wizards together comprised the White Council, each with his assigned color.

During late 1941, taking the Fellowship to Lothlórien, Tolkien brought another person onto this council of wizards.[896] A fragmentary and mostly illegible note mentioned "Galadrim" and "Lady" and "to White Council."[897] The note continued on to list a "Lord and Lady clad in white, with *white hair*." This introduced the newly invented Celeborn and Galadriel into the story. They appeared with little physical description beyond white hair and piercing eyes. Tolkien instead focused on their nature as Elves of great power dressed in white clothing designed to emphasize this quality. Galadriel soon announced to the Fellowship: "I was at the White Council" and "The lord and lady of Lothlórien are accounted wise beyond the measure of the Elves of Middle-earth..."[898] Tolkien again described her as "gleaming in white"; and for the first time as "tall and pale."

Tolkien's use of the term "wise" is notable because the terms "wizard" and "witch" both mean "wise."[899] And so in the final published text we find "Celeborn the Wise" and Galadriel is "[t]all and white and fair" and she lifts her "white arms" and Frodo tells her, "You are wise and fearless and fair, Lady Galadriel...." and she acknowledges, "Wise the Lady Galadriel may be..." but she is, in the end, "...a slender elf-woman, clad in simple white..." And it was during this period that Tolkien began to configure Gandalf's promotion to a White Wizard, when a note had Frodo peering into Galadriel's mirror and seeing there "a grey figure like Gandalf... in twilight but it seems to be clad in white. Perhaps it is Saruman."[900]

This equation of the color white with a council of wizards is interesting because Walter Skeat and James Britten's *Reprinted Glossaries and Old Farming Words* in 1879 included this fascinating entry on "White witches": "White witches, superior beings in human shape, who formerly inhabited the quarter of the island; with power (and will, when properly applied to) of counteracting the wicked intentions of the magic art. They are still said to inhabit the more extreme parts of the West of England...."[901]

In *The Hobbit* we find "a great council of the white wizards, masters of lore and good magic..." But these unnamed wizards were not yet characterized as incarnations of Middle-earth semi-deities. Given Tolkien's interest in elaborating on obscure fragmentary tradition, as well as his knowledge of Walter Skeat's writings and dictionaries in general, it is quite likely that he encountered the Skeat and Britten description of white witches. Their portrayal of white witches as "superior beings in human shape" provided a likely inspiration for Tolkien's later decision to incarnate his Middle-earth wizards from Maiar who assume human shape.

The Middle-earth wizard color chart could also have been adapted by Tolkien from 19th century literary sources. An equation between whiteness and good magic can be found in Sir Walter Scott's 1821 novel, *Kenilworth*, which featured a man variously described as an astrologer, cunning man, conjuror, and white witch. An attached glossary defined "white witch" as "a wizard or witch of beneficent disposition." Scott's fictional literary source was rooted in an actual historical tradition of British white witches – the association of "wizard" and "wise man" and "cunning man" appeared in William Holloway's 1840 dictionary of "provincialisms."[902]

Also during the period when Tolkien clad Galadriel "in simple white," his friend CS Lewis was apparently inventing his own version of a white witch in *The Lion, the Witch and the*

Wardrobe. The two often shared their work at meetings of the Inklings, and Lewis knew what Tolkien had written about Galadriel.[903] In addition, it is also evident that both writers drew inspiration from a novel by H. Rider Haggard, *She*. That book featured an immortal Queen garbed in white. In one scene, this Queen had a man peer into a "font-like vessel" to see images of the past in the water, and she denied that it was magic – a scene that surely helped to inspire the Mirror of Galadriel.[904]

Tolkien's comments about Galadriel in a 1971 letter also pointed to a possible influence of Virgin Mary imagery on the making of Galadriel.[905] And Michael Maher has suggested that Tolkien drew upon certain medieval religious texts – particularly a manuscript known as the "Loreto Litany" – for Mary imagery that he applied to Galadriel.[906] This is certainly possible. But the parallels that Maher described are so inexact and so general that they cannot be usefully termed "parallels" in any meaningful sense. And Verlyn Flieger has carefully parsed Tolkien's 1971 letter to show that is better read as a denial of any direct connection between Mary and Galadriel.[907] The Mary influence is weak, but perhaps it cannot be wholly discounted since Tolkien typically drew on diverse sources to create his characters and scenes.

Leslie Donovan mentioned and dismissed a comparison of Galadriel to "Homeric women" and instead detailed an argument that Tolkien had in mind Norse valkyrie imagery when he constructed aspects of Galadariel.[908] She argued that it was Tolkien's typical practice to reshape his source-material, and he took this approach to "the valkyrie tradition" in crafting Galadriel, eliminating certain aspects of that tradition and emphasizing aspects that "suit his own purposes[.]" Donovan pointed in particular to "allusions to light and radiance" and Galadriel's white raiment as a direct expression of a valkyrie-like radiance, and to the Elf Queen's association with a swan barge and valkyrie swan imagery. Donovan usefully reminded us of Tolkien's literary backcloth, and it seems likely enough that Tolkien had in mind some of these associations when he created Galadriel. But the chronology of these elements as they enter Tolkien's evolving world-making suggests a more complex history. Swanships and the White Council both appeared in Middle-earth before Galadriel, and so these pre-existing elements did not arise as elements flowing in concert from valkyrie-like associations.

Reviewing this chronology, the folkloric connotations seem much more significant than Norse or Christian references. During the late 1930s Tolkien conducted intensive research in folkloric fairytale literature. Deciding to constitute the White Council as a powerful force in Middle-earth, in 1940 he convened it first with wizards like Gandalf and Saruman, and then in 1941 he added Galadriel. This leaves open the more likely probability that Tolkien clothed her in white because he saw her from the beginning as a white witch and as a member of the White Council.

The entry for white witches in the Skeat and Britten dictionary is compelling as a likely influence on Tolkien because it conveyed actual British folkloric tradition, and Tolkien had a long-standing interest in making his legendarium relevant to the British sense of mythological identity. To make this connection we can point to Tolkien's awareness of British folklore literature and to his awareness of the work of Walter Skeat, who was active in the British Folk-Lore Society.

Another prominent member of the British Folk-Lore Society published a detailed account of white witches in 1908. In *Devonshire Characters and Strange Events*, Sabine Baring-Gould related a number of stories about English white witches, male and female, attesting, "I have seen and can testify to very notable and undeniable cures that they have effected."[909] These practitioners of folk magic were common in 19th century England. Baring-Gould noted that an article he published in a local newspaper "brought me at the lowest computation fifty letters from all parts of the country..."

One of his stories described a man who "went to the county capital to consult the White Witch" and there was shown "a glass of water" in which the face of a woman appeared, "that of a woman who lived not far from him." This woman, said the White Witch, "had overlooked his child" – the term "overlooked" here meant that the woman had cast a spell upon the daughter, making her "rather strange in her head." This magic is certainly evocative of Galadriel's Mirror. This was an actual account of British folk tradition.

We do not know beyond doubt that Tolkien ever looked at the Skeat and Britten dictionary or the Baring-Gould book. But the likelihood that Tolkien drew his White Council in part from British white witches diminishes the possibility that he had race in mind as a primary factor in attaching the moral symbolism of the color "white" to his White Council in *The Lord of the Rings*. This would move the matter away from the narratives of race and more deeply into the territory of traditional British folklore. This means that when Tolkien had Saruman the White betray Gandalf, he probably intended to show that in becoming a wizard of many colors, Saruman had abandoned the traditions of the British white wizard.

Another circumstance supports the possibility that Tolkien knew of the Baring-Gould white witches. In *Devonshire Characters and Strange Events*, the story that followed Baring-Gould's account of white witches in Britain opened with mention of the Corsairs of North Africa.[910] A few years after constituting the White Council, Tolkien inserted Corsairs into Middle-earth and later described them as "similar to the Mediterranean corsairs; sea-robbers with fortified bases."[911] Tolkien no doubt learned of the Corsairs from various sources, but a few parallels can be seen between Baring-Gould's Corsair and Tolkien's Corsairs.

The Baring-Gould story touched on the life of a man named Richard Peeke. It began by describing how "pirates of Algiers had for some years been very troublesome" along the coasts of Europe, and had been making "descents on the coasts of England and Ireland and had swept away people into slavery." Several "Christian powers" had deemed it necessary to attack Algiers "the principal port of these pirates." Richard Peeke was a sailor in the English fleet, and in 1621 they "sailed into the harbour of Algiers and set fire to the Moorish ships and galleys..." But "the Algerines succeeded in recovering all their ships with the exception of two, which burnt to the water's edge."

In Tolkien's original account of his Corsairs, Gimli the Dwarf described to Merry and Pippin his encounters with the Corsairs of Umbar.[912] These Corsairs "marched abroad" raiding and ravaging South Gondor. And Aragorn and his companions captured their lightly guarded fleet "save some ships that their masters set ablaze[.]" Aboard the Corsair ships were many slaves: "And on the ships the slaves rebelled. For the Corsairs of Umbar had in their ships many new-captured prisoners, and the oarsmen were all slaves, many taken in Gondor in petty raids, or unhappy descendants of slaves made in years gone by."

In the Baring-Gould story of Richard Peeke we find mention of slave raiding, an English attack, and the burning of a few ships of the Corsairs. Tolkien's story also described Corsair slavery, an attack by Aragorn and companions, and the burning of several Corsair ships. But the two tales part ways in their outcomes. In contrast to the failure of the English attack in the Peeke story, Aragorn and his companions prevailed and the slaves were freed, and the Corsairs fled "into the desert that lies north of Harad." The parallels between the two stories could have been extracted from other sources or invented by coincidence. But it is also arguable that Tolkien took note of the Richard Peeke story and deemed it useful. If so, he did not simply cut-and-paste his pirates from the Mediterranean to Middle-earth.

A point can be made about the association of the ideas of "wise man" and "cunning man." John Rhys published various accounts touching on Welsh wizards in his account of Celtic folklore. One *cwmshurwr* or conjuror came with an interesting decription: "The wizard was a *dyn llaw-harn*, 'a man with an iron hand[.]'"[913] Another is labeled a "cunning man," with an extended note on the term *cynnil* as signifying "'shrewd,' 'cunning,' or 'clever,' though it would probably come nearer the original meaning of the word to render it by 'smart[.]'"[914]

Tolkien's eventual portrayal of Saruman evoked this spectrum of description. Tom Shippey has associated the name "Saruman" with Old English *searu* "device, design, contrivance, art" and with *searo* "cunning."[915] And Shippey reminded us that

Tolkien had one character speak of Saruman as a wizard with "a mind of metal and wheels[.]" In addition, Tolkien translated the term "Isengard" as "the iron court."[916]

It is useful to emphasize that Tolkien's authorial strategy was one of adaptation, utilizing traditional elements and transforming them to fit his own narrative agenda, drawing inspiration from the historical world for his fantasy characters and events. To expect point-by-point reproduction is to miss the point. Tolkien did not aim at retelling history. He instead echoed the primary world in his secondary world – he produced a feigned history where he could apply his inventive imagination and his creativity. For this reason his Corsairs of Umbar were not thinly veiled Corsairs of 17th century Algiers; his wizards were not precisely cut from British folk traditions.

It would be misguided to divorce Tolkien's use of white symbolism entirely from the circumstances of his cultural world. He made a deliberate choice to imbue the colors "black" and "white" with esoteric moral qualities, and we must therefore consider what he intended; we must inquire into the degree to which his moral messaging aspired to influence our own calibrations of decency and identity.

In Tolkien's worldmaking we most often encounter blackness as a shallow moral quality, displaying a uniformity of evil, versus the contrasting diversity of whiteness and its emphasis on rectitude. It seems unlikely that Tolkien intended for his usage of whiteness in wizardry to convey racial identification as a primary intended symbolism, but this cannot be completely ruled out as a secondary message. Tolkien's audience believed in race. He accepted major premises of the racial social world.

Into this realm Tolkien summoned his White Council. One of his white wizards has endured death at the hands of a "dark" mildly Africanized Balrog. This wizard consequently assumes the burden and privilege of righteous insight; the other white wizard has betrayed this duty. Witnessing Saruman's abandonment of white robes, Gandalf favors tradition, "I liked white better." Tolkien's deep concern with Nazi Nordic racialism comes to mind as we listen to this exchange. We sense that Saruman has been busy lately "[r]uining, perverting, misapplying, and making for ever accursed, that noble northern spirit[.]" He has even gone so far as to ally himself with Mongol-type orcs. He sneers and rationalizes his breaking of the integrity of white light. And so Gandalf warns, "...he that breaks a thing to find out what it is has left the path of wisdom."[917] In his descent into evil, Saruman adopts a white hand as his symbol, further perverting his high calling as a white wizard.

Between these contending forces of good and evil we find Galadriel, the white witch of the Golden Wood. Galadriel has trodden her own complicated moral pathway in Tolkien's mind. Aligning herself with the darker forces of Elven history in order to rule in Middle-earth, she has nevertheless overcome the temptation to abandon her white elvish robes. She denies the Great Ring, remaining "a slender elf-woman, clad in simple white..."

Galadriel's spiritual reward is to escape her earthly burdens, the culmination of her long defeat, laying down the weight of wielding authority for the benefit of Elvendom. Taking ship for Valinor, she departs from Middle-earth. She sails for a magic realm where the gradations of moral darkness have been overcome; where there will be no more striving with enemies; where the swarthy and the sallow will no longer trouble the councils of the Wise.

Companions in Shipwreck

We can appreciate artistry without knowing anything of the artist. But when we consider how Tolkien proceeded with worldmaking, it is useful to ponder the nature of his inner life and how it shaped his creative choices, the productions of his imagination. This point is particularly clear when we consider Tolkien's private attitudes toward women and their consequent fictional circumstances in Middle-earth.

JRR Tolkien populated his tales of Middle-earth with many fascinating women, but the fifteen primary characters of *The Hobbit* and the nine primary characters of *The Lord of the Rings* do not include any females. This situation has properly led to much critical discussion about his creative choices regarding gender. A common theme is that the near-total absence of women in *The Hobbit* and the secondary nature of the handful of female characters in *The Lord of the Rings* must signify a profound male-centered regard, perhaps rooted in some form of misogynistic worldview.

Seeking to counter this criticism, Janet Croft and Leslie Donovan collected a number of fascinating essays in *Perilous and Fair: Women in the Works and Life of JRR Tolkien*.[918] The stated goal of this collection was "to remedy perceptions that Tolkien's works are bereft of female characters, are colored by anti-feminist tendencies, and have yielded little serious academic work on women's issues." The inclusion of a broad spectrum of valuable perspectives and analyses make this work indispensable for those who wish to investigate the topic of Tolkien and women.

So it is curious that very little attention is given in this collection to a detailed letter that Tolkien wrote in 1941 on women, sex, and marriage. One would think that such a document would attract much useful analysis and contemplation in any volume pertaining to women and Tolkien. But skimming *Perilous and Fair*, only a few brief moments are given to that letter. In a fine paper on Tolkien's relations with women in his early life and in academia, John Rateliff described the 1941 letter as "one of the most notorious things JRR Tolkien ever wrote..." This opinion does not seem a very promising characterization for any project designed to rescue Tolkien's image from criticism on women's issues. We can only wonder why the volume included no substantive consideration of the 1941 letter. But that letter offers some key insights into Tolkien's attitudes toward women.

Just a few months after composing that 1941 letter, Tolkien invented Galadriel as a member of the White Council. And three years later he came up with Éowyn, a princess of Rohan, and he sat down in 1946 to tell her story. As I argue below, it is useful to consider the 1941 letter and other aspects of Tolkien's biography when pondering Éowyn.

John Garth's *Tolkien and the Great War* described Tolkien's experience with what was then a mysterious and debilitating malady. In the spring of 1916 Tolkien married Edith Bratt; he soon thereafter set forth for the trenches of World War One. After just a few months as a soldier on the brutal battlefields of France, he became stricken with trench fever.[919] At the end of October 1916 Tolkien "was transferred to an officers' hospital a short distance from Beauval, at Gézaincourt" and then to "Le Touquet, and a bed at the Duchess of Westmorland Hospital." Next he took passage on a hospital ship, *Asturias*. By November 9 he found himself in a bed at the Birmingham First Southern General Hospital. Tolkien spent the next year falling in and out of trench fever and flu and convalescing in hospitals in Britain far from the front lines of the war. Garth provides little insight as to Tolkien's experiences at these hospitals, but it took several years for him to fully recover.

In 1917, racked by this intermittent illness, Tolkien wrote "The Tale of Tinúviel," a tragedy of love that became a major piece of his evolving legendarium. It is well-known that certain aspects of this story memorialize his relationship with his wife

Edith, drawing particularly on a moment that happened in the spring of 1917. After his initial recovery from trench fever, Tolkien was assigned duty at "an outpost of Humber Garrison near Thirtle Bridge at Roos... and Edith was able to live with him." There she danced and sang among the hemlocks. Tolkien wove this scene into his legendarium as a central enchantment in "The Tale of Tinúviel."

Tolkien wrote his first version of this story while convalescing for nine weeks during the summer of 1917 at Brooklands Officers' Hospital at Hull. This hospital nursing staff was managed by Margaret (Pakenham) Strickland-Constable.[920] She apparently spoke Swedish, Norwegian, German, French, and Danish. Given Tolkien's interest in language, it would not be surprising if he had some kind of brief friendship with her, but Strickland-Constable's diaries do not mention Tolkien.[921]

Several decades later Michael Tolkien, one of JRR's sons, joined the British military and in 1941 found himself in a hospital, recovering from an accident. There he fell in love with a nurse named Joan Griffiths. They soon announced their intention to marry. Their first son – also named Michael – was born in 1943. Many years later, this son recalled that the union was not a source of joy to JRR and Edith Tolkien.[922] Instead, they "disapproved of my father Michael's hasty wartime marriage to my mother." This opposition was due to "his lack of means and prospects" and to Joan's "uncultured, lower middle class" status, as well as her religious background in the Church of England rather than the Catholic Church. This family conflict "took the form of irate and pompous letters on either side…"

Preparing one such letter in early March 1941, JRR offered a lengthy disquisition on "earthly relationships."[923] It has a disheartening and gloomy tone. Tolkien felt that men and women could never be friends. He asserted that friendship "is virtually impossible between man and woman." Writing that "'friendship' has often been tried" and whether men and women draw together "for generous romantic or tender motives" or via "baser or more animal ones" inevitably "one side or the other nearly always fails." "The devil," Tolkien concluded, "is endlessly ingenious and sex is his favourite subject." These notions surely took shape early in his adult life and must have influenced his storytelling when it touched on matters of the heart. This makes his first full-length love story especially interesting.

We do not have the original 1917 version of "The Tale of Tinúviel"; Tolkien erased it and wrote over the sheets of paper in ink several years later. Whatever his original vision, it is a tale of peril and wonder. Looking for Edith in the tale, we find Tinúviel described as "[s]lender and very dark of hair" and her dancing inspired "dreams and slumbers" and she danced "at night when the moon shone pale[.]" John Garth quoted a 1971 letter that JRR wrote to son Christopher in which he similarly described Edith in her youth, the woman who inspired him to dream of Tinúviel: "In those days her hair was raven...."[924]

Beyond Edith Tolkien's dancing and singing in the springtime forest, she helped to shape "The Tale of Tinúviel" in another way. As John Garth described, Tolkien met Edith in 1908 when he was sixteen and she was nineteen, and they soon fell in love. Tolkien's guardian, Father Francis Morgan, "got wind of the romance and banned Tolkien from seeing Edith." It took another eight years before they married. And in "The Tale of Tinúviel" a smitten Beren is sent by Tinúviel's father to achieve an impossible quest as a condition for marriage. Beren succeeds, but it is a sad story.

Given the fact that Tolkien wrote this tragic love story in the course of his recovery from trench fever, it is notable that the most complete love story in *The Lord of the Rings* is that of Faramir and Éowyn, which unfolded in the Houses of Healing in Minas Tirith. It is interesting for its contrast to the tragedy of Beren and Luthien.

But what is even more interesting is that of all his characters in *The Lord of the Rings*, Tolkien identified most closely with Faramir. In a footnote attached to an incomplete draft letter written in January 1956, Tolkien wrote, "As far as any character is 'like me' it is Faramir."[925] This letter also mentioned that Tolkien gave Faramir a dream that played a crucial role in the development of his legendarium: "...when Faramir speaks of his private vision of the Great Wave, he speaks for me. That vision and that dream has been ever with me...." It seems that Tolkien intended to articulate a clear connection to Faramir.

In a letter fragment composed sometime in 1963, Tolkien spoke of Faramir as "motherless and sisterless" – like Tolkien himself – and of Faramir's character as "modest, fair-minded and scrupulously just, and very merciful."[926] And responding in this note to "[c]riticism of the speed of the relation or 'love' of Faramir and Éowyn" Tolkien began his explanation of Éowyn with this interesting observation: "It is possible to love more than one person (of the other sex) at the same time, but in different mode and intensity." He ended this letter with an insight drawn from his own life: "In my experience feelings and decisions ripen very quickly... in periods of great stress, and especially under the expectation of imminent death."

This sounds more intriguingly personal than Tolkien probably intended. But if Faramir is an echo of Tolkien, could Éowyn have been inspired in some part by a woman in Tolkien's life? The least speculative inspiration might be to listen for another echo of Edith Tolkien in the character of Éowyn, as with "The Tale of Tinúviel." A parallel is suggested in the way that Faramir and Éowyn fall in love in a hospital, and JRR and Edith conceived their first son while he was recovering from trench fever. But during Tolkien's various hospitalizations in 1916 and 1917, while married to Edith, in that time "of great stress" it seems that he somehow discovered that it was "possible to love more than one person[.]" This is his own account, though it isn't clear what he meant.

But this might explain certain aspects of his 1941 letter to son Michael. It is a detailed missive warning about the dangers of associating with women. The letter ends with autobiographical musings, and one fascinating passage seems to radiate a strong yearning to share unspoken personal experiences.

Tolkien begins with a theoretical "young woman" caught up in a sexual fervor, who then "may actually 'fall in love.'" In such a case "things are going to happen: and they may be very painful and harmful, if things go wrong." This seemingly represents an effort to share a bit of good advice, but it is followed with a peculiar apology: "Particularly if the young man only wanted a temporary guiding star and divinity (until he hitches his waggon to a brighter one), and was merely enjoying the flattery of sympathy nicely seasoned with a titillation of sex[.]" Tolkien then assures us that any such dalliance, if any such theoretical young man ever happened to get theoretically caught up in just such a theoretical scenario with a theoretical young woman, well, anyway, it was really "all quite innocent, of course, and worlds away from 'seduction.'"

This strange passage makes no sense as a flight of pure fancy. It could be read as an awkward skirting of Michael's particular circumstances. But it does sound somewhat like a thinly veiled confession of some kind. It would be understandable if Tolkien felt some impulse to confide in his son Michael, to explain his life – and to then decide that whatever happened simply felt impossible. In any case, we are left glimpsing a mysterious "shipwreck of love," as Tolkien put it.

In his own autobiographical Houses of Healing, Tolkien invited us to hear a magical echo of Edith in "The Tale of Tinúviel." In this way he poetically affirmed their marriage, transforming it into a legend of the First Age of Middle-earth. In the case of Éowyn, it is speculative to suggest that Tolkien meant for her to preserve veiled references to any actual person. Yet he openly acknowledged the echoes of himself in Faramir. And I believe that he enjoyed inserting hidden puzzles into his legendarium.

If an actual person inspired some aspect of Éowyn, it would be reasonable to look for this unknown woman somewhere in Tolkien's experience as a hospitalized soldier. It is interesting that Margaret Strickland-Constable was in charge of the nurses at Brooklands Officers' Hospital. According to the *The New Shorter Oxford English Dictionary*, the word "constable" refers to the "count (head officer) of the stable." In *The Peoples of Middle-earth* Tolkien wrote (p. 53) that the name Éowyn contained the "element éo-" which is "an old word meaning 'horse.'"

Tolkien selected this name long before he invented her stint in the Minas Tirith Houses of Healing. But perhaps the name suggested this plot development to Tolkien – up until 1946 his outlines all had Éowyn getting killed in the course of battling the Witch-King. So the change in her fortunes and the invention of the Houses of Healing entered the tale at the same moment. Was this new plot development derived from remembrance of some young nurse at Brooklands? Explaining the secrets of womanhood to son Michael in his 1941 letter, Tolkien's theory was that the "sexual impulse" made women "very sympathetic and understanding" with a "servient, helpmeet instinct" – echoing the very stereotype of a nurse. If Tolkien's affections turned to just such a "temporary guiding star," she is unknown now – or rather, she is only known to us through the romance of Faramir and Éowyn in the Houses of Healing.

Drawing upon the circumstances of his life to invent Middle-earth, Tolkien's creativity flowed through the inward lens of his personal moral judgments. To the extent that such introspections gazed upon the secrets of his love life, we really only know of his feelings for Edith. The Tolkien family has not released either Tolkien's private diaries or his correspondence with Edith. But the 1941 letter certainly leaves us with some rather dark conclusions about love: "A man has a life-work, a career, (and male friends), all of which could (and do where he has any guts) survive the shipwreck of 'love.'"

Where did that shipwreck come from? We may never know the full details. But it hints at a bittersweet voyage, with the tragedy of it memorialized in Tinúviel, and the sweetness of it commemorated in Éowyn's healing. Beren came to a tragic end, but Faramir lived happily ever after. If all these narrative threads are woven together in some part from aspects of Tolkien's inner world, perhaps it is best that we are given something that is merely glimpsed; a scene in the fading mist of a long-lost world. This is powerful magic.

A final point can be made about Tolkien's Houses of Healing. His 1941 letter focused on "the romantic chivalric tradition... as a product of Christendom." He regarded this religious element as "God's way of refining so much of our gross manly natures and emotion"; and he explained his view that women are "instinctively... monogamous" whereas "Men just ain't, not by their animal natures." Self-denial and suffering provide paths to the highest ideals that males can achieve in "a fallen world." In "The Houses of Healing" it is arguable that Tolkien has Aragorn embody the virtues of chivalric tradition. Éowyn suffers from a magical malady as debilitating as trench fever, and Aragorn summons her back from darkness, placing her hand in her brother's hand as she awakens. With this action, Tolkien reveals Aragorn as virtuous and wise – a kingly figure who has overcome his male animalistic nature.

In a later chapter, Tolkien revisits the Houses of Healing to bring together Faramir and Éowyn in an equally decorous tale of romance. And it is interesting that Tolkien identified with Faramir. Both he and Faramir suffered in war. In their Houses of Healing they both found occasion to explore their sexual selves. So when we visit Tolkien's fictional Houses of Healing, we find him pausing to consider model sexual behaviors for men.

Faramir marries a princess equal to his own station in life – a point felt by Michael Tolkien, who knew his parents had decided that his wife was "uncultured" and of "lower middle class" status. (Michael Tolkien wrote an autobiography that attempted "to make sense of and to some extent idealise the conflicts and confusions of his childhood..." But for reasons that are not given, his oldest son, also named Michael, termed the manuscript "unpublishable.") And JRR has both Aragorn and Faramir respond to Éowyn with measured wisdom – in the 1941 letter Tolkien warned that a "natural young woman... wants to become the mother of the young man's children." And so his fictional men proceed with care in handling Éowyn. We can only guess how Michael Tolkien read this story, given that he rushed into marriage.

As JRR Tolkien saw the matter, in the pre-Christian pre-Medieval realms of ancient Middle-earth, Aragorn and Faramir both prove unerring in adhering to ideals that echo chivalric tradition. And through them, Tolkien has a moral message for fallen animalistic males of the far future. With God and Christendom in hand, we men can indeed hope for some refinement of "our gross manly natures and emotion." As Tolkien noted in his 1963 draft letter about Faramir and Éowyn, the story "does not deal with a period of 'Courtly Love' and its pretences; but with a culture more primitive (sc. less corrupt) and nobler."

The mingling of biography with analysis of literary creativity is necessarily an art, not a science. In so doing, we must sometimes take journeys that wander beyond our familiar clarities – journeys to places that must first be glimpsed before they can be clearly seen. Secret paths of selfhood take us to the very edge of what we can know of ourselves, to whisper the far-off spells of selfhood.

For keepers of secrets, clarity must seem dark, foreboding. Perhaps at times Tolkien saw our love for one another and our human sexuality as a kind of hopeless shipwreck, for which we need divine intervention. But if so, this is only part of what he saw. Choosing to spend his life helping us all to voyage to magical realms, JRR Tolkien wished for hope in the world. And finding ourselves upon his distant quays, and boarding his magic ships to elsewhere, we encounter both sorrow and hope. But we can indeed do our best to learn better how to love one another; we can learn how to heal one another with love; we can keep on becoming whoever we become next in the journey.

Tolkien's Tree of Tales

Tolkien touched on his childhood literary interests in his essay "On Fairy-stories." Writing in 1943, after dismissing *Alice in Wonderland* and *Treasure Island,* he recalled: "Red Indians were better: there were bows and arrows (I had and have a wholly unsatisfied desire to shoot well with a bow), and strange languages, and glimpses of an archaic mode of life, and, above all, forests in such stories."[927]

Born in 1892, Tolkien grew up as the heir of academic attitudes that treated the cultural production of mythological literature as evolutionary. According to mythologist Christopher Vecsey, the eminent Victorian anthropologist, E.B. Tylor, "viewed myth as a reflection and indication of a certain stage of human thought which he termed 'animistic,' belonging to a stage of human development called 'primitive.'"[928] Seeing "primitive" people as enduring childlike representatives of an early evolutionary stage in human history, mainstream academicians decided "that only primitives maintain a working mythopoeic ability" – the ability to invent mythic master narratives and believe in myth. Mythologist Alan Dundes further explains the state of comparative mythology in this period, describing how researchers felt that they could glimpse "their own roots, their own ancestors" by studying "modern savage (primitive) people."[929] His judgment of the ideological basis for this belief system is severe: "These 'savages,' to continue to use the terrible ethnocentric, racist label, were living in the present just as the ancient forebears of the English, French, etc, must have lived in the past."

Racial Indians, no matter how elborate their cultural circumstances, always fell under this race-based rubric. It isn't clear the level of familiarity Tolkien would have had with the ethnographic discourse surrounding racial Indians, but even a passing acquaintance would have affirmed this cultural prejudice. A good example is that of George Bird Grinnell's 1911 *The Indians of To-day*, which begins, "When the white men first set foot in America, they found it inhabited by people who in the north were primitive, and whose development had been slow; for although man had inhabited the continent for many thousand years, his culture had progressed no further than that of the age of polished stone."[930]

An influential folklorist who shaped Tolkien's formative years was Andrew Lang. It is known that Tolkien in his youth was familiar with Lang's collections of fairytales, but we can't be entirely certain when Tolkien first encountered Lang's more academic writings on myth. In accordance with anthropological thinking of his day, Lang, in his 1884 *Custom and Myth*, separated world mythological traditions into those of "civilized men" versus what he termed the "savage mythologies" of "people in the savage state."[931] As with Tylor's evolutionary ranking system, Lang's arbitrary cultural appraisal reflected the pervasive influence of preferential ranking systems derived from racial taxonomies of the time – it is ironic that the untrue mythological origin stories of race provided the substance for the mythic narratives of civilized men. In such a context, Lang deemed his own cultural heritage and its roots to represent a normative character of "civil" and "civilized" society, whereas non-Europeans were treated as culturally stunted, lingering in a childlike state of "savagery" that his own folk had long ago abandoned.

Tolkien read *Custom and Myth* in the course of preparing "On Fairy-stories."[932] And given his acknowledged youthful interest in Lang, it is probably not coincidence that Lang and Tolkien both subscribed to the general tone of European and American orderings of humankind, categorized in both racial and cultural terms. Dimitra Fimi characterizes Tolkien's basic attitude as "hierarchical" – meaning that Tolkien divided and ranked his human social order in various ways in Middle-earth, but he tended to make manifest the widespread idea that some folk were more culturally developed than others.[933] Peering into *Traditions of the Skidi Pawnee*, Tolkien stared through a particular kind of lens that ranked culture along an evolutionary trajectory from unsophisticated "savagery" to the sophistications of "civilization." For Tolkien the qualities of "primitive" culture helped to imbue his storytelling with a sense of historical depth – his folk of a vanished past could be differentiated in cultural terms from contemporary people who saw themselves as Christian and civilized.

Formulating his own ideas about myth, Tolkien rejected aspects of this intellectual inheritance – as with the philological notions of F. Max Müller. In adopting this point of view, Tolkien drew in part upon the thinking of Andrew Lang, who countered philological mythography with a more folkloric view of myth. Seeing something necessary in myth, we might surmise that Tolkien found little sympathy for Müller's view that the invention of the "absurd tales" of myth occured in a historical time "of temporary insanity, through which the human mind had to pass."[934] Tolkien must also have been aware of Müller's early conflation of race and Aryan linguistics and his later rejection of that model.

But Tolkien embraced other aspects of traditional thinking about tradition, and he was careful to delineate his preferred meanings for the term "primitive." As I have noted earlier in this book, Tolkien set forth his early thinking on myth in an essay he wrote in 1914-1915, describing the Finnish *Kalevala* as "a collection of mythological ballads full of that very primitive undergrowth that the litterature of Europe has on the whole been cutting away and reducing for centuries..."[935] And sometime between 1919 and 1924 he added to his concept of "primitive undergrowth" a particularly significant note that guided his early years as a mythologist: "...I would that we had more of it left – something of the same sort that belonged to the English..."[936]

Tolkien felt that "the queer and strange, the unrestrained, the grotesque is not only interesting, it is valuable."[937] Attracted to this spirit of the *Kalevala*, Tolkien valued certain resonant qualities that likewise appear in Norse tradition: "...the quaint tales, the outrageous ghosts, the sorceries and by-tracks of human imagination and belief that crop out here and there..." Deciding that such elements in Homeric Greek epic had "properly been pruned away" he nevertheless felt "[i]t is not always necessary to purge it out altogether in order to attain to the Sublime." He concluded: "You can have your gargoyles on your noble cathedral, but Europe has lost much through too often trying to build Greek Temples."

For Tolkien, the necessary elements of mythic "primitive hero-story" included "glorious exaggerations" and a "child's delight[.]" For him myth meant "taking a holiday from the whole course of progress of the last three Milleniums" in order to become "wildly unhellenic and barbarous for a time[.]" Treating the creation of mythic master narratives in this fashion, Tolkien accepted the traditional academic project of constructing an artificial contrast between modern mythopoeic sensibility and primitive mythopoeic impulse. But rather than craft any sort of intellectual precision in his use of the term "primitive," Tolkien instead deferred to the race-based quality of meaning inherent in this contrast.

By the early 1940s, with his own private primitive mythmaking well advanced, Tolkien decided that for him the term "primitive" referred to pre-Christian folk living in an uncivilized state. This definition is made clear in "On Fairy-stories," where Tolkien determined that a certain Norse tale told of Thórr was a fairy story with a "primitive" quality – in a footnote Tolkien explained that he meant for "primitive" to apply to "peoples still living in an inherited paganism, who are not, as we say, civilised."[938] The fact that this definition entered the text of "On Fairy-stories" in 1943 indicates the degree to which Tolkien was thinking in that period about what "primitive" signified to him, as well as the peoples to whom the term could be applied.

Racial Indians were clearly on Tolkien's mind in 1943 when he referred to his childhood interest in "Red Indians."[939] Judging from his writings, this is the only time in his professional life that this seems to be explicitly true. The next year Tolkien again used the term "Red Indians" while complaining about a

"Yank burbling about 'Feudalism'": "...I said that an Englishman's relations with porters, butlers, and tradesmen had as much connexion with 'Feudalism' as skyscrapers had with Red Indian wigwams[.]"[940] Tolkien might well have known that the term "wigwam" is an Algonquin word, but he clearly didn't know that by 1944 Algonquin-speakers had a long record of building skyscrapers in New York City.

Whatever Tolkien knew of racial Indians in America, on those few occasions when he employed the phrase "Red Indians" he was probably invoking the kind of attitude that we find in Lang's 1884 *Custom and Myth*. There we find "Red Indians" on page 9, page 11, and on many other pages – Lang needed this colorful phrase to distinguish racial Indian myth from the mythology of India. In 1938-1939 Tolkien drew on *Custom and Myth* as well as Lang's collections of fairy stories to prepare the first version of "On Fairy-stories."[941] This was originally a lecture commemorating Lang, and Tolkien mentioned Lang's "adult study of mythology and folk-lore[.]"[942]

Tolkien described his early ambitions as a mythologist in a long letter he wrote in late 1951. There he said that "from early days" he felt "grieved by the poverty of my own beloved country: it had no stories of its own (bound up with its tongue and soil), not of the quality that I sought, and found (as an ingredient) in legends of other lands."[943] Listing various European literary traditions as models, he concluded, "I had a mind to make a body of more or less connected legend, ranging from the large and cosmogonic, to the level of romantic fairy-story... which I could dedicate simply to: to England; to my country." A few years later he affirmed again this agenda as a mythologist: "Having set myself a task... to restore to the English an epic tradition and present them with a mythology of their own: it is a wonderful thing to be told that I have succeeded[.]"[944]

In his 1951 letter Tolkien set forth observations that seem applicable to his likely attitudes toward Pawnee myth: "I am not 'learned' in the matters of myth and fairy-story, however, for in such things (as far as known to me) I have always been seeking material, things of a certain tone and air, and not simple knowledge." Celtic Arthurian myth he termed "powerful" with a "fair elusive beauty" but "too lavish and fantastical, incoherent and repetitive." It was also Christianized myth, which to him seemed a "fatal" flaw – the Christianization of Scandinavia illustrated for Tolkien the general effect that such cultural change could have on literary traditions and mythology.[945]

There is no doubt that Tolkien's lifelong agenda as a mythologist centered on the literary heritage of Europe, and more specifically on Northern European traditions. In 1947 he identified himself as "northern not only by descent (of little import) but by temper, taste, and such learning as I have scraped."[946] In even more specific personal terms he further mythologized his own identity as that of a Mercian of the English Midlands.[947] The sensibilities associated with this identity gave rise to major pieces of Middle-earth, both literary romance and backcloth.

Tolkien's preferred scholarly interests dictated his list of model legendariums in his 1951 letter: "...Greek, and Celtic, and Romance, Germanic, Scandinavian, and Finnish..." A first glance tends to highlight the nature of language groupings as Tolkien's guiding focus. But this list also suggests that he was drawn to the idea of mythology as storytelling that yields a narrative of identity based on shared legendry, a sense of communal selfhood rooted in literary traditions. It was the transmission of a shared group identity distinguished by language and historical tradition that drew his attention. Singling out the Finnish model as one that "greatly affected" him, Tolkien grasped the connection between language and national identity, but he also sensed that the absence of a coherent mythology was the element of impoverishment that he "felt to be missing" from the idea of being English.

In just the title of *Traditions of the Skidi Pawnee* Tolkien would have glimpsed these very articulations of culture and identity. Opening the book, he would have encountered what seemed an authoritative project to capture the mythic essences of what it meant to be Skidi Pawnee. To get a likely sense for how

Tolkien would have interpreted this experience, we can turn to a brief document he wrote in 1958. There he characterized his design of his early legendarium in cultural terms that he was familiar with, referring to "the oldest forms of the mythology – when it was still intended to be no more than another primitive mythology, though more coherent and less 'savage.'"[948] This is partly what he meant when he said in 1951 that he "always been seeking material, things of a certain tone and air..."

Tolkien's interest in "Red Indians" was incidental and superficial. Since his attitudes seem parallel to Andrew Lang's characterizations – at least in the use of terms like "primitive," "savage," and "Red Indian" – it makes sense that he also borrowed Lang's interpretive lens when he opened the pages of *Traditions of Skidi Pawnee*. If so, it was a casual application that replicated the trappings of Lang's ethnocentric racialism, but perhaps not always the heart of it – Tolkien felt free to contest Lang's modeling of what we know of "naked ancestors thousands of years ago[.]"[949] But there is no evidence that Tolkien found any cause to remodel Lang's Red Indians. So we might assume that Tolkien tended to absorb a particular valuation of culture when Lang portrays a Greek custom from antiquity and compares it to a contemporary American Indian custom, gazing with a sense of lofty insight upon primitives whose social crudities represent an arrested antiquarian culture worthy only of the lower forms of esteem: "That Greeks should dance about in their mysteries with harmless serpents in their hands looks quite unintelligible. When a wild tribe of Red Indians does the same thing, as a trial of courage, with real rattlesnakes, we understand the Red Man's motives, and may conjecture that similar motives once existed among the ancestors of the Greeks."[950]

Tolkien did not idealize the notion of "primitive." In a letter he wrote later in life he expressed the view that "'primitiveness' is no guarantee of value, and is and was in great part a reflection of ignorance."[951] Whether or nor this late opinion reflects his earlier usages of the term, his most consistent intended application seems antiquarian in nature. When Tolkien borrowed from Skidi myth, he surely interpreted this activity as borrowing from an arrested antiquarian culture in order to reconstruct his own version of long-vanished days of yore, enriching a tattered primitive past. But this also left him open to a perplexing dilemma. How would he explain this borrowing to the sophisticates in his world who wished for heroic legendry, for inspiring romance and myth relevant to their cultural self-image, only to discover that they have just been handed rattlesnakes still warm from the grasp of wild savages?

The logic that guided Tolkien's use of Skidi tradition was mythopoeic in nature. The Skidi legendarium would have provided for Tolkien an example of primitive savagery, and this quality drew Tolkien's interest because he yearned for an English mythology that had more of what he termed "primitive undergrowth" and he wished "we had more of it left – something... that belonged to the English[.]"[952] He turned to the Skidi material for such greenery because he knew that borrowings from non-English European tradition (like Norse and Finnish myth) would be noticed, and so these elements would fail to convey the right kind of homegrown English tone. Tolkien wrote in one 1936 essay: "Of English pre-Christian mythology we know practically nothing."[953] He added that "the fundamentally similar heroic temper of ancient England and Scandinavia cannot have been founded on (or perhaps rather, cannot have generated) mythologies divergent on this essential point." He had the option to transplant Norse greenery into the wilted mythic landscapes of England, and this would have plausibly fit the ancient English "heroic temper," but no one would have seen such mythological greenery as anything other than a patently invasive species.

Textual evidence reveals that Tolkien studied the Skidi legendarium carefully for practical ideas about how to craft the appropriate tone for his mythology. It had to be a "more coherent" but still "primitive" mythology. Traces of color borrowed from obscure Pawnee traditions would lend a desirable air of "primitive undergrowth." But in order for Tolkien's English mythology to be seen as "English," these borrowings could never be recognized as indigenous to any realm other than the realm of his own English imagination. For this reason he could never reveal his use of *Traditions of the Skidi Pawnee*.

With the logic of this project in mind, it seems difficult to justify a view of Tolkien as casually skimming *Traditions of the Skidi Pawnee*. He had reason to give thought to what he read. He had reason to draw material carefully from what he read. To be sure, to make serious use of *Traditions of the Skidi Pawnee*, Tolkien did not have to become an expert on Pawnee culture or history or language, or even of this one book. He simply had to absorb the basic imagery of song as a generative force, of a great spider making impassable cobwebs, of a little hairy man living in a hole, of talking eagles, of a shape-shifter with magic horses, of a man dying and resurrecting, of a flint monster slain by an arrow. With these "primitive" images in hand Tolkien the mythologist could meaningfully enrich the mythic textures of his Middle-earth while saying nothing of imports from distant "savage" Pawneeland.

Tolkien's own assessment of authorship as a creative process may find appeal to some as an explanation for how he made use of *Traditions of the Skidi Pawnee* – an alternate explanation to conscious borrowing. He noted that a story like *The Lord of the Rings* "grows like a seed in the dark out of the leaf-mould of the mind: out of all that has been seen or thought or read, that has long ago been forgotten, descending into the deeps."[954] The osmosis of cultural exposure is surely a process that is relevant to understanding both the general preferences and specific content of our cultural productions. Richard C. West reminds us that "Tolkien studied and taught myths and legends and fairy tales all his life, and they were an integral part of his mental furniture and imaginative make-up."[955]

Some may prefer to assume that Tolkien glanced through the pages of *Traditions of the Skidi Pawnee* on one or two occasions and retained enough for certain details to seep out into his later writings. Answering a reader's letter in 1938, Tolkien asserted that *The Hobbit* was "derived from (previously digested) epic, mythology, and fairy-story" but was "not consciously based on any other book[.]"[956] But comparative analysis of the extant evidence indicates that Tolkien consciously drew from the Skidi Pawnee stories. The level of correspondence between certain moments in his writings and certain moments in the Skidi stories indicates a deliberative process at work. Even Richard West concedes that "we can... be confident of a direct source [in Tolkien's writings] when he has borrowed a feature that is unique to some particular story[.]"[957]

Tolkien does not appear to have been so lightly concerned with his Pawnee sources that the Skidi tales simply slipped out of mind after he made use of them. It seems logical to discern an almost invisible aura of secrecy surrounding his use of the Skidi material. Toward this end, perhaps it can be postulated that his sense of nationalism and his sense of investment in the prerogatives of authorship together justified his choice to say nothing of the Pawnee stories. Tolkien acknowledged "the fascination of the desire to unravel the intricately knotted and ramified history of the branches on the Tree of Tales."[958] Source scholarship has established the great degree to which the "ramified history" of Tolkien's mythic derivatives is traceable to European sources – his Tree of Tales seems meticulously Eurocentric in character.

Until publication of the first edition of *Tolkien in Pawneeland*, scholarship on Tolkien's life typically showed little interest in the Red Indians he glimpsed in his youth. Since they never manifested themselves in any explicit way in his literary productions, it always seemed safe to assume that Red Indians were for Tolkien, at best, a passing boyhood fancy that left nothing more than a vague urge to shoot a bow. But Tolkien's casual notions about Red Indians were embedded in an interpretive theoretical matrix that defined his agenda as a mythmaker. During the year after I published Tolkien in Pawneeland, another prominent scholar published a fascinating paper arguing that Tolkien made use of Henry Longfellow's *The Song of Hiawatha* in various writings.[959]

Knowing now that even with his Eurocentric cultural agenda in mind, Tolkien still drew some of the greenery of his Tree of Tales from sources beyond Europe, we can fairly wonder how this impacts the inner truths of his storytelling. What does Tolkien's epic mythology signify in the world? Given the colossal popularity of his writings and associated films, this is an important question. For this reason, Tolkien's use of *Traditions of the Skidi Pawnee* is not a minor matter of incidental scholarly unraveling.

Tolkien in Pawneeland   ✳   Roger Echo-Hawk

Pawneeland in Middle-earth

To the extent that Tolkien wrestled with the symbolisms of selfhood and nationhood in his storytelling, with *Traditions of the Skidi Pawnee* in hand we can redefine the assumed Eurocentric meanings of those symbols. We can see more clearly his mythmaking as a mythology of the world. With this clarity of vision in hand, Middle-earth suddenly becomes less parochial and more global, and we glimpse the transcendent nature of myth as a narrative that transports us into unexpected journeys beyond our accustomed realms of wonder.

It should not be surprising that Tolkien read mythologies from lands beyond Europe. Indeed, it would be far more shocking to argue that he never opened any volume of myths pertaining to the rest of the world. But source scholarship on Tolkien's legendarium of the last forty years gives us the impression that Tolkien had little or no knowledge of anything beyond his favored parochial neighborhood on Planet Earth. What my argument really consists of, therefore, is to suggest that there is an actual grey rain-curtain to pull back, and when we pull it aside, we see Tolkien the mythologist at work upon very far shores. We see a scholar who roamed a broader world than the one he is typically permitted to roam.

But why should Tolkien keep to himself such wanderings? For one thing, Tolkien seemed to always feel that his mission as a writer had to do with serious matters pertaining to the cultural soul of his homeland and its European cultural environs. America was not in his mission statement. Moreover, Tolkien enjoyed putting hidden treasures and puzzles into his works. An excellent example of this occurs in his famous refusal to enlighten us as to the origins of Tom Bombadil. As Mark Hooker has shown, Tolkien took to his grave the knowledge that Tom Bombadil had something to do with a forgotten and somewhat flippant inscription on an old bell.[960]

During his years as the creator of Middle-earth, the evidence indicates that on a number of occasions JRR Tolkien picked up and studied *Traditions of the Skidi Pawnee*. The first of these moments occurred as early as 1914 when he invented Night the Spider. Then in 1919 when he wrote his creation story and birthed Ungoliont, he again made use of Pawnee tradition.

Importing Ungoliont from Pawneeland, Tolkien hinted that she was an exotic import: "even the Valar know not whence... she came..."[961] This obscuring of origin launched what would become a pattern. Tolkien took a vow of non-disclosure when it came to his Pawnee source-material, but he also took pleasure in crafting discursive placards declaring, "Here is an enigma; solve it if you can!"

Tolkien's Road of Death in *The Book of Lost Tales* – with its likenesses to the Pawnee Pathway of Departed Spirits – fell out of his legendarium by the time of his 1926 "Sketch of the Mythology" and subsequent *Quenta* of circa 1930. Through this excision, the fate of humankind after death became a mystery "not known to the Eldalië" and which "the Eldalië knew not."[962]

In 1930-1932 Tolkien returned to Pawneeland to extract building materials for Tom Bombadil, hobbits, Bladorthin, the stone-giants, Gollum, Beorn, the Mirkwood spiders, and Smaug. Along the way, Tolkien instituted the model he developed with Ungoliont. Introducing Gollum, Tolkien's narrator informs us, "I don't know where he came from or who or what he was."[963]

Tolkien next has Bladorthin speculate about Beorn's origin, and after setting forth several possibilities, the wizard concludes, "I can't say."[964] The context encourages us to read this as "I don't know"; but it is also possible to give a more literal reading of the statement as a refusal to tell. That is, Bladorthin "can't say" because Tolkien has sworn him to secrecy. Bent on his mission as a mythologist for England, Tolkien could never permit Bladorthin to openly acknowledge Beorn's Pawnee roots.

John Rateliff muses over Tolkien's choice to make Beorn a bear who can shape-shift versus making him a man who can become a bear, and he offers a convoluted explanation for what Tolkien meant by the statement that followed: "At any rate he is under no enchantment but his own."[965] It can be suggested that the secret answer is related to Tolkien's usage of material from the Skidi story, "The Boy, the Bears, and White Crow." In this story we find a man who can become a bear and a bear that can shape-shift into a horse, and Tolkien borrowed certain aspects of this Skidi enchantment, but he made no effort to exactly reproduce it. So Beorn is, in fact, under his own unique enchantment.

Invited by a reader in 1938 to clarify aspects of Smaug's history, Tolkien declined.[966] He taunted later researchers who would hunt for Smaug's sources, asking rhetorically, "...would not that be rather unfair to the research students? To save them trouble is to rob them of any excuse for existing." Whatever the source of his reluctance to reveal Smaug's origins, his reluctance did have the effect of keeping hidden the Skidi colorations in his tale of Smaug. In the same 1938 letter Tolkien adopted a somewhat similar tone regarding the origins of his hobbits, writing that he "had not thought of future researchers" and adding that he had "been made to see Mr. Baggins's adventures as the subject of future inquiry[.]"

Tolkien's most extensive borrowings from Pawneeland occurred in *The Hobbit*. He showed the manuscript to colleagues, and it proved interesting enough that a publisher issued the book in 1937. Many people read the book with enthusiasm. No one noticed the sprinkling of Pawnee elements; but it surely meant something to Tolkien – the transplanted Skidi "primitive undergrowth" had very usefully greened up the impoverished mythic soils of England.

In 1942 Tolkien borrowed from another Pawnee story to help tell the central tale of Gandalf's death and resurrection. And he restrained Gandalf from revealing too much about his Pawnee-derived death experience, permitting him to say only, "...I will not tell." Tolkien made his last arguable visit to Pawneeland in the early 1950s in the course of envisioning Gandalf's nature, though this could merely be an artifact of an incomplete documentary record, with the timing of his construction of Gandalf's death and his nature as Olórin occurring closer in time.

Speaking of Gandalf in response to questions from a reader, Tolkien wrote, "There are, I suppose, always defects in any large-scale work of art; and especially in those of literary form that are founded on an earlier matter which is put to new uses[.]"[967] This is certainly true of his use of Pawnee "earlier matter." But Tolkien then added that "...I have severely cut G's account of himself..." and "...I have purposely kept all allusions to the highest matters down to mere hints, perceptible only by the most attentive, or kept them under unexplained symbolic forms." This has to do, I would suggest, with Tolkien's religious aspirations, with his interwoven concepts of clear vision, eucatastrophy, fantasy, recovery, and, as he put it, "elucidation of the 'mythological' ideas in my mind."

In 1951 Tolkien asserted that the "great tales" of his legendarium "arose in my mind as 'given' things" and that "always I had the sense of recording what was already 'there,' somewhere: not of 'inventing'."[968] I read both a practical and a mystical sense in these words. He spent years absorbing the various European textual materials that then cast shining reflections into his tales, so as a practical matter the source material came together in a coherent way in his mind and the stories flowed readily to his hand. In a more mystical sense, Tolkien's theory of sub-creation was relational and religious. He believed that the Creator could choose to guide his hand as a vessel of sub-creation, and this Creator also had the power to subsequently make incarnate this sub-creation.[969] In "On Fairy-stories" he expressed the hope that "Redeemed Man" can "dare to guess that in Fantasy he may actually assist in the effoliation and multiple enrichment of creation" and "[a]ll tales may come true[.]"[970]

If, as I suggest in this analysis, Tolkien experimented with hinting at the "given things" from Pawnee stories – things borrowed from historical and mythical narratives – he never felt free to reveal this truth. He kept to himself the secret ingredients from far-off Vinland that enriched his "Fantasy." He preferred instead to ponder the degree to which his world-building might serve to express divine authorship.

Whatever the nature of his self-image as an author, Tolkien probably took for granted that discerning readers – and especially his peers in academia – would recognize some or most of his European source material. The Skidi sources were another matter. Pawneeland existed as a vaguely vanishing realm that bobbed at the far shores of the world that mattered to Tolkien and his colleagues. He had no reason to openly acknowledge his use of obscure Pawnee mythological materials – material that "was already 'there'" as a pre-recorded source of creative inspiration. But he could not resist the impulse to leave clues.

Launching into preparation of his legendarium, for example, Tolkien offered this intriguing listing of beasts in his earliest physical description of Valinor: "Beasts reveled there, deer among the trees, and herds of kine among its spaces and wide grass-lands; bison there were, and horses roaming unharnessed, but these strayed never into the gardens of the gods, yet were they in peace and had no fear, for beasts of prey dwelt not among them..."[971]

Wide grasslands? Bison? If we accept the fact that Tolkien utilized Pawnee source-material to inspire aspects of *The Book of Lost Tales*, it is then patently arguable that Tolkien intentionally placed these "wide grass-lands" and "bison" in purposeful conjunction. His phrase "gardens of the gods" is an idea that appears in the introduction to *Traditions of the Skidi Pawnee*. Evening Star plays a central role in Roaming Scout's creation story, and she "maintains a garden in which are fields of ripening grain and many buffalo, and from which spring all life."[972] This single sentence alone can account for Tolkien's portrayal above of Valinor.

By the time he wrote this description of Valinor in 1919, he had already composed his creation story and had told of Ungoliont, borrowing from Skidi tales.[973] Tolkien did not choose to cast this additional shadow of Pawneeland upon Middle-earth as an idle whim. Questing for vistas into the dim mists of history and forgotten meaning, Tolkien appreciated the art of discovery. He wafted a silhouette of Pawneeland into Valinor for his own unknown reasons. But he surely appreciated the inspiration of the Skidi stories, and in early 1919 he gave a lot of thought as to how to make use of Skidi construction material in his growing mythology.

Tolkien would have dismissed any suggestion of equating Valinor with America – this would run counter to his evolving interest in treating Valinor as a pre-Christian "heaven" with his wizards as a kind of "angel" who "are actually emissaries from the True West, and so mediately from God[.]"[974] But writing elsewhere that the Istari "came from over the Sea out of the Uttermost West" – and given the influence of Pawnee tradition on the making of Gandalf – perhaps it is arguable that Tolkien intended for a faint trace of Vinland to enter the magic of Valinor.[975] The poetry of "Uttermost West" evokes the lyrical mystery of Valinor, but "uttermost" might also hint at a more deeply hidden Pawneeland. Tolkien surely enjoyed the clever sleight-of-hand of slipping invisible echoes of Vinland into Valinor.

As time went on Tolkien's interest in Vinland waned. The phrase "wide plain" appears later in the *Quenta Noldorinea*, composed sometime around 1930, and the gardens of the gods reappear.[976] But the bison have gone the way of the buffalo, no more to be seen. And by later in the 1930s in the *Quenta Silmarillion* the "garden of the Gods" lingers, but the "wide grass-lands" have dwindled even more from "wide plains" to "the plains and woods of Valinor[.]"[977] By the 1950s these specific geographic features seem to have grown even vaguer, with mere mention of gardens and a "plain beyond the Pelóri" in the *Annals of Aman* in *Morgoth's Ring*, and with a "plain beyond the mountains" in the final *Silmarillion*, and no garden until Chapter Five, when we find very general "gardens of Valinor."[978]

By the 1950s Tolkien sensed that he had succeeded in creating a legendarium that would stand forth as a mythology for England, and under the spotlight of this success he may have regretted his choice to borrow from Pawneeland. During the various incarnations and revisions of *The Silmarillion*, the traces of Pawnee greenery in that book faded, dwindling into a forgotten leaf-mould under Tolkien's Tree of Tales. And in 1951 Tolkien expressed some regrets regarding *The Hobbit* – the work that was shaped most by Pawnee traditions. He wrote, "Some of the details of tone and treatment are, I now think... mistaken."[979]

He was probably referring here to the whimsical tone of *The Hobbit*, but he may have also felt that he went too far with some of the Pawnee material. In *The Hobbit* stone-giants are actual creatures known to Gandalf, and these creatures were very much indebted to Skidi tradition. But returning to the Misty Mountains in *The Lord of the Rings*, a moment comes when odd sounds and loose stones fall upon the Fellowship from the heights. With *The Hobbit* in mind, we expect stone-giants. One member of the party says, "You can call it the wind if you like, but I call it voices..."[980] To which Gandalf responds, "I do call it the wind[.]" Banishing the stone-giants into superstition, perhaps in hindsight Tolkien wished he hadn't borrowed so much from Skidi tradition.

By the end of his life Tolkien was an established popular author, and students of his work were beginning to study what he had done. Tolkien had always been dismissive and belittling of the project to excavate the carefully layered Middle-earth source material, but he was not above identifying his underlying sources when the mood struck. In one letter, for example, he referred to "Sigurd the Volsung, Oedipus, and the Finnish Kullervo" as the inspirations for "the tragic tale of Turin Túrambar and his sister Níniel[.]"[981] Tolkien also took the moment to target source scholarship and put down "people who like that sort of thing" because "it is not very useful[.]" He wished to keep hidden the Skidi Pawnee sources that enriched his legendarium, but he had diverse reasons for diminishing such research.

Tolkien spelled out in greater detail his attitude toward source scholarship in his essay "On Fairy-stories."[982] He pondered the question, "What is the origin of the fairy element?" Focusing on folklorists and anthropologists, Tolkien characterized their analytical inquiry as "using the stories not as they were meant to be used, but as a quarry from which to dig evidence, or information, about matters in which they are interested." And "ignorance or forgetfulness of the nature of a story (as a thing told in its entirety) has often led such inquirers into strange judgements" especially when it came to "recurring similarities[.]" He meant here to contest the idea that "any two stories that are built around the same folk-lore motive, or are made up of a generally similar combination of such motives, are 'the same stories'."[983]

I do not suggest that Tolkien drew from the Skidi legendarium in order to retell those stories. I do intend to assert that the existence of multiple correlated components in the Skidi legendarium and Tolkien's legendarium means that Tolkien deliberately drew from the Skidi stories, and these borrowed elements helped to shape stories and characters. It may well be a matter of personal judgment to decide which of these elements qualify as significant and which are trivial. But as Tolkien said: "It is precisely the colouring, the atmosphere, the unclassifiable individual details of a story, and above all the general purport that informs with life the undissected bones of the plot, that really count."[984] By any measure, the Skidi contributions to Tolkien's mythmaking deserve acknowledgment and are very significant.

Tolkien described the nebulous origins of fairytales as proceeding from a "Cauldron of Story" in which historical and imaginal elements lose context and reconfigure themselves within new narrative structures.[985] Delving through the misty strata of fairytale origins necessarily must be a speculative task performed from a desire to grasp the social "sources or material" of a story.[986] But since Tolkien's authorial process involved a comparable "Cauldron of Story," we can examine with more assurance and less speculation some of the likely ingredients of his soup.

A thriving industry of Tolkien source scholarship arose after his death, generating a very extensive literature on many fascinating topics. But this literature failed to yield insights into Tolkien's use of Pawnee traditions because no one looked for such insights, and *Traditions of the Skidi Pawnee* has never been reprinted and remains obscure. A significant variety of corresponding features exist between the Skidi Pawnee legendarium and Tolkien's Middle-earth legendarium. But since these are subtle weavings, not overt retellings, even had the book been re-issued and studied widely, most readers would have no doubt shrugged off as coincidence what seemed a chance parallel between creation myths. Tolkien successfully hid the New World in Middle-earth.

Tolkien did not aim at reproducing Pawnee culture in Middle-earth; he did not retell any Pawnee story; he did not lift passages from the mythology of Pawneeland. In his later years he gave thought to his own proprietary interests in his intellectual productions; and he much resented the very notion of fan fiction based on his legendarium, referring to one hopeful author as a "young ass."[987] For his part, Tolkien did not hesitate to draw from source-material in various ways, and he often refrained from crediting those sources.[988]

It is arguable that Tolkien merely engaged in usages that are inherent to typical creative processes of authorship, but some Pawnees may well choose to explore the nebulous moral boundaries of Tolkien's exploitation of proprietary Pawnee cultural productions. Traditional systems of regulating oral narratives were conjoined to religious systems that lay in tatters by the end of the 19th century in Pawneeland. And the awkward transition to American systems of literacy unfolded in a chaotic social environment. As Pawnees oriented themselves to the colliding conventions of this world, the social control of narrative property became less a matter of consensus and more an articulation of an unknowable future.

I suspect that Tolkien's motive for keeping quiet about using Pawnee stories also had something to do with his faith in his own creative integrity. As an author he had created Middle-earth; or rather, as Tom Shippey explains Tolkien's self-image as an author, the purview of his imagination ultimately derived from a purposeful Creator, and his legendarium might well reflect higher truths.[989] For this reason, what he saw as primitive Pawnee material served a lofty purpose, aiding a kind of mystical authorship summoned from his hand by the Author. And in less religious terms, Tolkien saw himself as an original author whose creativity often enough involved weaving together threads from disparate sources. In the end, however the Skidi stories came to hand, it was Tolkien's hand that did the lifelong labor of invention.

In our time on earth we tell stories and we want people to listen, and we are always influenced by stories that we admire; perhaps it would be somewhat useful to see Tolkien as an admirer of a certain quality in Pawnee tradition. As a storyteller Tolkien wished to enrich his tales from a Cauldron of Story containing the right flavors. The spices he found in Pawneeland were the kind of flavors that he deemed essential, not optional, for his particular mythic stew.

Beyond the savor of story, the assembling of narrative structures always has an anarchic component – a component that resists the orderly rule of social convention. Since storytelling functions to express the art of being human, its inherent nature is that it tends to flow everywhere – this process applied to Tolkien as an author, and it also applied to storytellers in Pawneeland. For this reason, the important essences of myth readily transcend national borders; myth has a shape-shifting magic that disregards even the most carefully maintained borders of cultural identity.

We may have specific notions about ownership of stories and ideas – ideas embedded in our social conventions and principles of law – but to assert that the esoteric meanings of any specific story can be successfully marked as the exclusive "property" of a nation or a cultural group is to underrate the powerful and fluid ambiguities of identity systems and of the art of storytelling. When Finland treats the *Kalevala* as its national epic, capable of defining Finnish identity, what does it mean when Tolkien borrows from the tragedy of Kullervo for his Middle-earth legendarium? When Tolkien borrows from the Finnish legendarium and from the Skidi legendarium, how can he be said to be engaged in the production of an "English" mythology?

This point is more than a literary curiosity. Tolkien's mythmaking is often described as having a global significance.

But it is difficult to reconcile this idea to his explicit focus on producing a Eurocentric literary legacy. It is fair to assume that such a literary quality can only be said to be culturally transcendent in the most general sense – every story we tell everywhere always has aspects of global applicability. It does not appear that Tolkien ever aspired for his mythmaking to have any worldwide significance. England and its cultural matrices occupied his thinking.

The processes by which stories arise are many, and the meanings we attach to their making and transmission are manifold, and when we tell our stories we have little choice about what others make of them and what they do with them. But one thing is clear. From the very beginning Middle-earth was never a project of exclusive cultural identity that just pertained to England, whatever Tolkien said on the matter. And Middle-earth today cannot be fairly characterized in terms of an exclusive Northern European cultural ecology, nor can it be meaningfully confined to Europe.

For the Pawnee people *Traditions of the Skidi Pawnee* can certainly serve functions related to the production of national Pawnee identity. The Skidi scholar James R. Murie created an extensive body of writings on Pawnee culture, and these works have helped to define the traditional basis for Pawnee history and will continue to be useful for this purpose.

But when Pawnee myth enters Tolkien's legendarium, and when Tolkien's English-myth-based-on-Pawnee-myth enters the world, it is clear that something beyond Pawnee identity has flowed from the heritage of Pawnee tradition. Given the diversity of uses that Tolkien found for Pawnee material, it is accurate to say that the transformative magic of Skidi traditional literature helped to elevate Tolkien's legendarium into a global mythology. Tolkien's mythmaking has not made us English. When we accept the relevance of Pawnee myth to Middle-earth, we embrace the idea that Tolkien gave us a mythology that is truly worldwide – a mythology that transcends the narrowing artifice of national cultural boundaries, and which we cannot readily contain or police with our notions of nationhood and ethnicity.

Acknowledging the Pawnee contribution to Middle-earth, we acknowledge that Pawnee mythology has participated meaningfully in global culture. The permeable interchange of culture creates its own abstract geography, its own unforeseeable maps of inner truths, and for this reason Middle-earth is rooted into the overburdened stone of our whole world. All of us together whisper its rumors of far realms. And when we quest for the secret symbolic essences of Tolkien's enchanted tales, we suddenly hear the mingled sighing of many mythological shores.

The Future of Race

We empower ourselves when we create our own ways of interpreting cultural touchstones, when we enliven the signifiers of society with meanings that connect us into community. But there remains the question of why Tolkien did not himself embrace a more global vision of Middle-earth. He launched his legendarium with the hope of chartering a sense of English mythological selfhood. And he expanded this to include integrative Anglo-Celtic cultural texturing. Both agendas unfolded from the geography of what he termed "northernness."

All these constructions ultimately defined his sense of racial identity. We can surmise that Tolkien felt little interest in redefining his mission to become a mythmaker for the wider world because he felt comfortably rooted in his own sense of Englishness and northernness. When he planted nasturtians and sunflowers in Bilbo's garden in 1938 he was summoning America into Middle-earth. But he wanted something specific and limited. From Pawneeland he imported touches of antiquarian texturing, something he deemed "primitive." This could never be explicit; he had no interest in expanding his legendarium into a mythology that he could dedicate to the world.

Tolkien's weaving of tradition into epic romance succeeded in giving rise to tales that would change the world. This process of deploying legend to shape social aspiration and inner mythic yearnings flowed into his wish to entertain his children with invented magical tales, shaping his aspirations as a novelist. He wrote legends of a lost world for Britain, and he invented fairytales for his children. But his vision ultimately remained parochial in nature.

In Tolkien's youth and early adulthood, British folklore was a thriving field of study. But that world had already faded by the time Tolkien inserted his hobbit into Middle-earth. Historian Richard Dorson characterized this fading as "one of the collateral tragedies of the Great War."[990] During those years some of the most prominent members of the group died, and the inner circle of British folklore dissipated. Worse, within the academy "folklore never gained academic acceptance." Anthropology flourished in some of the spaces that folklore created, but academic anthropologists "turned their backs on fairy tales."

In the shadow of this intellectual eclipse, Tolkien carried forward the fairytale flame of the defunct folkloric mission. His essay, "On Fairy-stories," articulated this sense of mission. The tone of his paper is certainly more folkloric than anthropological. But rather than collect or study folkloric materials – an approach that might not have advanced his academic career – Tolkien instead labored to transform existing myth and folklore into literary romance. Borrowing from dusty forgotten tomes, Tolkien carefully sifted fragmentary tradition. Taking in hand a diverse array of shining remnant threads from lost antiquity, Tolkien wove the dreamlike epic tapestry of his Middle-earth legendarium.

Tolkien's first "hobbit" materialized during the summer of 1930. The project to enliven his borrowed hobbit began with a single guiding association – a hobbit and a hole in the ground. This new "hobbit" arose from the blending of the Welsh hobbit and the British folkloric hob-hole – perhaps with some infusion from the Denham hobbit. In 1938 Tolkien wrote that he had no specific memory of inventing the term. But in that year, in the course of writing *The Fellowship of the Ring*, he made use of additional material from the Wright dictionary and perhaps from Skeat and Britten's *Reprinted Glossaries and Old Farming Words*. And he could not resist making the sly hidden reference to agricultural measures in his Baggins "Hundredweight Party."

In June 1955 Tolkien set forth two different stories of the origin of his hobbit. His story of the spontaneous composition of the first sentence in its entirety settled in as his standard external history to explain his hobbit – this development came with varying degrees of asertive clarity and occasional explicit claims of independent invention. But it is plainly arguable that we cannot accept Tolkien's account at face value.

Tolkien's hobbits were born from the hobs of English folklore and from the Welsh agricultural hobbit. But it was Tolkien's rich imagination and his process of mingling mythic essences that gave birth to their character and to the stories through which they roamed. Highlighting the Shire as a realm of country folk whose very name evoked a hidden reference to an agrarian context, Tolkien scattered into *The Lord of the Rings* various British agricultural references. His use of folk tradition replicated his mining of northern European mythological tradition, as well as the importing of colorful elements from America.

JRR Tolkien was born into a world that embraced race as a useful lens through which to view humankind. It should not be surprising that we can glimpse this fact in his early writings. The social mechanisms of race did not preoccupy Tolkien the mythmaker, but the assumptions of racial thinking did materialize in his storytelling. This is clear enough in *The Book of Lost Tales*, *The Lost Road*, and his tale of Númenor.

Tolkien's 1938 framing of the "wholly pernicious and unscientific race-doctrine" should be read as reflecting recent thinking about race in the British academy – we can assume that this comment reflected his awareness of the publication in 1935 of *We Europeans* by Julian Huxley and AC Haddon. But we must also reconcile this awareness to his use of race in preparing *The Lord of the Rings* during the years that followed.

Mindful of the challenge to race, for Tolkien the hyper-racialism of Nazi Germany provided a context to deploy that awareness, condemning Nazi ideological excesses and the extremity of their racial focus. But this did not mean that he was willing to abandon race. He instead experienced the social tension of an academic who could see the frailty of the intellectual justification for race yet accepted the colossal realities of racial practice. He negotiated a complex terrain that involved criticizing race and embracing it. This is still a common practice in academic culture today.

Tolkien was not locked into any single trajectory of culture. He made choices. As a man of his times, in the course of his life he could have rejected racial thinking; he could have devoted his imaginative energy to storytelling that really did defuse the power of race in the world. He had plenty of motivation for making such a choice, objecting to Nazi racialism. He chose otherwise.

That decision was common enough in those days, but not inevitable. During the same period when Tolkien was transforming the "dark-eyed" friend of Bill Ferny into "the squint-eyed southerner," Ashley Montagu was publishing a paper titled "Race and Kindred Delusions."[991] About the time Tolkien sat down to craft his first racialized orcs for his chapter "The Uruk-hai" – writing of "large, swart, slant-eyed Orcs" – Ashley Montagu was publishing his first book, *Man's Most Dangerous Myth: The Fallacy of Race*.[992]

Born in London in 1905, Montagu grew up in the same world that shaped Tolkien's early adulthood. He attended college in London, taking coursework with Charles Seligman – an anthropologist who would go on to assist Julian Huxley and AC Haddon in the writing of *We Europeans: A Survey of 'Racial' Problems*.[993] Montagu next studied with Franz Boas in New York, and during the late 1930s he decided to take up the growing anthropological mission to confront pro-race social traditions. In the preface to *Man's Most Dangerous Myth* Montagu took aim at his academic colleagues, "...I believe it is high time that the traditional concept of 'race' held by my professional brethren be dealt with frankly." For those who see Tolkien as a man of his times, locked into an inescapable logic on race, or who believe that Tolkien rejected racial thinking, the comparison with his contemporary Ashley Montagu should be helpful.

Tolkien infused color with much symbolic meaning in Middle-earth. He treated "white" as a frequent indicator of moral superiority, versus "black" and "sallow" as clear signifiers of moral inferiority. This strategy has naturally led many readers to see these choices as racially oriented, even as evidence of covert racism in Tolkien's attitudes. It is plain enough, in fact, that he did rely on racial stereotype in utilizing "Mongol-type" characteristics to mold his orcs and half-orcs, and that this usage referenced demeaning racial Asian imagery.

An extensive discourse exists on Tolkien's use of race, and a widely embraced consensus cites his seeming anti-race comments in his correspondence to conclude that Tolkien could not have been racist in his usages. We can indeed find storytelling in Middle-earth that is fundamentally opposed to the discriminatory divisions of bigotry. His pointed framing of dwarf versus elf prejudices is wonderfully transcended by the gradual bonding of Gimli the Dwarf and Legolas the Elf.

In November 2015 Michael Martinez posted an interesting discussion of Tolkien and race on the Tolkien Society blog: "Taboo Tolkien: The Nordicist Claim on Middle-earth Refuted." A few years before in 2012 Martinez had written an article in which he went so far as to acknowledge that the Mongol-type orcs "may be the only clear evidence of racism in Tolkien's fiction..." But now Martinez fumed that the topic of Tolkien and racism had drawn too many readers into a "neverending story of racist bias in *The Lord of the Rings*." Taking on the charge that Tolkien was "a Nordicist" Martinez asserted that search engines were delinquent in bringing up the various available rebuttals, so he recommended online works by two authors.

A little further searching proved distressing. I discovered that Wikipedia identified one of those recommended authors as "a supporter of Neo-Confederate policies in the Southern United States" who "has declared his support for the re-establishment of the Confederate States of America." Whether or not the research prepared by that scholar can be trusted, the truly significant issue is that the charge of racism has not died in Tolkiendom and it does not deserve to die. As Martinez and others have often enough observed, the accusation is typically based on a superficial reading of the uses of color in Tolkien's novels, with little or no reference to his other writings and to the larger social context. But the fact that the superficialities lead so many to feel a sense of discomfort means something – it means that we need in-depth scholarship asking how Tolkien made use of race.

In the vast analytical literature that has arisen on Middle-earth, it is arguable that affection for Tolkien's worldbuilding and respect for his scholarship has helped to deflect useful consideration of his racial usages. The absence of any in-depth analysis of his statements versus his literary uses of race within the relevant social context has hampered meaningful insight and constructive debate.

A sincere defensive enchantment typifies the ongoing project to protect Tolkien from his racialized orcs. Even when we see mention of his 1958 characterization, rather than wrestle with what it signifies, we are urged by some to believe that such wrestling will just prove needlessly tiresome because Tolkien's literary usages of race are merely meant to innocently mimic faux-medieval cultural texturing, and he was opposed to racism. By the early 21st century this became the established consensus in Tolkien studies and Middle-earth fandom. Within the circles of that world, those who would accuse Tolkien of harboring a racist streak could be dismissed as lacking factual insight, as non-scholars focused on superficial details that don't add up. And indeed, this was often true. Until recently the field of Tolkien studies has attracted little interest from scholars of race.

Since the late 1930s the academy on both sides of the Atlantic has been both a fount of challenges to race and a fount of affirmation for race. A vast literature confronting race in academia materialized during the final decades of the 20th century. One study of American textbooks showed that by the 1970s a consensus had taken shape in anthropology rejecting race as a useful explanation of human biological diversity.[994]

A fascinating 2001 paper by John Jackson has shown how one leading American physical anthropologist during the early 1960s secretly aided and encouraged pro-segregation racists.[995] The implication is that by then it was almost impossible for an academic scholar to be blatantly racist, to openly support the social agenda of racial separatism and white supremacy. One had to be subtle. One needed the option to deny an inclination to provide aid and comfort to white racists.

I see no evidence that Tolkien troubled himself with the complexities of academic politics on race. He seems to have been aware that the Huxleys and Montagus of his world had a good point, but he could nevertheless embrace race in that same world, acting to colorize his novels with his preferred subtleties of pro-race hierarchical logic. He could craft narratives of nuanced moral diversity when it came to his favored folk of Middle-earth, but nowhere do we find his racialized Mongol-type orcs transcending their narrow moral natures. And Tolkien felt little worry in 1958 when he suggested to a filmmaker that his racialized orcs should be portrayed as "Mongol-types."

Tolkien had a complicated set of attitudes toward race. Racial ideology can seem simple even when it generates an enormously variable and ever-changing spectrum of assumptions and practices in the world. In Tolkien's case we can see that his early life included acceptance of certain fundamental ideas about race that were widespread in Britain – ideas that can be glimpsed in his work, yet did not generate major narrative themes. During the late 1930s this changed. We see more explicit attention to race in his writings.

Our communal discourse on race, I believe, needs to explore the history of racial belief systems. We need to discuss the making of racial identity through racial bonding and the undoing of race. It is accurate to observe that race today is entrenched in the world. Racial identities feel real to practitioners. But in my corner of the world, as my personal and professional choice, I long ago chose to abandon racial identity. In so doing, I came to see that since racial identity is hinged on the practices of racial bonding, by abandoning those practices one can be non-racial.

Since World War Two millions of people in the world have slowly let go of adherence to racial identity systems, and many more millions hold weak attachments to race. The vast majority of these people do not know that an explicit non-racial narrative is possible in the world. But they do know that race is not very necessary in their daily lives.

The extant consensus in modern anthropology rejects the interpretation of racial identity systems as the logical outcome of biological realities. In academic scholarship racialism is interpreted as an expression of culture situated in history rather in timeless human biology. This view of race conflicts with the traditional faith-based practices of racial identity. In our social world today race exists as a pervasive historical belief system, a tradition-based cultural system in which adherents treat race as an inflexible inherited biological reality.

Since the late 20th century American society has configured a vast discussion on race that focuses on racial heirarchies and the consequent social production of racism. This kind of discourse traditionally favors the continued making of race as a matter of both private identity and social identity. But since the anthropological consensus on race argues that racism flows out of the historically empowered belief systems of race, this implies that enactment of racial bonding is what accounts for racism.

It is time to develop a conscious re-examination of old ideas about race, and to raise new issues that deserve a place in our talk on race. To what extent are people non-racial in their daily lives? How can non-racial identity consciousness coexist with social machinery that reproduces race on a vast scale? What role should race play in shaping the future? These are questions that deserve to be asked. And we can begin to rethink race by examining its history, by studying how race has been enacted in the world. In the end, since race is a belief system, it is possible to reject racial identity.

The essays on race in this book shed light onTolkien's attitudes; some might see this as a basis for judging whether he can be fairly labeled as a racist. But I have taken this journey to explore the world that gave rise to my world. To shape for myself the meanings that I wish to carry with me into my future, I must know what happened.

The examination of Tolkien's world and his choices gives us a necessary awareness of our own choices and challenges. He glimpsed the problem with race and even espoused anti-race idealism. But he still manufactured his monsters from the ingredients of non-white racial imagery, and it is difficult to understand how those monsters align with anti-race idealism. He sometimes sounded more like Alfred Rosenberg than like Julien Huxley or Ashley Montagu. When we examine what he did in the world, perhaps we can better judge for ourselves what we ought to do next.

I believe that race hurts us more than it helps us when it comes to identity and society. I believe that here at the beginning of a new millennium, ever-growing numbers of people are slowly becoming ever more non-racial. For those of us who choose to openly reject racial bonding, we must critique the making of race in the world; we must question the promotion of race in our storytelling.

And so we must not look away and refuse to ponder JRR Tolkien's racialized orcs, his semi-racial "black men," his hierarchy of golden-haired heroes. When we decide that we admire various qualities of Middle-earth, and when we bond with others through our appreciation of Tolkien the writer, we must add that his handling of race does matter. A great purpose is served by making sure that the dehumanizing machinery of race gets confronted in the literature that matters to us.

Whatever the history of race has given us, whatever Tolkien passed along to us in his writings, we should encourage one another to think carefully about what to do with race. When we understand how race has shaped the past, perhaps we can hope to discover different paths into another kind of future.

Tolkien in Pawneeland

Roger Echo-Hawk

ENDNOTES

Endnotes: Aryan Elves and the Nordic Roots of Númenor

[1] Joscelyn Godwin, *Arktos: The Polar Myth in Science, Symbolism, and Nazi Survival*, Adventure Unlimited, 1996, p. 47-61; Joscelyn Godwin, *Atlantis and the Cycles of Time*, Inner Traditions, 2011. Godwin's discussion of William Warren appeared in *Arktos*, p. 30-31. Her survey of Atlantology shows that the linking of the North Pole and Atlantis was established in other European writings long before the late 19th century.

[2] John Rhys, *Lectures on the Origin and Growth of Religion as Illustrated by Celtic Heathendom*, Williams and Norgate, 1892.

[3] Christina Scull and Wayne Hammond, *The JRR Tolkien Companion and Guide: Chronology*, Houghton Mifflin, 2006, p. 50, 52, 55, 59; Mark T. Hooker, *Tolkien and Welsh*, Llyfrawr, 2012, p. vii; Carl Phelpstead, *Tolkien and Wales: Language, Literature, and Identity*, University of Wales Press, 2011, p. xx, 137 endnote 14.

[4] John Rhys, *Lectures on the Origin and Growth of Religion as Illustrated by Celtic Heathendom*, Williams and Norgate, 1892, p. 631-632, also see p. 637-638.

[5] JRR Tolkien, *The Book of Lost Tales, Part One*, in *The History of Middle-earth, Volume I*, Christopher Tolkien editor, Houghton Mifflin, 1983, p. 56, 69-70, 100.

[6] JRR Tolkien, *The Book of Lost Tales, Part One*, Christopher Tolkien editor, 1983, p. 155.

[7] JRR Tolkien, *The Book of Lost Tales, Part One*, Christopher Tolkien editor, 1983, p. 166-169.

[8] JRR Tolkien, *The Book of Lost Tales, Part One*, Christopher Tolkien editor, 1983, p. 121.

[9] John Rhys, *Lectures on the Origin and Growth of Religion as Illustrated by Celtic Heathendom*, Williams and Norgate, 1892, p. 635.

[10] JRR Tolkien, *The Book of Lost Tales, Part Two*, in *The History of Middle-earth, Volume II*, Christopher Tolkien editor, Houghton Mifflin, 1984, p. 8, 42: Queen Wendelin is "Slender and very dark of hair" and "her skin was white and pale..." She is also known as Gwendeling and "was not elf or woman but of the children of the Gods..." Her daughter is (p. 10) "Tinúviel being a fairy" who (p. 11) has "bare white feet..." Also see discussion (p. 67) of the name "Morgoth," which Christopher Tolkien translated as "Black Strife." For humankind – as with Elves – Tolkien offered little physical description. In "Turambar and the Foalóke" we hear the story of Nienóri, who is frequently described as "fair" – a likely reference to beauty rather than skin tone, but at one point she is "the white maiden"; see JRR Tolkien, *The Book of Lost Tales, Part Two*, Christopher Tolkien editor, 1984, p. 111. Writing an essay circa 1930-1931 Tolkien referred to "the white people of the shores of Elfland"; see JRR Tolkien, *A Secret Vice: Tolkien on Invented Languages*, Dimitra Fimi and Andrew Higgins editors, HarperCollins, 2016, p. 30, 102. This appeared in a poem called "Nieninqe," literally "white tear" (see p. 56 endnote 75). The main character of this poem was "Nielikkilis" a child whose tears became snowdrops (endnote 76). Tolkien drew associations among the color white, snowdrops, and tears.

[11] JRR Tolkien, *The Book of Lost Tales, Part Two*, Christopher Tolkien editor, 1984, p. 165.

[12] JRR Tolkien, *The Book of Lost Tales, Part Two*, Christopher Tolkien editor, 1984, p. 173, 175, 192, 194, also see p. 216 where Glorfindel's name is translated as "Goldtress for his hair was golden."

[13] John Beddoe, *The Races of Britain*, Trübner, 1885, p. 268. In this book Beddoe presented extensive charts that he had compiled – his "Indices of Nigrescence" surveying the distribution of hair color and eye color in Britain.

[14] William Ripley, *Races of Europe: A Sociological Study*, Appleton, 1899, p. 467-470.

[15] The writing of "The Grey Havens" occurred in 1948, see JRR Tolkien, *Sauron Defeated*, in *The History of The Lord of the Rings, Part Four*, Christopher

Tolkien editor, Houghton Mifflin, 1992, p. 12-13. For the original version of the seed in Galadriel's gift-box to Sam see p. 108.

[16] For Galadriel's original white hair in late 1941 see JRR Tolkien, *The Treason of Isengard*, in *The History of The Lord of the Rings, Part Two*, Christopher Tolkien editor, Houghton Mifflin, 1989, p. 233. Christopher Tolkien noted that "this was early changed to make Galadriel's hair golden" (p. 256).

[17] JRR Tolkien, *Unfinished Tales*, Christopher Tolkien editor, Houghton Mifflin, 1980, p. 229-230.

[18] Simon Winchester, *The Meaning of Everything: The Story of the Oxford English Dictionary*, Oxford University Press, 2003, p. 206 footnote 7. The term "slip" here refers to a formal name for the research note system used by the *Oxford English Dictionary*. Winchester noted that OED rejected Tolkien's example of "the right to wallop one's own nigger" as racially offensive.

[19] JRR Tolkien, *The Book of Lost Tales, Part One*, Christopher Tolkien editor, 1983, p. 57; JRR Tolkien, *The Shaping of Middle-earth*, in *The History of Middle-earth, Volume IV*, Christopher Tolkien editor, Houghton Mifflin, 1986, p. 3.

[20] Rob Baker, April 11, 2012 blog post, "The Cenotaph, Alfred Rosenberg, Ada Emma Deane and the Ghost Hunter Harry Price," at *Another Nickel In The Machine*, viewed February 22, 2016. Baker described Rosenberg as "editor-in-chief of the Nazi daily newspaper *Volkischer Beobachter*" and as "one of the Nazi 'Big Five'" who was sent by Hitler to ascertain British sentiment toward Nazi Germany.

[21] Joscelyn Godwin, *Arktos: The Polar Myth in Science, Symbolism, and Nazi Survival*, Adventure Unlimited, 1996, p. 47-61; Joscelyn Godwin, *Atlantis and the Cycles of Time*, Inner Traditions, 2011. Rosenberg's *The Myth of the Twentieth Century* went into at least three printings in Germany by the end of 1931. I have relied on the James B. Whisker translation, circa 1980.

[22] JRR Tolkien, *Letters From Father Christmas*, Baillie Tolkien editor, Houghton Mifflin, 2004, p. 54.

[23] JRR Tolkien, *The Lost Road and Other Writings*, in *The History of Middle-earth, Volume V*, Christopher Tolkien editor, Houghton Mifflin, 1987, p. 7-10.

[24] The conversation between Tolkien and Lewis which inspired Tolkien to write *The Lost Road* occurred at an uncertain date, but Tom Shippey speculated that it probably happened sometime around February 1936; see Tom Shippey, "The Ransom Trilogy," in *The Cambridge Companion to CS Lewis*, Robert MacSwain and Michael Ward editors, Cambridge University Press, 2010, p. 237. Tolkien wrote at least three letters mentioning the genesis of *The Lost Road*; see Humphrey Carpenter, *The Letters of JRR Tolkien*, with the assistance of Christopher Tolkien, Houghton Mifflin, 2000 edition [original publication 1981], JRR Tolkien to Stanley Unwin, February 18, 1938, # 24, p. 29; Tolkien to Charlotte and Denis Plimmer, February 8, 1967, # 294, p. 378; Tolkien to Christopher Bretherton, July 16, 2015, # 257, p. 347. In the letter to Bretherton Tolkien mentioned his "Atlantis-haunting" dream and his efforts to write about it, culminating in "an abortive book" that was initiated "[w]hen C.S. Lewis and I tossed up..." Also see Humphrey Carpenter, *Tolkien: The Authorized Biography*, Houghton Mifflin, 1977, p. 170-172.

[25] JRR Tolkien, *The Legend of Sigurd and Gudrún*, Christopher Tolkien editor, HarperCollins, 2009, see p. 5 for Christopher Tolkien's guess that this project dated "perhaps to the earlier 1930s" and perhaps "near the end of 1931..."

[26] JRR Tolkien, *The Lost Road and Other Writings*, in *The History of Middle-earth, Volume V*, Christopher Tolkien editor, Houghton Mifflin, 1987, p. 11-12.

[27] JRR Tolkien, *The Lost Road and Other Writings*, Christopher Tolkien editor, 1987, p. 14. The same material I have quoted appeared in the second version of "The Fall of Númenor," slightly edited, see p. 24-25. In *The Lost Road* we find "lesser men," though none who "took the part of Morgoth" (p. 64-65); it was Manwë rather than "Fionwë son of Manwë" who endowed Men with riches and wisdom (p. 65); and there is only mention of "we have grown to be higher and greater than others of our race" (p. 65) rather than "other races of Men..."

[28] JRR Tolkien, *The Lost Road and Other Writings*, Christopher Tolkien editor, 1987, p. 38.

[29] Christina Scull and Wayne Hammond, *The JRR Tolkien Companion and Guide: Reader's Guide*, Houghton Mifflin, 2006, p. 651; see p. 649-656 for an essay on "Northernness." My quote from Marjorie Burns is from this essay. For a summary of the general idea of "northernness" see Elly R. Truitt, "Fantasy North," *Aeon*, 15 February 2016.

[30] William Ripley, *Races of Europe: A Sociological Study*, Appleton, 1899. For a brief discussion of this book and its influence see Ivan Hannaford, *Race: The History of an Idea in the West*, Woodrow Wilson Center Press, 1996, p. 329-330. Ripley defended the accepted model of three European races and objected to a project by a French anthropologist to define six races and four sub-races in Europe (see p. 597-606).

[31] AC Haddon and Julien Huxley, *We Europeans: A Survey of "Racial" Problems*, New York: Harper and Brothers, 1936, p. 139-140. Haddon and Huxley subsumed the "Mediterranean type" into a larger category that included "Nordic" and "Eurasiatic" subgroups (see p. 139-145). They also list the "three most characteristic types of European man" as Mediterranean, Eurasiatic, and Nordic (p. 50).

[32] Christina Scull and Wayne Hammond, *The JRR Tolkien Companion and Guide: Reader's Guide*, 2006, p. 668; for the comparison of Númenor to Nazi Germany they cite Christopher Tolkien's summary in JRR Tolkien, *The Lost Road and Other Writings*, in *The History of Middle-earth, Volume V*, Christopher Tolkien editor, Houghton Mifflin, 1987, p. 77.

[33] Humphrey Carpenter, *Tolkien: The Authorized Biography*, Houghton Mifflin, 1977, p. 144-145.

[34] Humphrey Carpenter, *Tolkien: The Authorized Biography*, 1977, p. 146-148.

[35] Carl Phelpstead, "Northern Courage," in *JRR Tolkien Encyclopedia: Scholarship and Critical Assessment*, Michael Drout editor, New York: Routledge, 2007, p. 461-462. For a survey of the expressions of "northern courage" in *The Lord of the Rings* see Liam Felsen, "Becoming Tolkien: Reading His Anglo-Saxon and Boethian Sources," in Leslie Donovan, editor, *Approaches to Teaching Tolkien's* The Lord of the Rings *and Other Works*, The Modern Language Association, 2015. p. 97-102.

[36] Christina Scull and Wayne Hammond, *The JRR Tolkien Companion and Guide: Chronology*, Houghton Mifflin, 2006, p. 159.

[37] JRR Tolkien, *A Secret Vice: Tolkien on Invented Languages*, Dimitra Fimi and Andrew Higgins editors, HarperCollins, 2016, p. 30, 102. The "white people" description appeared in a poem Tolkien wrote in Elvish with a

literal translation; the poem was titled "Nieninqe" meaning "snowdrop" / "white tear" (see p. 56 endnote 75 for discussion of this title).

[38] JRR Tolkien, "The Ambarkanta," in *The Shaping of Middle-earth*, in *The History of Middle-earth, Volume IV*, Christopher Tolkien editor, Houghton Mifflin, 1986, p. 238. Christopher published this paper together with writing dating to circa 1930 and later decided "The Ambarkanta" was written later and that it preceded the first notes on Númenor (see JRR Tolkien, *The Lost Road and Other Writings*, in *The History of Middle-earth, Volume V*, Christopher Tolkien editor, Houghton Mifflin, 1987, p. 9, 108; also see Christina Scull and Wayne Hammond, *The JRR Tolkien Companion and Guide: Reader's Guide*, Houghton Mifflin, 2006, p. 42, 283-284).

[39] Tolkien submitted his extant manuscript of *The Lost Road* to Allen & Unwin on November 15, 1937; see Christina Scull and Wayne Hammond, *The JRR Tolkien Companion and Guide: Reader's Guide*, Houghton Mifflin, 2006, p. 562.

[40] Humphrey Carpenter, *The Letters of JRR Tolkien*, with the assistance of Christopher Tolkien, Houghton Mifflin, 2000 edition [original publication 1981], Tolkien to Stanley Unwin, July 25, 1938, # 29, p. 37; this is just an excerpt from the actual letter.

[41] Humphrey Carpenter, *The Letters of JRR Tolkien*, 2000 edition [original publication 1981], Tolkien to Rütten & Loening Verlag, July 25, 1938, # 30, p. 37-38.

[42] Christine Chism, "Middle-earth, the Middle Ages, and the Aryan Nation: Myth and History in World War II," in Jane Chance, editor, *Tolkien the Medievalist*, Routledge, 2003, p. 63-92, see p. 63. Chism discussed Rosenberg at p. 72-75; she acknowledged (p. 74) that "there is no evidence that [Tolkien] read Rosenberg... or any other folkish racialist apologists for National Socialism..."

[43] Dimitra Fimi, *Tolkien, Race, and Cultural History*, Palgrave MacMillan, 2010, p. 136-137.

[44] My citations are to the first American edition of the book: AC Haddon and Julien Huxley, *We Europeans: A Survey of "Racial" Problems*, New York: Harper and Brothers, 1936, p. 120-122.

[45] Haddon and Huxley, *We Europeans: A Survey of "Racial" Problems*, 1936, p. 233-234.

[46] The third manuscript of "The Fall of Númenor" was prepared sometime during "a relatively early stage in the writing of *The Lord of the Rings*..."; see JRR Tolkien, *Sauron Defeated*, in *The History of The Lord of the Rings, Part Four*, Christopher Tolkien editor, Houghton Mifflin, 1992, p. 331. This version mentioned "evil men who had served Morgoth" (p. 332); it had "Fionwë son of Manwë" teaching the Men "and he gave them wisdom, and power, and life stronger than any others have of mortal race" (p. 332); and these Men were "more like to the Firstborn than any other of the kindreds of Men; yet they were less fair and less wise than the Elves, though greater in stature" (p. 334). The notable evolution here is that the word "races" appeared in the two previous manscripts, but it became "race" and "kindreds" in this third version.

[47] Humphrey Carpenter, *The Letters of JRR Tolkien*, with the assistance of Christopher Tolkien, Houghton Mifflin, 2000 edition [original publication 1981], excerpt from JRR Tolkien to Rhona Beare, # 230, June 8, 1961, p. 307.

[48] AC Haddon and Julien Huxley, *We Europeans: A Survey of "Racial" Problems*, New York: Harper and Brothers, 1936, p. 52-84 "Heredity as Applied to Man"; for quoted material see p. 55, 61, 69.

[49] E.R. Truitt, "Fantasy North," *Aeon*, 15 February 2016.

[50] Humphrey Carpenter, *The Letters of JRR Tolkien*, with the assistance of Christopher Tolkien, Houghton Mifflin, 2000 edition [original publication 1981], JRR Tolkien to Michael Tolkien, March 18, 1941, # 44, p. 55-56.

[51] Humphrey Carpenter, *The Letters of JRR Tolkien*, 2000 edition [original publication 1981], JRR Tolkien to WH Auden, # 163, June 7, 1955, p. 212.

[52] George Orwell, "North and South," Chapter 7 in *The Road to Wigan Pier*, Part 1, Victor Gollancz, 1937.

[53] Humphrey Carpenter, *The Letters of JRR Tolkien*, 2000 edition [original publication 1981], JRR Tolkien to Robert Murray, December 2, 1953, # 142, p. 172.

[54] Humphrey Carpenter, *The Letters of JRR Tolkien*, 2000 edition [original publication 1981], JRR Tolkien to Robert Murray, November 4, 1954, # 156, p. 205-206. For a comment about the First Age and Second Age as "a monotheistic world of 'natural theology'" and "the "Third Age' was not a Christian world" see JRR Tolkien to Houghton Mifflin, June 30, 1955, # 165, p. 220.

[55] Harry Lee Poe, "C.S. Lewis Was a Secret Government Agent," December 10, 2015, online at *Christianity Today*. Poe was able to obtain only a part of the Lewis recording.

[56] JRR Tolkien, *Beowulf: A Translation and Commentary*, edited by Christopher Tolkien, Houghton Mifflin Harcourt, 2014, p.163-164.

[57] Charlotte and Denis Plimmer, "The Man Who Understands Hobbits," *The Daily Telegraph*, March 22, 1968, reissued online as "JRR Tolkien: I never expected a money success," *The Telegraph*, October 21, 2015. Tolkien was interviewed by the Plimmers on the morning of November 30, 1966; see Christina Scull and Wayne Hammond, *The JRR Tolkien Companion and Guide: Chronology*, Houghton Mifflin, 2006, p. 681. Tolkien read a draft of the article in February 1967 and sent some corrections to the Plimmers; see Humphrey Carpenter, *The Letters of JRR Tolkien*, with the assistance of Christopher Tolkien, Houghton Mifflin, 2000 edition [original publication 1981], JRR Tolkien to Charlotte and Denis Plimmer, February 8, 1967, # 294, p. 372-378; Scull and Hammond *The JRR Tolkien Companion and Guide: Chronology*, p. 688-690, 721.

[58] Christina Scull and Wayne Hammond, *The JRR Tolkien Companion and Guide: Reader's Guide*, 2006, p. 665-679; also see 283-284, 657-664. For a detailed study of Tolkien's work on a narrative context for the Atlantis story in 1945-1946 see Verlyn Flieger, "Do the Atlantis story and abandon Eriol-Saga," *Tolkien Studies* 1, 2004, p. 43-68.

[59] Scull and Hammond, *The JRR Tolkien Companion and Guide: Reader's Guide*, 2006, p. 668; they cite Christopher Tolkien's summary in JRR Tolkien, *The Lost Road and Other Writings*, in *The History of Middle-earth, Volume V*, Christopher Tolkien editor, Houghton Mifflin, 1987, p. 77.

[60] Stuart D. Lee, "JRR Tolkien and The Wanderer: From Edition to Application," in *Tolkien Studies*, # 6, 2009, p. 189-211, see p. 195 note by Tolkien probably dating to circa 1942 (see chart p. 192).

⁶¹ Humphrey Carpenter, *The Letters of JRR Tolkien*, with the assistance of Christopher Tolkien, Houghton Mifflin, 2000 edition [original publication 1981], JRR Tolkien to Mrs E.C. Ossen Drijver, # 227, January 5, 1961, p. 303.

⁶² Humphrey Carpenter, *The Letters of JRR Tolkien*, 2000 edition [original publication 1981], JRR Tolkien to WH Auden, # 163, June 7, 1955, p. 213.

⁶³ Humphrey Carpenter, *The Letters of JRR Tolkien*, 2000 edition [original publication 1981], JRR Tolkien draft letter to Mr. Thompson, # 180, January 14, 1956, p. 232.

Endnotes: The Taylorian Traditions

⁶⁴ *Folk-Lore: A Quarterly Review*, volume 19, # 2, 1908, p. 129. Alfred Haddon's lantern lecture on the Skidi Pawnees was given at the monthly meeting of the Folk-Lore Society held February 19, 1908, and "The meeting terminated with a vote of thanks to Dr. Haddon for his lecture." The Chairman of the Folk-Lore Society that year was Dr. Moses Gaster, a professor at Oxford. Haddon's work as an anthropologist included ethnographic photography. To my knowledge, none of the photos he took during his 1906 visit to Pawneeland have appeared in any publication.

⁶⁵ *Proceedings of the Cambridge Antiquarian Society*, October 1906 to May 1907, volume 12, 1908, p. 113: "A. C. Haddon, Sc.D., F.R.S., read a paper on The Morning Star Ceremony of the Pawnee." This paper was given on Monday, May 27, 1907. A typescript with hand-written notes was edited and published by Philip Duke, "The Morning Star Ceremony of the Skiri Pawnee as Described by Alfred C. Haddon," *Plains Anthropologist*, volume 34, # 125, August 1989, p. 193-203. Excerpts from this publication appeared in Robert L. Hall, *An Archaeology of the Soul: Native American Indian Belief and Ritual*, University of Illinois Press, 1997, p. 86-94. Citing Murie's notes at the Field Museum, Hall listed Haddon's traveling companions as Edward Seler, Paul Ehrenreich, and William Jones. Haddon could have given this paper on other occasions or talks on the topic, but we only know of the 1907 and 1908 presentations.

⁶⁶ AC Haddon, "Recent Publications of the Bureau of American Ethnology," *Nature*, May 10, 1906, p. 30-33. Haddon concluded this review with a pointed observation on Britain: "When one looks at the bulk of ethnological matter published by the United States Government, and realises the

enormous value to student of these full, accurate, and well-illustrated memoirs, one cannot but feel ashamed of our own Government, which, possessing every opportunity and inducement to study and report upon our own native races, does absolutely nothing."

[67] George A. Dorsey [and James R. Murie], *Traditions of the Skidi Pawnee*, Houghton Mifflin, 1904. Dorsey took sole credit for editing this collection of narratives, but the bulk of the collecting and all of the translating was done by James R. Murie. Between 1899 and 1903 anthropologist George Dorsey worked with Murie to collect and translate oral traditions from Skidi storytellers. A note (p. 359) specified that Dorsey's editing focused on "correction of grammatical errors" and it referred to "Indian interpreters," but only Murie was mentioned in Dorsey's preface: "In all the work I have relied largely upon the assistance of James R. Murie, a well-educated Skidi half-breed, without whose services it is probable that the present collection would not have been made." Murie's father was an American from Scotland. *Traditions of the Skidi Pawnee* featured stories told by 28 Skidis – a significant percentage of living adult Skidis of that time. A 1903 census listed about 266 members of the Skidi Band (National Archives, Record Group 75, Microcopy 595, Records of the Bureau of Indian Affairs, Pawnee Census 1903). The Skidi are one of four bands of the Pawnee Nation. The Pawnees have a reservation in Oklahoma and scattered properties in Nebraska.

[68] John Rhys, *Celtic Folklore: Welsh and Manx*, two volumes, Oxford: Clarendon Press, 1901; see volume 2, p. 683-684 footnote 1: "I am chiefly indebted to my friend, Professor A. C. Haddon for references to information as to the dwarf races of prehistoric times."

[69] *Folk-Lore: A Quarterly Review*, volume 16, 1905, p. 116-118, book review by N.W. Thomas of *Traditions of the Skidi Pawnee*, edited by George A. Dorsey.

[70] Christina Scull and Wayne Hammond, *The JRR Tolkien Companion and Guide: Chronology*, Houghton Mifflin, 2006, p. 13, 40. Scull and Hammond do not mention even a single volume associated with Tolkien's early years that could pertain to "Red Indians."

[71] Scull and Hammond, *The JRR Tolkien Companion and Guide: Chronology*, 2006, p. 41. Scull and Hammond noted that "Tolkien felt indebted to Craigie, both for his tutelage and for having in late 1918 arranged a post for

Tolkien... on the staff of the *Oxford English Dictionary*" (Scull and Hammond, *The JRR Tolkien Companion and Guide: Reader's Guide*, 2006, p. 190-191).

[72] Verlyn Flieger and Douglas A. Anderson, *Tolkien On Fairy-stories*, HarperCollins, 2008, p. 55; JRR Tolkien, "On Fairy-stories," in *Tales from the Perilous Realm*, Houghton Mifflin, 2008, p. 355. This comment about "Red Indians" does not appear in either "Manuscript A" or "Manuscript B" of "On Fairy-stories," so it must date to the preparation of "Manuscript C" in 1943. This means that it was a late insertion into the paper, adding a personal touch to Tolkien's intellectual analysis of fairytale literature.

[73] Flieger and Anderson, *Tolkien On Fairy-stories*, 2008, p. 309. A brief mention of Red Indians also occurs in JRR Tolkien, *The Monsters and the Critics and Other Essays*, edited by Christopher Tolkien, Houghton Mifflin, 1984, see "On Translating Beowulf," p. 57: Tolkien observed that a translator should not avoid words pertaining to chivalry, because the men of Beowulf were indeed men of "chivalrous courts." "If there be any danger of calling up inappropriate pictures of the Arthurian world, it is a less one than the danger of too many warriors and chiefs begetting the far more inept picture of Zulus or Red Indians." This essay with its casual mention of Red Indians was written in early 1940 (Christina Scull and Wayne Hammond, *The JRR Tolkien Companion and Guide: Reader's Guide*, 2006, p. 784).

[74] Humphrey Carpenter, *Tolkien: The Authorized Biography*, Houghton Mifflin, 1977, p. 47-48.

[75] Carpenter, *Tolkien: The Authorized Biography*, 1977, p. 47. The poem was "Wood-sunshine," written in July 1910. Carpenter cited a poem by Francis Thompson as a possible inspiration for the fairy scene in "Wood-sunshine," but John Garth was unable to identify any "obvious verbal echoes" (John Garth, "The road from adaptation to invention: How Tolkien Came to the Brink of Middle-earth in 1914," *Tolkien Studies* 11, 2014, p. 11). Consideration of Tolkien's early fairy conceptions appeared in Dimitra Fimi, "'Come sing ye light fairy things tripping so gay': Victorian Fairies and the Early Work of JRR Tolkien," in *Working With English: Medieval and Modern Language, Literature and Drama*, Volume 2, 2005-2006, p. 10-26; Dimitra Fimi, *Tolkien, Race and Cultural History: From Fairies to Hobbits*, Palgrave Macmillan, 2010, p. 13-20.

[76] JRR Tolkien, *The Story of Kullervo*, edited by Verlyn Flieger, HarperCollins, 2015, "On 'The Kalevala' or Land of Heroes," p. 77-78 (this publication

reprints JRR Tolkien, "'The Story of Kullervo' and Essays on Kalevala," transcribed and edited by Verlyn Flieger, *Tolkien Studies*, volume 7, 2010, p. 211-278).

[77] John Garth, "The road from adaptation to invention: How Tolkien Came to the Brink of Middle-earth in 1914," *Tolkien Studies* 11, 2014, p. 18-21, 28-30.

[78] JRR Tolkien, *The Story of Kullervo*, edited by Verlyn Flieger, 2015, "On 'The Kalevala' or Land of Heroes," p. 68 (also see endnote p. 92). Tolkien's mention of Vinland in this text was brief: "You feel like Columbus on a new Continent or Thorfinn in Vinland the good."

[79] JRR Tolkien, *The Book of Lost Tales, Part Two*, in *The History of Middle-earth, Volume II*, Christopher Tolkien editor, Houghton Mifflin, 1984, p. 261-262.

[80] Christina Scull and Wayne Hammond, *The JRR Tolkien Companion and Guide: Chronology*, Houghton Mifflin, 2006, p. 97. The dating of Tolkien's manuscripts is not always very clear, but Scull and Hammond believe that he began to write the first prose tales of his Middle-earth mythology in late 1916 or during the first half of 1917.

[81] JRR Tolkien, *The Book of Lost Tales, Part One*, Christopher Tolkien editor, 1983, p. 45. Christopher Tolkien observed that the only specific evidence for dating the writing of "The Music of the Ainur" to early 1919 appears in a letter that his father wrote in 1964 (see Humphrey Carpenter, *The Letters of JRR Tolkien*, with the assistance of Christopher Tolkien, Houghton Mifflin, 2000 edition [original publication 1981], p. 345). Christopher explained (p. 52) that for *The Book of Lost Tales* he published the second draft of "The Music of the Ainur," an expanded version of the first draft. Opinions on the dating of this manuscript to early 1919 appear in Scull and Hammond, *The JRR Tolkien Companion and Guide: Chronology*, 2006, p. 107; Scull and Hammond, *The JRR Tolkien Companion and Guide: Reader's Guide*, 2006, p. 123.

[82] Verlyn Flieger email to Roger Echo-Hawk, August 15, 2013. In August Flieger visited Oxford University and the Taylorian and sent this report to me: "...I did verify that the 1904 edition of *Traditions of the Skidi Pawnee* was acquired by the Taylor Institute Library in Oxford at the time of publication, and has been there ever since. I was able to look at it; it's a handsome volume, but with no indications of who might have read it."

[83] Tolkien took the Classical studies track when he started at Oxford in 1911, but John Garth has also noted Tolkien's study of Latin at his previous school, see Garth, "The road from adaptation to invention: How Tolkien Came to the Brink of Middle-earth in 1914," *Tolkien Studies* 11, 2014, p. 3. In 1908 Tolkien obtained an English-Latin dictionary to assist with his studies (see Liverpool Hope Library blog, "Unusual Provenance Discovery in Special Collections," March 18, 2016). Tolkien inscribed the copy with his name, date, and "KES," referring to King Edward's School where he had been a student since autumn 1900. At a 1909 "annual Latin Debate" at King Edward's School, Tolkien dubbed himself with a Latin name carefully designed for both personal meaning and humor in punning.

[84] Scull and Hammond, *The JRR Tolkien Companion and Guide: Chronology*, 2006, p. 28, 31, 32, 34, 36, 50, 52, 54.

[85] Scull and Hammond, *The JRR Tolkien Companion and Guide: Chronology*, 2006, p. 39.

[86] Scull and Hammond, *The JRR Tolkien Companion and Guide: Chronology*, 2006, p. 41; Scull and Hammond, *The JRR Tolkien Companion and Guide: Reader's Guide*, 2006, p. 190-191. William Craigie published several papers in the Folk-Lore Society journal in 1898; see William Craigie, "Evald Tang Kristensen, A Danish Folklorist," *Folk-Lore: A Quarterly Review*, volume 9, # 3, September 1898, p. 194-224; "Some Highland Folklore," p. 372-379. Craigie was listed as a member of the Folk-Lore Society in the 1898 volume.

[87] The Taylorian Librarian and her staff reviewed the extant partial loan records and were unable to locate any record showing that Tolkien borrowed the library's copy of *Traditions of the Skidi Pawnee*, or that anyone at Oxford checked out the book (Jill Hughes email to Roger Echo-Hawk, October 23, 2013). No record exists in their partial files showing that Tolkien ever checked out any book in their system.

[88] Humphrey Carpenter, *The Letters of JRR Tolkien*, with the assistance of Christopher Tolkien, Houghton Mifflin, 2000 edition [original publication 1981], JRR Tolkien to Edith Bratt, undated letter written in October 1914, # 1, p. 7.

[89] Scull and Hammond, *The JRR Tolkien Companion and Guide: Chronology*, 2006, p. 106-107.

[90] Scull and Hammond, *The JRR Tolkien Companion and Guide: Chronology*, 2006, p. 153.

[91] Scull and Hammond, *The JRR Tolkien Companion and Guide: Chronology*, 2006, p. 162.

[92] Scull and Hammond, *The JRR Tolkien Companion and Guide: Chronology*, 2006, p. 216.

[93] Scull and Hammond, *The JRR Tolkien Companion and Guide: Chronology*, p. 252, 253-254.

[94] John Garth, "The road from adaptation to invention: How Tolkien Came to the Brink of Middle-earth in 1914," *Tolkien Studies* 11, 2014, p. 1-44.

[95] Tom Shippey, *The Road to Middle-earth*, Houghton Mifflin, 2003, p. 348.

[96] John Garth, "The road from adaptation to invention: How Tolkien Came to the Brink of Middle-earth in 1914," *Tolkien Studies* 11, 2014, p. 1-44; see p. 1-3.

[97] JRR Tolkien, *The Book of Lost Tales, Part One*, in *The History of Middle-earth, Volume I*, Christopher Tolkien, editor, Houghton Mifflin, 1983, p. 204-206; Christina Scull and Wayne Hammond, *The JRR Tolkien Companion and Guide: Reader's Guide*, Houghton Mifflin, 2006, p. 579-580. Scull and Hammond also suggest (p. 568) that Tolkien may have drawn inspiration from a poem by George MacDonald called "The True History of the Cat and the Fiddle."

[98] Mark Atherton, *There and Back Again*, I.B. Tauris, 2012, p. 220. For Shippey's consideration of Tolkien's Man in the Moon poems see Tom Shippey, *The Road to Middle-earth: How JRR Tolkien Created a New Mythology*, Houghton Mifflin, 2003, p. 36-38.

[99] James Hardy, editor, *The Denham Tracts*, Volume II, published by David Nutt 1895; Folk-Lore Society, volume 35, 1895, p. 55-57. A general survey of English texts related to the Man in the Moon can be found in a paper by Thomas Honegger, "The Man in the Moon: Structural Depth in Tolkien," in *Root and Branch: Approaches Towards Understanding Tolkien*, Thomas Honegger editor, 2005 [1999], p. 9-70, viewed online at Academia 11/15/2015.

[100] Christina Scull and Wayne Hammond, *The JRR Tolkien Companion and Guide: Reader's Guide*, Houghton Mifflin, 2006, p. 653; also see Stuart D. Lee,

"JRR Tolkien and The Wanderer: From Edition to Application," in *Tolkien Studies*, # 6, 2009, p. 204-205. Tolkien notated the word "make" in the quote with this addition: "I might say 'subcreate', indicating that if successful the result may be new (in art), though all its material is given."

Endnotes: In the Land of Magic

[101] Tolkien family accounts involving spiders appear in Humphrey Carpenter, *The Letters of JRR Tolkien*, with the assistance of Christopher Tolkien, Houghton Mifflin, 2000 edition [original publication 1981], p. 217, #163, June 7, 1955; John D. Rateliff, *The History of the Hobbit, Part One: Mr. Baggins*, Houghton Mifflin, 2007, p. 342 endnote 14; Scull and Hammond, *The JRR Tolkien Companion and Guide: Reader's Guide*, 2006, p. 973; Michael Drout, *JRR Tolkien Encyclopedia: Scholarship and Critical Assessment*, p. 668, entry on "Tolkien, Michael (1920-84)." In a 1957 radio show Tolkien said his children motivated him to write a chapter in *The Hobbit* using spider villains; see JRR Tolkien, *The Annotated Hobbit*, annotated by Douglas A. Anderson, Houghton Mifflin, 2002, p. 210.

[102] John D. Rateliff, *The History of the Hobbit, Part One: Mr. Baggins*, 2007, p. 334.

[103] A giant spider monster can be found in Chapter 21 of L. Frank Baum's *The Wonderful Wizard of Oz* (1900).

[104] Two good summaries of Tolkien's spider monsters make no mention of his original spider; see John D. Rateliff, *The History of the Hobbit, Part One: Mr. Baggins*, 2007, p. 326-334; Christina Scull and Wayne Hammond, *The JRR Tolkien Companion and Guide: Reader's Guide*, Houghton Mifflin, 2006, p. 973-976.

[105] JRR Tolkien, *The Book of Lost Tales, Part Two*, in *The History of Middle-earth, Volume II*, Christopher Tolkien editor, Houghton Mifflin, 1984, p. 261-262.

[106] John Garth, "The road from adaptation to invention: How Tolkien Came to the Brink of Middle-earth in 1914," *Tolkien Studies* 11, 2014, p. 18-21, 28-30. Verlyn Flieger prefers a less specific date for the writing of "The Story of Kullervo," putting it more broadly between 1912 and 1916; see JRR Tolkien, *The Story of Kullervo*, edited by Verlyn Flieger, HarperCollins, 2015, p. xii-xiii.

[107] Tolkien took up the tale of Eärendel sometime in 1919-1920 and prepared various outlines and notes, but he never wrote the actual legend see JRR Tolkien, *The Book of Lost Tales, Part Two*, Christopher Tolkien editor, 1984, p. 252-267. The earliest outline, which Christopher Tolkien labeled "scheme B" does not much resemble the circa 1914 note. There is no mention of Iceland, Greenland, or Night the Spider. In "outline C" we find elements of the 1914 note, including these notes: "Driven west. Ungweliantë. Magic Isles. Twilit Isle." Christopher Tolkien found this encounter with Ungweliantë "curious" (p. 256) due to the orientation to the west, but this followed the 1914 notes. A "scheme D" does not seem to mention Ungweliantë, but she reappeared in "outline E" under a different name, Wirilómë. It does not appear that these various notes contain any mention of a land of strange men.

[108] JRR Tolkien, *The Story of Kullervo*, edited by Verlyn Flieger, HarperCollins, 2015, p. 68; JRR Tolkien, "'The Story of Kullervo' and Essays on Kalevala," edited by Verlyn Flieger, *Tolkien Studies*, volume 7, 2010, p. 246; also quoted in Christina Scull and Wayne Hammond, *The JRR Tolkien Companion and Guide: Reader's Guide*, Houghton Mifflin, 2006, p. 440. Tolkien's essay, "On 'The Kalevala' or Land of Heroes," exists in a handwritten manuscript. The essay was prepared for two talks given by Tolkien in November 1914 and February 1915. A typescript of this essay was prepared by Tolkien circa 1919-1921, and it revised the comment on the New World and Vinland: "We will avoid the Peak in Darien, if only for the reason that I at any rate am not remaining silent about/upon it – still you do feel like a Columbus landing on a new continent, a Thorfinn Karlsefni in a Vinland the Good – and better off, for your new heroic acquaintances are better fun than Skraeling or Red Indian." See JRR Tolkien, *The Story of Kullervo*, edited by Verlyn Flieger, 2015, p. 101.

[109] JRR Tolkien, *The Book of Lost Tales, Part Two*, Christopher Tolkien editor, 1984, p. 267-268.

[110] JRR Tolkien, *The Story of Kullervo*, edited by Verlyn Flieger, 2015, p. 113-114; JRR Tolkien, "'The Story of Kullervo' and Essays on Kalevala," edited by Verlyn Flieger, *Tolkien Studies*, volume 7, 2010, p. 269-270.

[111] JRR Tolkien, *The Story of Kullervo*, edited by Verlyn Flieger, 2015, p. 71. JRR Tolkien, "'The Story of Kullervo' and Essays on Kalevala," edited by Verlyn Flieger, *Tolkien Studies*, volume 7, 2010, p. 248; also quoted in Christina Scull and Wayne Hammond, *The JRR Tolkien Companion and Guide: Reader's Guide*, Houghton Mifflin, 2006, p. 441.

[112] JRR Tolkien, *The Story of Kullervo*, edited by Verlyn Flieger, 2015, p. 105; JRR Tolkien, "'The Story of Kullervo' and Essays on Kalevala," edited by Verlyn Flieger, *Tolkien Studies*, volume 7, 2010, p. 264; also quoted in Scull and Hammond, *The JRR Tolkien Companion and Guide: Reader's Guide*, 2006, p. 441.

[113] JRR Tolkien, *The Story of Kullervo*, edited by Verlyn Flieger, 2015, p. 106; JRR Tolkien, "'The Story of Kullervo' and Essays on Kalevala," edited by Verlyn Flieger, *Tolkien Studies*, volume 7, 2010, p. 266.

[114] John Box, "The Death of Spider-Woman," in George A. Dorsey [and James R. Murie], *Traditions of the Skidi Pawnee*, Houghton Mifflin, 1904, p. 39-44. This story and the preceding "How the Buffalo Went South" (which also pertained to Spider Woman) were both narrated by John Box.

[115] Christina Scull and Wayne Hammond, *The JRR Tolkien Companion and Guide: Reader's Guide*, Houghton Mifflin, 2006, p. 974.

[116] Verlyn Flieger, "Tolkien, Kalevala, and 'The Story of Kullervo,'" in JRR Tolkien, *The Story of Kullervo*, edited by Verlyn Flieger, HarperCollins, 2015, p. 133. Here Flieger concluded that Tolkien's retelling of the the Finnish tale of Kullervo "was an essential step on Tolkien's road from adaptation to invention that resulted in the 'Silmarillion.'" Also see Scull and Hammond, *The JRR Tolkien Companion and Guide: Reader's Guide*, 2006, p. 445, where they noted that Tolkien deemed the writing of his prose version of the *Kalevala* "a step leading to *The Silmarillion*."

[117] Verlyn Flieger, "Tolkien, Kalevala, and 'The Story of Kullervo,'" in JRR Tolkien, *The Story of Kullervo*, edited by Verlyn Flieger, 2015, p. 139. Flieger outlined a lengthy history of scholarly recognition of Tolkien's tranformational creative process, beginning with a 1981 analysis by Randel Helms, who took note of Tolkien "learning to outgrow an influence, transform a source" to Anne Petty in 2004 noting how Tolkien "drew on earlier sources" to apply his own "organization and textualization to the story elements" (see p. 134-135).

Endnotes: Worlds of Song

[118] Roaming Scout's earlier name "Tah-whoo-kah-tah-wee-ah" appears in 1914 testimony given by a Skidi elder (Pawnee Agency, Oklahoma, Realty

Office, Allotment File 345 Roaming Scout or Pawnee Tom, Eli Shotwell testimony, July 10, 1914). A manuscript by anthropologist Alice Fletcher prepared sometime around 1902 has this explanation of the name "Roaming Scout" – probably derived from James Murie and Roaming Scout: "The name Ki-ri-kí-ri-su ra-ká-wa-ri means running or roaming scout. Ki-ri-kí-ri-su, scout; ra-ká-wa-ri, roaming, walking, running, under the arching dome of the sky" (National Anthropological Archives, Alice Fletcher Papers, Box 28, Item 95, "Authority," undated typescript). Linguist Douglas Parks renders the name as Kirikiirisu Rakaawarii, meaning Scout Roaming the World, explaining that Rakaawarii "is based on the verb stem kaawarii, which means 'going around inside, roaming in (an enclosed space),' but in personal names has the metaphorical meaning 'roaming under the vault of the Heavens'" (Douglas R. Parks and Lula Nora Pratt, *A Dictionary of Skiri Pawnee*, 2008, University of Nebraska Press, p. 11).

[119] Roaming Scout, "Dispersion of the Gods and the First People," in George A. Dorsey [and James R. Murie], *Traditions of the Skidi Pawnee*, 1904, p. 3-14. Murie and Dorsey classed this story as a "Cosmogonic" narrative, a historical account relating to "origins, rituals, especially ceremonies, or to life beyond the grave."

[120] JRR Tolkien, *The Book of Lost Tales, Part One*, in *The History of Middle-earth, Volume I*, Christopher Tolkien editor, Houghton Mifflin, 1983, p. 45-63, "The Music of the Ainur." Christopher Tolkien published here the second manuscript of this story, written in ink, which expanded on a first draft "hastily pencilled and much emended[.]" Citing a letter written by Tolkien in 1964, Christina Scull and Wayne Hammond have concluded that the first draft in pencil of "The Music of the Ainur" was written between December 1918 and June 1919, probably early within this time-frame; see Christina Scull and Wayne Hammond, *The JRR Tolkien Companion and Guide: Reader's Guide*, Houghton Mifflin, 2006, p. 123.

[121] JRR Tolkien, *The Book of Lost Tales, Part One*, Christopher Tolkien editor, 1983, p. 52, 64. The Skidi story begins with Tirawa saying, "Each of you gods I am to station in the heavens;" and then situating "the Sun" and "Moon" and various stars. Tolkien's first draft mentioned the sun and moon, but his second draft deleted this passage (see endnote 7, p. 60; compare to text on p. 57). With Eriol's question (p. 64) "stations" appears in conjunction with mention of "the Sun" and "the Moon." In both creation stories "stations" is applied to the deities made by each creator.

[122] JRR Tolkien, *The Shaping of Middle-earth*, in *The History of Middle-earth, Volume IV*, Christopher Tolkien, editor, Houghton Mifflin, 1986, p. 78.

[123] For the "Ainulindalë" of the 1930s see JRR Tolkien, *The Lost Road and Other Writings*, in *The History of Middle-earth, Volume V*, Christopher Tolkien, editor, Houghton Mifflin, 1987, see "Quenta Silmarillion," p. 155-166. For the "Ainulindalë" of the 1950s see JRR Tolkien, *Morgoth's Ring, the Later Silmarillion, Part One*, in *The History of Middle-earth, Volume X*, Christopher Tolkien, editor, Houghton Mifflin, 1993, p. 3-44.

[124] JRR Tolkien, *The Book of Lost Tales, Part One*, Christopher Tolkien editor, 1983, p. 52, 63.

[125] JRR Tolkien, *The Book of Lost Tales, Part One*, Christopher Tolkien editor, 1983, p. 53.

[126] JRR Tolkien, *The Book of Lost Tales, Part One*, Christopher Tolkien editor, 1983, p. 54.

[127] JRR Tolkien, *The Book of Lost Tales, Part One*, Christopher Tolkien editor, 1983, p. 56.

[128] JRR Tolkien, *The Book of Lost Tales, Part One*, Christopher Tolkien editor, 1983, p. 62

[129] JRR Tolkien, *The Book of Lost Tales, Part One*, Christopher Tolkien editor, 1983, p. 58.

[130] George A. Dorsey [and James R. Murie], *Traditions of the Skidi Pawnee*, Houghton Mifflin, 1904, p. 330 endnote 14; JRR Tolkien, *The Book of Lost Tales, Part One*, in *The History of Middle-earth, Volume I*, Christopher Tolkien, editor, Houghton Mifflin, 1983, p. 58, 62, 113.

[131] JRR Tolkien, *The Book of Lost Tales, Part One*, Christopher Tolkien editor, 1983, p. 62.

[132] Humphrey Carpenter, *The Letters of JRR Tolkien*, with the assistance of Christopher Tolkien, Houghton Mifflin, 2000 edition [original publication 1981], p. 7, # 1, JRR Tolkien to Edith Bratt, undated letter written in October 1914.

[133] JRR Tolkien, *The Story of Kullervo*, edited by Verlyn Flieger, HarperCollins, 2015; JRR Tolkien, "'The Story of Kullervo' and Essays on Kalevala," edited by Verlyn Flieger, *Tolkien Studies*, volume 7, 2010, p. 211-278.

[134] Christina Scull and Wayne Hammond, *The JRR Tolkien Companion and Guide: Reader's Guide*, Houghton Mifflin, 2006, p. 31-32; Michael David Elam, "The Ainulindalë and J.R.R. Tolkien's Beautiful Sorrow in Christian Tradition," *Seven: An Anglo-American Literary Review*, volume 28, 2011, p. 61-78; Nicholas Birns, "The Stones and the Book: Tolkien, Mesopotamia, and Biblical Mythopoeia," posted July 15, 2011, viewed online at Academia 11/15/2015, paper published in *Tolkien and the Study of His Sources*, Jason Fisher editor, McFarland, 2011, p. 45-68.

[135] Carpenter, *The Letters of JRR Tolkien*, 2000 edition [original publication 1981], # 131, 1951, p. 143-161; see p. 144 where Tolkien describes the "Arthurian world" as a literature that is "involved in, and explicitly contains the Christian religion."

[136] JRR Tolkien, *The Legend of Sigurd and Gudrún*, Christopher Tolkien, editor, HarperCollins, 2009, p. 23-26.

[137] The formative nature of Tolkien's experiences in the First World War is described in detail by John Garth in his excellent *Tolkien and the Great War: The Threshold of Middle-earth*, Houghton Mifflin, 2003.

[138] John D. Rateliff, *The History of the Hobbit, Part One: Mr. Baggins*, Houghton Mifflin, 2007, p. 64 endnote 28.

[139] Marjorie Burns has suggested that Tolkien set an echo of Snorri Sturluson's *Gylfaginning* into the framing structure of "The Music of the Ainur"; see Marjorie Burns, "Old Norse Literature," in Michael Drout, *JRR Tolkien Encyclopedia: Scholarship and Critical Assessment*, New York: Routledge, 2007, p. 475.

Endnotes: Daughters of a Dark Moon

[140] Dan Jibréus, "The Long Journey of White Fox," *Nebraska History*, volume 95, #2, Summer 2014, p. 107.

[141] John Box held three names in his life: Ru tsi ra su re sa ru, Man Treated Royally; Kiwakuu Pahut, Red Fox; and Good Sun; see Martha Royce Blaine,

Some Things Are Not Forgotten: A Pawnee Family Remembers, University of Nebraska Press, 1997, p. 12. Blaine wrote that Box "was said to have been born about 1844" (p. 14); and another document recorded that he was born about 1845 (*Identification and Description of the Lands Covered by Selections and Allotments, 1893*, Government Printing Office, p. 9). John Box died on November 8, 1925 (Pawnee Agency, Oklahoma, Realty Office, Allotment File 42 John Box).

[142] After the publication of *Traditions of the Skidi Pawnee* Murie continued to work in partnership with John Box, mentioning him in 1916 as a priest and paying him for help with Skidi ceremonial songs (American Museum of Natural History, Department of Anthropology Archives, Correspondence File 357, James R. Murie letter to Clark Wissler, March 3, 1916).

[143] John Box, "How the Buffalo Went South," in George A. Dorsey [and James R. Murie], *Traditions of the Skidi Pawnee*, Houghton Mifflin, 1904, p. 36-38. Dorsey and Murie identified John Box under the name "Fox" (see p. 335 endnote 72). For a Kitkahahki Pawnee version of this story see White Sun, "The Buffalo and Red-Spider-Woman's Daughter," in George A. Dorsey [and James R. Murie], *The Pawnee Mythology*, Carnegie Institution, 1906 [see Bison Books edition 1997], p. 211-213. This version of the story referred to Spider Woman as "Old red painted woman," and she dwells in the south at "the center of the land..." The buffalo trample her as she sinks into the earth, and she becomes "a vine with a little squash on it[.]"

[144] "The Theft of Melko and the Darkening of Valinor" appeared in JRR Tolkien, *The Book of Lost Tales, Part One*, in *The History of Middle-earth, Volume I*, Christopher Tolkien, editor, Houghton Mifflin, 1983, p. 140-161. According to Christina Scull and Wayne Hammond the original version of this story was written probably in early 1919, and probably after "The Music of the Ainur" (Scull and Hammond, *The JRR Tolkien Companion and Guide: Reader's Guide*, Houghton Mifflin, 2006, p. 124).

[145] JRR Tolkien, *The Book of Lost Tales, Part One*, Christopher Tolkien editor, 1983, p. 151. This first adventure with Ungoliont unfolded on p. 151-153.

[146] Charlotte and Denis Plimmer, "The Man Who Understands Hobbits," *The Daily Telegraph*, March 22, 1968, reissued online as "JRR Tolkien: I never expected a money success," *The Telegraph*, October 21, 2015. Tolkien was interviewed by the Plimmers on the morning of November 30, 1966; see Christina Scull and Wayne Hammond, *The JRR Tolkien Companion and Guide:*

Chronology, Houghton Mifflin, 2006, p. 681. Tolkien read a draft of the article in February 1967 and complained that it contained information that was "totally inaccurate," and he sent some corrections to the Plimmers; see Scull and Hammond *The JRR Tolkien Companion and Guide: Chronology*, p. 688-690, 721. The article says that Tolkien pointed out that female and male monsters differ, and he mentioned a spider that must be Shelob: "She is a sucking, strangling, trapping creature." The idea of spider monsters trapping their enemies was a theme that began in 1914 with Night the Spider and continued in all his later spiders.

[147] For an opinion that monstrous spiders are "virtually nonexistent in traditional Germanic literature" see Joe Abbott, "Tolkien's Monsters: Concept and Function in The Lord of the rings (Part II) Shelob the Great," *Mythlore* 60, Winter 1989, p. 40. Abbott believed that Tolkien intended for Ungoliant to have been a Maia (p. 41). In a comprehensive summary of Norse influences on Middle-earth Marjorie Burns made no mention of any Norse inspiration for Ungoliant or other Tolkien spider-monsters; see Marjorie Burns, "Old Norse Literature," in Michael Drout, *JRR Tolkien Encyclopedia: Scholarship and Critical Assessment*, New York: Routledge, 2007, p. 473-479 – the entry for "Ungoliant" in this encyclopedia (p. 687) made no mention of any spider myth source-material. A 2014 survey of Norse influences on Middle-earth did not mention spiders: Tommy Kuusela, "In Search of a National Epic: The use of Old Norse myths in Tolkien's vision of Middle-earth," in *Approaching Religion*, volume 4, # 1, May 2014, p. 25-36.

[148] A one-line mention in the *Kalevala* of spider poison can be found in John Crawford's 1889 translation of Runo IX, but this brief listing did not appear in the WS Kirby translation. Celtic folklore and myth make randon mention of spiders, but with no evident source that could have inspired Night the Spider / Ungoliont. It is not clear what Tolkien intended in referencing spiders as "the particular terror of northern imaginations."

[149] JRR Tolkien, *The Book of Lost Tales, Part One*, Christopher Tolkien editor, 1983, p. 151, 154, 200, 214. The Pawnee story orienting Spider Woman to North and South echoes Keresan Pueblo mythology that identifies the North as an origin point and the South as a destination; see Carol Patterson-Rudolph, *On the Trail of Spider Woman: Petroglyphs, Pictographs, and Myths of the Southwest*, Ancient City Press, 1997, p. 7-9. The Pawnee story associated Spider Woman with "the centre of the earth," and in some versions of the Keresan Pueblo myth, Spider Woman plays a role in an emergence origin story, with the first people emerging from inside the earth.

[150] George A. Dorsey [and James R. Murie], *Traditions of the Skidi Pawnee*, Houghton Mifflin, 1904, p. 335, endnote 74. For more information on Spider Woman see p. 351-352 endnote 228 and p. 354 endnote 245. In these Pawnee accounts of Spider Woman it is interesting that she stands in polar opposition to Ungoliont. Spider Woman is the source of sweet spring water upon mountains and hillsides, whereas Ungoliont indulges an insatiable appetite for sucking up light, "applying even her lips... and sucking away" the "fiery radiance" of the Two Trees (JRR Tolkien, *The Book of Lost Tales, Part One*, Christopher Tolkien editor, 1983, p. 153).

[151] JRR Tolkien, *Morgoth's Ring, the Later Silmarillion, Part One*, in *The History of Middle-earth, Volume X*, Christopher Tolkien, editor, Houghton Mifflin, 1993, p. 97-98, 100.

[152] "Roverandom," in JRR Tolkien, *Tales from the Perilous Realm*, Houghton Mifflin, 2008, p. xiv (for the date of composition), 27 (for the association of spiders and mountains); also see p. 30, 43, 44).

[153] JRR Tolkien, *The Book of Lost Tales, Part One*, Christopher Tolkien editor, 1983, p. 270-271.

[154] JRR Tolkien, *The Lays of Beleriand*, in *The History of Middle-earth, Volume III*, Christopher Tolkien editor, Houghton Mifflin, 1985, p. 11, 111-112.

[155] John Box, "The Death of Spider-Woman," in George A. Dorsey [and James R. Murie], *Traditions of the Skidi Pawnee*, 1904, p. 39-44. This story and the preceding "How the Buffalo Went South" (which also pertained to Spider Woman) were both narrated by John Box. A second story features various elements of "The Death of Spider Woman," see John Box, "The Basket Game, Or the Woman in the Moon," in George Dorsey [and James R. Murie], *The Pawnee Mythology*, 1906, Carnegie Institution of Washington, publication # 59, Bison Books 1997 reprint, University of Nebraska Press, p. 233-236.

[156] For an excellent regional survey of Spider Woman traditions and iconograpy see Carol Patterson-Rudolph, *On the Trail of Spider Woman: Petroglyphs, Pictographs, and Myths of the Southwest*, Ancient City Press, 1997. David Leeming and Jake Page described Spider Woman as a "personalized" goddess in *The Mythology of Native North America*, University of Oklahoma Press, 1998, p. 11; for her cosmogonical aspect see p. 27-33, 90, 91, 103; for references to her folkloric fantasy aspect see p. 92, 148. She is both a divinity

of cosmogonical myth and a character of fantasy storytelling. Among the Sioux, Spider Man (Iktome) is a trickster fantasy figure; see Richard Erdoes and Alfonso Ortiz, *American Indian Myths and Legends*, Pantheon Books, 1984, p. 335, 337-339, 339-341, 358-359, 372-374, 381-382. One survey of Spider cosmogonic stories noted a distribution pattern that included the Pacific Island, East Asia, and India; and in North America, Spider Woman was especially prevalent in the Southwestern United States (Anna Birgitta Rooth, "Creation Myths of the North American Indians," in Alan Dundes, editor, *Sacred Narrative: Readings in the Theory of Myth*, University of California Press, 1984, p. 175-176).

[157] The two tales in *Traditions of the Skidi Pawnee* narrated by John Box about Spider Woman display notable differences. In "How the Buffalo Went South" Spider Woman is the divine daughter of Moon and Sun, and she obstructs the buffalo, but is not particularly evil. In "The Death of Spider-Woman" she is a murderous character, vanquished by two sons of Sun and Moon. This diversity of portrayal reflects varying modes of tale transmission and purpose, rooted in complex narrative traditions. The cosmogonical Spider Woman is most often a benign or benevolent deity, as in the story of Taihipirus (Roaming Scout, "The Moon Medicine," p. 199-203, see p. 201). A note to this story (endnote 228, p. 351-352) explained that the Moon is a cosmogonical Spider Woman associated with human origins. An endnote to "How the Buffalo Went South" (endnote 74, p. 335) informed us that many Spider Women existed "under the direct influence of the Moon" and "their influence was uniformly good[.]" But the humanized Spider Woman in "The Death of Spider-Woman" was a magical sorceress, an evil figure in Pawnee fantasy storytelling. A note to a story told by Bright Eyes (endnote 69, p. 334) suggested that Witch Woman is "not to be confounded with the Spider-Woman." The *stoo* (Witch Woman) is a cannibal sorceress with animal magic. A note to "The Death of Spider-Woman" (endnote 78, p. 335-336) seeks to reconcile the confusion by explaining that the evil sorceress in the story is a Witch Woman who became a Spider Woman after being exiled to the Moon. But the story itself makes no such distinction. A note to another story (endnote 245, p. 354, referencing story on p. 231) depicted Spider Woman as a shapeshifter able to "transform herself into a deer and vice versa"; she is here termed *statatciks* or Deer Ears Spider and is "under the direct influence of the Moon." Spider Woman in *Traditions of the Skidi Pawnee* thus holds diverse aspects of character as a celestial divinity, an earthly figure of mystery and power, and as an evil fantasy sorceress. This is the spectrum of ideas that Tolkien could have encountered in these Skidi traditions.

[158] Carl Phelpstead, *Tolkien and Wales: Language, Literature, and Identity*, University of Wales Press, 2011, p. 92. The poem quoted is Tolkien's "The Lay of Aotrou and Itroun."

[159] George A. Dorsey [and James R. Murie], *Traditions of the Skidi Pawnee*, Houghton Mifflin, 1904, p. 334 endnote 69.

[160] JRR Tolkien, *The Return of the Shadow*, in *The History of The Lord of the Rings, Part One*, Christopher Tolkien editor, Houghton Mifflin, 1988, p. 121.

[161] JRR Tolkien, *The Treason of Isengard*, in *The History of The Lord of the Rings, Part Two*, Christopher Tolkien editor, Houghton Mifflin, 1989, p. 90-94.

[162] Tolkien's imagery in this version of "Errantry" must harken back to "The Theft of Melko" in *The Book of Lost Tales, Part One*, where we first encounter Ungoliont in her dark cavern "as the ancient books say, and here on a time were the Moon and Sun imprisoned..."; see JRR Tolkien, *The Book of Lost Tales, Part One*, in *The History of Middle-earth, Volume I*, Christopher Tolkien, editor, Houghton Mifflin, 1983, p. 151. This in turn must refer to a story that Tolkien never wrote, inspired in some way by the *Kalevala*, Runo XLIX, which concerns the captivity of the sun and moon in a copper mountain; see *Kalevala: The Land of Heroes*, W.F. Kirby translator, J.M. Dent & Company, 1907, volume 2, p. 205-214.

[163] JRR Tolkien, *The Book of Lost Tales, Part One*, Christopher Tolkien editor, 1983, p. 151-152.

[164] English census records online give Arthur Tolkien's date of birth as about 1857, and Mabel Suffield was born about 1870. During the early 1870s they both lived in suburbs of Birmingham.

[165] Verlyn Flieger and Douglas A. Anderson, *Tolkien On Fairy-stories*, HarperCollins, 2008, p. 55; JRR Tolkien, "On Fairy-stories," in *Tales from the Perilous Realm*, Houghton Mifflin, 2008, p. 355. This comment about "Red Indians" does not appear in either "Manuscript A" or "Manuscript B" of "On Fairy-stories," so it must date to the preparation of "Manuscript C" in 1943.

Endnotes: Saru and Sári and the Sun

[166] JRR Tolkien, *The Book of Lost Tales, Part One*, in *The History of Middle-earth, Volume I*, Christopher Tolkien editor, Houghton Mifflin, 1983, p. 174-206. Christopher Tolkien described the surviving original of "The Tale of the Sun and Moon" as "a manuscript in ink over an erased pencilled original, but toward its end... it becomes a primary manuscript in ink with the pencilled draft extant in another book." Christopher Tolkien decided to "shorten" this complicated manuscript "without omitting any detail of interest."

[167] Christina Scull and Wayne Hammond, *The JRR Tolkien Companion and Guide: Reader's Guide*, Houghton Mifflin, 2006, p. 125.

[168] *Kalevala: The Land of Heroes*, W.F. Kirby translator, J.M. Dent & Company, 1907, volume 2, p. 189-197. In 1914 and 1915 Tolkien prepared two illustrations that referenced Runo 47; see Scull and Hammond, *The JRR Tolkien Companion and Guide: Reader's Guide*, 2006, p. 440-441.

[169] JRR Tolkien, *The Story of Kullervo*, edited by Verlyn Flieger, HarperCollins, 2015, p. 73-74; JRR Tolkien, "'The Story of Kullervo' and Essays on Kalevala," edited by Verlyn Flieger, *Tolkien Studies*, volume 7, 2010, p. 249.

[170] John Garth, "The road from adaptation to invention: How Tolkien Came to the Brink of Middle-earth in 1914," *Tolkien Studies* 11, 2014, p. 25, 28.

[171] JRR Tolkien, *The Book of Lost Tales, Part One*, in *The History of Middle-earth, Volume I*, Christopher Tolkien editor, Houghton Mifflin, 1983, p. 183-184.

[172] JRR Tolkien, *The Book of Lost Tales, Part One*, Christopher Tolkien editor, 1983, p. 186-187; the name "Sári" also appeared on p. 193, 195, 198, 215-216, 218, 221-222, and appendix p. 265.

[173] JRR Tolkien, *The Book of Lost Tales, Part One*, Christopher Tolkien editor, 1983, p.189-193.

[174] JRR Tolkien, *The Book of Lost Tales, Part One*, Christopher Tolkien editor, 1983, p. 202, 215; also see p. 194-195. Tolkien had plans for the love story between Urwendi and Fionwë – it would have major consequences in the future (p. 219), but this myth never got written.

[175] JRR Tolkien, *The Book of Lost Tales, Part One*, Christopher Tolkien editor, 1983; for the names "Children of Ilúvatar" and "Children of Men" see p. 57, 59; for "Gilfanon's Tale" see p. 229-245.

[176] JRR Tolkien, *The Book of Lost Tales, Part One*, Christopher Tolkien editor, 1983, p. 233, 236-237.

[177] JRR Tolkien, *The Shaping of Middle-earth*, in *The History of Middle-earth, Volume IV*, Christopher Tolkien editor, Houghton Mifflin, 1986, p. 11-75.

[178] JRR Tolkien, *The Shaping of Middle-earth*, Christopher Tolkien editor, 1986, p. 20.

[179] JRR Tolkien, *The Shaping of Middle-earth*, Christopher Tolkien editor, 1986, p. 97-99, 170-171.

[180] JRR Tolkien, *The Shaping of Middle-earth*, Christopher Tolkien editor, 1986, p. 269, 295.

[181] JRR Tolkien, *The Shaping of Middle-earth*, Christopher Tolkien editor, 1986, p. 262-293.

[182] JRR Tolkien, *The Lost Road and Other Writings*, in *The History of Middle-earth, Volume V*, Christopher Tolkien editor, Houghton Mifflin, 1987, p. 118.

[183] JRR Tolkien, *The Shaping of Middle-earth*, Christopher Tolkien editor, 1986, "The Ambarkanta," p. 235-261; see quote at p. 237. Christopher Tolkien originally placed "The Ambarkanta" around 1930, and later decided that it actually dated to circa 1935-1937 (see JRR Tolkien, *The Lost Road and Other Writings*, in *The History of Middle-earth, Volume V*, Christopher Tolkien editor, Houghton Mifflin, 1987, p. 9, 108; also see Christina Scull and Wayne Hammond, *The JRR Tolkien Companion and Guide: Reader's Guide*, Houghton Mifflin, 2006, p. 42, 283-284).

[184] JRR Tolkien, *The Lost Road and Other Writings*, Christopher Tolkien editor, 1987, p. 200. The material quoted in this paragraph appears at p. 241, 241-242, 242, 245.

[185] Roaming Scout, "The Children-of-the-Sun Society," in George A. Dorsey [and James R. Murie], *Traditions of the Skidi Pawnee*, Houghton Mifflin, 1904, p. 57-59.

[186] George A. Dorsey [and James R. Murie], *Traditions of the Skidi Pawnee*, 1904, p. 339 endnote 115. In the story, the young men "talked contrariwise," performing the opposite of what they said. In the story they confronted a "large water serpent" and destroyed it with stones that exerted "the power of lightning." Then a talking eagle gave feathers to them, advising, "put them upon your head and wear them always." Each man thereafter donned a feather as a society badge.

[187] Roaming Scout, "Dispersion of the Gods and the First People," in George A. Dorsey [and James R. Murie], *Traditions of the Skidi Pawnee*, 1904, p. 4.

[188] George A. Dorsey [and James R. Murie], *Traditions of the Skidi Pawnee*, 1904, p. 6.

[189] George A. Dorsey [and James R. Murie], *Traditions of the Skidi Pawnee*, 1904, p. 339 endnote 114.

[190] JRR Tolkien, *The Book of Lost Tales, Part One*, in *The History of Middle-earth, Volume I*, Christopher Tolkien, editor, Houghton Mifflin, 1983, p. 246-247.

[191] JRR Tolkien, *The Book of Lost Tales, Part One*, Christopher Tolkien editor, 1983, p. 265.

[192] John Garth, "The road from adaptation to invention: How Tolkien Came to the Brink of Middle-earth in 1914," *Tolkien Studies* 11, 2014, p. 25, 28. Also see JRR Tolkien, *The Story of Kullervo*, edited by Verlyn Flieger, HarperCollins, 2015, p. 15-21, 27-32; JRR Tolkien, "'The Story of Kullervo' and Essays on Kalevala," edited by Verlyn Flieger, *Tolkien Studies*, volume 7, 2010, p. 220, 236, 240, 245. This early set of writings by Tolkien features a name – and variants of the name – that Tolkien adapted or invented for his main character: Sāri, Sāari, and Saari. Tolkien did not provide a translation for this name. In the 2015 edition Flieger noted (p. xii-xiii) the "problematic" dating of this manuscript, which she put "as nearly as can be ascertained, some time during the years 1912-1914" – a letter written in October 1914 mentioned the writing of the story.

[193] *Kalevala: The Land of Heroes*, W.F. Kirby translator, J.M. Dent & Company, 1907, volume 2, p. 208, line 140.

[194] John Garth, "The road from adaptation to invention: How Tolkien Came to the Brink of Middle-earth in 1914," *Tolkien Studies* 11, 2014, p. 28.

[195] JRR Tolkien, *The Book of Lost Tales, Part One*, in *The History of Middle-earth, Volume I*, Christopher Tolkien, editor, Houghton Mifflin, 1983, p. 185-186.

[196] JRR Tolkien, *The Book of Lost Tales, Part One*, Christopher Tolkien editor, 1983, p. 192.

[197] JRR Tolkien, *The Lays of Beleriand*, in *The History of Middle-earth, Volume III*, Christopher Tolkien, editor, Houghton Mifflin, 1985, p. 11.

[198] George A. Dorsey [and James R. Murie], *Traditions of the Skidi Pawnee*, Houghton Mifflin, 1904, p. xix.

[199] JRR Tolkien, *The Book of Lost Tales, Part One*, Christopher Tolkien editor, 1983, p. 187.

[200] JRR Tolkien, *The Book of Lost Tales, Part One*, Christopher Tolkien editor, 1983, p. 66.

[201] George A. Dorsey [and James R. Murie], *Traditions of the Skidi Pawnee*, 1904, p. xix.

[202] Roaming Scout, "Dispersion of the Gods and the First People," in George A. Dorsey [and James R. Murie], *Traditions of the Skidi Pawnee*, 1904, p. 5-6.

[203] JRR Tolkien, *The Book of Lost Tales, Part One*, Christopher Tolkien editor, 1983, p. 98.

[204] JRR Tolkien, *The Book of Lost Tales, Part One*, Christopher Tolkien editor, 1983, p. 66, 94.

[205] JRR Tolkien, *The Book of Lost Tales, Part One*, Christopher Tolkien editor, 1983, p. 264. During the 1920s Tolkien listed and abandoned several names built from the roots of Palúrien: Bladorinand and Belaurien (JRR Tolkien, *The Lays of Beleriand*, in *The History of Middle-earth, Volume III*, Christopher Tolkien, editor, Houghton Mifflin, 1985, p. 160).

[206] Clive Tolley's 1980 *Mallorn* paper is quoted in Christina Scull and Wayne Hammond, *The JRR Tolkien Companion and Guide: Reader's Guide*, Houghton Mifflin, 2006, p. 442.

Endnotes: The Mythology of Mischief

[207] Roaming Scout, "Lightning Visits the Earth," in George A. Dorsey [and James R. Murie], *Traditions of the Skidi Pawnee*, Houghton Mifflin, 1904, p. 14-20.

[208] Roaming Scout, "Lightning Visits the Earth," in George A. Dorsey [and James R. Murie], *Traditions of the Skidi Pawnee*, 1904, p. 17: "The gods in the heavens saw him, and they were satisfied, and they wished that Lightning should remain upon the earth, and all the Stars wished that things could be as they were, save one Star in the Southeast. This Star, Skiritióhuts, Fool-Coyote, was jealous of the power of the Bright-Star."

[209] JRR Tolkien, *The Book of Lost Tales, Part One*, in *The History of Middle-earth, Volume I*, Christopher Tolkien, editor, Houghton Mifflin, 1983, p. 53-54.

[210] JRR Tolkien, *The Book of Lost Tales, Part One*, Christopher Tolkien editor, 1983, p. 144-145; quote appears at 146.

[211] JRR Tolkien, *The Book of Lost Tales, Part One*, Christopher Tolkien editor, 1983, p. 76-77.

[212] JRR Tolkien, *The Book of Lost Tales, Part One*, Christopher Tolkien editor, 1983, p. 212-213.

[213] George A. Dorsey [and James R. Murie], *Traditions of the Skidi Pawnee*, 1904, p. xix, 57. Drawing from information provided by Roaming Scout and James R. Murie, Alice Fletcher left an interesting note on the Milky Way (National Anthropological Archives, Alice Fletcher Papers, Box 28, Item 95, undated typescript). The name for the Milky Way is given as Ru-ha-rú-tu-ru-hut, referring to a bright white windy celestial expanse. This "is the path taken by the spirits of the dead as they pass along driven by the wind which dwells at the north on their way to their abode where the star stands midway the east and west at the south." And "most of the people linger in their death through sickness, so the path they tread is the long stretch that we see of this path across the heavens, while the short path is that made by those whose life is cut short by sudden death, as in battle." An account

given by James R. Murie to Natalie Curtis names the Milky Way "The Pathway of Departed Spirits" since "after death the spirit passes on this pathway to the Southern Star, the abiding place of the dead" (Natalie Curtis, *The Indians' Book*, Dover Publications, 1968 [originally published 1907, 1923], p. 99). Pratt and Parks render the Skidi name for the Milky Way as Rakiiraruhuuturuuhat (Douglas R. Parks and Lula Nora Pratt, *A Dictionary of Skiri Pawnee*, 2008, University of Nebraska Press, p. 214). Other communities in North American also envisioned the Milky Way as a path of the dead; see George Bird Grinnell, *The Story of the Indian*, 1908 [1895], D. Appleton and Company, p. 216. Grinnell briefly touched on the Cheyenne "Spirit Road" and the Blackfeet "Wolf Road" and he observed, "Most tribes called it the Ghost's Road."

[214] Kristine Larsen, "Myth, Milky Way, and the Mysteries of Tolkien's Morwinyon, Telumendil, and Anarrima," *Tolkien Studies*, volume 7, 2010, p. 197-210; quote appears at 207.

[215] JRR Tolkien, *Morgoth's Ring, the Later Silmarillion, Part One*, in *The History of Middle-earth, Volume X*, Christopher Tolkien, editor, Houghton Mifflin, 1993, p. 160.

[216] John Garth review of *Parma Eldalamberon* 15, in *Tolkien Studies* 3, 2006, viewed online on John Garth website. Both publications were out of print (October 2015), but Garth posted his review on his website. The review contained a glimpse of Tolkien's story about the Milky Way: "Finding that Watling Street, the Roman road from Dover to Chester, shared its name with the Milky Way, he devised a myth of terrestrial and celestial road-building that would explain this, involving race rivalry, treachery, and redress by the gods." Garth noted: "These are early ideas, barely surviving in *The Book of Lost Tales*, yet now we see what must surely be the very first, barely recognisable conception of Fëanor as he was forged by Tolkien (as Eärendil sprang partly out of references to the obscure Wade) from a key figure in northern myth."

[217] JRR Tolkien, *The Book of Lost Tales, Part One*, in *The History of Middle-earth, Volume I*, Christopher Tolkien, editor, Houghton Mifflin, 1983, p. 76.

[218] JRR Tolkien, *The Book of Lost Tales, Part One*, Christopher Tolkien editor, 1983, p. 71.

[219] JRR Tolkien, *Morgoth's Ring, the Later Silmarillion, Part One*, in *The History of Middle-earth, Volume X*, Christopher Tolkien, editor, Houghton Mifflin, 1993, p. 159. Marjorie Burns has suggested that in creating stars from sparks Tolkien had in mind Norse myth "where Odin and his brothers use sparks from the fire realm, Múspell, to create stars that wander and stars that are free to move" (Marjorie Burns, "Old Norse Literature," in Michael Drout, *JRR Tolkien Encyclopedia: Scholarship and Critical Assessment*, New York: Routledge, 2007, p. 476). Missing from this parallel is any link between stars and death, as we find in Pawnee tradition and in Tolkien's mythology.

[220] JRR Tolkien, *The Book of Lost Tales, Part One*, Christopher Tolkien editor, 1983, p. 131.

[221] JRR Tolkien, *The Book of Lost Tales, Part One*, Christopher Tolkien editor, 1983, p. 251.

[222] JRR Tolkien, *The Lost Road and Other Writings*, in *The History of Middle-earth, Volume V*, Christopher Tolkien editor, Houghton Mifflin, 1987, p. 182-183.

[223] JRR Tolkien, *The Lost Road and Other Writings*, Christopher Tolkien editor, 1987, p. 1.

[224] John D. Rateliff, *The History of the Hobbit, Part Two: Return to Bag-End*, Houghton Mifflin, 2007, p. 510.

[225] Rateliff, *The History of the Hobbit, Part Two: Return to Bag-End*, 2007, p. 691.

[226] John D. Rateliff, *The History of the Hobbit, Part One*, 2007, p. 45; Christina Scull and Wayne Hammond, *The JRR Tolkien Companion and Guide: Reader's Guide*, Houghton Mifflin, 2006, "Addenda and Corrigenda" for p. 638.

[227] JRR Tolkien, *The Annotated Hobbit*, annotated by Douglas A. Anderson, Houghton Mifflin, 2002. p. 46.

[228] John D. Rateliff, *The History of the Hobbit, Part One*, 2007, p. 143-145, 151 endnote 17. Douglas Anderson suggests that the stone-giants "can be interpreted as a type of troll" (JRR Tolkien, *The Annotated Hobbit*, annotated by Douglas A. Anderson, 2002, p. 104). He pointed to Tolkien's mention of "Stone-trolls," but this mention only appeared in Tolkien's later writings.

When Tolkien invented his stone-giants, he was more clearly thinking of some kind of monstrous giant.

[229] John D. Rateliff, *The History of the Hobbit, Part One*, 2007, p. 128.

[230] Roaming Scout, "Lightning Visits the Earth," George A. Dorsey [and James R. Murie], *Traditions of the Skidi Pawnee*, Houghton Mifflin, 1904, p. 14-20; see quoted material at p. 14, 15, 15-16.

[231] John D. Rateliff, *The History of the Hobbit, Part One*, 2007, p. 231-232.

[232] Well-Fed Captured Woman, "The Deluge," in George A. Dorsey [and James R. Murie], *Traditions of the Skidi Pawnee*, 1904, p. 23-24. Numerous versions of this story exist in Pawnee tradition. In this account, the giants "were like gods; they could perform miracles; they felt that they were just as good as any of the gods in the heavens. When the Sun came up from the east, they called it names[.]"

[233] George A. Dorsey [and James R. Murie], *Traditions of the Skidi Pawnee*, 1904, p. 338 endnote 105.

[234] Humphrey Carpenter, *The Letters of JRR Tolkien*, with the assistance of Christopher Tolkien, Houghton Mifflin, 2000 edition [original publication 1981], # 232, November 4, 1961, p. 309; Christina Scull and Wayne Hammond, *The JRR Tolkien Companion and Guide: Reader's Guide*, Houghton Mifflin, 2006, "Switzerland," p. 992-995. A detailed account of Tolkien's 1911 visit to Switzerland appears in a 1967 letter, but with no mention of a thunderstorm or a "bad night" (*The Letters of JRR Tolkien*, # 306, circa fall 1967, p. 391-393). Tolkien's thunder-battles could have drawn upon scenes in an H. Rider Haggard book; see Dale Nelson, "Literary Influences, Nineteenth and Twentieth Centuries," in Michael Drout, *JRR Tolkien Encyclopedia: Scholarship and Critical Assessment*, New York: Routledge, 2007, p. 369-370. But no mention appeared in this Haggard novel of "stone-giants." Tolkien could have mixed his inspirational materials here.

Endnotes: Coyote Bombadil

[235] Humphrey Carpenter, *The Letters of JRR Tolkien*, with the assistance of Christopher Tolkien, Houghton Mifflin, 2000 edition [original publication 1981], #144, April 25, 1954, p. 174.

[236] Christina Scull and Wayne Hammond, *The JRR Tolkien Companion and Guide: Reader's Guide*, Houghton Mifflin, 2006, p. 23.

[237] JRR Tolkien, *The Return of the Shadow*, in *The History of The Lord of the Rings, Part One*, Christopher Tolkien, editor, Houghton Mifflin, 1988, p. 115-116. The first Bombadil poem appeared in its entirety in JRR Tolkien, *The Adventures of Tom Bombadil*, edited by Christina Scull and Wayne Hammond, HarperCollins, 2014, p. 130-131, 138-140.

[238] Scull and Hammond, *The JRR Tolkien Companion and Guide: Reader's Guide*, 2006, p. 23; JRR Tolkien, *The Adventures of Tom Bombadil*, edited by Christina Scull and Wayne Hammond, HarperCollins, 2014, p. 131.

[239] JRR Tolkien, *The Book of Lost Tales, Part One*, in *The History of Middle-earth, Volume I*, Christopher Tolkien editor, Houghton Mifflin, 1983, p. 57.

[240] JRR Tolkien, *The Book of Lost Tales, Part One*, Christopher Tolkien editor, 1983, p. 66. For another mention of "aged spirits that journeyed from Ilúvatar with him who are older than the world" see p. 99. The passage goes on to say, "Still is the world full of these in the days of light, lingering alone in shadowy hearts of primeval forests..."

[241] John Rhys, *Lectures on the Origin and Growth of Religion as Illustrated by Celtic Heathendom*, Williams and Norgate, 1892, p. 104-106.

[242] Scull and Hammond, *The JRR Tolkien Companion and Guide: Reader's Guide*, 2006, p. 191.

[243] JRR Tolkien, *The Book of Lost Tales, Part One*, Christopher Tolkien editor, 1983, p. 94 – in this passage the terms Eldar, Gnome, and Shoreland Piper all refer to Elves.

[244] JRR Tolkien, *The Book of Lost Tales, Part One*, Christopher Tolkien editor, 1983, p. 108.

[245] JRR Tolkien, *The Book of Lost Tales, Part One*, Christopher Tolkien editor, 1983, p. 106.

[246] JRR Tolkien, *The Book of Lost Tales, Part One*, Christopher Tolkien editor, 1983, p. 115, 120.

[247] JRR Tolkien, *The Book of Lost Tales, Part Two*, in *The History of Middle-earth, Volume II*, Christopher Tolkien editor, Houghton Mifflin, 1984, p. 8, 10.

[248] JRR Tolkien, *The Book of Lost Tales, Part Two*, Christopher Tolkien editor, 1984, p. 8, 76.

[249] JRR Tolkien, *The Book of Lost Tales, Part Two*, Christopher Tolkien editor, 1984, p. 10.

[250] JRR Tolkien, *The Shaping of Middle-earth*, in *The History of Middle-earth, Volume IV*, Christopher Tolkien editor, Houghton Mifflin, 1986, p. 21, 23.

[251] JRR Tolkien, *The Shaping of Middle-earth*, Christopher Tolkien editor, 1986, p. 78.

[252] JRR Tolkien, *The Shaping of Middle-earth*, Christopher Tolkien editor, 1986, p. 85.

[253] JRR Tolkien, *The Shaping of Middle-earth*, Christopher Tolkien editor, 1986, p. 263.

[254] JRR Tolkien, *The Return of the Shadow*, in *The History of The Lord of the Rings, Part One*, Christopher Tolkien, editor, Houghton Mifflin, 1988, p. 115-116. The first Bombadil poem appeared in its entirety in JRR Tolkien, *The Adventures of Tom Bombadil*, edited by Christina Scull and Wayne Hammond, HarperCollins, 2014, p. 130-131, 138-140.

[255] Mark T. Hooker, *The Hobbitonian Anthology*, Llyfrawr, 2009, p. 64.

[256] Mark T. Hooker, *The Hobbitonian Anthology*, Llyfrawr, 2009, p. ix. In the early 1960s, rewriting "The Adventures of Tom Bombadil" to add mention of the Withywindle in the Shire, Tolkien produced another supporting piece of the puzzle in the geography of both Middle-earth and England. Studying maps of the English countryside northeast of Oxford, Hooker discovered that west of the River Avon, between Buckland and Bredon Hill (we are invited to read here: "Bree Hill"), is a locale called "The Dingle" (*A Tolkienian Mathomium*, p. 11-13). In this revision of "The Adventures of Tom Bombadil," Tolkien situated Tom's realm "where the Withywindle / ran from a grassy well down into the dingle." And introducing this poem, Tolkien now used "the Dingle" as the name for "the wooded valley of the

Withywindle[.]" "Dingle" has a double meaning. It is both a deep shady hollow and the ringing of a bell. It is apparent that Tolkien intended for his invented countryside to echo familiar landscapes – the campus of Oxford University and its bell in Tom Tower.

[257] Discussion on the dating of "The Adventures of Tom Bombadil" can be found in Christina Scull and Wayne Hammond, *The JRR Tolkien Companion and Guide: Reader's Guide*, Houghton Mifflin, 2006, p. 23; an early version of this poem was published in 1934, and it appears in Hammond and Scull, *The Lord of the Rings: A Reader's Companion*, Houghton Mifflin, 2005, p. 124-127. It also appeared in JRR Tolkien, *The Adventures of Tom Bombadil*, edited by Christina Scull and Wayne Hammond, HarperCollins, 2014, p. 123-137. In this edition Scull and Hammond note that excerpts from the early version of "The Adventures of Tom Bombadil" were written in Elvish script in five texts, and it is the script that has been dated to 1931. This implies that the poem was in existence by sometime in 1930-1931.

[258] John Mackay Wilson, *Tales of the Borders*, volume 3, 1851, published by Robert Martin, p. 272-274: stories of kelpies and water-wraiths. On p. 273: "…we must not confound the kelpie and the water-wraith, as has become the custom in these days of incredulity. No two spirits, though they were both spirits of the lake and the river, could be more different. The kelpie invariably appeared in the form of a young horse; the water-wraith in that of a very tall woman, dressed in green, with a withered, meager countenance, ever distorted by a malignant scowl."

[259] John Rhys, *Celtic Folklore: Welsh and Manx*, Volume One, 1901, Oxford University Press, "Undine's Kymric Sisters," p. 1-74. Goldberry wears green clothing, but the first mention of the clothing of the "Lake Lady" (p. 16) described her as "a lady in white[.]" Another account of a Lake Maiden mentioned "her long yellow hair" (p. 17) like Goldberry. In general the Welsh tales do not sound much like Goldberry, but the association with water is noteworthy.

[260] John M. Bowers, "Tolkien's Goldberry and *The Maid of the Moor*," in *Tolkien Studies 8*, 2011, p. 23-36.

[261] Goldberry's character as transitional in Tolkien's legendarium has been noted by John Garth, as reflected in a term that appeared in a text on Elvish language. Garth cited *nindari* "river-maid" in a text contemporary with the

first appearance of Goldberry (John Garth review essay, *Tolkien Studies* 11, 2014, p. 225-241, see p. 230-231).

[262] Mark T. Hooker, *Tolkien and Wales*, Llyfrawr, 2012, "The Daughter of the River," p. 74-78.

[263] John Rhys, *The Welsh People*, New York: Macmillan, 1900, p. 58-59.

[264] JRR Tolkien, *The Monsters and the Critics and Other Essays*, edited by Christopher Tolkien, Houghton Mifflin, 1984, see "On Translating Beowulf," p. 60. This essay was written early 1940 (Christina Scull and Wayne Hammond, *The JRR Tolkien Companion and Guide: Reader's Guide*, Houghton Mifflin, 2006, p. 784).

[265] R.C. Maclagan, "'The Keener' in the Scottish Highlands and Islands," *Folk-Lore: A Quarterly Review*, volume 25, March 1914, p. 84-91.

[266] Goldberry's green gown and silver-green clothing appeared in the 1934 version of "The Adventures of Tom Bombadil"; see Hammond and Scull, *The Lord of the Rings: A Reader's Companion*, Houghton Mifflin, 2005, p. 127.

[267] JRR Tolkien, *The Return of the Shadow*, in *The History of The Lord of the Rings, Part One*, Christopher Tolkien, editor, Houghton Mifflin, 1988, p. 117.

[268] Roger Echo-Hawk, *Tolkien in Pawneeland*, 2013, p. 57-64; George Dorsey [and James R. Murie], *Traditions of the Skidi Pawnee*, Houghton Mifflin, 1904.

[269] Cheyenne Chief, "The Story of Coyote," in George A. Dorsey [and James R. Murie], *Traditions of the Skidi Pawnee*, Houghton Mifflin, 1904, p. 239-253.

[270] Cheyenne Chief, "The Story of Coyote," in George A. Dorsey [and James R. Murie], *Traditions of the Skidi Pawnee*, 1904, p. 244. Cheyenne Chief may have woven together several Coyote stories into a longer episodic tale.

[271] Cheyenne Chief, "The Story of Coyote," in George A. Dorsey [and James R. Murie], *Traditions of the Skidi Pawnee*, 1904, p. 249-250.

[272] Humphrey Carpenter, *Tolkien: The Authorized Biography*, Houghton Mifflin, 1977, p. 162. Carpenter did not cite any source for Tolkien's reference to Rackham as a possible inspiration for the Bombadil tree-adventure. Tolkien wrote letters in 1957 and 1961 that briefly mentioned

Rackham's drawings. But none of his extensive comments on Bombadil mention the artist.

[273] Cecil J. Sharp, *English Folk-Carols*, London: Novello & Company, 1911, p. 5-6.

[274] Newly Made Chief Woman, "Coyote Rescues a Maiden," in George A. Dorsey [and James R. Murie], *Traditions of the Skidi Pawnee*, 1904, p. 254-259. Murie and Dorsey wrote down seven stories from this storyteller. She was the daughter of a doctor named Scabby Bull, who was "a great medicine-man among the Skidi, and who had many stories to tell about the different animals." This biographical note appears in George Dorsey [and James R. Murie], *The Pawnee Mythology*, 1906, Carnegie Institution of Washington, publication # 59, also Bison Books reprint, University of Nebraska Press, 1997, p. 460; also see 142. A story about Scabby Bull, told by Wonderful Sun, appears in *Traditions of the Skidi Pawnee* at p. 231-238. Roaming Scout had a brother named Scabby Bull but it is not clear if this was the same man as the father of Newly Made Chief Woman.

[275] Andrew Lang, *Essays in Little*, London: Henry and Company, 1891, p. 146. This Lang mention of barrowwights is quoted in Wayne Hammond and Christina Scull, *The Lord of the Rings: A Reader's Companion*, Houghton Mifflin, 2005, p. 137.

[276] JRR Tolkien, *Beowulf: A Translation and Commentary*, edited by Christopher Tolkien, Houghton Mifflin Harcourt, 2014, p.163-164.

[277] Hammond and Scull, *The Lord of the Rings: A Reader's Companion*, 2005, p. 126; JRR Tolkien, *The Adventures of Tom Bombadil*, edited by Scull and Hammond, HarperCollins, 2014, p. 127.

[278] JRR Tolkien, "Chaucer as Philologist: The Reeve's Tale," *Transactions of the Philological Society* 1934, London: David Nutt, A.G. Berry, 1934, p. 1-70.

[279] James Halliwell, *A Dictionary of Archaic and Provincial Words*, in two volumes, London: John Russell Smith, 1846, p. 931.

[280] Joseph Wright, *English Dialect Dictionary*, Oxford: Henry Frowde, 1905, Volume 6 T-Z, p. 490.

[281] James Hardy, editor, *The Denham Tracts*, Volume I, London: David Nutt 1892; Folk-Lore Society, volume 29, 1891, p. 166, 245-246.

[282] Spotted Horse, "Coyote and the Rolling Stone," in George A. Dorsey [and James R. Murie], *Traditions of the Skidi Pawnee*, Houghton Mifflin, 1904, p. 260-265. Spotted Horse told four stories that appeared in *Traditions of the Skidi Pawnee*.

[283] George A. Dorsey [and James R. Murie], *Traditions of the Skidi Pawnee*, 1904, p. xxii.

[284] Michael Drout, *JRR Tolkien Encyclopedia: Scholarship and Critical Assessment*, p. 668, entry on "Tolkien, Michael (1920-84)."

[285] JRR Tolkien, *The Return of the Shadow*, in *The History of The Lord of the Rings, Part One*, Christopher Tolkien editor, Houghton Mifflin, 1988, p. 112, 125, 126.

Endnotes: The Almost Forgotten Hobbits

[286] James Hardy, editor, *The Denham Tracts*, Volume II, published by David Nutt 1895; Folk-Lore Society, volume 35, 1895, p. 79. For consideration of *The Denham Tracts* and its mention of hobbits see Katharine Briggs, *A Dictionary of Fairies*, 1976, p. 93-94; Donald O'Brien, "On the Origin of the Name 'Hobbit'," *Mythlore* 60, Winter 1989, p. 32-38; Tom Shippey, *The Road to Middle-earth*, 2003, p. 66; Douglas Anderson in JRR Tolkien, *The Annotated Hobbit*, annotated by Douglas A. Anderson, Houghton Mifflin, 2002, p. 9; John D. Rateliff, *The History of the Hobbit, Part Two: Return to Bag-End*, Houghton Mifflin, 2007, p. 841-865; Dustin Eaton, "The Denham Tracts," in Michael Drout, *JRR Tolkien Encyclopedia: Scholarship and Critical Assessment*, New York: Routledge, 2007, p. 121; Tom Shippey, "The Ancestors of the Hobbits: Strange Creatures in English Folklore," *Lembas Extra*, 2011, p. 97-106.

[287] Donald O'Brien, "On the Origin of the Name 'Hobbit'," *Mythlore* 60, Winter 1989, p. 32-38. O'Brien took note (p. 33, 38 endnote 18) of how Roderick Sinclair cited the Briggs mention of the Denham hobbit in a May 1977 issue of *Amon Hen* 26 on p. 12.

[288] Tom Shippey, *The Road to Middle-earth*, Houghton Mifflin, 2003, p. 66.

[289] As late as 2007 the *OED* was still ignoring the existence of the Denham hobbit; see Dustin Eaton, "The Denham Tracts," in Michael Drout, *JRR Tolkien Encyclopedia: Scholarship and Critical Assessment*, Routledge, 2007, p. 121.

[290] Donald O'Brien made brief mention of the Welsh unit of agricultural measure in his paper "On the Origin of the Name 'Hobbit'," *Mythlore*, volume 16, # 2, Number 60, Winter 1989, p. 32-38. Michael Livingston provided an extended discussion of this aspect of the term with numerous examples in "The Myths of the Author: Tolkien and the Medieval Origins of the Word *Hobbit*," *Mythlore*, volume 30, 2012, p. 129-146.

[291] John C. Morton, *A Cyclopedia of Agriculture*, in 2 volumes, London: Blackie and Son, 1863, Volume 2.

[292] Walter W. Skeat and James Britten, editors, *Reprinted Glossaries and Old Farming Words*, London: Trübner & Company, Part 4, Reprinted Glossaries Parts 18-22, 1879, p. 171; James Britten, *Old Country and Farming Words: Gleaned from Agricultural Books*, London: Trübner & Company, 1880.

[293] Joseph Wright, *English Dialect Dictionary*, Oxford: Henry Frowde, 1905, Volume 3 H-L, p. 183, "hobbit" appeared with this addition: "Also written hobit."

[294] James Hardy, editor, *The Denham Tracts*, Volume I, published by David Nutt 1892; Folk-Lore Society, volume 29, 1891; James Hardy, editor, *The Denham Tracts*, Volume II, published by David Nutt 1895; Folk-Lore Society, volume 35, 1895.

[295] James Hardy, editor, *The Denham Tracts*, Volume II, published by David Nutt 1895; Folk-Lore Society, volume 35, 1895, p. 77-80.

[296] The Denham list of folkloric creatures has been reprinted and discussed in many places. See Donald O'Brien, "On the Origin of the Name 'Hobbit'," *Mythlore* 60, Winter 1989, p. 37; John Rateliff's *The History of the Hobbit* featured the list in *Part Two*, 2007, p. 841-865, and the 2011 edition of that book included an earlier version of the list (see Merlin DeTardo, "The Year's Work in Tolkien Studies 2011," in *Tolkien Studies*, volume 11, 2014, p. 262.)

[297] Humphrey Carpenter, *The Letters of JRR Tolkien*, with the assistance of Christopher Tolkien, Houghton Mifflin, 2000 edition [original publication 1981], Tolkien to Waldman undated letter circa 1951, # 131, p. 144.

[298] Verlyn Flieger and Douglas A. Anderson, *Tolkien On Fairy-stories*, HarperCollins, 2008, p. 177; also see note p. 197. Here Tolkien listed materials in Andrew Lang's *Blue Fairy Book* that included chapbook tales of "Jack and Dick Whittington" and "Jack and Babes." It is possible that this is the kind of material that he referenced in his 1951 letter.

[299] For mention of this Folk-Lore Society publication series see Richard Dorson, *The British Folklorists*, University of Chicago Press, 1968, p. 233.

[300] A discussion on Tolkien's "A Middle English Vocabulary" appeared in Christina Scull and Wayne Hammond, *The JRR Tolkien Companion and Guide: Reader's Guide*, Houghton Mifflin, 2006, p. 586-589.

[301] John D. Rateliff, *The History of the Hobbit, Part Two: Return to Bag-End*, Houghton Mifflin, 2007, p. 847.

[302] Rateliff, *The History of the Hobbit, Part Two*, 2007, p. 848. Rateliff elsewhere discussed the possibility that Tolkien drew from *The Denham Tracts* in his use of the term "carrock"; see Rateliff, *The History of the Hobbit, Part One*, 2007, p. 263-265.

[303] William Holloway, *A General Dictionary of Provincialisms*, London: John Russell Smith, 1840, p. 83.

[304] James Halliwell, *A Dictionary of Archaic and Provincial Words*, in two volumes, London: John Russell Smith, 1846, p. 452-453.

[305] Christina Scull and Wayne Hammond, *The JRR Tolkien Companion and Guide: Chronology*, Houghton Mifflin, 2006, p. 41; Scull and Hammond, *The JRR Tolkien Companion and Guide: Reader's Guide*, 2006, p. 190-191.

[306] Raymond Chambers was listed as a member of the Folk-Lore Society in *Folk-Lore: A Quarterly Review*, volume 31, 1920, p. iii; Humphrey Carpenter, *The Letters of JRR Tolkien*, with the assistance of Christopher Tolkien, Houghton Mifflin, 2000 edition [original publication 1981], Tolkien to Furth, August 31, 1937, # 15, p. 20.

[307] Two major works on the Welsh aspects of Tolkien's legendarium that make no mention of the Welsh agricultural hobbit are Carl Phelpstead, *Tolkien and Wales: Language, Literature, and Identity*, University of Wales Press, 2011; Mark T. Hooker, *Tolkien and Wales*, Llyfrawr, 2012. Phelpstead gives an excellent in depth survey of Tolkien's interest in Welsh materials. Hooker delves into a variety of Welsh dimensions in Tolkien's novels. Both books are excellent surveys of Tolkien's Welsh usages. I have the impression that Hooker has written elsewhere about the Welsh agricultural hobbit, but I have not seen that publication.

[308] James Hardy, editor, *The Denham Tracts*, Volume I, published by David Nutt 1892; Folk-Lore Society, volume 29, 1891, p. 108.

[309] Charles P.G. Scott "The Devil and his Imps: an Etymological Inquisition," in *Transactions of the American Philological Association* 1895, volume 26, p. 79-146. This paper featured unusual spellings reflecting a seeming effort to conventionalize practical spellings.

[310] The influence of Joseph Wright on Tolkien is discussed in Humphrey Carpenter, *Tolkien: The Authorized Biography*, Houghton Mifflin, 1977, 37, 55-56; Scull and Hammond, *The JRR Tolkien Companion and Guide: Reader's Guide*, 2006, p. 1125-1126; John Rateliff, "The Missing Women: JRR Tolkien's Lifelong Support for Women's Higher Education," in Janet Brennan Croft and Leslie Donovan, editors, *Perilous and Fair: Women in the Works and Life of JRR Tolkien*, Mythopoeic Press, 2015, p. 47-51.

[311] Humphrey Carpenter, *The Letters of JRR Tolkien*, with the assistance of Christopher Tolkien, Houghton Mifflin, 2000 edition [original publication 1981], Tolkien to E.M. Wright, February 13, 1923, # 6, p. 11.

[312] Christina Scull and Wayne Hammond, *The JRR Tolkien Companion and Guide: Reader's Guide*, Houghton Mifflin, 2006, p. 1126.

[313] Carl Phelpstead, *Tolkien and Wales: Language, Literature, and Identity*, University of Wales Press, 2011, p. 15.

[314] Joseph Wright, *English Dialect Dictionary*, Oxford: Henry Frowde, 1905, Volume 3 H-L, p. 183-185.

[315] Joseph Wright, *English Dialect Dictionary*, Oxford: Henry Frowde, 1905, Volume 3 H-L, p. 185. John Rateliff points out that Wright's citations of *The*

Denham Tracts was "frequent" see Rateliff, *The History of the Hobbit, Part One*, 2007, p. 264.

[316] William Holloway, *A General Dictionary of Provincialisms*, London: John Russell Smith, 1840, p. 80; James Halliwell, *A Dictionary of Archaic and Provincial Words*, in two volumes, London: John Russell Smith, 1846, p. 453.

[317] Charles P.G. Scott "The Devil and his Imps: an Etymological Inquisition," p. 79-146, in *Transactions of the American Philological Association* 1895, volume 26.

[318] Joseph Wright, *English Dialect Dictionary*, Oxford: Henry Frowde, 1905, Volume 3 H-L, p. 185.

[319] Joseph Wright, *English Dialect Dictionary*, Oxford: Henry Frowde, 1905, Volume 6 T-Z, p. 124, 130.

[320] John D. Rateliff, *The History of the Hobbit, Part Two: Return to Bag-End*, Houghton Mifflin, 2007, p. 475-476.

[321] Rateliff, *The History of the Hobbit, Part Two*, 2007, p. 513.

[322] Rateliff, *The History of the Hobbit, Part Two*, 2007, p. 549.

Endnotes: Tolkien's Hobbit Origin Stories

[323] Humphrey Carpenter, *The Letters of JRR Tolkien*, with the assistance of Christopher Tolkien, Houghton Mifflin, 2000 edition [original publication 1981], Tolkien to editor of the *Observer*, January or February 1938, published February 20, # 25, p. 30; John D. Rateliff, *The History of the Hobbit, Part Two: Return to Bag-End*, Houghton Mifflin, 2007, p. 855-858. Tolkien's earliest known comments on the origin of his hobbits appeared in JRR Tolkien letter to Arthur Ransome, December 15, 1937, in Alaric Hall and Samuli Kaislaniemi, "'You tempt me grieviously to a mythological essay': JRR Tolkien's Correspondence with Arthur Ransome," in Jukka Tyrkkö, Olga Timofeeva, Maria Salenius, editors, *Ex Philogia Lux: Essays in Honour of Leena Kahlas-Tarkka*, Helsinki: Société Néophilologique, 2013, p. 261-280; for a transcription of the letter see p. 265-266. This mentioned an absence of any internal hobbit origin story in his mythology: "As for hobbits no high legends deal with their origin, and having no better information I am inclined to claim them as a pleasant if miniature variety of our own kind, or

of some related strain." No evidence has come forward to show that Tolkien ever used the term "hobbit" in any writing prior to *The Hobbit*.

[324] Illustrating a true homophone, John Rateliff points to "weak" and "week" – two words that sound the same and have very similar spellings but enclose entirely different meanings; see John D. Rateliff, *The History of the Hobbit, Part Two: Return to Bag-End*, Houghton Mifflin, 2007, p. 863 endnote 2. They are not the same words at all, though they bear strong similarities.

[325] Humphrey Carpenter, *The Letters of JRR Tolkien*, with the assistance of Christopher Tolkien, Houghton Mifflin, 2000 edition [original publication 1981], Tolkien to Stanley Unwin, March 4, 1938, # 26, p. 35.

[326] John D. Rateliff, *The History of the Hobbit, Part Two: Return to Bag-End*, Houghton Mifflin, 2007, p. 849.

[327] John D. Rateliff, *The History of the Hobbit, Part One: Mr. Baggins*, Houghton Mifflin, 2007, p. 9. Another possible reference to the crop-related nature of the Welsh hobbit is weakly implied on the previous page when Bilbo struck the Dwarves as being "more like a grocer than a burglar!"

[328] For an example of a 19th century British discussion of wireworms see John Curtis, *Farm Insects*, Blackie and Sons, 1860, p. 152-210.

[329] JRR Tolkien, *The Return of the Shadow*, in *The History of The Lord of the Rings, Part One*, Christopher Tolkien editor, Houghton Mifflin, 1988, p. 15.

[330] JRR Tolkien, *The Return of the Shadow*, Christopher Tolkien editor, 1988, p. 22.

[331] Humphrey Carpenter, *The Letters of JRR Tolkien*, with the assistance of Christopher Tolkien, Houghton Mifflin, 2000 edition [original publication 1981], Tolkien to Milton Waldman, undated letter circa late 1951, # 131, p. 158; Tolkien to Allen & Unwin, December 12, 1955, # 178, p. 230. For a discussion of the pastoral quality of Tolkien's hobbits see Philip Irving Mitchell, "Conceptions of the Pastoral in *The Fellowship of the Ring*," in Leslie Donovan, editor, *Approaches to Teaching Tolkien's* The Lord of the Rings *and Other Works*, The Modern Language Association, 2015. p. 108-110.

[332] Carpenter, *The Letters of JRR Tolkien*, 2000 edition [original publication 1981], Tolkien to Rayner Unwin, July 3, 1956, # 190, p. 250.

[333] Carpenter, *The Letters of JRR Tolkien*, 2000 edition [original publication 1981], Tolkien to Deborah Webster, October 25, 1958, # 213, p. 288.

[334] JRR Tolkien, "Nomenclature of *The Lord of the Rings*," 1967, in Christina Scull and Wayne Hammond, *The Lord of the Rings: A Reader's Companion*, Houghton Mifflin, 2005, p. 768.

[335] John Rhys, *Lectures on the Origin and Growth of Religion as Illustrated by Celtic Heathendom*, Williams and Norgate, 1892, p. 204.

[336] JRR Tolkien, *The Return of the Shadow*, in *The History of The Lord of the Rings, Part One*, Christopher Tolkien editor, 1988, p. 112, 114 endnote 1.

[337] Joseph Wright, *English Dialect Dictionary*, Oxford: Henry Frowde, 1905, volume 6, T-Z, p. 525-526. It is interesting that Wright's definition for "withywind" also cited Morton's 1863 *A Cyclopedia of Agriculture*, which contained the Welsh agricultural hobbit.

[338] JRR Tolkien, "Nomenclature of *The Lord of the Rings*," 1967, in Christina Scull and Wayne Hammond, *The Lord of the Rings: A Reader's Companion*, Houghton Mifflin, 2005, p. 779.

[339] JRR Tolkien, *The Return of the Shadow*, in *The History of The Lord of the Rings, Part One*, Christopher Tolkien editor, Houghton Mifflin, 1988, p. 132.

[340] JRR Tolkien, *The Return of the Shadow*, in *The History of The Lord of the Rings, Part One*, Christopher Tolkien editor, 1988, p. 132-133.

[341] In Skeat and Britten's *Reprinted Glossaries and Old Farming Words* (Walter W. Skeat and James Britten, editors, *Reprinted Glossaries and Old Farming Words*, London: Trübner & Company, Part 4, Reprinted Glossaries Parts 18-22, 1879) we find a number of terms that will sound familiar to Tolkien readers, including Combe (p. 10), Archet (p. 30), Dumbledore (p. 34), Quickbeam (p. 39), Moots and Moot (associated with trees p. 40, 152), Nuncle (p. 41), Staddle (p. 44), Withwind and Withy (p. 47), Deadman (p. 62, also see p. 141), Lob (p. 70), and Nob (p. 104). In the Skeat and Britten dictionary withwind was defined as a "climbing plant, common in hedges; a species of the convolvulus, or bindweed"; and withy was identified as "the willow" (Walter W. Skeat and James Britten, editors, *Reprinted Glossaries and Old Farming Words*, London: Trübner & Company, Part 4, Reprinted Glossaries

Parts 18-22, 1879, p. 47). It is also possible that Tolkien drew from the Skeat and Britten volume to manufacture the term "Withywindle" in 1938, but then consulted Wright's dictionary to prepare the 1967 "Nomenclature."

[342] Christina Scull and Wayne Hammond, *The JRR Tolkien Companion and Guide: Chronology*, Houghton Mifflin, 2006, p. 39, 49, 51.

[343] Joseph Wright, *English Dialect Dictionary*, Oxford: Henry Frowde, 1898, Volume 1 A-C.

[344] Scull and Hammond, *The JRR Tolkien Companion and Guide: Chronology*, 2006, p. 118; Christina Scull and Wayne Hammond, *The JRR Tolkien Companion and Guide: Reader's Guide*, Houghton Mifflin, 2006, p. 966; Tom Shippey, entry for *A New Glossary of the Dialect of the Huddersfield District*, in Michael Drout, *JRR Tolkien Encyclopedia: Scholarship and Critical Assessment*, New York: Routledge, 2007, p. 457.

[345] JRR Tolkien, *The Return of the Shadow*, in *The History of The Lord of the Rings, Part One*, Houghton Mifflin, 1988, p. 132.

[346] Joseph Wright, *English Dialect Dictionary*, Oxford: Henry Frowde, 1905, Volume 5, R-S, p. 714-715. In British agriculture a staddle served as the foundation of a corn or hay-rick, but they could also be "trees reserv'd at the felling of woods for growth for timber" (Walter W. Skeat and James Britten, editors, *Reprinted Glossaries and Old Farming Words*, London: Trübner & Co., Part 4, Reprinted Glossaries Parts 18-22, 1879, p. 44, 46, 90).

[347] JRR Tolkien, "Nomenclature of *The Lord of the Rings*," 1967, in Christina Scull and Wayne Hammond, *The Lord of the Rings: A Reader's Companion*, Houghton Mifflin, 2005, p. 776.

[348] JRR Tolkien, *The Return of the Shadow*, in *The History of The Lord of the Rings, Part One*, Christopher Tolkien editor, Houghton Mifflin, 1988, p. 133.

[349] Walter W. Skeat and James Britten, editors, *Reprinted Glossaries and Old Farming Words*, London: Trübner & Company, Part 4, Reprinted Glossaries Parts 18-22, 1879, p. 30.

[350] JRR Tolkien, "Nomenclature of *The Lord of the Rings*," 1967, in Christina Scull and Wayne Hammond, *The Lord of the Rings: A Reader's Companion*, Houghton Mifflin, 2005, p. 765.

³⁵¹ JRR Tolkien, *The Return of the Shadow*, in *The History of The Lord of the Rings, Part One*, Christopher Tolkien editor, 1988, p. 132-133, 151, 165.

³⁵² Joseph Wright, *English Dialect Dictionary*, Oxford: Henry Frowde, 1898, Volume 1, A-C, p. 705; JRR Tolkien, "Nomenclature of *The Lord of the Rings*," 1967, in Christina Scull and Wayne Hammond, *The Lord of the Rings: A Reader's Companion*, Houghton Mifflin, 2005, p. 767.

³⁵³ Joseph Wright, *English Dialect Dictionary*, Oxford: Henry Frowde, 1905, Volume 1, A-C, p. 723.

³⁵⁴ Walter W. Skeat and James Britten, editors, *Reprinted Glossaries and Old Farming Words*, London: Trübner & Company, Part 4, Reprinted Glossaries Parts 18-22, 1879, p. 10, 13, 87.

³⁵⁵ JRR Tolkien, *The Return of the Shadow*, in *The History of The Lord of the Rings, Part One*, Christopher Tolkien editor, Houghton Mifflin, 1988, p. 141 endnote 4.

³⁵⁶ Joseph Wright, *English Dialect Dictionary*, Oxford: Henry Frowde, 1905, Volume 3, H-L, p. 635; Walter W. Skeat and James Britten, editors, *Reprinted Glossaries and Old Farming Words*, London: Trübner & Co., Part 4, Reprinted Glossaries Parts 18-22, 1879, p. 70.

³⁵⁷ Joseph Wright, *English Dialect Dictionary*, Oxford: Henry Frowde, 1905, Volume 4, M-Q, p. 284-285; Walter W. Skeat and James Britten, editors, *Reprinted Glossaries and Old Farming Words*, London: Trübner & Company, Part 4, Reprinted Glossaries Parts 18-22, 1879, p. 104.

³⁵⁸ Walter W. Skeat and James Britten, editors, *Reprinted Glossaries and Old Farming Words*, London: Trübner & Company, Part 4, Reprinted Glossaries Parts 18-22, 1879, p. 171; James Britten, *Old Country and Farming Words: Gleaned from Agricultural Books*, London: Trübner & Company, 1880.

³⁵⁹ Joseph Wright, *English Dialect Dictionary*, Oxford: Henry Frowde, 1905, Volume 3 H-L, p. 281.

³⁶⁰ JRR Tolkien, *The Return of the Shadow*, in *The History of The Lord of the Rings, Part One*, Christopher Tolkien editor, Houghton Mifflin, 1988, p. 251, 309; see

Mark Hooker, *The Hobbitonian Anthology*, p. 160-164 for a detailed survey of English usages for hundredweight.

[361] JRR Tolkien, *The War of the Ring*, in *The History of The Lord of the Rings, Part Three*, Christopher Tolkien editor, Houghton Mifflin, 1990, p. 144 for date; p. 149 and 166 endnote 9 for description of the first use of halfling.

[362] Humphrey Carpenter, *The Letters of JRR Tolkien*, with the assistance of Christopher Tolkien, Houghton Mifflin, 2000 edition [original publication 1981], Tolkien to RW Burchfield, September 11, 1970, # 316, p. 405.

[363] Joseph Wright, *English Dialect Dictionary*, Oxford: Henry Frowde, 1905, Volume 3 H-L, p. 30. Wright listed these alternate versions of "halfling": haaflan; hafflang; hafflin; haflin; half-lang, hauflin; hawflin; hoafen; hoaflin.

[364] See *The Two Towers*, "The Black Gate is Closed." Christopher Tolkien's discussion of the writing of this chapter in the spring of 1944 does not make clear whether the sentence about Frodo was written then or added later, see JRR Tolkien, *The War of the Ring*, in *The History of The Lord of the Rings, Part Three*, Christopher Tolkien editor, Houghton Mifflin, 1990, p. 121-130.

[365] JRR Tolkien, *The War of the Ring*, Christopher Tolkien editor, 1990, p. 36, 44 endnote 29; Christina Scull and Wayne Hammond, *The JRR Tolkien Companion and Guide: Reader's Guide*, Houghton Mifflin, 2006, p. 536.

[366] Tom Shippey, *The Road to Middle-earth*, 2003, p. 66.

[367] For dating of the manuscript to the late 1940s see JRR Tolkien, *The Peoples of Middle-earth*, in *The History of Middle-earth, Volume XII*, Christopher Tolkien editor, Houghton Mifflin, 1996, p. 28, 54 endnote 1. For the quote on inventing the term "hobbit" see p. 49.

[368] JRR Tolkien, *The Peoples of Middle-earth*, Christopher Tolkien editor, 1996, p. 10, 49, 69.

[369] Humphrey Carpenter, *The Letters of JRR Tolkien*, with the assistance of Christopher Tolkien, Houghton Mifflin, 2000 edition [original publication 1981], Tolkien to WH Auden, June 7, 1955, # 163, p. 215.

[370] Humphrey Carpenter, *The Letters of JRR Tolkien*, 2000 edition [original publication 1981], Tolkien undated notes prepared for Houghton Mifflin, circa June 1955, # 165, p. 219 footnote.

[371] The date of "circa September 1956" for this interview by Ruth Harshaw is given in Rateliff, *The History of the Hobbit, Part One*, 2007, p. xii; but the date of January 15, 1957 is given in Christina Scull and Wayne Hammond, *The JRR Tolkien Companion and Guide: Chronology*, Houghton Mifflin, 2006, p. 499. Scull and Hammond note that Harshaw had some difficulty in understanding Tolkien.

[372] JRR Tolkien unpublished letter dated October 26, 1958 to Mrs. LM Cutts; see Tolkien Gateway online.

[373] Christina Scull and Wayne Hammond, *The JRR Tolkien Companion and Guide: Reader's Guide*, Houghton Mifflin, 2006, p. 385-386, 387.

[374] Richard Plotz interview, Scull and Hammond, *The JRR Tolkien Companion and Guide: Reader's Guide*, 2006, p. 388.

[375] Charlotte and Denis Plimmer interview with Tolkien, quoted in John D. Rateliff, *The History of the Hobbit, Part One: Mr. Baggins*, Houghton Mifflin, 2007, p. xiii; Christina Scull and Wayne Hammond, *The JRR Tolkien Companion and Guide: Chronology*, Houghton Mifflin, 2006, p. 681, 688-690, 721; Tom Shippey, *The Road to Middle-earth: How JRR Tolkien Created a New Mythology*, 2003, Houghton Mifflin, p. 67.

[376] Rateliff, *The History of the Hobbit, Part One*, 2007, p. xii; Scull and Hammond, *The JRR Tolkien Companion and Guide: Chronology*, 2006, p. 715, 716-717.

[377] Humphrey Carpenter, *The Letters of JRR Tolkien*, with the assistance of Christopher Tolkien, Houghton Mifflin, 2000 edition [original publication 1981], Tolkien to RW Burchfield, September 11, 1970, # 316, p. 404.

[378] Carpenter, *The Letters of JRR Tolkien*, 2000 edition [original publication 1981], Tolkien to Roger Green, January 8, 1971, # 319, p. 406-407.

[379] John D. Rateliff, *The History of the Hobbit, Part Two: Return to Bag-End*, Houghton Mifflin, 2007, p. 841-865.

[380] John D. Rateliff, *The History of the Hobbit, Part One: Mr. Baggins*, Houghton Mifflin, 2007, p. 48.

[381] Carpenter, *The Letters of JRR Tolkien*, 2000 edition [original publication 1981], # 25, circa February 1938, p. 30.

Endnotes: Treasures of Tradition

[382] JRR Tolkien, *The Adventures of Tom Bombadil*, edited by Christina Scull and Wayne Hammond, HarperCollins, 2014, p. 240-251. In 1961 Tolkien wrote of "Iúmonna Gold Galdre Bewunden" that the entire poem "was in fact inspired by a single line of ancient verse"; see Humphrey Carpenter, *The Letters of JRR Tolkien*, with the assistance of Christopher Tolkien, Houghton Mifflin, 2000 edition [original publication 1981], Tolkien to Pauline Gasch, December 6, 1961, # 235, p. 312.

[383] Carpenter, *The Letters of JRR Tolkien*, 2000 edition [original publication 1981], Tolkien to editor of the *Observer*, January or February 1938, published February 20, # 25, p. 31.

[384] The earliest extant version of Chapter One of *The Hobbit* described Bilbo as a "burglar" – see John D. Rateliff, *The History of the Hobbit, Part One: Mr. Baggins*, Houghton Mifflin, 2007, p. 8, 10. Donald O'Brien also took note of an interesting entry in one Scottish dictionary (published in 1960) that is interesting, but coincidental to Tolkien's decision to cast his new hobbit as a burglar. Defining "Hub... also hob" the dictionary defined the term as an accusation of "dishonesty" or theft, citing "*A hobbet thief,* a veritable thief" (Donald O'Brien, "On the Origin of the Name 'Hobbit'," *Mythlore* 60, Winter 1989, p. 34). It remains a remote possibility that Tolkien could have encountered some Scottish source with this usage.

[385] JRR Tolkien, *Beowulf: A Translation and Commentary*, Christopher Tolkien editor, Houghton Mifflin, 2014, p. 77-78.

[386] Tolkien drew attention to an Old English term in *Beowulf* that has the dragon there "sniffing along the stone" and this must have given rise to Tolkien's description of Smaug sniffing for Bilbo – see discussion on this point by Mary Faraci, "'I wish to speak': Tolkien's voice in his *Beowulf* essay," in Jane Chance, editor, *Tolkien the Medievalist*, Routledge, 2003, p. 58-59.

[387] JRR Tolkien, *Beowulf: A Translation and Commentary*, Christopher Tolkien editor, Houghton Mifflin, 2014, p. 350-353.

[388] John D. Rateliff, *The History of the Hobbit, Part Two: Return to Bag-End*, Houghton Mifflin, 2007, p. 667.

[389] Joseph Wright, *English Dialect Dictionary*, Oxford: Henry Frowde, 1905, Volume 3 H-L; Donald O'Brien, "On the Origin of the Name 'Hobbit'," *Mythlore* 60, Winter 1989, p. 32-38; Michael Livingston, "The Myths of the Author: Tolkien and the Medieval Origins of the Word *Hobbit*," *Mythlore*, volume 30, 2012, p. 129-146.

[390] Humphrey Carpenter, *The Letters of JRR Tolkien*, with the assistance of Christopher Tolkien, Houghton Mifflin, 2000 edition [original publication 1981], Tolkien to editor of the *Observer*, January or February 1938, published February 20, # 25, p. 31.

[391] JRR Tolkien, *Beowulf: A Translation and Commentary*, edited by Christopher Tolkien, Houghton Mifflin, 2014, p. 351.

[392] Humphrey Carpenter, *The Letters of JRR Tolkien*, 2000 edition [original publication 1981], Tolkien to Stanley Unwin, December 16, 1937, # 19, p. 26.

[393] The Katherine Briggs summary of "The Hobyahs" was reprinted by Donald O'Brien, "On the Origin of the Name 'Hobbit'," *Mythlore* 60, Winter 1989, p. 34, 38 endnote 27.

Endnotes: British Folklore and Tolkien

[394] Campbell, Dasent, and Hartland all receive mention in one list of works consulted by Tolkien circa 1939-1943; see Verlyn Flieger and Douglas A. Anderson, *Tolkien On Fairy-stories*, HarperCollins, 2008, p. 306-311.

[395] *Folk-Lore: A Quarterly Review*, volume 25, March 1914, p. 8.

[396] John Garth, *Tolkien and the Great War*, 2003, p. 119. Tolkien's first book manuscript was *The Trumpets of Faerie*, a collection of poems.

[397] A later incarnation of the David Nutt imprint published a paper by Tolkien: JRR Tolkien, "Chaucer as Philologist: The Reeve's Tale," *Transactions of the Philological Society* 1934, London: David Nutt (A.G. Berry)

1934, p. 1-70. See JRR Tolkien, *The Return of the Shadow*, in *The History of The Lord of the Rings, Part One*, Christopher Tolkien editor, Houghton Mifflin, 1988, p. 382 for mention of Chaucer's Reeve's Tale 1939.

[398] JRR Tolkien, *The Annotated Hobbit*, annotated by Douglas A. Anderson, Houghton Mifflin, 2002, p. 8.

[399] Humphrey Carpenter, *The Letters of JRR Tolkien*, with the assistance of Christopher Tolkien, Houghton Mifflin, 2000 edition [original publication 1981], Tolkien to Allen & Unwin, December 12, 1955, # 178, p. 230.

[400] E.A. Wyke-Smith in *The Marvelous Land of the Snergs*, 2006, originally published 1928, Dover Publications.

[401] Simon J. Cook, "Concerning Hobbits," December 16, 2014, online at *The History Vault*; see John Rhys, Untitled Address of the President of the Anthropology Section of the BAAS, dated September 6, 1900, in *Report of the Seventieth Meeting of the British Association for the Advancement of Science*, London: John Murray, 1900, p. 884-896.

[402] Simon Cook, "Changing Faces of Britain's Natives," January 22, 2015, online at *English Historical Fiction Authors*, viewed January 24, 2015. The 1902 John Buchan novelette was titled "No-Man's-Land" – a term which Tolkien applied to Middle-earth, but not to hobbit realms.

[403] John Buchan, *The Watcher by the Threshold and other Tales*, London: Thomas Nelson, 1922, originally published 1902, p. 37.

[404] John Rhys, *Celtic Folklore: Welsh and Manx*, two volumes, Oxford: Clarendon Press, 1901, Volume One, p. 286-289, 323-353. Rhys made frequent mention of his participation in the British Folk-Lore Society and various publications of that society.

[405] John D. Rateliff, *The History of the Hobbit, Part One: Mr. Baggins*, Houghton Mifflin, 2007, p. 29.

Endnotes: Wizard of the Great Grasslands

[406] JRR Tolkien, *The Annotated Hobbit*, annotated by Douglas A. Anderson, Houghton Mifflin, 2002, p. 287; John D. Rateliff, *The History of the Hobbit, Part Two: Return to Bag-End*, Houghton Mifflin, 2007, p. 48-53.

[407] Rateliff, *The History of the Hobbit, Part Two: Return to Bag-End*, 2007, p. 53.

[408] JRR Tolkien, *The Shaping of Middle-earth*, in *The History of Middle-earth, Volume IV*, Christopher Tolkien editor, Houghton Mifflin, 1986, p. 262, 268.

[409] JRR Tolkien, *The Shaping of Middle-earth*, Christopher Tolkien editor, 1986, p. 296.

[410] JRR Tolkien, *The Shaping of Middle-earth*, Christopher Tolkien editor, 1986, p. 330.

[411] JRR Tolkien, *The Shaping of Middle-earth*Christopher Tolkien editor, 1986, p. 298; also see p. 329, 334.

[412] Curly Head, "Death of the Flint-Monster: Origin of Birds," in George A. Dorsey [and James R. Murie], *Traditions of the Skidi Pawnee*, Houghton Mifflin, 1904, p. 29.

[413] JRR Tolkien, *The Book of Lost Tales, Part One*, in *The History of Middle-earth, Volume I*, Christopher Tolkien editor, Houghton Mifflin, 1983, p. 232-233.

[414] Christina Scull and Wayne Hammond, *The JRR Tolkien Companion and Guide: Reader's Guide*, Houghton Mifflin, 2006, p. 571-572. Josef Madlener's postcard image of the wizard that helped shape Bladorthin is published in JRR Tolkien, *The Annotated Hobbit*, annotated by Douglas A. Anderson, Houghton Mifflin, 2002, between p. 178-179.

[415] Humphrey Carpenter, *The Letters of JRR Tolkien*, with the assistance of Christopher Tolkien, Houghton Mifflin, 2000 edition [original publication 1981], JRR Tolkien to Stanley Unwin excerpt, December 7, 1946, # 107, p. 119; John D. Rateliff, *The History of the Hobbit, Part Two: Return to Bag-End*, Houghton Mifflin, 2007, p. 715.

[416] John D. Rateliff, *The History of the Hobbit, Part One: Mr. Baggins*, Houghton Mifflin, 2007, p. 8.

[417] Rateliff, *The History of the Hobbit, Part One: Mr. Baggins*, 2007, p. 43 endnote 12.

[418] Rateliff, *The History of the Hobbit, Part Two: Return to Bag-End*, 2007, p. 670.

[419] Rateliff, *The History of the Hobbit, Part One: Mr. Baggins*, 2007, p. 235.

[420] Roaming Scout, "Lightning Visits the Earth," in George A. Dorsey [and James R. Murie], *Traditions of the Skidi Pawnee*, Houghton Mifflin, 1904, p. 14-20, see p. 14.

[421] Rateliff, *The History of the Hobbit, Part Two: Return to Bag-End*, 2007, p. 514.

[422] Rateliff, *The History of the Hobbit, Part One: Mr. Baggins*, 2007, p. 94-96.

[423] Douglas Anderson has identified a source from Icelandic tradition that likely inspired Tolkien's trolls who turn to stone in sunlight (JRR Tolkien, *The Annotated Hobbit*, annotated by Douglas A. Anderson, Houghton Mifflin, 2002, p. 80-82). Tom Shippey identified another enlightening source, comparing Thor in the Norse "Alvismál" with Gandalf – both trick opponents who become transformed into stone at dawn (Tom Shippey, *The Road to Middle-earth: How JRR Tolkien Created a New Mythology*, 2003, Houghton Mifflin, p. 75). An online forum, "Parallels between Middle-earth and Norse Myths" at *Minas Tirith Forums* (viewed on August 26, 2013) also contains a post by Wandering Tuor that repeats Shippey's finding. A prose version is available in Kevin Crossley-Holland, *The Norse Myths*, Pantheon Books, 1980, p. 143-146. These sources do not explain the elements in Tolkien's tale that echo Roaming Scout's "Lightning Visits the Earth."

[424] John D. Rateliff, *The History of the Hobbit, Part One: Mr. Baggins*, Houghton Mifflin, 2007, p. 130.

[425] George A. Dorsey [and James R. Murie], *Traditions of the Skidi Pawnee*, Houghton Mifflin, 1904, p. 339 endnote 116. An interesting note on the magic power of flint can be found in Field Museum of Natural History, George Dorsey / James R. Murie Field Notes, Box A-2, "Medicine-Man" undated typescript (circa 1906): "The medicine-man's power to cure or heal is distinguished... from his power to mesmerize or hypnotize, known as pihkawiu (flint arm, hence strong arm). By means of this latter power he may destroy the will of another, and so either crush his enemy or place the will of his patient under his own that his animal power during his singing over him will go to the soul of the patient and bring out the evil influence. This mesmeric power, from the word pikawiu, is comparable to the magic power of a flint arrow or bullet in its ability to cut off life, and the medicine-

man believes in his ability to throw this power into another man as one would shoot an arrow into an enemy."

[426] JRR Tolkien, *The Legend of Sigurd and Gudrún*, Christopher Tolkien, editor, HarperCollins, 2009, p. 22-23.

Endnotes: Gollum the Mysterious Being

[427] Cheyenne Chief, "The Story of Coyote," in George A. Dorsey [and James R. Murie], *Traditions of the Skidi Pawnee*, Houghton Mifflin, 1904, p. 239-253, see p. 253.

[428] Cheyenne Chief, "The Hairy Man," in George A. Dorsey [and James R. Murie], *Traditions of the Skidi Pawnee*, Houghton Mifflin, 1904, p. 304. This story is included among "Animal Tales" which feature a number of fictional tales, but it seems more of a historical oral tradition, and it is unlikely that Skidi listeners would have deemed it fictional. Dorsey and Murie acknowledged in their introduction to *Traditions of the Skidi Pawnee* (p. xxiii) that their classification decisions met with only "partial success." Dorsey and Murie's notes include a brief mention of "hairy dwarfs" (Field Museum of Natural History, Dorsey / Murie Field Notes, Box A-2, Material Culture, "Medicine-Man," typescript, p. 9): "[I]n the medicine-man ceremonies were certain ones known as Kitscoa, funny people or imitators. They dress grotesquely, bedaub their bodies with mud, wear masks, made either of corn husks, rawhide, feathers or wood... It seems to have been their duty to perform strange antics during the ceremonies to amuse the people, especially do they imitate in a mocking spirit the more serious performance. They are sometimes spoken of as hairy dwarfs, or supernatural beings who have mysterious ways of whom the people are afraid for they make loud cries in the night, and should they be seen it [is] a sure sign of bad luck." Another story told by John Buffalo in *Traditions of the Skidi Pawnee* briefly mentions "wonderful dwarfs" (p. 95), but it doesn't provide any discussion of them. In Oklahoma I have heard many stories about "little people." My uncle, Myron Echo Hawk, believed that his wife was killed by little people.

[429] My original conclusions on the Pawnee influence on the opening of *The Hobbit* appeared in the first edition of my book, *Tolkien in Pawneeland*, December 2013, p. 70-71.

[430] Christina Scull and Wayne Hammond, *The JRR Tolkien Companion and Guide: Reader's Guide*, Houghton Mifflin, 2006, p. 23.

[431] JRR Tolkien, *The Annotated Hobbit*, annotated by Douglas A. Anderson, Houghton Mifflin, 2002, p. 5-12.

[432] Scull and Hammond, *The JRR Tolkien Companion and Guide: Reader's Guide*, 2006, p. 385-393.

[433] John D. Rateliff, *The History of the Hobbit, Part One: Mr. Baggins*, Houghton Mifflin, 2007, p. xiii. Rateliff's logic does not rely on the childhood memories of Tolkien's children, recorded late in life, as does that of Scull and Hammond, who favor 1929 as a late date of origin, so I favor Rateliff's view that the opening line and first chapter of *The Hobbit* were most likely written during 1930.

[434] Cheyenne Chief, "The Hairy Man," in George A. Dorsey [and James R. Murie], *Traditions of the Skidi Pawnee*, Houghton Mifflin, 1904, p. 304.

[435] John D. Rateliff, *The History of the Hobbit, Part One: Mr. Baggins*, Houghton Mifflin, 2007, p. 8.

[436] Rateliff, *The History of the Hobbit, Part One: Mr. Baggins*, 2007, p. 29.

[437] John Rhys, *Celtic Folklore: Welsh and Manx*, two volumes, Oxford: Clarendon Press, 1901, Volume One, p. 286-289, 323-353.

[438] JRR Tolkien, *The Shaping of Middle-earth*, in *The History of Middle-earth, Volume IV*, Christopher Tolkien editor, Houghton Mifflin, 1986, p. 78, 85.

[439] John D. Rateliff, *The History of the Hobbit, Part One: Mr. Baggins*, Houghton Mifflin, 2007, p. 157 – the other quotes from this volume in this paragraph are from p. 156, 155, and 155; Cheyenne Chief, "The Hairy Man," in George A. Dorsey [and James R. Murie], *Traditions of the Skidi Pawnee*, Houghton Mifflin, 1904, p. 304.

[440] Newly Made Woman Chief, "Speak-Riddles and Wise-Spirit," in George A. Dorsey [and James R. Murie], *Traditions of the Skidi Pawnee*, Houghton Mifflin, 1904, p. 300-301.

[441] White Eagle, "Contest Between Witch-Woman and Beaver," in George A. Dorsey [and James R. Murie], *Traditions of the Skidi Pawnee*, Houghton Mifflin, 1904, p. 301-302.

[442] John D. Rateliff, *The History of the Hobbit, Part One: Mr. Baggins*, Houghton Mifflin, 2007, p. 154.

[443] Rateliff, *The History of the Hobbit, Part One: Mr. Baggins*, 2007, p. 166.

[444] Rateliff, *The History of the Hobbit, Part One: Mr. Baggins*, 2007, p. 168, 187. "Glip" appears in JRR Tolkien, *The Annotated Hobbit*, annotated by Douglas A. Anderson, Houghton Mifflin, 2002, p. 119. Anderson notes "though it is undated it was probably written around 1928." The significance of the name Glip is unclear. But *The New Shorter Oxford Dictionary* lists "glit" and "gleet" as "Slimy, sticky, or greasy matter" and as discharge from a wound.

[445] JRR Tolkien, *The Return of the Shadow*, in *The History of The Lord of the Rings, Part One*, Christopher Tolkien editor, Houghton Mifflin, 1988, p. 75. See p. 78-81 for the first fully developed draft of what became "The Shadow of the Past," with emphasis on Gollum.

[446] JRR Tolkien, *The Return of the Shadow*, Christopher Tolkien editor, 1988, p. 84-85 endnote 7.

[447] JRR Tolkien, *The Return of the Shadow*, Christopher Tolkien editor, 1988, p. 86.

[448] John D. Rateliff, *The History of the Hobbit, Part One: Mr. Baggins*, Houghton Mifflin, 2007, p. xxxviii; JRR Tolkien, *The Annotated Hobbit*, annotated by Douglas A. Anderson, Houghton Mifflin, 2002, p. 6-7.

[449] Verlyn Flieger and Douglas A. Anderson, *Tolkien On Fairy-stories*, HarperCollins, 2008, p. 249-250; JRR Tolkien, *The Annotated Hobbit*, annotated by Douglas A. Anderson, Houghton Mifflin, 2002, p. 7.

[450] Humphrey Carpenter, *The Letters of JRR Tolkien*, with the assistance of Christopher Tolkien, Houghton Mifflin, 2000 edition [original publication 1981], # 163, June 7, 1955, p. 215 footnote; JRR Tolkien, *The Annotated Hobbit*, annotated by Douglas A. Anderson, Houghton Mifflin, 2002, p. 7.

[451] E.A. Wyke-Smith, *The Marvelous Land of the Snergs*, 2006 [originally published 1928], Dover Publications, p. 7.

[452] Carpenter, *The Letters of JRR Tolkien*, 2000 edition [original publication 1981], # 25, circa February 1938, p. 30, 34-35.

Endnotes: Beewolf and Beorn and the Bear-boy

[453] "Sellic Spell" was published in JRR Tolkien, *Beowulf: A Translation and Commentary*, Christopher Tolkien editor, 2014, p. 355-414. A set of five or so manuscripts preserve the composition of "Sellic Spell." Christopher Tolkien believes that "Sellic Spell" was written by his father during the early 1940s, and Douglas Anderson and Verlyn Flieger suggest that the story might have originated in the spring or summer of 1943 (see JRR Tolkien, *Beowulf: A Translation and Commentary*, Christopher Tolkien editor, Houghton Mifflin Harcourt, 2014, p. 359; Verlyn Flieger and Douglas A. Anderson, *Tolkien On Fairy-stories*, HarperCollins, 2008, p. 100).

[454] Verlyn Flieger and Douglas A. Anderson, *Tolkien On Fairy-stories*, HarperCollins, 2008, p. 46, and see p. 38 and 100.

[455] Verlyn Flieger and Douglas A. Anderson, *Tolkien On Fairy-stories*, HarperCollins, 2008, p. 122-135. Tolkien's research for "On Fairy-stories" began in late 1938 and gave rise to the version of the paper that he read in early 1939, and it is apparent that he returned again to the paper in 1943 and conducted another intensive period of research to expand the paper.

[456] Verlyn Flieger and Douglas A. Anderson, *Tolkien On Fairy-stories*, 2008, p. 38.

[457] Verlyn Flieger and Douglas A. Anderson, *Tolkien On Fairy-stories*, 2008, p. 100.

[458] Margaret Hunt, translator, *Grimm's Household Tales*, volume 2, London: George Bell, 1884, # 91, "The Elves," p. 24-28.

[459] RW Chambers, *Beowulf: An Introduction to the Study of the Poem*, Cambridge University Press, 1921, p. 370.

[460] Margaret Hunt, translator, *Grimm's Household Tales*, volume 2, London: George Bell, 1884, # 166, "Strong Hans," p. 253-259.

[461] JRR Tolkien, *Beowulf: A Translation and Commentary*, Christopher Tolkien editor, 2014, p. 395.

[462] Verlyn Flieger and Douglas A. Anderson, *Tolkien On Fairy-stories*, HarperCollins, 2008, p. 306-307; RW Chambers, *Beowulf: An Introduction to the Study of the Poem*, Cambridge University Press, 1921, p. 370.

[463] Verlyn Flieger and Douglas A. Anderson, *Tolkien On Fairy-stories*, HarperCollins, 2008, p. 100.

[464] Douglas Anderson, "RW Chambers and *The Hobbit*," *Tolkien Studies*, # 3, 2006, p. 137-147; RW Chambers, *Beowulf: An Introduction to the Study of the Poem*, Cambridge University Press, 1921, p. 62-68, 365-381 – the second edition of the book appeared in 1932.

[465] The Chambers summary of "Ivashko Medvedko" was translated from AN Ifanasief, *Narodnuiya Russkiya Skazki*, Moscow, volume I, 1860, p. 6.

[466] Douglas Anderson, "RW Chambers and *The Hobbit*," *Tolkien Studies*, # 3, 2006, p. 143. Tolkien in a 1944 letter noted his lack of fluency in Russian, "I can't write Russian..."; this seems to refer to a project involving a Polish vocabulary, see Carpenter, *The Letters of JRR Tolkien*, JRR Tolkien to Christopher Tolkien, January 18, 1944, # 55, p. 67.

[467] Post Wheeler, *Russian Wonder Tales*, 1912, "Little Bear's-Son," p. 249-271.

[468] Douglas Anderson, "RW Chambers and *The Hobbit*," *Tolkien Studies*, # 3, 2006, p. 143, 145 endnote 15.

[469] Roger Echo-Hawk, *Tolkien in Pawneeland*, 2013, p. 89-94, "Werebear Shape-Shifters." For this present chapter, "Werebear Shape-Shifters" has been merged with a post on my *Pawneeland* blog, "Tolkien's Marvelous Tales," posted December 28, 2014.

[470] John D. Rateliff, *The History of the Hobbit, Part One: Mr. Baggins*, Houghton Mifflin, 2007, p. 256-260, 281 endnote 7. Also see Tom Shippey, *The Road to Middle-earth: How JRR Tolkien Created a New Mythology*, 2003, Houghton Mifflin, p. 80; JRR Tolkien, *The Annotated Hobbit*, annotated by Douglas A. Anderson, Houghton Mifflin, 2002, p. 165.

[471] Yellow Calf, "The Boy, the Bears, and White Crow," in George A. Dorsey [and James R. Murie], *Traditions of the Skidi Pawnee*, Houghton Mifflin, 1904, p. 138-146. James Yellow Calf was born about 1863 and died in 1914

(*Identification and Description of the Lands Covered by Selections and Allotments, 1893*, Government Printing Office, p. 9). Murie and Dorsey set down five stories told by Yellow Calf; four appeared in *Traditions of the Skidi Pawnee*. In "The Boy, the Bears, and White Crow" a poor boy follows a father grizzly bear to a cave in a cedar grove, and there he is given power. He chooses a black bear cub for a companion and it is transformed into a "fine black horse." The grizzly gives him another gray horse which is implied to be a mountain lion. Returning to his community, the poor boy encounters an evil leader who tries to steal a slain buffalo from him. They fight, each man turning into various bears. "The horse broke loose and ran to the cinnamon bear and began to stamp on it with its forelegs. The bear was killed." Thus is the evil leader slain. The young skinchanger becomes the new leader. He says the former evil leader had a white crow that would now frighten away the buffalo. At a council a man fills a pipe and offers the young skinchanger his daughter. They smoke, agreeing to the terms. The skinchanger has one condition: "Seeing my ponies upon the hill, never touch or scold them." Next he tries to capture the white crow. He doesn't succeed until he meets "a great tarantula" who gives him a ball of spider silk. His mother-in-law hits the black horse on the forehead with a stick and it transforms into a bear. The skinchanger in his tipi is aware of what happened to the magic horse, and he says, "Did me wrong!" He runs out, becoming a bear, and the two bears begin killing people. They decide they must return to the father grizzly's cave in a cedar grove.

[472] John D. Rateliff, *The History of the Hobbit, Part One: Mr. Baggins*, Houghton Mifflin, 2007, p. 232.

[473] Reading about the Pawnee bear cub, Tolkien would have had in mind that the Norse story *Hrolf Kraki's Saga* focused on a man named "Bjarki" – this name means "little bear."

[474] John D. Rateliff, *The History of the Hobbit, Part One: Mr. Baggins*, Houghton Mifflin, 2007, p. 232. It is interesting that Tolkien made use of the name "Beorn" in an early writing dating after circa 1917, and this Beorn is the brother of "Eoh" – Old English for "horse" (JRR Tolkien, *The Book of Lost Tales, Part Two*, in *The History of Middle-earth, Volume II*, Christopher Tolkien, editor, Houghton Mifflin, 1984, p. 290-291).

[475] John D. Rateliff, *The History of the Hobbit, Part One: Mr. Baggins*, Houghton Mifflin, 2007, p. 266-268.

[476] John D. Rateliff, *The History of the Hobbit, Part One: Mr. Baggins*, 2007, p. 231.

[477] John D. Rateliff, *The History of the Hobbit, Part One: Mr. Baggins*, 2007, p. 240.

[478] John D. Rateliff, *The History of the Hobbit, Part One: Mr. Baggins*, 2007, p. 35-36, 240.

[479] Good Chief, "Long-Tooth-Boy," in George A. Dorsey [and James R. Murie], *Traditions of the Skidi Pawnee*, Houghton Mifflin, 1904, p. 89-94. Good Chief died in 1905, and Dorsey and Murie described him as "the oldest chief of the Skidi" whose "father, in turn was in his time hereditary head chief of the Skidi and was the keeper of the chief's bundle" (George Dorsey [and James R. Murie], *The Pawnee Mythology*, 1906, Carnegie Institution of Washington, publication # 59, also Bison Books reprint, University of Nebraska Press, 1997, p. 86).

[480] George A. Dorsey [and James R. Murie], *Traditions of the Skidi Pawnee*, Houghton Mifflin, 1904, p. 344 endnote 151. The deadly breath of the bear in Good Chief's "Long-Tooth-Boy" matches a moment in "The Boy, the Bears, and White Crow" when two shape-shifting bears "blew their breath at the people and killed them" (p. 145).

[481] JRR Tolkien, *Letters From Father Christmas*, Baillie Tolkien editor, Houghton Mifflin, 2004, p. 57, also see p. 61.

[482] John D. Rateliff, *The History of the Hobbit, Part One: Mr. Baggins*, Houghton Mifflin, 2007, p. 240.

[483] George A. Dorsey [and James R. Murie], *Traditions of the Skidi Pawnee*, 1904, p. 359 endnote 299; this note is in reference to a bear dance mentioned on p. 313.

[484] John D. Rateliff, *The History of the Hobbit, Part One: Mr. Baggins*, 2007, p. 238.

[485] John D. Rateliff, *The History of the Hobbit, Part One: Mr. Baggins*, 2007, p. 243.

[486] John D. Rateliff, *The History of the Hobbit, Part One: Mr. Baggins*, 2007, p. 241.

[487] John D. Rateliff, *The History of the Hobbit, Part One: Mr. Baggins*, 2007, p. 253-268, 452; Mark T. Hooker, *Tolkien and Wales*, Llyfrawr, 2012, p. 180-181.

[488] JRR Tolkien, *The Monsters and the Critics and Other Essays*, Christopher Tolkien editor, Houghton Mifflin, 1984, see "Sir Gawain and the Green Knight," p. 73.

[489] JRR Tolkien, *Beowulf: A Translation and Commentary*, Christopher Tolkien editor, 2014, p. 147.

[490] JRR Tolkien, *Beowulf: A Translation and Commentary*, Christopher Tolkien editor, 2014, p. 249.

[491] JRR Tolkien, *Beowulf: A Translation and Commentary*, Christopher Tolkien editor, 2014, p. 249.

[492] Tolkien believed that *Beowulf* was originally composed between 670 and 735 CE, see Michael Drout, "Beowulf: Tolkien's Scholarship," in Michael Drout, *JRR Tolkien Encyclopedia: Scholarship and Critical Assessment*, Routledge, 2007, p. 59-60.

[493] A 1937 mention of Tolkien's wish to reflect a "northern atmosphere" cultural quality in his private mythmaking can be found in Humphrey Carpenter, *The Letters of JRR Tolkien*, with the assistance of Christopher Tolkien, Houghton Mifflin, 2000 edition [original publication 1981], Tolkien to Furth, August 31, 1937, # 15, p. 21.

Endnotes: To Distant Lands and Back Again

[494] For an excellent synthesis of Tolkien's use of Norse literature in the making of his Middle-earth legendarium see Marjorie Burns, "Old Norse Literature," in Michael Drout, *JRR Tolkien Encyclopedia: Scholarship and Critical Assessment*, Routledge, 2007, p. 473-479.

[495] JRR Tolkien, *The Lost Road and Other Writings*, in *The History of Middle-earth, Volume V*, Christopher Tolkien, editor, Houghton Mifflin, 1987. Christopher Tolkien reviewed the evidence for when his father wrote *The Lost Road* and concluded that it was probably begun in 1936 and terminated

in late 1937 (p. 7-10). JRR's notes planning future chapters for the book appear at p. 77 – this is where mention of Vinland occurred. Christopher included an index with this entry (p. 454): "*Vinland* Old Norse name for America[.]" Tolkien's interest in Norse literature gave rise to an essay around 1926 called "Introduction to the 'Elder Edda'" (JRR Tolkien, *The Legend of Sigurd and Gudrún*, Christopher Tolkien, editor, HarperCollins, 2009, p. 13-15, 16-32). In the years that followed he wrote two epic poems based on Norse legend.

[496] JRR Tolkien, *The Lost Road and Other Writings*, in *The History of Middle-earth, Volume V*, Christopher Tolkien editor, Houghton Mifflin, 1987, p. 12. See p. 9 for a discussion asserting that these various manuscripts about Númenor date to the period 1936-1937 and evolved into the *Akallabêth*.

[497] JRR Tolkien, *The Lost Road and Other Writings*, Christopher Tolkien editor, 1987, p. 17-18.

[498] JRR Tolkien, *The Lost Road and Other Writings*, Christopher Tolkien editor, 1987, p. 28. The mention of America in these early manuscripts on Numenor reappeared in the next revision dating to sometime before February 1942; see JRR Tolkien, *Sauron Defeated*, in *The History of The Lord of the Rings, Part Four*, Houghton Mifflin, 1992, p. 331-340, 338, 339.

[499] Early manuscript material for *The Hobbit* and useful textual clarification appears in John D. Rateliff, *The History of the Hobbit*, two volumes, Houghton Mifflin, 2007.

[500] "Eirik the Red's Saga," translated by Keneva Kunz, in *The Sagas of Icelanders: A Selection*, edited by Örnólfur Thorsson, 2000, p. 653-674. Aud the Deep-minded was the granddaughter of "Bjorn Buna, an excellent man from Norway." She settled in Iceland where she lived at first with her brother Bjorn.

[501] "Eirik the Red's Saga," translated by Keneva Kunz, in *The Sagas of Icelanders: A Selection*, edited by Örnólfur Thorsson, 2000, p. 667-668. The beached whale incident was framed in the saga as "payment for a poem" about Thor, made by a man named Thorhall, who said, "Didn't Old Redbeard prove to be more help than your Christ?"

[502] John D. Rateliff, *The History of the Hobbit, Part One: Mr. Baggins*, Houghton Mifflin, 2007, p. 303, 347.

[503] Rateliff, *The History of the Hobbit, Part One: Mr. Baggins*, 2007, p. 383.

[504] JRR Tolkien, *The Lays of Beleriand*, in *The History of Middle-earth, Volume III*, Christopher Tolkien editor, Houghton Mifflin, 1985, p. 1-4. The earliest extant version of "The Lay of the Children of Húrin" was apparently composed most broadly between about 1919 and 1925.

[505] JRR Tolkien, *The Lays of Beleriand*, Christopher Tolkien editor, 1985, p. 11; also see 111-112. The wine of Dor-Winion then appears "at the table of Thingol" in Doriath (p. 17; also see p. 118).

[506] JRR Tolkien, *The Lays of Beleriand*, Christopher Tolkien editor, 1985, see p. 94 footnote associating the date of 1923. Here Christopher states his view that the manuscript "was made at Leeds," dating no later than 1925.

[507] JRR Tolkien, *The Lays of Beleriand*, Christopher Tolkien editor, 1985, p. 111.

[508] JRR Tolkien, *The Lost Road and Other Writings*, in *The History of Middle-earth, Volume V*, Christopher Tolkien editor, Houghton Mifflin, 1987, p. 333-334. Tolkien's decision to situate Dorwinion in the *Quenta Silmarillion* must have been made before *The Hobbit* was accepted for publication in late 1936. With publication of *The Hobbit*, Tolkien had to give up the idea of locating Dorwinion in Tol Eressëa.

[509] John D. Rateliff, *The History of the Hobbit, Part One: Mr. Baggins*, Houghton Mifflin, 2007, p. 418.

[510] Rateliff, *The History of the Hobbit, Part One: Mr. Baggins*, 2007, p. 417-420.

[511] JRR Tolkien, *The Fall of Arthur*, Christopher Tolkien, editor, Houghton Mifflin Harcourt, 2013, p. 125-168.

[512] JRR Tolkien, *The Lost Road and Other Writings*, in *The History of Middle-earth, Volume V*, Christopher Tolkien editor, Houghton Mifflin, 1987, p. 46.

[513] JRR Tolkien, *The Lost Road and Other Writings*, Christopher Tolkien editor, 1987, p. 45.

Endnotes: Unraveling Spider Silk

[514] John D. Rateliff, *The History of the Hobbit, Part One: Mr. Baggins*, Houghton Mifflin, 2007, p. 229.

[515] The listing of "swans" and "Mirkwood" in Tolkien's "First Outline" for *The Hobbit* surely refers to the Norse "Volundarkvida"; see *The Poetic Edda*, Carolyne Larrington translator, Oxford University Press, 1996, p. 102-108. This poem told of three swans who shape-shifted into women and who dwelt in a forest known as Mirkwood – one of these swan-women married the main character, who was poetically compared to a "lord of elves." Whatever possible adventure these swan-women may have suggested to Tolkien for *The Hobbit*, they got set aside, and no mention of them occurred in any of the manuscripts that survive.

[516] John D. Rateliff, *The History of the Hobbit, Part One: Mr. Baggins*, 2007, p. 308-309.

[517] Rateliff, *The History of the Hobbit, Part One: Mr. Baggins*, 2007, p. 308, 320 endnote 22.

[518] Rateliff, *The History of the Hobbit, Part One: Mr. Baggins*, 2007, p. 335-337.

[519] Good Chief, "Long-Tooth-Boy," in George A. Dorsey [and James R. Murie], *Traditions of the Skidi Pawnee*, Houghton Mifflin, 1904, p. 89-94, see p. 93 for mention of the use of magic spider silk.

[520] Yellow Calf, "The Boy, the Bears, and White Crow," in George A. Dorsey [and James R. Murie], *Traditions of the Skidi Pawnee*, Houghton Mifflin, 1904, p. 138-146.

[521] "Errantry" was reprinted in the early 1960s in *The Adventures of Tom Bombadil*; see JRR Tolkien, *The Adventures of Tom Bombadil*, edited by Christina Scull and Wayne Hammond, HarperCollins, 2014, p. 55-60, 155-167; also JRR Tolkien, *Tales from the Perilous Realm*, Houghton Mifflin, 2008. The history of the poem appears in JRR Tolkien, *The Treason of Isengard*, in *The History of The Lord of the Rings, Part Two*, Christopher Tolkien editor, Houghton Mifflin, 1989, p. 84-109. Christopher Tolkien did not offer a date for the first draft of "Errantry," but he noted that his father "read it to the original 'Inklings' in the early 1930s." Christina Scull and Wayne Hammond noted the existence of manuscript versions of the poem written in an

"'Elvish' script which has been dated to c. 1931"; see JRR Tolkien, *The Adventures of Tom Bombadil*, edited by Christina Scull and Wayne Hammond, HarperCollins, 2014, p. 162.

[522] JRR Tolkien, *The Treason of Isengard*, Christopher Tolkien editor, 1989, p. 85.

[523] JRR Tolkien, *The Treason of Isengard*, Christopher Tolkien editor, 1989, p. 85-87.

[524] Jason Fisher website, *Lingwë: Musings of a Fish*, "The Origins of Tolkien's 'Errantry' – Part 2," post dated October 1, 2008 (website viewed Monday, May 6, 2013).

[525] Verlyn Flieger and Douglas A. Anderson, *Tolkien On Fairy-stories*, HarperCollins, 2008, p. 30, 177, 210, 214; JRR Tolkien, "On Fairy-stories," in *Tales from the Perilous Realm*, Houghton Mifflin, 2008, p. 319.

[526] JRR Tolkien, *The Treason of Isengard*, in *The History of The Lord of the Rings, Part Two*, Christopher Tolkien editor, Houghton Mifflin, 1989, p. 93.

[527] John Box, "How the Buffalo Went South," in George A. Dorsey [and James R. Murie], *Traditions of the Skidi Pawnee*, Houghton Mifflin, 1904, p. 36-38. From the outset Tolkien might have had in mind things Skidi in "Errantry," as evidenced in the first draft, written circa 1930-1931. There we find references to "a little grasshopper" and "webs of all the attercops" – imagery mildly reminiscent of a Skidi story in which Spider Woman was defeated and exiled to the moon, carried by grasshoppers; see John Box, "The Death of Spider-Woman," in George A. Dorsey [and James R. Murie], *Traditions of the Skidi Pawnee*, Houghton Mifflin, 1904, p. 39-44. The grasshoppers in Tolkien's poem were deleted from later drafts.

[528] JRR Tolkien, *The Treason of Isengard*, in *The History of The Lord of the Rings, Part Two*, Christopher Tolkien editor, Houghton Mifflin, 1989, p. 330-333; JRR Tolkien, *The War of the Ring*, in *The History of The Lord of the Rings, Part Three*, Christopher Tolkien editor, Houghton Mifflin, 1990, p. 104.

[529] JRR Tolkien, *The War of the Ring*, in *The History of The Lord of the Rings, Part Three*, Christopher Tolkien editor, Houghton Mifflin, 1990, p. 106.

[530] Yellow Calf, "The Boy, the Bears, and White Crow," in George A. Dorsey [and James R. Murie], *Traditions of the Skidi Pawnee*, Houghton Mifflin, 1904, p. 145.

[531] John D. Rateliff, *The History of the Hobbit, Part One: Mr. Baggins*, Houghton Mifflin, 2007, p. 472, 478-479, 571 endnote 4, 569, 583, 623-625.

[532] Rateliff, *The History of the Hobbit, Part One: Mr. Baggins*, 2007, p. 618-619, 642-643.

Endnotes: The Old Thrush's Secret

[533] Curly Head, "Death of the Flint-Monster: Origin of Birds," in George A. Dorsey [and James R. Murie], *Traditions of the Skidi Pawnee*, Houghton Mifflin, 1904, p. 24-30.

[534] Humphrey Carpenter, *The Letters of JRR Tolkien*, with the assistance of Christopher Tolkien, Houghton Mifflin, 2000 edition [original publication 1981], p. 345, # 257, July 16, 1964. Describing Tolkien's early interest in dragons, Carpenter singled out Andrew Lang's *Red Fairy Book* and the "tale of Sigurd who slew the dragon Fafnir" and he also mentioned a story Tolkien wrote circa 1899 about a dragon (see Humphrey Carpenter, *Tolkien: The Authorized Biography*, Houghton Mifflin, 1977, p. 22-23).

[535] John D. Rateliff, *The History of the Hobbit, Part Two: Return to Bag-End*, Houghton Mifflin, 2007, p. 525-534; Carl Phelpstead, *Tolkien and Wales: Language, Literature, and Identity*, University of Wales Press, 2011, p. 66-68; Christina Scull and Wayne Hammond, *The JRR Tolkien Companion and Guide: Reader's Guide*, Houghton Mifflin, 2006, p. 215-222.

[536] Rateliff, *The History of the Hobbit, Part Two: Return to Bag-End*, 2007, p. 549.

[537] Rateliff, *The History of the Hobbit, Part Two: Return to Bag-End*, 2007, p. 559.

[538] Rateliff, *The History of the Hobbit, Part Two: Return to Bag-End*, 2007, p. 496, 498-502.

[539] Curly Head, "Death of the Flint-Monster: Origin of Birds," in George A. Dorsey [and James R. Murie], *Traditions of the Skidi Pawnee*, Houghton Mifflin, 1904, p. 29.

⁵⁴⁰ John D. Rateliff, *The History of the Hobbit, Part Two: Return to Bag-End*, Houghton Mifflin, 2007, p. 483-489.

⁵⁴¹ JRR Tolkien, *The Book of Lost Tales, Part Two*, in *The History of Middle-earth, Volume II*, Christopher Tolkien, editor, Houghton Mifflin, 1984, p. 69; Christina Scull and Wayne Hammond, *The JRR Tolkien Companion and Guide: Reader's Guide*, Houghton Mifflin, 2006, p. 123-124. The original composition of "Turambar and the Foalókë" occurred sometime around early 1918, but it isn't clear when the surviving text was prepared because it is known to be the second draft and not the first.

⁵⁴² JRR Tolkien, *The Book of Lost Tales, Part Two*, Christopher Tolkien editor, 1984, p. 69.

⁵⁴³ John Garth, *Tolkien and the Great War: The Threshold of Middle-earth*, Houghton Mifflin, 2003, p. 220-221. Garth cites JRR Tolkien, *The Book of Lost Tales, Part Two*, Christopher Tolkien editor, 1984, p. 172, 176 from "The Fall of Gondolin." This was Tolkien's first tale, written in early 1917 (Christina Scull and Wayne Hammond, *The JRR Tolkien Companion and Guide: Reader's Guide*, Houghton Mifflin, 2006, p. 121). Garth's comparison of Tolkien's dragons to WWI tanks refers to mention in this tale of "dragons of fire and serpents of bronze and iron" and Melkor's destructive "things of iron" (p. 176).

⁵⁴⁴ John Garth, *Tolkien and the Great War: The Threshold of Middle-earth*, Houghton Mifflin, 2003, p. 267. Garth shares many insights into probable parallels between Tolkien's WWI experiences and aspects of his fictional universe. He also cautions that Tolkien's "statements on the influence or otherwise of the First World War on *The Lord of the Rings* are few and wary" (p. 310), but "some of his memories must have invigorated [*The Hobbit*]" (p. 307). These observations are applicable to Tolkien's fiction in general.

⁵⁴⁵ Humphrey Carpenter, *The Letters of JRR Tolkien*, with the assistance of Christopher Tolkien, Houghton Mifflin, 2000 edition [original publication 1981], p. 30, # 25, circa February 1938.

⁵⁴⁶ John D. Rateliff, *The History of the Hobbit, Part Two: Return to Bag-End*, Houghton Mifflin, 2007, p. 523-524.

⁵⁴⁷ A magic arrow named "Dailir" is discussed in Rateliff, *The History of the Hobbit, Part Two: Return to Bag-End*, 2007, p. 558-559, 564 endnote 6; see JRR

Tolkien, *The Lays of Beleriand*, in *The History of Middle-earth, Volume III*, Christopher Tolkien editor, Houghton Mifflin, 1985, p. 42, 45.

[548] Rateliff, *The History of the Hobbit, Part Two: Return to Bag-End*, 2007, p. 549.

[549] Cheyenne Chief, "Black and White (A Love Story)," in George Dorsey [and James R. Murie], *Traditions of the Skidi Pawnee*, Houghton Mifflin, 1904, p. 308-325. See p. 309 for discussion of arrows made by Skidi priests and "painted with dark blue paint, so that they were black" – these were used for "making that buffalo holy"; then p. 310: "...as the buffalo threw out its front leg, the boy pulled his bow-string, loosed the arrow, and shot the buffalo in the soft place under the shoulder, so that the arrow went through the heart."

[550] John D. Rateliff, *The History of the Hobbit, Part Two: Return to Bag-End*, Houghton Mifflin, 2007, p. 689; also see p. 776.

[551] Rateliff, *The History of the Hobbit, Part Two: Return to Bag-End*, 2007, p. 550.

[552] Rateliff, *The History of the Hobbit, Part Two: Return to Bag-End*, 2007, p. 619.

[553] John Garth, "The road from adaptation to invention: How Tolkien Came to the Brink of Middle-earth in 1914," *Tolkien Studies* 11, 2014, p. 1-44.

[554] Rateliff, *The History of the Hobbit, Part Two: Return to Bag-End*, 2007, p. 647.

[555] Rateliff, *The History of the Hobbit, Part Two: Return to Bag-End*, 2007, p. 678.

[556] Rateliff, *The History of the Hobbit, Part Two: Return to Bag-End*, 2007, p. 683.

[557] Yellow Calf, "The Boy, the Bears, and White Crow," in George A. Dorsey [and James R. Murie], *Traditions of the Skidi Pawnee*, Houghton Mifflin, 1904, p. 138-146.

Endnotes: Messengers of Tirawa and Manwë

[558] John D. Rateliff, *The History of the Hobbit, Part One: Mr. Baggins*, Houghton Mifflin, 2007, p. 219-224.

[559] Roaming Scout, "Dispersion of the Gods and the First People," in George A. Dorsey [and James R. Murie], *Traditions of the Skidi Pawnee*, Houghton Mifflin, 1904, p. 8: ""Let us now let the man know that he shall become a

warrior, and that upon his back he shall wear the Swift Hawk, to tell him of the office of a warrior." The hawk as a messenger of Morning Star is discussed at p. 330 endnote 14.

[560] JRR Tolkien, *The Book of Lost Tales, Part One*, in *The History of Middle-earth, Volume I*, Christopher Tolkien editor, Houghton Mifflin, 1983, p. 58; also see p. 62, 113.

[561] In *Traditions of the Skidi Pawnee* the creation story (p. 8) tells us that to men is given "the Swallow, who is the messenger bird for the gods in the west." And various endnotes mention the meadowlark (p. 333 endnote 45: "The meadow lark is often spoken of as the messenger or errand boy of the Evening Star") and the bluebird (p. 330 endnote 18: "Attached to each of these pipes, as found in the sacred bundles, is generally the skin of a bluebird, which is regarded as the messenger between Tirawa and men, and thus, from its position on the pipe, is able not only to carry the sacrifice to Tirawa, but also the prayers of men"; and p. 333 endnote 50: "Presumably a bluebird, which is usually regarded as the messenger or errand boy of Tirawa").

[562] "The Young Eagle and His Grandmother," told by White Crow Feathers, in George Dorsey [and James R. Murie], *Traditions of the Skidi Pawnee*, Houghton Mifflin, 1904, p. 175.

[563] JRR Tolkien, *The Book of Lost Tales, Part One*, Christopher Tolkien editor, 1983, p. 176-177.

[564] George A. Dorsey [and James R. Murie], *Traditions of the Skidi Pawnee*, 1904, p. 330 endnote 15.

[565] JRR Tolkien, *The Book of Lost Tales, Part One*, in *The History of Middle-earth, Volume I*, Christopher Tolkien, editor, Houghton Mifflin, 1983, p. 73. Tolkien's "Sorontur King of Eagles" appears in "The Coming of the Valar," a myth that Tolkien wrote during the same period as "The Music of the Ainur" (Christina Scull and Wayne Hammond, *The JRR Tolkien Companion and Guide: Reader's Guide*, Houghton Mifflin, 2006, p. 123-125). Tolkien's eagles lingered through the different iterations of *The Silmarillion*, as Christopher Tolkien has noted, quoting from the final version (*The Book of Lost Tales, Part One*, p. 89): "cf. *The Silmarillion* p. 110: 'For Manwë to whom all birds are dear, and to whom they bring news upon Taniquetil from Middle-earth, had sent forth the race of Eagles'..."

[566] JRR Tolkien, *The Lost Road and Other Writings*, in *The History of Middle-earth, Volume V*, Christopher Tolkien editor, Houghton Mifflin, 1987, p. 38; also see p. 47, 62, 78.

[567] JRR Tolkien, *The Lost Road and Other Writings*, Christopher Tolkien editor, 1987, p. 87.

[568] JRR Tolkien, *The Lost Road and Other Writings*, Christopher Tolkien editor, 1987, p. 77.

[569] JRR Tolkien, *The Lost Road and Other Writings*, Christopher Tolkien editor, 1987, p. 75.

[570] Examples of stories that concern talking eagles in *Traditions of the Skidi Pawnee* include "The Children-of-the-Sun Society," told by Roaming Scout, p. 57-59; "The Boy Who Conquered the Buffalo," told by Curley Head, p. 109-111; and "The Girl Who Grieved for Her Brother," told by Cheyenne Chief, p. 304-306. A story that the Skidi would have heard as purely fictional is told by "Big-Medicine-Man" (also known as Big Doctor or George Esau), "Coyote and Eagle," p. 270-271.

[571] Wonderful Buffalo, "Origin of the Few-Buffalo-Dancers Society," in George Dorsey [and James R. Murie], *Traditions of the Skidi Pawnee*, Houghton Mifflin, 1904, p. 68-69.

[572] Bright Eyes, "The Man Who Visited Spirit Land," in George Dorsey [and James R. Murie], *Traditions of the Skidi Pawnee*, Houghton Mifflin, 1904, p. 69-71. An endnote qualifies this story comparing a magic golden eagle to the Creator as "an individual belief" (p. 342 endnote 127). In portraying his eagles in *The Hobbit*, Tolkien used for his model a drawing of a golden eagle from a book published in 1919 (JRR Tolkien, *The Annotated Hobbit*, annotated by Douglas A. Anderson, Houghton Mifflin, 2002, p. 160).

[573] George Dorsey [and James R. Murie], *Traditions of the Skidi Pawnee*, Houghton Mifflin, 1904, p. 347 endnote 173.

[574] JRR Tolkien, *The Annotated Hobbit*, annotated by Douglas A. Anderson, Houghton Mifflin, 2002, p. 156-157. To illustrate Chaucer's treatment of a "talkative eagle" Anderson presents two excerpts from Chaucer's "The House of Fame."

[575] JRR Tolkien, *Morgoth's Ring, the Later Silmarillion, Part One*, in *The History of Middle-earth, Volume X*, Christopher Tolkien editor, Houghton Mifflin, 1993, p. 409.

Endnotes: Bombadil Reborn

[576] Humphrey Carpenter, *The Letters of JRR Tolkien*, with the assistance of Christopher Tolkien, Houghton Mifflin, 2000 edition [original publication 1981], Tolkien to Stanley Unwin, # 17, October 15, 1937, p. 24.

[577] Carpenter, *The Letters of JRR Tolkien*, 2000 edition [original publication 1981], Tolkien to Stanley Unwin, #19, December 16, 1937, p. 25-27.

[578] JRR Tolkien, *The Book of Lost Tales, Part Two*, in *The History of Middle-earth, Volume II*, Christopher Tolkien editor, Houghton Mifflin, 1984, p. 10.

[579] JRR Tolkien, *The Return of the Shadow*, in *The History of The Lord of the Rings, Part One*, Christopher Tolkien editor, Houghton Mifflin, 1988, p. 42-43.

[580] Humphrey Carpenter, *The Letters of JRR Tolkien*, with the assistance of Christopher Tolkien, Houghton Mifflin, 2000 edition [original publication 1981], Tolkien to CA Furth, #33, August 31, 1938, p. 40-41.

[581] Christina Scull and Wayne Hammond, *The JRR Tolkien Companion and Guide: Chronology*, Houghton Mifflin, 2006, p. 220.

[582] JRR Tolkien, *The Return of the Shadow*, in *The History of The Lord of the Rings, Part One*, Christopher Tolkien editor, Houghton Mifflin, 1988, p. 111-112.

[583] R.C. Maclagan, "'The Keener' in the Scottish Highlands and Islands," *Folk-Lore: A Quarterly Review*, volume 25, March 1914, p. 84-91.

[584] Goldberry's green gown and silver-green clothing appeared in the 1934 version of "The Adventures of Tom Bombadil"; see Wayne Hammond and Christina Scull, *The Lord of the Rings: A Reader's Companion*, Houghton Mifflin, 2005, p. 127.

[585] JRR Tolkien, *The Return of the Shadow*, in *The History of The Lord of the Rings, Part One*, Christopher Tolkien editor, Houghton Mifflin, 1988, p. 117.

[586] JRR Tolkien, *The Return of the Shadow*, Christopher Tolkien editor, 1988, p. 120.

[587] R.C. Maclagan, "'The Keener' in the Scottish Highlands and Islands," *Folk-Lore: A Quarterly Review*, volume 25, March 1914, p. 90.

[588] Humphrey Carpenter, *The Letters of JRR Tolkien*, with the assistance of Christopher Tolkien, Houghton Mifflin, 2000 edition [original publication 1981], Tolkien to Naomi Mitchison, #144, April 25, 1954, p. 174.

[589] JRR Tolkien, "Nomenclature of *The Lord of the Rings*," 1967, in Christina Scull and Wayne Hammond, *The Lord of the Rings: A Reader's Companion*, Houghton Mifflin, 2005, p. 779.

[590] JRR Tolkien, *The Return of the Shadow*, in *The History of The Lord of the Rings, Part One*, Christopher Tolkien editor, Houghton Mifflin, 1988, p. 235.

[591] Humphrey Carpenter, *The Letters of JRR Tolkien*, with the assistance of Christopher Tolkien, Houghton Mifflin, 2000 edition [original publication 1981], Tolkien to Katherine Farrer, August 7, 1954, # 148, p. 183.

[592] JRR Tolkien, *The Return of the Shadow*, Christopher Tolkien editor, 1988, p. 244 and p. 38.

[593] Peter Gilliver and colleagues suggest that Tolkien may have drawn from the OED for his understanding of the history of nasturtians. See Peter Gilliver, Jeremy Marshall, and Edmund Weiner, *The Ring of Words: Tolkien and the Oxford English Dictionary*, Oxford: Oxford University Press, 2006, p. 169-170.

[594] John Gerard, *The Herball or Generall Historie of Plantes*, 1636, p. 252.

[595] Joseph Wright, *English Dialect Dictionary*, Oxford: Henry Frowde, 1905, volume 6, T-Z, p. 526. Skeat and Britten's *Reprinted Glossaries and Old Farming Words* refers to bindweed as "Withwind"; see Walter W. Skeat and James Britten, editors, *Reprinted Glossaries and Old Farming Words*, London: Trübner & Company, Part 4, Reprinted Glossaries Parts 18-22, 1879, p. 47.

[596] Christina Scull and Wayne Hammond, *The JRR Tolkien Companion and Guide: Reader's Guide*, Houghton Mifflin, 2006, p. 25; Hargrove, "Tom

Bombadil," in Michael Drout editor, *JRR Tolkien Encyclopedia*, 2007, p. 670-671.

[597] Andrea Mathwich, "Goldberry: Servant or Master of Bombadil?" in *Forgotten Leaves: Essays from a Smial*, Jessica Burke and Anthony Burdge editors, Myth Ink Books, 2015, p. 46-49. This essay described a debate on the nature of Tom Bombadil sponsored by a Tolkien fan group on Thursday, May 22, 2014 at the Barbed Wire Books Hobbit Hole in Longmont, Colorado. Andrea brought snacks from Goldberry's table; Linda Echo-Hawk sang a song she had just composed, using a poem spoken by Bombadil about Goldberry; and Bill Kelso recorded the debate.

[598] John Garth review essay, *Tolkien Studies* 11, 2014, p. 225-241, see p. 230-231: "Curious survivals in the 1930s are the terms *wingi* 'mermaid, foam-maid' and *nindari* 'river-maid,' which form a bridge between the 'fays' who accompany the Valar in *The Book of Lost Tales* and the Maiar who do so in later versions of the legendarium. The term nindari particularly brings to mind Goldberry, whose first appearance... was closely contemporary with 'Declension of Nouns.'"

Endnotes: Holes and Houses and Hills

[599] John D. Rateliff, *The History of the Hobbit, Part One: Mr. Baggins*, Houghton Mifflin, 2007, p. 28.

[600] Christina Scull and Wayne Hammond, *The JRR Tolkien Companion and Guide: Reader's Guide*, Houghton Mifflin, 2006, p. 54. Tolkien drew a number of versions of The Hill (JRR Tolkien, *The Annotated Hobbit*, annotated by Douglas A. Anderson, Houghton Mifflin, 2002, p. 46, 62-63, after 178). All show a dome-shaped hill rising above an inset doorway and windows with a tree that moves up to the top of the hill.

[601] George A. Dorsey [and James R. Murie], *Traditions of the Skidi Pawnee*, Houghton Mifflin, 1904, p. xiv-xvi.

[602] JRR Tolkien, *The Return of the Shadow*, in *The History of The Lord of the Rings, Part One*, Christopher Tolkien editor, Houghton Mifflin, 1988, p. 110, 130. Christopher Tolkien cited a letter dated August 31, 1938 (p. 109, 110) reporting that JRR had made good progress in his new story, and this is interpreted to mean that the story had "passed through the Old Forest by

way of the Withywindle valley, stayed in the house of Tom Bombadil, escaped from the Barrow-wight, and reached Bree."

[603] JRR Tolkien, *The Return of the Shadow*, Christopher Tolkien editor, 1988, p. 132.

[604] JRR Tolkien, *The Return of the Shadow*, Christopher Tolkien editor, 1988, p. 137, 154.

[605] Humphrey Carpenter, *The Letters of JRR Tolkien*, with the assistance of Christopher Tolkien, Houghton Mifflin, 2000 edition [original publication 1981], # 19, December 16, 1937, p. 26.

[606] JRR Tolkien, *The Return of the Shadow*, Christopher Tolkien editor, 1988, p. 42-43.

[607] JRR Tolkien, *The Return of the Shadow*, Christopher Tolkien editor, 1988, p. 110-115.

[608] JRR Tolkien, *The Return of the Shadow*, Christopher Tolkien editor, 1988, p. 117.

[609] JRR Tolkien, *The Return of the Shadow*, Christopher Tolkien editor, 1988, p. 121.

[610] Simon J. Cook, "Concerning Hobbits," online essay at *The History Vault*, December 16, 2014.

[611] Christina Scull and Wayne Hammond, *The JRR Tolkien Companion and Guide: Chronology*, Houghton Mifflin, 2006, p. 50, 52, 55, 59; Mark T. Hooker, *Tolkien and Welsh*, Llyfrawr, 2012, p. vii; Carl Phelpstead, *Tolkien and Wales: Language, Literature, and Identity*, University of Wales Press, 2011, p. xx, 137 endnote 14.

[612] John Rhys, Untitled Address of the President of the Anthropology Section of the BAAS, dated September 6, 1900, in *Report of the Seventieth Meeting of the British Association for the Advancement of Science*, London: John Murray, 1900, p. 884-896.

[613] John Rhys, *The Welsh People*, New York: Macmillan, 1900. For my quotes on the pre-Celtic "Aborigines" see p. 12-14.

[614] JRR Tolkien, *The Return of the Shadow*, Christopher Tolkien editor, 1988, p. 117, 121.

[615] John Rhys, *The Welsh People*, 1900, p. 53. Rhys made mention in his chapter "The Pictish Question" in *The Welsh People* of "an old woman of fabulous age called Bera, Béara, or Béirre" who attained "the status of a witch or wise woman... not quite to that of a goddess." This raises the possibility that Tolkien drew from Rhys to construct the name "Goldberry" at circa 1930-1931 in the course of writing "The Adventures of Tom Bombadil."

[616] John Rhys, *Celtic Folklore*, volume 2, Welsh and Manx, Oxford: Clarendon Press, 1901, p. 659-663; see quoted material at p. 662.

[617] In Tolkien's first version of the Council of Elrond, Elrond did not know about "this strange Bombadil"; see JRR Tolkien, *The Return of the Shadow*, Christopher Tolkien editor, 1988, p. 401.

[618] John Rhys, Untitled Address of the President of the Anthropology Section of the BAAS, dated September 6, 1900, in *Report of the Seventieth Meeting of the British Association for the Advancement of Science*, London: John Murray, 1900, p. 886-888.

[619] David MacRitchie, *The Testimony of Tradition*, Kegan Paul, Trench, Trübner, 1890, p. 101-118.

[620] Mark T. Hooker, *A Tolkienian Mathomium*, Llyfrawr, 2006, p. 189-190.

Endnotes: The Enchanted Feather

[621] JRR Tolkien, *The Treason of Isengard*, in *The History of The Lord of the Rings, Part Two*, Christopher Tolkien editor, Houghton Mifflin, 1989, p. 211.

[622] JRR Tolkien, *The Treason of Isengard*, Christopher Tolkien editor, 1989, p. 430.

[623] Christina Scull and Wayne Hammond, *The JRR Tolkien Companion and Guide: Chronology*, Houghton Mifflin, 2006, p. 252-253; JRR Tolkien, *The Treason of Isengard*, in *The History of The Lord of the Rings, Part Two*, Houghton Mifflin, 1989, p. 1, 430-431.

[624] Bright Eyes, "The Man Who Visited Spirit Land," in George A. Dorsey [and James R. Murie], *Traditions of the Skidi Pawnee*, Houghton Mifflin, 1904, p. 69-71. On p. 334 endnote 60 Bright Eyes is identified as the "wife of Yellow-Calf." In 1892 James Yellow Calf was married to a woman named Green Calf, age 51 (*Identification and Description of the Lands Covered by Selections and Allotments, 1893*, Government Printing Office, p. 9). Bright Eyes was the teller of four stories in this volume and four more stories in *The Pawnee Mythology*, published in 1906. In that book, a footnote on p. 139 identifies her further as "a Skidi woman, who, at the time of her death recently, was the keeper of the Big-Black-Meteoric-Star bundle." A 1903 census lists Yellow Calf alone, suggesting that Green Calf had died by then. Elsewhere Big Crow is identified as the keeper of that bundle (and as a grandson of Big Knife), suggesting that Bright Eyes was a close relative (George Dorsey [and James R. Murie], *The Pawnee Mythology*, 1906, Carnegie Institution of Washington, publication # 59, also Bison Books reprint, University of Nebraska Press, 1997, p. 38 footnote). Three keepers of this bundle are listed in one document prepared by James R. Murie and George Dorsey: Cheyenne Chief (heir), Yellow Calf, and Mark Rutter (Big Crow) keeper (Field Museum of Natural History, George Dorsey / James R. Murie Field Notes, Box 3, "Society & Religions" undated typescript circa 1906). The inclusion of Yellow Calf here implies strongly that Bright Eyes and Green Calf were the same person. Rutter was born about 1858 (*Identification and Description of the Lands Covered by Selections and Allotments, 1893*, Government Printing Office, p. 12), so he could have been a son of Green Calf, who was born about 1841. If we identify Green Calf as Bright Eyes, keeper of the Big Black Meteoric Star Bundle, then it makes sense that when she died in 1903 the bundle would have gone to Big Crow, with her husband Yellow Calf retaining keepership rights as well.

[625] JRR Tolkien, *The Book of Lost Tales, Part One*, in *The History of Middle-earth, Volume I*, Christopher Tolkien editor, Houghton Mifflin, 1983, p. 212-213.

[626] JRR Tolkien, *The Book of Lost Tales, Part One*, Christopher Tolkien editor, 1983, p. 264.

[627] George A. Dorsey [and James R. Murie], *Traditions of the Skidi Pawnee*, Houghton Mifflin, 1904, p. xix, 57.

[628] JRR Tolkien, *The Treason of Isengard*, in *The History of The Lord of the Rings, Part Two*, Christopher Tolkien editor, Houghton Mifflin, 1989, p. 431.

[629] Humphrey Carpenter, *The Letters of JRR Tolkien*, with the assistance of Christopher Tolkien, Houghton Mifflin, 2000 edition [original publication 1981], p. 203, # 156, November 4, 1954. On one occasion when Tolkien discussed the meaning of Gandalf's death experience, he chose to also revisit his creation story, which, as I argue in a previous chapter, drew upon the Skidi Pawnee creation story: "But the nature of the gods' knowledge of the history of the World, and their part in making it (before it was embodied or made 'real') – whence they drew their knowledge of the future, such as they had, is part of the major mythology" (Humphrey Carpenter, *The Letters of JRR Tolkien*, with the assistance of Christopher Tolkien, Houghton Mifflin, 2000 edition [original publication 1981], p. 203, # 156, November 4, 1954). By this time Tolkien had rewritten his creation story away from the Skidi myth; but having drawn from that narrative, it might not be coincidental that it would have come to mind as he mused on Gandalf's spiritual enhancement.

[630] Bright Eyes, "The Man Who Visited Spirit Land," in George A. Dorsey [and James R. Murie], *Traditions of the Skidi Pawnee*, Houghton Mifflin, 1904, p. 70-71.

[631] George A. Dorsey [and James R. Murie], *Traditions of the Skidi Pawnee*, Houghton Mifflin, 1904, p. 341-342 endnote 125.

Endnotes: A Very Peculiar Letter

[632] Roaming Scout, "Dispersion of the Gods and the First People," George A. Dorsey [and James R. Murie], *Traditions of the Skidi Pawnee*, Houghton Mifflin, 1904, p. 9, 10, 11. Both dream and vision occur in this creation story. In the first instance of dream-knowledge (p. 9), Closed Man is taught how to make a hoe "by the Moon, in a dream." Next Evening Star "came to the man in a vision and told him that a time was coming when she should give him a holy bundle[.]" After the man uses the bundle and makes a sacrifice, "in the night, [Evening Star] visited the man in a vision." She visits him for many nights. At a later time after the man encounters other people in the world Evening Star "came to Closed-Man again, in a vision" (p. 10). The message is for unifying all the people. Finally, another man told Closed Man of his experience, "that [Evening Star] had come to him in a vision and that he had learned the different ceremonies and songs belonging to the bundles..." (p. 11).

[633] George A. Dorsey [and James R. Murie], *Traditions of the Skidi Pawnee*, 1904, p. 331 endnote 24.

[634] JRR Tolkien, *The Book of Lost Tales, Part One*, in *The History of Middle-earth, Volume I*, Christopher Tolkien, editor, Houghton Mifflin, 1983, p. 13. Christina Scull and Wayne Hammond, *The JRR Tolkien Companion and Guide: Chronology*, Houghton Mifflin, 2006, p. 97.

[635] JRR Tolkien, *The Book of Lost Tales, Part One*, Christopher Tolkien editor, 1983, p. 66, 71.

[636] JRR Tolkien, *The Book of Lost Tales, Part One*, Christopher Tolkien editor, 1983, p. 74.

[637] JRR Tolkien, *The Lost Road and Other Writings*, in *The History of Middle-earth, Volume V*, Christopher Tolkien, editor, Houghton Mifflin, 1987, p. 50.

[638] JRR Tolkien, *The Lost Road and Other Writings*, in *The History of Middle-earth, Volume V*, Christopher Tolkien, editor, Houghton Mifflin, 1987, p. 52.

[639] Christina Scull and Wayne Hammond, *The JRR Tolkien Companion and Guide: Reader's Guide*, Houghton Mifflin, 2006, p. 494-498.

[640] "Leaf By Niggle," JRR Tolkien, *Tales from the Perilous Realm*, Houghton Mifflin, 2008, p. 285.

[641] Verlyn Flieger and Douglas A. Anderson, *Tolkien On Fairy-stories*, HarperCollins, 2008, p. 122; Christina Scull and Wayne Hammond, *The JRR Tolkien Companion and Guide: Reader's Guide*, Houghton Mifflin, 2006, p. 686-687.

[642] Verlyn Flieger and Douglas A. Anderson, *Tolkien On Fairy-stories*, 2008, p. 122.

[643] Verlyn Flieger and Douglas A. Anderson, *Tolkien On Fairy-stories*, 2008, p. 122.

[644] Christina Scull and Wayne Hammond, *The JRR Tolkien Companion and Guide: Reader's Guide*, Houghton Mifflin, 2006, p. 687; Christina Scull and Wayne Hammond, *The JRR Tolkien Companion and Guide: Reader's Guide*, "Addenda and Corrigenda" for p. 683-689.

[645] Verlyn Flieger and Douglas A. Anderson, *Tolkien On Fairy-stories*, 2008, p. 35; JRR Tolkien, "On Fairy-stories," in *Tales from the Perilous Realm*, Houghton Mifflin, 2008, p. 327.

[646] Verlyn Flieger and Douglas A. Anderson, *Tolkien On Fairy-stories*, 2008, p. 132, 134.

[647] Verlyn Flieger and Douglas A. Anderson, *Tolkien On Fairy-stories*, 2008, p. 35; JRR Tolkien, "On Fairy-stories," in *Tales from the Perilous Realm*, 2008, p. 327.

[648] Verlyn Flieger and Douglas A. Anderson, *Tolkien On Fairy-stories*, 2008, p. 59; JRR Tolkien, "On Fairy-stories," in *Tales from the Perilous Realm*, 2008, p. 361-371.

[649] Verlyn Flieger and Douglas A. Anderson, *Tolkien On Fairy-stories*, 2008, p. 110.

[650] Verlyn Flieger and Douglas A. Anderson, *Tolkien On Fairy-stories*, 2008, p. 245-246.

[651] Verlyn Flieger and Douglas A. Anderson, *Tolkien On Fairy-stories*, 2008, p. 59; JRR Tolkien, "On Fairy-stories," in *Tales from the Perilous Realm*, 2008, p. 361-371.

[652] Verlyn Flieger and Douglas A. Anderson, *Tolkien On Fairy-stories*, HarperCollins, 2008, p. 77; JRR Tolkien, "On Fairy-stories," in *Tales from the Perilous Realm*, Houghton Mifflin, 2008, p. 387.

[653] Verlyn Flieger and Douglas A. Anderson, *Tolkien On Fairy-stories*, 2008, p. 67-69; JRR Tolkien, "On Fairy-stories," in *Tales from the Perilous Realm*, 2008, p. 371-375.

[654] Verlyn Flieger and Douglas A. Anderson, *Tolkien On Fairy-stories*, 2008, p. 192-194, 265.

[655] Humphrey Carpenter, *The Letters of JRR Tolkien*, with the assistance of Christopher Tolkien, Houghton Mifflin, 2000 edition [original publication 1981], JRR Tolkien to Christopher Tolkien, November 7-8, 1944, # 89, p. 100.

[656] Humphrey Carpenter, *The Letters of JRR Tolkien*, 2000 edition [original publication 1981], JRR Tolkien to Peter Hastings draft letter, September 1954, # 153, p. 189.

[657] JRR Tolkien, *Sauron Defeated*, in *The History of The Lord of the Rings, Part Four*, Christopher Tolkien editor, Houghton Mifflin, 1992, p. 145-327. Discussion of the dating of *The Notion Club Papers* can be found at p. 145-147.

[658] Verlyn Flieger, "Do the Atlantis story and abandon Eriol-Saga," *Tolkien Studies* 1, 2004, p. 43-68, see quote at p. 58.

[659] Humphrey Carpenter, *The Letters of JRR Tolkien*, 2000 edition [original publication 1981], JRR Tolkien to WH Auden, # 163, June 7, 1955, p. 213.

[660] Tom Shippey, *The Road to Middle-earth: How JRR Tolkien Created a New Mythology*, 2003, Houghton Mifflin, p. 285.

[661] George A. Dorsey [and James R. Murie], *Traditions of the Skidi Pawnee*, Houghton Mifflin, 1904, p. 331 endnote 24.

Endnotes: Olórin in the Uttermost West

[662] Verlyn Flieger and Douglas A. Anderson, *Tolkien On Fairy-stories*, HarperCollins, 2008, p. 35; JRR Tolkien, "On Fairy-stories," in *Tales from the Perilous Realm*, Houghton Mifflin, 2008, p. 327.

[663] JRR Tolkien, *The War of the Ring*, in *The History of The Lord of the Rings, Part Three*, Christopher Tolkien editor, Houghton Mifflin, 1990, p. 145, 153.

[664] Christina Scull and Wayne Hammond, *The JRR Tolkien Companion and Guide: Reader's Guide*, Houghton Mifflin, 2006, p. 751.

[665] JRR Tolkien, *Morgoth's Ring, the Later Silmarillion, Part One*, in *The History of Middle-earth, Volume X*, Christopher Tolkien editor, Houghton Mifflin, 1993, p. 147.

[666] JRR Tolkien, *The Lost Road and Other Writings*, in *The History of Middle-earth, Volume V*, Christopher Tolkien editor, Houghton Mifflin, 1987, p. 162.

[667] JRR Tolkien, *Morgoth's Ring, the Later Silmarillion, Part One*, Christopher Tolkien editor, 1993, p. 3-6, 41.

[668] JRR Tolkien, *Morgoth's Ring, the Later Silmarillion, Part One*, Christopher Tolkien editor, 1993, p. 15.

[669] JRR Tolkien, *The Silmarillion*, Houghton Mifflin, 1977, p. 31; JRR Tolkien, *Unfinished Tales*, Houghton Mifflin, 1980, p. 397.

[670] JRR Tolkien, *Unfinished Tales*, 1980, p. 388-402. Christina Scull and Wayne Hammond, *The JRR Tolkien Companion and Guide: Reader's Guide*, Houghton Mifflin, 2006, p. 432-434; Christina Scull and Wayne Hammond, *The JRR Tolkien Companion and Guide: Reader's Guide*, "Addenda and Corrigenda" for p. 432.

[671] Christina Scull and Wayne Hammond, *The JRR Tolkien Companion and Guide: Chronology*, 2006, p. 638-639, 684.

[672] JRR Tolkien, *Unfinished Tales*, Houghton Mifflin, 1980, p. 396.

[673] JRR Tolkien, *Unfinished Tales*, 1980, p. 396.

[674] Christina Scull and Wayne Hammond, *The JRR Tolkien Companion and Guide: Reader's Guide*, "Addenda and Corrigenda" for p. 432.

[675] George A. Dorsey [and James R. Murie], *Traditions of the Skidi Pawnee*, Houghton Mifflin, 1904, p. 331 endnote 24.

[676] Verlyn Flieger and Douglas A. Anderson, *Tolkien On Fairy-stories*, HarperCollins, 2008, p. 77; JRR Tolkien, "On Fairy-stories," in *Tales from the Perilous Realm*, Houghton Mifflin, 2008, p. 387.

[677] Verlyn Flieger and Douglas A. Anderson, *Tolkien On Fairy-stories*, 2008, p. 59; JRR Tolkien, "On Fairy-stories," in *Tales from the Perilous Realm*, 2008, p. 361-371.

[678] Verlyn Flieger and Douglas A. Anderson, *Tolkien On Fairy-stories*, 2008, p. 110. The *Oxford English Dictionary* definition for "fancy" refers to "things not present."

[679] JRR Tolkien, *Unfinished Tales*, Houghton Mifflin, 1980, p. 396; Christina Scull and Wayne Hammond, *The JRR Tolkien Companion and Guide: Reader's Guide*, Houghton Mifflin, 2006, p. 432-434; Christina Scull and Wayne

Hammond, *The JRR Tolkien Companion and Guide: Reader's Guide*, "Addenda and Corrigenda" for p. 432.

[680] JRR Tolkien, *The Peoples of Middle-earth*, in *The History of Middle-earth, Volume XII*, Christopher Tolkien editor, Houghton Mifflin, 1996, p. 386.

[681] Humphrey Carpenter, *The Letters of JRR Tolkien*, with the assistance of Christopher Tolkien, Houghton Mifflin, 2000 edition [original publication 1981], p. 201, # 156, November 4, 1954.

Endnotes: Tolkien's Mongol-type Orcs

[682] Walter Y. Evans-Wentz, *The Fairy-Faith in Celtic Countries*, Oxford University Press, 1911, p. 166-167.

[683] Humphrey Carpenter, *The Letters of JRR Tolkien*, with the assistance of Christopher Tolkien, Houghton Mifflin, 2000 edition [original publication 1981], Tolkien to Forrest Ackerman, undated June 1958, # 210, p. 274.

[684] For a good summary of Tolkien's early pre-racial goblins / orcs, see John D. Rateliff, *The History of the Hobbit, Part One: Mr. Baggins*, Houghton Mifflin, 2007, p. 137-143; also see JRR Tolkien, *The Return of the Shadow*, in *The History of The Lord of the Rings, Part One*, Christopher Tolkien editor, Houghton Mifflin, 1988, p. 437 endnote 35.

[685] JRR Tolkien, "Goblin Feet," in *Oxford Poetry 1915*, edited by G.D.H.C and T.W.E. [Gerald Crow and T.W. Earp], Oxford: Blackwell, 1915, p. 64-65. Tolkien abandoned the tone and imagery of this early poem as he developed his fantasy elves and goblins, and he came to regret having published "Goblin Feet."

[686] Christina Scull and Wayne Hammond, *The JRR Tolkien Companion and Guide: Reader's Guide*, Houghton Mifflin, 2006, p. 568. They drew on Tolkien's 1939 draft of "On Fairy-Stories" for the note regarding the "mixture of German and Scottish flavours" that entered into MacDonald's "classic goblin."

[687] JRR Tolkien, *The Book of Lost Tales, Part Two*, in *The History of Middle-earth, Volume II*, Christopher Tolkien editor, Houghton Mifflin, 1984, p. 14.

[688] JRR Tolkien, *The Book of Lost Tales, Part Two*, Christopher Tolkien editor, 1984, p. 99.

[689] JRR Tolkien, *The Book of Lost Tales, Part Two*, Christopher Tolkien editor, 1984, p. 159-160. The term, "glamhoth," became interchangeable with "goblin" and "orc" in Tolkien's verse narratives of the early 1920s; see, for example, JRR Tolkien, *The Lays of Beleriand*, in *The History of Middle-earth, Volume III*, Christopher Tolkien editor, Houghton Mifflin, 1985, p. 34. In Tolkien's descriptions at this early date, the terms "subterranean," "granite," and "deformed" evoke the goblins and "cobs" of George MacDonald in *The Princess and the Goblin*, London: Strahan & Company, 1872. MacDonald's goblins dwelt underground and had cobs that were deformed animals. For more on this comparison, see Jason Fisher, "Reluctantly Inspired: George MacDonald and JRR Tolkien," in *North Wind: A Journal of George MacDonald Studies*, volume 25, 2006, p. 113-120.

[690] JRR Tolkien, *The Book of Lost Tales, Part Two*, in *The History of Middle-earth, Volume II*, Christopher Tolkien editor, Houghton Mifflin, 1984, p. 79, 166. Ivan M. Granger referred me to a poem by Christina Rossetti, and I found that Tolkien's early comparison of orcs to cats echoed one goblin described in that poem. In "Goblin Market" some "goblin men" pass through a "haunted glen" and "One had a cat's face"; see Christina Rossetti, *Goblin Market, The Prince's Progress, and Other Poems*, London: Macmillan & Company, 1879 edition [originally published 1863], p. 3, 4, 13.

[691] JRR Tolkien, *The Shaping of Middle-earth*, in *The History of Middle-earth, Volume IV*, Christopher Tolkien editor, Houghton Mifflin, 1986, p. 12, 82.

[692] JRR Tolkien, *A Secret Vice: Tolkien on Invented Languages*, Dimitra Fimi and Andrew Higgins editors, HarperCollins, 2016, p. 32, 57-58 endnote 82.

[693] JRR Tolkien, *The Return of the Shadow*, in *The History of The Lord of the Rings, Part One*, Christopher Tolkien editor, Houghton Mifflin, 1988, p. 437 endnote 35.

[694] JRR Tolkien, *Beowulf: A Translation and Commentary*, edited by Christopher Tolkien, Houghton Mifflin, 2014, p.163-164. The content of Tolkien's *Beowulf* note on *orcnéas* most likely dates to the early 1930s. Also see JRR Tolkien, "Nomenclature of *The Lord of the Rings*," 1967, in Christina Scull and Wayne Hammond, *The Lord of the Rings: A Reader's Companion*, Houghton Mifflin, 2005, p. 761-762 for a late discussion on the term "orc."

[695] "The Last Tale: The Fall of Númenor," in JRR Tolkien, *The Lost Road and Other Writings*, in *The History of Middle-earth, Volume V*, Christopher Tolkien, editor, Houghton Mifflin, 1987, p. 24, also see 212, 233.

[696] JRR Tolkien, *The Lost Road and Other Writings*, Christopher Tolkien editor, 1987, p. 280.

[697] JRR Tolkien, *Sauron Defeated*, in *The History of The Lord of the Rings, Part Four*, Christopher Tolkien editor, Houghton Mifflin, 1992, p. 31.

[698] Tolkien's 1958 mention of "Mongol-types" appeared in Humphrey Carpenter, *The Letters of JRR Tolkien*, with the assistance of Christopher Tolkien, Houghton Mifflin, 2000 edition [original publication 1981], Tolkien to Forrest Ackerman, undated June 1958, # 210, p. 274. Tolkien's writings have been selectively released by the Tolkien Estate, which controls access to Tolkien's papers. An official biography by Humphrey Carpenter was published during the 1970s, approved by the Tolkien Estate; see Humphrey Carpenter, *Tolkien: The Authorized Biography*, Houghton Mifflin, 1977. For an excellent consideration of Carpenter's perspective on this biography see Douglas Anderson, "Obituary" for Carpenter in *Tolkien Studies* # 2, 2005, p. 217-224. Carpenter wrote that his first draft of the biography was "deemed unacceptable by the Tolkien family..." His second version proved more acceptable, but in hindsight he felt he went too far to please the family: "What I'd actually done was castrated the book, cut out everything which was likely to be contentious."

[699] Asya Pereltsvaig and Martin W. Lewis, *The Indo-European Controversy: Facts and Fallacies in Historical Linguistics*, Cambridge University Press, 2015, p. 23: "Gobineau and his successors claimed that the original Aryans lost their racial essence as they spread from their homeland and interbred with lesser peoples. The resulting mixture supposedly led to degeneration and loss of vigor."

[700] Asya Pereltsvaig and Martin W. Lewis, *The Indo-European Controversy: Facts and Fallacies in Historical Linguistics*, Cambridge University Press, 2015, p. 21-25.

[701] Ivan Hannaford, *Race: The History of an Idea in the West*, Woodrow Wilson Center Press, 1996, p. 305-306.

[702] JP Mallory, *In Search of the Indo-Europeans: Language, Archaeology and Myth*, Thames and Hudson, 1989, p. 267, 269.

[703] For an excellent summary of Max Müller's influence on the study of myth see Richard Dorson, *The British Folklorists*, University of Chicago Press, 1968, p. 160-186.

[704] Verlyn Flieger and Douglas A. Anderson, *Tolkien On Fairy-stories*, HarperCollins, 2008, p. 41-42, also see 181-182.

[705] Humphrey Carpenter, *The Letters of JRR Tolkien*, with the assistance of Christopher Tolkien, Houghton Mifflin, 2000 edition [original publication 1981], JRR Tolkien to Michael Tolkien, March 18, 1941, # 44, p. 55-56.

[706] Ivan Hannaford, *Race: The History of an Idea in the West*, Woodrow Wilson Center Press, 1996, p. 326-327.

[707] G. Elliot Smith, untitled address to the Anthropology Section of the BAAS, September 5, 1912, in *Report of the Eighty-Second Meeting of the British Association for the Advancement of Science*, London: John Murray, 1913, p. 577.

[708] Humphrey Carpenter, *Tolkien: A Biography*, Houghton Mifflin, 1977, p. 13. Here Carpenter discussed a family group photo that included "a house-boy named Isaak" and a family tradition about an incident when Isaak "stole little John Ronald Reuel[.]" Carpenter may also had in mind a 1944 letter written by JRR; see Humphrey Carpenter, *The Letters of JRR Tolkien*, with the assistance of Christopher Tolkien, Houghton Mifflin, 2000 edition [original publication 1981], Tolkien to Christopher Tolkien, April 18, 1944, # 61, p. 73. In this 1944 letter Tolkien recalled his mother talking about "'local' conditions" in South Africa – conditions that seem to refer to the status of racial blacks, since he added, "The treatment of colour nearly always horrifies anyone going out from Britain" and it is unfortunate that "not many retain that generous sentiment for long." This letter suggests a moral objection to South African apartheid. It is unclear what news Tolkien heard that motivated him to mention "anyone going out from Britain" to South Africa.

[709] *Encyclopedia Britannica*, Cambridge: University Press, 1911, volume 19, p. 344.

[710] Louis Menand, *The Metaphysical Club: A Story of Ideas in America*, New York: Farrar, Straus and Giroux, 2001, p. 389-390; Leonard Harris and Charles Molesworth, *Alain L. Locke: The Biography of a Philosopher*, University of Chicago Press, 2008, p. 59-78.

[711] Leonard Harris and Charles Molesworth, *Alain L. Locke: The Biography of a Philosopher*, University of Chicago Press, 2008, p. 71.

[712] Edwin Black, *War Against the Weak: Eugenics and America's Campaign to Create a Master Race*, New York: Thunder's Mouth Press, 2003, p. 207-234.

[713] Michael W. Perry, *Lady Eugenist: Feminist Eugenics in the Speeches and Writings of Victoria Woodhull*, Seattle: Inkling Books, 2005, see reproductions of news articles from *Pall Mall* and *Evening Standard*, p. 16-17.

[714] GK Chesterton, *Eugenics and Other Evils*, London: Cassell and Company, 1922, preface.

[715] Tolkien knew Chesterton's work as early as 1908 when he donated two of Chesterton's books to his school library; see Christina Scull and Wayne Hammond, *The JRR Tolkien Companion and Guide: Chronology*, Houghton Mifflin, 2006, p. 13. For mention of GK Chesterton in Tolkien's essay, "On Fairy-stories," see Verlyn Flieger and Douglas A. Anderson, *Tolkien On Fairy-stories*, HarperCollins, 2008, p. 57 and note on p. 109, p. 84 and note on p. 114-115, p. 89 and note on p. 116; editorial note p. 130; p. 153 deleted text; Manuscript A passages: p. 189, 189-190, 192-193, notes p. 202-204; Manuscript B passages: p. 236, 237-238, 242.

[716] GK Chesterton, *Eugenics and Other Evils*, London: Cassell and Company, 1922, p. 15, 140, 142.

[717] Anonymous article, *The Seaman*, National Sailors' and Firemen's Union, volume 1 # 40, Friday, May 1, 1914, p. 6 (online record, University of Warwick, University Library, Modern Records Centre). The cited speech by Joseph Havelock Wilson was paraphrased here by the anonymous reporter.

[718] Anonymous article, *The Seaman*, volume 1 # 40, Friday, May 1, 1914, p. 8 (online record, University of Warwick, University Library, Modern Records Centre).

[719] The 1883 Francis Galton definition of eugenics is quoted in Clare Hanson, *Eugenics, Literature and Culture in Post-war Britain*, Routledge, 2013, p. 2.

[720] The 1904 Francis Galton definition of eugenics is quoted in Ivan Hannaford, *Race: The History of an Idea in the West*, Woodrow Wilson Center Press, 1996, p. 330 citing two publications by Galton in 1904 and 1905.

[721] JRR Tolkien, *The Book of Lost Tales, Part One*, in *The History of Middle-earth, Volume I*, Christopher Tolkien editor, Houghton Mifflin, 1983, 147, 175.

[722] JRR Tolkien, *The Book of Lost Tales, Part Two*, in *The History of Middle-earth, Volume II*, Christopher Tolkien editor, Houghton Mifflin, 1984, p. 3-68, the quote is from p. 10. Queen Gwendeling is described as having white skin (p. 8), and her daughter Tinúviel is also described that way (p. 11).

[723] JRR Tolkien, *The Book of Lost Tales, Part Two*, in *The History of Middle-earth, Volume II*, Christopher Tolkien, editor, Houghton Mifflin, 1984, p. 165.

[724] GK Chesterton, *Eugenics and Other Evils*, London: Cassell and Company, 1922, p. 180.

[725] Humphrey Carpenter, *The Letters of JRR Tolkien*, with the assistance of Christopher Tolkien, Houghton Mifflin, 2000 edition [original publication 1981], Tolkien to Peter Hastings, draft letter dated September 1954, # 153, p. 194.

[726] Dimitra Fimi, *Tolkien, Race and Cultural History: From Fairies to Hobbits*, Palgrave Macmillan, 2010, p. 146-147. Another encyclopedia discussion of Tolkien and "Hierarchy" focuses on Christian ideology associated with the "Great Chain of Being" and the internal rankings of sentient beings in Middle-earth, but it offers no consideration of Tolkien's attitudes toward race and racial hierarchies; see David Oberhelman, "Hierarchy," in *JRR Tolkien Encyclopedia: Scholarship and Critical Assessment*, edited by Micael Drout, Routledge, 2007, p. 271-272. Entrenched post-WW2 racial bias against blacks in Britain was evidenced by a 1950s survey of 100 women students at Oxford and Cambridge, 84 of whom reported they "would not be willing to marry an African"; see Clare Hanson, *Eugenics, Literature and Culture in Post-war Britain*, Routledge, 2013, p. 101.

[727] Carl Phelpstead, *Tolkien and Wales: Language, Literature and Identity*, Cardiff: University of Wales Press, 2011, p. 15.

[728] William Ripley, *Races of Europe: A Sociological Study*, Appleton, 1899. Ripley acknowledged the assistance of British anthropologist Alfred Haddon. For a brief discussion of this book and its influence see Ivan Hannaford, *Race: The History of an Idea in the West*, Woodrow Wilson Center Press, 1996, p. 329-330.

[729] John Rhys, *The Welsh People*, New York: Macmillan, 1900, p. 35 footnote 1.

[730] Simon J. Cook, "English history, British identity, Aryan villages: 1870-1914," online at *Academia*, viewed January 20, 2014.

[731] Dimitra Fimi, *Tolkien, Race, and Cultural History*, Palgrave MacMillan, 2010, p. 136-137.

[732] Elazar Barkan, *The Retreat of Scientific Racism: Changing concepts of race in Britain and the United States between the world wars*, Cambridge University Press, 1992 [reprinted 1996], p. 302-304.

[733] My citations are to the first American edition of the book: AC Haddon and Julien Huxley, *We Europeans: A Survey of "Racial" Problems*, New York: Harper and Brothers, 1936.

[734] Elazar Barkan, *The Retreat of Scientific Racism: Changing concepts of race in Britain and the United States between the world wars*, Cambridge University Press, 1992 [reprinted 1996], p. 296.

[735] Elazar Barkan, *The Retreat of Scientific Racism: Changing concepts of race in Britain and the United States between the world wars*, Cambridge University Press, 1992 [reprinted 1996], p. 302.

[736] Jonathan Marks, "Let's Move on from Race," 2009, viewed online March 14, 2012. During the early 1960s the challenge to race posed by *We Europeans* lost ground in the United States under the leadership of anthropologist Carleton Coon and the lawyers of the American Bar Association, who drew on Coon in an effort to obstruct the civil rights movement. See Vincent Sarich and Frank Miele, *Race: The Reality of Human Differences*, Westview Press, 2004, p. 94.

[737] AC Haddon and Julien Huxley, *We Europeans: A Survey of "Racial" Problems*, New York: Harper and Brothers, 1936, p. 73.

[738] AC Haddon and Julien Huxley, *We Europeans: A Survey of "Racial" Problems*, New York: Harper and Brothers, 1936, p. 147-151.

[739] Humphrey Carpenter, *The Letters of JRR Tolkien*, with the assistance of Christopher Tolkien, Houghton Mifflin, 2000 edition [original publication 1981], Tolkien to Stanley Unwin, July 25, 1938, # 29, p. 37.

[740] AC Haddon and Julien Huxley, *We Europeans: A Survey of "Racial" Problems*, New York: Harper and Brothers, 1936, 47-49, 72-74.

[741] Humphrey Carpenter, *The Letters of JRR Tolkien*, with the assistance of Christopher Tolkien, Houghton Mifflin, 2000 edition [original publication 1981], JRR Tolkien to Michael Tolkien, March 18, 1941, # 44, p. 55-56.

[742] Christine Chism, "Middle-earth, the Middle Ages, and the Aryan Nation: Myth and History in World War II," in Jane Chance, editor, *Tolkien the Medievalist*, Routledge, 2003, p. 63-92, see p. 63-64.

[743] Christine Chism, "Middle-earth, the Middle Ages, and the Aryan Nation: Myth and History in World War II," in Jane Chance, editor, *Tolkien the Medievalist*, Routledge, 2003, p. 72, 74.

[744] Clare Hanson, *Eugenics, Literature and Culture in Post-war Britain*, Routledge, 2013, p. 94-106.

[745] Humphrey Carpenter, *The Letters of JRR Tolkien*, with the assistance of Christopher Tolkien, Houghton Mifflin, 2000 edition [original publication 1981], Tolkien to Forrest Ackerman, undated June 1958, # 210, p. 274.

[746] Michael Martinez, "Is It True There Is Racism in *The Lord of the Rings*?" November 29, 2012, viewed online at middle-earth.xenite.org on September 14, 2014. Martinez wrote here that Tolkien "doesn't imply that the Orcs were Mongols or that the Mongols were Orcs – rather, he used a nightmarish caricature of Mongols as an archetype for a fearfully menacing enemy that would evoke the kind of terror once associated with the Mongols."

[747] Dimitra Fimi, *Tolkien, Race, and Cultural History*, Palgrave MacMillan, 2010, p. 155-157.

[748] Sandra Straubhaar, "Ethnic Diversity and Imperial Arrogance: Changing Attitudes toward Miscegenation and Multiculturalism in Tolkien's Middle-earth," paper dated March 20, 2003, online at *Academia*, viewed on January 29, 2014, p. 18. This paper saw publication: Sandra Straubhaar, "Myth, Late Roman History and Multiculturalism in Tolkien's Middle-earth," in Jane Chance editor, *Tolkien and the Invention of Myth: A Reader*, University Press of Kentucky, 2005, p. 101-117.

[749] *Encyclopedia Britannica*, Volume 9, 1911, entry for "Ethnology and ethnography," p. 851.

[750] Verlyn Flieger and Douglas A. Anderson, *Tolkien On Fairy-stories*, HarperCollins, 2008, p. 307. I don't know which edition of *Encyclopedia Britannica* Tolkien consulted for his 1938-1943 research project, but the comprehensive 11th edition published in 1911 would have been widely available.

[751] JRR Tolkien, *The Return of the Shadow*, in *The History of The Lord of the Rings, Part One*, Christopher Tolkien editor, Houghton Mifflin, 1988, p. 139, 142 endnote 13.

[752] JRR Tolkien, *The Return of the Shadow*, in *The History of The Lord of the Rings, Part One*, Christopher Tolkien editor, Houghton Mifflin, 1988, p. 309, 336.

[753] John Rhys, *Celtic Folklore: Welsh and Manx*, two volumes, Oxford: Clarendon Press, 1901, Volume Two. Rhys referred to fairy folk in Welsh tradition as having sallow skin; see p. 660, 667. He also referred to the study of "skulls and skins" (p. 664) and "swarthy long-skulls" (p. 666) and mathematical skills (p. 663-665) comparing fairy folk to Basque, and "swarthy brats" and "a swarthy population" (p. 668). Rhys made clear his own judgment of "superior physique of the more powerful population" constituting "blond babies" versus "dark complexion" and "swarthy brats." Rumor of fairy ancestry – which Rhys interpreted as aboriginal ancestry – provided reason in Wales for a quarrel "fought out with fists[.]" Rhys associated with this aboriginal / fairy ancestry (p. 668-669) "a swarthy population of short stumpy men occupying the most inaccessible districts of our country."

[754] Wayne Hammond and Christina Scull, *The Lord of the Rings: A Reader's Companion*, Houghton Mifflin, 2005, p. 153-154.

755 Joseph Jacobs, *English Fairy Tales*, London: David Nutt, 1890, p. 211-214.

756 Walter W. Skeat and James Britten, editors, *Reprinted Glossaries and Old Farming Words*, London: Trübner & Company, Part 4, Reprinted Glossaries Parts 18-22, 1879, p. 79.

757 John Beddoe, *The Races of Britain*, Trübner, 1885, p. 9.

758 Joseph Wright, *English Dialect Dictionary*, Oxford: Henry Frowde, 1905, Volume 5 R-S, p. 710.

759 Walter Johnson, *Folk-Memory or the Continuity of British Archaeology*, Oxford at the Clarendon Press, 1908, p. 52. The quote on the Chinese occurred in a chapter titled "Folk-Memory and Racial Continuity." These characteristics of eye-shape seemed to the author "to mark off the old 'Eskimo' or 'Palaeolithic' type."

760 Anonymous article, *The Seaman*, National Sailors' and Firemen's Union, volume 1 # 40, Friday, May 1, 1914, p. 6 (online record, University of Warwick, University Library, Modern Records Centre). The cited speech by Joseph Havelock Wilson was paraphrased here by the anonymous reporter.

761 Humphrey Carpenter, *The Letters of JRR Tolkien*, with the assistance of Christopher Tolkien, Houghton Mifflin, 2000 edition [original publication 1981], Tolkien to Stanley Unwin, October 13, 1938, # 34, p. 41.

762 JRR Tolkien, *The Treason of Isengard*, in *The History of The Lord of the Rings, Part Two*, Christopher Tolkien editor, Houghton Mifflin, 1989, p. 192.

763 JRR Tolkien, *The Treason of Isengard*, in *The History of The Lord of the Rings, Part Two*, Christopher Tolkien editor, Houghton Mifflin, 1989, p. 205 endnote 5.

764 JRR Tolkien, *The Treason of Isengard*, in *The History of The Lord of the Rings, Part Two*, Christopher Tolkien editor, Houghton Mifflin, 1989, p. 194.

765 JRR Tolkien, *The Treason of Isengard*, in *The History of The Lord of the Rings, Part Two*, christopher Tolkien editor, Houghton Mifflin, 1989, p. 202.

766 JRR Tolkien, *The Treason of Isengard*, in *The History of The Lord of the Rings, Part Two*, Christopher Tolkien editor, Houghton Mifflin, 1989, p. 330-339.

[767] Ivan Hannaford, *Race: The History of an Idea in the West*, Woodrow Wilson Center Press, 1996, p. 177.

[768] Simon J. Cook, "Concerning Hobbits," online essay at *The History Vault*, December 16, 2014.

[769] Christina Scull and Wayne Hammond, *The JRR Tolkien Companion and Guide: Chronology*, Houghton Mifflin, 2006, p. 50, 52, 55, 59; Mark T. Hooker, *Tolkien and Welsh*, Llyfrawr, 2012, p. vii; Carl Phelpstead, *Tolkien and Wales: Language, Literature, and Identity*, University of Wales Press, 2011, p. xx, 137 endnote 14.

[770] John Rhys, Untitled Address of the President of the Anthropology Section of the BAAS, dated September 6, 1900, in *Report of the Seventieth Meeting of the British Association for the Advancement of Science*, London: John Murray, 1900, p. 884-896.

[771] Christina Scull and Wayne Hammond, *The JRR Tolkien Companion and Guide: Chronology*, Houghton Mifflin, 2006, p. 39, 49, 51.

[772] WLH Duckworth, "On Anthropological Observations made by Mr. F. Laidlaw in the Malay Peninsula (Skeat Expedition)," in *Report of the Seventieth Meeting of the British Association for the Advancement of Science*, London: John Murray, 1900, p. 909-910.

[773] WLH Duckworth, "On Crania collected by Mr. J. Stanley Gardiner in his Expedition to Rotuma," in *Report of the Seventieth Meeting of the British Association for the Advancement of Science*, London: John Murray, 1900, p. 910.

[774] Humphrey Carpenter, *The Letters of JRR Tolkien*, with the assistance of Christopher Tolkien, Houghton Mifflin, 2000 edition [original publication 1981], Tolkien to Forrest Ackerman, undated June 1958, # 210, p. 274.

[775] JRR Tolkien, *The Treason of Isengard*, in *The History of The Lord of the Rings, Part Two*, Christopher Tolkien editor, Houghton Mifflin, 1989, p. 379. Christopher Tolkien noted here that his father would occasionally "doodle" words taken "from a newspaper that lay beside him" as he worked on the manuscript. This is his interpretation of the source of the words "Chinese bombers" and "Muar River" and "Japanese attack in Malaya[.]" Also see Christina Scull and Wayne Hammond, *The JRR Tolkien Companion and Guide:*

Chronology, Houghton Mifflin, 2006, p. 251 for mention of these "references to the Muar River and the Japanese attack on Malaya[.]" It is most logical that Tolkien set down these notes on a single occasion in late January 1942, inspired by a newspaper.

[776] JRR Tolkien, *The Treason of Isengard*, in *The History of The Lord of the Rings, Part Two*, Christopher Tolkien editor, Houghton Mifflin, 1989, p. 387, endnote 1. Christopher Tolkien cites the dates of "7-8 December 1941" and "16 January 1942" for the events referenced in his father's doddles on the Muar River and the Japanese invasion of Malaya.

[777] JRR Tolkien, *The Treason of Isengard*, in *The History of The Lord of the Rings, Part Two*, Christopher Tolkien editor, Houghton Mifflin, 1989, p. 382, 386.

[778] JRR Tolkien, *The Treason of Isengard*, in *The History of The Lord of the Rings, Part Two*, Christopher Tolkien editor, Houghton Mifflin, 1989, p. 410.

[779] JRR Tolkien, *The Treason of Isengard*, in *The History of The Lord of the Rings, Part Two*, Christopher Tolkien editor, Houghton Mifflin, 1989, p. 379.

[780] Walter Skeat, *Malay Magic*, London: Macmillan, 1900.

[781] "Malay Peninsula," in *Encyclopedia Britannica*, volume 17, Cambridge University Press, 1911 edition, p. 473.

[782] Tolkien amplified his 1942 characterization of diverse orcs in materials prepared during the late 1940s for the preface and appendices of *The Lord of the Rings*. He wrote that their "barbarous and unwritten speech" became diversified "into as many jargons as there were groups or settlements of Orcs"; and "the evil Power" experimented with cross-breeding Trolls and "the larger Orcs." See JRR Tolkien, *The Peoples of Middle-earth*, in *The History of Middle-earth, Volume XII*, Christopher Tolkien editor, Houghton Mifflin, 1996, p. 35-36.

[783] "The Malay," in *Encyclopedia Britannica*, volume 17, Cambridge University Press, 1911 edition, p. 475-476.

[784] JRR Tolkien, "The Choices of Master Samwise," *The Two Towers*. The drafting of this chapter seems to have occurred in various stages in 1942 and 1944, but the date of the insertion of an oblique reference to orkish pirates is not clear from the published manuscript materials in JRR Tolkien, *The*

Treason of Isengard, in *The History of The Lord of the Rings, Part Two*, Christopher Tolkien, editor, Houghton Mifflin, 1989, p. 330-339; JRR Tolkien, *The War of the Ring*, in *The History of The Lord of the Rings, Part Three*, Christopher Tolkien editor, Houghton Mifflin, 1990, p. 183-226.

[785] Tolkien wrote the first draft of "Flotsam and Jetsam" sometime during the second half of 1942 – he noted in a letter written at the end of that year that he had reached this chapter; see Humphrey Carpenter, *The Letters of JRR Tolkien*, with the assistance of Christopher Tolkien, Houghton Mifflin, 2000 edition [original publication 1981], Tolkien to Stanley Unwin, December 7, 1942, # 47, p. 58. Also see JRR Tolkien, *The War of the Ring*, in *The History of The Lord of the Rings, Part Three*, Houghton Mifflin, 1990, p. 59 endnote 10: "Flotsam and Jetsam" was written after June 1942. Publishing an account of the writing of this chapter, Christopher Tolkien did not present the original draft comments on half-orcs, saying only (p. 52) that this passage is "much the same" as the finished text.

[786] Tolkien revisited his half-orcs later in the final chapters of *The Lord of the Rings*, where they play a more direct role in the development of the plot – in "The Scouring of the Shire," written in 1948, we encounter more of these half-orcs; see JRR Tolkien, *Sauron Defeated*, in *The History of The Lord of the Rings, Part Four*, Christopher Tolkien editor, Houghton Mifflin, 1992, p. 13. The homecoming hobbits "were disturbed to see half a dozen large ill-favoured Men lounging against the inn-wall; they were squint-eyed and sallow-faced." These Men brought to Sam's mind "that friend of Bill Ferny's at Bree[.]" And we soon meet "a squint-eyed rascal calling the Ring-bearer 'little cock-a-whoop'."

[787] Humphrey Carpenter, *The Letters of JRR Tolkien*, with the assistance of Christopher Tolkien, Houghton Mifflin, 2000 edition [original publication 1981], Tolkien to Christopher Tolkien, August 12, 1944, # 78, p. 90.

[788] Anonymous article, *The Seaman*, National Sailors' and Firemen's Union, volume 1 # 40, Friday, May 1, 1914, p. 6 (online record, University of Warwick, University Library, Modern Records Centre). The cited speech by Joseph Havelock Wilson was paraphrased here by the anonymous reporter.

[789] Robert Tally Jr, "Let Us Now Praise Famous Orcs: Simple Humanity in Tolkien's Inhuman Creatures," *Mythlore*, Issue 111/112, Volume 29, # 1/2, Fall/Winter 2010, p. 17-28.

[790] Humphrey Carpenter, *The Letters of JRR Tolkien*, with the assistance of Christopher Tolkien, Houghton Mifflin, 2000 edition [original publication 1981], Tolkien to Christopher Tolkien, May 25, 1944, # 71, p. 82.

[791] Clare Hanson, *Eugenics, Literature and Culture in Post-war Britain*, Routledge, 2013.

[792] Clare Hanson, *Eugenics, Literature and Culture in Post-war Britain*, Routledge, 2013, p. 1. Tolkien mentioned William Beveridge in one letter; see Humphrey Carpenter, *The Letters of JRR Tolkien*, with the assistance of Christopher Tolkien, Houghton Mifflin, 2000 edition [original publication 1981], JRR Tolkien to Christopher Tolkien, August 22, 1944, # 79, p. 91. Beveridge was then serving as Master of University College, Oxford, and Tolkien mentioned his frequent appearance in news reports.

[793] Clare Hanson, *Eugenics, Literature and Culture in Post-war Britain*, Routledge, 2013, p. 68; Humphrey Carpenter, *The Letters of JRR Tolkien*, with the assistance of Christopher Tolkien, Houghton Mifflin, 2000 edition [original publication 1981], JRR Tolkien to Michael Tolkien, January 12, 1941, # 42, p. 48, 437 endnote 42. Tolkien mildly belittled Haldane in a 1937 letter: "We are not in Pembroke expected to descend to the level of a J.B.S. Haldane." See Tolkien to GE Selby, December 14, 1937, transcription online at Tolkien Gateway, viewed July 8, 2015.

[794] For letters written by JRR Tolkien to Naomi Mitchison see Humphrey Carpenter, *The Letters of JRR Tolkien*, with the assistance of Christopher Tolkien, Houghton Mifflin, 2000 edition [original publication 1981]: Tolkien to Naomi Mitchison, December 18, 1949, # 122, p. 133-134; Tolkien to Naomi Mitchison, April 25, 1954, # 144, p. 173-181; Tolkien to Naomi Mitchison, September 25, 1954, # 154, p. 196-199; # 155, a draft passage from # 154, p. 199-200; excerpt, Tolkien to Naomi Mitchison, June 29, 1955, # 164, p. 217; excerpt, Tolkien to Naomi Mitchison, December 8, 1955, # 176, p. 228-229 – a transcript of this entire letter is available online; excerpt, Tolkien to Naomi Mitchison, October 15, 1959, # 220, p. 300; p. 445 endnote for letter 154; another letter from Tolkien to Mitchison is known, but not published, dated November 8, 1959. According to Hammond and Scull's online addendum to *The JRR Tolkien Companion and Guide*, dated 10 April 2014, Tolkien wrote in this November 1959 letter that his vacation to Bournemouth was due to Mitchison.) Tolkien knew of Mitchison as early as 1915 when poems they wrote appeared together in an issue of *Oxford Poetry*. (*Oxford Poetry 1915*, edited by G.D.H.C and T.W.E. [Gerald Crow and T.W. Earp], Oxford:

Blackwell, 1915; see Naomi M. Haldane "Awakening of the Bacchae," p. 22; JRR Tolkien "Goblin Feet," p. 64-65. This was a very early publication for Tolkien.

[795] Christina Scull and Wayne Hammond, *The JRR Tolkien Companion and Guide: Reader's Guide*, Houghton Mifflin, 2006, p. 592-593.

[796] Humphrey Carpenter, *The Letters of JRR Tolkien*, with the assistance of Christopher Tolkien, Houghton Mifflin, 2000 edition [original publication 1981], Tolkien unsent draft letter to CS Lewis, circa 1943, # 49, p. 62.

[797] Julian Huxley quoted in Simon Frankel, "The Eclipse of Sexual Selection Theory," in *Sexual Knowledge, Sexual Science: The History of Attitudes to Sexuality*, edited by Roy Porter and Mikuláš Teich, Cambridge University Press, 1994, p. 167.

[798] Julian Huxley, "The Vital Importance of Eugenics," *Harper's Monthly Magazine*, volume 163, August 1931, p. 326.

[799] Daniel Kevles, *In the Name of Eugenics: Genetics and the Uses of Human Heredity*, University of California Press, 1985, p. 113-134.

[800] JRR Tolkien, *Morgoth's Ring, the Later Silmarillion, Part One*, in *The History of Middle-earth, Volume X*, Christopher Tolkien editor, Houghton Mifflin, 1993, p. 73-74, 78, 109-110, 123-124.

[801] JRR Tolkien, *Morgoth's Ring, the Later Silmarillion, Part One*, in *The History of Middle-earth, Volume X*, Christopher Tolkien, editor, Houghton Mifflin, 1993, p. 406, 408-424.

[802] JRR Tolkien, *Morgoth's Ring, the Later Silmarillion, Part One*, in *The History of Middle-earth, Volume X*, Christopher Tolkien editor, Houghton Mifflin, 1993, p. 415-421. Tolkien's final notes on orcs came sometime after early November 1969, see p. 421-424.

[803] JRR Tolkien, *Morgoth's Ring, the Later Silmarillion*, Christopher Tolkien editor, 1993, p. 416.

[804] "The Grey Annals," JRR Tolkien, *The War of the Jewels, the Later Silmarillion, Part Two*, in *The History of Middle-earth, Volume XI*, Christopher Tolkien

editor, Houghton Mifflin, 1994, p. 12. The Avari were Elves who never made it to Valinor.

[805] JRR Tolkien, *The War of the Jewels, the Later Silmarillion, Part Two*, Christopher Tolkien editor, 1994, p. 15-17, 36, 52-53, 56-60, 72-79, 82, 84-86, 89, 94-97.

[806] Christina Scull and Wayne Hammond, *The JRR Tolkien Companion and Guide: Chronology*, Houghton Mifflin, 2006, p. 510-511.

[807] Humphrey Carpenter, *The Letters of JRR Tolkien*, with the assistance of Christopher Tolkien, Houghton Mifflin, 2000 edition [original publication 1981], see various letters written between September 7 1957 and June 1958, p. 260-277.

[808] Christina Scull and Wayne Hammond, *The JRR Tolkien Companion and Guide: Chronology*, Houghton Mifflin, 2006, p. 522, 524.

[809] Christina Scull and Wayne Hammond, *The JRR Tolkien Companion and Guide: Chronology*, Houghton Mifflin, 2006, p. 524-525, 526, 527-529.

[810] AC Haddon and Julien Huxley, *We Europeans: A Survey of "Racial" Problems*, New York: Harper and Brothers, 1936, p. 73.

[811] Michael Organ, "Tolkien's *Japonisme*: Prints, Dragons and a Great Wave," *Tolkien Studies* 10, 2013, p. 105-122; viewed at Research Online 11/15/2015. Organ made no mention of Tolkien's Mongol-type orcs in his analysis. Tolkien's 1914 purchase of Japanese prints is given very brief notice in Humphrey Carpenter, *Tolkien: The Authorized Biography*, Houghton Mifflin, 1977, p. 69.

[812] Anonymous article, *The Seaman*, National Sailors' and Firemen's Union, volume 1 # 40, Friday, May 1, 1914, p. 6 (online record, University of Warwick, University Library, Modern Records Centre). The cited speech by Joseph Havelock Wilson was paraphrased here by the anonymous reporter.

[813] Anonymous article, *The Seaman*, volume 1 # 40, Friday, May 1, 1914, p. 8 (online record, University of Warwick, University Library, Modern Records Centre).

[814] JRR Tolkien, *Morgoth's Ring, the Later Silmarillion, Part One*, in *The History of Middle-earth, Volume X*, Christopher Tolkien editor, Houghton Mifflin, 1993, p. 415-421. Tolkien's final notes on orcs came sometime after early November 1969, see p. 421-424.

[815] William Ripley, *Races of Europe: A Sociological Study*, Appleton, 1899, p. 462. Ripley rejected the European "Turanian" aborigine hypothesis and favored an alternate view involving an ancient aboriginal "long-headed" population and an invading "broad-headed" population – perhaps Scythians.

[816] Max Müller, *Chips from a German Workshop*, in two volumes, Longmans Green, 1868, volume 1, p. 65.

[817] George Dasent, *Popular Tales from the Norse*, second edition, Edinburgh: David Douglas, 1903, p. xxv. In his "Preface" Müller specified that "Turanians" included Finns and Mongolians (Müller, *Chips from a German Workshop*, 1868, volume 1, p. xiv). For a general survey of referencing of Mongolic people in British Victorian folklore see Carole Silver, *Strange and Secret Peoples: Fairies and Victorian Consciousness*, Oxford University Press, 1999, p. 43-50.

[818] George Dasent, *Popular Tales from the Norse*, 1903, p. xxxii.

[819] JRR Tolkien, *The Shaping of Middle-earth*, in *The History of Middle-earth, Volume IV*, Christopher Tolkien editor, Houghton Mifflin, 1986, p. 12.

[820] David MacRitchie, *The Testimony of Tradition*, Kegan Paul, Trench, Trübner, 1890, p. 1-11.

[821] David MacRitchie, *The Testimony of Tradition*, Kegan Paul, Trench, Trübner, 1890, p. 174-175, also see p. 143-144 footnote 1.

[822] David MacRitchie, *The Testimony of Tradition*, Kegan Paul, Trench, Trübner, 1890, p. 190-193.

[823] Walter Y. Evans-Wentz, *The Fairy-Faith in Celtic Countries*, Oxford University Press, 1911 – for the reference to "Mongol type" folk in Cornwall see p. 166-167. Evans-Wentz summarized and dismissed David MacRitchie's theories about fairies as Skraeling Finn-men; see p. xxii-xxiii. John Rhys

contributed a short essay on Welsh fairy lore to Evans-Wentz's book; see p. 135-137.

[824] Tolkien's 1958 mention of "Mongol-types" appeared in Humphrey Carpenter, *The Letters of JRR Tolkien*, with the assistance of Christopher Tolkien, Houghton Mifflin, 2000 edition [original publication 1981], Tolkien to Forrest Ackerman, undated June 1958, # 210, p. 274. The official Tolkien biography by Humphrey Carpenter appeared during the 1970s, approved by the Tolkien Estate; see Humphrey Carpenter, *Tolkien: The Authorized Biography*, Houghton Mifflin, 1977.

[825] For an excellent consideration of Carpenter's perspective on his biography of Tolkien see Douglas Anderson, "Obituary" for Carpenter in *Tolkien Studies* # 2, 2005, p. 217-224. Given the fact that Tolkien's writings have not been made fully available to researchers by the Tolkien Estate, it is impossible to guess whether unreleased papers contain further details shedding light pertaining to racial Asians. Christina Scull and Wayne Hammond have noted that "the most private of Tolkien's surviving papers remain private..." (Christina Scull and Wayne Hammond, *The JRR Tolkien Companion and Guide: Chronology*, Houghton Mifflin, 2006, p. x). Their vast and important erudition on Tolkien is rooted in (p. xv) the mentorship of Christopher Tolkien and the permission of the Tolkien Estate for the use of "copyright and permissions to quote from Tolkien's writings." We can only guess how these factors have shaped their scholarship.

[826] Patrick Curry, *Defending Middle-earth, Tolkien: Myth and Modernity*, Houghton Mifflin, 2004 [1997], for Curry's entire consideration of racism see p. 30-31. Also see Patrick Curry, "Tolkien and His Critics: A Critique," in Thomas Honegger editor, *Root and Branch: Approaches towards Understanding Tolkien*, Walking Tree, 2005 [1999], p. 75-139.

[827] Christina Scull and Wayne Hammond, *The JRR Tolkien Companion and Guide: Reader's Guide*, Houghton Mifflin, 2006, p. 791-794.

[828] Wayne Hammond and Christina Scull, *The Lord of the Rings: A Reader's Companion*, Houghton Mifflin, 2005, p. 153-154 for discussion of "squint-eyed"; and p. 375-380 discussion of orcs in "The Uruk-Hai."

[829] Tom Shippey, "Literature, Twentieth Century: Influence of Tolkien," in *JRR Tolkien Encyclopedia: Scholarship and Critical Assessment*, Michael Drout editor, New York: Routledge, 2007, p. 382.

[830] Robert Tally Jr, "Let Us Now Praise Famous Orcs: Simple Humanity in Tolkien's Inhuman Creatures," *Mythlore*, Issue 111/112, Volume 29, # 1/2, Fall/Winter 2010, p. 20.

[831] Dimitra Fimi, *Tolkien, Race and Cultural History: From Fairies to Hobbits*, Palgrave Macmillan, 2010, p. 154-158. Advising on the teaching of Tolkien and race a few years later, Fimi decided to further boil down her already minimal book discussion on Tolkien's racialized orcs, managing to fit the entire topic into this endnote: "Other relevant discussion points are the idea of the noble savage, interracial marriage, and racial characteristics of the Orcs (see Fimi 150-157)..."; see Dimitra Fimi, "Teaching Tolkien and Race," in *Approaches to Teaching Tolkien's* The Lord of the Rings *and Other Works*, Leslie Donovan editor, MLA, 2015, p. 144-149. It is puzzling why she would advise the teaching of Tolkien and race in this fashion, minimizing Tolkien's most explicit use of real world racial thinking, and choosing such a veiled and oblique reference to his Mongol-type modeling. It is difficult to see how this strategy would be helpful to anyone who wants to truly understand the topic at hand.

[832] Jason Fisher, review of Dimitra Fimi's *Tolkien, Race and Cultural History*, viewed September 14, 2015 online on the review page of the Mythopoeic Society, review originally published in *Mythlore* 111/112, Volume 29, # 1 and 2, 2010 Fall/Winter. Fisher's quote from Fimi was excerpted from a longer statement on p. 157 of her book.

[833] Jonathan Marks, "Solving the riddle of race," in *Studies in History and Philosophy of Biological and Biomedical Sciences*, 2016, p. 1-4; the quote is from p. 3. Marks also made honorable mention of *We Europeans* as "influential" (p. 2): "For the early conjunction of evolutionary and racial theory, one should probably look rather at the influential 1935 book *We Europeans*..."

[834] Dimitra Fimi, "Teaching Tolkien and Race," in *Approaches to Teaching Tolkien's* The Lord of the Rings *and Other Works*, Leslie Donovan editor, MLA, 2015, p. 148.

[835] James McNelis, "Teaching the Critical Debate over *The Lord of the Rings*," in *Approaches to Teaching Tolkien's* The Lord of the Rings *and Other Works*, Leslie Donovan editor, MLA, 2015, p. 44-49. McNelis is listed as "professor of English at Wilmington College, Ohio." Beyond the papers by Fimi and

McNelis, this collection of essays contains only one other brief mention of the topic of race (p. 88).

[836] Christine Chism, "Middle-earth, the Middle Ages, and the Aryan Nation: Myth and History in World War II," in Jane Chance, editor, *Tolkien the Medievalist*, Routledge, 2003, p. 66-67.

Endnotes: Tolkien's Black Men

[837] JRR Tolkien, *A Secret Vice: Tolkien on Invented Languages*, Dimitra Fimi and Andrew Higgins editors, HarperCollins, 2016, p. 65, "Essay on Phonetic Symbolism."

[838] For drawings of black goblins in Tolkien's Father Christmas letters see JRR Tolkien, *Letters From Father Christmas*, Baillie Tolkien editor, Houghton Mifflin, 2004, letters for 1933, 1938.

[839] Tolkien's 1935 drawing of a stylized black-skinned doll or child is directly positioned beside this comment: "Hope you enjoy the PANTOMIME"; this refers to a traditional English Christmas performance, a fairytale theater enactment.

[840] Tolkien wrote his first mention of "black Men" in late August 1938; see JRR Tolkien, *The Return of the Shadow*, in *The History of The Lord of the Rings, Part One*, Christopher Tolkien editor, Houghton Mifflin, 1988, p. 151; on p. 152 "those black fellows" appeared.

[841] JRR Tolkien, *The Return of the Shadow*, in *The History of The Lord of the Rings, Part One*, Christopher Tolkien editor, Houghton Mifflin, 1988, p. 151, 339, 340, 344.

[842] James Hardy, editor, *The Denham Tracts*, Volume II, published by David Nutt 1895; Folk-Lore Society, volume 35, 1895, p. 77-78. In addition to to "hobbits" and "black-men," one additional term could have been adapted by Tolkien: night-bats to shadowbats in *Roverrandom*.

[843] Joseph Wright, *English Dialect Dictionary*, Oxford: Henry Frowde, 1898, Volume 1 A-C, p. 284.

[844] Several possible examples of "black-men" appear in James Hardy, editor, *The Denham Tracts*, Volume II, London: David Nutt 1895; Folk-Lore Society,

volume 35, 1895; see p. 276, where a "big dark man" appears, very frightful, and p. 277-278 where a man gets lost and meets "a gentleman dressed in black" with cloven feet.

[845] James Hardy, editor, *The Denham Tracts*, Volume II, published by David Nutt 1895; Folk-Lore Society, volume 35, 1895, p. 77-78.

[846] Joe Louis quoted in Paul Gilroy, *Against Race: Imagining Political Culture Beyond the Color Line*, Cambridge Massachusetts: The Belknap Press, 2000, p. 168.

[847] Simon Winchester, *The Meaning of Everything: The Story of the Oxford English Dictionary*, Oxford University Press, 2003, p. 206 footnote 7discusses Tolkien's OED slip regarding the word "wallop" and the illustration of usage. Winchester wrote that Tolkien's "seniors at the Dictionary thought it too offensive (and insufficiently illustrative) and so did not use it."

[848] J.H. Balfour Browne, *South Africa: A Glance at Current Conditions and Politics*, Longmans Greene, 1905. On p. 89 Balfour-Browne mentioned a "phrase of obloquy which we used to justify the war" – meaning a slogan that helped to motive the British to prosecute the Second Boer War. The statement characterized Boers as wishing to be "free to whip their niggers." This is probably a version of the phrase that Tolkien documented in his 1919 slip for the *Oxford English Dictionary*: "the right to wallop one's own nigger." For an example of the use of the phrase in debates about South Africa see *The Parliamentary Debates*, volume 77, October 20, 1899, p. 445: "Last evening I somewhat rudely contradicted the right hon. the Colonial Secretary, when he said that the real object of the Great Trek was because the Boers had been robbed of their liberty to 'wallop their own niggers.' That statement was a gross falsehood."

[849] Humphrey Carpenter, *The Letters of JRR Tolkien*, with the assistance of Christopher Tolkien, Houghton Mifflin, 2000 edition [original publication 1981], Tolkien to Stanley Unwin, July 25, 1938, # 29, p. 37.

[850] Dimitra Fimi, *Tolkien, Race, and Cultural History*, Palgrave MacMillan, 2010, p. 136-137.

[851] Stuart D. Lee, "JRR Tolkien and The Wanderer: From Edition to Application," in *Tolkien Studies*, # 6, 2009, p. 189-211, see p. 195 note by Tolkien probably dating to circa 1942, and see chart p. 192.

[852] Humphrey Carpenter, *The Letters of JRR Tolkien*, with the assistance of Christopher Tolkien, Houghton Mifflin, 2000 edition [original publication 1981], Tolkien to Naomi Mitchison December 8, 1955, # 176, p. 229; Tolkien interview with Denys Gueroult January 20, 1965, quoted in Zak Cramer, "Jewish Influense in Middle-earth," *Mallorn*, volume 44, August 2006, p. 9-16; for a comparison of the Dwarvish language with Hebrew see Magnus Åberg, "An Analysis of Dwarvish," in *Adra Philology 1*, edited by Anders Stenström, Arda Society, 2007, p. 42-65. Renee Vink has argued that Tolkien's insertion of Jewish colorations into his dwarves occurred after the writing of *The Hobbit*, and evidence for anti-Semitism in this portrayal is weak; see Renee Vink, "'Jewish' Dwarves: Tolkien and Anti-Semitic Stereotyping," viewed online at Academia 11/14/2015 – this paper is not dated but it appears to be the same paper that appeared in *Tolkien Studies* 10, 2013, p. 127-157.

[853] Patrick Curry, "Tolkien and His Critics: A Critique," in Thomas Honegger editor, *Root and Branch: Approaches towards Understanding Tolkien*, Walking Tree, 2005 [1999], p. 75-139.

[854] Margaret Sinex, "'Monsterized Saracens,' Tolkien's Haradrim, and Other Medieval 'Fantasy Products,'" *Tolkien Studies*, volume 7, 2010, p. 175-196.

[855] Audrey Smedley and Brian Smedley, *Race in North America: Origin and Evolution of a Worldview*, Westview Press, 2012, p. 98-99.

[856] M. Lindsay Kaplan, "The Jewish Body in Black and White in Medieval and Early Modern England," in *Philological Quarterly*, volume 92, # 1, 2013, p. 41-65.

[857] E.R. Truitt, "Fantasy North," *Aeon*, 15 February 2016.

[858] Audrey Smedley and Brian Smedley, *Race in North America: Origin and Evolution of a Worldview*, Westview Press, 2012, p. 94. Other researchers suggest that Elizabethan London could have had a significant population of residents from Sub-Saharan Africa, with one scholar counting 89 references to Africans, with an extrapolated potential population as high as 900 (see Jacob Selwood, *Diversity and Difference in Early Modern London*, Ashgate, 2010, p. 10 footnote 32).

[859] Anu Korhonen, "Washing the Ethiopian white: Conceptualizing black skin in Renaissance England," in *Black Africans in Renaissance Europe*, TF Earle and KJP Lowe editors, Cambridge University Press, 2005, p. 94-112, quote from p. 110.

[860] Wayne Hammond and Christina Scull, *The Lord of the Rings: A Reader's Companion*, Houghton Mifflin, 2005, p. 343; also see discussion of black symbolism on p. 566-567.

[861] *Brothers Grimm's Household Tales*, Volume 2, translated by Margaret Hunt, London: George Bell and Sons, in two volumes, 1884, p. 28-34.

[862] Verlyn Flieger and Douglas A. Anderson, *Tolkien On Fairy-stories*, HarperCollins, 2008, p. 307.

[863] Humphrey Carpenter, *The Letters of JRR Tolkien*, with the assistance of Christopher Tolkien, Houghton Mifflin, 2000 edition [original publication 1981], Notes on WH Auden's review, circa 1956, # 183, p. 243.

[864] JRR Tolkien, *The Lost Road and Other Writings*, in *The History of Middle-earth, Volume V*, Christopher Tolkien editor, Houghton Mifflin, 1987, p. 91.

[865] Humphrey Carpenter, *The Letters of JRR Tolkien*, with the assistance of Christopher Tolkien, Houghton Mifflin, 2000 edition [original publication 1981], JRR Tolkien to Michael Tolkien, July 29, 1966, # 289, p. 369-370.

[866] JRR Tolkien, *The Book of Lost Tales, Part One*, in *The History of Middle-earth, Volume I*, Christopher Tolkien editor, Houghton Mifflin, 1983, p. 261. For an early translation of "Morgoth" as "Black Strife" see JRR Tolkien, *The Book of Lost Tales, Part Two*, in *The History of Middle-earth, Volume II*, Christopher Tolkien editor, Houghton Mifflin, 1984, p. 67. Also see JRR Tolkien, *A Secret Vice: Tolkien on Invented Languages*, Dimitra Fimi and Andrew Higgins editors, HarperCollins, 2016, p. xxiii-xxiv.

[867] JRRTolkien, "Sigelwara Land," *Medium Ævum*, volume 1, # 3, December 1932, p. 183-196; JRRTolkien, "Sigelwara Land," *Medium Ævum*, volume 3, # 2, June 1934, p. 95-111. For a brief note by Christopher Tolkien on these papers see JRR Tolkien, *The Treason of Isengard*, in *The History of The Lord of the Rings, Part Two*, Christopher Tolkien editor, Houghton Mifflin, 1989, p. 439 endnote 4 referencing terms used on p. 434-435.

[868] Tom Shippey, *The Road to Middle-earth: How JRR Tolkien Created a New Mythology*, Houghton Mifflin, 2003, p. 42. LJ Swain also noted the "apparent" connection between the "Sigelware" and Balrogs; see LJ Swain, "Exodus, Edition of," in *JRR Tolkien Encyclopedia: Scholarship and Critical Assessment*, Michael Drout editor, New York: Routledge, 2007, p. 181.

[869] Tolkien created his Balrogs between 1916 and 1920 in the course of writing "The Fall of Gondolin"; see JRR Tolkien, *The Book of Lost Tales, Part Two*, in *The History of Middle-earth, Volume II*, Christopher Tolkien editor, Houghton Mifflin, 1984, p. 144-220, "The Fall of Gondolin." The leader of the Balrogs is Gothmog, the son of Melko; see JRR Tolkien, *The Book of Lost Tales, Part Two*, Christopher Tolkien editor, 1984, p. 183, and see JRR Tolkien, *The Book of Lost Tales, Part One*, Christopher Tolkien editor, 1983, p. 93, Christopher notes: "...Melko has a son ('by Ulbandi') called Kosomot; this, it will emerge later, was Gothmog Lord of Balrogs, whom Ecthelion slew in Gondolin." Tolkien provided an explanation of the root-meaning of the term "balrog" as (roughly) an evil felon: JRR Tolkien, *The Shaping of Middle-earth*, in *The History of Middle-earth, Volume IV*, Christopher Tolkien editor, Houghton Mifflin, 1986, p. 209; for internal etymology of the term see JRR Tolkien, *The Lost Road and Other Writings*, in *The History of Middle-earth, Volume V*, Christopher Tolkien editor, Houghton Mifflin, 1987, p. 377, 384, 404.

[870] JRR Tolkien, *The Lays of Beleriand*, in *The History of Middle-earth, Volume III*, Christopher Tolkien editor, Houghton Mifflin, 1985, p. 100, 296.

[871] JRR Tolkien, *The Lays of Beleriand*, in *The History of Middle-earth, Volume III*, Christopher Tolkien editor, Houghton Mifflin, 1985, p. 7, 98.

[872] JRR Tolkien, *The Shaping of Middle-earth*, in *The History of Middle-earth, Volume IV*, Christopher Tolkien editor, Houghton Mifflin, 1986, p. 93; JRR Tolkien, *The Lost Road and Other Writings*, in *The History of Middle-earth, Volume V*, Christopher Tolkien editor, Houghton Mifflin, 1987, p. 233. For the likely initial translation of the name "Morgoth" as "Black Strife" see JRR Tolkien, *The Book of Lost Tales, Part Two*, in *The History of Middle-earth, Volume II*, Christopher Tolkien editor, Houghton Mifflin, 1984, p. 67.

[873] JRR Tolkien, *The Treason of Isengard*, in *The History of The Lord of the Rings, Part Two*, Christopher Tolkien editor, Houghton Mifflin, 1989, p. 197. Tolkien added a note to this draft (p. 199), a reminder to revise the "description of Balrog" to make it more nebulous in form, just an impression of a "man's shape."

[874] Christina Scull and Wayne Hammond, *The JRR Tolkien Companion and Guide: Chronology*, Houghton Mifflin, 2006, p. 252-253; JRR Tolkien, *The Treason of Isengard*, Christopher Tolkien editor, Houghton Mifflin, 1989, p. 1, 430-431.

[875] JRR Tolkien, *The Treason of Isengard*, in *The History of The Lord of the Rings, Part Two*, Christopher Tolkien editor, Houghton Mifflin, 1989, p. 194.

[876] LJ Swain, "Exodus, Edition of," in *JRR Tolkien Encyclopedia: Scholarship and Critical Assessment*, Michael Drout editor, New York: Routledge, 2007, p. 181.

[877] Christopher Tolkien did not include the full passage where the black half-trolls first appeared in the early manuscript material; he instead mentioned a rewritten passage that listed Gothmog, the Variags of Khand, and "the black 'half-trolls' of Far Harad"; see JRR Tolkien, *The War of the Ring*, in *The History of The Lord of the Rings, Part Three*, Christopher Tolkien editor, Houghton Mifflin, 1990, p. 369. He included few clues useful for dating the material in the chapter, but preceding textual material was written after October 1944 (p. 312), so the original version of this passage seems to have been written sometime toward the end of 1944 or later. At the end of November 1944 JRR sent to Christopher completed manuscripts of "Shelob's Lair" and "The Choices of Master Samwise," and he described later material as having been "written or sketched"; see Humphrey Carpenter, *The Letters of JRR Tolkien*, with the assistance of Christopher Tolkien, Houghton Mifflin, 2000 edition [original publication 1981], Tolkien to Christopher Tolkien, November 29, 1944, # 91, p. 104. This suggests that the making of his "black people like half-trolls" could have happened during November or December of 1944. In the final published version of "The Battle of the Pelennor Fields" Tolkien referred to "black people like half-trolls" and later in the chapter he mentioned colorless "troll-men."

[878] Tom Shippey's argument that Tolkien meant for his folk of Far Harad to reflect Anglo-Saxon ideology and not his own view of Africans can be found in Dimitra Fimi, "Teaching Tolkien and Race," in *Approaches to Teaching Tolkien's* The Lord of the Rings *and Other Works*, Leslie Donovan editor, MLA, 2015, p. 146. Shippey's argument appeared for a time on the publisher's website and can be treated as an official effort to insulate Tolkien from charges of racism.

[879] Margaret Sinex, "'Monsterized Saracens,' Tolkien's Haradrim, and Other Medieval 'Fantasy Products,'" *Tolkien Studies*, volume 7, 2010, p. 178-183, 187-188.

[880] For Tolkien's characterization of the Gondorians as resembling Egyptians with Hebraic theology see Humphrey Carpenter, *The Letters of JRR Tolkien*, with the assistance of Christopher Tolkien, Houghton Mifflin, 2000 edition [original publication 1981], Tolkien to Rhona Beare, October 14, 1958, # 211, p. 281; and see p. 283 footnote for reference to 6000 year time frame from the fall of Mordor to the present.

[881] Humphrey Carpenter, *The Letters of JRR Tolkien*, with the assistance of Christopher Tolkien, Houghton Mifflin, 2000 edition [original publication 1981], Tolkien to Christopher Tolkien, April 18, 1944, # 61, p. 73. According to Humphrey Carpenter's brief introductions to a sequence of 1944 letters, Christopher left for South Africa in January 1944 "to train as a pilot"; and in April had arrived "at a camp in the Transvaal."

[882] J.H. Balfour Browne, *South Africa: A Glance at Current Conditions and Politics*, Longmans Greene, 1905, p. 30-39; also see p. 43-52 for a discussion of Chinese laborers in South Africa; see p. 79-93 for a discussion of the Bantu and Boer history.

[883] Humphrey Carpenter, *The Letters of JRR Tolkien*, with the assistance of Christopher Tolkien, Houghton Mifflin, 2000 edition [original publication 1981], JRR Tolkien to Christopher Tolkien, January 18, 1945, # 95, p. 108. The book Tolkien referenced in this letter was Frank Stenton, *Anglo-Saxon England*, Oxford at the Clarendon Press, 1943.

[884] AC Haddon and Julien Huxley, *We Europeans: A Survey of "Racial" Problems*, New York: Harper and Brothers, 1936, p. 229.

[885] Clare Hanson, *Eugenics, Literature and Culture in Post-war Britain*, Routledge, 2013, p. 99-101. Hanson noted that the riots were centered on an assault on a "mixed race couple by a gang of white youths [.]" A news report in 2002 cited recently declassified police reports showing that the police knew the Notting Hill civil unrest was racially motivated but suppressed that information (Alan Travis, "After 44 years secret papers reveal truth about five nights of violence in Notting Hill," *The Guardian*, Saturday 24 August 2002). The police reports showed that the rioting was "triggered by 300- to 400-strong 'Keep Britain White' mobs[.]"

[886] For brief comments on the negative response of British mainstream society to American popular music of the mid-1950s see Philip Norman, *John Lennon: The Life*, Ecco, 2008, p. 84-85, describing John Lennon's early musical world and "adult Britain's hatred and terror of rock 'n' roll and the resolve to stamp it out..."; also see p. 93-94. A slightly younger Keith Richards became aware of American music and often had no idea what race the musicians might be, and he describes a London of the early 1960s filled with enclaves of American music "purists"; see Keith Richards with James Fox, *Life*, Little Brown, 2010, p. 72, 82-83.

[887] Humphrey Carpenter, *The Letters of JRR Tolkien*, with the assistance of Christopher Tolkien, Houghton Mifflin, 2000 edition [original publication 1981], JRR Tolkien to Christopher Bretherton, July 16, 1964, # 257, p. 345. Tolkien knew of the prospect of a Beatles film based on *The Lord of the Rings*; see Christina Scull and Wayne Hammond, *The JRR Tolkien Companion and Guide: Chronology*, Houghton Mifflin, 2006, p. 740, where Rayner Unwin assured Tolkien in 1968 that the Beatles were probably not involved in plans for a film. The negotiations for Tolkien's film rights also involved discussions on a second film concept involving Heinz Edelmann, the Art Designer for *Yellow Submarine*. For mention of this animated film see Christina Scull and Wayne Hammond, *The JRR Tolkien Companion and Guide: Chronology*, Houghton Mifflin, 2006, p. 737, quote by Tolkien in January 1969 of his distaste for art samples by Heinz Edelmann as "the lowest point in foul vulgarity." Scull and Hammond suggested that the samples could have been from *Yellow Submarine*. Edelmann recalled that after completing *Yellow Submarine* he was involved in a project to make an animated movie based on *The Lord of the Rings*, but "We never got the rights and the finance" (Heinz Edelmann radio interview with Robert Hieronimus, October 28, 1993; transcript viewed online 11/30/2015). According to David Hughes, the style would have featured less color, with the story as "a sort of operatic impression" modeled on Akira Kurosawa (David Hughes, *Tales from Development Hell*, 2011; viewed online 12/1/2015). Since Edelmann's vision for the film differed from *Yellow Submarine* it seems unlikely that the samples that Tolkien received (and despised) were from that film.

[888] Christina Scull and Wayne Hammond, *The JRR Tolkien Companion and Guide: Chronology*, Houghton Mifflin, 2006, p. 735. Joy Hill's reminiscence seems to apply most directly to visits she had with Tolkien after he moved to Poole in August 1968 (see p. 731).

Endnotes: The White Wizards

[889] John Rateliff, *The History of the Hobbit, Part One: Mr. Baggins*, Houghton Mifflin, 2007, p. 48: "Certainly the phrase 'Gandalf the Grey' is never used in *The Hobbit*..."

[890] John Rateliff, *The History of the Hobbit, Part Two: Return to Bag-End*, 2007, p. 696 endnote 4.

[891] JRR Tolkien, *The Treason of Isengard*, in *The History of The Lord of the Rings, Part Two*, Houghton Mifflin, 1989, p. 22. This mention of the White Council came in a draft of material that eventually became "The Shadow of the Past." It seems clear that Tolkien was repeating an idea from *The Hobbit* with no added depth just yet. Gandalf tells Frodo: "Let me see – it was after the White Council in the South that I first began to give serious thought to Bilbo's ring." The passage went on to mention "wizards" but without any detail.

[892] JRR Tolkien, *The Treason of Isengard*, Christopher Tolkien editor, 1989, p. 34.

[893] JRR Tolkien, *The Treason of Isengard*, Christopher Tolkien editor, 1989, p. 70, note dated August 26-27, 1940: "The wizard Saramond the White [written above at the same time: Saramund the Grey] or Grey Saruman[.]"

[894] JRR Tolkien, *The Treason of Isengard*, Christopher Tolkien editor, 1989, p. 82: "Yes, I, Gandalf the Grey...." This is the first use of this name. The manuscript may have been written after August 1940 or during that period.

[895] JRR Tolkien, *The Treason of Isengard*, Christopher Tolkien editor, 1989, p. 132: Radagast says to Gandalf: "It was Saruman the [Grey>] White..." This phrase is repeated again. Then: "Radagast the Grey [in pencil> Brown]. Thereafter on this page and the next we find Saruman the White, Gandalf the Grey, and Radagast the Brown. It was here in the late 1940 manuscript that Tolkien settled the wizard color chart. This is Saruman's declaration to Gandalf about breaking white into many colors. See p. 138 endnote 26 and p. 140 endnotes 42 and 43.

[896] The Galadriel chapters and notes were written on paper dated August 1940 in one complete manuscript, much emended and rewritten; see JRR Tolkien, *The Treason of Isengard*, Christopher Tolkien editor, 1989, p. 217.

Christopher Tolkien described (p. 261) a typescript he made of part of the chapter in early August 1942, and cites the probable composition date of late 1941 for the original materials of this chapter. For an estimate of "towards the end of 1941" as the date of authorship of the Lothlórien chapters see Christina Scull and Wayne Hammond, *The JRR Tolkien Companion and Guide: Chronology*, Houghton Mifflin, 2006, p. 250.

[897] JRR Tolkien, *The Treason of Isengard*, Christopher Tolkien editor, 1989, p. 233.

[898] JRR Tolkien, *The Treason of Isengard*, Christopher Tolkien editor, 1989, p. 246-251.

[899] JRR Tolkien, *The Treason of Isengard*, Christopher Tolkien editor, 1989, p. 405 endnote 23: Christopher Tolkien notes that *wicce* and *wicca* both are Old English terms for witch, with *wicca* masculine and *wicce* feminine.

[900] JRR Tolkien, *The Treason of Isengard*, Christopher Tolkien editor, 1989, p. 250.

[901] Walter W. Skeat and James Britten, editors, *Reprinted Glossaries and Old Farming Words*, London: Trübner & Company, Part 4, Reprinted Glossaries Parts 18-22, 1879, p. 100.

[902] William Holloway, *A General Dictionary of Provincialisms*, London: John Russell Smith, 1840, p. 190: "WISE-MAN, A wizard. In the south a conjuror is called a Cunning-man." Tolkien might have had these conceptions and terms in mind as early as the mid-1920s, as we can see in an undated text that followed *The Book of Lost Tales*. In a short fragment we find a description of Melko as "cunning and very deep in wisdom..." (see JRR Tolkien, *The Shaping of Middle-earth*, in *The History of Middle-earth, Volume IV*, Christopher Tolkien editor, Houghton Mifflin, 1986, p. 3; Christopher Tolkien did not offer any clear dating for the fragment I have quoted from about Melko, but it seems to pertain to the mid-1920s or slightly later). This use of "cunning" and wisdom" together might be coincidence, but it could show that by the 1920s Tolkien was giving some kind of thought to English folkloric wizards and the nature of magic power.

[903] Humphrey Carpenter, *The Letters of JRR Tolkien*, with the assistance of Christopher Tolkien, Houghton Mifflin, 2000 edition [original publication 1981], Tolkien to Stanley Unwin, December 7, 1942, # 47, p. 58.

[904] Hammond and Scull cite a 1981 paper by John Rateliff connecting Galadriel's mirror to Ayesha's mirror; see Wayne Hammond and Christina Scull, *The Lord of the Rings: A Reader's Companion*, Houghton Mifflin, 2005, p. 321. The influence of H. Rider Haggard's *She* on diverse aspects of *The Lord of the Rings* has been widely noted in Tolkien scholarship; see Hammond and Scull, *The Lord of the Rings: A Reader's Companion*, 2005, p. 88-89, 312-313, 325, 664. A series of fascinating papers by Mark Hooker in *A Tolkienian Mathomium* point to a spectrum of influences on Tolkien of Haggard's novels, see Mark T. Hooker, *A Tolkienian Mathomium*, Llyfrawr, 2006, p. 123-159. Tolkien is reported to have "ranked Haggard very highly" as reported by Roger Lancelyn Green in Douglas Anderson, editor, *Tales Before Tolkien: The Roots of Modern Fantasy*, New York: Ballantine Books, 2003, p 133. And in a 1966 interview Tolkien said "I suppose as a boy *She* interested me as much as anything"; see Hammond and Scull, *The Lord of the Rings: A Reader's Companion*, 2005, p. 313.

[905] Humphrey Carpenter, *The Letters of JRR Tolkien*, with the assistance of Christopher Tolkien, Houghton Mifflin, 2000 edition [original publication 1981], Tolkien to Ruth Austin, January 25, 1971, # 320, p. 407.

[906] Michael Maher, SJ, "A land without stain," in Jane Chance, editor, *Tolkien the Medievalist*, Routledge, 2003, p. 225-236.

[907] Verlyn Flieger, "But What Did He Really Mean?" *Tolkien Studies* 11, 2014, p. 153.

[908] Leslie Donovan, "The Valkyrie Reflex in JRR Tolkien's *The Lord of the Rings*," in Jane Chance, editor, *Tolkien the Medievalist*, Routledge, 2003, p. 106-132; reprinted in Janet Brennan Croft and Leslie Donovan, editors, *Perilous and Fair: Women in the Works and Life of JRR Tolkien*, Mythopoeic Press, 2015, p. 221-257.

[909] S. Baring-Gould, *Devonshire Characters and Strange Events*, London: John Lane, 1908, p. 70-83 "White Witches."

[910] Sabine Baring-Gould, *Devonshire Characters and Strange Events*, London: John Lane, 1908, p. 84 "Manly Peeke."

[911] Wayne Hammond and Christina Scull, *The Lord of the Rings: A Reader's Companion*, Houghton Mifflin, 2005, p. 466 mention of Umbar; p. 522

mention of corsairs of Umbar; p. 755 "Nomenclature" entry for "Corsairs": "They are imagined as similar to the Mediterranean corsairs; sea-robbers with fortified bases."

[912] JRR Tolkien, *The War of the Ring*, in *The History of The Lord of the Rings, Part Three*, Christopher Tolkien editor, Houghton Mifflin, 1990, p. 413.

[913] John Rhys, *Celtic Folklore: Welsh and Manx*, two volumes, Oxford: Clarendon Press, 1901, volume 1, p. 19; other wise men are mentioned on p. 256, 257, 264. Also see a story about an English cunning man in volume 2, p. 458-462.

[914] John Rhys, *Celtic Folklore: Welsh and Manx*, two volumes, Oxford: Clarendon Press, 1901, Volume One, p. 264.

[915] Tom Shippey, *The Road to Middle-earth: How JRR Tolkien Created a New Mythology*, Houghton Mifflin, 2003, 170-171.

[916] JRR Tolkien, "Nomenclature of *The Lord of the Rings*," 1967, in Christina Scull and Wayne Hammond, *The Lord of the Rings: A Reader's Companion*, Houghton Mifflin, 2005, p. 772.

[917] Sometime in late 1940 Tolkien settled the arrangement of the White Council and during the same period came up with the early versions of the exchange between Gandalf and Saruman; Tolkien's observations about Nazi Nordic racialism are found in a March 1941 letter; and the invention of Galadriel as a member of the White Council happened later in 1941. (For the letter see Humphrey Carpenter, *The Letters of JRR Tolkien*, with the assistance of Christopher Tolkien, Houghton Mifflin, 2000 edition [original publication 1981], JRR Tolkien to Michael Tolkien, March 18, 1941, # 44, p. 55-56.)

Endnotes: Companions in Shipwreck

[918] Janet Brennan Croft and Leslie Donovan, editors, *Perilous and Fair: Women in the Works and Life of JRR Tolkien*, Mythopoeic Press, 2015.

[919] Trench fever was recognized as an illness by 1916, but its etiology remained a mystery for several years thereafter.

[920] United Kingdom, National Archives, East Riding of Yorkshire Archives and Records Service; Strickland-Constable Family. Viewed online 15 August 2012.

[921] In November 2012 I published an early version of this essay on the blog of a Tolkien fan group. Researcher Dave Hanson left a comment about his recent research on the Strickland-Constable diaries. She made no mention of Tolkien.

[922] Michael Tolkien, "Lecture on JRR Tolkien Given to the University of St. Andrews Science Fiction and Fantasy Society on 2nd May, 1989" (viewed online Friday, June 21, 2013). This Michael Tolkien was a son of Michael Tolkien and grandson of JRR.

[923] Humphrey Carpenter, *The Letters of JRR Tolkien*, with the assistance of Christopher Tolkien, Houghton Mifflin, 2000 edition [original publication 1981], JRR Tolkien letter to son Michael Tolkien, # 43, 6-8 March 1941, p. 48-54. An excellent summary on the topic of women and marriage in Tolkien's world – together with a consideration of this 1941 letter – can be found in Christina Scull and Wayne Hammond, *The JRR Tolkien Companion and Guide: Reader's Guide*, Houghton Mifflin, 2006, p. 1107-1123.

[924] John Garth, *Tolkien and the Great War: The Threshold of Middle-earth*, Houghton Mifflin, 2003, p. 238.

[925] Humphrey Carpenter, *The Letters of JRR Tolkien*, 2000 edition [original publication 1981], JRR Tolkien draft letter to Mr. Thompson, # 180, January 14, 1956, p. 232.

[926] Humphrey Carpenter, *The Letters of JRR Tolkien*, 2000 edition [original publication 1981], JRR Tolkien draft letter to unknown fan, # 244, circa 1963, p. 323-324.

Endnotes: Tolkien's Tree of Tales

[927] Verlyn Flieger and Douglas A. Anderson, *Tolkien On Fairy-stories*, HarperCollins, 2008, p. 55; JRR Tolkien, "On Fairy-stories," in *Tales from the Perilous Realm*, Houghton Mifflin, 2008, p. 355. This comment about "Red Indians" does not appear in either "Manuscript A" or "Manuscript B" of "On Fairy-stories," so it must date to the preparation of "Manuscript C" in 1943.

[928] Christopher Vecsey, *Imagine Ourselves Richly*, Crossroad Publishing, 1988, p. 10.

[929] Alan Dundes, *Sacred Narrative: Readings in the Theory of Myth*, University of California Press, 1984, p. 72.

[930] George Bird Grinnell, *The Indians of To-day*, Duffield, 1911, p. 11. Grinnell was one of the most well-known ethnographers of the period.

[931] Andrew Lang, *Custom and Myth*, 1884, Longmans, Green and Company, p. 1, 3.

[932] Verlyn Flieger and Douglas A. Anderson, *Tolkien On Fairy-stories*, HarperCollins, 2008, p. 308.

[933] Dimitra Fimi, *Tolkien, Race and Cultural History: From Fairies to Hobbits*, Palgrave Macmillan, 2010, p. 141-159.

[934] Müller quoted in Christopher Vecsey, *Imagine Ourselves Richly*, Crossroad Publishing, 1988, p. 10.

[935] JRR Tolkien, *The Story of Kullervo*, edited by Verlyn Flieger, HarperCollins, 2015, p. 71. JRR Tolkien, "'The Story of Kullervo' and Essays on Kalevala," edited by Verlyn Flieger, *Tolkien Studies*, volume 7, 2010, p. 248; also quoted in Christina Scull and Wayne Hammond, *The JRR Tolkien Companion and Guide: Reader's Guide*, Houghton Mifflin, 2006, p. 441.

[936] JRR Tolkien, *The Story of Kullervo*, edited by Verlyn Flieger, 2015, p. 105; JRR Tolkien, "'The Story of Kullervo' and Essays on Kalevala," edited by Verlyn Flieger, *Tolkien Studies*, volume 7, 2010, p. 264; also quoted in Scull and Hammond, *The JRR Tolkien Companion and Guide: Reader's Guide*, 2006, p. 441.

[937] JRR Tolkien, *The Story of Kullervo*, edited by Verlyn Flieger, 2015, p. 71. JRR Tolkien, "'The Story of Kullervo' and Essays on Kalevala," edited by Verlyn Flieger, *Tolkien Studies*, volume 7, 2010, p. 248. This quote and the material that follows in this paragraph are from Tolkiens early manuscript dated to circa 1914-1915.

[938] Verlyn Flieger and Douglas A. Anderson, *Tolkien On Fairy-stories*, HarperCollins, 2008, p. 44, 224-226; JRR Tolkien, "On Fairy-stories," in *Tales from the Perilous Realm*, Houghton Mifflin, 2008, p. 339.

[939] Flieger and Anderson, *Tolkien On Fairy-stories*, 2008, p. 55; JRR Tolkien, "On Fairy-stories," in *Tales from the Perilous Realm*, 2008, p. 355.

[940] Humphrey Carpenter, *The Letters of JRR Tolkien*, with the assistance of Christopher Tolkien, Houghton Mifflin, 2000 edition [original publication 1981], # 58, April 3, 1944, p. 69.

[941] Verlyn Flieger and Douglas A. Anderson, *Tolkien On Fairy-stories*, HarperCollins, 2008, p. 308; Christina Scull and Wayne Hammond, *The JRR Tolkien Companion and Guide: Reader's Guide*, Houghton Mifflin, 2006, 683-689.

[942] Verlyn Flieger and Douglas A. Anderson, *Tolkien On Fairy-stories*, HarperCollins, 2008, p. 51; JRR Tolkien, "On Fairy-stories," in *Tales from the Perilous Realm*, Houghton Mifflin, 2008, p. 350.

[943] Humphrey Carpenter, *The Letters of JRR Tolkien*, with the assistance of Christopher Tolkien, Houghton Mifflin, 2000 edition [original publication 1981], Tolkien to Milton Waldman, # 131, circa late 1951, p. 143-161 (see quote at 144),

[944] Humphrey Carpenter, *The Letters of JRR Tolkien*, with the assistance of Christopher Tolkien, Houghton Mifflin, 2000 edition [original publication 1981], # 180, January 14, 1956, p. 230-231.

[945] JRR Tolkien, *The Legend of Sigurd and Gudrún*, Christopher Tolkien, editor, HarperCollins, 2009, p. 23-26.

[946] Christina Scull and Wayne Hammond, *The JRR Tolkien Companion and Guide: Reader's Guide*, Houghton Mifflin, 2006, p. 962; also see p. 244-248.

[947] Carl Phelpstead, *Tolkien and Wales: Language, Literature, and Identity*, University of Wales Press, 2011, p. 110-116.

[948] JRR Tolkien, *Morgoth's Ring, the Later Silmarillion, Part One*, in *The History of Middle-earth, Volume X*, Christopher Tolkien, editor, Houghton Mifflin, 1993, p. 370.

[949] Verlyn Flieger and Douglas A. Anderson, *Tolkien On Fairy-stories*, HarperCollins, 2008, p. 54; JRR Tolkien, "On Fairy-stories," in *Tales from the Perilous Realm*, Houghton Mifflin, 2008, p. 354.

[950] Andrew Lang, *Custom and Myth*, 1884, Longmans, Green and Company, p. 9.

[951] Humphrey Carpenter, *The Letters of JRR Tolkien*, with the assistance of Christopher Tolkien, Houghton Mifflin, 2000 edition [original publication 1981], # 306, circa fall 1967, p. 394.

[952] JRR Tolkien, "'The Story of Kullervo' and Essays on Kalevala," edited by Verlyn Flieger, *Tolkien Studies*, volume 7, 2010, p. 264; also quoted in Christina Scull and Wayne Hammond, *The JRR Tolkien Companion and Guide: Reader's Guide*, Houghton Mifflin, 2006, p. 441.

[953] JRR Tolkien, *Beowulf: The Monsters and the Critics*, Christopher Tolkien, editor, Houghton Mifflin, 1984, p. 21.

[954] Christina Scull and Wayne Hammond, *The JRR Tolkien Companion and Guide: Reader's Guide*, Houghton Mifflin, 2006, p. 273.

[955] Richard C. West 2003 paper quoted in Scull and Hammond, *The JRR Tolkien Companion and Guide: Reader's Guide*, 2006, p. 969.

[956] Humphrey Carpenter, *The Letters of JRR Tolkien*, with the assistance of Christopher Tolkien, Houghton Mifflin, 2000 edition [original publication 1981], # 25, February 20, 1938, p. 31.

[957] Richard West 2003 paper quoted in Scull and Hammond, *The JRR Tolkien Companion and Guide: Reader's Guide*, 2006, p. 969.

[958] Verlyn Flieger and Douglas A. Anderson, *Tolkien On Fairy-stories*, HarperCollins, 2008, p. 39; JRR Tolkien, "On Fairy-stories," in *Tales from the Perilous Realm*, Houghton Mifflin, 2008, p. 332.

[959] John Garth, "The road from adaptation to invention: How Tolkien Came to the Brink of Middle-earth in 1914," *Tolkien Studies* 11, 2014, p. 1-44.

Endnotes: Pawneeland in Middle-earth

[960] Mark T. Hooker, *The Hobbitonian Anthology*, Llyfrawr, 2009, p. 643-671.

[961] JRR Tolkien, *The Book of Lost Tales, Part One*, in *The History of Middle-earth, Volume I*, Christopher Tolkien editor, Houghton Mifflin, 1983, p. 151.

[962] JRR Tolkien, *The Shaping of Middle-earth*, in *The History of Middle-earth, Volume IV*, Christopher Tolkien editor, Houghton Mifflin, 1986, p. 21, 100.

[963] John D. Rateliff, *The History of the Hobbit, Part One: Mr. Baggins*, Houghton Mifflin, 2007, p. 154-155, 166.

[964] Rateliff, *The History of the Hobbit, Part One: Mr. Baggins*, 2007, p. 231-232.

[965] Rateliff, *The History of the Hobbit, Part One: Mr. Baggins*, 2007, p. 232, 247 endnote 15, 259-260.

[966] Humphrey Carpenter, *The Letters of JRR Tolkien*, with the assistance of Christopher Tolkien, Houghton Mifflin, 2000 edition [original publication 1981], # 25, circa February 1938, p. 30.

[967] Humphrey Carpenter, *The Letters of JRR Tolkien*, with the assistance of Christopher Tolkien, Houghton Mifflin, 2000 edition [original publication 1981], # 156, November 4, 1954, p. 201.

[968] Humphrey Carpenter, *The Letters of JRR Tolkien*, with the assistance of Christopher Tolkien, Houghton Mifflin, 2000 edition [original publication 1981], # 131, Tolkien to Milton Waldman, circa late 1951, p. 145.

[969] Tom Shippey, *The Road to Middle-earth: How JRR Tolkien Created a New Mythology*, 2003, Houghton Mifflin, p. 285; Christina Scull and Wayne Hammond, *The JRR Tolkien Companion and Guide: Reader's Guide*, Houghton Mifflin, 2006, p. 982-984.

[970] Verlyn Flieger and Douglas A. Anderson, *Tolkien On Fairy-stories*, HarperCollins, 2008, p. 78-79; JRR Tolkien, "On Fairy-stories," in *Tales from the Perilous Realm*, Houghton Mifflin, 2008, p. 389.

[971] JRR Tolkien, *The Book of Lost Tales, Part One*, in *The History of Middle-earth, Volume I*, Christopher Tolkien, editor, Houghton Mifflin, 1983, p. 75.

[972] George A. Dorsey [and James R. Murie], *Traditions of the Skidi Pawnee*, Houghton Mifflin, 1904, p. xix. As Roaming Scout's creation story makes clear (p. 5), Evening Star's Garden is a mystical celestial realm, established before the earth was itself formed from a quartz crystal (see p. 329 endnote 7 which refers to p. 5). Tirawa bestows upon her a generative power, "You shall be known as Mother of all things; for through you all beings shall be created."

[973] Christina Scull and Wayne Hammond, *The JRR Tolkien Companion and Guide: Reader's Guide*, Houghton Mifflin, 2006, p. 123-124.

[974] Humphrey Carpenter, *The Letters of JRR Tolkien*, with the assistance of Christopher Tolkien, Houghton Mifflin, 2000 edition [original publication 1981], p. 202, 207, # 156, November 4, 1954; # 268, January 19, 1965, p. 354.

[975] JRR Tolkien, *Unfinished Tales*, Houghton Mifflin, 1980, p. 388.

[976] JRR Tolkien, *The Shaping of Middle-earth*, in *The History of Middle-earth, Volume IV*, Christopher Tolkien editor, Houghton Mifflin, 1986, p. 80, 85, 87.

[977] JRR Tolkien, *The Lost Road and Other Writings*, in *The History of Middle-earth, Volume V*, Christopher Tolkien editor, Houghton Mifflin, 1987, p. 222, 224.

[978] JRR Tolkien, *Morgoth's Ring, the Later Silmarillion, Part One*, in *The History of Middle-earth, Volume X*, Christopher Tolkien editor, Houghton Mifflin, 1993, p. 55; JRR Tolkien, *The Silmarillion*, Houghton Mifflin, 1977, p. 38, 59.

[979] Humphrey Carpenter, *The Letters of JRR Tolkien*, with the assistance of Christopher Tolkien, Houghton Mifflin, 2000 edition [original publication 1981], # 131, Tolkien to Milton Waldman, circa late 1951, p. 159.

[980] JRR Tolkien, *The Return of the Shadow*, in *The History of The Lord of the Rings, Part One*, Christopher Tolkien editor, Houghton Mifflin, 1988, p. 423-424.

[981] Humphrey Carpenter, *The Letters of JRR Tolkien*, with the assistance of Christopher Tolkien, Houghton Mifflin, 2000 edition [original publication 1981], # 131, Tolkien to Milton Waldman, circa late 1951, p. 150.

[982] Verlyn Flieger and Douglas A. Anderson, *Tolkien On Fairy-stories*, HarperCollins, 2008, p. 38; JRR Tolkien, "On Fairy-stories," in *Tales from the Perilous Realm*, Houghton Mifflin, 2008, p. 331-334.

[983] Flieger and Anderson, *Tolkien On Fairy-stories*, 2008, p. 38; JRR Tolkien, "On Fairy-stories," in *Tales from the Perilous Realm*, 2008, p. 331.

[984] Flieger and Anderson, *Tolkien On Fairy-stories*, 2008, p. 39; JRR Tolkien, "On Fairy-stories," *Tales from the Perilous Realm*, 2008, p. 332. A version of this passage also appears in JRR Tolkien, *The Legend of Sigurd and Gudrún*, Christopher Tolkien, editor, HarperCollins, 2009, p. 31: "Far more important than the names of the figures, or the origins of the details of the story (except where this helps us to understand what is unintelligible or to rescue a text from corruption) is the atmosphere, colouring, style."

[985] Flieger and Anderson, *Tolkien On Fairy-stories*, 2008, p. 44-47; JRR Tolkien, "On Fairy-stories," in *Tales from the Perilous Realm*, 2008, p. 340-344.

[986] Flieger and Anderson, *Tolkien On Fairy-stories*, 2008, p. 40; JRR Tolkien, "On Fairy-stories," in *Tales from the Perilous Realm*, 2008, p. 333.

[987] For Tolkien's concerns about copyright see Humphrey Carpenter, *The Letters of JRR Tolkien*, with the assistance of Christopher Tolkien, Houghton Mifflin, 2000 edition [original publication 1981], # 258, August 2, 1964, p. 349; also see # 271, May 25, 1965, p. 356; # 273, p. 358. For Tolkien's comment on a proposal by an unknown writer to compose fan fiction see Humphrey Carpenter, *The Letters of JRR Tolkien*, with the assistance of Christopher Tolkien, Houghton Mifflin, 2000 edition [original publication 1981], # 292, December 12, 1966, p. 371.

[988] An instance of Tolkien's uncited source material is his close reproduction of an eagle illustration from a 1919 publication; see JRR Tolkien, *The Annotated Hobbit*, annotated by Douglas A. Anderson, Houghton Mifflin, 2002, p. 160.

[989] Tom Shippey, *The Road to Middle-earth: How JRR Tolkien Created a New Mythology*, 2003, Houghton Mifflin, p. 285; Christina Scull and Wayne Hammond, *The JRR Tolkien Companion and Guide: Reader's Guide*, Houghton Mifflin, 2006, p. 982-984.

Endnotes: The Future of Race

[990] Richard Dorson, *The British Folklorists*, University of Chicago Press, 1968, p. 440.

[991] JRR Tolkien, *The Return of the Shadow*, in *The History of The Lord of the Rings, Part One*, Christopher Tolkien editor, Houghton Mifflin, 1988, p. 309, 336. Ashley Montagu, "Race and Kindred Delusions," *Equality*, volume 1, # 7, 1939, p. 20-24.

[992] JRR Tolkien, *The Treason of Isengard*, in *The History of The Lord of the Rings, Part Two*, Christopher Tolkien editor, Houghton Mifflin, 1989, p. 408-410. Ashley Montagu, *Man's Most Dangerous Myth: The Fallacy of Race*, Columbia University Press, 1942.

[993] Elazar Barkan, *The Retreat of Scientific Racism: Changing concepts of race in Britain and the United States between the world wars*, Cambridge University Press, 1992 [reprinted 1996], p. 302-304.

[994] Alice Littlefield, Leonard Lieberman, and Larry T. Reynolds, "Redefining Race: The Potential Demise of a Concept in Physical Anthropology, *Current Anthropology*, volume 23, # 6, December 1982, p. 641-652; reprinted in E. Nathaniel Gates editor, *Critical Race Theory: The Concept of "Race" in Natural and Social Science*, Garland 1997 / Routledge 2013, p. 105-116. This paper is a study of the treatment of the race concept in 58 American textbooks.

[995] John P. Jackson Jr, "'In Ways Academical': The Reception of Carleton S. Coon's *The Origin of Races*," *Journal of the History of Biology*, volume 34, # 2 Summer 2001, p. 247-285. This paper details how Carleton Coon worked in secret with Carleton Putnam to shape a political attack on Boasian anti-race scholarship during the early 1960s, and the subsequent furor in which Coon tried to silence critics, threatening lawsuits and pushing for administrative censure.

****

Presentations of portions of *Tolkien in Pawneeland*:

Real Myth & Mithril
Longmont, Colorado
May 19, 2013

Mythcon 44
Lansing, Michigan
July 14, 2013

Barbed Wire Books
Longmont, Colorado
September 18, 2014

Real Myth & Mithril
Niwot, Colorado
April 25, 2015

Mythcon 46
Colorado Springs, Colorado
August 1, 2015

****

Early versions of several chapters are online
at *Pawneeland*

For further information
visit *Tolkienland*

Swanship

fabled creatures slowly wander
to the other side of the spell

beyond the end of the myth

let us invent new likenesses
for cryptic symbols of selfhood

for this journey and this joy
we will face our fears

we will wish one another well
so now let us take our leave

sailing through rumors in the mist
I will never forget what happened

CPSIA information can be obtained at www.ICGtesting.com
Printed in the USA
BVOW08s0611070816

458211BV00003B/115/P